Pro Football
Expansion II

Part Two of a Trilogy

Published by Jim Gardner

This book is fiction.

ISBN: 9798366119795

Pro Football Expansion II

Part Two of a Trilogy

Jim Gardner

This trilogy is dedicated to the late Phil Roache, my English teacher during my junior year at Covina High School in Covina, California, who helped me to discover my aptitude as a writer. He also taught me a thing or two about football as my first high school football coach.

Also dedicated to Craig Howes, my expository writing professor during my senior year at the University of Hawaii who helped me to refine those skills.

If you like this literary work, give substantial credit to the aforementioned men. If you don't like it, you can conclude that I should have paid more attention to these two fine men.

Many thanks to my youngest brother Steve who provided valuable assistance in the editing and publication of this work.

Also thanks to my younger Mike who wasn't in a position to help with the publication but he did say nice things about my work.

Thanks also to Reggie for being such a terrific son.

CHAPTER ONE
A New Look At An Old Friend

Something was gnawing at me. Perhaps it was a premonition or something left undone. Whatever it was, it kept me from getting a good night's sleep. I was out of bed before five o'clock on that Friday morning in February, 1977.

To refresh your memory, I was a pro football player for the Hawaiians of the National Football League and a graduate student at the University of Hawaii. I had spent much of my childhood in a lower income section of Azusa, California, until my family moved almost 20 miles away to middle class Montebello the summer before I started high school.

For the record, Azusa was not and is not a bad place. I simply happened to live in a rough section of the community where one fought for survival. The kids who were weaker or smaller often couldn't have lunch at school because there was no shortage of bullies willing to relieve them of their lunch money or sack lunches. Other items commonly stolen included bicycles, skateboards, baseball gloves, jackets, gym clothes and anything else that wasn't nailed down.

Even textbooks were commonly stolen. Despite the fact that the kids doing the stealing had virtually no use for even their own textbooks, it was done for the sheer joy of stealing from a weaker kid to allegedly prove one's manhood.

At the time I thought that the bullies were tough. Now I understand just how cowardly they were. There is no bravado involved in preying on a vulnerable kid.

Where did I fit in in the grand scheme of things?

I got into my share of fights. I was small for my age and that worked to my disadvantage until I had a growth spurt when I was about 13. I had to deal with the bigger kids who tried to prey on me but fate seemed to smile upon me. I never lost my lunch money or anything else. I got through that phase my life relatively unscathed.

Well, there was the stabbing when I was 12. One morning, specifically on November 22, 1963, which would prove to be a very tragic day in America, a friend and I spotted two kids who appeared to be about our age but turned out to be freshmen at a high school in neighboring Covina trying to relieve my friend's eight-year-old brother of his lunch money. Instinctively we squared off against the two bullies.

My friend and I were doing pretty well. We were getting the best of the cowardly bullies whom we found were ditching school that day. After I knocked my opponent down and turned to face my friend's opponent, my opponent snuck up behind me and stabbed me in the back with a switchblade.

That incapacitated me for a few months and forced me to repeat seventh grade because I had to miss so much school. At least my friend's younger brother was able to hang on to his lunch money.

Fate was kinder in Montebello. This jaded kid met a compassionate football coach who cared enough to mold him into a pretty good quarterback as well as a defensive back, punter and placekicker.

At the time I thought I was simply a high school student having fun. If anything, my sights were set on becoming a professional baseball player while my parents tried to drum the notion of a military career into my head. I was more than slightly surprised when I started hearing from college football and baseball coaches during my junior year at South Valley High School. Some sent telegrams or letters while some sent representatives or called on the phone. Some even showed up personally including John McKay and Rod Dedeaux from USC and Tommy Prothro from UCLA.

Fortunately I had my high school coach, Marcus Farnwell, to guide me through. The attention I received was overwhelming and I wasn't prepared. Farnwell advised me to focus on the schools whose representatives talked about education and sports while disregarding those who offered bribes of cars, money and other material goods. Some schools, which will remain nameless, did attempt the aforementioned bribes. I guess I was a hot item although I should point out that McKay , Dedeaux and Prothro attempted no such bribes.

They came from all over. In late December, 1968, I answered the front door of my home and found a stocky, grandfatherly type on the porch.

"Jay Dockman?" the man inquired with a smile as wide as the Grand Canyon.

"Yes?"

"I'm Woody Hayes."

I admit that I was impressed once he explained who he was. At the time I didn't really follow college football except for USC and UCLA so I wasn't familiar with Ohio State. A few days later Ohio State would break my heart by pulverizing USC in the Rose Bowl although that was not the reason I didn't choose Ohio State.

As time went on the recruiting intensified. One day later in my junior year I was pulled out of class and summoned to the administration office to be introduced to the legendary Bear Bryant of Alabama.

Through the last two years of high school I heard from every school in the Pac-8 as well as schools such as Texas, Georgia, Kentucky, Syracuse, Tennessee, Michigan State, Arizona State, Texas A&M, Michigan, Miami and several other major colleges. Some recruited me for football, some for baseball and some were amenable to allowing me to play both sports. Even religious schools such as Brigham Young University, SMU and Notre Dame expressed interest although I was neither LDS, Methodist nor Catholic.

4

All along I was fairly certain I would pick USC although I was open to others. I ultimately did attend USC my freshman year where I played JV football as a defensive back and baseball as a first baseman and outfielder.

The University of Hawaii never tried to recruit me. I still managed to secure a transfer to Hawaii after one year at USC. I loved attending USC and the prestige of being a part of such a nationally respected athletic program. I admit that I wasn't happy being used as a defensive back instead of a quarterback although that only played a minimal role in my decision to leave USC. Primarily I desired to get away from my Southern California roots to be more on my own and experience something different. Hawaii also didn't feel that I could be used as a quarterback but the coaching staff offered me an opportunity to play in the offensive backfield.

Fate smiled upon me again when the World Football League was founded. I was in my final undergraduate semester when I was drafted by the Hawaiians of the World Football League. I was also drafted at that time by the Dallas Cowboys and in baseball by the Boston Red Sox. It might have seemed like an automatic choice but it wasn't. I considered all three possibilities.

Dallas probably wasn't a serious contender. If I was going to play football I wanted to stay in Hawaii. It was primarily a matter of baseball being my favorite sport and football offering me an opportunity to stay at what had become my home and remain close to my girlfriend. I had come to Hawaii thinking it was simply a place to go to get my college degree while enjoying life elsewhere for a few years. I didn't dream that I would settle there but it had become my home by the time I graduated.

Hawaii obviously had the home field advantage among the three teams. I opted to play football in the WFL.

On October 22, 1975, the WFL folded. Hawaii no longer had a pro football team. I no longer had a job.

But fate smiled again. The NFL was already planning to expand into Tampa and Seattle. About six weeks after the WFL folded the NFL announced that it would also add Memphis and Hawaii into the 1976 expansion.

Just the same, it wasn't a merger. It was expansion and all four teams were to pad their rosters through the expansion draft, the rookie free agent draft and free agent signings. Those who had played for the WFL teams in Memphis and Hawaii could not remain with those teams if another NFL team held the rights to them.

The Dallas Cowboys technically held the NFL rights to me. Fortunately the team was willing to negotiate.

The Cowboys got Hawaii to surrender a number one draft choice for me; a semblance of a coup for the Cowboys since they didn't take me until the third round when they drafted me in 1974. The only thing that mattered was I was staying home.

So on this February, 1977, morning I had played three years for the Hawaiians; two in the WFL and one in the NFL. At the age of 25 life was good except for something enigmatic which compelled me to get out of bed well before dawn.

The sudden inability to sleep was not unprecedented. There were Sunday mornings during the season when I rose at about this time despite the fact that I had set my alarm clocks for a slightly later time. In Hawaii our home games started at either ten or eleven o'clock, depending on whether the rest of the country was on daylight or standard time. The TV networks had overwhelming clout.

But this wasn't football season. It wasn't even Sunday. I simply didn't feel like sleeping.

For the record, our first regular season game for the 1977 season was exactly seven months away. We would open up in New Orleans and have our home opener a week later against Buffalo.

That was when we would start proving that 1976 was no fluke. We were 7-7 in 1976; a mediocre record under normal circumstances but phenomenal for an expansion team. We definitely had everybody's attention. We won more games than the three other expansion teams combined. One more victory and we would have doubled their combined total.

Heck, we had better records than 12 of the previously established NFL teams and an identical record to one of the others. Along the way we defeated three playoff contenders and the team that ultimately won the Super Bowl.

A lot of doubters didn't believe we could top that in 1977. I couldn't wait to prove those cynics wrong.

Or was I simply looking forward to the start of the regular season so that I could leapfrog past training camp? The regular season would be preceded by two months of training camp at the Kaneohe Marine Corps Air Station. That was an intense experience of two-a-days prior to our first exhibition game as well as meetings, films, boredom and an assortment of coaches ranting and raving about our alleged ineptitude. It was as if the coaches were all closet Marine Corps drill instructors.

All the while I would watch the preseason roster dwindle down until roughly two-thirds of those who entered camp were no longer a part of the team. Although I had had a fairly decent 1976 season, there was no guarantee that I would still be around for the opening kickoff. Throughout my career I never took for granted having the team made.

Perhaps that was the reason I looked forward to opening day in New Orleans. If I was there it would mean that I had survived training camp and made the team. That didn't mean that I couldn't be placed on waivers during the season so my vow was to work hard from day one all the way through the final play of the final game.

But training camp was still more than four months away. I was in my first semester as a graduate student. My top priorities for the offseason were to keep myself in good physical shape, make good progress toward my master's and have some fun, generally in that order although not always.

Hawaiians head coach Chuck Walker spotted me at the university a few days earlier. When I applied for graduate school and was accepted during the season I didn't make a big deal out of it among my teammates and coaches. Very few of them knew my plans. Walker was among those who didn't know.

"Hi, Coach," I greeted when our paths crossed near Sakamaki Hall. "What are you doing here?"

"Just talking to the football coaches about some possible free agents. What's with the armload of books?"

"Oh, I'm working on my master's."

Walker raised his eyebrows. He seemed pleasantly surprised.

"Well good, good," he said, beaming. "I like to see athletes take an interest in academics. Too many get scholarships and waste the opportunity to get the education that's supposed to go along with the opportunity to play sports. It makes me sick when they waste four years of college like that."

It also made me sick. I knew of a few teammates from the Hawaiians who had gone through college with very little time in the classroom. I also recalled a few of my college teammates who never took academics seriously.

Perhaps it was because of the battles I'd had with my parents who believed I was sabotaging America by choosing college over Vietnam that I took academics so seriously. All I really know is I had been very grateful for the opportunity to play college football and baseball while earning my bachelor's degree. I was among the privileged class on an athletic scholarship but, unlike many of my peers across the country, I went to class, did my homework and passed my tests.

Being up at an early hour, I took a shower while the coffee brewed. As soon as I was dressed I poured myself a cup and opened a textbook to begin work on a research project. The very second I was settled in the phone rang.

There was only one reason why the phone would ring at five o'clock in the morning. My roommate, Bill, was needed at the restaurant where he was assistant manager. His previous shift ended only five hours earlier and now they needed him again.

"Bon matin," I greeted cheerily when I picked up the phone. "Le maison de l'etudiant."

"Huh?" replied a puzzled caller whom I immediately recognized as Kathy Ching; a very cute young lady of Chinese ancestry whom I first met when we were both undergraduates.

"Tu as besoin de parler l'etudiant?"

"Jay?"

"Qui?"

"Jay, speak English," Kathy requested laughingly. "Can I speak to Bill?"

"Is it really necessary?" I asked.

"It is, I'm afraid," she replied apologetically. "The other assistant called in sick again. We need Bill to fill in."

There was one very good reason why the other assistant called in sick. It was in direct correlation with the discos having closed only about an hour earlier. He was too drunk and/or too tired and/or too lazy to report for his scheduled shift. It happened two or three times a month. It was ostensibly one of the perks of being an assistant manager at a restaurant owned by members of one's own family.

I knocked on Bill's bedroom door.

"Yeah, I'm awake," he called in a tone that told me he knew why the phone had rung.

"Sorry, pal. Looks like it was disco night for Troy again."

"I'm going to kill that son-of-a-bitch one of these days," I heard Bill mutter before he picked up the extension in his bedroom.

Bill had been a wide receiver at the University of Hawaii, playing his final season during my rookie year as a pro. He was invited to try out for the Hawaiians as a free agent after he graduated in 1975 but decided he had had enough of football. He felt his future would be more secure if he took up an offer to use his business administration degree to be an assistant manager at a Waikiki restaurant. At times like this he probably wished he had given pro football a shot.

At least I saw no reason to believe my day would be interrupted. I had planned to do research at the university and then have a workout at a gym in Pearl City. That night I was planning to go to the Blaisdell Arena to watch the University of Hawaii basketball team take on Centenary.

The phone rang. It was six o'clock; a seemingly strange hour for a phone call. I couldn't think of any reason for the phone to ring at this hour.

"Hello?"

"Jay?"

"Yeah?"

"This is Chris," said the voice on the other end.

"Chris?"

"Chris Alexander."

Christopher Allen Alexander had been another college teammate. He had been a tight end who played two years at the University of Hawaii after two years at Citrus Junior College in Glendora, California, which also happens to be my birthplace. He was a part of the same graduating class as me. . . .

Except Chris never graduated. He racked up enough credits at Citrus to transfer to the University of Hawaii as a junior. During his first year he did the bare minimum to maintain his eligibility and did practically nothing his senior year. He was placed on academic probation after the fall, 1973, semester after his grade point average dropped to 1.6 but seemed undaunted. He registered for the spring semester but never went to class. He had used up his football eligibility so, in his mind, why bother?

That painted a partial picture of Chris. He was still a good friend and generally a nice guy except he did have a way of getting under a person's skin.

I had seen Chris only once in the previous two years. I might have been more happy to hear from him except I was baffled by the fact that he had my unlisted phone number. I was still not necessarily sorry to hear from him although he also wasn't on my list of people from whom I was hoping to hear. I didn't even know he was still in Hawaii.

But six o'clock in the morning?

Perhaps it really had been a premonition.

Or a foreboding.

"It looks like you've done pretty well for yourself," Chris commented. "I've been following your career."

"Thanks," I replied modestly. "How's everything with you?"

"Not too good, really. I got screwed out of football, I don't have a job and I just had a minor accident. Would you believe I even have to use food stamps?"

"That bad, huh?" I said lackadaisically.

"It's a bummer, man!"

I didn't want to be unsympathetic. It was still hard to feel sorry for Chris. Perhaps he had had his share of bad breaks but he was the type to embellish and insist he was never culpable.

Chris wanted for us to go to the beach that morning. My plans were already made but he was adamant.

"C'mon, man. I haven't seen you in a helluva long time."

Knowing the futility of resisting when I wasn't necessarily averse to seeing him again, I consented to spend part of the day with him. Had I been totally averse to meeting with him again I would have had no problem telling him so but a part of me still considered him to be a friend and wanted to see him.

"Far out," he said. "Can you pick me up?"

"What happened to that new Firebird you had last time I saw you?"

"Ah, I missed a few payments and those (expletive deleted) at the bank repossessed it."

That was vintage Chris, I thought as I bit my lip to keep from laughing. He always found a way to place culpability elsewhere for his lack of responsibility. His car had been financed through what was marketed by the bank as a "pay any day loan." That meant that a customer could make a payment on any day during the month the payment was due. In Chris's mind that meant he could pay any day of his own choosing even if it was six months later.

I got directions to Chris's place which was a little more than a mile away from me and resumed my research work. Obviously I wouldn't be going to the university that day. I still had enough material at home to make the day productive. The beauty of being a graduate student was that you didn't have to spend much time in the classroom.

As I did my research work I was distracted. I did a lot of thinking about Chris. He was a genuinely nice guy but one who tended to believe the world owed him a living and so much more.

One of the reasons why Chris washed out of school was because he figured he would have a long, illustrious career in pro football. That would be followed by the inevitable enshrinement in the Pro Football Hall of Fame. He was never drafted but managed to secure a free agent tryout with Denver.

Chris was a fringe player, at best, who wasn't even a starter much of the time in college. It was a miracle that somebody from the NFL was willing to give him a chance. Expert opinions, not my own, were that the longest Chris would last was halfway through the exhibition season and that was a stretch. He was a decent college tight end when he was in there but had about as much chance of making an NFL team as a gopher snake outfighting a mongoose.

Just the same, I admired Chris for finding an opportunity to try. There was always a chance that he might actually make the team if he made the most of the opportunity.

Unfortunately in the Denver camp he was overheard referring to members of the coaching staff in a series of expletives within the first few days. His tirade was just the excuse the coaching staff needed to cut down the preseason roster. He was immediately placed on waivers with no takers, having the dubious distinction of being the first player cut by the Broncos that season.

Fortunately for Chris it was 1974. This was the dawning of the WFL. Although the WFL season had already begun, Chris was signed by the Detroit Wheels.

Chris being Chris, he still couldn't keep his mouth shut. As a seasoned veteran of a fraction of an NFL training camp, which ostensibly meant that the Wheels should have been grateful just to have him, he showed up with the attitude that he knew more about football than the coaches. After about three days of his criticism, which was about how long he lasted with the Broncos, they cut him before he experienced so much as a single play as a pro. His talent, marginal though it may have been, was wasted.

10

But Chris had been a good and somewhat loyal friend. I kept that in mind as I pulled up to the curb outside of Chris's apartment building. It was a very rundown dwelling in Honolulu's McCully section.

"Don't let this place throw you," Chris commented from his apartment. "I'm only here in transient. I'll be moving to a better place as soon as I get everything together."

I didn't comment but silently agreed that it would be a good idea for Chris to move. The place he lived in appeared to be about ten years overdue for being condemned and razed.

Chris didn't look much better than his apartment did. Although I remembered him as one who normally didn't take the initiative to work out during the offseason, I was surprised by how out of shape he had gotten. He didn't look like he had ever been a tight end, having weakened and developed a gut. His once stylishly cut reddish hair was now oily and tied in a ponytail that ran to the middle of his back.

"What beach we going to?" Chris asked once we were en route.

"Waikiki, I guess."

"Why Waikiki?" he asked, sounding as if there was something about Waikiki that offended him.

"It's close."

"Yeah but it's too crowded. There's the tourists and. . . ."

"Well where do you suggest we go?" I asked, now becoming very sorry my old friend had tracked me down.

"How about Haleiwa?"

"That's clear up on the North Shore. I don't have time to drive all the way up there."

"Okay, how about Kailua? That's close."

"That's way over the Pali. Why go there when Waikiki is just down the road?" I answered, also feeling that the closer the beach, the sooner I could be done with him. I already knew that I wanted to spend as little time as possible with Chris in the future. His welcome wore thin in a hurry.

"Okay," he replied bitterly. "How about . . . ?"

"How about Waikiki?" I intervened lightly to help me maintain my cool. "This is my car and I'm the one who's driving and Waikiki is where we're going."

Chris finally seemed resigned to his perceived dismal fate. He suggested that I pull in front of a liquor store so that we could pick up a six pack.

"Now that's a good idea," I said brightly as I stopped the car in front of a liquor store on Kalakaua Avenue although I normally didn't drink that early in the day. "I'll keep the engine running and you run inside, okay?"

"Sure. Oh, can I borrow some money? All I have on me is food stamps."

I held my tongue as I slipped Chris a fin.

"What kind should I get?" he asked although I would soon wonder why he even bothered asking.

"Bud."

"Ah, whaddya want Bud for?"

"That's the kind I drink," I responded, thinking that was reasonable enough.

"Man, I don't want Bud," he said, twisting his face as if Budweiser was as inviting as the cough medicine his mother used to give him.

"Well I'm the one who's buying and I want Bud."

"How about Michelob?"

"How about Bud?"

"I don't want Bud," he whined.

"If it means that much to you, get Michelob."

Chris triumphantly went into the liquor store while I fumed. Chris had always been on the pushy side, I knew, although that trait seemed to be infinitely more prevalent now. It appeared to define his entire personality at this juncture whereas before his traits also included warmth, generosity and general courtesy.

I could sense that I was in for a very long day even if my reunion with Chris lasted only an hour. If this was truly the way Chris turned out I was going to do whatever I could to avoid him in the future. I didn't want to be unkind but I didn't need a friend like him.

We went to the grassy section of Fort DeRussy. For what seemed like the first time since I answered the phone that morning Chris didn't argue or make any demands. It was actually a fairly easy choice since the grassy section of Fort DeRussy was the only place in Waikiki where one could lie on the beach and drink legally. It was federal property that was open to the public although its primary purpose was as a recreation center for military personnel. Fort DeRussy had also served as an R&R center during the Vietnam War.

"Basically I'm just a student right now," I told Chris during the course of our conversation. "I'm working for my master's at the university. I also work out to stay in shape and I have my TV show every week."

"Not to mention picking up a lot of chicks," Chris added almost enviously.

I shrugged and waved the allegation off. I dated my share of women although I didn't consider myself to be more of a ladies' man than anybody else. In college Chris had actually done reasonably well with the ladies although his attempts at establishing lasting relationships had a way of falling short. I suspected that the culpability was on Chris's shoulders but it wasn't necessarily always that way.

Chris wasn't doing much with his life. He still talked about wanting to be a pharmacist, as he did during the two years I had known him in college, although I doubted that he ever would. Judging from the way he acted and the way he talked, his life was engulfed with drugs and alcohol. He spoke freely about cocaine and other things he was into. He smoked marijuana on a daily basis, seemed to drink more than I had ever known him to and was generally a mess.

I didn't want to judge Chris harshly. I had my share of indulgences. I wasn't averse to drinking a few beers and I was obviously a cigarette smoker. In college and even during the first part of my WFL career I indulged in marijuana on rare occasions. It was something I looked back on with regret later in life when I finally understood how useless such indulgences are. There is absolutely nothing cool by smoking, drinking and smoking marijuana. There is everything to gain by abstaining from those vices.

As wrong as my indulgences might have been for me, I was a veritable teetotaler compared to Chris. His indulgences seemed to dominate Chris's life. On top of that, he had recently been in a minor accident and was prescribed valium. That didn't mix well with beer and anything else he might have ingested that day. He was not averse to testing the limits of his body's endurance.

"You still surf?" Chris asked as he opened his third beer while I was still on my first.

"I went surfing at Sunset last week. I go a few times a month in the offseason. I'll get fined five-thousand dollars if I get caught surfing at any time between the start of training camp and our final game of the season."

"How come?" Chris asked with a distasteful look on his face.

"They don't want me getting hurt. It'll hurt the team if I get hurt. Once we start training camp I don't have much time for surfing anyway."

Being from Southern California, Chris had surfed in some of the same spots I had in high school. One of our favorite topics of conversation after we first met in 1972 was about our individual experiences at places such as Newport, Huntington, Santa Monica and Malibu. He and I had also gone surfing together a few times in college.

That recollection reminds me of one Sunday early in my final semester as an undergraduate when Chris and I were surfing near Makapu'u Point. Among the other surfers in the area was Donald Stroup; the oceanography professor from the university. I had him as a sophomore but Chris took his course only during the previous semester. That was during his final semester of eligibility when he was making only cameo appearances in the classroom.

I didn't spot Professor Stroup until Chris paddled over to him. The professor was only about 30 feet away.

"Don't you teach oceanography at the university?" I heard Chris ask.

"Uh, yes I do," the bearded professor replied while looking at Chris as if trying to place him. Each oceanography class was comprised of a few hundred students in Spalding Hall. The classroom resembled a movie theater with a capacity of 400. The professor and his graduate assistants addressed the class through a microphone on a stage.

With so many students in the class, there was no way for the professor to recall the overwhelming majority of them. Usually when a professor is spotted by an obscure former student it means that a compliment is coming.

"Ya flunked me, ya bastard," Chris said bitterly and paddled back toward me. I recall wanting to pretend that I had never met Chris in my life and managed to catch a wave before Chris got back to me. Although I doubted that Stroup had any idea of who I was, it was definitely an embarrassing moment that I will probably never forget.

Oceanography grades were based solely on three exams. Somehow it never occurred to Chris that the way to pass those exams was by actually going to class and studying.

But this was Chris. It was never his fault. He was genuinely surprised that he didn't pass the course ostensibly based solely on the merit of his football scholarship. Attendance, taking notes, studying and passing exams were for other students. Chris apparently believed that his work as a tight end for the football team taught him everything he needed to know about oceanography.

Unfortunately for Chris, it didn't work that way. He probably believed that the administration, which had the audacity to insist that Chris do something other than play football to graduate, was in cahoots with the same charlatans who didn't award him automatic induction into the Pro Football Hall of Fame just for being Chris Alexander.

But that was Chris in spades. It was the NFL's loss when Denver cut him and nobody claimed him. In his mind there was probably also a direct correlation between the day the Detroit Wheels let him go and the day the World Football League folded.

Still, Chris had been my friend and a good one at one time. I was reminding myself of that fact in perpetuity as the day wore on. That was probably the only thing that prevented me from excusing myself on the pretext of using the men's room and hightailing it to my car.

At the beach we continued to talk about old times. There were football games we had played, postgame parties at Papa's Pizza on Lewers Street, a gambling scandal that did not involve Chris and me but marred an otherwise outstanding season for the team, some of the people we had known and a few other topics.

Being heterosexual males, we also checked out the female scenery. There didn't seem to be much to look at except for some older military wives with children. It wasn't that they lacked pulchritude but they seemed to be in their 30s and 40s. That was old for two men in their mid-20s.

There was one young lady about ten yards away who bore a certain amount of appeal. She was wearing a red and blue two-piece bathing suit

14

and her long blonde hair was pinned in a bun at the nape. She seemed oblivious to her surroundings, focusing her attention on her paperback book.

Periodically men in the area approached her and tried to win her company. All were politely turned away.

I paid her little mind. Chris, however, seemed to believe she was planted there strictly for him.

"What do you think of her?" Chris asked.

"She's okay," I replied ambivalently. "Not that fantastic, though."

"I'm going to take a shot at her."

I made a sweeping motion with my hand to let Chris know he had my blessing. He grabbed a beer and walked over to her. It was amusing to watch the lady smile politely and shake her head a few times before Chris returned in defeat.

"Well?" I asked wryly.

"Well first I offered her a beer," he began, "and she turned it down. Then I asked her if she wanted to smoke a joint and she turned that down."

"Gee!" I remarked in mock despair. "How could you have struck out after great opening lines like that?"

Chris didn't respond verbally. He made a distasteful face in the direction of the young lady as if to suggest that she had the wrong attitude. To him it was almost as if his opening lines mandated that she immediately discard her clothing, lie on her back and cry out, "Take me, take me!"

From that point on the young woman was pretty well forgotten. Chris and I talked about other issues. There was practically nothing that Chris was currently into that interested me but I dealt with it.

Sometime early that afternoon I suggested we leave. Chris somehow deduced that that was an invitation to spend the afternoon at my place. I had actually still been planning to go to the gym. Instead I reluctantly decided to accommodate Chris.

We picked up our gear. Instead of heading directly to my car, something enigmatic drove me to the young lady. It was as if there was a magnet attached to her that suddenly activated. She was pulling up a pair of cutoff blue jeans as I approached since she was also preparing to leave.

"Excuse me," I said. "Are you a military dependent or something?"

"Eh?"

"Are you a military dependent?" I repeated.

"Oh, no," she replied, looking me over. "I'm here on holiday from Canada."

"Oh? Well maybe you'd like to get together for a drink or something before you go."

"Well, gee. I don't know."

"It's perfectly innocent," I assured her although the words seemed to flow from my mouth without any preconceived thought. I was still surprised that I had approached her at all. "Why don't you give me the name of your hotel and I'll try to give you a call tomorrow? We can talk about it then."

She gave me the name of her hotel and the room number. She said she looked forward to my call.

"Oh, what's your name?" I asked.

"Annica."

"Annica," I repeated as I wrote the information inside a matchbook, very familiar with the name since I had dated a beautiful tourist from Sweden with that name during my junior year at the university. "Scandinavian?"

"Eh?"

"Your name. Are you of Scandinavian ancestry?"

"Oh, yes. My grandparents came over from Sweden."

It was incredibly strange. Earlier I felt relative ambivalence for the pretty young lady. Suddenly I felt a strong attraction to her. My movements and words seemed totally involuntary. It was as if I was fated to spend time with her.

Annica was, I believed, still just another Canadian visitor. Winter was Canadian tourist season in Hawaii since this was their retreat from the cold. In November I had had a very pleasant experience with a lovely young lady named Bonnie from Burnaby, British Columbia that was previously documented. In January I had a pleasant evening with a visitor from Calgary named Karen and another pleasant evening with a nurse from Edmonton named Tamara. Now I find myself about to get to know somebody named Annica from a part of Canada still unknown to me.

"You know that wasn't the first time you did that to me, don't you?" Chris remarked somewhat enviously as I started my car.

"First time I did what?"

"Getting a chick to go out with you after I struck out with her."

"What makes you so sure she'll go out with me?"

"C'mon, Jay. You practically swept her off her feet."

"I don't know about that," I said. "Whatever may have attracted her was in the approach, that's all."

"I guess my approach didn't turn her on," Chris remarked dejectedly.

"I guess not."

"But what was wrong with it?"

"Chris, no halfway decent woman in her right mind is going to fall for a total stranger whose opening line is an offer to share a joint with her. That might have worked five or six years ago but not now."

"I don't see why not."

16

I shook my head. It seemed pointless to try to explain things to him. Chris could be a very thoughtful, compassionate individual. This day was a perpetual reminder that he could also be an overbearing, convoluted pain in the derriere.

On the way to my place we stopped for more beer. That was Chris's idea although the beer wound up being on me. Once again money prevailed over food stamps.

Bill was home when we got there. That made things easier for me. He knew Chris since we had all been teammates and had even shared an off-campus house together. I was glad to see Bill since I didn't feel like putting up with Chris alone.

With the plethora of roommates who came and went at what became known as the Manoa Zoo during our college days, the time when our tenures as housemates overlapped was only about seven or eight months. I was the only one who stayed from the first day in August, 1972, to the final day in December, 1974. Chris was a charter tenant who stayed for about a year and-a-half. Bill didn't move in until April, 1973, and stayed for a little more than a year although he had been a frequent visitor before and after that. During the final six months I actually had the three-bedroom house to myself as I began my pro football career.

The three of us spent a good part of the afternoon talking about old times and the potpourri of people we had known in our undergraduate days. Most of those who hung out at the Manoa Zoo were athletes although not all were football players. Those who didn't play football were on the baseball or basketball teams and there were also some non-athletes who hung out.

And, of course, there was no shortage of girls who stopped by. It wasn't as if we were staging orgies although there were wild rumors of such. We simply had several females as friends who stopped by as well as those who were girlfriends.

For that matter, there was an assortment of non-students who stopped by. The place had a very magnetic effect. There was a period when the Manoa Zoo was practically an unincorporated state landmark.

One of the more interesting, if not blatantly pathetic, characters to reside at the Manoa Zoo for the first few months of 1973 was a slender individual from Wisconsin named Mike Fisher. He was a good student who knew very little about sports although he professed to be an authority on virtually everything. He worked as an aide for the football team during my junior and senior years and received a tuition waiver even though he professed to come from a very affluent family.

Mike, like the rest of us, liked to party and did fit in in that respect. Nobody as far as I could tell looked down on him for not being athletic although he seemed to feel inferior to the jocks and always tried to play himself up. He chronically lied about being personal friends with a plethora

17

of celebrities including several members of the Green Bay Packers and Milwaukee Brewers, owning luxury vehicles, summers in Europe and, especially, being irresistible to the opposite sex. He was notorious for disappearing overnight on occasion and then coming back with tales about a comely female who appeared out of nowhere and invited him to spend the night with her.

The fact is, Mike was a good looking guy who was usually fun to have around. He also dressed well and was very intelligent. Through all of his fabrications I could see another side to him. Unlike Chris and others I knew, he was very serious about academics. I had to give him that much credit.

Mike's biggest flaw was his mouth. He was a veritable megalomaniac who not only lied about his own alleged glories, he would also tell lies about people behind their backs.

"I really wish that we had told Jerry we would have liked him fine just the way he was," I offered somewhat somberly during the course of the conversation with Chris and Bill. "He would have been okay had he been willing to simply be himself."

Mike graduated one semester after I did. The last we heard at that point, he was attending the University of Michigan as a graduate student and had married a girl from his hometown.

At least that is what somebody had heard through 1977. With Jerry we could never be totally sure. All of his convoluted lies made him a veritable pest.

An interesting footnote to this is I encountered Mike Fisher a few years after this conversation took place. While I was in Green Bay to play the Packers, Mike found out where the team was staying and contacted me.

Although I was apprehensive, I agreed to meet with him and was pleasantly surprised by how he had turned out. He had earned a master's degree from the University of Michigan and was inching his way toward his doctorate. At the time he was teaching political science at a community college not too far from Green Bay.

The story of Mike's marriage to his hometown sweetheart also turned out to be very true. I was very happy to meet the former Carlene McGregor who had known Mike when she was two years behind him in high school although they never dated then. She was a very congenial, petite young woman with long dark brown hair. She had given birth to their son a few months before and later added two daughters.

During a private moment between Mike and me he expressed his remorse for his exaggerations in Hawaii. He admitted that part of his motivation was the way he felt insecure while hanging around the athletes he had gotten to know. He had learned to be content by simply being himself.

Of course I forgave him. I was only too happy to befriend Mike Fisher now that he was content to be himself. I got together with him and his family whenever I played in Green Bay and saw them in Hawaii when they came to visit.

Getting back to the subject of pests, Chris accompanied me to the University of Hawaii basketball game after inviting himself along. That meant, of course, that I was buying his ticket since it wasn't *Food Stamp Night* at the Blaisdell Arena.

Had Chris not invited himself along I wouldn't even have had to purchase my own ticket since I had a media pass. Being the gracious host, I purchased two tickets to ensure that we had seats together. It was tempting to buy just his and use my media pass to sit in the press box without him.

Nah, I thought. We were having our reunion for this one day and then we could go our separate ways. This day was his. Tomorrow I could get my life back.

The Rainbows played a good game. The basketball program was about to go on two-years' probation because of some infractions uncovered a year earlier so the team was struggling with the exodus of the previous team. The team still clicked on rare occasions and on this night appeared almost unbeatable.

That's the way it was for the Rainbows' 1976-77 season. There were nights when everything fell into place and nights when everybody shot bricks. Being a loyal alumnus, I continued my support. Unfortunately history eventually showed that things would get worse before they would get better.

"Hey, there's Franco Harris," Chris pointed out brightly during the contest.

"Where?" I asked cynically.

"Over there on the right."

I thought that the beer and valium and whatever else Chris had ingested was causing him to hallucinate but he turned out to be right. Sitting on the floor section a few rows from the court was the Steeler running back I actually felt honored to have somebody of his stature watching my alma mater's basketball team.

"Why don't we go talk to him?" Chris suggested.

"Why? You don't know him."

"But you do."

"I do not. We haven't played the Steelers yet. I've never met him."

"Okay but I'll bet he knows who you are. You should go introduce yourself to him so we can talk to him."

Whether Harris knew who I was or not, I didn't know and didn't really care. Somewhere in the future we would meet on the gridiron. On this night I was content to leave him alone and allow him to enjoy the basketball game. There was no sense in having two active NFL players suffering by being in Chris's presence. I would handle that ignominious task for both of us. Franco could thank me later.

Chris enjoyed the game. Our seats were behind one of the baskets near the Rainbows' entrance to their locker room since I wasn't about to spring for more expensive seats for Chris's benefit. When the game ended in favor of Hawaii he ran over to the area close to the locker room entrance and slapped the players on the back as they passed.

It had been an exceptionally good game so some of the players didn't mind the pats on the back. A few of them even accepted Chris's handshakes. A few others bore understandably puzzled looks as if they were wondering who the exuberant lunatic was.

I made it a point to keep my distance during this exhibition. I was also wondering who the exuberant lunatic was. He bore some resemblance to somebody I had known a few years earlier but I could no longer be sure. For all of his flaws in college, he was impeccable then compared to what he had become.

CHAPTER TWO
Carol

I couldn't get Chris home soon enough. Once I had gotten him to his abode I retreated to mine and heaved a sigh of relief that my very long day with him was over. My patience had been tested to the max.

Bill had to work early in the morning so he had already gone to bed by the time I got home. Despite the fact that I was exhausted after getting virtually no sleep the night before, I took advantage of the fact that I had the living room to myself. I spent some time reading and thinking about the day's events.

Primarily I thought about Chris. I was ambivalent about seeing him again. He had been a close friend at one time but not anymore. I still didn't want to simply abandon him.

Just the same, he seemed to be out of control. I didn't feel that I could associate with him if he was going to run amok with his drug use. Even the prescribed valium was something he seemed to be taking recreationally and carelessly. He even tried to persuade me to take some earlier that day.

Perhaps this day's reunion was it. I may have turned him off when I refused to smoke marijuana with him. He seemed very surprised and possibly even appalled when I told him I no longer engaged in the vice. I had tried it a few times during my junior and senior years of high school and indulged a little more often in college, including several times with Chris, but that was all behind me at this juncture.

Regardless, I had no intention of initiating further contact with Chris. I figured I would try to be kind while keeping my distance. I was definitely not going to alter my plans for his whimsical demands again. The world may have owed him a life of prosperity but I didn't owe him a thing.

As I lit a cigarette I noticed the name and hotel information of the young lady I had met earlier that day written inside the matchbook I was using. At least my reunion with Chris hadn't been a total waste of time. The next day I would probably call this Canadian Aphrodite who'd said she was looking forward to my call. It amused me to recall that my former college teammate had crashed and burned in his attempt to woo her before I fared a little better.

Being a reasonably normal heterosexual male, I was always attracted to beautiful women. During the basketball game I spent time watching the Rainbow cheerleaders going through their routines. There definitely were some attractive ladies on the squad. If a game was boring, as some of them were this season, especially when UCLA castoff Gavin Smith's shooting went cold, I could always check out the cheerleaders.

That brought back memories of the relationship I'd had with a cheerleader a few years earlier. Carol Jeanne Lafayette was, to me, the epitome of pulchritude. In laymen's terms, she was "a fox" although there was a lot more to her than that. What augmented her physical appeal was that she was even more beautiful on the inside. She was a very virtuous, intelligent young woman.

I went into my bedroom and opened the drawer of my nightstand and pulled out a framed 8x10 photo of Carol. This was something she had taken specifically for me shortly before I went to my first pro football training camp in Riverside, California. She was leaning against a palm tree at Maunalua Bay with her long golden blonde hair blowing in the breeze. Her smile displayed a perfect set of teeth. Her mere being defined virtue in the most veritable sense.

Carol and I met near the end of summer school prior to my senior and her sophomore year at the University of Hawaii. She was Canadian; born in Vancouver and raised in White Rock, British Columbia, until she and her family moved to Hawaii when she was 14. Her family was Catholic although not especially active in the faith. She lived in the Hawaii Kai section of Honolulu and went to the Catholic Maryknoll High School prior to entering the University of Hawaii.

I have to admit to having felt insecure about being with a girl like Carol. From the moment I met her she seemed too good to be true. In the early stage of our relationship I couldn't accept the notion that she was sincere. I figured that a nice virtuous girl like her was going to dump a jaded guy like me at any moment.

That, of course, was very stupid and self-defeating. I still couldn't seem to be able to help considering Carol to be very much out of my league. I simply wasn't sure of how to handle being in a relationship with somebody like her and didn't know what to expect. Dating back to when I was about eleven, I had been with countless females for various lengths of time but had never really had a serious relationship. I had played the hand I believed I had been dealt by portraying a hustler out for a good time. I had the confidence to pick up girls. I did not have the confidence to delve into a relationship for an extended length of time.

Making this epic even more stupid, I was so convinced that Carol was going to kiss me off that I eventually slept around a little. I may have gotten good grades in the classroom but it was obvious that I wasn't always smart. My pride superseded my determination to work at making our relationship successful. I rationalized to myself that my infidelity would ease the pain when Carol decided to terminate the relationship like I figured she would do.

It would come as no surprise that my infidelity was what almost destroyed an otherwise ideal relationship. The entire matter came to a head after a football game less than two months after Carol and I first met.

22

I had had a good first half. I caught five passes for 98 yards and a touchdown. I had also rushed three times for 17 yards.

At halftime the opposing coach ostensibly assigned a man to stick to me like a magnet during the second half. No matter where I lined up, he was directly opposite.

It wasn't that I was being defended that caused a stir. It was that the defender was employing illegal tactics to keep me under control. He was apparently trying to see how much he could get away with without being penalized. Since the officials acted as if they were oblivious to the whole thing he was able to get away with a lot.

"Watch number 45," I told an official after one play. "He's holding."

That was putting it mildly. My opponent was grabbing my jersey, trying to trip me, grabbing my facemask and doing whatever else he felt like trying to get away with doing. He had a subtle way of committing these infractions but the officials still should have noticed. Hawaii's coaching staff sure noticed and was hollering about it so the officials should also have noticed. I later learned that the play-by-play announcer was talking about it so it was even obvious in the press box which was located at the top of the bleachers.

Midway through the third quarter I rushed around right end. My nemesis made a clean tackle, then planted his knee into my gut as he got up.

"Don't tell me you didn't see that," I said, gasping since the defender had knocked the wind out of me.

"See what?" the official countered. He was either blind, stupid or an alumnus of the other school. When one of our coaches suggested exactly that to him he finally threw up his yellow flag. We were nailed for unsportsmanlike conduct.

Toward the end of the quarter we were driving. I started out on a post pattern when this defensive back suddenly stuck his arm out and clotheslined me. He actually swung his arm in such a manner that his fist went right into my throat, knocking me flat on my back.

I slowly got up. I also knew that I had reached my breaking point. The smart thing to do would have been to take myself out of the game until I had cooled off. When one is as angry as I was the smart thing is rarely considered.

On the very next play, which was a sweep around left end on the opposite side of where I had formed up, I was off like a shot at the snap. I ran directly toward the defender and gave him a left uppercut to the jaw. He went down in a heap.

"Play right!" I barked as I hovered over him, pointing my finger down at him as he laid quivering on the ground. "Play right or get the hell out of the game!"

Unfortunately it was me who was getting out of the game. The yellow flag at my feet was thrown in my honor. The 15-yard penalty for unnecessary roughness nullified our 12-yard gain. I was also ejected; relegated to the bench for the remainder of the game.

As soon as I realized that I was ejected I went ballistic for all present at Honolulu Stadium to see. My colorful vernacular led to another yellow flag. An additional 15 yards was being tacked on for unsportsmanlike conduct.

Angrily I slowly walked off the field as I worked on regaining my poise. Carol, who was behind the bench with her cheerleading colleagues, was looking down at the ground. She had to have seen what I was going through.

Suddenly Carol raised her head. She was looking straight at me with eyes that appeared to be shooting knives. The beautiful emerald-colored eyes that could normally light up the darkest of nights were suddenly not the least bit enticing.

"Don't take it so hard, chickie," I muttered sarcastically to myself. "It's not your problem."

I disregarded Carol. I sat on the bench and focused on *watching* the rest of the game.

One of the coaches came over and, in a very non-judgmental way, asked me how I was doing. He understood what I had been through but he didn't want any more trouble. He instructed me to leave the field as quickly as possible after the game. The coaching staff didn't want any confrontations with the other team.

And so I immediately left the field after the final gun. I didn't sprint off but I also didn't walk. I simply wanted to get away from Honolulu Stadium as quickly as possible and put the entire incident behind me. The only consolation was that we did actually win the game to remain undefeated.

I took a long hot shower and felt a little better. I eschewed the inquiring sportswriters the best I could with "no comment" being the most profound reply they could get from me. I didn't want coverage of the incident to supersede the actual game. I was hoping they wouldn't say anything at all but I knew it would get at least a blurb.

After I got dressed I left the locker room determined to have a pleasant evening with Carol. Chris Alexander asked me if I was going to Papa's Pizza where a large part of the team congregated after a game but I declined in favor of something more private with Carol. I figured I might have to answer for my action at practice on Monday but I still had what little was left of Saturday and all day Sunday to enjoy life. Nothing appealed to me more than Carol did.

Outside the locker room I looked for Carol. She wasn't chatting with the other girls in the area the way she normally did. When I finally spotted her she was standing with her back to me near the exit which led to Isenberg Street.

"Careful, Jaybird," my teammate and 1977 roommate Bill Trimble warned discreetly. "She's really pissed."

24

"She is? At me?" I inquired, surprised.

"Who else?"

That made no sense. My actions were totally provoked.

"That's stupid. The guy was getting away with murder out there. She ought to be angry at him and the officials."

"I know."

"Some of us tried to talk to her," added Sandy, a cute blonde political science major who was dating Bill at the time. "I think deep down she understands but she's too upset."

I looked apprehensively at Carol as she remained frozen by the gate. I figured I could simply explain everything to her, or so I hoped. With her cheerleading obligations it seemed possible that she never saw what precipitated my action.

"What can I say?" I said to Bill and Sandy and a few others in the area. "It's my problem. I'll deal with it."

As I headed toward Carol a few more of my teammates looked at me with expressions that seemed to be either pitying me or wishing me luck. The fact that I had an angry girlfriend seemed to be the worst kept secret in Honolulu.

"Ready to go?" I asked Carol nonchalantly in a clumsy attempt to defuse the situation.

Carol said nothing. She handed me the key to my car and briskly walked ahead of me to where she had parked it in the lot behind the stadium. Since I was required to spend Friday night and all day Saturday sequestered with the team before each game I always let her take my green 1967 Volkswagen home with her after school on Friday. That way the vehicle would be there for a quick getaway after the game.

I opened the passenger door. Carol got in without a word before I went around to the driver's side. She still hadn't even looked at me or acknowledged in any way that I existed.

"That was a stupid thing to do!" she barked as soon as I was seated and about to close my door.

"What are you talking about?" I asked calmly in a futile attempt to extinguish Carol's fire.

"You know darn well what I'm talking about!"

"No. I can't say that I do."

"Getting yourself thrown out of the game, as if you didn't know. Way to go, smart guy!"

"Carol, if you let me explain I'd. . . ."

"You don't have to explain anything to me, creep!"

"Watch whom you're calling a creep," I retorted, starting to lose my patience.

"I'll call you anything I want, creep!"

I didn't respond. I knew that one of us had to get things under control and I was certain it wasn't going to be her. I had to find a way to maintain my composure. That meant pausing to collect myself when I felt myself getting angry.

Name-calling was not Carol's style. She was a very virtuous young lady who rarely spoke ill of anybody. She even found nice things to say about President Nixon as a person even though she disliked him as a politician. The name-calling was simply indicative of how upset she was.

We sat in silence for several minutes. The only sounds to be heard were faint sounds of pins being knocked down at the bowling alley behind us on the other end of the parking lot.

"Carol, I'm probably going to catch hell for this at practice on Monday. I don't need it from you, too."

"Why not?" she asked sharply. "You deserve it."

"Look!" I snapped, starting to lose my patience again. "The guy was obviously planted to do whatever he could get away with doing. I had a fairly good first half so they put this guy in the game to go one-on-one with me. Wherever I lined up, he was there. He grabbed my shirt, he tried to trip me, he clotheslined me with his fist and he kneed me in the gut once after he tackled me. Am I supposed to let him get away with all that? I suppose you'd be happier if the guy paralyzed me."

"If you were half as smart as you obviously think you are you would have told the referee."

Carol still hadn't looked at me. That was annoying, to say the least. Although it would have been totally out of character for her, I wondered if she was getting some type of sadistic pleasure out of refusing to consider my position. I had no idea of how badly she was hurting inside over this which, as it turned out, merely exacerbated another issue that had yet to be broached.

Carol suddenly lurched forward. She placed her face in her hands.

"Oh, cher Dieu," she said softly as if in prayer. "Pourquoi est-ce que j'ai avoir un homme si malade?"

Carol and I had been together for about two months. Obviously there were a lot of things I didn't know about her.

Like the fact that she was fluent in French.

Perhaps I should have known. It made sense since her parents were both born and raised in Quebec. I simply never gave it any thought. She was also close to fluent in German but this was the first time I had ever heard her speak anything but English. This French monologue continued for a long moment.

Of course there were several things that Carol didn't know about me.

Like the fact that I was also fluent in French and understood every word that she said. Whether she had spoken French consciously or not, I didn't know. What she had done was utter a somewhat frantic prayer to God. As she did so you can bet that she wasn't thanking Him for my presence in her life. She was actually dressing me down to Him.

Carol's monologue in French was something I found amusing since she apparently believed she was insulting me without my knowledge. I had to practically bite my lip off to keep from laughing out loud. I actually considered responding in French, then thought better of it.

"By the way, I think you should know that I did tell the ref but he ignored me," I said in a calm manner that was probably uncharacteristic for somebody who had just been insulted in a foreign tongue. "He said he never saw anything even though I'm sure he was lying. The coaches and several other people saw it and were trying to point out what this guy was doing so how was it that he could claim that he didn't see anything? I'm sorry for what I did and for the way it hurt you but I'm even more sorry that you won't even listen."

Silence!

Cold silence!

It was annoying. Carol simply sat silent and stared out the windshield.

"If you don't want to have anything to do with me like it seems, why are you sitting in my car?" I asked dejectedly. "Why didn't you ride home with your family?"

"They went to Maui for the weekend. I guess that was too much for you to remember. Isn't it nice that they have athletic scholarships so that Neanderthals can go to college without the benefit of brains?"

"Well excuse me, your majesty. Couldn't you have taken the bus? Or would it have betrayed your bourgeois image if you'd been seen utilizing public transportation?"

My remark was unkind but I wasn't taking it back. She wasn't the one who initially stuck the dagger in me but she was definitely twisting it. I didn't have to take the verbal abuse.

Carol remained silent for a moment until she could no longer contain herself and started to cry. It baffled me that my iniquity could have upset her as much as it seemed to. I was about to find out that this was a mere drop in the bucket. There was a lot more to this than a simple uppercut on the gridiron.

"You're nothing, Dockman," she sobbed. "When I first started dating you somebody told me you were no good but I didn't listen. I was told that all you cared about were sports, sex and parties. I didn't believe it but now I think I do. That's okay for you because next year you'll probably be playing professional football or baseball and you'll become a big star and. . . . "

"What's wrong with being a professional athlete?" I asked.

"Nothing! Seriously nothing! But that's all you'll ever be. There's so much more to life than that but you don't care about the things that really count."

That hurt. I didn't believe it was true although, in retrospect, perhaps I did come across as being a little too full of myself back then. I was young and my life often did revolve around sports so maybe it was simply a matter of not fully comprehending what was truly important. I wasn't necessarily insensitive to those things although I probably wasn't as sensitive as I should have been.

"I've stuck by you," she added meekly as tears descended from her eyes. My heart honestly broke for her. I wanted to reach out to try to comfort her but I was afraid she would push me away and arouse my ire again. "I've been loyal to you even though it's given me a reputation that I don't need and. . . ."

"You don't have a reputation."

"Don't be so sure. Yesterday I was in Kuykendall Hall waiting for my English lit class when I heard some guys talking about some of the football players and their girlfriends. They were in the men's room but I could hear them out in the hall and so could everybody else. One guy said, and I quote, 'Dockman's screwing that blonde on the cheerleading squad.'"

I recalled her downtrodden feelings after her English lit class the day before. Prior to then I had walked her to Kuykendall Hall and she had been in extremely upbeat spirits. Although she had tried to hide it, I could tell when I saw her afterward that something was upsetting her.

"Actually he didn't exactly say that you were screwing me," she added. "He used a verb that was much cruder. I just can't use that word."

The fact is, Carol and I had never had sex together. I suspected that she was a virgin although neither or us ever broached the subject. I found out later that my suspicions were correct.

"Is that what was wrong with you yesterday afternoon?" I asked, having gently tried to persuade her to open up and she tried to convince me that a test she had just taken drained her more than anticipated. I didn't believe her but I didn't pursue the matter any further.

Carol nodded.

"Why didn't you tell me?" I asked.

"What good would it have done?"

"I don't know. But I care about you. I need to know about something like this. You were violated."

Carol didn't respond. She appeared puzzled about something.

"Who said it? I'll kill him."

"No you won't," Carol replied in a somewhat exasperated voice. "It doesn't matter. It wasn't a football player so don't go interrogating your teammates. Just let it go. I can live with it since I know the truth. It doesn't matter."

"What do you mean it doesn't matter,'?" I asked strongly. "Nobody has the right to talk about you like that. There's no excuse for it."

Once again Carol said nothing. I was wondering if she was blaming me.

"I never said anything that would make somebody say something like that."

"I'm sure you didn't," she agreed, sounding sincere but still upset. "I know you wouldn't say something like that."

It had to have been Mike Fisher. As soon as she quoted the offending phrase I could vividly hear the words coming out of his mouth. If that weren't enough, the fact that she knew it wasn't a football player indicated that she recognized the voice.

Fisher had a class in Kuykendall Hall at the same time as Carol's English lit class. There was a plethora of circumstantial evidence against him that I considered to be overwhelming.

"I don't want you to pursue this any further," she insisted. "I appreciate your willingness to defend me but it's not necessary. That remark is not what's wrong now anyway."

I was willing to more than simply defend her. I was even willing to die for her if it came to that. At the moment it seemed as if I was going to die *because* of her . . . and what did she mean by the last remark?

"I'm also sorry for what I said about your athletic scholarship," she continued. "You're a good student because you work hard academically and I admire you for that but I don't know if you're going to amount to anything outside of sports."

"Why do you say that?"

"I don't know," she replied. "I don't even know what kind of a boyfriend you are or if you even want to be my boyfriend. I've stood by you even though you've been to bed with other girls and. . . ."

"What makes you think I've been to bed with other girls?"

"Well you're not exactly discreet about it," she replied almost frantically, looking at me for the first time. I noticed the redness in her eyes from crying. "You know that hot dog place across from the university?"

"Lum's?" I responded evenly, knowing I was busted as soon as she referred to that particular establishment.

"Yes, Lum's," she said firmly. "It's very popular with students, as you so obviously know, and you've been picking up girls there and leaving with them to . . . to do what you do with loose girls."

This explained a lot. I suddenly felt like a blithering idiot.

"So you were on my case because of something I did on the football field when what's really bothering you is that I was with one or two other girls."

"You've been with more than one or two," she retorted, "but that's not what's bothering me. What bothers me is that I believed it was possible you wouldn't turn out to be what I was told you were but apparently I was wrong . . . and . . . and I feel like a total fool for giving you the benefit of the doubt. You are what you are and if that makes you happy. . . ."

She couldn't continue. She was crying too hard. I realized that I had seen things solely from my own perspective. I hadn't been able to accept the possibility that I might actually have mattered to Carol and that my extracurricular actions were hurting her. Beneath the cocksure facade of a reasonably good student-athlete lurked an individual considerably less self-confident and lacking in common sense.

Eventually I found out that this dilemma had been building up inside Carol for quite some time. One cynical friend of hers whom I had yet to meet had been observing my antics at Lum's and reporting them to her. The friend seemed to be getting sadistic pleasure out of this after previously insisting that I would do what I wound up doing.

Carol opted not to act impulsively when pondering what to do about me. She had even consulted a priest a few days earlier; a priest I happened to know although Carol didn't know that I knew him until the priest told her. She ultimately decided that on this very evening she would broach the subject of my infidelity in a rational manner, feeling it was time to lay down a few ground rules about fidelity while also being willing to forgive me.

That was the plan, anyway. Seeing the way I was being handled during the second half of the football game upset her considerably. My retaliation simply turned out to be what finally ignited her fuse.

For the record, I had only cheated on Carol three times although there were other times Carol's friend had observed me leaving with coeds but all I was doing in those cases was giving them rides to their homes or dorms. My infidelity was something that only began recently but that justifies nothing. Once would have been too many. I had something positively wonderful in my life and didn't want to blow it. I was kicking myself for having been so stupid.

We sat silently for several minutes. I truly felt for Carol, hating myself for what I had put her through. She had actually believed in me for reasons I could not comprehend. She was, I reasoned, the best thing that ever happened to me. My own insecurity convinced me that I was going to lose her anyway so I did exactly what could have been defined as sabotaging my own opportunity for veritable romantic bliss.

I figured that nothing was going to be resolved on this night. At least she seemed more composed and was no longer crying. I believed she could drive home okay. I took the ignition key off the ring and placed it in the ignition.

"Drive home carefully," I directed and quickly took off on foot before she could respond, cutting through Moiliili Field which was on King Street diagonally across from the stadium so that she wouldn't be able to follow me in the car. I even stayed for several minutes to make sure she wouldn't be waiting for me on the Beretania Street side.

I didn't go home right away but stopped instead at the university. I spent an hour or two sitting on a bench outside Kuykendall Hall which had been a favorite meditation spot for me dating back almost to the day that I officially became a student at the university. It was ideal because I could sit on a bench by the vending machines while enjoying a view of the Waikiki skyline. Perhaps out of self-pity I bought too many cups of coffee from the vending machine and smoked too many cigarettes while pondering my dilemma.

The other inhabitants of the Manoa Zoo went to Makapu'u Beach early the following morning. They requested my company but I politely declined. I stayed home by myself and watched NFL football on TV although I didn't pay much attention to it. I wanted to be there in case Carol came by or called. I knew she would return my car but was that the end of the line for us? I worried about the possibility of losing her.

Early that afternoon I answered a knock at the front door. It was Carol. She was wearing a brightly colored dress. Although she wasn't an especially active Catholic, she went to church that morning and took Holy Communion while in search of spiritual strength and guidance.

"Can we talk?" she asked softly. There was a pleading look in her eyes.

And so we talked. Somehow we found the maturity to agree to erase any negatives from the past and move forward. It turned out we had both been plagued by trepidation and handled those things in our own ways.

We simply hadn't communicated. We both vowed to change that. I swore that I would never again allow my insecurities to cause me to cheat on her.

That meant total abstinence from what most people my age believed was extremely important back then. Although we didn't discuss this, I knew that Carol wasn't ready to surrender her virtue and I was more than okay with that. Those who had known me would have found it impossible to believe that I was abstaining from sex had they known but that wasn't going to be my problem.

What mattered to Carol and me was simply being together and being grateful for what we had. If I had been given a choice between a harem of every other attractive female on campus or a monogamous relationship with Carol it would have been an easy choice. I was content with Carol.

I suppose it may have been after the first practice following my infamous uppercut that I came to truly understand how significant the little things are. We practiced on Cooke Field while the cheerleaders practiced on the track surrounding the field. The workout was light and without pads since it was the first workout after a game.

The cheerleaders broke up their practice shortly before ours ended. Carol stayed and sat on the bottom row of wooden bleachers, meaning she was present when the team met at midfield for the workout's final words before "Everybody but Dockman" was dismissed.

As Carol sat on the sideline I dealt with my nonjudicial punishment. I ran a series of sprints, grass drills and other physical exercises designed to discourage me from repeating my infraction.

I wasn't happy about having Carol witnessing my punishment although her presence served as a reminder that there was a better side of life waiting for me. The coaches weren't happy about my being punished in front of her since they were not trying to humiliate me. One of the coaches sat with her for a few minutes and explained to her that the staff had preferred not to levy any punishment at all since I had merely responded to some flagrant rule violations which had been ignored by the officials. The coaches felt like they had to do something since my act was witnessed by so many people including one prudish member of the Board of Regents who tried to persuade the coaches to kick me off the team. There was a lot of pressure on the coaches to do something. This way they could say they took care of the situation and let the matter drop.

Eventually I was excused after getting a very compassionate talking to by the coaching staff. I went to the bleachers and sat next to Carol.

"Did you enjoy that?" I asked, trying to be jocular but that was probably shielded by how weary I was.

Carol simply reminded me that the ordeal was over. As I noticed how profusely I was perspiring, as one is apt to do while working out in Hawaii's humidity, Carol reached behind her. She opened a small ice chest she had hidden behind her and presented me with an ice cold bottle of Gatorade.

"Where'd this come from?" I asked.

"I just twitched my nose and there it was," she replied lightly. It was a seemingly frivolous gesture that really wasn't frivolous at all. Just the fact that she thought of something like that meant more than one can describe.

But that was Carol. She gave from the heart and only wanted what came from the heart. I could buy out an entire jewelry store and it wouldn't have meant a thing to her if my heart wasn't in it. If I took a few seconds to pick her a simple flower she would effervesce with gratitude. She epitomized the notion that it was the thought that counted.

From that point on we had a very warm and loving relationship. Our class schedules ran almost simultaneous so that was convenient. We often got together for liquid refreshment between classes. We also spent several hours studying together, especially for finals and midterms, and quizzed each other. We also enjoyed picnics, drive-in movies, trips to the ice cream store, watching television, going to the beach and simply being together.

I also got along very well with Carol's parents and two younger sisters. It was even Carol's father who had introduced us although I am not certain that he intended to plant the seed for a romantic relationship. He accepted me and was never unkind, as opposed to fathers of other girls I had encountered who eyed me suspiciously as if I perpetually had carnal desires on my mind. He trusted Carol and, however ill-advised it might have been with the reputation I allegedly had, he trusted me. In the Lafayette household I was always treated like one of the family.

Later in the football season I ran a cross pattern during the first half of a game at Honolulu Stadium. The pass was high so I had to leap up to get it. As I was getting my hands on the ball a defensive back hit me below the waist, causing me to pinwheel over and land on my head before rolling over on my back. It wasn't a malicious hit but I was in a vulnerable position. As a defensive back in high school and college freshman I had made a few hits like that myself.

I was momentarily unconscious. When I opened my eyes I was looking in the face of the team trainer who was kneeling over me. Behind him were what seemed like about a thousand concerned faces but were actually only a handful belonging to Coach Dave Holmes and a few teammates. Behind them were the stadium lights.

"Move your feet," the trainer instructed.

"Wha'," was my groggy response.

"Wiggle your feet," he said.

I was barely coherent enough to understand what he wanted. I wiggled my feet back and forth while the trainer looked relieved. I was still too groggy at the time to understand that he was checking me for paralysis.

The trainer held his hand up.

"How many fingers do you see?" he asked.

"All I see is the lights," I replied.

He shifted his position to block the lights with his body and then repeated the question.

"Uh, three?" I answered although to this day I have no idea how many fingers he was showing.

"Okay, we're going to send you to Queen's to get checked out."

"Where?"

Before I could inquire further I found myself being placed on a stretcher and into an ambulance that I didn't notice had pulled up on the field. I was told that the fans at the game and even my teammates and some of my opponents gave me a nice round of applause as I was being placed in the ambulance although I didn't notice. At that moment I barely knew my name and where I was.

A doctor in the emergency room at Queen's Hospital checked me out. I was diagnosed with a mild concussion but no other injuries. I was told that I needed to take it easy for a few days but would be okay to play in our game the following week, pending clearance from the team medical staff.

When I walked out to the waiting area of the emergency room I wasn't sure if I should have been surprised to see Carol there. She had gotten permission to scrub her cheerleading duties and ran all the way to where she had parked my car to follow me to Queen's although she said she would have left even without permission. What did surprise me was seeing

Carol's family there. They were at the game and left to travel to Queen's as soon as I was taken away. Carol's youngest sister Denise even cried when I was placed in the ambulance.

"Are you okay, honey?" Carol asked as soon as I appeared, wrapping her arms around my waist while undaunted by the white t-shirt I was wearing that was still moist from perspiration while I carried my green game jersey with my shoulder pads inside. The amorous term she used was a first for either of us although I loved the sound of it and it would become a regular part of our vernacular.

"I'm okay," I replied gratefully, returning the embrace with my free arm.

"You gave us quite a scare," Carol's dad remarked.

I looked at Carol's family gratefully as I released my embrace. At that moment I noticed Denise. Although she had stopped crying, I noticed the redness of her eyes and there was still some moisture on her cheeks.

"Hey, you don't have to worry about me," I said compassionately.

"It really shook her up," Carol's mom replied.

"Ah, I didn't mean to do that," I answered, gently stroking Denise's hair as she cracked a weak smile. "I really appreciate your concern, though. I need fans like you."

Although an official from the athletic department was present to get a report on me and transport me back to the stadium if I wasn't being held for observation, I rode back with Carol. It was my car but I didn't feel like driving. As we were getting on the H-1 Freeway I told Carol how surprised I was to see her family in the emergency room.

"Why?" she replied somewhat curtly. "Haven't you noticed the way everybody treats you when you come by? You're like a member of the family. Did you really expect them to just sit in the stadium and calmly watch the game after you were taken away in an ambulance?"

Suddenly I felt very stupid. The flagrantly obvious hadn't set in until that moment, I guess.

It was Christmas that provided one of the most poignant experiences of my relationship with Carol and her family. It actually began a few days earlier when I agreed to take Carol to the Sears at the Ala Moana Center so that she could buy a new dress for Midnight Mass. I figured that it would be a very expeditious process since my idea of a shopping spree was finding a pair of blue jeans or shirt that I liked, trying it on and then making my purchase in less than a half-hour. With Carol I finally understood why my sister was gone for about two or three hours and sometimes more whenever my mom took her to a local shopping mall to purchase clothing. The larger the purchase, the longer the excursion.

Carol carefully sifted through the dresses on the rack. Some she passed on quickly while others she studied meticulously. Occasionally she would take one off the rack that she deemed "in the running" and hold it in front of her in front of a mirror, then turn and ask me how I thought she looked.

"Fine, I guess," was my lethargic response each time. As far as I was concerned, Carol would have looked beautiful if she was dressed in burlap.

Rather than take umbrage, Carol always smiled somewhat teasingly. She seemed to be enjoying my insouciant attitude. By this time we were secure enough in our relationship that we could tease each other as long as we didn't take it too far. Since I was very befuddled but not angry, Carol seized the opportunity.

Eventually she narrowed her selection down to three dresses. She took them to the fitting room to try the dresses on while I felt conspicuous standing by myself in the women's section. Even that process seemed to take forever as Carol meticulously inspected each dress in the mirror while she was wearing it before coming out, doing a slow pirouette and asking my opinion before getting my typical insouciant response.

Finally, miraculously before the store closed, Carol decided on a dress that satisfied her. It was a peach-colored long sleeve pleated dress with a floral pattern, collar and belt.

Much to my surprise, once Carol had purchased the dress she announced that she had to go purchase shoes that matched the dress. When we got to the shoe section she very quickly found a pair of medium heels that matched the dress perfectly, pointing out her selection to the high school-aged male working that day. He very quickly measured Carol's foot, then went into the back to find a pair in Carol's size. Carol tried them on and made her purchase, meaning only about a ten minute visit to the shoe department.

"Just like that?" I asked in mock sarcasm. "Don't you want to check out every pair in the place first? There's some white tennis shoes over there that might go good with the dress. I think they might also have a pair of cowboy boots that you'll like."

"That won't be necessary," Carol replied lightly. "I don't like to spend a lot of time shopping."

"Oh," I said in mock weariness.

Feeling somewhat relieved that I no longer felt incarcerated at Sears, Carol and I stopped at Coco's Coffee Shop for lunch. That was when I found out that Midnight Mass would not be complete for Carol unless I went with her. Fortunately I had a hole card.

"I have to work on Christmas Eve," I pointed out since I would be tending bar at the Rose And Crown like I had done over the summer before football workouts began.

"But you get off at eleven o'clock that night," she retorted.

"I'm not a Catholic."

"You don't have to be Catholic. You know that I rarely go to church but Midnight Mass has always been very special to me. It is a very special observance of the birth of Our Savior and it would mean the world to me if you would go with me."

I said nothing. I didn't have a suitable response. I could understand Carol extending the invitation but I couldn't understand why she was so adamant when I politely declined. It was just a church service that she liked to attend.

"It will mean a lot to Father McBride if you go," Carol added.

That got my attention. Father Gerald McBride was a priest from a parish near the university. I knew him because it wasn't unusual to find him watching the football team practice. He was a very gregarious man in his mid-40s and one I enjoyed talking to on many occasions.

"You know Father McBride?" I asked.

"Yes and I happen to know that you do, too. I've known for a couple of months now."

Carol explained that she and her family first knew Father McBride when they were still up in Canada. He was actually their parish priest and had baptized Carol and her two sisters when they were infants. He also administered the first Holy Communions to Carol and her sister Michelle before transferring out of the parish to a locale unknown to the Lafayettes.

After the Lafayettes moved to Hawaii in 1968 Carol ran into Father McBride when he happened to be paying a call at Maryknoll High School in Honolulu. It was a very pleasant surprise for both of them since Carol and her family thought very highly of Father McBride and the feeling was mutual. Although the Lafayettes didn't live in the same parish, on the rare occasions that they attended church they went to McBride's parish. He even administered the first Holy Communion to Denise when she came of age in 1971, continuing a tradition of performing the rite for all of the Lafayette girls although in a totally different country for Denise.

Carol explained to me how she had gone to the church on her way to her waitress job in the Continental Coffee Shop at the Ala Moana Center to pray for guidance one day when she and I were having trouble getting our relationship on track. When Carol finished praying she sat back in the pew. Father McBride then appeared and greeted her congenially. She was so startled by his sudden presence that she immediately broke down in tears.

At Father McBride's prompting, Carol met with him in his office. This was two days before our confrontation after I decked a cornerback who was employing dirty tactics to keep me under control. Carol unburdened herself to him about my infidelity, wondering if she should dump me. Father McBride suggested that forgiveness was a possibility if she could get me to repent and give her my fidelity.

"We might not be sitting here right now if it weren't for Father McBride," Carol said. "I was so confused and he helped me to clear my head. I really didn't know what to do. If he hadn't come along I might have broken it off with you."

I nodded thoughtfully. I liked Father McBride and knew he liked me but I didn't know until this point that Carol had a long history with him and that he played a pivotal role in keeping us together. He didn't tell her not to dump me but simply gave her an alternative to consider.

"Okay, I'll go to Midnight Mass," I said. "I'll come straight from the Rose And Crown. Save me a seat."

"No, I'll have my parents drop me off at the Rose And Crown," she answered.

"You don't have to do that. I promise to be there. I won't stand you up."

"I know. I trust you. I just want to walk in with you."

We went back and forth on this for a few more minutes. Although I didn't feel it was necessary to impose on Carol's parents to detour into Waikiki to drop her off before the mass, I agreed to have her meet me at my workplace.

At shortly before eleven o'clock on Christmas Eve Carol showed up at the Rose and Crown. The joint was packed with rowdies celebrating the birth of Our Savior by getting hammered. Many did the same thing for St. Patrick's Day, Cinco de Mayo, Groundhog Day or simply because it was one of the seven days of any given week.

Carol caught my eye and smiled sweetly as she stood at the door. She looked absolutely radiant in her brand-new dress. Her makeup included matching lipstick and nail polish and her long hair had been set in soft curls. She was living proof that it was possible to improve on perfection.

I was mixing a bourbon and water and looked around the crowded bar. There were no seats available but I only had five minutes left. I waved to let her know I would be ready shortly.

Right at the stroke of eleven I left my post behind the bar. I took some time to clean up and change my shirt. Carol and I then left, finding parking not readily available in the area of the church. We had to park about three blocks away, then walked briskly to the church where Carol's sister Michelle was waiting at the door. She escorted us to where Carol's parents had saved us seats in the second pew from the front.

Had Carol known on Saturday when she gently twisted my arm to get me to attend what she learned that afternoon, she said she might not have asked me to come. She got a call from somebody from the church advising her that a featured soloist had developed a sore throat. Carol was asked if she minded filling in.

Carol loved to sing although she was apprehensive about singing a solo in front of me. I knew that she had sung in her high school choir but I had never heard her sing at this point.

The opportunity to sing a beautiful hymn superseded her apprehension. She readily agreed to sing. However, she didn't tell me she was going to do it.

At one point in the mass Carol abruptly rose from her seat. She went up to the pulpit and, to an organ accompaniment and my shock, she belted out the most beautiful version of *O Holy Night* that I had ever heard. Her voice bore an uncanny resemblance to that of Judy Collins. I was absolutely mesmerized.

Carol never looked at me during her solo. She told me later she was too nervous. She said she was afraid she would screw it up if she looked at me. Her solo was so impeccable and beautiful that a few people were even moved to tears.

When Carol finished she returned to her seat. She was smiling but appeared very flustered.

"You are absolutely incredible," I said softly as I grabbed her hand. I held it for the rest of the mass.

The Lafayettes' car was parked in the main parking lot. They gave me a ride to where I had parked my car.

I returned to the church. The chapel was empty except for a few stragglers. I found Father McBride standing at the front of the chapel.

"So nice to see you here tonight, my friend," he said with his ever-present smile.

"I'm glad I came. I'm not a Catholic but Carol twisted my arm. I'm glad she did."

"Carol's a very wonderful young lady. You and she look like a very nice couple."

"Thank you," I replied. "I guess I owe you a lot of thanks. I know that Carol consulted you when she and I were having difficulties. I'm really grateful for what you did."

Father McBride shook his head.

"I was just there for her to unburden herself," he said, appearing to be careful not to go into any detail since Carol was in sanctuary when she met with him. "It was up to the two of you to make it work. I wasn't in a position to tell her what to do."

I nodded.

"Well I appreciate your help regardless. Do you remember the last time I saw you just after a preseason workout and I told you that I had met a very special lady?"

"I certainly do. I'm glad to see that it was Carol. She's a wonderful girl from a wonderful family. Be good to her and I know that she'll be good to you."

"I will," I said willingly.

Father McBride blessed me by making the sign of the cross. Although I wasn't a part of his religion, I respected him and his faith and appreciated the gesture.

Christmas Day was even better. I arrived at the Lafayette home during the latter part of the morning. There was always a warm feeling in the house but the warmth was especially prevalent on this occasion.

Gifts were exchanged. I provided modest but thoughtful gifts befitting somebody on a college football scholarship to Carol's parents and two sisters while being slightly more extravagant with the gifts I bought for Carol. I also received very thoughtful gifts from Carol and her family. There was also Christmas music being played on the stereo and a wonderful dinner consisting of baked ham and an assortment of trimmings with pumpkin pie for dessert.

At about nine o'clock I announced my departure. Carol escorted me to my car which was parked on the street in front of the house.

Carol and I stood by the driver's side door and chatted. We were holding hands until I pulled her close and embraced her around the waist while she held me tightly around my neck and rested the side of her face against my chest. I loved the feel of her body against mine, savoring the movements of her chest as she softly breathed. I ran one hand up and down her back while she lightly scratched the back of my neck with her long nails.

This Christmas was obviously very special but there was still some unfinished business. It wasn't anything new but it involved an unexpressed thought. I was probably as apprehensive about expressing myself as she had been before she sang her solo at Midnight Mass.

"Carol, I love you."

There had been several young women who passed through my life over the years; a few of whom I may have even thought I loved. It wasn't until this date at the age of 22 years, two months and two days that I realized I was truly *in love*. I probably knew it a month before that and a month before that and even a month before that. I may even have known it that day in August when I first noticed Carol and couldn't take my eyes off of her as she and her colleagues practiced their cheerleading routines on the track at Cooke Field. I definitely felt something that day that I had never felt before.

Carol didn't offer an immediate response. She simply tilted her head back and looked at me with a tight grin. Her eyes seemed to sparkle but she didn't speak.

Inwardly I started to panic. I had meant what I said because it was very true but perhaps Carol wasn't ready for that yet. Perhaps she thought that the four months we had been together was not a sufficient amount of time to arrive at such a conclusion.

Carol opened her mouth slightly and looked at me amorously, then planted a soft sweet kiss on my lips and held it for several seconds while tightening her grip around my neck. She then tilted her head back again and looked me in the eye.

"I've always loved you, Jay."

In May, 1974, I left for my first pro training camp in Riverside, California; the only time the Hawaiians ever trained outside of Hawaii. Just prior to that I stood in front of a jeweler at the Ala Moana Center while waiting for her to get off work at the coffee shop on the lower level. I was looking at some engagement rings, thinking seriously about proposing to Carol before I left. I knew that I was ready to commit myself.

No, I thought. I was just starting my career and Carol still had two years before graduation. I decided it would be prudent to wait even though, emotionally, I was ready to marry her at that moment.

I called Carol during the early stage of camp and wrote two letters to her but she only answered my first letter. I was concerned about the lack of communication but tried not to dwell on it. I knew that she was taking some tough courses in summer school and that may have been getting the bulk of her attention. I figured I would first focus on making the team. She and I could work things out when the team returned to Hawaii after our first two games in Orlando, Florida, and Anaheim, California.

A few days prior to our trip to Florida I was told that I had made the team. I tried to call Carol with the news and discovered that her phone had been disconnected. The thrill of making the team had suddenly lost some of its zest.

Somehow I avoided the temptation to panic and immediately fly back to Hawaii. I knew Carol well enough to know that there was a legitimate reason for this sudden enigma. I got through the games in Orlando and Anaheim well enough, despite the fact that we lost both games, and flew with the team to Honolulu.

When I got home I immediately drove out to Carol's house. There was no need to even pull into the driveway. The house was vacant and up for sale. It was as if I had spent most of the previous year on some type of hallucinogen that made me only imagine a wonderful relationship with a beautiful blonde and her family.

It wasn't as if I could not have found out where Carol had gone. It also wasn't a matter of my not caring. I simply figured that the next move was hers since she had taken the initiative to leave town without telling me.

A neighbor of Carol's, Stacy Miyamoto who also happened to be Carol's best friend, offered to tell me where she had gone but I told her not to. I figured it was up to Carol, not Stacy, to let me know. I missed her terribly and always hoped she would turn up but I figured that she needed to sort things out in her own way. I was assured by Stacy, who was in contact with Carol, that Carol was healthy so that was all that really mattered. I told Stacy that if Carol was ever in a bad situation that I would drop whatever I was doing and rush to her aid regardless of where in the universe she happened to be. Unless that happened I was leaving it up to Carol.

This was obviously not a conventional breakup. I knew Carol too well to believe that she had left me maliciously. The concise explanation was that my departure was hard on her and then her father, who was an executive at Canadian Pacific Airlines, was abruptly transferred to the

40

mainland to complicate matters for her. She went to a locale unknown to me at the time to sort things out and wound up staying there.

I waited for Carol for as long as I could. At the end of 1974 I decided to do some soul-searching for a few months in Southern California. I even allowed myself to be set up on a blind date and found it to be very unsatisfying. Aside from that, I dated nobody between Carol's departure and through all of 1975.

By the time 1976 rolled around I had pretty well given up on Carol and felt obligated to start dating again. As a consequence, I reacquired the ladies' man reputation I'd had before Carol came into my life. I suppose I earned it although I didn't consciously cultivate it and wasn't proud of it. It simply seemed like the only way to deal with the loneliness I wasn't necessarily consciously aware that I was experiencing.

By early 1977 Carol was primarily a memory from the past. I still missed her more than I realized and was still curious about her disappearance but I bore no animosity toward her. Somehow I had the clarity to understand that she must have had issues which she needed to sort out. I had needed her and never stopped loving her and my disappointment from her sudden absence was beyond comprehension. Still, whatever it was that she apparently needed was greater than my need for her presence.

At least that was what I told myself.

CHAPTER THREE
Comeuppance

What I would experience during the first part of 1977 was ostensibly my comeuppance. The year began routinely enough with my quest for a master's degree tacked on to my social life and strict routine to be in shape for the football season. There would prove to be obstacles provided by Chris Alexander and, as it turned out, the young Canadian woman I met on the beach.

Dealing with Chris really wasn't that difficult. I could see what he had become within the first few minutes of us reestablishing our friendship. I had actually seen it developing even back in the days of the Manoa Zoo. It was simply much more prevalent in 1977.

Chris may have fallen on some hard times which did not leave me unsympathetic. Those hard times were still largely his own doing. They were the result of his past mistakes and the fact that he was doing little to rectify those mistakes or to improve himself. According to Chris, life owed him. He never literally said that but that was his attitude.

Just the same, Chris was primarily an annoying obstacle and not much else. Over the next few months I heard a lot from him although I never again altered any plans for him and, for the record, it was never me who initiated the contact. If he wanted to do something and I had other plans, which I usually did, I declined without being rude.

Chris spent a lot of time at my place the final few weeks before he moved to Arizona in May. Although Bill and I considered his intrusions annoying, we consoled ourselves with the fact that he would soon be leaving. That probably seems like a fine way to feel about somebody who had once been a close friend but Chris truly had become little more than a drugged out parasite. He was totally out of control and there was nothing anybody could do for him as long as he wasn't going to take the initiative to help himself.

Late in May Chris had a late flight to Los Angeles where he would catch a connection to Arizona. Loyal friend that he was, Chris decided that Bill and I would be heartbroken if he didn't spend his final day in Hawaii with us.

This was probably the only day in Bill's life when he would have been thrilled to have been called in to work on his day off. Had that happened Chris would have had nowhere to go when he showed up unannounced at my condo that morning since I had left for the gym and didn't return home until that afternoon. -

Bill initially felt panic when Chris showed up at the door with two suitcases in hand. His impression was that Chris had unilaterally decided that he was going to move in with us for the duration of his stay in Hawaii.

That was also my initial impression when I got home and spotted the suitcases in the living room.

"What's this?" I asked, considering the possibility of having to physically remove Chris from the premises or else getting the police to do it.

"Oh, I'm leaving tonight," Chris replied.

I don't know if my relief showed. Until that day Bill and I hadn't been apprised of the exact date that Chris was leaving. We also were not certain that he wouldn't change his mind before the day arrived. We both silently made it a point not to do anything that would encourage Chris to stay in Hawaii, especially since he no longer had any place to go. If he changed his mind about leaving, our condo unit was not going to be an option.

Chris still had a series of errands to run. He naturally decided that Bill and I owed it to him to run him around town. Had it been an ordinary day we probably would have told him to find his own way. Since he was leaving we patiently pasted our smiling faces on while we drove him around and silently counted the minutes before he would depart. They were very looooooooooooong minutes.

Of course Chris also expected one or both of us to take him to the airport. He hinted occasionally but never came out and said so and neither Bill nor I was going to volunteer. Had he asked directly he would not have liked the answer. Chris's welcome was worn very thin. I was tired and had no intention of taking him.

Chris's flight was scheduled to depart at about 10:30. Throughout the evening he sat in our living room watching TV with Bill and me, drinking our beer and occasionally wondering out loud how long the drive to the airport would be.

Bill and I didn't ignore Chris. We also didn't respond to his hints. When his flight was 20-25 minutes from its scheduled departure he finally accepted the fact that neither Bill nor I had any intention of taking him to the airport. He had no choice but to arrange his own transportation.

As a final magnanimous gesture, Bill and I allowed Chris to use our phone. The first call he made was to arrange to have a taxi pick him up. He then called the airline and inquired about his flight.

"Hold the plane," he actually said. "I'm on my way."

After that Chris shook hands with Bill and me, picked up his suitcases and departed. Bill and I didn't even see him to the elevator, let alone to the sidewalk below. Whatever we were watching on TV seemed more important.

A few minutes later I looked over the lanai to Ala Wai Boulevard 14 floors below just in time to see Chris getting into a cab. His flight was scheduled to depart about 15 minutes later. The drive to the airport from this part of Waikiki was at least 20 minutes and longer if the cab driver opted for Ala Moana Boulevard instead of the freeway.

We never heard from Chris again. My guess is he spent that night sleeping at the airport. He was scheduled to be on the airline's final flight to Los Angeles that night before catching his connection to wherever he was going in Arizona and there was no way he was going to make it on time.

Knowing Chris, he was probably deeply shocked to discover when he got to the airport that the airline didn't hold a jumbo jet full of people strictly on his order. After all, *life owed him.*

On the bright side, at least he left Bill and me with a laugh. We both found it hysterically funny that Chris obviously believed the airline would hold a plane just because he said he was on his way.

"I can hear him now," I cracked. "'But I told you to hold the plane.' Believe me, that is exactly what he did if he missed his flight."

"Perhaps he'll file a formal complaint with the FAA," Bill lightly suggested.

I wouldn't have put it past Chris. How can one depend on an airline if its flights depart at their scheduled times?

Chris got a semblance of the last word, though. Several days after his departure the phone bill came. Bill and I always split the standard user fee and paid for our own long-distance calls. This time we also wound up having to split extra costs. Chris had used our phone to make long distance calls to California and Arizona without our knowledge. We had allowed him to use our phone when he needed to make a local call but he apparently decided that meant we didn't mind if he made long distance calls, including some very lengthy ones, as well. Long distance calls in 1977 were much more costly than they came to be in later years. Ironically whenever he wanted to make a local call, which cost nothing, he always asked permission to use the phone.

It wasn't that the surprise charges put Bill and me in debt. We were simply put off by Chris unilaterally deciding that we were willing to spend our money on him. The phone bill alone justified our refusal to drive him to the airport.

But Chris was primarily a petty annoyance. A pretty 22-year-old female from Peachland, British Columbia, Canada, filled the major impediment role.

To this day I have no clue pertaining to what compelled me to approach Annica Pettersson in the first place that day at Fort Derussy. She was very pretty but it wasn't as if pulchritude was a rare find. All I know is something magnetic seemed to pull me toward a young woman I had paid little attention to until I suddenly found myself addressing her.

After my initial encounter with Annica I still didn't know if I would ask her out. I did, though, believe we would go out for a maximum of one evening.

I won't go into detail more graphic than necessary. What I will say is we fell fast for each other; something that surprised me and probably her. We began something we did not want to end. I even impetuously invited her to move in with me for a little while and she readily agreed, actually indefinitely postponing her trip home. Inviting her to take up residency with me was unlike anything I had ever done before and I'm positive that it wasn't like her to accept such an invitation. The invitation came without any premeditation during a passionate romp on Waikiki Beach and the shock of my extending the invitation was superseded by an even greater shock that she readily accepted.

The romance itself did not serve as an impediment to my routine. She understood that I had responsibilities. I continued my workouts and studies. I also continued my TV show except in this case she always went to the studio with me. I also played in a local baseball league on Sundays and she accompanied me to my games.

Aside from my local obligations, I did my best to keep her entertained. I took her to various local beaches, nightclubs, restaurants and other local attractions. We had a great time together.

We knew all along that eventually she would have to go home. We did discuss the possibility of her coming on a more permanent basis later in the year.

"I'll probably come back in October," she said during one of our discussions, "on the 23rd."

The date she mentioned was my birthday. It was a nice gesture although not necessarily realistic. For starters, I figured she would probably forget me once she was settled back home. Even if she did return she would have had to settle on a new date if she wanted me to pick her up at the airport.

"I won't be here on the 23rd," I pointed out. "We'll be playing in Atlanta."

"Atlanta?"

"Yes, Atlanta, Georgia," I clarified; tempted to explain where Georgia was but thinking it better to assume she knew where Georgia was instead of running the risk of insulting her intelligence. "We play the Atlanta Falcons on that date."

"Oh? Well wouldn't they rather come here and play?" she asked.

Obviously Annica was a little naive. She wasn't stupid. She simply wasn't especially worldly, having lived her life primarily in a rural setting and barely getting through high school. Her three older siblings all went to college but she hung up the textbooks as soon as she was finished with high school.

Annica's naivete was what probably encouraged her to accept the invitation to move in with a man she barely knew although I didn't think about it at the time. She had some apprehension but generally trusted me. It wasn't a wise move on her part but I can honestly say that I was careful not to betray that trust. Moral issues aside, I was very good to her.

After about four weeks I took Annica to the airport and she returned home. Throughout her stay she maintained her claim that she would return later that year. She also wanted me to take some time and pay her a visit in Peachland. She practically begged me to visit.

I doubted that the romance would survive. I had strong feelings for her although I suspected that she would get comfortable in her native environment and move on. I figured that she would forget me even before we could discuss the possibility of my visit. I was good with that if that was the way she wanted it.

As I watched Annica's orange Canadian Pacific 747 fly away I realized it was possible that Annica would not forget me once she returned to Peachland. I silently vowed that I would give her my fidelity and otherwise do my part to make the relationship last. That included finding a window of opportunity to spend some time with her in her native environment if she still wanted me to.

It was admittedly a very unconventional romance. I never was one to analyze things based on what people normally did.

Chris was obviously still in Honolulu the entire time Annica was with me. Somehow I managed to avoid him most of that time although he appeared occasionally.

Looking back, the entire matter disappoints me. I didn't understand why such activity was considered immoral back then. At the time God was simply somebody I believed existed and Jesus Christ was somebody who died on the cross so that I could sin without worrying about my ultimate fate regardless of how I lived my life. In 1977 I looked at myself as fairly righteous and invincible. I don't want to preach or judge anybody else but I obviously had a different moral compass back then.

The truth is, despite the reputation as a ladies' man that I inherited without soliciting, my ultimate goal was to find the right woman and marry her and raise a family with her. I didn't like the reputation I had as a ladies' man although I also wasn't going to settle down with somebody who didn't seem right for me. A few years earlier I was fairly certain that I had found my ideal spouse but that ended without prior warning. I was wondering now if Annica was my ideal companion. She wasn't as sophisticated or educated as Carol, or even most of the other women I dated for that matter, but I didn't see that as an impediment. My relationship with Annica felt perfectly natural and I was willing to let myself go to wherever it took me.

When Annica left Hawaii she insisted that she was going to write to me as soon as she got home. I didn't expect anything that quickly but when 10-12 days passed without a single word I decided to allow Annica to simply be a wonderful memory and move forward.

"Have you worked out the details on your trip to Canada yet?" Don Simmons asked as we drank a beer at a dive officially named Davy Jones' Locker but was affectionately referred to as *The Toilet*.

"I'm not going," I replied without emotion.

"Why not?"

"Well, you know. She spent about a month with me and it was great for both of us. Now she's back in Canada and I haven't heard from her. I figure she's just moving on."

"Not necessarily."

"Hey, it's okay," I said. "I loved having her with me and I hope she enjoyed it, too. Throughout the entire time until just before I put her on the plane she tried to persuade me to go visit her. Since she hasn't written, even to answer the letter I wrote to her the day after she left, I figure it's time to move on."

Don took a swig of his beer. He paused and pondered for a moment.

"Perhaps she's just not a letter writer," he suggested. "You should probably contact her and ask her if she still wants you to go up there. That way, at least you'll know."

I still didn't believe it was necessary. As I said, I was living a totally different life back then; a product of the Woodstock Generation. It is pretty pathetic to recall that Annica and I had essentially shared our lives for a month or so and both seemed willing to casually write the entire experience off once we parted company. I suppose we were products of our generation. We apparently didn't understand, or wouldn't admit, that to find true meaning in life one has to live in a more committed relationship.

The next day I realized that I wasn't ready to write the experience off so casually. I decided to write to her one more time, then went one better and called her. I had set aside a week at the end of April exclusively for a sojourn out of Hawaii and I wanted to know *right now* if Annica still wanted me to visit on her turf. If she did I would first spend a couple of days with my family in Southern California since I was already planning that visit and spend the rest of the time with her.

Annica wasn't home when I called. She was playing in a badminton tournament. I left a message with one of her brothers who happened to be heading to that same tournament. About 15 minutes later the phone rang.

"Jay?" she cried out ecstatically when she heard my voice. She sounded out of breath.

"Annica?"

"Oh, Jay. I ran all the way to the phone because I couldn't wait to find out if you were coming. Are you coming?"

Whatever doubts I may have had about Annica's feelings for me were erased. She seemed to want my presence very badly. I very happily made arrangements to fly up to Canada to meet with her at the end of April.

The visit to my family went well. I also got to spend time with a few old friends and even made a trip to Dodger Stadium to see the Dodgers who were off to a flying start.

After enjoying my time in California I anxiously looked forward to being with Annica again. Annica was naive, somewhat insecure and not well-educated but I didn't care. I accepted her for what she was without being condescending. For the first time in three years I was romantically connected to somebody in what was at least a semblance of a committed relationship.

The day I headed up to Canada was a day as long as a day preceding a Monday night football game. In both cases the day is spent with a focus on a single event. I flew on Western Airlines from Los Angeles to San Francisco and then Vancouver before a Pacific Western 737 transported me to Kelowna. All the way I thought of Annica and the wonderful time I was hoping to have with her. I also fretted some about whether I would make a good impression on her family.

Less than 24 hours after I lovingly embraced and kissed Annica at the Kelowna Airport I was at that same airport to return to Vancouver alone and confused. The Annica I had known and may even have loved in Honolulu was a stark contrast to the spoiled brat I visited in Peachland. Rather than go into graphic detail, I will primarily say that she was very selfish and unappreciative of my effort which was comprised of a lot of time, trouble and expense largely at her tenacious request. In a very short time she blindsided me with a barrage of insults, condemning me for actually making such a trip for her benefit. I wasn't there to put myself on a pedestal as a hero but I also never dreamed that I would be condemned for doing something nice for her, especially since she practically begged me to do it.

It was all I could do to maintain my poise. She had been warm and wonderful in Honolulu; the kind of woman who could please most men. Once I encountered her on her own turf she had morphed into the wicked witch of the Pacific Northwest. I couldn't leave Peachland soon enough.

For a short time after my return flight I sat in shock at the airport in Vancouver. I was angry. I was bruised. I wondered if I was somehow emasculated by the young woman whose mentality had transgressed into that of a spoiled three-year-old.

All the while I looked at her in a desperate search for the sweet lady I had known in Honolulu. I tried to ascertain if it was remotely possible that the lady in Honolulu could actually have been connected in any way to the female I found in Canada. The two females looked the same but Snow White had morphed into Lizzie Borden. Fortunately she didn't have an ax within reach.

"I'm a bitch!" she insisted at one point.

I did not feel compelled to argue. I also was not going to obsequiously stick around and put up with the abuse. I left, getting the last word in but not feeling any better because of it. While the entire mess was on her, I couldn't help but feel temporarily emasculated since there was no way that I could have prepared myself for what Annica had become and I went through a period when I wondered if it was remotely possible that I was to blame. It took a little while before I could convince myself that Annica's attitude was not a reflection on anything I had done wrong or my masculinity. I knew better but one can't help but wonder what one may have done to have led one to be put through an ordeal like that.

What I considered doing as I pondered at Vancouver International was return immediately to Honolulu since I no longer had any real purpose in Canada. Unfortunately that didn't seem like a good idea. It was widely known among my peers why I had gone to Canada. An early return would have generated too many questions that I didn't feel like answering.

I checked into the Howe Street Villa Hotel where I would house myself until my regularly scheduled departure a few days later. To ensure that the experience wasn't a total loss, I spent much of the daylight hours running through the streets of Vancouver. It would be interesting to try to calculate how many miles I covered running up and down Granville Street between my hotel and the airport. I wasn't simply jogging but running at full sprints most of the time. A lot of it was uphill.

Subconsciously, however, the reason I ran the way I did was to try to work the pain of betrayal out of my system. As I mentioned, despite all of the talk about me being a ladies' man, I preferred to find the right woman and settle down with her. It obviously wasn't Annica but the experience made me wonder if I was fated to never find such an inamorata.

On my first night in Vancouver I found a nightclub I liked around the corner from my hotel. I went there every night for the remainder of my stay. I worked off my anxieties by dancing with some of the local ladies on a strictly platonic basis.

"What's a good looking guy from Hawaii doing in a place like Vancouver by himself, eh?" an attractive woman of about 30 asked.

It was hard to respond to that. It was meant as a compliment but it actually made me all too cognizant of how I wound up in Vancouver by myself. Any knowledgeable person would insist that Annica was not worth the agony and that was very true. I was still in shock in the early stage of sudden betrayal.

While I was in Vancouver I thought about a local lady I had dated in Honolulu almost six months earlier. I didn't know where she lived but I did know where she worked. I wondered if I should drop in on her.

No, I thought. We'd had a wonderful experience during our nights together. Although I considered Bonnie to be infinitely more worthwhile than Annica at this point, I did not want Bonnie to see me in my current frame of mind.

Besides, what Bonnie and I once had was probably destined to end where it did and forever remain a cherished memory. I figured she had moved on and may have even found somebody who would prove to be a permanent fixture in her life. Even if that wasn't the case, Bonnie was not somebody I should look up only after my experience with somebody else didn't work out. Bonnie was too good a lady to be sought out only as an alternative.

Although I wasn't necessarily cognizant of it at the time, it was after I returned to Honolulu that Annica proved to be a major impediment. I returned very jaded although I tried not to show it.

Physically it could be argued that Annica didn't affect me adversely at all. I worked out probably even harder than I would have under normal circumstances. It was, like my days in Vancouver, a subconscious effort to work off my inner turmoil as well as stay in shape.

On the other hand, I was emotionally spent and abused myself. I smoked a lot more than I had previously. Although I did not become a chronic drunk, I drank more than I normally would have. Simply put, I found it virtually impossible to care.

Somehow I managed to do well in school. Had this happened during my undergraduate days I might have found this to be more of a struggle since the undergraduate curriculum requires more time in the classroom. As a graduate student I worked more independently in research and typing up my findings. It was harder to concentrate on my work after my Canadian calamity but I got through it. It helped that I was near the end of the semester. I had already completed the overwhelming majority of my work by the time I set foot in Canada.

What I wondered was if I was condemned to remain single for the rest of my life. A few years earlier I had lost Carol in a non-malicious but enigmatic way. Now Annica suddenly didn't want me essentially because I was willing to be nice to her and treat her with a respect that other men might never have shown her previously. It wasn't as if Carol and Annica were the only two girlfriends I had ever had. They were simply the only two where I'd wondered if I might have been destined to have a long future with them.

With Annica I was seeing how long we could last, being open to the possibility of staying together or distance driving us apart. With Carol, as I mentioned previously, I had actually begun looking at engagement rings in anticipation of a day down the road when I could ask her to marry me. In both cases I wound up alone and in shock after surprise endings to the relationships.

By June I was in my recovery phase. I was still somewhat jaded but moving on. In late May I attended the Hawaiians minicamp, which was always held at Stanford University since the area near San Francisco was considered to be a neutral location for those of us who lived in Hawaii and those who were scattered around the rest of the country, and succeeded in becoming mentally ready for the football season.

One smart move I made was asking Don Simmons to act as my agent. He was initially reluctant but finally agreed to represent me, welcoming the challenge of becoming a sports agent. He was a good choice, I knew, since he was the type of guy who could talk a great white shark into surrendering to its prey. I wound up signing a five-year contract that I will refer to as "lucrative" and let it go at that. It wasn't something that made me a millionaire since salaries for professional athletes still hadn't reached that pinnacle but it did give me a strong sense of financial security.

By June I had also decided it was time to get away from the Waikiki scene on a residential basis. My condominium was up for sale. I had just closed a purchase on a two-bedroom condominium in Hawaii Kai and would move in on July 1; four days before the start of training camp. I would also be a solo occupant. I allowed Bill to remain in my Waikiki condo for as long as it remained unsold.

All things considered, I was feeling reasonably good in early June while shopping at Kahala Mall. I was still bruised but recovering. My life was about to change for the better.

Actually I had just arrived at the mall with no purpose other than to look around to see if there was anything that appealed to me when I stopped dead in my tracks after entering from the parking lot on the Waialae Avenue side. A strange feeling washed over me as I looked straight ahead about ten yards. Sitting on a bench across from the Orange Julius was a very familiar woman with long golden blonde hair.

At least she looked familiar from the rear. As I pondered whether to proceed and see if she was whom I thought she was she raised her right hand to scratch the back of her head. There was no mistaking the gold bracelet around her wrist. I had given it to her.

I took a few tentative steps until I was directly behind her, moving slightly to the left to ensure that the bracelet and hair were attached to the right face. My heart was pounding. I even considered leaving.

"Carol?"

Impulsively she turned her head in my direction. She turned slightly pale as soon as she recognized me. She moved her mouth slightly as if she wanted to speak, but couldn't, then held her hand over her mouth and took a deep breath. She seemed more shocked to see me than I was to see her.

I hesitated. Dozens of thoughts ran through my mind. I felt the need to proceed carefully.

After a period where we looked at each other for what seemed like an eternity, I sat next to her. In an effort to keep our business in the crowded shopping mall private, I asked her in French where she had been.

"Hilo," she replied barely loud enough for me to hear.

Once we started the dialogue we became a little less uncomfortable with each other although there was still a heavy barrier between us. I wanted to ask her why she had left virtually without a trace, which I had every right to do. Something told me that this was not the time.

51

What she eventually told me was that shortly after my departure the airline her father worked for suddenly transferred him to San Francisco.

That much I already knew although I hadn't known the specific location. Now that I knew I wondered how close I had come to running into her father over the previous couple of months. I had stopped in San Francisco on my way to Canada and flew round trip to San Francisco in May for minicamp.

The departure of Carol's parents and two sisters placed an extremely heavy weight on Carol's shoulders since those she was closest to were moving on. She stayed behind in Honolulu to complete the first summer session at the university, even residing at the Manoa Zoo since she was its primary caretaker while I was at training camp anyway, but opted to forego the second summer session. Instead she flew down to Hilo to visit a friend from her Maryknoll days and sort things out in her mind.

Carol said she had wanted to contact me to confide in me. Unfortunately this was long before the cell phone era so reaching me would have been extremely difficult. She also didn't want to disrupt my quest to make the team. She knew that too big a distraction could spell the difference between making the team and unemployment.

Even the most unflappable of people have their trials. Carol rarely lost control of herself but the departure of her family was incredibly traumatic for her. It would have been less difficult for her had I been in town but, as it was, I was in California and she had been counting on her family to keep her company while she awaited my return. The stress of whether I would make the team augmented the stress of not having her family nearby. It was unfortunate that this was the one time that the Hawaiians didn't train in Hawaii.

There was another critical issue involved in her decision to head down to Hilo. That was something she and I would discuss later. I suspected it but didn't broach the subject during our initial encounter.

Time passed in the more laid back environment in Hilo and so did the time when she felt she would be welcome in Honolulu. When she decided she had stayed too long without letting me hear from her she tried to make the most of the situation by completing work toward her bachelor's degree at the University of Hawaii's Hilo campus. She stayed on the Big Island because she believed I would not welcome her back.

Of course she couldn't escape my presence. She watched me play football whenever our games were on television and read about me in the paper. She also became a regular viewer of my TV show when I started doing that, swearing each week that she was going to stop tuning in. She said she never found the strength to resist.

Carol returned to Honolulu to visit a few times but only saw me once. As was already mentioned, she and her friend Stacy Miyamoto were in attendance the previous September when we hosted Denver. That meant she was even there to witness my first NFL touchdown.

It was only a few days prior to my spotting her at Kahala Mall that Carol returned to Honolulu to live. She was hired as a French instructor at the university and had rented a condominium on Kinalau Place in the Makiki section of Honolulu. It was close to a bus stop which was handy because she had sold her car before she left the Big Island and didn't have a new car yet.

"How are you getting home?" I asked.

"The bus."

"No you're not. I'll drive you."

I grabbed Carol's packages before she could consider protesting and led her out to the parking lot. She gasped when she spotted my Porsche. She was with me when I got the car as part of my signing bonus with the WFL Hawaiians. Not only was she my first passenger but she actually sat in the car before I did. After I was handed the keys the day of my signing I opened the passenger door to let her in before getting in on the driver's side for the first time.

"Can I take you to dinner tonight?" I blurted impulsively, superseding whatever temptation there was to simply take her home with a casual "see ya later." I still wasn't sure if I was asking her for a date or simply offering to take an old friend to dinner.

Carol hesitated. I feared hearing about a new boyfriend.

"Okay," she replied.

It was, I suppose, a date although not an especially romantic one. We talked about things that had happened since we had last seen each other. Among the topics were President Nixon's resignation, Patty Hearst's incarceration, her family's relocation, the NCAA investigation of the University of Hawaii basketball team, the fall of Saigon and President Carter's beer-guzzling brother.

Carol also knew about Annica. It was the price I paid for being a public figure since a lot of people knew my business. While I was in Canada newspaper columnist Dave Donnelly decided it was his duty to report my alleged romance with Annica while wondering in print if matrimony was in my near future. Ironically Donnelly's blurb appeared the day after my tumultuous departure from Annica's abode.

"It was very bizarre," I explained without getting too graphic. I was too embarrassed, I suppose, to admit to being burned. "It was nice, I guess, but in the end it wasn't worth the time and effort."

Peachland was part of British Columbia's Okanagan region. Carol knew the area well. Her family used to vacation in the Okanagan on occasion while the Lafayettes were still living in Canada.

Throughout dinner I looked into Carol's beautiful green eyes. I was torn between being elated that she was with me and fearful that she would disappear again. Did I dare even remotely considering another romantic relationship with Carol?

I realized that night that I had never stopped loving Carol. I also knew, however subconsciously, that she had never stopped loving me. There was love in her eyes that I could see. It was mixed in with apprehension and trepidation. That was probably the same thing she saw in my eyes.

What I was tempted to do was take Carol in my arms and hold her until the sun came up. I wanted to assure her that everything would be all right. I wanted to simply disregard her three-year hiatus and pick up where we left off.

I knew that was not possible. For one thing, I was scared. It is impossible to explain. I just know that I was. I didn't know it at the time but, in retrospect, I was definitely scared.

She was also scared. I think she was afraid that I might try to avenge her disappearance. She felt as if she had betrayed me but she truly hadn't. She simply got caught in a trap as a result of being human enough to act irrationally. For all of the pain she had caused me to feel, I knew she didn't cause it deliberately. Carol wasn't that type of person.

I was happy to be with Carol again. For all of the tormenting pain I'd experienced in Canada, I was even relieved that my romance with Annica didn't last. Carol was always the great love of my life. There was a level of happiness that only she could provide.

Our first night out was a good start; at least for two people who had their guards up. It was going to take some time. I silently vowed to give myself exclusively to Carol while trying to move at a comfortable pace. I was hoping she felt similar about me.

The details and reasons for Carol's three-year absence did not come out on this night. They would come much later. I wasn't in any hurry. I was with the woman I knew I wanted to be with forever and was thrilled.

But, again, I was apprehensive. Did I dare get close to her? I wondered. I had lost her once and that had devastated me. Losing her a second time would have destroyed me.

After dinner I took Carol home. After escorting her to the door of her 17th floor unit I kissed her for the first time in more than three years. It was a somewhat cordial, courtesy kiss we exchanged instead of the more passionate kisses from before. We looked at each other as if we were both wondering where we would go from there. Neither of us was certain.

Before I went home I drove out to Hawaii Kai and sat by the water at Maunalua Bay. It suddenly dawned on me while I was there that my reunion with Carol took place on Annica's 23rd birthday. I wondered if perhaps in some cosmic way it was necessary for me to experience Annica before finding Carol again.

I took a few moments to compare Carol and Annica. The two young women were born exactly one month apart. Despite the fact that Annica

54

was a month older, Carol was at least a few years more mature. I was definitely getting the better end of the deal if Carol was back to stay.

When I got home Bill had returned home from work. He had already left for work when I got home that afternoon. He didn't know about Carol being back in town.

"Been on a date, I see," Bill said.

"How'd you know that?"

"Well, you've been known to do that occasionally."

"I suppose," I replied. "You'll never believe who I took out tonight."

"Annica," he guessed jocularly.

I hesitated and looked at Bill in a bemused way.

"Be serious," I said. "Think back a few years."

Bill looked thoughtful for a moment.

"That doesn't exactly narrow it down," he said lightly.

Suddenly the expression on his face indicated that he had flashed on something.

"Not Carol," he said.

"Yes, Carol."

"Wow. Where'd she come from all of a sudden?"

And so it went. I had taken my lumps. My hope now was that I could gravitate toward a much happier life.

I was up until about three in the morning. Before I went to bed I wrote Carol a letter. It was one I hoped to give to her someday. It was a matter of whether we got on track.

It would be easy to assume that Carol and I simply picked up where we left off. It wasn't that simple. I don't know if it's possible for any couple to routinely pick up after a three-year hiatus. It probably depends on the circumstances surrounding the separation and reunion and everything that happened in the interim.

Our lives were obviously different by this time. We were no longer a couple of campus sweethearts. Much of her focus was on getting her teaching career underway. I was less than a month from the beginning of my fourth pro football training camp.

We did what we were obligated to do regarding the other facets of our lives and saw each other a few times a week. There was moderate affection but also a barrier between us that kept it casual. We both knew it would take time before we could truly connect. I was apprehensive about getting too attached partially because my downfall with Annica was still a recent painful memory despite the fact that I tried to have it no longer affect me. I was also subconsciously afraid of getting close to Carol and having her disappear on me again.

At least I handled my insecurity better than I did when we started dating in college. I didn't deal with it by messing with other women the way I did in college. I would be good to Carol while still resisting the urge to get too close right away. There was a lot of discomfort in gradually adjusting to being together again.

CHAPTER FOUR
Training Camp 1977

To the average fan football is something that begins during the first exhibition game and climaxes at the Super Bowl or Pro Bowl. To me, at least since I turned pro, football was 12 months a year. I don't want to embellish my dedication, maturity or intelligence but when I committed myself to play pro football I gave serious thought to how good a career I wanted to have.

What I decided was to be absolutely the best I could be. Whether I was cut in my first training camp or had a Hall of Fame career, I was going to dedicate myself to doing my absolute best.

During the summer between my junior and senior years in college I read George Plimpton's Paper Lion. I had seen the movie when it came out in 1969 but never read the book until 1973. It was an autobiographical account of Plimpton, at the age of 36, working out as a rookie quarterback for the Detroit Lions.

One part that stayed with me, possibly because I read it while playing college football and was being referred to as a pro prospect, was when one rookie was cut immediately after a workout. Although he might not have ultimately made the team anyway, the reason he was cut so early was because he allowed himself to get out of shape. He simply wasn't prepared for training camp. I wasn't about to let that happen to me.

While not wanting to be cut because I allowed myself to get out of shape, I also realized that how well I did once I had made the team was contingent on how hard I worked all year. Regardless of whether I got cut, was strictly a substitute and/or a special teams player, or a member of the taxi squad, I wanted to have such a status only if that was the peak of my abilities. I didn't want to sit on the bench or watch football only from the bleachers or on TV while knowing that I hadn't worked hard enough. Whatever I achieved, it would be because I was willing to work hard.

Was it for the love of the game or an ego trip?

I definitely loved the game and respected it. Football provided me an opportunity to earn a living while playing on a level that most men never realize. There was a price to pay for the privilege and there were many negatives that most people wouldn't understand associated with football. The positives made it all worth the price.

Yet I won't deny that my ego played a role. I got a thrill out of knowing that people enjoyed watching me play. I loved being a starter on an NFL team and being considered one of the top players in the game throughout my career. I loved being cheered in Honolulu and would have been crushed had I been booed in Honolulu. I loved it when the fans booed me in

Philadelphia or any other city I visited if the reason was simply because I wore an enemy team's colors.

Something new would be added to our home games in 1977. Two dozen young women between the ages of 20 and 25 plus six alternates would be selected to be Hawaiian cheerleaders. A tryout camp was scheduled to begin in July for about 100 women who applied. In September the 24, plus the six alternates, would make their debut prior to our home opener against Buffalo.

The uniforms would not be as provocative as those of the Dallas Cowboy cheerleaders. The uniforms would be comprised of red pleated cheerleader mini-skirts and red tops with brown and white trim. The tops would reveal no cleavage although the uniform would include bare midriffs. Also to be included were white, knee-high boots.

"To tell you the truth, I really hadn't given it much thought," Walker replied guardedly when a reporter asked what he thought about the addition of cheerleaders. "Will they be enough to make the fans forgive us if we don't play well?"

I wasn't averse to having cheerleaders. I also didn't see them as a major enhancement. I recalled having a playful argument with Carol when we were together in college. After we had won about our first half-dozen games Carol started kidding me about how it was all because of her and her cheerleading colleagues.

"You guys would be lost without us," she teased. "It's our cheerleading that causes you guys to play better."

"Is that right?" I shot back with equal levity. "Then at least I'll know whom to blame if we finally lose a game."

The Hawaiian cheerleaders were to perform before and during every home game. During halftime they would do choreographed routines with whatever band happened to be performing.

None of the players and coaches had anything to do with the selection process. The cheerleaders were reportedly to be selected on the basis of talent, poise, intelligence, character and availability for rehearsals and games. All of them had to have other means of support since the pay was a paltry 30 dollars a game.

Unlike their counterparts in Dallas, our cheerleaders were not discouraged from fraternizing with the players although it also was not encouraged. If a player and cheerleader happened to link up romantically, they were not to allow it to show on the field. Any encounter on the field could not extend beyond routine courtesy.

To keep costs down, the cheerleaders would not perform during exhibition games or road games. The only road game they would perform at was the Super Bowl if we ever got there.

The alternate cheerleaders would be in their uniforms and paid the same 30 dollars per game. They would also be the ones to present leis to all

58

players and coaches prior to the home opener against Buffalo at midfield during the pregame introductions of the entire roster. They would also present the leis prior to each subsequent game except the introductions were limited to whichever starting unit was to be introduced and any players that were added to the roster since our previous home game. During the actual games they would sit in the dugout seats behind the south end zone between the two baseball dugouts and be ready to fill in should one of the regular cheerleaders be injured or otherwise unable to continue.

In the interest of being gracious hosts, our visiting teams would be asked in advance if they wanted leis for their starters who were to be introduced. Some would and some would not.

As planned, I moved into my new condominium on July 1. It was a very liberating experience. The facility was so secure that there was even a guard shack at the entrance where visitors needed to check in. The twin-tower facility also had a swimming pool for each tower, a putting green, outdoor jacuzzis, a cabana and a workout facility.

My unit was on the ninth floor. It had a reasonably large living room and a separate dining area. There was also a modest sized kitchen, two bedrooms, two bathrooms and a washer and dryer. Out the windows of the living room and master bedroom there was a nice view of Maunalua Bay which was a mile or so away.

As luck would have it, my Waikiki condominium sold in a hurry. Bill wound up renting a unit on Kuhio Avenue in Waikiki. He moved the same day as me. We spent virtually the entire day helping each other move.

I didn't have much time to enjoy my new dwelling. I barely had time to unpack and organize my new furniture before having to leave for training camp. I packed a modest wardrobe to take with me. The clothing was of the casual assortment such as blue jeans and bermuda shorts since I didn't anticipate going anywhere where one was expected to dress up although I did include a few aloha shirts to wear while I was prerecording my TV show. I also included an assortment of athletic garments including three pairs of gym shorts, an assortment of T-shirts and several pairs of white athletic socks.

Also included were four brand new pairs of shoes that I would wear on the field. Two pair were white all-purpose shoes with rubber cleats that I would use during games played on artificial turf. The other two were white regulation football cleats that I would use on grass fields.

Why four pairs?

Not everybody had that many. Many would show up with one pair of each or two of one and one of the other. Occasionally I saw players who wore only the all-purpose shoes.

I preferred to have an extra pair of each. That way if the shoe wore out I would always have a spare pair. I would rotate each pair during training camp to ensure that all four pairs were broken in properly before the exhibition season. This was especially necessary for the cleats since those were much heavier than the all-purpose shoes.

Like the year before, training camp officially began on July 5. Walker thought it would be extremely unpatriotic to force the team to go through its first workouts on Independence Day. The rookies were required to report on July 2 but Walker gave them July 4 off after two full days of physicals, meetings and workouts. All personnel were to be at the Kaneohe Marine Corps Air Station by midnight leading into July 5.

Camp took on a different ambience the night of July 4 this time. I knew a lot more people than I did the year before. There were still a lot of new faces since we were starting with 115 players including 54 rookies; two of whom were cut by other teams during the 1976 preseason. We were still an established team with a reputation in the NFL for playing well.

Back for another shot was defensive end Kyle McWherter. He was with us in 1976 after four years in Kansas City but was cut early in the season when Jon Jurgens was activated. Unfortunately he found no takers when he was placed on waivers and was welcomed back to Hawaii in 1977. He was a good player whom I admired for his determination and relentlessness.

Out of 83 colleges, the University of Hawaii was once again the most represented with seven alumni in camp. This included three rookie free agents in safety Patrick Yokum, linebacker Brad Kuiwa and defensive tackle Kimo Pume. There was also local representation in rookie free agent linebacker Pat Morales from Laie who played for Kahuku High School and then played his college football at BYU.

Among the other colleges, USC, UCLA and San Diego State had four alumni in camp. Washington State, Syracuse and Missouri had three and 12 others had two.

There were also two Ivy League alumni; both rookie free agents. Defensive tackle Jerry Urmanski was from Colgate and tailback Duke Turlock was from Yale.

Almost seven months earlier we completed our maiden NFL season with a victory in Cleveland. All but four players from that final game were back in camp. Center Phil Hoddesson had retired, guard Jim Kohl was sold to Memphis, halfback Gary Giametti was traded to San Diego and linebacker Bob McWilliams was traded to Baltimore. Some from the 1976 team would be cut during camp but nobody was cut during the offseason.

I arrived in camp at about eleven o'clock. There was never a curfew for the veterans on the night we were to report aside from the requirement that we be physically present in the compound by midnight. I sat on the lawn outside our living quarters and drank a couple of beers while chatting with several teammates from the year before. There were a lot of handshakes among the veterans since there were several who did not live in Hawaii

60

during the offseason. We were together as a unit for the first time since December since a few had valid reasons to be excused from minicamp.

The first official day was the usual potpourri of physicals, equipment distribution and other seemingly frivolous activity. That night we had our first camp meeting. All 115 players and eleven coaches crammed into the meeting room normally used by the offense. Roughly half were forced to stand since there were only 65 seats which included desktops on which to diagram our plays in our playbooks.

Walker stood at the podium at the front of the room and smiled. He was wearing an orange polo shirt with the Hawaiians logo on the left breast. Throughout camp he wore an assortment of polo shirts, aloha shirts, T-shirts and dress shirts. Throughout my career he always wore a polo shirt with the team logo the night of the first meeting. I never found out if this was to instill a first impression or simply superstition.

The steady hum of conversation ended. All eyes were on Walker. We were Walker's children. In his own way he loved every one of us. Over the next two months he would have to send roughly two-thirds of his current batch of children away. He didn't relish that but it had to be done. His job was to keep only those who could best serve the team.

"Good evening, men. For those I haven't met, I am Coach Chuck Walker and I welcome you to the Hawaiians. I sincerely hope you enjoyed the offseason but that you kept yourselves in shape because it's time to go to work."

"What I am going to say is something I will say every year at the opening meeting for as long as I am the coach. It doesn't matter to me how you came to the team. Some of you are seasoned veterans in your primes. Some of you are here after being released or traded by other teams and many of you are rookies. The bottom line is you are here because you have earned the opportunity to try to make this team. Nobody gave you anything you didn't deserve. You have earned the right to be here."

Walker paused. I think he wanted to let his previous remarks settle in. It was a confidence builder.

"A lot of cuts will be made between now and the beginning of the season," Walker continued in a more somber manner. "It is never a pleasant task to tell a player he will no longer be with us. Those who represent the team will be those who most deserve the privilege."

Walker leaned against the podium. He pointed his index finger toward the Hawaiian hopefuls.

"Your job is to dedicate yourself to making this team," he emphatically stressed. "Your job is to be here in excellent condition. Your job is to give it everything you've got during workouts. Your job is to pay attention during meetings and learn your assignments. Your job is to follow the rules. That is the only way you can benefit from the experience. Don't allow yourself to get cut because you didn't do what you should have done. Those who try to slide by cheat themselves by not living up to their potential."

Walker stepped back. He smiled momentarily and then continued.

"My job and the job of the other coaches is to lead this team. We are here to see to it that everybody gets a fair opportunity. It doesn't matter to us who you are. Nobody is guaranteed a spot on this team. Our job is to do our best to see to it that everybody gets a fair shot. If we didn't feel you deserved a fair opportunity to make the team you wouldn't have been signed in the first place."

Walker segued to introductions of the coaching staff. There were two new faces in 1977. Jim Potter was our new offensive coordinator, replacing Mike Tipton who left to take a head coaching job at a college in Maryland. Also added was linebacker coach Alan Rizzo, taking the place of Max Crawford. Crawford was still with us as defensive coordinator after seeing double-duty the previous season when the racist ideals of our original defensive coordinator led to his dismissal and Crawford's increased caseload.

The subject of race was touched on. Walker explained that racism would not be tolerated. He pointed out that nobody would be at an advantage or disadvantage based on race.

Then came the subject of places that were off limits. It was primarily places where gambling was known to take place. Many of the places Walker cited were in the vicinity of Hotel Street which was Hawaii's version of Skid Row back in 1977. It would eventually be cleaned up but it was the epitome of sleaze back then.

"Now let me tell you what we're up against," Walker continued as he slowly walked around the room, looking his players over. "Last year we were seven and seven. Normally that's a so-so record. Mediocrity is for losers but it was a damned good record for an expansion team. You guys who were with us showed a lot of heart by putting that record together, especially since you had to win the last two games on the road in relatively cold weather to reach that pinnacle. Along the way you even beat the team that eventually won the Super Bowl. Imagine that. The only team that beat Oakland last year was a lowly expansion team from Hawaii."

"But we can no longer glorify ourselves by what we did last year. This is a new beginning and the bar has been raised. Your performance last year caused everybody to sit up and take notice. If anybody made the mistake of taking this team lightly, they won't this year. You showed the world that the Hawaiians were a legitimate team who could play with the best but now you're going to have to be that much better just to duplicate last year's record."

Walker hesitated. He frowned and pointed.

"And I'll tell you this. I won't accept seven and seven this year. You're not an expansion franchise anymore. We are out to be winners, playing one

62

game at a time but still with a goal of getting to the Super Bowl. If we feel that the way to achieve our maximum possible level of excellence is by having a roster comprised exclusively of rookies, that's exactly the way we'll do it."

"The Super Bowl is six months away," Walker pointed out in conclusion. "We will get there by taking it one step at a time. It starts with training camp."

Back to the routine. I loved training camp. I also hated training camp.

Looking back, I only thought I hated training camp. It was a grueling ordeal to test our endurance. Six days a week until the beginning of exhibition season we dealt with two workouts a day. Conditioning, rushing drills, passing drills, blocking drills and tackling drills were all part of our everyday routine. Naturally that was accompanied by the sounds of padded bodies colliding, grunts, whistles, quarterbacks calling signals and coaches barking out a plethora of chastising remarks.

Along the sidelines were witnesses. Members of the media were often on hand. Also present were Marine Corps personnel. Some brought their wives or girlfriends and in some cases there were Marines bringing their children out to watch us go through our paces. That usually meant we were hounded for autographs after each workout. Some guys thought the autograph requests were annoying while others were more amenable. I personally didn't mind, especially with the kids.

There were down times although the periods were short. From Monday morning through the second workout on Saturday there were breaks in the routine only long enough to get a little rest. Thoughts of lying on the beach or taking a nice scenic drive were nixed since the breaks weren't long enough to make such a venture worthwhile. Our days included mandatory weightlifting sessions and our presence at meals was also mandatory. Since we were on the same schedule as the year before, our schedule included meetings Monday through Friday evenings which lasted until about nine o'clock.

At one time I wondered how our regimented routine compared with that of Marine Corps recruits. The only advantage I could see that we had was that we had opportunities to venture away, even if only briefly. We could also stay away all day on Sunday. Those of us with permanent local homes could spend Saturday nights at home.

That's not to mention that we weren't forced to get our heads shaved on arrival. We also didn't march or stand snap inspections. Any horror stories about sadistic football coaches were child's play compared to some of the stories I was told about some Marine Corps drill instructors.

If there was an advantage of being a Marine Corps recruit, it was that they only went through basic training once. For a pro football player every season begins with football's version of basic training.

But training camp, grueling though it may have been, really wasn't bad. I enjoyed the camaraderie of my peers. I also enjoyed the anticipation of a new season. Each season my two primary goals were to make the team and to help my team win the Super Bowl. Training camp was simply the first necessary step.

Like the previous season, I had to drive into Honolulu after our Monday night meeting to videotape my TV show that would be shown the following night. What I had done to keep the show fresh and topical was give it a slight change of format. This was inspired, surprisingly enough, by the show that was taped to be shown during my ill-fated trip to Canada in April.

I had left Hawaii on a Saturday morning. Since there was no substitute host available I taped my show on Friday. That was premature for a show comprised of a week's worth of sports highlights. I could fudge a day or two if I needed to but four days in advance was too soon.

What I did was get a few Hawaii Islanders on that show. We spent time talking about hopes for the baseball season which had just begun. The players also got to talk about their baseball backgrounds on both the amateur and professional levels.

I enjoyed the interview format although I didn't want to lose the highlight segment. What we decided was to do exclusively sports highlights during weeks of heavy sports activity. During weeks when there was a reduction of sports activity, at least of local interest, we went almost exclusively to the interview format.

During training camp we tried to do primarily the interview format. There were still highlight clips incorporated into most shows, especially when we were able to get clips of the Hawaii Islanders who were enroute to their third consecutive division championship.

Quarterback Steve Bender was my guest on the first show that would be videotaped during the 1977 training camp. This was actually during the second week of camp since I was able to prerecord my show that ran the day camp opened the day before. Steve and I got into my Porsche after the Monday evening meeting and headed into Honolulu.

Steve went directly into makeup when we arrived at the Kapiolani Boulevard facility. I rushed into a voice recording studio to quickly view the selected sports highlights and decide what I wanted shown before I narrated over the highlights. Once that was taken care of we knew how much time we had available for the interview segment.

I got a quick dab of pancake on my face and took my seat in the studio next to Steve. I had selected topics I wanted to discuss and briefed Steve so that he could think about what he wanted to say. I also invited him to make a suggestion about a highlight from his career that he wanted to discuss. It was critical that we be as organized as possible since we had to be back in our rooms by midnight.

"Good evening. Welcome to Sportsrap," I said when the studio portion of the taping began. "I'm your host, Jay Dockman, and with me tonight is the quarterback for the Hawaiians, Steve Bender."

"Steve, thanks for being on the show," I continued as I turned slightly to face him. "Now last week we started another training camp. This is the fourth of my professional career but you've been around a little longer than me. How many does this make for you?"

"This is my 16th, Jay."

"Geez," I sighed and it wasn't fake. Given what I knew about training camps from my comparably young career, I couldn't imagine enduring that many. "What is it that keeps you going back?"

The primary camera was switched. There was a tight shot of Steve as he responded.

"Well, Jay. I don't know that I can narrow it down to just one or two things. I do enjoy football and feel that I am still in pretty good shape. Last year we had what would be classified as a mediocre record by normal standards but it was pretty sensational for an expansion team. I'd like to see how much we can improve on that. I can honestly say that I don't think I've gone to camp with this much enthusiasm since my rookie year in 1962."

Steve proved to be an excellent guest. He had a lot to say and was very articulate. He was very comfortable in front of the camera.

Since the show now ran at 8:30 on Tuesday nights, that meant Hawaii Islander home games were not even half over as we approached the end of the show. Like the year before, what we did was tape four different tight shots of me to be inserted near the end of the show coming out of the final commercial break.

"And how are the Islanders doing tonight?" I asked as I looked into the camera and paused. "Hey, that's great. I hope they hang on."

Of course that was contingent on the Islanders winning at the time. During the actual telecast a graphic with the score would appear after I asked the question and the response obviously was as if I could actually see the graphic.

"And how are the Islanders doing tonight?" I asked as we taped a second segment. "Oh," I responded with a trace of disappointment, "but the game's not over yet. Let's hope they can come back."

A third segment was taped in the event of the game being tied at the time. The fourth was a simple announcement that the Islanders had been rained out.

As it turned out in this case, the Islanders were down 5-2 at the time of the show. They would ultimately lose 12-4 to the Salt Lake City Gulls.

If the Islanders were on the road their games were usually over by the time the show ran. We still taped these segments but naturally did them in the past tense. We also did a few clips in the present tense in case a game on the mainland was going extra long. It was very unlikely but still possible.

Among the changes from 1976 was that the team revised its training camp roommate system. In 1976 the team wanted the captains to room together, which didn't pose a problem, but the team wanted all other roommates assigned by position. This also included the roommate assignments for preseason road games.

It wasn't necessarily unusual for teams to try to room people by position. There are also reasons why such a system is not practical. One is because some positions have an odd number of players. Another is because two players assigned to a room might not be compatible.

The previous year it wasn't impractical to assign roommates. We were an expansion team in its first year so most of even the non-rookies didn't know each other especially well. Many had squared off against each other and a few had even been teammates but there were only a few cases when players came to camp and teamed up with personal friends.

During the previous camp I had the misfortune of being assigned to room with Robert Shibata. The reason he was my roommate was because he and I were the only halfbacks with pro experience. The other three were rookies and housed in a barracks with the other rookies.

The problem with rooming with Shibata was that he hated me. His contempt for me was obvious from day one. Some of my teammates speculated that it was out of jealousy. I simply ignored him. When I tried to congenially introduce myself at the start of training camp and was told where I could go and what I could do with myself when I got there before his salutation was capped off by calling me a slang term for a homosexual, I never spoke to him again that I recall.

In retrospect, I think his problem was that his chances for making the team were not good. Some of my teammates concurred with that assessment. Had Shibata not decided to abruptly leave the team on his own he almost definitely would have been waived. Since he took it upon himself to walk out the night before our exhibition game in Memphis the team didn't even have to make his travel arrangements.

Shibata's departure worked out well for me. During what little was left of camp I didn't have a roommate. For our final exhibition game in Green Bay rookie Gary Giametti was assigned to room with me. Whenever we traveled during the regular season we didn't have roommates.

Giametti was not somebody I would have picked on my own since there were guys I knew better than him. We still got along well during our brief overnight tenure as roommates. I don't believe, however, that rooming two men together simply because they play the same position has any impact on how well they play.

Probably the most awkward pairing during the 1976 preseason road games was quarterbacks Frank Joseph and Joe Billingsley. Joseph was a rowdy individual who smoked and drank. Billingsley was a somewhat devout LDS member. Billingsley did not always epitomize how one of the LDS faith should behave but he also wasn't especially comfortable having a roommate who liked to smoke and drink.

Such pairings became obsolete in 1977. The veterans were allowed to choose their own roommates. This meant that childhood friends Russ Allen and Norm Richards could room together. Bender asked Billingsley to be his roommate, meaning that the two quarterbacks could be together by choice and Bender could serve as Billingsley's mentor to prepare him for when he would take over as our starting quarterback. Joseph roomed with Ben Blakely who had the same rowdy interests as Joseph.

Marv Nelson asked me to be his roommate. I was trying to decide among Marv, Ed Jennings and my former college and WFL teammate Rich Hasegawa and made my decision simply because Marv asked me. In all subsequent training camps Marv remained as my roommate until he retired as a player and moved into the coaching ranks.

There were still instances when roommates were assigned. This affected those who were either undecided or else had no preference.

I happened to see the first cut of training camp take place. Walker continued his compassionate tradition of making all cuts except for disciplinary cases after breakfast. The victims got a good night's sleep and good breakfast before meeting with the Grim Reaper. Anybody who left breakfast without being stopped just outside the dining hall lived to play another day.

Assistant coach Greg Wilson resumed his dubious role of preliminary hatchet man. Those of us who had been through camp before were all too familiar with what it meant when Wilson lurked outside the dining hall. Some of the fringe players lingered inside the dining hall as if hoping to will Wilson away.

"Morning, Coach," I greeted Wilson cheerfully.

"Good morning, Jay," he replied without cheeriness. He knew he was on a dismal mission and didn't feel like smiling. He wasn't much of a coach but he also wasn't without a heart.

I could afford to be optimistic on that particular morning. My first six days of training camp had gone well. I was 25, in good physical shape, playing hard and coming off a good season. My time to worry would not come until later as long as I continued to work hard. The ones getting cut at this juncture were only the most hopeless of cases.

Just the same, I always got jittery whenever I spotted Wilson lurking. I suppose it was probably because I felt bad for the casualty, felt bad for Wilson and Walker for having to undergo such an unpleasant undertaking, worried that one of the casualties would be a personal friend and even felt somewhat insecure about my own chances.

I was a few feet beyond Wilson when I stopped to talk to Russ Allen, Norm Richards and Marv Nelson. That was when I saw Wilson stop a rookie free agent tackle from Northwest Missouri named Gene Pettigrew. He was instructed to get his playbook and report to Walker's office.

The look on Pettigrew's face told me he knew exactly what was going down. He smiled when Wilson called his name as he approached. His facial muscles sagged when he found out what Wilson wanted. He made the long walk to the rookie barracks to retrieve his playbook and report to Walker. He would return to the barracks one more time to gather his possessions and then be driven to the airport.

Wilson left his perch as soon as Pettigrew had been rerouted to Walker. That meant that Pettigrew was going to be the only casualty that day. Unlike the previous year when four players had the indignity of being the first casualties, Pettigrew had the ignominious distinction of being the only man let go when the first cut of 1977 was made. He wouldn't even have a fellow casualty to talk to on the way to the airport.

"The man just let himself get out of shape," Marv muttered as we watched the woebegone Pettigrew make his melancholy sojourn.

Marv's observation was right on the mark. If I had been expected to name three people as likely candidates to be the first cut for lack of conditioning, Pettigrew definitely would have been near the top of that list. He had to have been a decent college player or else he would not have been signed in the first place. When he signed as a free agent he ostensibly visualized stardom in the NFL and spent time celebrating when he should have focused on staying in shape. Hooking on in the NFL is difficult enough as it is. It is virtually impossible for those who allow themselves to report to camp out of shape.

Walker was in one of his more charming moods at our morning workout. One of his biggest pet peeves was people who showed up out of shape. Since Pettigrew was on his way home, Walker had to vent his hostilities on us.

"Kerner, what's with you? Did you retire after last season? Hit that hole! Hit that hole!"

"What the hell kind of pass was that, Joseph? If you're going to complete the pass you have to at least throw it in the same county as the receiver."

"I can't believe you, Dockman," Walker bellowed after a pass bounced off of my fingertips. "Did you break your hands signing your new contract?"

"Dammit, McDaniel! What kind of tackle was that? Hit the ball carrier! Don't make love with him!"

The words alone were not indicative of unusual behavior by Walker. It was what followed that suggested that Pettigrew's dilemma was eating

Walker up. Often his criticism was followed by, "I sent Pettigrew home this morning. You're going to be next if you don't shape up."

Normally a cut didn't affect Walker this adversely. Walker hating cutting players who simply weren't good enough to make the team and those forced out by a lack of roster space was simply a necessary evil. A man cut because he reported out of shape or utilized some other method of taking things lightly had a way of getting under his skin.

The cuts continued as training camp progressed. I always felt bad seeing players who had been cut. Many of my teammates also did although it was a very conflicting feeling. We felt helpless and often wanted to express sincere regrets although it felt incredibly awkward. We also felt great relief that it wasn't us.

In most cases a player cut would never play pro football again. A few would resurface with other teams or even be called back to the Hawaiians later. Some would dedicate an entire year to getting in better shape and returning for another try, occasionally with success.

And there are those rare instances when somebody cut by one team resurfaces with another and becomes a superstar. The most glaring example I know of involved a rookie quarterback cut by the Pittsburgh Steelers. That quarterback resurfaced a year later with the Baltimore Colts and wound up in the Pro Football Hall of Fame. One had to wonder how hard they were kicking themselves in Pittsburgh where the Steelers' first-ever NFL championship didn't come until the season after Johnny Unitas retired.

With so many rookies in camp there were always those whom I never got a chance to know. They simply didn't last long enough and during the early stages of camp there was always a barrier between the rookies and veterans. Until the number of total prospects was whittled down, the rookies and veterans even worked out separately most of the time. Most of the interaction during the earliest days of camp was limited to meetings and meal times.

Occasionally there would be somebody in camp, not necessarily a rookie, who was nearly impossible to figure out. Occasionally it was somebody whose skills or dedication seemed to be lacking and made me wonder how he managed to be in camp. Other times it was a personality thing.

In 1977 it was a personality thing involving a rookie halfback named Dave Rossi. He was born and raised in San Francisco and played football at San Jose State after two years at a local junior college. His father had reportedly been an alcoholic who died when Rossi was in elementary school. His mother managed an Italian restaurant her family had owned since the 1930s.

This was actually Rossi's second pro training camp. He tried out as a free agent with the 49ers the year before. He was cut about halfway through the exhibition season.

Rossi was with the 49ers when they opened the exhibition season with us the previous year. Apparently the trip to Hawaii impressed him. He reportedly was related to somebody who knew Walker. He was signed as a free agent the day before our minicamp started.

I suspected that Rossi would make the team if evaluated on the basis of his performance and not his personality. I doubt, though, that he would have made the team had Gary Giametti not been traded. He simply appeared to be the best among those trying to make the other halfback spot, assuming I would make the team again. He was reasonably fast and was a fairly good receiver. There was still nothing spectacular about him. He simply seemed to be slightly better than the others.

Rossi was one of the cockiest rookies I ever encountered. He came across as one who would have been shocked to learn that they weren't already preparing a space for him in the Pro Football Hall of Fame. He was almost as bad as my old friend Chris Alexander although Rossi was at least willing to work toward his goals.

Just about everybody was aware of Rossi's presence almost from the moment he reported. Something in the way he combed his hair and dressed made me think of James Dean. He gave the impression that he believed he was the one everybody on the team would want for a best friend, would want to invite to dinner and, above all, would be the only one we could count on to score the winning touchdown in the Super Bowl. His overall cocksure nature was actually comical.

Rossi had no inhibitions when dealing with team personnel including the coaches. He approached everybody as if he had known them for years. From day one he was talking about what he thought might be fun when we opened the regular season in New Orleans and how he looked forward to playing in San Francisco in December as if he already had the team made. It probably would not have surprised me to learn that he had already made several thousand dollars' worth of purchases on the assumption that he would be receiving a Super Bowl check.

I have to admit, though, that I didn't dislike Rossi. I didn't necessarily trust him but I actually found him hard not to like.

One thing about Rossi that I found both annoying and amusing was that it didn't matter to him what position a person played. He had ideas which he passed along to help each person he felt needed his mentoring. It didn't matter if it was a rookie or a ten-year veteran. He always seemed to have a suggestion or two.

I was not immune. There were times when he decided he needed to counsel me. It wasn't as if I was above constructive criticism but, as the incumbent starter with three years of pro experience, I didn't believe that a rookie who had yet to play a single down in a regular season NFL game had any business telling me how to play.

What amazed me most of all was how he managed to maintain his eligibility through four years of college. He did not seem the least bit like the type to spend time in the classroom.

I never asked Rossi about it but I would bet that he found some way to cheat his way through college. It wasn't necessarily any school's fault. I simply believe that he probably got away with having somebody take care of frivolous details such as homework and exams. If he wrote essays and term papers the way he talked he would have flunked out on the basis of grammar alone.

Put another way, he spent four years in college and didn't learn a thing.

As always, the best part of training camp was getting sprung on Saturdays. I recalled how much I had enjoyed it the previous year since I could abandon most of my thoughts about football for a little more than 24 hours. In 1976 I utilized the time to sit in solitude, take a long drive, walk on a beach and sleep in my own bed. These are things we often take for granted.

A special feeling washed over me when I got into my car and drove off the base. That alone made me feel human again.

This is not to suggest that I didn't get into my car and go places during the rest of the week. I did but rarely. The routine was so regimented that I could never travel very far or be gone for very long. About the only real opportunity was a three-hour window between our evening meeting and midnight curfew. Every Monday night I raced into Honolulu to record my TV show but that was an obligation, not a luxury, and I was finding it very inconvenient. On the other nights I usually stayed in camp. Occasionally I did leave just to get away for even a short time.

When I was sprung on Saturday afternoon it was a different matter. I could leave without having to worry about curfew for more than 24 hours.

From 1977 on I lived in Hawaii Kai and usually took the same route when I was sprung if I wasn't heading straight into town to go to an Islander baseball game. It was the only time during the week that I saw the Kailua business district in the daytime. Although I did occasionally drive through for a brief exile during the week, it was only on Saturdays that I truly felt as if I was a part of the same world as the merchants and patrons.

When I reached Castle Hospital I turned left and headed east on Kalanianaole Highway. I would pass the Hawaii Youth Correctional Facility and Women's Correctional Facility before reaching the Enchanted Lake section of Kailua on the left. This was a pleasant suburban area often referred to by locals as "Enchanted Lakes" even though there is only one lake.

The highway turned to one lane in each direction once I reached Waimanalo. The area had a country ambience which is hard to describe. A familiar landmark was a local style fast food facility called Frankie's Drive-

In on the right. A little further down would be Bellows which was a small oceanfront Air Force facility. Beyond that is a place known as Sherwood Forest, so named for its multitude of trees, with horse stables and an open field directly across the highway.

Eventually I would reach Waimanalo Beach Park which included a typical public park with playground equipment in the area leading to the beach. Shortly after that the ocean would be directly next to the highway with Rabbit Island (Manana Island) majestically placed a mile or so offshore; so named because of its resemblance to a rabbit with its ears down. I would also pass the Oceanic Institute before reaching Makapu'u Beach with Sea Life Park directly across the highway.

I often unconsciously smiled at the sight of people swimming in the ocean or lying in the sand at the beaches in Waimanalo and Makapu'u. It was a very tranquil sight, as was the sight of the hang gliders overhead.

How wonderful it was to feel free again. The refreshing trip home generally took 35-45 minutes, depending on the traffic. I made good money as a football player and I loved my career. It still wasn't a simple or idyllic life. There was an enormous price to pay for the privilege. The rigors of camp were a heavy part of that price.

For about 30 hours or so I could revel in something more akin to what was really important in life. I had a peace of mind I didn't always experience while struggling to get through a week of two-a-days and everything that went with it.

Obviously when I returned to camp I had given up a lot of my freedom although I did enjoy the camaraderie of my teammates. I had to deal with the isolation from society, possible career threatening injuries, being worked to the bone and the possibility of being cut.

One of the Marines I met during the 1977 training camp was a corporal named Peter Lay. He was from Whittier, California, which wasn't too far from where I had lived in Montebello. He sought me out because he remembered me from high school since South Valley had played against his high school's football team.

Peter graduated from high school in 1972, meaning he was a sophomore when I was a senior. He went to Rio Hondo Junior College for a couple of years, worked a couple of jobs and then decided to begin a three-year stretch in the Marines; the last year of which was spent at the Kaneohe Marine Corps Air Station after a year and-a-half on Okinawa.

One Saturday I was preparing to leave when I spotted Peter. He was to meet some friends in Kailua so I gave him a lift.

"This is always so refreshing," I commented as we exited the base. "For six full days it's football, football, football. It's always nice to spend the day away."

"Yeah, I guess you don't get much time to yourself," Peter remarked.

"Not enough to really do anything. Through the days of two-a-days, meetings and everything else you think about what isn't all that far away but seems like light years away. There are beaches, shopping centers, movie theaters and other places nearby. Even my condo is only about 18 or 19 miles away but it all seems like an alien world."

Peter said he understood exactly what I meant. He recollected the day in November, 1974, when he began basic training. Although most of that first day was spent looking pretty much like a civilian at the AFEES station in Los Angeles, he didn't feel like a free man. It was also difficult to ride the bus from Los Angeles to San Diego and watch all of the civilian facilities go by.

"I know I volunteered for the Marines but I hated the thought of being locked up for boot camp," Peter said.

One of the most difficult things Peter had to endure was going through extremely harsh physical drills. This was done with commercial aircraft taking off just over the fence at San Diego International Airport. A wire fence was the only thing that separated the area where Peter was being worked to the bone and the airport tarmac.

"You've got those damned drill instructors screaming and yelling at you," he lamented, "and you can see those planes taxiing and taking off. It was always tempting to climb the fence, find a way to get on the plane and fly to wherever that plane was going."

Suddenly the rigors of training camp didn't seem quite so harsh.

At least until I returned.

One thing that was different in 1977 was that I had Carol back in my life. This was obviously a welcome difference. I called her once or twice a week after the evening meeting.

That doesn't sound like much but this was 1977. This was a few years before every other person on the planet owned a cell phone. In order to talk to Carol I had to find a vacant pay phone on a base full of Marines and dozens of NFL hopefuls.

It also comes back to our just resuming our relationship after a three-year hiatus. I still needed time in solitude when I could be away from camp, or so I believed, and Carol understood.

We still had time to spend together. If the Islanders were home we always went to their games which was never a problem since Carol liked baseball and understood how sitting comfortably at a baseball game was a pleasant way of mentally recuperating from the rigors of camp. It was even while I was playing baseball in college that Carol first noticed me.

Carol and I also had time to go to dinner together. Despite my aversion to eating in public facilities after spending the week eating with dozens of football players, I recognized Carol's need to go out to eat even if it was a casual place like Bob's Big Boy or Sizzler. The important thing was that I was on a brief sabbatical and could spend some time with Carol.

There was still a barrier between Carol and me. I didn't mistreat her in any way although I had unwittingly drawn a demarcation line which limited how close I would allow her to get to me. I was afraid to give myself fully to her partially because that was essentially what I had done for Annica only a few months earlier and got burned specifically for being willing to be open, sincere and unselfish.

It didn't make sense that I was apprehensive about Carol over what Annica did. I knew that life was dealing me a much better hand by bringing Carol back to me. My relationship with Annica probably had been fated to end down the road anyway but I stuck with her for as long as it seemed right. Perhaps it would have officially ended on my end when Carol turned up or perhaps time and distance would have driven Annica and me apart. All I know is it ended in about as humiliating a fashion as one can imagine. The memory of that carried into my relationship with Carol.

Of course Carol wasn't without culpability. She was still the woman who left without a trace a few years earlier. Although I knew Carol well enough to know that she didn't do so maliciously, I still feared the possibility of it happening again.

Perhaps there was no reason to compare Carol and Annica. Both were physically very beautiful so they had that in common. They were also the only two women who had had relationships with me intense enough for me to ponder whether there might be a lifetime future between us. In both cases they ended in ways which left me baffled.

But Carol was back. I loved her. I always had and always would. I simply had trouble showing it under the circumstances. I was very confused, I think.

Carol didn't know what to think. My distance made her wonder if she was being punished for her disappearance. It did play a role, of course, but neither of us realized the primary culprit was Annica. I hadn't even gone into any detail regarding my less-than-amicable parting with Annica. I recalled telling Carol something to the effect of what part of her anatomy I believed Annica had stuck her head but not much else. I was too proud to admit to Carol that I had gone so far out of my way for Annica's benefit and wound up humiliated.

After our meeting the night before our public scrimmage we held an impromptu talent night in the courtyard of our compound. It was something Russ Allen suggested about three days earlier and was planned out by Allen, Norm Richards, Ted Dietrich, Steve Bender, Marv Nelson, Jeff Kerner, Clint Abraham and me.

Attendance was not mandatory although almost everybody including the coaches attended. It was our version of *The Gong Show* which was popular at

74

the time although I never understood why since I thought the show was pretty stupid. Bender served as master of ceremonies. Marv was the lone judge. His "gong" was a large pot that he struck with a ladle.

Allen and Richards started the night as a bluegrass duo. Russ was an outstanding banjo player and Norm was fairly good on guitar. If they needed the work they were probably good enough as a duo to be hired at one of the local dives.

At least they were good enough if they didn't try to sing. They did good renditions of *Dueling Banjos* and *Foggy Mountain Breakdown* which were instrumentals. It was prearranged that they would then start singing *Rocky Top* and Marv would gong them away after the first few bars. Those few bars convinced virtually everybody that Russ and Norm should never aspire for careers as singers.

Almost everybody was advised that they could be arbitrarily selected to perform so that they could think of something to do. Bender would call on whomever he happened to spot. That individual would do something brief and usually off the wall until he was finished or gonged off.

"We would like to welcome Neil Carver to our show to display his talent," Bender announced, much to the surprise and possible chagrin of Carver, a rookie quarterback out of Mississippi.

Carver dutifully moved to the front and did his act. He laid on his back and raised his arms and legs, gradually moving them closer to his body to impersonate bacon frying.

That lasted about five seconds. Marv gave him the gong.

Mixed in were skits which featured a semblance of organization. Defensive tackle Hank Prendergast was a part of an extremely small minority of possibly one who could actually sing. The witty six-year African-American veteran out of Southeast Missouri stood erect and held his hand over his heart before belting out his version of *God Bless America*.

God bless the Hawaiians
Team that I love
Stand beside them
And guide them
Through the night with the coach from above.
From Hawaii, to Miami, to Los Angeles,
Gray with smog.
God bless the Hawaiians
My team sweet team
God bless the Hawaiians
My team sweet team

Later I was part of a skit with Dietrich and Abraham that was actually largely plagiarized from a skit done in Detroit several years earlier. and described in George Plimpton's *Paper Lion*. Dietrich portrayed Walker and Abraham played a rookie. I hung out of sight throughout most of the routine.

Rookie: You wanted to see me, Coach?

Walker: Yes, rookie. We've been going over our roster and realized that you figure very prominently in our plans.

Rookie: Really? Oh, this is so exciting. Does this mean I'm going to start?

Walker: No, idiot. You figure in our plans by not being on the team. We can't win with you on the roster.

Rookie: But Coach, I work really hard. I'll try harder.

Walker: Sorry, rook. It just won't work. You're slow, you're fat, you couldn't block your way through mashed potatoes and your breath would gross out a skunk.

Rookie: (on his knees) Oh, please. Give me one more chance.

Walker: Sorry, rook. There just isn't room for you. The traveling secretary has your ticket home. (hollering) Mr. Okuda.

At this point I appeared. I was carrying an ax that was borrowed from the Marines. I was wearing a pillowcase with eyeholes over my head as an executioner's hood.

Walker: Give the rookie his ticket home.

Okuda : Yes, Coach.

I grabbed the rookie's arm and led him to the chopping block which was actually a chair. As I raised the ax Walker closed the bit by saying to the rookie, "Best of luck in your future."

The few "organized" acts were spaced out among the arbitrary selections. We hoped that would hold everybody's interest and it seemed to.

Rookie safety Jim Vorsino from Indiana had an interesting routine.

"I'm going to rehearse the beer commercials I'm going to do after my career is over."

He opened a can of beer, chugged it down in about five seconds and then belched.

Mark Black was called. He did an impromptu ballet for about ten seconds and was mercifully gonged away.

One of the funnier bits involved Eric Hamer. He announced that he was going to perform *Telephone Man*, probably the corniest song to hit the charts in 1977 (giving Gabe Kaplan's *Up Your Nose* a run for its money), with his armpits.

Eric ostensibly thought he would be gonged quickly. He started, then looked over at Marv, then continued. He looked over at Marv and nodded his head to encourage him to gong him off.

Everybody was laughing because Eric looked extremely uncomfortable. He continued, then stopped and looked hopefully at Marv.

"No, no," Marv said loud enough for everybody to hear. "Keep going. I like this."

It was a fun night. Roughly half of those present would not be around when the regular season started. This gave them a recollection about which they could smile.

July 30 was the day of our annual scrimmage. By this time there were 94 players left in camp. After 25 days the only ones cut were those the coaching staff ascertained had absolutely no chance of being of any benefit to the team. Walker gave everybody as much time as he could but there were those he simply knew would never make it. Films, scouting reports and recommendations were no substitute for what Walker and his aides saw in front of them.

Like the year before, I felt compelled to venture off by myself after lunch. I drove into Kailua's business district and pulled into a small shopping center. I bought an afternoon newspaper from the rack outside the Holiday Mart and then went inside the A&W next door and bought a hamburger, fries and root beer. Although my mind was on the scrimmage and I checked my watch every two or three minutes, I did manage to lose myself in the newspaper.

Of course there was an update on the team. I didn't bother reading it. This sojourn into Kailua was a sanctuary. Whatever was in the article wasn't anything I didn't already know. I divorced myself from the Hawaiians during my brief sabbatical.

Reading about the outside world, there was an article about the possibility of Lyndon Johnson stealing his election to the U.S. Senate in 1948. There was a question about 200 allegedly fake ballots.

Trade tensions between the U.S. and Japan were heating up. It was also the second anniversary of the disappearance of Jimmy Hoffa.

In Hawaii three men were arrested on the island of Kahoolawe. This was the uninhabited island the military had been using for target practice, much to the chagrin of the native-Hawaiian population. It wasn't unusual in those days for somebody of Hawaiian blood to sneak onto the island to protest the bombing.

In sports, the first NFL exhibition game of the season was scheduled for that day. The Jets and Bears would be squaring off for the Hall of Fame Game in Canton, Ohio. Being inducted into the Pro Football Hall of Fame were Bart Starr, Forrest Gregg, Frank Gifford and Bill Willis.

Vic Bernal and Eddie Watt teamed up to pitch the Hawaii Islanders to a 5-4 win over the Tucson Toros. Bernal had been pitching out of the bullpen. Manager Dick Phillips said that Bernal had just earned his way back into the starting rotation.

My favorite team, the Los Angeles Dodgers, had just scored a 4-1 victory in Montreal in a game that was halted after seven innings because of rain. I was feeling good about the Dodgers' 13-game lead over Cincinnati in the National League West. Although the Reds were essentially the same team that had swept the New York Yankees in the World Series the previous season, I was confident that the Dodgers would not blow their sizable lead the way they did in 1951.

Reading the newspaper at the A&W was my way of killing time before the scrimmage. Other players utilized other methods. Bender went grocery shopping with his wife. Several other guys took naps or watched television. Dave Shuford, Eric Hamer, Frank Joseph and Rich Hasegawa had a small stakes poker game. Ed Jennings and Mark Black actually did nine holes of golf with a couple of Marines.

I was back in camp by four o'clock. That was more than enough time to get taped and dressed. The buses would be leaving at 5:30 after the two sides had briefings from their respective head coaches.

"Ready to go?" I asked a Black rookie from UCLA named Chuck Hebron.

"I guess. I don't remember being this nervous in college and I even played in the Rose Bowl."

"Just remember. You got this far. That means you've done pretty well. Just keep playing hard."

I had to be guarded in my encouragement. First of all, I didn't want to give him enough of a push so that he would wind up taking a friend's job away. Secondly, he would be on the opposite team during the scrimmage. Thirdly, this third-round draft choice was a linebacker and I didn't want to build up his confidence so much that he would wind up pulverizing me.

As we took the drive to the scrimmage site of Kailua High School we were once again greeted by a smattering of cheers along the way. On Kalaheo Avenue a few fans in their yards spotted us and waved. When we reached Kailua's business district there were a few horns honking, arms waving from inside cars and index fingers raised just like the year before. After one full NFL season our fans still seemed to like us.

Not every fan was enlightened. One woman in her early 20s spotted the bus stopped for a red light on Kuulei Street at Oneawa Street.

"Who are you guys playing tonight?" she asked from the sidewalk fronting a local dry cleaner.

"Ourselves," Kerner called. "We're going to beat ourselves."

"Just like we did in Denver last year," Hayer added.

It had been a relatively quiet bus to this point. Kerner's and Hayer's responses cracked everybody up including the coaches. It even cracked everybody up on the other bus which was right behind us and close enough for almost everybody to hear the exchange.

Of course not everything was equitable in the pro football world. Kerner and Hayer were seasoned veterans still close to the top of their games. They could get away with occasional witticisms like that. Had those remarks come from fringe players. . . .

Like the year before, we were greeted with enthusiasm when we reached the scrimmage site. It was another overflow crowd for this charity event. The previous year the spectators didn't have any idea of what kind of team we would be. After our mediocre but outstanding for an expansion team showing in 1976, our fans knew we were dead serious about our football.

The cheers washed over me as we ran on the field. It was another breath of fresh air. The scrimmage was another milestone since we were playing in front of the general public again. Although it was only a preseason scrimmage, it was another giant leap toward the start of what I hoped would be an outstanding season.

There were 91 active players for the scrimmage. There had been 19 cuts including the two Ivy Leaguers. Two had left camp including tight end Danny Klaas who had been on the taxi squad in 1976 and was having marital problems. The remaining three were out with injuries although two of them were expected to be healthy in time for our first exhibition game against the Giants the following week.

Carol was there. She was with her best friend, Stacy Miyamoto. I couldn't see either of them and had no idea of where they were sitting but I knew they were there.

I had a reasonably good scrimmage. I rushed twice for eleven yards. I had three receptions for 104 yards including a 72-yard touchdown pass from Joseph. During the special teams phase I had one punt return for eleven yards and a kick return for 27 yards.

Overall it seemed like a good scrimmage. It wasn't a bad way to end the first phase of camp. Unfortunately there were those who wouldn't see the second phase.

CHAPTER FIVE
The Exhibition Season

Monday's cuts were almost sadistic. Ten hopefuls had to pack their bags. This included two players who had been rookies with us in 1976. Fullback Danny Edwards and tight end Craig Kamanu were among four players cut with prior NFL experience. Also among the casualties was Kimo Pume; the rookie free agent defensive tackle from the University of Hawaii.

Some of the cuts stung. We still couldn't afford to get caught up in our grief. It was time to move on.

Although we were still technically in our training camp mode, we had done away with the two-a-days and could focus primarily on future opponents. It was exciting since we could look forward to an actual encounter with a rival in a bona fide NFL stadium.

The absence of two-a-days did not mean liberated afternoons. It was still a regimented schedule. Twice a week we had safety valve workouts for players designated as emergency backups. I continued my role as emergency quarterback and also got some work in as a punter. I hadn't punted since high school but I was still able to put together some fairly good punts.

The safety valve sessions were not contact sessions. They were done simply to familiarize the emergency backups with the plays. There were only a handful of us affected by this anyway. Guard Bill Stanek ran some plays at fullback, tackle Vince Daniels worked out at guard and linebacker Kevin Zanakis ran plays at tight end. Hasegawa worked out at tailback and Hamer ran patterns as a wide receiver.

These drills were run primarily for my benefit since an emergency quarterback was considered to be the most vital of the safety valve positions. It was less difficult to improvise at the other positions. A team might as well leave the field if the regular quarterbacks go down and there is nobody who can fill in.

Other players were called out for these drills to give a semblance of a feel of game conditions. It was done with the only real contact coming when offensive players hit the dummies held by the defensive players. There were occasions of incidental contact when defensive backs and receivers bumped in a joint effort to reach a pass. They were careful not to go too hard.

During the 1976 training camp I worked at quarterback only occasionally during the regular practice sessions. I only learned a handful of plays; just enough basic rushing and pass plays to carry us through in the unlikely event that I was needed.

In 1977 I spent more time working out at quarterback with these twice-weekly special sessions and would continue at least once a week during regular workouts throughout the season. Every play our regular quarterbacks could run, I could run.

I loved these sessions. My devotion to football could be traced to my days as a high school quarterback. This was almost like reviving an old friend who had been left for dead for a few years. It was exhilarating to discover that I could still roll out or drop back and fire bullets on short pass routes and still had the touch to complete long passes. I also still had the moves and timing to hand off on rushing plays; something that isn't as simple as it appears.

"Geez, Jay," Allen remarked after I completed about half-a-dozen consecutive passes. "You missed your calling. You could lead Tampa Bay to the Super Bowl if you were the Bucs' quarterback."

"I'm sure their current crop of quarterbacks would be thrilled to hear you say that," backs and receivers coach Craig Bennici cracked.

"Helluva pass, Jay," Hasegawa commented, having returned after being the recipient of the previous pass. "They should've had you throwing more passes in college. Maybe we could've beat Nebraska."

"Nebraska?" I replied lightly, knowing that Rich couldn't have been especially serious about our 1971 encounter with the team that would win the National Championship. "They beat us 45-3. What difference would a few passes from me have made?"

Aside from these special sessions, we also had mandatory weightlifting sessions and film sessions in the afternoons. These included films of our upcoming opponents.

We obviously couldn't watch films of the Giants' previous preseason game since they were also about to begin their exhibition season. We did, however, have films of them from the previous season. I am sure it was no coincidence that we saw films of a game the Giants actually won in 1976 to prevent us from getting cocky about their 3-11 season. On Wednesday afternoon we watched the Giants beat the Lions late in the 1976 season.

This is not to say that Walker didn't give us afternoons off. He made it a point to give us an afternoon off during the week whenever possible, meaning we could leave after lunch but had to be back in time for dinner. Walker believed that a little extra freedom at this stage meant better performances overall and I believe he was right. It was a breath of fresh air. Some guys took care of personal business, some spent time with family, some did recreational things and some simply lounged around.

In my case it varied. I recall spending time on a nearby beach. I also enjoyed the base bowling alley a couple of times. Once I went to Don Simmons' house which was only about a mile away and spent the afternoon watching television.

I never ventured too far away despite the temptation to go into Honolulu. Carol was working and I would also have to deal with the heavy afternoon traffic on my way back. There was enough to do in the general vicinity of camp to ease the tension.

The week leading to our first exhibition game was a long one. It is what happens when one focuses on a single significant event. Although the game was only five days away from when our workweek began on Monday, it seemed as if it would come in a totally different lifetime.

We left Hawaii shortly after lunch on Thursday. Unlike the regular season when we always flew out of Honolulu International Airport, it was simply a matter of boarding the gray military buses that transported us to the tarmac on the base where our chartered DC-8 awaited.

What is interesting is that a watchdog group eventually demanded an audit to see how much of the taxpayers' money was used to fund the Hawaiians' use of the Marine base. It was reported a year earlier that before any lease could be signed the Hawaiians had to agree to cover their own expenses ranging from the construction of the training facility to employment of off duty Marine personnel to the use of the military buses but apparently the group forgot or didn't believe the report. Once again the audit showed that the only money the taxpayers spent on us was when they bought tickets to our games.

As was often the case when I flew, I read. I rarely flew without picking up a newspaper. It also wasn't unusual for me to take along a magazine and/or at least one book.

In this case I was reading *The Godfather*. Rich Grummon had the hardback edition which he loaned me.

At this juncture I still hadn't even seen the movie. Back when *The Godfather* was current I rarely went to movies. I usually spent my free time in more active pursuits such as dancing, surfing and other beach activities, and sporting events. Occasionally I went to movies but they were never my first choice.

The book had me riveted. I rarely put it down during the long flight to New York. It convinced me that someday I was going to have to see the movie. Eventually I did after I bought it on VHS a decade or so later.

We arrived in New York sometime after dawn on Friday. I guess it was about nine before I was asleep in my hotel room. Because of the number of players still on the active roster, we had to double up. Just like in camp, I roomed with Marv.

It was the typical road routine of the NFL Hawaiians. I took a nap and grabbed a quick bite to eat. From there we traveled into New Jersey for a modest workout at the Meadowlands. Then it was dinner with the per diem we were given and a midnight curfew.

So here I was in the Big Apple. As I had learned in the past, visiting a city did not mean that I would actually see the city. I was there strictly to play football. I didn't see any Broadway shows or Yankee Stadium or any of the other attractions. I saw the Empire State Building and Statue of Liberty only from the seat of the aircraft.

There were landmarks that I did see up close. I recall the Hudson River and Holland Tunnel. While these landmarks might have been veritably New York, they were hardly what brought people to the city.

In the locker room of the Meadowlands I put on a pair of gym shorts, a Los Angeles Dodger T-shirt and hat, and my white all-purpose shoes. We were approaching the two-hour mark before kickoff.

I pondered about my tradition. Since my third game as a pro I ran laps around the field exactly two hours before kickoff.

But Carol was back in my life. She had disappeared prior to the start of my pro career and my initial purpose of the run was to simply appear to be loosening up while scanning the bleachers for her.

By the second season I had given up on ever finding her, yet I continued the ritual. In many cases I was running before the fans were allowed in the stadium so there was no point in looking for her.

Just the same, I had continued the ritual. Without fail in each of my first three seasons I was running laps two hours before kickoff. It had become a ritual if not a superstition.

And so two hours before kickoff at the Meadowlands I was running laps around the field. I decided it was too much a part of me to discontinue. The ritual was now in its fourth season. It would remain through the final game of my career.

We lost the toss. That meant seven consecutive exhibition games where we lost the toss. That was also the number of exhibition games in the Hawaiians' NFL history.

The only reason this really mattered was that I expected to play from scrimmage only through the first quarter. If we started the game on offense that meant I would have more opportunities to play.

Not that it really mattered statistically. It was simply a tune-up for most of the veterans. For some of the veterans and virtually all of the rookies it was an opportunity to show what they could do under game conditions. The later we got into the game, the more likely we were to see players who wouldn't be with us in New Orleans six weeks later.

For the record, I had a relatively unspectacular day. I rushed once for five yards. I also had one reception for nine yards and returned a kick for 23 yards.

My best showing was my one punt return. Late in the second quarter I fielded a punt near the left sideline at the Hawaii 32. I headed upfield to the Hawaii 46 where I was knocked out of bounds. It was pretty good but not spectacular.

Bender had a yawnable day. While I played only through the first quarter except for kick and punt returns which also had me on the field in the second quarter, Steve only played one series. He had a 16-yard completion to Dietrich, one incompletion and one interception. He was on the field for all of eight plays.

The rest of the first half was awarded to quarterbacks Billingsley and Joseph. Billingsley had a long series and then Joseph wound up with a series that didn't last. Walker sent Joseph back out for another series that ended the half with a field goal.

Billingsley overall looked pretty good. He began a drive at our one after the defense managed a tough goal line stand. The offense under him ultimately moved 91 yards to the New York eight.

Joe was then sacked for an eight-yard loss. After that he was under pressure again and threw the ball away for an interception. Obviously he needed to work on his poise under pressure.

It still wasn't a bad outing for the second-year quarterback from BYU. He completed seven of ten passes for 57 yards.

Joseph also had a reasonably good outing. He completed three of six passes for 52 yards. It was a nice homecoming for him after playing the first seven years of his career with the Jets.

As expected, those of us who played the first half were allowed to shower and dress at halftime. At that point we were down 7-3. It was 14-3 when I returned to the field in the third quarter.

We had started the opening drive of the half at our own 14. On the very first play Neil Carver threw a pass that was picked off at the 25 and returned to the one. One play later the Giants rushed for a TD.

Near the end of the third quarter we scored a field goal. Near the end of the fourth quarter an 80-yard drive was climaxed by an eight-yard touchdown pass from Steve Garibaldi to Dave Rossi. That narrowed the gap to 14-13.

Unfortunately our onside kick attempt was too long. The Giants ran out the clock.

"There are some guys playing their hearts out out there," I overheard Walker remark along the way.

He was right. From my vantage point on the bench it was obvious that players on both sides were giving their all. A lot of careers were on the line.

Stats showed that Carver settled down after his interception. In a dozen attempts he completed seven passes for 114 yards.

Garibaldi had a respectable outing. The rookie free agent from Syracuse completed five passes in eleven attempts for 49 yards with no interceptions and one touchdown.

Only three cuts were made before we prepared for our next matchup. All were rookie free agents. We were well under the roster limit for that point and Walker wasn't going to make cuts simply for the sake of making cuts. All but the three unfortunates would get at least one more opportunity to showcase themselves when we took on Memphis on Monday night at Aloha Stadium.

There was some question about our quarterback situation. Bender and Billingsley seemed secure, barring a total collapse. Billingsley could be erratic but the coaching staff seemed to believe he would develop. They must have seen something in him or else they wouldn't have taken him as early as the second round a year earlier.

Offensive tackle was our most top-heavy position. There were six returnees from the previous season including one who spent 1976 on the taxi squad. Also in the mix was Pete Kimmitt; our top draft choice out of UCLA.

Defensive end was also heavily stocked. We had five from 1976 including Kyle McWherter. He was the type of player Walker loved. It would have been easy for the African-American defensive end from Murray State to hang it up. Instead he refused to concede that he was through after four seasons and part of a fifth in the NFL.

Also at defensive end was Whitey Stansell. He was taken in the fourth round from Kansas State. Although Walker was sincere when he stressed that nobody was guaranteed anything regardless of how they were acquired, it is difficult to cut a rookie taken that early in the draft.

There would be three players on the shelf for Monday's game. Center Stuart Arroyo broke his leg prior to the scrimmage and would be out almost until the end of the exhibition season. Linebacker Chuck Hebron was out with a sore shoulder. Wide receiver Joe Schary would miss out with an ankle injury.

It looked like a good crowd, I observed during the pregame warmup, especially for a preseason game. One never knows what to expect in a game like this. The game is competitive although this early in the preseason it is comprised primarily of rookies and others simply trying to make the team.

We always tried to win but the early preseason games could often be boring for the fans. Those projected to start during the regular season would play the first quarter and possibly into the second. Then it becomes a battle for playing time for everybody else.

This is why it was such a pleasant surprise to see so many people at the stadium. Perhaps the fans had simply been yearning for pro football which hadn't been played in Hawaii since November.

It didn't hurt that the team sold so many season tickets. Exactly 40,000 season tickets were sold. That compared to about 27,000 in 1976. The team cut off season ticket sales at 40,000 to leave about 10,000 available for individual game purchases.

I suppose our 7-7 record in our maiden 1976 season left a good impression, especially since we usually played well in defeat. Probably all but a few of 1976's season ticket holders bought season tickets in 1977. Officials said they probably could have sold at least 5,000 more if they'd wanted to.

But this was a preseason game and there were two different season ticket packages. One was for all games while the other was strictly for regular season games. Individual game tickets in 1977 were 15 dollars for sideline seats and ten dollars for end zone seats. There was a slight discount for those who purchased season tickets for the regular season. There was a slightly larger discount for those who bought the all-games package.

The fact that we sold 40,000 season tickets surprised a lot of people including those who set the ceiling. They believed that the demand being that high was hypothetical. They set the ceiling in the unlikely scenario that the hypothetical happened. That left 10,000 unsold to ensure that as many people as possible could enjoy the Hawaiians in person. Our fans would understand if all of our games wound up sold out if the sellouts included a reasonable number of walk-up tickets. They wouldn't understand and would lose interest in us if only those willing to buy season tickets were able to see us in the flesh.

As it turned out, the Hawaiians initiated special policies for individual game tickets. Nobody could purchase more than ten tickets per game and could not buy tickets more than two games in advance. This made it harder on the scalpers and prevented a few hundred people from hogging the remaining tickets. Half of the individual game tickets were not made available until seven days prior to the game.

By the looks of the crowd, it appeared to me that almost everybody buying season tickets bought the full package. I found out later that roughly 85 percent purchased the full package. That was roughly 34,000. We were a hot item.

We kept a streak alive. We lost the toss. That meant all eight exhibition games in Hawaii's NFL history.

Our fellow expansionists seized the moment. Ostensibly undaunted by our projected starting defense, they started on their own 23 and moved slowly but surely downfield. There were no extremely long gains. They simply did enough to sustain the drive and chew up a substantial portion of the clock.

The Grizzlies climaxed their drive with a five-yard run into the end zone. The extra point gave them a 7-0 lead. With 5:58 left in the first quarter I was finally going to take the field.

We put together an impressive drive of our own. Along the way I caught two passes for a combined total of 30 yards. With us on the Memphis 25

Larry Scott ran a sweep around right end to the eleven. He broke three tackles along the way, much to the delight of the crowd.

On the next play I carried off right tackle. I was hammered at the line and coughed up the ball. Memphis recovered at the nine.

With 1:17 left in the first quarter Bender was through for the night. His token appearance included three completions in four attempts for 37 yards.

Memphis's drive carried into the second quarter. This time it didn't reach the end zone. Richards forced a fumble that Zanakis recovered at the Hawaii 37.

That got the crowd back into it. Billingsley took over at quarterback. I stayed in along with Kerner, Scott, Dietrich and the other starters.

On the first play Billingsley showed that he wasn't ready to dethrone Bender. Under heavy pressure, his pass to Dietrich was intercepted at the Memphis 46. The defensive back got all the way to the Hawaii 32.

The truth be told, Billingsley's pass was nowhere near Dietrich. With the heat on he pretty much put the ball up for grabs just like he did when he threw an interception the previous week against the Giants.

"You've got to relax out there," Walker told Billingsley. "Take the hit. A sack is always better than an interception."

Memphis scored again to climax a relatively short drive. The Grizzlies led 14-0 with 10:38 left in the first half.

I felt sick. That probably matched the way the team looked thus far. I didn't like losing, even during a preseason game, but the score didn't really bother me. What did bother me was that we were not playing well. At this stage it was primarily our projected starters against their projected starters. That meant that we were being buried by a team that won only two games in 1976.

Memphis kicked off. I fielded the kick a yard deep in the end zone.

This was my highlight of the night. I headed upfield following quality blocks from my teammates. Along the way I broke three tackles. I finally went down at the Hawaii 42 when a Grizzly grabbed me from behind around the waist and yanked me down.

I went down pretty hard but quickly bounced up with no ill effects. I hoped that return made up for my fumble.

As it turned out, I was through for the night on plays from scrimmage. Walker sent in backups for Scott, Kerner and me.

Billingsley was still in there. He was scheduled to rotate evenly with Joseph for the majority of the half. Since Billingsley's first drive lasted only one play Walker sent him back in.

Joseph was not amused. He didn't say anything but was visibly angry. He was expecting to go in.

At least Billingsley rebounded from his interception. He completed both passes he attempted on this drive. That included a 26-yard touchdown pass to tight end Chester McCracken; a second-round draft choice from Texas A&I.

We were down 28-7 at halftime. I had one more kick return for 24 yards to give me 67 yards between the two returns.

Billingsley and Joseph had unspectacular stats at quarterback. Billingsley had two completions in three attempts for 51 yards including the aforementioned interception and touchdown. Joseph had four consecutive completions for a relatively meager 29 yards sandwiched between two interceptions.

Despite the fact that the starters did not put together especially stellar performances, we got to shower and change at halftime. It wasn't that Walker was being generous. He probably simply preferred to have us sitting in the baseball dugouts and dugout seats between the dugouts. That meant less congestion on the bench while the rookies and fringe players got their licks in.

I was hungry. I went up the stairs underneath the stadium to the concourse and bought myself a couple of hot dogs and a beer and went back down the stairs. I consumed my food and drink while sitting in the Islander dugout with some of my teammates.

It wasn't against team rules to get refreshments. What was unclear was whether it was permissible to get beer. Nobody ever said it wasn't allowed. Guys like Black, Joseph, Blakely and a few others almost always had two or three beers during the second halves of these games before loading up on Tic Tacs.

Memphis still led 28-7 at the start of the fourth quarter. The Grizzlies expanded their lead to 35-7 while the Hawaiian wannabes fought for their careers, managing a field goal to narrow the gap to 35-10. On the final play of the game Earl Landers, a rookie free agent tailback from North Carolina, caught a swing pass from Carver. He ran a few yards before eluding a defender by diving into the end zone. The extra point made it a 35-17 loss.

The fans were hoping for a comeback victory or at least a closer game. Near the end we continued doing a lot of rushing plays and routine pass plays instead of a hurry-up offense comprised of quick passes. There were some boos from the crowd.

"The scoreboard means very little at this stage of the exhibition season," Walker was quoted as saying in one of the local newspapers. "The fans have to understand that we're trying to give them a good football game but our primary concern at the moment is evaluating the talent. We couldn't say that we gave these running backs a fair shot if we went to the air on every play. We need to see what they can do under game conditions. We like to win but it's not as imperative right now as it will be during the season."

The article then went into more description of the game.

"There were some bright spots," Walker admitted. "Overall I don't believe we played a good game."

That was an understatement. We really stunk up the place. The most glaring statistic was that we turned the ball over seven times; five on interceptions and two on fumbles.

So strange it seemed to have a Tuesday off. Only once before had the NFL Hawaiians had a Tuesday off. That was the previous October after we played our Monday night game in Oakland.

But this was a fluke when we played on a Monday night during the preseason. To avoid rush hour traffic the kickoff did not take place until seven o'clock. The game was televised only in Memphis so Grizzly fans got to see the game if they were willing to stay up almost until dawn. Throughout my entire career this was the only time we ever had a Monday preseason game.

One advantage to having Tuesday off was that I could do my TV show live. Having to race into Honolulu on Monday, prerecord the show and get back to base before curfew was getting very old. The live show still mandated a lot of work, especially when I had to grope for highlights of our encounter with the Grizzlies, but it was far less stressful than the Monday night routine.

Part of my afternoon was spent downtown. I had made an appointment to get a haircut at Fritz Andre in the Davies Pacific Center on Merchant Street. I was nearing my destination when a serious sounding newscaster came on the radio.

"Rock and roll star Elvis Presley . . . is dead."

Sad news although not earth-shattering for me. I had liked Elvis all right and respected him for his impact but had never been fanatical about him. The murder of John Lennon a few years later was more difficult for me to handle. I knew people, however, who were devastated by the death of Elvis.

"What do you think of ol' Elvis?" I asked Joe as he cut my hair.

"What do you mean 'old Elvis'?" Joe asked lightly, being roughly the same age as Elvis.

"Well, I don't mean he was old," I said. "I'm just saying it's too bad about him."

"Why? What happened?"

I was sorry I spoke. I felt awkward having to tell Joe and fellow stylists Fritz and Lloyd that Elvis Presley had died. None of them were into Elvis any more than I was as far as I knew. It still felt awkward.

After I got my hair cut it seemed like I heard nothing but Elvis on the radio. Perhaps that's all I remember but it seems like Elvis was all over the dial. Songs, interviews and personal reflections seemed to dominate the air waves.

When we returned to work on Wednesday there were four fewer people in camp. Four rookie free agents were told after breakfast to report to Walker with their playbooks.

This included Garibaldi. I figured that either he or Carver would have to go just to get the quarterback population down to four. Garibaldi completed only four passes in 13 attempts for 52 yards over the two games. Although Carver had thrown two interceptions, his seven completions in 12 attempts for 102 yards and a touchdown over the two games gave him the nod over Garibaldi. He would still need to dramatically improve his performance if he wanted to last much longer.

If it was any consolation, at least Garibaldi and the three other former hopefuls were spared the wrath of Walker during the film session. He was merciless because we truly did not play well. In the offensive film session I can't think of anybody he didn't lambaste at least once. Some of the guys probably would have gladly switched places with Elvis.

"I'm glad there are four weeks left before the season opener," Walker remarked when the offense and defense were together after the sessions. "I realize that these early exhibition games are not about winning or losing but I expected more of you, especially those of you who were with us last year. We are definitely not ready."

That stung. Although nothing was directed at me personally, being a part of that allegedly elite fraternity brought out the guilt in me. Football coaches, especially those with parts of Vince Lombardi rubbed off on them, have a way of belittling a man's self-worth.

"The defense surrendered huge chunks of real estate," Walker continued, referring primarily to the starting unit. "As far as the offense goes, those seven turnovers were downright disgusting. In order to win games you have to maintain possession."

Walker chewed us out pretty good.

Of course we deserved it.

"It was almost a sellout crowd Monday night," Walker pointed out as he entered the home stretch of his interminable chastising session. "I don't know the exact attendance but it was more than 48,000. More than 48,000 paid good money to be bored to death. If you guys don't play better in Houston and Seattle you're going to be playing before 50,000 empty seats when the Raiders come to town."

On the subject of Houston, that was our next destination with a relatively short week to prepare. We had our typical training camp schedule from Wednesday morning through Friday afternoon and then we flew to Houston, arriving just in time for a quick nap on Saturday morning before a light workout at the Astrodome.

"Wow!" I gasped.

That was my first expression after setting foot on the field at the Astrodome. It was actually my second time in this indoor facility since I had played here once in the WFL days but I was still impressed. I had watched baseball and football games in the 12-year-old facility on TV over the years but one cannot grasp the true splendor without experiencing it up close and personal.

Unlike outdoor facilities, the Astrodome used cushion seats to provide extra comfort for its patrons. The high ceiling was painted white since the original transparent dome resulted in too much glare for baseball players trying to track down fly balls. That caused the natural grass to die since there was no longer any sunlight to aid in its growth, forcing officials to scramble for a deal to install what became known as "Astroturf."

It was ultimately decided that artificial turf was superior to natural grass. Stadia such as Busch Stadium and Candlestick Park replaced grass with artificial turf while newly-built stadia, including Aloha Stadium in 1975, would include artificial turf.

Later it would be determined that artificial turf was not superior to natural grass. Excepting facilities with non-retractable domes, artificial turf would be replaced by natural grass at most stadia. Aloha Stadium would be one of the few holdouts.

We were still on a roll. We lost the toss for the ninth consecutive time in preseason. It almost seemed as if we had as much chance of winning the toss in a preseason game as President Carter had of getting his brother Billy to give up beer.

This time it paid to lose the toss. Eric Guinn put out a booming kick that was fielded four yards deep in the end zone. Hamer nailed the return man at the eleven.

Our starting defense, which Walker never hesitated to remind during the week that it was "an embarrassment to the NFL," dug in and was virtually impenetrable. Three plays later the Oilers faced fourth and 14 at their own seven.

That enabled me to take the field and stop marveling at the roof, the scoreboard and the air conditioning unit. I was extremely hyped to get started. After I took my position just inside the 50 I jumped up and down several times while waiting for the Oiler punting unit to break its huddle.

I fielded the punt at the Hawaii 44. Had I made a fair catch we still would have had very good field position. I decided to make a run for it.

It wasn't much of a gamble. I picked up at least five yards before I had any kind of a challenge. I managed to cut slightly to the left and put an end to that.

I was finally brought down at the Houston 26. Five plays later I rushed into the end zone from the three. We had a 7-0 lead with 11:27 left in the first quarter. It was also the first time we ever led during the 1977 preseason.

With less than a minute to play in the first quarter Bender threw his first touchdown pass of the preseason. It was a 26-yarder to Dietrich which was also Ted's first touchdown reception of the preseason. That gave us a 14-7 lead.

We suffered a casualty midway through the second quarter. It appeared that Jim Morrissey was going to be out of action for at least a couple of weeks. He injured his shoulder, meaning he was definitely out for the rest of the game. The true extent of his injury would not be known until later.

The Oilers kicked a 39-yard field goal to end the half. That cut our lead to 14-10. More extreme fireworks ignited earlier in the quarter.

In hindsight, I suppose we should have known something would develop. From the time that Rossi dropped Billingsley's pass near the end of the first half until we went to the locker room at halftime, Billingsley could be heard muttering under his breath. I happened to be nearby on the sideline and heard him mutter Rossi's name a few times. This was accompanied by language that probably had Brigham Young spinning in his grave.

Rossi should have caught the pass. It wasn't an especially difficult pass to catch. Just the same, even the best receivers drop passes they should easily catch. Vision momentarily obstructed by a defender or something in the crowd, turning toward the ball too late, misinterpreting the ball's trajectory or simply having too much time to think about it are among the causes for miscues. It is unfortunate but it happens.

I spotted Rossi about 20 feet from where Billingsley was using a vernacular which made us forget he had been on a church mission only five years earlier. Rossi grabbed a cup of Gatorade, chugged it down, crumbled the cup and slammed it down. His body language, vocal language, flushed face and bulging veins told me he was at least as upset with himself as Billingsley was.

"Take it easy, man," I said when I reached Rossi.

"I can't," Rossi replied angrily. "I shoulda had that (expletive deleted) ball. I never drop those. Never!"

"Sure you do," I said calmly, placing my hands on his shoulder pads to look him in the eye. "Everybody does. I do. Dietrich does. Lynn Swann does. Drew Pearson does. The trick is to not let it affect you next time. You've got to put it behind you."

Rossi was calming down a little but was still upset. Of course he had a lot riding on his performance. He had already experienced the crestfallen sensation of being cut once. Whether it was a lack of ability, a lack of conviction, attrition or his cocky attitude that led to his dismissal from the 49ers the year before, I knew not. All I knew was he desperately wanted to be a Hawaiian when we opened the regular season in New Orleans.

In the short time I had known Rossi he had given me a multitude of reasons to dislike him. He was two-faced, had a big mouth and he had a demented sense of humor. I liked him anyway.

Sort of.

"Let me tell you something," I said paternally. "I know exactly how you feel. Last November in Philadelphia I dropped a pass in the end zone. It was the last play of the game and we would have won had I caught the pass. Don't think I didn't feel like crap after that."

Rossi looked at me with traces of relief and even gratitude on his face. Although he was competing for my job, I felt compelled to help him. Perhaps I didn't truly consider him to be a threat to my status. He talked with the cocksure nature of an All-Pro future Hall of Famer but in reality he was simply good enough to have a legitimate shot at playing in the NFL.

When the half ended we filed into the locker room. Some of the stragglers were still coming in when Billingsley greeted Rossi with a hard right to the jaw.

Rossi had no way of knowing what was coming and went down. He sprang up quickly. Both players were restrained before any more punches were thrown.

"What the hell do you think you're doing, Billingsley?" Walker asked sternly as he stood toe to toe with the brash quarterback. "What do you think you're doing?"

Billingsley said nothing. He simply shook his head.

"What did Rossi do to deserve that?" Walker demanded to know. "Is this because he dropped a pass?"

Billingsley looked at the floor and nodded softly.

"That's the most pathetic excuse I've ever heard for hitting a man," Walker said, trying to keep his voice down. "That little episode will cost you 500 dollars. You will also shower, get dressed and spend the rest of the game here in the locker room. When the game ends you are to immediately go sit on the bus. I don't want to see you until we get to the airport."

We all thought that Walker was through for the moment. He wasn't.

"Let me tell you something else, Mr. Perfect. If you still think that what you just did was justified, you let me know. For every pass you throw that misses its target I will personally hold your arms together so that your intended receiver can take a shot at you. As long as you believe you were right to hit a teammate simply for dropping a pass you are going to have to take what you dish out."

Walker threw down the cigarette he was smoking, crushed it out with his foot and put a fresh cigarette in his mouth as he stormed away. I could see that his hands were shaking as he lit the new cigarette. In all the years I knew Walker, I can't recall too many times when he was more angry.

"You okay, man?" Jennings asked Rossi while I opened the lid to my Marlboro pack so that Rossi and then Jennings could help themselves.

"Yeah, I'm okay," Rossi replied bitterly. "Ah'm gonna get that little son of a bitch."

"Let it go," Allen directed. "Walker handled it. Your job is to try to make the team. Let it go."

Very little was said for the rest of halftime. The starters were through for the night so we showered, dressed and watched the second half from the sidelines.

Rossi played reasonably well in the second half. At least he didn't drop any passes.

In the end we finally had a preseason victory, 24-20. With playing time pretty well divided up, nobody had a spectacular day. I carried twice for nine yards and had one reception for six yards. My best stat was two punt returns for 30 yards.

The eyes were on the quarterbacks although not because of Billingsley. It is still worthy of note that he was the only quarterback of the four with a poor performance that day. He had one completion in seven attempts and one interception for 21 yards. It still would have been a poor performance even had Rossi caught the pass.

Bender was solid in his quarter of work. He completed all four passes he attempted for 65 yards and a touchdown.

Also throwing a touchdown pass was Joseph who completed five of seven passes for 49 yards and no interceptions. Carver completed two out of three for 28 yards and one interception.

Halfway through the exhibition season there was no reason to believe that Bender would not be our starting quarterback when we opened in New Orleans three weeks later. Only an injury or a total collapse would leave him on the bench.

As far as the backup situation went, it seemed to be up for grabs. I didn't realize how poorly Billingsley had played until I read the newspaper in Honolulu the next day. I wondered if whatever unofficial guarantees he might have had as a second-round draft choice were null and void because of his dismal game and what he did to Rossi.

Overall Billingsley's stats were okay. Through three games he had completed ten passes in 20 attempts for 129 yards. He had thrown one touchdown pass but had three passes picked off.

Joseph had 12 completions in 19 attempts for 130 yards. He also had one touchdown to his credit with two interceptions.

No less impressive was Carver. He had 16 completions in 27 attempts for 244 yards and a touchdown. His biggest impediment toward making the team was that he had thrown four interceptions.

Just the same, he was looking reasonably good.

So was Joseph.

If we could disregard the Houston game, so was Billingsley.

The space between the Houston game and when we had to return to camp at midnight seemed to pass in the wink of an eye. Our plane landed at the Kancohe Marine Corps Air Station at a little after eleven o'clock so I was back home at a little after midnight.

On Monday I got up, did some laundry, took a nap and prepared the finishing touches for my TV show. I then went to Carol's where she whipped up a nice pork chop dinner for us.

After that I went to the studio to prerecord the next night's TV show. I preferred to go to the Islander game where I could relax but I had my obligation. As I drove back to the Marine base I swore that I would not do the show during the following year's training camp. The show was once a blessing but it was more of an inconvenience by this time.

When cuts were made on Tuesday all four quarterbacks were still with us. Although Billingsley's value may have dropped a little in Houston, I didn't believe Walker was going to get rid of him based on one poor performance. He had it in him to be a decent NFL quarterback.

It must have been a major relief to Carver to still be with us. Early in the fourth quarter his first pass was intercepted and returned 17 yards for a touchdown, narrowing our lead to 21-20. It was only his second play from scrimmage and there were tears welling in his eys as he returned to the sideline. That alone told me how badly he wanted to make the team.

Like the rest of the projected starters, by this time I was on the sideline watching in street clothes. I was standing with Marv, McDaniel and Stanek when Carver sat on the bench and wiped his face with a towel. He hadn't been in long enough to have worked up a sweat. He was wiping away tears.

"Shake it off, Carv," Allen encouraged from nearby.

Bender sat next to Carver and put his arm around him. I couldn't hear what Bender was saying but it was obvious that he was trying to encourage him. After 15 seasons Bender still hadn't forgotten what it was like to be a rookie hoping for an opportunity to play pro football.

But Carver did not get the ax. He would be with us in Seattle on Sunday.

Four true rookies, one technical rookie who was on our taxi squad in 1976 and three veterans did get the ax on Tuesday. That reduced our roster to 67 including the injured Stuart Arroyo. He was expected to be ready in time for our final exhibition game.

Among those cut were three with ties to Hawaii. Linebacker Pat Morales, who had played for Kahuku High School before his college career at BYU, was sent packing. Another rookie free agent cut was safety Patrick Yokum from Walla Walla, Washington, who had played for the University of Hawaii. He had been my college teammate for one season since he was a freshman when I was a senior.

The final player with previous Hawaii ties to get cut was more of a shock. Defensive tackle K.T. Smith, who had been with us in 1976, was let go. He graduated from the University of Hawaii one year ahead of me before a pro career that would take him to Denver in the NFL and Birmingham in the WFL before returning him to Hawaii.

"You've got to be kidding," was my remark when I first set foot on the field at the Kingdome prior to our light workout on Saturday afternoon.

I suppose I shouldn't have been surprised. I caught a good look at the Kingdome from the team bus on Interstate 5. It didn't look nearly as big as the Astrodome did from the outside but I probably thought it was only an illusion. When I saw it from the inside the reality hit me.

The Astrodome was palatial. The Kingdome was a place to be avoided if one was claustrophobic. It was obviously larger than Honolulu's Blaisdell Arena but the most major sport played at the Blaisdell was basketball. The Kingdome featured baseball and football.

I had been awestruck by the Astrodome. I was probably disgusted with the Kingdome. The construction of the Kingdome was not Seattle's finest hour.

"The veterans will play at least through the first half," Walker told us in the locker room prior to the kickoff. "I want to give everybody a good look but we have to start building momentum for the season. Keep in mind that you're still with us because you deserve to be. Don't get discouraged. If you get discouraged your game will suffer. Everybody in this room has a shot at making this team."

That was important to Walker. He wanted everybody at their best. They couldn't be at their best if they were down on themselves. If they weren't at their best Walker couldn't get a true look at them.

We broke a string. We actually won the opening toss. It was the first time in ten preseason games.

Having the ball first did not seem to hurt us any. We started at our own 22 after Hasegawa fielded the opening kickoff a yard deep in the end zone and returned it to the 22. We then continued to march the length of the field.

On second and goal from less than a yard out I went in motion from right to left. Bender took the snap and fired a pass to me in the left slot. I sidestepped a defender and practically waltzed into the end zone.

We scored again in the first quarter on Guinn's 46-yard field goal. On the ensuing kickoff the Seattle return man fielded the ball at the one. Rookie Jim Vorsino shot downfield and brought the return man down at the eleven.

For the record, we scored again on our third possession which ran partway into the second quarter. It was Guinn again kicking a 57-yard field goal. That was the longest field goal in the Hawaiians' brief history although it was also unofficial since this was only preseason. It may also have been bad news for Phil Gerhardt, the rookie free agent kicker from Wisconsin. He had kicked three field goals in as many tries, as had Guinn, but his only long field goal was 46 yards.

It wasn't Gerhardt's job to win. It was more like Guinn's to lose. He was the incumbent. With the exception of one game in 1976, he had been very dependable. As good as Gerhardt looked, I doubted that he would be with us in New Orleans. With Guinn's 57-yarder I doubted that he would even be with us the following week against Oakland.

With Bender connecting with Dietrich late in the half for a 15-yard touchdown, our lead was expanded to 20-0. That was the way it was at halftime. It appeared to me that both of our first units were coming together. The offense had two touchdowns and two field goals in five possessions. The defense never let the Seahawks get past midfield.

Granted, we were playing a team that had only won twice in 1976. None of the teams we had played thus far had winning records in 1976. We had to have had one of the weakest preseason schedules in NFL history when factoring in previous season records. The Oilers had the best record among the four we had played thus far with five victories in 1976 including their victory over us. The Giants, Grizzlies and Seahawks had seven wins and 35 losses among them.

Just the same, there was something in the way we were playing. The units were coming together.

Bender had played the entire first half, as scheduled. He had ten completions in 20 attempts with no interceptions for 150 yards and two touchdowns.

The only subpar performance among the starters was that of Scott. He picked up only 20 yards in eight carries with his first three carries netting him no yards. Take away those three carries and he had a more respectable 20 yards on five carries.

I had 17 yards on two carries. That went with my three receptions for 40 yards and a touchdown. Dietrich had five receptions for 81 yards and a touchdown.

Walker surprised us by letting most of the first half starters shower and dress at halftime. It wasn't really expected this late in the preseason. Rather than go to the sideline when I was dressed, I first went to the concourse with Dave Shuford, our center from Notre Dame whom we acquired for Bob McWilliams in a trade with the Baltimore Colts.

We watched the third quarter and part of the fourth on the concourse. There were TV screens which enabled us to watch the action while enjoying a beer.

Buying the beer was interesting. Dave and I got in line behind the only patron at the moment; a man who appeared to about 70. I thought I was hallucinating when the stocky African-American woman dispensing the beer asked to see his ID. He showed it without complaint.

"Two beers, please," I requested, still unsure if I had seen correctly.

"Can I see an ID, please?"

I immediately understood as I pulled out my driver's license. Everybody regardless of age had to show an ID. I didn't know if it was a Kingdome policy or simply the vendor's policy. All I know is it seemed like a good idea to eliminate the hassle of trying to ascertain who should be carded and who shouldn't.

"Oh, Hawaii," the woman said brightly as she inspected my driver's license. "I guess you came all the way over here to see your team play."

"Uh, yeah," I responded as I accepted my license back while the vendor started pouring the two beers.

"You're lucky," she said. "Your team's a lot better than ours. Do you go to the games a lot."

"I've been to all of them so far," I replied casually while Dave tried not to laugh out loud.

By the end of the game Gerhardt had kicked field goals of 29 and 35 yards. Those were our only scores of the second half. We wound up with a 26-7 victory.

What was noteworthy was that Joseph played ahead of Billingsley. Whether Billingsley's poor performance the week before was a factor was unknown.

Regardless, both quarterbacks saw limited action. Joseph completed two passes in three attempts for 31 yards. Billingsley completed two passes in five attempts for 22 yards. Neither threw an interception.

Carver didn't play at all. I tried not to read anything into that but it didn't look good for him. I am sure he had to be wondering where his career was going.

During the flight home I worked up the nerve to ask Walker what he was planning for Tuesday afternoon.

"Why?" he asked firmly but not with hostility.

"Well, you know that I do this TV show on Tuesday nights that is prerecorded on Monday nights," I replied, trying to be careful to word myself properly. I felt as if I was asking Walker for a special favor and I hated to do that. "Anyway, the Islanders are in a hot pennant race against the team they're playing against right now. If I can go into town on Tuesday afternoon to tape the show it will be more up to date."

Walker stared at me for a good ten seconds. I am not sure if he was trying to discourage me from altering the routine. Tuesday was usually the afternoon he gave us off during the exhibition season after our morning workout but not always. I was simply hoping to give him a reason to make this week the norm.

"I don't know how you can play football with these outside interests," he muttered.

"Have I ever given you less than 100 percent?" I asked.

Walker paused and admitted that I had never been a slacker. He then admitted that he had been planning to give us Tuesday afternoon off anyway. He also reminded me to be careful not to get so wrapped up in my outside interests that it would become detrimental to my future as a football player.

There was no problem there. I was conscious of being a football player first. Although I still hadn't told anybody, I was growing even more certain that I would not be doing the TV show during the 1978 preseason.

It was close to midnight on Sunday night when I set foot in my condo again. I went to sleep almost as soon as I got there. I wanted to get up early in the morning to make the most of my day off.

And I did. I started by taking Carol to breakfast at the Columbia Inn. I was having a terrible craving for pancakes but I didn't want to go to the trouble of making them myself and I also didn't want Carol to have to put herself out. Instead I treated her to breakfast before she had to go teach at the university.

I went back home and tried to fix my place up. It suddenly dawned on me why my days off hadn't seemed especially restful. I had just moved in prior to training camp and hadn't had a chance to do much with my condo.

Not that there was a lot that I could do, I guess. It was a matter of getting the right furniture and putting it in place. Since I had virtually no interior decorating skills it was more of a challenge.

That night Carol and I went to Aloha Stadium to see the Hawaii Islanders in a double-header against the Spokane Indians; then the AAA farm club of the Milwaukee Brewers while the Islanders were still operated by the San Diego Padres. It was the Islanders' final home series of the season and they began the night holding a slim one-half game lead over Spokane in their division.

The Islanders swept the twin-bill by identical 5-3 scores. The Indians went with the long ball, hitting six home runs during the two games but all of them were solo shots. The Islanders' lead was extended to two-and-a-half games.

Five rookies and two veterans had played their final games with the Hawaiians. Two days after our game in Seattle the seven finished breakfast and were told to go see Walker and take their playbooks. That is akin to a gangster being told he is being "taken for a ride." There is nothing enigmatic pertaining to what is about to happen in either case.

The casualties included two alumni of the University of Hawaii. Rookie linebacker Brad Kuiwa was sent home to Waimanalo. Sent home to Kahuku was defensive end Edmund Kupau, our 25th round draft choice from 1976. Both were fine football players. We had simply reached the point where numbers mandated that we release NFL caliber players.

I happened to run into both men before they left camp. I had known them both in college since their careers overlapped mine although Kuiwa's by only one year. Kupau was two years behind me so I had known him better, especially since he had also played one season with me on the Hawaiians.

"It was great while it lasted," Kupau remarked with a smile of resignation. "I was the last player drafted last year and nobody expected me to make the team. I guess I'm lucky I got as far as I did."

Walker would be the first to dispute Kupau's contention of luck. Walker maintained until the day he died that he never kept a player who didn't deserve to play for him. Nobody was *lucky* to be on the team.

Kupau and Kuiwa were told to stay in shape; that a spot could open for them. Both still doubted that they would ever play for the Hawaiians again. Kupau was planning to see if there might be an opportunity with another NFL team. Kuiwa, who was virtually untried in the NFL, was planning to check out the prospects in Canada.

Suddenly Hasegawa and I were the only University of Hawaii alumni on the roster. The only other player with Hawaii football ties prior to the NFL expansion was Hamer who had played one season with the WFL Hawaiians before also being a part of the NFL Hawaiians.

The newspaper reported some good news for a former University of Hawaii player. K.T. Smith, who was cut by the Hawaiians a week earlier, had signed with Miami. That meant he would be playing reasonably close to his home in Warner Robins, Georgia. He would also be opposing us during the third week of the season.

Our active roster was down to 58. Center Stuart Arroyo was returning to action but two others were sidelined by injuries. Wide receiver Joe Slater had broken his elbow. Defensive tackle Hank Prendergast had a broken ankle. Both were expected to be out for about six weeks.

As expected, I prerecorded my TV show on Tuesday afternoon. Figuring prominently were highlights from the Seattle game. The studio was also able to get a clip of Lou Brock stealing a base against the San Diego Padres the night before; something that would not have been available had we taped the show on Monday night. It was Brock's 893rd stolen base. That broke Ty Cobb's major league record.

I was also able to give a glowing account of the Islanders' sweep from the night before. I could not have been as effective had I not been at the stadium to witness it.

"And how are the Islanders doing now?" I asked.

This was our usual segment where the graphic would appear in front of me. As always, four different responses were taped to cover if the Islanders were winning, losing, tied or if the game was rained out. Rain wasn't likely but one never knew in Hawaii.

"This is the Islanders' final home game of the regular season," I pointed out. "They began tonight with a two and-a-half game lead over Spokane. Their fate is in their own hands."

The Raiders were in town. Not only were they the defending Super Bowl champions, they were the first team we would see in the preseason who had a winning record in 1976.

It was good that it worked out this way. To play a team of the Raiders' caliber at this point would provide a good barometer for us. Both teams would be using primarily starters who should have been in close to midseason form. A good performance against the Raiders would suggest that we were about ready for the season.

Those were my thoughts as I ran my pregame laps. It felt good to be home again and in the great outdoors. I realized that the next time we left town we would be playing for keeps.

Of course that was based on the assumption that I would make the team. We still had Rossi and Gene Marceau vying for my spot. Perhaps Walker would keep them and not me.

In the limited time I had played I had six carries for 31 yards and seven receptions for 85 yards. On the assumption that I had the team made, it was a battle for the other spot. Marceau had three carries for nine yards while Rossi had one carry for one yard. Rossi led in receptions with seven for 52 yards compared to Marceau's four for 27 yards.

It was hard to pick a winner. Neither had spectacular stats. If there was anything that might give somebody an edge, Rossi seemed more likely to throw a good downfield block.

But Marceau wasn't as cocky.

"I want to play as many of you as I can," Walker announced in the locker room prior to when we would take the field before kickoff. "We also have to focus on shifting the momentum to the upswing going into the season. The starters will play at least three quarters with the same kind of substitutions we would make in a regular season game. After that, we'll see. We'll do everything we can to get you some playing time."

As we ran on the field I thought about how our regular season opener was only two weeks away. It seemed like an eternity.

I glanced up into the bleachers as I approached our sideline. I had left Carol two tickets. I spotted her near the top of the orange seats with Stacy Miyamoto.

According to Carol, she and Stacy became best friends about five minutes after Carol arrived at her new house in 1968. Carol was standing in the yard of her Hawaii Kai home checking out the palm trees and Koko

101

Crater when Stacy walked by and introduced herself. The bond was immediate.

Hawaii won the toss.

"Wow, we're on a roll," I remarked.

"Huh?" said Mark Black who had been standing next to me.

"We won the toss. That's two in a row."

Black looked at me and shook his head. His expression indicated that he may have thought that I was insane.

"You keep track of when we win the toss?" he asked.

I shook my head and dropped the subject. I couldn't explain how I knew our preseason coin toss record. I wasn't even sure of why I knew.

There were some interesting highlights of our encounter with the team that marred our final home game of 1976. Hawaii drew first blood from the Oakland ten. Grummon caught a touchdown pass eight yards deep in the end zone to climax a sustained drive. Oakland was called for pass interference but we obviously declined. Walker almost went into cardiac arrest when the referee announced that we were accepting the penalty, then corrected himself. We led 7-0 with 5:03 left in the first quarter.

On the first play of the second quarter Oakland punted into the end zone. It might not have got to the end zone had I not laid a pretty good block on the wideout. He tried to sidestep me, then tried to leap over me. That was when I drove myself into him and flipped him over.

The wideout sprang up and shoved me. I hesitated and then took a step toward him. Hasegawa got between us.

"Come on, man. Take it easy," Rich said to the wideout, holding his arms out to keep us apart. "We know how badly you want to make this team. Take it easy."

Suddenly I felt pity for the wideout. He was probably fighting for a spot on the roster. I had kept him from making a big play that could have helped his chances.

Still, I had a job to do. I couldn't hold back for his benefit. As long as I was on the field I had to give it my all.

There was no scoring through most of the second quarter. I don't believe it was ineptitude on the parts of the offenses. It seemed to be primarily the superior work of the two defenses. We were going at each other as if it was already Super Bowl XII. Since we were trading conferences and divisions with Seattle for some reason, it was possible that we would face Oakland in the Super Bowl.

With Oakland driving Rodgers recovered a fumble at the Hawaii 38. If we could march down the field in a timely manner we could take a 14-0 lead into the locker room at halftime.

We were looking good and the crowd was into it. Scott was chewing up huge chunks of real estate. I then rushed off left tackle for eleven yards to give us a first and goal at the seven.

Walker sent Rossi in to spell me for a play or two. I watched from the sideline as Bender dropped back to pass. He spotted Rossi in the end zone.

A defensive tackle hit Bender's arm as he threw. The ball fluttered toward the right corner of the end zone. A defensive back covering Dietrich adjusted and made a diving catch. The Raiders had first and ten at the 20. There was 3:58 left in the half.

It was good defense that caused the turnover. It also seemed to fire up their offense. Ken Stabler methodically moved his team downfield. They scored on an eight-yard pass with six seconds left in the half.

Obviously one play can figure substantially. We could have had a 14-0 lead at halftime or, at worst, a 14-7 lead. Instead we went into the locker room with a 7-7 tie.

There would be no halftime shower. As Walker had said before the game, the starters would play at least three quarters.

Walker made one change. To the surprise of nobody, Bender was finished for the afternoon. Walker wanted Bender to play only long enough to sharpen his skills for the season. He had six completions in ten attempts for 98 yards with one touchdown and one interception.

The other three quarterbacks were to rotate. They actually drew straws to determine the order. The rotation would be Carver, Billingsley and Joseph.

Black intercepted a pass at the Hawaii 37 to set up our first series of the third quarter. Initially it appeared that the seventh year pro out of Oklahoma was going to go all the way. A desperate lunge by Stabler knocked Black out of bounds at the 12.

Needless to say, the crowd loved it. The 46,105 cheered as if they didn't know it was only a preseason game. It was as if we were playing with vengeance on our minds for Oakland defeating us in our final home game of 1976 and ruining our chance for a winning season. We were 36 feet from retaking the lead.

Carver's luck at drawing straws earned him an opportunity he hadn't had in our previous preseason games. He got into the game with the starters still at the other ten positions. The 22-year-old rookie was calling the plays before a group of veterans with between three and ten years of pro experience.

Scott got us halfway to the goal line with a six-yard rush up the middle. On second down Carver rolled to his left and tried to hit Grummon in the end zone. Unfortunately he overcompensated for the fact that he was rolling away from his natural side and his pass was off the mark. The pass was picked off in the end zone.

I don't think there was any rookie who put so much heart into his performance that preseason than Carver did. It was obvious from day one that he was determined to make the team. He worked and worked and worked.

Obviously he was devastated. He stood off to the side and avoided eye contact, looking upward as if he was trying to find a pretty girl in the uppermost part of the stadium on the opposite side. He was shellshocked.

Was the interception Carver's death blow?

All I knew was that it didn't look good for him. Bender looked great and Joseph was doing well. I was also certain that Billingsley was still being groomed as the quarterback of the future. At least Carver was likely to get another shot before the final gun.

Billingsley didn't waste his chance. Starting from the Hawaii 33, he drove us downfield for a touchdown.

Theoretically he drove us to two touchdowns. Scott plunged in from the one but that was nullified by a holding penalty. The score was still tied and we had second and goal from the eleven.

Two plays later it was fourth and goal from less than a yard out. I went off right tackle into the end zone to put us ahead with 2:51 left in the third quarter.

Exactly 90 seconds later we scored again. Zanakis forced a fumble at the Oakland 34. Rodgers scooped it up and returned it to the 17.

Three plays later we had third and nine at the 16. Joseph hit Grummon inside the five. Two giant steps later he was in the end zone. We had a 21-7 lead with 1:21 left in the third quarter.

That was it for the projected starters. I wouldn't even be returning punts and kickoffs. All I had to do was bask in the sunshine until the game was over.

There were still some sparkling performances. One of them was from Jerry Reiser, a tailback from Western Michigan who had spent the previous season on injured reserve after being taken from Houston in the 33rd round of the expansion draft. Following an Oakland field goal, Reiser fielded the kickoff at the one and returned it 50 yards to the Oakland 49.

This led to another opportunity for Carver. On third and nine he completed a 17-yard pass to Mitch McGovern but little else went his way. His final pass was in and out of the hands of Phillip Pappas, our eleventh-round draft choice from Wisconsin.

Midway through the final period Oakland narrowed the gap to 21-17 on a 16-yard touchdown pass. The Raiders then started another drive on their own 45 with 2:16 left after a 32-yard return of a 50-yard punt. The drive climaxed with a ten-yard scoring pass. The Raiders had a 24-21 lead with two seconds left.

Oakland kicked off. It was a low kick and was fielded by Ozzie Roberts on the three. He reached the 27 before being brought down. That was it.

In the locker room I noticed Carver sitting in front of his locker. He was hanging his head as if he was wearing the Hawaiians uniform for the final time. I am sorry to say I believed he was. It wasn't a reflection on him as a quarterback and it definitely was not a reflection of his heart. It was simply a matter of a lack of space for him.

But his fate wouldn't be confirmed until Tuesday morning. After I showered, dressed and rode the bus to the Marine base I was sprung for about 30 hours. I wanted to spend that time living as normal a life as possible.

Carol whipped up a good stir-fry dinner for Stacy and me. It was good to see Stacy since I had rarely seen her over the previous year. Like me, she was a graduate student but was attending Northern Arizona University. She would be flying to Flagstaff the next day.

When Carol abruptly moved to the Big Island in 1974 it was almost as hard on Stacy as it was on me. Not only could Stacy not see her best friend on an almost daily basis, she could see how much Carol's departure was tearing me up. I hid my emotions pretty well but Stacy knew me well enough and cared enough to see through the facade during the first difficult months of life suddenly without Carol.

None of this was discussed at dinner. We talked about football, which was inevitable. Stacy talked about her studies and how much she enjoyed her temporary relocation to Arizona. Carol talked about teaching at the university. Stacy and Carol also went back in time and giggled about some of the things they did as teenagers.

At one point Carol excused herself to use the bathroom. Stacy looked at me in a way that suggested that she knew what I was going through. She was happy that Carol and I were together. She also seemed to know that Carol and I truly hadn't bonded. Somehow I sensed that that was what Stacy wanted to say.

I recalled about three years earlier. Stacy told me she honestly believed that Carol and I would someday be together again. She was one of two people to tell me that with Don Simmons being the other a few months later. That prophecy seemed to be coming true although there was a long way to go.

Stacy and Carol were hanai sisters. The love between them was unsurpassable. Both would have done virtually anything for the other.

In all due respect to the sister I did have, I almost considered Stacy to be my sister. She and I had had a very loving friendship dating back about five years which was about a year before I met Carol. If somebody half-German, one-quarter British, one-eighth Hispanic and one-eighth Seminole could have a full-blooded Japanese woman for a sister, Stacy truly was my sister.

Monday was Labor Day. I avoided labor. Carol and I went on a picnic at Kapiolani Park with the crowd from Arthur's; a businessperson's lounge in Downtown Honolulu that Don Simmons had introduced me to shortly before my sojourn to Canada. I spent a large part of the day playing softball. There was also a good food spread, a little beer and camaraderie among friends who had absolutely nothing to do with football.

It was great to be something other than a pro football player for a day. I loved being a football player but I wouldn't have had I had to be one 24/7. Like most jobs, there was a time to dedicate myself to my work and a time to let go.

Of course it was impossible to break completely away.

"How do the Hawaiians look?"

That was a question I was asked in about a dozen different ways.

"Okay, I guess. It's hard to tell. The roster isn't set yet."

Ambiguity seemed to be the way to go. I knew we were not incapable of winning the Super Bowl. I also knew we were not incapable of duplicating Tampa Bay's woeful 1976 season.

By midnight I was back in camp. I hated returning after a day of freedom. It was always that way throughout my career. The final week of training camp always seemed the longest. After Sunday's game I would ride the bus back to base, grab my things and be officially sprung from camp. We would still use the facility during weeks before road games on grass but I would be free to go home after each day's work was done.

But first I had to deal with that long final week.

And then there was the matter of whether I would make the team.

On that note, four rookies found out after breakfast on Tuesday morning that they would no longer be with us. This included defensive end Whitey Stansell, our fourth round draft choice from Kansas State whom I thought would be hard to cut. It probably looked promising for him when Kupau was cut the week before. What did him in was the awe-inspiring play of Kyle McWherter. With Jim McDaniel, Jon Jurgens and Gavin Pratt seeming secure in their places it may have come down to a choice between Stansell and McWherter. Stansell played well but McWherter was on fire. It was as if he was making up for the nine games he missed after being cut in 1976.

Stansell played up to expectation and there was a good chance he would turn up with another team. For the moment he would be home in Hays, Kansas, by the end of the day.

As it would work out, Stansell would wind up with the Bears by the end of the week. That meant we would see him in Chicago in November.

Getting back to the present, the other three rookies cut were free agents. This included Carver.

106

Carver was smiling when I saw him. He looked both relieved and disappointed. He pushed himself to the limit. Unfortunately the odds were always against him.

"You tried," Allen told him outside the barracks where the rookies bunked. "You gave it your best shot. Don't be hanging your head."

"You did a really good job," Bender added. "You've got nothing to be ashamed of."

"Shop around when you get home," Allen suggested. "There might be somebody in the NFL looking for a backup quarterback. You also might find an opening in Canada."

Carver smiled an uneasy smile. He shook hands with the six of us who happened to be there. He then picked up his luggage and headed to the van that would transport him, Stansell, center Paul Dalrymple and fullback Keith Whitney to the airport.

In the four preseason games in which Carver saw action he completed 17 of 31 passes for 261 yards and one touchdown. He also threw five interceptions which obviously didn't help his chances.

And so we were down to 54 plus three out with injuries. The final cut would keep at least eleven more off of the active roster. Some would stay with us on the taxi squad. The rest would sever their ties with the team.

Kickoff is at one o'clock tomorrow," Walker announced at our Saturday night meeting. "Breakfast is at 8:30. The bus leaves at 9:45 sharp. I want everybody to give it their all. We want that momentum for when we kick off the season in New Orleans next week."

Walker paused. I am not sure if he was collecting his thoughts or kicking himself for mentioning New Orleans when we had to face the Lions first. Normally Walker and everybody else refrained from mentioning any future game except for the one we were to play next.

"We'll be having a team meeting on Monday morning at nine," Walker continued. "No workout but a meeting. We'll go over the agenda for the week. Everybody be on time."

Why the meeting?

Partially for the reason Walker expressed. Primarily it was so that everybody would be together on the day of the final cuts. The team had to submit its final roster on Monday. If everybody was scattered around the island the unfortunates might find out about their being cut through the media. Walker didn't want anybody finding out that way.

There was some radical revamping of the special teams for this final preseason matchup. Most of the projected starters, including myself, would not be on any of the special teams. This was meant to give the rookies and fringe players as much opportunity to play as possible. The reason was allegedly a secret but most of us knew anyway.

This meeting ended right on schedule at nine o'clock. I was feeling remarkably content and confident. I was positive I had the team made although I didn't say so. I was very aware of my stats through the first five games. I would have to screw up beyond imagination to get cut.

I called Carol to say hello. I continued my practice of being friendly without speaking too affectionately. I knew that I loved Carol more than I could ever love any other woman. I also knew that when she left town without telling me that she honestly never meant to hurt me. Just the same, I couldn't get myself to let my guard down completely. Something diabolical had me convinced that Carol might eventually disappear with no explanation again if I allowed her to get too close too soon.

It was a quiet night at training camp. Different groups of people sat around talking quietly among themselves. I actually sat and talked with Rossi and Marceau; meaning the three of us fighting for what we believed would be two roster spots. One of us would be gone 48 hours later unless the odd man out wound up on the taxi squad. There was no way that all three of us would be on the active roster.

Rossi talked about his upbringing. He was his parents' only child and was seven when his alcoholic father died. He grew up in the vicinity of San Francisco's legendary Haight and Ashbury. He had played baseball in youth leagues since that is what most boys did. Like me, he didn't play organized football until he reached high school.

Although Rossi must have been a pretty good football player in high school, I doubt that he experienced the glories he described. I never accepted his contention that he averaged ten yards per carry as a running back. Had he been that good John McKay at USC would have gone after him and ignored Ricky Bell.

One interesting claim that Rossi made was that he had known Janis Joplin. She died while he was a junior in high school but he was definitely from the neighborhood where he could have come into contact with her.

"Once I saw her so wasted that I thought she was gonna pass out on the sidewalk," Rossi said. "I saw her mostly when she was straight. She was really nice when she was straight. Once I told her I wanted to go into show business. She just looked at me and said, 'No you don't, Dave. Get your education and make something of yourself.'"

It sounded somewhat credible. Janis obviously wasn't in a position to dispute his claim.

Marceau didn't even come close to matching Rossi's pretentiousness. One wouldn't describe him as taciturn but one also couldn't describe him as extremely vocal.

In high school Marceau had been a three-sport star, lettering in football, basketball and baseball. Football had always been his favorite sport which he started playing when he was nine. His favorite player had been Paul Hornung. His favorite coach had been Vince Lombardi.

Ultimately Marceau played football at Portland State. That was close to his hometown of Camas, Washington.

"It's east of Vancouver," Marceau explained of Camas. "I lived on a hill and could stand in my front yard and look across the Columbia River to Oregon."

Marceau was our 12th and final draft choice. One could argue that Marceau had an edge over Rossi since Rossi was signed as a free agent. Unfortunately for Marceau, a 12th round draft choice is not necessarily favored over a free agent. If the coaching staff wanted somebody unpretentious then Marceau would be an easy choice. I still believed, though, that Rossi was the better player.

I was doing my pregame laps at eleven o'clock. Our kickoff was later than normal for a Sunday home game although that was no big deal. We didn't have the marquee value of the Cowboys, Steelers, Rams and Raiders so this preseason matchup was televised only in Detroit and vicinity. It was a local telecast for the Lions so CBS had no control over our starting time.

It amazed me how good I felt. I was more excited than I thought I would be. Although it was only a preseason game, this one would be played almost entirely as if it was a regular season game. We needed to be sharp to have good momentum going into the season.

What was also different was that the two end zones were painted. Normally this would have waited for the regular season but the University of Hawaii opened its season the night before. In the north end zone were replicas of the University of Hawaii and Hawaiians helmets. In the south end zone were replicas of the Detroit Lions and University of New Mexico helmets.

This is it, I thought as I finished my final lap. The final tune-up before we started playing for keeps. Training camp would officially be over by the end of the day. I would sleep in my own bed that night. I would sleep in my own bed every night until Friday when I would spend the night flying to New Orleans.

I was dressed and ready to go. I sat in front of my locker and drank a cup of Gatorade shortly before we would take the field before kickoff. As had been the case the previous year, I was flanked by Kerner and Rodgers in the locker room.

We were still carrying two kickers; Guinn and Gerhardt. The advantage seemed to be to Guinn. He had made three out of four field goal attempts. His miss was from 53 yards but he made the aforementioned one from 57 yards.

Gerhardt had also done well, converting on five out of six. His longest was from 46 yards. His miss was from 31 yards.

I suppose it came down to Guinn's longest field goal being eleven yards longer than Gerhardt's since both were pretty equal when it came to kickoffs. Both had only one miss but Guinn's was 22 yards longer than Gerhardt's. Guinn was also the incumbent and still in his prime.

But that could all change. It may have depended on the kind of day the two had against the Lions. Guinn simply seemed to have the tiebreaker advantage.

Of course there were the two fighting for my position. I maintained my belief that the job would be won by Rossi unless Walker decided to go with somebody a little easier to handle. From the very beginning Rossi talked like he had the team made.

"When we get to New Orleans. . . . "

That was a common way for Rossi to start a sentence. He didn't seem to believe it was possible that the coaching staff wouldn't have as high opinion of him as he obviously did.

Rossi was probably right. He still shouldn't have gotten so presumptuous. Marceau was not a bad football player. There was no way to know what Walker was thinking.

Perhaps Walker would keep Rossi and Marceau and get rid of me. I made it a point never to think of myself as indispensable.

We reverted back to our old ways. We lost the toss. That made ten out of 12 exhibition matchups in our brief NFL history.

Guinn kicked off toward the south end zone. It was a booming kick that was fielded seven yards deep in the end zone. Guinn's chances for making the team went up another notch.

The Detroit return man may have been desperate to make the team. He decided to run the kick out. If he got past the 20 his stock would go up.

Defensive tackle Jerry Dodd, our fifth-round draft choice out of Miami, nailed him at the 16. He also forced a fumble. The Lions recovered but the hopes of one return man may have been dashed.

Of course the play didn't hurt Dodd's chances for making the team. Walker's job would be more difficult if he was thinking about cutting Dodd.

Early in the second quarter we took a 10-0 lead. That came when Scott ran a sweep around left end. He scampered 24 yards for a touchdown.

With about five minutes left in the half we had third and five at the Detroit 45. Bender dropped back and unleashed a pass to me. I made a diving catch at the 28, got up and fought for three more yards. That gave us another first down.

Walker sent Rossi in. I trotted to the sideline. Walker was beaming.

"That's the way to play it!" Walker exclaimed, whacking my shoulder pad with the palm of his hand. "That's what I like to see!"

After two plays I returned to action. The drive climaxed with a three-yard pass from Bender to Scott. We had a 17-0 lead with 2:04 left in the half.

As I grabbed a cup of Gatorade I felt strangely at peace. Perhaps it was triggered by Walker's approbation. I somehow felt invulnerable. For that moment all was well in my world.

Gerhardt kicked off. The kick was taken a yard deep in the end zone. The Lions' return man ran it out.

Suddenly I spotted Hasegawa. He was shooting downfield at a pace that would have made Jesse Owens proud. He wound up with a clear shot of the return man at the eleven where he hammered him.

"Yeah, baby! Way to go, Rich!" I hollered almost involuntarily as soon as my fellow University of Hawaii alum leveled the enemy. I suppose his chances for making the team had just increased.

During the second half I thought about the fun I was having. I suppose the 17-0 lead helped. I played hard on the field but felt practically no stress on the sideline. The score seemed to mean nothing because there was no playoff berth at stake. I was eagerly anticipating the start of the season.

While on the sideline I paid little attention to the defense. I quietly joked with some of my teammates and stole glances into the crowd. I even nodded and smiled at a couple of friends I spotted when I normally tried to avoid eye contact with the spectators.

The Lions finally got on the scoreboard with 5:19 left in the third quarter. That narrowed the gap to 17-7. Exactly 25 seconds later our lead was cut to 17-14 when Bender's pass to Dietrich was picked off and returned 43 yards for a touchdown.

I didn't feel so loose anymore. Suddenly I wasn't having so much fun.

"What the hell was that?" Walker asked sternly, standing with his hands on his hips as Bender reached the sideline.

Bender said nothing. The films would show that it wasn't exactly Bender's fault. The defensive back simply made a great play. He read the play and timed it perfectly. It happens.

It didn't take us long to widen the gap. Two plays to be exact after the kickoff was downed in the end zone. Bender hit me at the Hawaii 39. I raced the remaining 61 yards to give us a 24-14 lead; a 77 yard play.

Running that play was like being hypnotized. It was after I crossed the goal line that I noticed the 44,702 cheering spectators. At the time I was focused only on trying to reach the end zone. Afterward I recalled seeing the people in the end zone seats jumping up and down and hearing the cheers of the entire stadium but I was not aware of all of that at the time.

We were playing to win. Just the same, Walker did a lot of shuttling in and out during the fourth quarter, especially among the backs and receivers. There were opportunities for guys to get final glimmers of hope.

Guinn kicked a 22-yard field goal to give us a 27-14 lead with 6:18 left. It was only a chip shot but it could have decreased his chances of making the team had he missed.

111

Gerhardt got another opportunity to display his kicking off capabilities. He got off a high kick that was taken on the goal line. The return man fielded the ball cleanly and headed upfield.

Hasegawa must have been the invisible man on kick returns that day. He was down the field so fast that it appeared as if nobody made any effort to block him. The return man tried to veer away but Rich got his arms around him and wrestled him to the ground on the eleven-yard line.

The crowd loved it. So did everybody on our sideline. Walker was all aglow. It appeared that Hasegawa had just proved his worth to the team.

One has to give the Lions credit. They didn't quit. They drove downfield and scored on an eight-yard pass with 32 seconds left, narrowing the gap to 27-21. Their onside kick failed so we wound up winning to even our preseason record at 3-3.

CHAPTER SIX
Off and Running

Our preseason stats were posted at the camp site. I was surprised to see how well I had done. I had rushed 14 times for 80 yards. My yardage total was second only to Scott who picked up 237 yards on 47 carries.

What also surprised me was that I had led the team in receptions and receiving yards. I caught 16 passes for 277 yards. Dietrich was a close second with 15 receptions for 260 yards.

Obviously I had fairly impressive stats. I was still queasy about the possibility of being cut. I felt almost like a mouse in a rattlesnake cage.

The roster, as expected, was dramatically reduced on Monday morning. Wilson manned his usual post outside the dining facility. He sent several players to Walker with their playbooks.

Gerhardt got the ax. It wasn't a shock although it wasn't a reflection on his kicking. Guinn simply beat him out.

As I expected, Rossi was staying and Marceau was cut loose. As undisciplined as Rossi was, he was the better player.

Tackle Sterling Burgess was waived. The six-year veteran who had gone to the Pro Bowl once during his five years with Green Bay was slowed by old injuries. There were no takers. Walker told him to keep himself in shape since it was always possible that he would be needed later.

Guard Greg Henry was also waived. He was claimed by San Diego. This would be his third tenure in San Diego since he began his career with the Chargers in 1973, then played for the Southern California Sun of the WFL in 1974 before returning to the Chargers in 1975. He had spent most of 1976 with us on the taxi squad.

One cut that few saw coming was that of Joseph. He made a decent showing in preseason, completing 15 of 24 passes for 176 yards and two touchdowns and two interceptions. His numbers were slightly better than those of Billingsley but Billingsley was still earmarked for the future. Walker apparently decided to go with two quarterbacks to give us room for a player at another position.

The news took Joseph by surprise. I know because I happened to be walking out of the dining hall with Hasegawa just ahead of Joseph and Blakely. Rich and I greeted Wilson cheerily as he stood at his grim reaper post, then heaved sighs of relief when Wilson returned the greeting in the cordial manner of one preparing to give bad news to somebody other than yourself.

I happened to look back as Wilson stopped Joseph. The expression on Joseph's face indicated that he had no idea that this was coming. He probably figured that he was safe once we got down to three quarterbacks.

Most of us thought we would be going with three quarterbacks like we did in 1976.

Among the other casualties were wide receiver Mitch McGovern who spent 1976 on the taxi squad after being signed as a free agent out of Kentucky and Jerry Dodd although they weren't cut. McGovern was placed on injured reserve with a knee injury while Dodd suffered a neck injury that put him on injured reserve. That meant that both were out for the season. Dodd's injury was career threatening.

There were a lot of relieved individuals as we gathered for our team meeting. I took a seat and realized I was sitting next to McWherter.

"Congratulations, man. It's good to see you," I said, shaking his hand.

The five-year veteran from Murray State shrugged sheepishly and cracked a partial smile.

"It feels good to be here," he said. "Unfortunately some good players are going home today. I know how they feel. I've been there."

Our active roster, as mandated by the NFL, was down to 43. The roster was comprised of 31 with NFL experience, three with WFL and NFL experience, one with Canadian Football League experience and there were eight rookies.

"Congratulations, men," Walker said to open the brief meeting among 43 active players as well as those who were injured, designated for the taxi squad and the rest of the coaching staff. "The final roster is set. You have earned the privilege to represent the Hawaiians in 1977. How long this lasts depends on you. Changes can still be made because of injuries or players who don't produce. My recommendation is that you give it everything you've got throughout the season."

I happened to notice Rossi sitting two seats to my left. I hoped he understood how fortunate he was. He was a good football player but was still fortunate that he didn't have stiffer competition in training camp. His biggest break came when the team traded Gary Giametti to San Diego during the offseason. There was no way that he would have beat Giametti out.

Rossi was a decent-enough running back, I suppose, although not spectacular. He also wasn't going to be especially useful in long pass situations. He could catch the short passes all right. Anything longer than ten or 15 yards he didn't handle well. He was willing to try to fight for the extra yard or two but didn't seem to be as tough to bring down as Giametti was.

"Would you mind working with Rossi to help him become a better player?" Walker asked me after our workout on Tuesday.

"I don't really mind, " I replied, feeling that Rossi was no threat to my status as a starter, "but how do you help somebody who knows how everybody else should play his position? The guy hasn't played a single

114

down in a regular season game and already he thinks he's All-Pro at a dozen different positions."

Walker chuckled at that. He said I was probably right. Although he never said so, he was probably regretting the Giametti trade.

Among those also with us was a tall blonde, balding individual named Henri Dubois. He was French-Canadian from Ste Martine, Quebec, which is roughly halfway between Montreal and New York State.

Dubois played four years for Edmonton and two years for Montreal in the Canadian Football League after graduating from McGill Universite. After getting a reluctant blessing from his former team, he shopped around the NFL for an opportunity to play. Memphis, Detroit, Cincinnati and New Orleans all expressed interest before Dubois settled on Hawaii.

Of course there were no guarantees of him making the team when he reported. Walker gave his blessing for his signing after watching films of him in action. He wasn't signed as a foreign novelty. He was signed because Walker felt that he was a legitimate candidate.

There was one particular concern the team needed to address before signing him. Did Dubois speak English?

Fortunately he was bilingual. His native language was French but he was adept at English. Occasionally he had trouble with slang terms although not enough to be an impediment.

Dubois was a tough competitor on the field and a pretty nice guy off the field. He rented an apartment on Kuhio Avenue on the east end of Waikiki and was reportedly a very popular patron of the Rose and Crown Pub in King's Alley; the same pub where I tended bar the summer prior to my senior year in college.

We were adding a new position for 1977. This was what we referred to simply as the Gatorade Coach.

As the name implies, this was a token position manned by young boys and occasionally girls. The duties consisted entirely of remaining behind a table on the sideline and keeping a supply of cups of Gatorade ready for the players.

This was a fun position. It gave those selected a chance to assist the team and observe the game from ground level. That also often meant hearing player discussions, coach discussions and being up close when Walker reacted adversely to a play or an official's call. Often the Gatorade Coach could hear some very colorful language.

In most cities there was a relative or an acquaintance of somebody who could fill the position. Our first Gatorade Coach would be 12-year-old Kenny Nelson. This was Marv's nephew.

The Gatorade Coach had to adhere to certain rules. For safety reasons he or she was only allowed in the area directly behind the bench and Gatorade table. He or she was also not to speak to a player unless the player spoke to him or her first since the players had to concentrate on the game. Most importantly, the Gatorade supply was to never run out.

Of course the position was very unofficial. Nobody who filled the role was on the payroll. It was a paid position since the players and coaches each kicked in a buck or two. The Gatorade Coach generally walked away with a minimum of 60 dollars. Occasionally, especially after an especially good game when spirits were light, the players were extremely generous and a Gatorade Coach could pocket as much as 200 dollars or even more for a few hours of work.

Going from Hawaii Kai to Aloha Stadium during rush hour can be a real bear. Kalanianaole Highway traffic was usually heavy and so was the traffic when the highway turned into the H-1 Freeway. I usually left by about 7:15 to be ready to go at nine. I always arrived with plenty of time to spare but it was better to be early than late.

Friday's practice was extra special. It would be our last full-padded workout prior to our first regular season game. Afterward we would fly to New Orleans.

What was different this season was that we could actually drive ourselves to the airport. A space had been reserved for us near Air Service to leave our cars when playing on the road. Not having to scramble for rides to the airport was one fewer distraction.

Our nine o'clock meeting was very brief. That was usually the case late in the week. Rarely was anything new installed two days before a game. That was why it was a meeting of the entire team instead of the offense and defense breaking into separate groups.

"Men," Walker began with a huge smile on his face. "I've got a really good feeling inside me. We put together a pretty good team last year and I have no doubt that this year's team will be even better."

Walker paused, possibly thinking he should save the pep talk for 48 hours and more than 4,000 miles later. I know he had me pumped up and we were only going to practice.

Rather than continue the hype, Walker went over the itinerary again to make sure everybody understood. We would fly to New Orleans after the day's workout, check into the hotel, sleep for a few hours, work out at the Superdome, have dinner at our leisure, have a midnight curfew, have a team breakfast at 7:30 on Sunday morning and play the Saints at noon. We would return home immediately after the game.

"How do you think we're going to do?" Prendergast asked Marv in the locker room after we had dressed and headed to the field at Aloha Stadium.

Marv smiled and nodded.

"A lot better than last year," he replied confidently. "We did real good last year and that was special. If everybody does what he is capable of doing we can go all the way."

116

Marv had excellent instincts. He was at least as adept as Walker in analyzing potential. That was part of the reason why he eventually became such a good coach.

"How do you think it'll feel playing in New Orleans again?" I asked.

"Hell, I don't have any bad feelings for New Orleans or anybody there. I'd rather be here but I wish the Saints well."

Marv paused. He pondered a moment.

"At least I wished them well last year," he added. "They've got some good people there and I was always rooting for them to win. I can't really do that this year because they're in the same division as us."

We had a very spirited workout. The veterans were anxious to get another season underway. The rookies had leaped a formidable hurdle by making the team and on Sunday would be initiated into a very exclusive fraternity.

Walker was on his best late in the week behavior. He hollered if somebody was too slow or made a mistake but he didn't go into hysterics. He was also quick with the compliments if somebody did something especially well.

After practice I showered, dressed and drove to the airport. Dave Shuford caught a ride with me. We were expected to share rides since some of the players, especially those new to the team, didn't have cars yet. A local dealer would provide cars for those who needed them in an advertising exchange after we returned from New Orleans.

Dave was a very complex individual. He was gregarious, intelligent, cocksure, compassionate and a prankster. He was married with two kids but lived a lot like a single person although he didn't cheat on his wife or neglect his kids as far as I knew. His wife Gail was more introverted and didn't mind that her husband had a weekly poker night or liked to have a night out with the boys on occasion. He was the breadwinner and ostensibly a pretty loyal husband and father.

"I'm really going to like playing for this team," Dave remarked as we headed down Kamehameha Highway alongside Pearl Harbor. "There's some really good people on this team."

"Did you like the guys you played with in Baltimore?" I asked.

"Oh, sure. Great guys, really. There's just something a little extra special about this group. They all seem to get along pretty well and are really dedicated to winning."

"Walker would kill us if we weren't."

"Yeah, I know. In a lot of ways he reminds me of Lombardi."

I wondered how Dave could have made the comparison. He was a senior at Notre Dame when Vince Lombardi died.

"Did you know Lombardi?" I asked.

"No. I met him once but I never knew him. There were some guys I met who had played for him on the Packers and they told me about him. He ran his players into the ground. He also would have given up everything he owned to help one in trouble."

I nodded. I had heard that type of thing about Lombardi. He wasn't the pariah he was often made out to be.

At least not always.

"Did you know that Walker coached under Lombardi for a few years?" I asked.

"No, I didn't. Are you serious?"

"Very. He coached for a few years in Green Bay. He doesn't consciously emulate Lombardi but he is a lot like Lombardi was. He holds Lombardi in pretty high esteem. Bender and Dietrich both played for Lombardi in Washington and they say they can see how some of Lombardi rubbed off on Walker."

We talked more about Walker and the team as we headed down Nimitz Highway. I turned right on Lagoon Drive, then right on Aolele Street to where I would park my car and board the DC-8. A truck had already transported our luggage and equipment from Aloha Stadium to the airport so all we had to do was park the car and board the plane.

It was about four o'clock in the morning, local time, when we touched down in New Orleans. That translated to about eleven o'clock Friday night, body time. We filed off the plane as quickly as possible and boarded the waiting bus. Our luggage was also put on the bus. A truck stood by to transport the football gear to the Superdome.

It was well after daybreak when we were finally settled in our hotel rooms. I settled down for a nap since we were scheduled for a light workout at the Superdome that afternoon. It was all part of Walker's master plan to get us to adjust to the local environment as quickly as possible.

Walker's way was effective. The long flights provided us with time for a few hours of sleep before a light workout. That meant we would probably be too tired to do anything but sleep the night before the game.

Or so Walker hoped.

I rose at about eleven, went to a coffee shop for a modest breakfast and boarded the bus to the Superdome. It was another milestone toward finally getting the season underway.

The workout was a simple walkthrough without pads. At most, it was an opportunity to brush up on our assignments. At the very least, it was an opportunity to kill time while keeping some of our rowdier players off Bourbon Street. We all seemed anxious to start the game. If we weren't ready by this time, we never would be.

118

"Which sport are you playing?" Walker asked me lightly in the locker room, referring to the T-shirt and baseball cap I was wearing from the Los Angeles Dodgers.

I actually had about half-a-dozen Dodger T-shirts and a couple of caps I had picked up during my most recent visit to Dodger Stadium. As was mentioned previously, I had a tradition that would carry throughout my career. During every final walkthrough before a game I wore a Dodger T-shirt and cap. I was also decked out in this attire when I ran my pregame laps and wore a Dodger T-shirt under my uniform during every game. I also wanted to wear the cap on the sideline during games but it was against NFL rules to wear any cap that was not officially from the team for which one played.

When I stepped on the field of the Superdome I was truly awed by its majesty. The Astrodome had impressed me but the Superdome was even more palatial. Catching my eye was the gondola high above the field which featured TV screens to give those sitting up high a better view of the action. The highest seats extended even higher than the highest seats in the Astrodome.

"Hey, Marv," I called since this had once been his home field. "Those seats way up there. Do they issue oxygen masks with those seats?"

The Superdome was overwhelming. It seemed like a mansion in an upscale neighborhood. The Astrodome was from the same neighborhood but with owners in a slightly lower tax bracket. Seattle's Kingdome, comparably, was a doghouse.

Walker and the rest of the coaches were in a good mood. So was the entire team. We were giddy in anticipation of our first regular season game of 1977.

"Work it off," Walker instructed. "I want you anxious to go tomorrow but don't take it too far. Too much excitement creates too many mistakes."

Walker enjoyed watching baseball. Being from the Midwest, he was a Cardinal fan. He utilized his knowledge of baseball when he addressed me during the workout by using names of the current Los Angeles Dodgers.

"All right, Dusty Baker. Way to hustle."

"Good job, Don Sutton."

"Way to move, Dave Lopes."

"Hey, Penguin. That's the way to do it."

Near the end of the workout Bender slightly overthrew a pass to me. I leaped up and barely got my fingertips on the ball before it dropped incomplete.

"Now are you going to tell me that Steve Garvey wouldn't have caught that?" Walker asked jocularly.

"Hell yes," I replied with equal levity. "I'm three or four inches taller than Garvey."

That cracked a few people up including Walker. We were loose because we were confident. There was still enough tension among us to suggest that we weren't overconfident.

I ran into Marv in the hallway of the hotel at about 11:30. He had just returned to the hotel after spending the evening with a few relatives. He had grown up in Mississippi but played college football in Louisiana at Grambling before his nine often frustrating years with the Saints. He had two beers with him.

"Ready to go?" he asked, handing me one of the beers.

"As ready as I'll ever be," I replied. "I can't wait to get started."

Marv and I talked for a few minutes in the hall. As anxious as we both were, the long flight and the beer acted as a sedative for us. We were both in our rooms and sound asleep before midnight.

Kickoff was at noon. I was up before 5:30. I took a shower and got dressed and ran into Kerner in the hall. He and I went downstairs for coffee, being joined by Marv, Bender, Dietrich, Ed and Clint.

We sipped our coffee and looked at each other. Occasionally somebody would bring up something pertinent to the game. Very little was said aside from that.

I noticed a couple of men glaring at us from across the room. I wasn't sure if they were diehard Saints fans or a couple of Klansmen or KKK sympathizers who objected to the sight of our integrated table. I figured that if it was the latter, Marv and Clint had more class, character and intelligence than either of those men could ever hope to have.

During the pregame warmup I occasionally glanced across the field to where the Saints were warming up. At one point I was standing next to Marv.

"What do you think?" I asked. " . . . think we can take these guys?"

"We damn well better," he replied in a tone that was dead serious. "I didn't come all this way to lose. I got enough of that when I was here before."

I understood although I couldn't see things from the same perspective as Marv. Our attitude was always that we don't travel a long distance to come up short. Marv never had trouble getting psyched up for a game but he equated New Orleans solely with losing. That gave him extra incentive. He loved his former teammates, coaches, fans and the city in general but nine years in New Orleans produced too much losing.

It was an amazing contrast. We had been in the NFL for one year and the Saints had been in for ten. We were still considered to be the better team. Vegas favored us by ten and-a-half points.

Of course we couldn't focus on any of that. If we simply assumed we were going to win based on such frivolity we were destined to start 1977 with a very devastating loss. We were determined to go against the Saints with the same intensity we would use against the Steelers, Raiders, Rams, Cowboys or any other championship caliber team.

I sat in front of my locker while waiting to take the field prior to kickoff. I gazed at the uniform I was wearing and marveled at the whiteness of it with its colored trim. Although I had worn essentially the same uniform for six exhibition games and a scrimmage, it seemed more special this time. Somehow it seemed to have a regular season luster.

My teammates sat around and went through their pregame rituals. In retrospect, the guys who had been with us a year earlier but were now gone were practically forgotten. Guys like the traded Gary Giametti and retired Phil Hoddeson didn't seem to exist anymore. Only those in the room mattered at this point.

"All right, men," Walker called as he stood in the middle of the room. "We now officially enter 1977. Last year is history. Oakland won the Super Bowl, Tampa Bay didn't win at all and we had a pretty good season under the circumstances. It's all a dead issue now. Today you begin a new chapter. I expect it to be a good one."

Walker paused. His expression seemed to be a smirk of confidence as he nodded and looked us over.

"We're looking to have a better season than last year. If Tampa Bay wins just one game they will have improved. Oakland can improve on last year by having a perfect season."

I was suddenly reminded that the Raiders' quest for a perfect season was destroyed by my teammates and me. Walker seemed to be reminded of that as well.

"Of course the Raiders are probably also thinking that they might make it since they don't have us on their schedule this year," he added lightly.

Walker's remark created muffled laughter. He wanted us to take the game seriously. He also wanted us loose.

"We're looking to improve," Walker continued. "Let me remind you again that the bar is high. Seven and seven would be outstanding for teams like Tampa Bay, Seattle, Memphis and even New Orleans. It would be mediocre for us this year. We've already reached that pinnacle."

"What I want is to make the playoffs," Walker added as he walked around the room, looking each of us in the eye. "You were selected to play for this team because you are the ones we believe can get us to the next level. If we make the playoffs we can get to the Super Bowl."

Perhaps it was the Superdome itself that inspired Walker. This was where the Super Bowl was going to take place in January. Otherwise it seemed more than a little premature to talk about the Super Bowl before the opening kickoff of our second season.

But we knew Walker was going somewhere with this.

"Wherever we go," he continued, standing in the middle of the room again, "it starts today. We play this season one game at a time, one quarter at a time, one play at a time. Let's start the season by playing hard, playing smart and playing well. If you play the way I know you can there is no way the Saints can beat you. Let's start the season right and enjoy that plane ride home."

With that we let out a collective roar and headed out of the locker room. Everybody went to the sideline except for the starting offense. We stayed near the tunnel until we were introduced to the crowd. We were amused by the boos that greeted each player as his name was called. Marv got the loudest boos, being a former Saint, but there were also a few discernable cheers.

We had the same captains as the previous season; Bender, Marv, Rodgers and Allen. When Marv's name was announced there was another smattering of applause although the crowd was primarily ambivalent. There were also a few negative remarks that could be heard on our sideline.

"How good can they be? They got one of our rejects."

"You stink, Nelson!"

"Too bad you can't play for a good team, Marv!"

Marv was in the middle of the field and didn't hear any of the remarks. The latter remark was the most interesting. Our 1976 record was better than any single-season record the Saints ever had in their ten-year history. Exactly what was their definition of a "good" team?

"What do the fans here know about a good team?" Prendergast wondered lightly as he sat on our bench in street clothes and game jersey; himself a former Saint. "They've never had one."

"You probably have to admire their loyalty, I suppose," Jennings said. "Ten years of losing seasons and they still support the team."

This exchange took place while the coin was being tossed. As was the case in the 1976 opener, we lost the toss.

"That's the only thing we're going to lose today," I remarked to Carl Hayer.

I was still disappointed. My regular season debut would have to wait until the defense was finished. Just the same, I knew that my time would come. I had a full NFL season under my belt. I had become a little more patient than I was during our season opener a year earlier.

There was an adrenaline rush as our kicking unit got into place. Guinn teed up the ball and awaited the referee's signal. The adrenaline seemed to be felt by virtually all of my teammates. Everybody seemed excited.

The red shirt wearing a headset near the sideline got his signal from CBS and pinwheeled his arm and left the field. The referee blew his whistle to start the game.

"Here we go," I said as I watched from the sideline.

"A great season starts now," Allen offered.

"Let's do it," I heard McDaniel say.

"Here we go, guys," said Kerner.

Guinn kicked off and another rush went through my system. The ball arched up and was taken about four yards deep in the end zone. The return man started up, hesitated and then downed the ball. Officially the 1977 season had started but was still zero seconds old.

"Aw, c'mon! Run it out, you clown!" Marv hollered jocularly. "You just blew your chance to return the opening kickoff for a touchdown!"

Marv would know. Not only was he there, he was among those running interference as John Gilliam returned the opening kickoff for a touchdown. Ten years later there wasn't much else on the Saints' highlight reel.

We settled down and watched as the Saints tried to score. The Saints picked up a first down, then faced third and five at their own 44. Their hopes for a second first down were dashed when Zanakis sacked the quarterback at the 35, setting off a huge roar from those of us on the sideline while drowning out the groans and expletives coming from the crowd. Our collective attitude was at the right level.

"Punt return unit!" Walker called.

The time had come for me to play ball. I took my place in the general vicinity of the 25. I was suddenly so nervous that I wasn't certain that I wanted to have my first play of the season on the punt return unit. A kick return or a play from scrimmage would have been easier on the nerves but a punt was more difficult to handle. I feared the possibility of muffing the ball so much that I considered letting the ball drop untouched before the punt was even up in the air.

As soon as the ball was punted I forgot my fears and got into position to field the ball. I caught it on the 28 and headed upfield. I had to zigzag a little but managed to fight my way to the 36. Eight yards is not a bad return on a punt. Not great but not bad.

I bounced up enthusiastically. I had gotten my first licks in for 1977. I was effervescent as I joined my offensive colleagues near the 25 where we would huddle.

"This is our first drive of the season," Bender remarked in the huddle. "Let's take it all the way in."

It took us only one play to get past midfield. Bender hit Dietrich near the right sideline at the New Orleans 43. Ted got all the way to about the 25 before being knocked out of bounds.

Unfortunately Ted had stepped on the sideline at the 40. That was where we would continue our drive.

"Okay, okay. Good job," Bender said. "That's not a bad start."

The blitz was on during the next play. Bender tried to hit Scott on a safety valve just before he was hit. Unfortunately the ball was just out of Scott's reach and dropped untouched.

We made up for it on the next play. Bender hit me over the middle at the 28. I broke a tackle at the 27 and got all the way down to the 15 before two defenders hit me simultaneously. We were 45 feet from our first score of the season.

The Saints' total losses were more than double their total victories over their ten-year existence but they were playing like they wanted to turn it around. We were going to the air again but the Saints put a heavy rush on Bender. He managed to scramble away and even picked up a yard before stepping out of bounds at the 14.

We did a play-action fake on the next play. Bender got into position and cocked his arm, spotting Kerner at about the five.

A defensive tackle deflected the pass and it veered off course, arching up and downfield toward the right. A linebacker covering the flat dove for the ball and came up with the interception at the eight. Dietrich fell on top of him to prevent him from getting up and running.

It is hard to accept being that close and coming away with nothing. Eleven offensive players dejectedly ran toward our sideline. The roar of the crowd echoing through the enclosed facility made it worse for us. The crowd was drowning out the groans and expletives coming from our sideline.

"It's okay. It's okay," Walker said, slapping a few of us on our rears as we went by. "They made a good play. These things are going to happen sometimes. Put it behind you. We'll get there next time."

Walker knew how we felt. Chastising us after one promising series went awry was not going to help although he wasn't always that understanding. He was also right about the Saints making a good play. It happens.

The Saints got off to an inauspicious start. They were called for illegal procedure prior to the snap. That gave them a first and 14 at the four.

"All right," Shuford remarked. "That's halfway to a safety. I'll settle for the two points. Then we get the ball back and get our touchdown."

The Saints dashed our hopes for a safety on the first play. They completed a pass at the 20. The receiver got to the 23 before Rodgers and Blakely brought him down.

Like the Saints' previous drive, the first first down would also be the last. They once again faced a third and five; this time at the 28. A pass near midfield was then batted down by Dubois.

"C'est si bon, Henri! Tres bien!" I cheered as I headed toward the field, giving Dubois accolades in his native language. "Magnifique, mon homme!"

I took my place in front of the Hawaii 30 for the punt. This time I had to backpedal a little. The films would show that for the second consecutive time I fielded the punt at the 28.

There were fewer obstructions this time. I shot straight forward. I wasn't touched until I was hit and dropped at the Hawaii 39.

124

My instincts told me we would score this time although the first play would hardly testify to that. Scott ran off left tackle and picked up one paltry yard.

The next play was better. Bender hit me near the right sideline at the New Orleans 45. I managed two more yards before being wrestled out of bounds.

We continued picking up chunks of yardage. On a second and three at the 23 Scott fought his way to the 20. The officials stopped the clock with 4:19 left in the quarter to measure.

It was short but the Saints got us the first down by getting called for encroachment. We were confident enough to believe we could score without the philanthropy but we weren't too proud to accept the gift. That took the ball to the 15.

This time we were determined to not be denied. On a Kailua left Scott was hit behind the line, then broke free. He managed to fight his way to the eleven.

We went to the air on the next play. Bender got set but there were no open receivers. He wisely threw the ball out of the end zone. It was third and six.

I hated the thought of having to settle for a field goal although it was better than nothing and definitely better than another turnover. I preferred that we convert on this play, at least enough to get another first down.

There wouldn't be a first down. Bender hit Kerner about three yards deep in the end zone. With 2:39 left in the first quarter we were on the board for the first time in 1977. The extra point made it 7-0.

Of course it felt good to get that first score under our belts. We were a little loose on the sideline.

"We're not going to let you get in the game," Dietrich lightly told our punter, Ray Jablonski.

"It's all right with me. I'll still get paid," Jablonski kidded back.

After the ensuing kick was downed in the end zone the Saints continued an ephemeral tradition of getting one first down and one first down only. It was our pass interference infraction on Dubois that got it for them at the New Orleans 39. On the very next play a pass in their left flat was intercepted by Zanakis at the New Orleans 44. The Z-man returned the ball to the 35 before going down.

"All right!" I cried out, jumping from my seat and pulling on my helmet as I ran to the field. "Here we go, Hawaii! Here we go!"

It was very exciting. We clearly had the momentum. Now we had to avoid losing it. We could put this game away by the end of the third quarter if we kept it up.

But it wasn't easy. After two rushes we had third and two at the 27. We figured the Saints would be looking for a rush so Bender called a pass. He wound up sacked at the 35 just as time was running out in the first quarter.

125

It was a disappointment but I fought off the negative feelings as I ran to the sideline. The season was young. The Saints were determined to turn their fortunes around. They were not incapable of making big plays. They might not have been a very good team but they had good players.

At least Guinn came through for us at the start of the second quarter. His 52-yard field goal attempt was true to give us a 10-0 lead.

Critics could argue that the ensuing kick return was an example of why the Saints hadn't had a winning season. The kick somehow had an unbelievable hang time and was fielded at the three. The return man only got to the eight before Hasegawa drove him down. That brought our sideline to life.

"Way to go, Rich!"

"All right, Hasegawa!"

"Yeah, Hasegawa! You da man! You da man!"

The Japanese-American was all smiles as he returned to the sideline. The first to shake his hand was Walker who then slapped him on the back. Nobody was smiling more broadly than Walker. Game films would show that the Saints' kick return unit treated him as if he wasn't even there. Nobody seemed to be anywhere near him as he sprinted toward the return man. No doubt the players on the Saints return team got an earful as they watched the game films.

The futile kick return was the type of thing that could have compelled the Saints to wave the white flag. Instead they made a determined march. Three first downs later they would have the ball on the Hawaii 49. It was their furthest penetration of the day.

They wouldn't get much further. A two-yard rush was followed by a two-yard loss when Allen tackled a running back behind the line. After an incompletion they had fourth and ten.

I took my place on the ten. I thought about the fun I was having. Although we only had a ten-point lead, I felt as if it was insurmountable. All we had to do was keep scoring, control the clock and prevent the Saints from scoring. It was a pretty bold thought relatively early in the second quarter but there was something about the Hawaiians' collective attitude that had me convinced that we couldn't be beat.

But hey, I was having a great time.

The punt was to my left. The punter was trying to kick it out of bounds deep in our territory but he didn't put enough on it. I fielded the ball on the 14 about two yards from the sideline. I was tackled at the 21.

It wasn't my best return but it would do. I bounced up and headed to the huddle, clapping my hands and expressing encouragement to my colleagues as they arrived. I was happy with the way the team was looking during the opening minutes of the season.

126

Our drive got off on the wrong foot when Abraham jumped prior to the snap. He seemed to be the team's biggest offender on this type of penalty. We had first and 15 at the 16 before we could get started.

Scott swept around left end to the 18. I then went off left tackle to the 22. It was third and nine.

There was no mystery about what was next. Bender met a heavy rush but still got the pass off. I caught the ball near the right sideline at the 28. I managed to get to the 36 to give us the first down we needed.

We picked up 42 yards on the next play. Bender handed off to me and I ran as if sweeping around left end. I had the option of rushing or passing and spotted Grummon downfield. I hit him at the New Orleans 41. He was finally caught from behind at the 22.

That was an awesome feeling. I had thrown an almost perfect pass, hitting Grummon right where he held his hands out right in front of him. It was great to know that I still had the touch. Dating back to my first game as a high school quarterback, it always gave me a rush to throw a completion, especially a long one.

The momentum continued. Bender hit Dietrich at the two. It was perfect execution since Ted had to jump as he headed toward the sideline. He managed to get both feet down before stepping out of bounds. We were pounding on the door.

Those final six feet were tough. Bender tried to hit me in the end zone and the pass was nearly intercepted. A pass to rookie tight end Chester McCracken was then caught near the back of the end zone but McCracken came down with one foot behind the end line. It was third and goal at the two.

We went back to the running game. Scott went through the right. He was still standing when he reached the end zone. With the extra point we had a 17-0 lead with 5:43 left in the half.

For the moment I could relax as I sat on the bench and enjoyed my cup of Gatorade. I was cognizant of the Saints having plenty of time to catch us. It was still a three-score game. I believed we had the game won as long as we didn't screw up and give it away.

Thanks to a short kick, the Saints had their best field position of the day to start a drive at their own 32. After a first down they found themselves with third and five at the Hawaii 49. Their hopes of getting any further were dashed when Jennings sacked the quarterback at the New Orleans 46.

Man we were hot! I realize that the Saints didn't have much of a season in 1976 and weren't expected to be much better in 1977 but I wasn't thinking about that. All I cared about was how awesome we seemed to be.

As I ran on the field for the punt I could almost sense the crowd's thoughts. It was relatively quiet in the palatial sold-out Superdome. The patrons had to be thinking it was going to be another season of futility for them. That had to be a depressing thought with a little more than two minutes left in the first half of the first game of the season.

At least the punter earned his paycheck. The punt went out of bounds at the Hawaii eleven. With 1:57 left in the half we had reached the two-minute warning.

In retrospect, we were a little too full of ourselves in the huddle as Bender talked to Walker on the sideline. We were laughing a little and that probably wasn't unnoticed by the Saints' defensive unit. For whatever the reason, the Saints hadn't had much success in their history but their roster was full of bona fide professionals. Our cocksure attitude with a mere 17-point lead could have been the spark to fire them up.

If they were fired up, we quickly smothered the flames. Grummon caught a short pass at the 14 and steamrolled his way to the 20 to give us second and one. Kerner then got us the first down with several yards to spare by rushing up the middle.

Trying to tackle Kerner is sometimes like trying to tackle a rolling boulder. He was built like a tank and defenders sometimes seemed to bounce off of him.

Of course he had help. There were several downfield blocks along the way. I hit one guy in the numbers near midfield to knock him out of the play as Kerner ran by. I could have thrown another block but Kerner was ten yards ahead of me by the time I bounced up from the aforementioned block that took the defender and me down.

Kerner was finally brought down at the Saints 28. It was a 52-yard run. With 1:14 to play in the half I was not thinking field goal. I believed we had a great shot at the full seven.

Of course I always thought that way.

There was one casualty on the play. Stanek injured his knee throwing a downfield block. After our trainer attended to him for a few minutes he limped off the field while receiving polite applause. He would be out for the rest of the game but would be back in action the following week.

Once Stanek was off the field the clock started again. We hurried up to the line and Scott rushed off right tackle to the 26. We called time with 1:03 left in the half.

It appeared that I had my first touchdown of the season on the next play. I caught a pass near the right sideline at the ten. I raced all the way to the end zone. I had to straight-arm a defender near the five and, in doing so and without realizing it, stepped out of bounds at the four. At least we had a first down with 51 seconds left in the half.

Bender tried to hit Dietrich in the end zone on the next play. For the second time he almost had a pass intercepted in the end zone. The defensive back made a good play by stepping in front of Dietrich. He batted the ball forward but couldn't catch up to it. The clock was stopped with 42 seconds left.

We had a better result on the next play. Bender hit Grummon about two yards deep in the end zone. With the extra point we had extended our lead to 24-0. The clock was down to 34 seconds.

I was smiling broadly on the sideline as I drank a cup of Gatorade. The more we played, the more impressed I was with my teammates. I was enjoying myself so much that it surprises me that I wasn't already absolutely certain that we would be back in New Orleans in January for the Super Bowl.

The Saints opted to run out the clock and the two teams went into their respective locker rooms. I chugged another cup of Gatorade and then, after a visit to the urinal, drank a Pepsi. I was feeling pretty good but had returned to earth and was feeling more cautious. If we could score 24 points in the first half, why couldn't the Saints score at least that many in the second half? We had to overcome whatever temptation we may have had to become complacent. If we blew this one it was going to be the longest plane ride of my life.

Walker seemed to be thinking the same way.

"We've still got to be aggressive," he stressed before we returned to the field. "A 24-point lead might be insurmountable in high school but not in the NFL. We have to wear them down. They want to get back in this game and you can't allow that to happen. We have to score and control the clock."

We wouldn't have to wait for our first scoring opportunity. The advantage of losing the opening coin toss was that we would be receiving the kick to open the second half. I stood on the goal line along with Hasegawa. Several yards ahead of me was Dave Rossi who was about to see his first action in an NFL regular season game. As flaky as Dave was, I knew he would go all out.

The kicker put everything he had into it. Hasegawa caught the ball eight yards deep in the end zone and immediately downed it. We had a first down at the 20. Rossi's official NFL debut was most unspectacular.

We began the half by trying to make a statement. Dietrich and I shot downfield as if we were going out for a Hail Mary pass. Bender overthrew me by about five yards at the about the New Orleans 40. I made a desperation dive forward but still came up a few yards short. All I managed to do was scrape up both arms on that blasted artificial turf.

"(Expletive deleted)," I muttered.

From there we appeared to pick up from where we left off at halftime. Scott and Kerner picked up huge chunks of yardage and a Saints facemask penalty gave us a first down at the Hawaii 48. I then ran a sweep around left end to give us second and four at the New Orleans 46. Scott followed with another sweep around right end to give us a first down at the 40.

That was where the drive stalled. Scott went up the middle for four yards and Bender completed a pass to Dietrich at the 24. Unfortunately the completion was nullified by an illegal motion penalty that gave us a second and eleven at the 41. Before I knew it we had fourth and eleven and I was running off the field.

Jablonski was going to have his first punt of the season. He went for the coffin corner and was a little long. The punt bounced into the end zone to give the Saints a first down at the 20.

It was obvious but not a surprise that the Saints made some adjustments at halftime. They were moving the ball, picking up large chunks at a time. In no time at all they had their furthest penetration of the day with a first down at the Hawaii 25.

A one-yard rush and two incompletions later the Saints had little choice but to try a field goal. Our defense seemed to have woken up and slammed the door on them. I could sense the Saints' offensive unit's frustration as it left the field.

That frustration was compounded by the field goal attempt, no doubt. It was a 41-yarder. It split the uprights but underneath the crossbar. We had the ball at the Hawaii 24 and still held a 24-0 lead with 5:07 left in the third quarter.

In no time we were moving upfield again. I did my part on second and nine from our 39, catching a pass at the New Orleans 39 and taking it down to the 33. On third and inches at the 23 I went off right tackle and fought my way to the 21 to give us our third first down of the drive.

We continued from there. A series of rushes by Scott and Kerner gave us another first down at the six with less than a minute to play in the quarter. A sweep around left end by Scott that got us a mere yard to the five was the final play of the quarter.

As we changed sides I didn't see any evidence that any substantial part of the crowd had given up and gone home. I wasn't looking especially hard for that but chunks of empty seats are good indicators that many of those in attendance had had enough. It appeared that the New Orleans faithful was hoping for a miracle. I was hoping we could take it in and force an exodus.

Scott's sweep around right end to start the final period got us all the way to the one. Kerner then finished the job, going up the middle and forcing his way into the end zone. Some of us, including myself, helped the officials by raising our arms.

As I joined a few of my teammates in congratulating Kerner I happened to glance up at the scoreboard. I noticed that the score hadn't changed. I also noticed the line judge talking to the referee.

Dietrich was offside. Instead of a touchdown, we had third and goal from the six. I could almost feel the heat of Walker's boiling blood.

We tried to get it in again. Bender's pass to McCracken was batted down in the end zone. Dejectedly the offensive players not on the field goal team ran off the field.

I happened to be running alongside Dietrich. As we neared the sideline I noticed the scowl on Walker's face. His eyes seemed to be shooting daggers at Dietrich.

"I'm sorry, Coach," Dietrich said.

"Yeah, we're all sorry, Dietrich, but you just cost us a touchdown!" Walker barked loud enough to be heard through part of the lower section of the quiet arena behind our bench. I happened to look in that direction and noticed some of the spectators starting to laugh. It was probably the most entertaining part of the game the fans in that section experienced to this point. They didn't have much other cause for enjoyment that day.

At least we got something out of the drive. Guinn converted on a 23-yard field goal attempt. Our lead was now 27-0 with 13:59 left.

Despite the apparent setback, we were feeling pretty good. Even Dietrich was up. I could see him stifling laughter. The chastising he got from Walker struck him as funny although it wouldn't have had this been a tight game. He was careful not to face Walker while his face bore such an amused expression.

Actually there were a few of us who found Walker's belittling retort amusing. Allen was at the Gatorade table and taking a sip and had a mouthful of Gatorade that shot out of his mouth when Walker's response cracked him up. Walker's words and Allen's response broke me up so I turned my back to keep Walker from catching me taking things lightly. It was all symbolic of our collective mood since we were confident that the game was securely in our hip pockets.

We almost iced the game completely on the kickoff. The kick was fielded on the four but Hasegawa once again was downfield in a hurry. He actually hit the ball carrier at the nine, forcing a fumble. After a few seconds the Saints had recovered their own fumble at about the point of contact.

By this time the defense may have been tired or simply confident enough not to play with the earlier intensity. Whatever the case, the Saints put together a pretty good drive. They methodically moved downfield although with very little hope of a comeback, especially since they were also chewing up the clock.

The Saints finally scored on an eleven-yard pass to trail 27-7 with 5:33 left. The crowd responded appropriately although there didn't seem to be much enthusiasm. It almost seemed as if we were playing in front of the crowds in the Tom Slick cartoons which let out a lethargic "Yea."

To the surprise of nobody, the Saints tried an onside kick. Also to the surprise of nobody, we had nothing but ball handlers on our kick return unit. It was Dietrich who recovered the kick at the 50, perhaps redeeming himself for his faux pas on our previous drive.

We weren't concerned with scoring. We just wanted to run out the clock. Only one more pass was thrown when we faced second and eleven at the

New Orleans 38. This was intended to prevent the Saints from keying on the run. I caught the pass at the 21 and was brought down at the 17.

Shortly after that Walker sent in the backups. Billingsley went in at quarterback. Grant Collier, acquired from San Diego in the Giametti trade, went in at fullback, Ozzie Roberts took over at tailback and Rossi replaced me.

We finally turned the ball over on downs at the seven with 1:12 left. The Saints, to their credit, tried to put up another score. That was thwarted after a few plays when James Malick intercepted a pass at the Saints 21 and returned the ball to the 15. With 39 seconds left Billingsley took a couple of snaps and that was it. We had won our second consecutive season opener.

The postgame locker room was jubilant. We had started the season on a positive note. We were tied for first place in the NFC West.

Bender offered the postgame prayer. After that Walker, smiling as wide as the room itself, held up a football.

"Game ball," he said. "There were a lot of great performances. Zanakis made a couple of key plays and Hasegawa was brutal on a couple of kickoffs and, overall, it was a tremendous team effort. I think the game ball should go to somebody who spent a lot of time here in New Orleans without really knowing what it was like to win."

At that point he flipped the ball to Marv. It was a fitting reward for his return to the city where he had toiled for nine years.

"All right, men," Walker continued as he stood in the midst of a few dozen radiant men. "That was a good way to start the season."

A collective roar went up. It died down quickly so that Walker could continue.

"I want you to enjoy this. We'll have a great flight home and you've got all day tomorrow to savor this. Next week we've got a tough game at home with Buffalo. We'll start worrying about that on Tuesday."

As it turned out, Scott narrowly missed out on a 100-yard game. He had 21 carries for 93 yards. Kerner wasn't far behind with 70 yards on only eight carries. As one who was used primarily for his blocking skills and short yardage ability, the 70 yards represented a career high for him.

I started the season with a 100-yard reception game. I caught six passes for 127 yards.

What is interesting is that I had the only two receptions of the second half. However, there were only five official pass attempts. For most of the second half we were focusing on trying to run down the clock.

The flight home was very short. Timewise it was no shorter than scheduled but it seemed to take no more than an hour or two to fly from New Orleans to Honolulu. Everybody walked up and down the aisle, cheerily engaging in conversation with everybody else.

It should come as no surprise that football players can become a little silly after a lopsided victory. Dietrich heard at least a few times about how we would have had an even bigger margin of victory but he "cost us a touchdown."

Of course everybody was very careful not to mock Walker unless he was out of earshot.

I was near the back of the plane talking to Kerner, Allen and Richards. We were laughing and congratulating ourselves for being the greatest football players on the greatest team in the world. That was when Larry Westfall, a rookie guard from Kansas, approached us with a smile as wide as Texas.

"Man, that was some job we did against the Saints, wasn't it?" the radiant Westfall asked rhetorically.

"I would say it was okay, wouldn't you, Jay?" Allen responded lightly.

"Not bad, not bad," I replied in feigned nonchalance. "Perhaps a six on a scale of ten."

Westfall was still smiling but looked confused.

"It looked good on the scoreboard," Allen said. "The real tale will be told when we watch the films on Tuesday."

"Ah, the films," Kerner chimed in. "Did you make any mistakes today?"

"Well, I don't think so," Westfall replied tentatively. "I did kind of miss a block on a kick return."

"That's going to be your moment in the spotlight," I said. "Walker is going to show that over and over again."

"Believe me," Kerner added, "you're going to almost be sorry you decided to be a pro football player."

Westfall looked like he found it hard to believe what we were telling him. Why would such a brilliantly played game turn out so badly on film?

"Believe me, rook," Allen continued. "When we watch the films on Tuesday the coaches are going to rant and rave and make you feel about two inches tall. You'll leave the session wondering if you only imagined that we won this game."

What I didn't discover until the next day was that our victory was a milestone . . . for the Saints . . . and a dubious one. It was the 100th loss for the Saints since their inception a decade earlier.

CHAPTER SEVEN
Buffalo Roams In

During the films on Tuesday the coaches ranted and raved and made us feel like we were two inches tall. We left the session wondering if we'd only imagined that we had won the game.

The veterans knew that this was the way it was. It was a ploy to bring us down to earth after a one-sided victory and make us want to be even better in the next game.

I was dumb enough to believe I was immune from criticism. I blocked well, returned three punts for 26 yards and rushed three times for 12 yards. As I previously mentioned, I also caught the aforementioned six passes for 126 yards and completed the only pass I threw for 42 yards.

The latter was where I got berated. Walker didn't seem to care for my choice of receivers.

Walker ran the clip back and forth a few times. The play was a Moloka'i option left. I lined up in the slot and went into motion on cue. On the snap Dietrich, playing wide to the right, ran a streak pattern. Grummon, lined up tight on the left, ran a flag.

Bender took the snap and faked a handoff to Kerner up the middle, then bootlegged to his right where he handed off to me on a reverse. I spotted Grummon open downfield and fired a picture-perfect pass to him.

"What's wrong with this play, Jay?" Walker asked sternly.

Walker ran the play back and forth a couple more times before I gave him an honest answer.

"I don't know," I said. "It looks pretty good to me."

"It does, huh? You passed to Grummon and he picked up about 40 or 50 yards but look at Dietrich there. He's got six points written all over him."

When Bender handed me the ball it appeared to the defense that the play was a run all the way. That caused the defensive backs who had been covering Grummon and Dietrich to move in, allowing Grummon and Dietrich to get open.

Dietrich was deep enough so that a well-thrown pass was earmarked for six points. Grummon was not nearly as deep or as fast as Dietrich and the defender who had been covering Dietrich was able to adjust and pursue Grummon before bringing him down after I had passed to him.

"So why didn't you pass the ball to Dietrich?" Walker asked.

"Because I didn't see him," I replied firmly, thinking that was reasonable enough.

"But you knew what pattern Dietrich was running, didn't you?"

"Yes but I still didn't see him. I saw Grummon and he was open."

The unfortunate thing in a situation like this is that the rules don't allow a timeout so that everybody has to freeze to enable the ball carrier to take a minute to ponder his options. Decisions have to be made in a fraction of a second. A 42-yard gain is usually grounds for celebration.

Walker knew I was right, I was sure. He just needed time to accept it. He didn't speak to me the rest of the day . . . unless an icy glare is an effective means of communication.

After the films we changed for a light workout and moved to the field. Westfall came over to where I was talking to Russ Allen, Marv Nelson and James Malick.

"You guys weren't kidding on the plane the other day," Westfall said in amused disbelief. "I found it hard to believe we won that game with the way Walker was harping at everybody."

"That's the psychological makeup of the way things are around here," I casually told him although inwardly I was furious at Walker. "The bigger the margin of victory, the worse we get treated during films."

"Ain't it the truth," Allen remarked lightly, having experienced similar diatribes in the defensive film session. "If we win by 50 points the coaches will start having people shot for their so-called miscues."

Dietrich was nearby doing stretching exercises and heard the exchange.

"Well I'm going to have Jay shot," he jocularly remarked. "I didn't get to score a touchdown and it's all his fault."

"But you also cost us a touchdown," Marv reminded Dietrich, cracking everybody up including Dietrich.

Dietrich's and Marv's remarks might not have been especially funny under normal circumstances. These circumstances weren't normal. We were all fairly tense after our haranguing film sessions. Dietrich's and Marv's, as well as Allen's, remarks gave us a light laugh and loosened us up a little.

But I was still fuming.

One thing that concerned me was the possibility of not starting on Sunday. I stood my ground when Walker lambasted me because I knew I was right. Walker still had the final say on who played and who didn't. Was he so bullheaded that he would bench me over something like that? Perhaps my standing my ground was the shot in the arm Rossi needed for his career.

By Wednesday my fears were assuaged. Walker was speaking to me again. He even gave me a compliment or two during practice.

"All right, Dockman!" he called out jubilantly when I blasted through the hole on an off-tackle play. "That's great hustle!"

At the end of Friday's workout Walker walked off the field with me.

"You know, Jay, it isn't always easy for a coach to admit he's wrong but I was definitely wrong the other day. If you see a man open, pass the ball to him. If you hesitate the opportunity might be gone a second or two later. You did the right thing by passing to Grummon on Sunday."

"Thanks, Coach," I replied gratuitously. I admired him for his willingness to admit his mistake.

Our workout on Saturday was what we would normally expect the day before a game. It was primarily a formality. We made last minute adjustments, especially since there were a couple of lineup changes. Kerner was out with a foot injury so Collier would be starting at fullback. Gavin Pratt would be starting at right defensive end by virtue of beating out Jon Jurgens. This was the type of thing that could go back and forth throughout the season.

It was like a dress rehearsal. I was in my traditional Dodger attire that had become my trademark. A few times I noticed Walker looking at me and shaking his head with an amused expression on his face.

We walked through our assignments. Our workout ended before noon.

Saturday night was the annual "Meet The Hawaiians" banquet. Like the year before, it was held at the Ala Moana Hotel. This time we met in the Plumeria Ballroom.

There were some rules for the team to abide by. First of all, everybody was required to attend. This included coaches, taxi squad members, injured personnel and a few others aside from those on the active roster. If somebody's wife was having a baby or there was some other emergency that person could be excused but there was no begging off without a legitimate reason.

Unlike the previous year when we were required to wear something "casually dressy," this time we had been issued team blazers. These were the same shade of brown as our jerseys and featured the Hawaiians logo on the pocket. We had the option of wearing a dress shirt or aloha shirt underneath but the blazer was an absolute must.

This being 1977, it wasn't considered a big deal that many of the players and coaches smoked. I have always been ashamed to admit that I was still among those who indulged in the deadly vice. We were allowed to smoke although they asked that those of us who did smoke to try to keep it to a minimum. Walker couldn't very well prohibit us from smoking since he was a smoker himself.

We were put on our honor to abide by the two-drink maximum. Football players are human and many obviously drink. They still didn't want anybody getting drunk, especially at an event such as this. Getting drunk and making themselves and the team look bad was discouraged in very strong language.

One thing I discovered was that only the players, coaches and other team personnel ate for free. I knew that the general public had to pay but didn't know that any guests of the players and coaches were also subjected to the 15-dollar fee. This included wives, girlfriends and anybody else.

I didn't mind shelling out 15 bucks for Carol. I was simply taken by surprise. It was a charity event. Somebody was going to benefit from my alleged philanthropy.

136

The players and their guests were once again assigned seats in the front and the rest of the guests selected seats toward the rear. Carol and I were assigned to sit at a large round table with Marv and Karla Nelson, Mark Black and his date, newlyweds Rich and Carolyn Grummon, and Eric Hamer and his date. The table next to us included Jennings, Rossi, Blakely, Rodgers, Kerner and guests. It was obvious that the smoking players were clumped together.

After we found our seats I went to the bar to get a glass of wine for Carol and a beer for myself. Hasegawa came over to me.

"Hey, Jay. Isn't that Carol? Your girlfriend in college?"

At that moment I realized how unexposed to the team Carol had been. We had only been reunited for about three months although most of that time I spent in training camp. There had been no arbitrary encounters with teammates away from training camp when Carol was with me.

Carol had gone to our preseason scrimmage and home exhibition games but had no contact with the team itself. Our schedule was so regimented that there were no pregame or postgame gatherings like there were during the regular season. During the games she met a few wives but they might have written her off as just one of my dates.

I didn't speak much about Carol during camp, if at all. That was partially due to the lack of time for socializing. I was also apprehensive because I wasn't sure of how Carol and I would ultimately wind up and I avoided making any announcements that might build up a relationship that I wasn't sure would last.

"You've got a good memory," I said to Rich. "She hasn't been around for more than three years."

I took Rich to our table to reintroduce him and Carol. Although Rich and I usually were normally not part of the same social circle in college, we had been friends and she did remember him.

It was the prototype banquet. No host cocktails, dinner and the program. It was an outstanding meal; tossed salad, prime rib, steamed rice (as I previously mentioned, I was not a rice eater but they prepared it so well at the Ala Moana Hotel that I tolerated it after I loaded it with pepper), mixed vegetables and rolls and butter. Dessert was apple crisp.

The team's majority owner, Cec Heftel, flew to Hawaii from Washington where he was serving his first term as the representative from Hawaii's First Congressional District. He gave a very concise speech, thanking the fans for their support and saying that he looked forward to a season that would prove to be even better than 1976. There wasn't a single trace of hot air despite him being a politician. After his speech, which probably wasn't even five minutes long, he yielded to master of ceremonies Les Keiter who was once again our radio play-by-play announcer. Keiter then introduced Coach Walker.

Like the previous year, Walker was a very congenial speaker. He introduced the rest of the coaching staff and then the players in numerical order including those out with injuries. Unlike the previous year when an oversight prevented the taxi squad members from being introduced, Walker included them in the introductions. He said something very positive about each player which impressed those in attendance and, he hoped, boosted our confidence just enough as players. At the very least, he massaged our egos.

"Number ten, Steve Bender," he said to cue kicker Eric Guinn to sit and Bender to stand. "This is our starting quarterback for the second year in a row. We got him from San Francisco in the expansion draft and he proved to be an outstanding acquisition. Steve's now in his 16th season but he looks like he is still in his prime."

"Number 12, Joe Billingsley," Walker segued as Bender sat and Billingsley stood while the audience gave polite applause. "We drafted him last year out of Brigham Young University. You don't see much of him now because he's Bender's backup but he's developing very well. If Bender goes down I have every confidence that Joe will fill in admirably. He's definitely our quarterback of the future."

Joe probably needed the glowing approbation. He often showed a chip on his shoulder even though he was a vital part of the team. Sometimes his surly disposition made him easy to dislike.

"Number 22, Jay Dockman," Walker called a little later as I stood and Carl Rodgers sat while I got my polite applause. "He's a local favorite from the University of Hawaii who played his high school ball in California. He is one of the most versatile players on the team if not in the NFL. He's primarily a receiver who will also rush a few times a game. He's also proven himself to be an excellent passer who can even fill in at quarterback if necessary."

"Number 24, Jeff Kerner," Walker said to cue me to sit and Jeff to stand. " . . . "

And so it went. Player after player was introduced to polite applause and a few kind words.

The last item on the agenda was the showing of a highlight film which Walker narrated. It was comprised primarily of 1976 highlights but a few highlights from the exhibition season and even the previous week's game in New Orleans were included.

My ego was padded when my 63-yard screen pass touchdown from our Monday night game in Oakland was included. I appeared frequently but that was the best segment , at least to me, where I was included.

"Howard Cosell was furious that we were included in the Monday night schedule," Walker remarked about the Oakland game. "I think we did a pretty fair job of humbling him. As you probably know, that isn't easy to do."

I suddenly noticed Keiter at the head table. He seemed to be stifling laughter. He had worked with Cosell while with ABC in New York and was in full agreement.

It didn't necessarily surprise me that my 42-yard pass to Grummon the previous week was included. What surprised me was Walker's description of it. Since the film was of TV footage and not the panaramic shot from game films the viewers couldn't see Dietrich wide open downfield.

"This is Jay Dockman firing an excellent pass to Rich Grummon last week in New Orleans," Walker said. "What you can't see is Ted Dietrich wide open downfield for a sure touchdown. I got on Jay about that but he was absolutely right and I was wrong since all he could see was Grummon. If you see a man open, that's when you've got to throw the ball. There's no time to stop and look for a better option."

I didn't feel it was necessary for Walker to get into that.

But I appreciated it.

When it was over I handled a few autograph requests but got out as quickly as I politely could. I wanted to shift my focus to the Buffalo game.

Carol met about a dozen of my teammates. She had heard a lot about Marv and Ed who were probably my two closest friends on the team and found them to be as congenial as I had described. She enjoyed the senses of humor of Shuford, Allen and Grummon. She was also impressed with the sincere congeniality of McDaniel, Hayer and Bender.

"Who was that blonde guy again?" she asked as we drove away from the hotel.

"Which blonde guy?"

"The one at our table."

"Oh, Mark Black. He's our left cornerback."

"Okay," she said. "He seemed kind of. . . . I don't know. Kind of full of himself, I guess. Very cocky."

I nodded and grinned. I got along with Mark but Carol was right about him.

"He's a little different," I conceded. "I don't have any problem with him but, yeah, he's kind of unique. He's one of those guys who went to college on a football scholarship and did everything but go to class."

"Really?"

"Well, according to him, he went to Oklahoma for four years and left with the academic equivalent of a high school sophomore. He actually brags about that. He was even more flippant about school than my old friend Chris was."

"Chris?" Carol responded reflectively. "You mean Chris Alexander?"

I nodded.

"Yeah, I remember him from the Manoa Zoo. Nice guy but a little strange at times. Whatever happened to him? Do you know?"

"The last I heard, he was in Arizona," I said, hoping she wouldn't ask for details since I didn't feel like talking about Chris.

"Do you ever hear from him?" she asked.

"Nope."

And that was the last we spoke of Chris that night, thank God.

I got Carol home at a little before ten o'clock. I was feeling hyper but knew it was a good idea to not stay out late. After all, I had a football game about 12 hours later.

"What time do you have to get up?" Carol asked as I prepared to head home.

"I'll set the alarms for about 5:30. I'll probably get up on my own about an hour or so prior to that."

I rolled out of bed at 4:22. I had laid down at about 11:30 and eventually got to sleep. I woke up at 1:13, 2:20, 3:05, 3:47 and finally 4:22.

While the coffee brewed I showered and dressed. I was back in my old groove of getting out of bed and wanting to play football *right this minute*.

At about 6:15 I went to the parking garage and got in my car. I started driving out of the twin-tower dwelling in Hawaii Kai's Hahaione Valley.

"Stick it to the Bills," a guard cheerily called as I drove past the guard shack to the street.

About 20 minutes later I had picked Carol up and continued toward the stadium. She was one of five guests I would have at the game. Also getting complimentary tickets were my former roommate Bill, his alleged girlfriend Cherie (she believed they were forever while he took it one day at a time), Don Simmons and his girlfriend Eileen. It wasn't easy getting that many tickets for the home opener. It still surprises me that I did.

Ticket allocations varied from team to team. The Hawaiians system was that the Stadium Authority gave the team 200 tickets for a group of seats in the orange section at midfield behind the Hawaiians bench. Each player, coach and team official was automatically given two tickets. Those who had children were given extras to accommodate the entire family.

Those who were not going to use any of their allotted tickets were expected to return them. This was because there were always requests for extras. Those were given out on a first come, first served basis.

The 200 tickets for the team were not designated by seat or row numbers. They were printed specifically to designate the holder as a guest of the team. This entitled the holder to sit in the reserved section. The lack of seat assignments enabled ticket holders to choose their own seats in this section.

Once the 200 tickets were gone any player wanting extra tickets had to dig into his own pocket. He could buy tickets for seats directly below the complimentary seats at face value. Tickets for the orange rows stretching from the front row to the row directly below the complimentary section did not become available to the general public until 24 hours before kickoff or until the rest of the sideline seats were sold out, whichever came first.

I was fortunate to get my three extra tickets before the 200 designated freebies were gone. By Tuesday it had become obvious that our home opener would be a sellout in short order. We were all told to buy any extra tickets we needed because tomorrow would be too late. The minute the other sideline seats were sold the remaining unpurchased seats in the orange section would be taken to the box office for walkup sales.

As it was, our home opener was officially sold out by about 10:30 on Wednesday morning. We beat the deadline to lift the television blackout by almost 24 full hours. In 1976's home opener we beat the deadline only by about an hour.

I entered the stadium parking lot through gate 4 which was located on Salt Lake Boulevard near Kamehameha Highway. I parked in the players' section and escorted Carol through the tunnel to the field in the north end zone.

Our last regular season game at Aloha Stadium was ten months earlier. Suddenly it seemed as if it had only been the previous week. The early morning atmosphere and stadium ambience made it seem as if all that had happened since November was compressed into a few days.

Of course there would be telltale differences. The team would feature some new faces and some of the old faces were gone. I was also now with Carol.

The north end zone looked identical to 1976 with the Hawaiians helmet and University of Hawaii helmet flanking large block letters spelling HAWAII. The University of Hawaii helmet in 1977 was white with a muscular Hawaiian warrior running with a football inside a rainbow. It was a design adopted the year after I graduated and I liked that design better than the logo a few years later which featured UH at the upper end of a rainbow. Both designs I liked infinitely better than the nauseating black uniforms the team would adopt in 1999. Black simply was not symbolic of Hawaii.

We crossed the length of the field and walked through the south end zone with the ALOHA in block letters painted in. On the mauka side was a painted replica of Buffalo's helmet, which was white in 1977. On the opposite side was the University of Idaho helmet; the University of Hawaii's previous night's opponent.

I took Carol to the hospitality room where several teammates, coaches, wives, girlfriends and children were congregating. Carol helped herself to a good breakfast at the buffet. I limited myself to my usual small portion of fruit, juice and coffee.

"That's all you're going to eat?" Carol asked.

141

"If I eat this other stuff it's going to wind up on the turf the first time I get hit," I replied lightly.

Besides, I never had much of an appetite before a game. I only ate what little I did because I didn't want to play on an empty stomach.

I did my usual pregame ritual of running my laps and warming up with my teammates. In the locker room, after Hayer led us in *The Lord's Prayer*, Walker addressed the team. He was more concise this time.

"All right, men. Buffalo's going to be tough but we can take them. All we have to do is play 60 minutes of tough, smart football. This is the home opener. Let's give our hometown fans what they want."

With that we filed out to the south end zone. Since this was the home opener, all coaches and players were to be introduced individually. The nonstarters, including those out with injuries, were introduced in numerical order, then the starting defense and starting offense. We ran through two lines each of 12 cheerleaders to midfield where the six alternate cheerleaders handed out leis.

During the introductions most of the Buffalo players took their place on the makai sideline. After our introductions were completed, Buffalo's starting defense was introduced. For the remainder of the season the visiting team's designated unit would be introduced before our designated unit was introduced. Since the entire team was introduced for the home opener the Hawaiians showed the Bills the courtesy of not having their unit introduced before having to wait through the Hawaiians entire team introductions.

Nanakuli High School's band marched to the center of the field to play the *National Anthem*. Like the previous year, all high school bands wanting to perform before a game and during halftime were invited to sign up. All bands were then randomly selected and assigned a home game in the order in which they were drawn.

In Nanakuli's case it was a holdover from 1976. Nanakuli was chosen the previous season to perform at our first home playoff game if it actually came to that. Since we didn't host a playoff game, Nanakuli was moved to the 1977 home opener.

Roosevelt's and Kahuku's bands were selected for home playoff games in 1977. If we didn't host a playoff game they would be the first two bands for 1978 home games.

The coin toss went off at 9:55, as scheduled. For the second time in as many weeks we lost the toss. That meant that the beginning of the contest was once again a test of my patience as well as our defense.

"Okay, kickoff team. Take the field," Walker directed. "This is our time to shine, men. Everybody be up for this. Don't take this team lightly."

142

I wasn't taking anybody lightly. I just wanted to get on the field. I was hoping the defense would make quick work of the Bills to enable me to get my first licks in.

It appeared initially that my wait was going to be shorter than anticipated. Guinn's kick was fielded at the two. The Buffalo return man got to the 24 before taking a hard shot from defensive tackle Ken Gilbert.

"Fumble!"

There wasn't much of a scramble. Buffalo quickly recovered right about where the fumble took place. My hopes had only been up for a second or two.

It still didn't take long. A rush for no gain and two incomplete passes terminated Buffalo's opening drive. I was on the field with 14:12 left in the first quarter.

I took my place on the Hawaii 35. While I waited for the Buffalo punting unit to break its huddle I stole a glance into the bleachers. Carol was sitting in the second row from the top of the orange seats. This is the lowest section of the stadium although the orange seats extend for several rows so Carol was high enough for an unobstructed view. As the punting unit got into position I could see that Carol's eyes were glued to me as she sat flanked by Karla Nelson and Pam Bender.

Once the ball was snapped I focused on the task at hand. The punt soared in my direction. I caught the ball at the 37 and, sensing room to run although I couldn't hear Rich Hasegawa coaching me from about ten yards ahead of me, I charged forward.

I managed to sidestep one white jersey on about the 45. I wasn't so fortunate when I encountered another white jersey. He caught me at about the 48 but I fought his momentum and stayed up. That bought me another yard before another Bill joined in and the two brought me down at the Hawaii 49. It was a great place to begin our first drive.

It was a very satisfying return. The 12 yards were better than average but what made me feel really good was the quality of the return. I could easily have gone down on the 47 or 48 but I refused. The difference from the extra effort was still no more than six feet. Sometimes that is the difference between seven points and no points. Every yard is vital.

As it was, we needed 153 feet for our first score. Collier erased nine of those feet with his first carry of the game, blasting through the middle to the Buffalo 48. Scott then picked up four yards around right end to give us third and three at the 44.

The initial plan was to go to the air. Bender saw something he didn't like and called an audible.

Whatever Bender saw or sensed was right on. Scott picked up 14 yards off left tackle to give us a first down at the 30, drawing a huge roar from the crowd.

"All right, Larry! That's the way to do it!" I cried enthusiastically as I helped him to his feet.

"Don't forget to credit the line," he replied with his trademark crooked smile as he and I headed toward the huddle. "Those guys opened a hole as wide as the Grand Canyon."

Three plays from scrimmage and we were already in field goal range. Naturally nobody from our side wanted a field goal.

After Scott's one-yard gain up the middle we went to the air for the first time. I made a leaping catch near the left sideline inside the ten and was wrestled down at the four. It was first and goal and our fans continued to be extremely vocal.

"Right on, Jaybird!" Grummon remarked enthusiastically as he helped me to my feet. "That was a catch for the highlight reels."

There were a few more compliments and pats on the back as we huddled near the 15. Bender told me he thought the pass was too high and would fly out of bounds. It didn't seem like an especially difficult catch to me but two days later I would see how spectacular it looked on the game films.

Back to action, the Bill defense put on a heavy rush. Bender got a quick short pass off to Grummon but it was batted down at the line.

It was more of the same on second down. This time the receiver was Joe Schary, our sixth round draft pick out of Illinois. That was also batted down; this time in the end zone.

Another pass was called and Bender once again saw a rush of white jerseys. Steve rolled to his right. I was directly in front of him about eight yards deep in the end zone but he crossed the line of scrimmage before he saw me. He continued forward and dove into the end zone just inside the pylon as I joined a few of my teammates, as well as the officials, in signaling a touchdown.

Abraham and I helped Steve to his feet while the crowd continued a sustained roar. The play was more proof that Steve played as if he was still in his prime. If he kept playing like that it would be a long time before Billingsley would come off the bench.

Bender gave the ball to Clint who spiked it. We ran off the field in triumph.

The extra point climaxed the 51-yard drive. We led 7-0 with 11:19 left in the first quarter.

I grabbed a cup of Gatorade from the table between our two benches. Before I moved away I saw Bender approaching and grabbed another cup.

"Here," I said, holding a cup out to him. "Let me buy you a drink."

I was feeling pretty loose although I had to be careful. We still had to play another 56 minutes and 19 seconds.

Guinn's kickoff was fielded a yard deep in the end zone. Buffalo put forth a fairly effective wedge. The return man was past the 20 before any of

144

my teammates could even get close. He was still on his feet at the 30; not being hit until defensive tackle Jess Palumbo, a rookie free agent from Texas, hit him from his right side at the 37.

"Fumble!"

The ball popped loose and hit the ground. A mixture of brown jerseys and white jerseys jumped after it. Although I couldn't see the ball, the mass of humanity indicated that the ball was gradually moving toward the south end zone.

It seemed to take forever to sort through the pile of players near the 30. I thought I was going to suffocate from holding my breath. The stadium seemed eerily silent.

The referee raised up from the pile. He pointed toward the south end zone, drawing still another enormous roar from the crowd. We had first down at the 29. Dubois got credit for the recovery.

"Magnifique, Henri! Magnifique!" I exclaimed as our paths crossed, slapping fives as I headed to our huddle.

This is the kind of thing a team has to capitalize on. We wasted no time in getting started. Bender hit Dietrich at the four. Ted had to go into a slide to catch it since the ball was losing altitude. A defender touched him at the point of the catch to prevent further advancement.

I helped Ted to his feet. As we jogged to where we would huddle we took note of the crowd. There were a lot of happy smiling faces clapping and yelling their exultation.

"Don't you just love the sound of our fans?" Ted remarked.

"Let's keep them happy," I replied.

On the next play Bender hit Grummon on a quick slant at the two. Rich went down just shy of the goal line.

Collier then went up the middle on the next play and ran into a wall of white jerseys. Wanting to make the most of his opportunity to start in place of the injured Kerner, he continued his momentum and just managed to get past the goal line to draw another explosion from the fans as well as his teammates.

Things were obviously going our way. In two possessions we had traveled a combined total of 80 yards. That was enough for a 14-0 lead with 10:02 left in the quarter. Like the week before, it was a matter of playing our game.

Guinn seemed to get caught up in the moment on the kickoff. He kicked the ball out of the end zone for a touchback.

"You weren't supposed to do that, Eric," Dave Shuford remarked lightly when Guinn returned to the sideline. "You're supposed to let them have a return. That way we can force another fumble."

Buffalo began its drive by going up the middle to the 27. It was the first play from scrimmage, out of only four, where the Bills gained yardage.

The Bills picked up a couple of first downs, even crossing midfield which was not a surprise since the Bills seemed to have a superior running game. On second and six from our 42 McDaniel dropped the ball carrier for a one-yard loss. Blakely then knocked down a pass at about the 25 to send the Bills' punting unit on the field.

Of course that also sent me on the field. I stood on the seven and waited for the punt. It seemed very unlikely that the punt would be one I could return.

The punt was up. I could tell that the ball was going to be slightly over my head. I raised my hand to decoy the wideouts into thinking I was making a fair catch to try to slow them up, then ran forward as soon as the ball passed overhead.

As I turned around I could see that the ball had taken a high bounce. One of the wideouts caught the ball and froze in his tracks at the three. He made a great play. We had to cover 97 yards to get a score this time.

We huddled at the rear of the north end zone. Bender looked confident as he prepared to call a play.

"We've gone from one end of the field to the other before," he reminded us. "There's no reason why we can't do it now. This game belongs to us."

Scott rushed up the middle and picked up all but 96 of the yards we needed for our next touchdown. I then carried on a Waimanalo right, breaking a couple of tackles before going down at the 18. I didn't want it to go to my head but for the moment I was feeling pretty good about myself, especially when I took note of the cheering of the crowd.

"All of these fans are going to be hoarse by the time the game ends," I remarked to Grummon as he helped me to my feet.

We now had some breathing room. Scott gave us a little more by picking up five yards around right end. He picked up one more on the following play, then fumbled.

Fortunately he recovered his own fumble. It was third and four at the Hawaii 24.

"Hey, don't do that, man" Grummon remarked lightly to try to ease Scott's mind as our huddle was forming. "Only Buffalo is allowed to fumble today."

"We even encourage them to," Bender added before getting down to business and calling the play.

Bender took the snap, dropped back and looked for Grummon. Rich flared out to the 29, positioning himself beyond the first down marker on the right. Bender fired and. . . .

Interception!

A Bill linebacker stepped in front of Grummon. He picked off the pass and headed for the end zone. Marv pursued him and tackled him but not until reaching the end zone. I was about ten yards further downfield than

Grummon and on the opposite side at the time of the pick so all I could do was helplessly watch and then dejectedly move to our sideline. On one play the Bills were back in the game. Our spirits weren't so light anymore.

"Shake it off, men. Shake it off," Walker directed.

I grabbed a cup of Gatorade and quickly chugged it down. After the extra point I had to take the field again. We held a 14-7 lead with 32 seconds left in the first quarter. The Bills were not only back in the game but they suddenly had the momentum.

"It happens. It happens," offensive coordinator Jim Potter reminded us although I think he was primarily focused on keeping Bender's confidence up since he was the most disgruntled about his mistake. "Show these guys that you're undaunted by this. Just come right back and score again. That'll be another giant step toward victory."

I don't know if my spirits were lifted substantially but I knew that Potter was right. As I took my place on the goal line of the north end zone I looked up at the scoreboard. We still held a 14-7 lead and we were getting the ball. Despite the recent setback, our position was better than Buffalo's.

It took some doing to get the momentum back. Hasegawa fielded the kickoff in the end zone and downed the ball. Dietrich then jumped prematurely to give us a first and 15 at the 15. Scott then went off left tackle and was stuffed at the line to close out the quarter. I hoped we weren't unraveling.

Bender went to confer with Walker on the mauka sideline and the rest of us straggled toward the south side of the field. We spoke in hushed tones as we moved because the Bills' defense was moving in the same direction and we didn't want them hearing us. With us experiencing a hiccup in our offensive production after getting off to a flying start, we were primarily trying to encourage each other. We still had the lead as well as the ball against a team that finished 2-12 in 1976. Sometimes it is hard to get motivated against a team like that so we were pumping each other up although nobody was talking about the Bills' 1976 record. We had to believe they would have a better team in 1977.

We began the second quarter with an incomplete pass. We finally got on track on the next play when Bender hit me with a pass near the mauka sideline at the 31. I got up to the 37 before I was pushed out of bounds and into the arms of Mark Black and Russ Allen before I would have had to leap over our bench.

"Thanks, guys," I said lightly before turning to return to the field.

"Don't mention it, Jaybird," Allen replied.

"That's what we're here for," Black said simultaneous with Allen's remark.

"Good job, Jay," Walker remarked as I ran past him.

Our third down conversion got our fans back into the game and worked wonders for our confidence. I hoped it also helped to deflate Buffalo's confidence.

We methodically moved downfield. A mixture of rushes and passes picked us up a couple of first downs. A defensive holding penalty gave us a second and two at the Buffalo 32.

I got the call on a sweep around right end. Following my protection, I managed to get us another first down with a yard to spare at the 29.

Two plays later we were at the 19. Time was called to measure. We were about three inches short of the first down.

Walker allowed Bender to call the play. I think he figured they would be looking for a fullback or tailback up the middle. Instead he called a Waimanalo left which had me carry off left tackle. I picked up a yard to give us a first down at the 18. The interception that produced Buffalo's only score to this point was virtually forgotten.

After two rushes by Scott we had first and goal at the three. It was then Scott who was called on to take us the rest of the way although it wasn't easy. He swept around left end to the one, then carried up the middle to inches from the goal line.

Buffalo was called for a facemask. That moved the ball half the distance to the goal line. In this case that was about two or three inches.

It was Scott getting the call again; this time in the air. He went up the middle on a play-action fake. Bender then passed over the middle in the end zone and hit Scott right on the numbers. We had succeeded in doing what Potter encouraged us to do.

Guinn's extra point was true. We had our two-touchdown lead back with 6:52 left in the half.

It may have been another step toward victory. From Buffalo's perspective it seemed to simply be another obstacle to overcome. They weren't wailing, retreating to the locker room or waving white flags and it didn't appear as if their coach was threatening to lace their Gatorade with cyanide. They seemed to take the field with the attitude that they could overcome a two-touchdown deficit.

"The Bills seem to believe they can still win this game," I overheard Abraham remark.

"The fools," Kerner replied lightly from his post in street clothes and game jersey behind our bench.

The Bills started in a semblance of a hole. Guinn's kickoff was fielded about five yards deep in the end zone. The return man came out and was met by Hasegawa near the ten. He managed to briefly sidestep Hasegawa but Rich stayed with him, dragging him down by the shoulder pads at the 13.

"Yeah, Rich!" I yelled although I don't think too many people heard me above the roar of the crowd. Rich was primarily a backup but he definitely knew how to get his moments in the spotlight. Players like that are very vital to the team.

The Bills, being professionals, still seemed undaunted. They went to work and picked up huge chunks of yardage. After three first downs they had a third and eight at the Hawaii 40. By this time the clock was running with roughly three minutes left in the half. I was hoping for an incomplete pass that would not only force them to punt or try a field goal of about 57 yards but would also stop the clock to give us more time to chalk up another score.

We didn't send in the nickel defense. Although we figured the Bills would pass, it was no secret that they had a superior running game. A nickel or dime defense might have made us too vulnerable to the run. Walker decided to keep our standard defense in.

They went to the air. They didn't try to get just enough for a first down the way we expected but tried to get a little more than that. Blakely had his man well covered but it wasn't enough. The receiver outleaped Blakely near the 20. Blakely then brought him down at the 19. Had he got away it would have been a sure six points for the Bills.

Out of frustration I muttered a few words that I would rather not repeat. At least I had the discipline to keep my voice down. As was mentioned previously, the space between the sideline seats and our bench area at Aloha Stadium was not very large. Anything slightly louder than normal conversation could be heard in the front rows. The fans in those seats heard more than their share of profanity since not all of our players were discreet but I tried to be mindful of the fans' presence.

My downtrodden spirits lasted only one play. Allen intercepted a pass over the middle at the 14. He ran like a fullback as 48,967 cheered him on. He broke no fewer than three tackles before a trio of Bills finally brought him down at the Hawaii 49. That was the same spot where we began our first drive of the game.

"That's great field position," Walker pointed out as the offense ran on the field. "You guys should be able to put something on the board."

Our momentum might actually have been slightly deflated. We were hyped to go and discovered that we were at the two-minute warning. The clock showed 1:52.

As Bender stayed behind to converse with Walker the remaining ten members of the offense wistfully took our places in the huddle. At the same time I discreetly looked at the Buffalo defense and tried to read what was going through their minds. I wanted to believe there was nothing positive there. I was hoping they were writing the game off as a lost cause and couldn't wait to get back home. What a long trip to Buffalo they were destined to have.

When play resumed the Bills almost took the ball right back. Bender fired a pass to Dietrich at about the 35. Unfortunately a defensive back batted it back toward the line of scrimmage and another defensive back managed to get his hands on it before it hit the ground. Fortunately for us he wasn't able to get a solid grip on the ball and it fell incomplete. The clock was stopped with 1:44 showing.

I went around left end on the next play. Thanks to some outstanding blocking, I wound up with a lot of room to run. I had picked up about eight yards before any defender managed to put so much as a hand on me. I got all the way to the Buffalo 37 before I was finally brought down. To preserve the two timeouts we had left we went to the line without a huddle.

Bender hit Grummon near the left sideline at the 26. Rich immediately stepped out of bounds. This not only gave us another first down but it stopped the clock with 1:23 left.

Two incomplete passes sandwiched around an illegal procedure penalty gave us a third and 15. The clock showed 1:06. A field goal would have been all right but, as always, we wanted to get the full allotment. We were not yet ready to trade the touchdown in for a field goal.

Bender hit me near the right sideline at the 14 which was good enough for another first down. A defensive back tried to wrestle me down at that spot to keep me in bounds. I still managed to fight my way out to stop the clock with 57 seconds left.

"Dietrich!"

That came from Schary, the rookie wide receiver from St. Charles, Missouri. Walker was sending him in with a play. Dietrich went out.

The play was botched. It was a 3 Mililani left but Bender stumbled after taking the snap and wasn't able to make a clean handoff. He ran to his right, spotted Schary who had shifted his position from near the end zone to back toward the line to try to help block and Bender got a pass off to him. Schary caught the ball at the 12 and was immediately brought down. We used our second timeout with 48 seconds left.

I didn't envy Bender. It was his faux pas that blew the play although we did manage to get two yards out of it. I still didn't envy him having to go talk to Walker. There was no way around meeting with Walker after we called a timeout.

Walker didn't appear too upset. I looked back from our huddle and saw Walker talking with his hand on Bender's shoulder. He had to have known that Bender wasn't the first quarterback to stumble after taking a snap. I recalled doing it a few times during my tenure as a high school quarterback. You simply have to complete the play and go from there.

The next play was an incomplete pass when Bender threw the ball just out of my reach in the end zone. That gave us a third and eight with the clock stopped at 40 seconds.

Bender met a heavy rush on the next play but still managed to pass me the ball at the ten. Unfortunately I was only able to get as far as the six. That left us two yards short of a first down. The issue now was whether to try to pick up the last two yards on fourth down and risk not scoring or simply go for the field goal.

We decided to go for the points. A field goal would turn a two-score game into a three-score game. We let the clock run down to three seconds and burned our final timeout. Guinn came on with the rest of the field goal unit and put it through from 23 yards out before both teams went to their locker rooms for halftime. Our fans gave us generous applause as we left the field.

"This game isn't over," Walker cautioned before we returned to the field. "We still have 30 minutes to play. The Bills are going to be determined to come back. You can't let down."

I knew Walker was right. I sat directly in front of my locker and fought off any feelings of complacency. I still couldn't help but feel as if the game was over and needed to change my attitude. It definitely was not over.

"We do have something going for us," Walker added. "We've got the momentum and we'll be receiving the kickoff. Let's use it to our advantage and put this game away as soon as possible."

We returned to the field amid enthusiastic cheers. Those cheers washed away the feelings of complacency. Our fans were counting on us. They could forgive us for losing a tough game but not if we blew a sizable halftime lead. We could not let our fans down.

I stood on the goal line with my lone remaining college teammate. Hasegawa and I slapped fives, as usual.

"Let's do it," he said with a confident smile.

"Yes, let's do it," I replied and took my place.

The kick was up. It was heading Rich's way. As he was fielding the kick four yards deep in the end zone I encouraged him to return it and shot forward. I managed to throw a decent block near the 20. It wasn't my best block but it was enough to keep the man out of the play. As it was, Rich was brought down by another defender at the 20.

We went to work. After an incomplete pass intended for Dietrich Bender hit me at the 33. I got as far as the 37 to give us our first first down of the second half.

Scott and Collier each picked up five yards to give us another first down. Scott then picked up an additional five on a sweep to give us a second and five at the Buffalo 48. Bender then hit me on a safety valve at the 46. I got to the 41 to give us our third first down of the drive.

Thus far we were doing exactly what we needed to do. We were moving downfield and using up a lot of time. The clock wasn't a factor at this point but it would come into play sooner if we continued to expand our lead.

It was Scott again, picking up ten yards between two carries. The chain came out and we had another first down. Our fans were elated.

Ozzie Roberts came in to spell Scott for a couple of plays. He carried off left tackle for four yards to the Buffalo 27. That was followed by a pass to Dietrich at the seven. Ted fought for two more yards to give us a first and goal at the five.

The fans loved what they were seeing. They were obviously very vocal. Their roaring approbation contributed to our confidence level.

Collier suddenly seemed to have a magnet in his pants pulling him toward the south end zone. At least that was what Walker suggested during the film session two days later. He first jumped before the snap to move us back to the ten. After Scott rushed to the six Collier was hit for a one-yard loss to give us third and goal at the seven. Our confidence level may have diminished a little.

We went to the air. Bender hit Grummon at the two. Rich dove into the end zone to give us our fifth score in six possessions. Each of our six possessions had actually ended in scores but one of the scores was for our opponent. Our confidence level was on the rise again.

As expected, Guinn converted on the extra point. We had a 31-7 lead with 7:21 left in the third quarter. Barring a miraculous turnaround, somebody was going to have a very loooooooong flight to Buffalo.

Once again I had to fight the feeling of complacency. We had a 24-point lead which seemed comfortable but I knew we couldn't rely on that. Even Buffalo's recent history which meant that they were essentially the polar opposite of the Oakland Raiders was not something to take seriously. The Bills were comprised of professional football players. If they believed they could come back and overtake us, it was possible.

I did my best to stay focused. I did my usual ritual of grabbing my cup of Gatorade. I sat on the bench with my game face on.

Guinn kicked off. The Buffalo return man fielded the ball two yards deep in the end zone. He hesitated, then ran out. He met Dubois near the ten.

"Fumble!"

That was the Bills' third fumble on kickoffs. I didn't see the fumble but the action near the hit indicated that McDaniel wasn't lying when he yelled that there was a fumble.

"Get the ball!" I cried out, jumping to my feet. "Get it! Get it! Get it!"

Unfortunately the Bills maintained possession. They had a first down at the 13.

"Damn," Dietrich remarked lightly. "I told Guinn to put more axle grease on the ball."

The Bills managed a first down at the 33 but didn't do much else. They had a third and four at the 39 and attempted a pass which Blakely nearly intercepted. He had the ball in his hands and then dropped it. He later admitted that he made the mistake of starting to run before fully possessing the ball.

It didn't matter. We were still getting the ball back. I took my position on about the 20 to await the punt.

I didn't have to go far to field the punt. I took a couple of steps and caught the ball at the 21. I managed to elude a defender near the 25 and another before the 30. I was finally brought down at the 32.

This was what we needed, I figured. Even if we didn't score we could kill a substantial amount of time. I hoped that the fans could accept the fact that we weren't likely to throw too many passes.

Scott got us off to a flying start by going up the middle to the 39. He then went around left end to give us a third and one at the 41.

Unfortunately Collier went off right tackle and slammed into a wall of white jerseys for no gain. With 3:08 remaining in the third quarter Ray Jablonski was finally going to have to justify his paycheck. It was the second consecutive week that he didn't see action until the second half.

The truth is the game was over. Buffalo put together a reasonably good drive but that was climaxed by a 50-yard field goal attempt early in the fourth quarter that fell short. Neither team scored again.

After the errant field goal attempt I had my final carry of the day, picking up five yards. The only other time I would touch the ball was when I made a fair catch of a punt at the Hawaii 21 about halfway through the final period.

There was one relatively significant event early in the fourth quarter. Two plays after my final carry Scott picked up eleven yards. It was announced over the public address system that Scott had passed the 100-yard mark. Officially he had 105 at that point. He would wind up with 107 yards on 23 carriers.

After my fair catch Walker sent in the reserves. Billingsley went in at quarterback and Collier stayed at fullback since he didn't have the luxury of a backup. Ozzie went in for Scott, Rossi replaced me, Schary went in for Dietrich, McCracken spelled Grummon and there were also substitutions on the line.

The backups put together a fairly impressive drive. They picked up five first downs which prevented the Bills from getting the ball again. The final first down was at the Buffalo 20 with about a minute left. That was when Walker told Billingsley to simply drop to his knee a couple of times to run out the clock. Had the backups scored earlier it would have been acceptable. At this point it would have been running up the score. Walker was never one to do that.

As winning postgame lockers are apt to be, ours was extremely jubilant. We had two victories in as many tries. We hoped that meant momentum for the following week in Miami.

"All right," Walker called as he stood in the middle of the noisy locker room. "First thing's first. Who wants to volunteer to give the prayer."

After a moment's hesitation, Billingsley volunteered. Walker then addressed the team.

"That was an outstanding effort. Good execution. Heads up football all the way."

With Walker's approbation we roared our approval. In the locker room after cleanly winning a football game may be one of the times when a group of men can justify being absolutely full of themselves.

"Now," Walker continued. "I want to give away two game balls this week. The first goes to the man whose interception late in the first half may have been what kept our opponents out of the game for good."

Walker tossed the ball to Allen. It was another opportunity to roar our approval.

"One more," Walker called out to quiet us down. "We had to make a substitution. From where I stood it looked to me like this man did a great job of rising to the occasion. We traded away a pretty good teammate to get him but I think he fills his role very well."

Walker tossed the second ball to Collier. As we roared our approval, there could be very little argument that he deserved the accolade. Although his stats would show eleven carries for only 26 yards, it was his work as a blocker that played a major role in why Scott was able to rush for 107 yards. As the only regular fullback available, he couldn't ask for a breather without going to a safety valve.

"We go to Miami next," Walker continued. "I hope you play just as hard and just as well there as you did last week and today. Our goal is to go to the Super Bowl. We've taken two giant leaps toward achieving that goal."

Another collective roar. This contrasted the relative silence nearby in the Buffalo locker room. The Hawaii Visitors' Bureau would accuse us of not showing the aloha spirit to the tourists.

"One more thing," Walker said. "This year we're providing a postgame buffet in the hospitality room after each home game. You and your guests are all welcome."

That was welcome news. The previous season only breakfast was provided and that was something the players couldn't really enjoy so close to gametime. Obviously the team's account executives persuaded somebody to provide us with postgame munchies in exchange for advertising in the program.

It was a superb buffet. There was roast beef, ham and turkey for sandwiches, different types of bread and condiments, tossed salad, potato salad, baked beans, different cheeses, fruit and chocolate cake. What it amounted to was an indoor picnic.

I ate two roast beef sandwiches and an assortment of side dishes. Something like this provided the team with a little more unity. The pregame atmosphere in the hospitality room was okay but it didn't have a cohesive

154

effect. We needed an opportunity to congregate and unwind in an environment devoid of stress.

After we left the stadium Carol and I stopped briefly at her place so that she could pick up a bathing suit. We then went to my place where we could change clothes and spend the rest of the afternoon in the pool area.

Carol and I swam and basked in the sun. We also spent time in one of the jacuzzis. Although we didn't discuss anything especially personal in the jacuzzi, we spoke primarily in French. This was a tactic we began in college whenever we wanted to keep our conversation as private as possible.

Speaking in French did not guarantee that nobody would understand us. We were still careful not to get too personal when conversing near other people. Speaking French simply meant it was less likely that our conversations would go beyond ourselves.

This being a Sunday afternoon, there were a lot of people in the pool area. Many of those present had seen the game on TV. A few had even been to the game.

"Great game, Jay," a dark-haired man of about 35 commented while Carol and I were conversing in the jacuzzi. "A couple of catches you made were sensational."

"Thanks," I replied as graciously as possible. "I'm glad you enjoyed the game."

I didn't know many of the people in the pool area but they all seemed to know me. Throughout the afternoon I was complimented by different people who had seen the game. Obviously one should not become a pro football player if one wishes to remain anonymous, especially in a small place like Hawaii. The longer I played football, the more I was recognized by football fans all over the state. There was no place between South Point and Hanalei where I could go without being recognized. It was even remotely possible that I would be recognized on Ni'ihau although my lack of Hawaiian blood prevented me from ever going there.

As gregarious as I was, I was never one who was comfortable when compliments were heaped on me. It was nice when people said something nice about my performance and it was better than having them make disparaging remarks. I still preferred to politely thank them for their compliment and move on to other business instead of spending a lot of time talking about myself.

"You've got quite a fan club here," Carol remarked after we went up to my unit for dinner.

"Apparently so," I said somewhat wearily. "And I had never even seen most of those people we saw today."

The fact is, I always liked football best when I played well and I loved the cheers of the home crowd. I also wasn't dumb enough to actually be surprised if a fan, especially in Hawaii, recognized me.

Yet there was still a part of me that wished I could play the best football of my life and then slip into oblivion until the next game.

CHAPTER EIGHT
Tropics East

Normally I tried to avoid making commercials during the season. They could be a distraction and I already had enough of those. They also had to be shot on Mondays most of the time since Mondays normally were my only days completely devoid of football. I didn't relish having obligations on my only day off, especially since I spent a large part of the day doing research in preparation for getting my master's degree and also making most of my preparations for my Tuesday night TV show.

There were exceptions. In 1976 Marv and I shot a milk commercial that was revived as soon as we began playing exhibition games. In 1977 I consented to do a spot for a growing local eatery called Zippy's.

At eight o'clock on Monday morning I showed up at the Makiki Zippy's on King Street and met the film crew. When everything was ready I was seated at a table where a mahimahi plate lunch was placed in front of me. This was the standard Hawaiian plate lunch which included a scoop of macaroni salad and a scoop of white rice. Since I would not be eating the food during the commercial, it wasn't necessary for me to mention that I didn't care for rice and preferred potatoes. Rice was a local staple in Hawaii.

As soon as the camera was rolling I put a bite of mahimahi on a fork and brought it toward my mouth. That was when a prerecorded voice of radio personality Stephen B. Williams interrupted me.

VOICE: Jay Dockman. What are you doing here?
JAY: Just having a little lunch.
VOICE: But I didn't know pro football players ate at Zippy's.
JAY: The smart ones do.
VOICE: But why Zippy's?
JAY: Well, where else can you go with such an outstanding variety of food from which to choose?
VOICE: I see. And what's your favorite?
JAY: Well, um, today it's mahimahi. Tomorrow, maybe the roast beef.

It took only three takes to do it. I did the lines well enough but the first take went 35 seconds, the second went 31 seconds and the third went 29 seconds. It wasn't necessarily an innovative spot but it served its purpose. I was used for the obvious name recognition and put out the word that Zippy's featured a variety of favorites.

After the season I made another spot for Zippy's. In that case I was standing at the counter waiting for a takeout order when an unseen female whose name I never caught asked for my autograph.

Like the first spot, I looked directly into the camera, giving the impression that I was looking the voice talent in the eye. She asked me if I ate at Zippy's often, to which I replied, "I've been eating at Zippy's since my days with the Bows."

"Bows" was a common referral to Rainbows as the University of Hawaii athletic squads were referred to during my tenure. The claim to have eaten at Zippy's since my college days was true although slightly embellished. There were only two Zippy's in Hawaii when I arrived and the number of times I ate at Zippy's during my three undergraduate years could be counted on the fingers of my hands. My favorite local eatery in those days was Chunky's which was more convenient since it was located across the street from the old Honolulu Stadium and was much closer to the university than any existing Zippy's.

But I definitely liked Zippy's and still do.

We had two victories in as many tries. For the first time in our history including the two WFL seasons the Hawaiians were 2-0. We began the season by matching our longest winning streak of 1976. We were actually on a four-game winning streak since the only time we won two in-a-row in 1976 was right at the end of the season.

Victories are victories. They look impressive in the standings. It still wasn't as if we began the season by toppling championship caliber teams. The victories at the end of 1976 which helped keep the Bengals and Browns out of the playoffs were far more impressive than our two victories over a couple of 1976 doormats to start 1977.

Still, our first two games were victories and that was all that really mattered. Our fellow expansion teams in Seattle, Memphis and Tampa were 0-2 in 1977 although we were no longer considered to be in their category. We were on schedule to duplicate Miami's 17-0 from five seasons earlier although expecting us to duplicate that feat was more than a slight stretch. We did have sole possession of first place in our division, one game ahead of the Rams and Falcons and two games ahead of the 49ers and Saints.

We were feeling good when we arrived at the Kaneohe Marine Corps Air Station on Tuesday morning. We would be practicing at the base this week since grass was replanted at the Orange Bowl after seven seasons of artificial turf. I don't believe we were especially cocky but we were happy. First place feels pretty good. There were enough beaming smiles for the entire team to do an Ultra Brite commercial.

Walker wasn't going to be a part of the commercial. He came in with a scowl on his face. He immediately brought us down to earth.

"What are you guys so happy about?" he demanded to know.

Suddenly the room was deadly silent. Nobody dared speak.

"I don't know why you guys are acting so full of yourselves. You may have won two games but you haven't played anybody tough yet. You

158

definitely couldn't have thought Buffalo would be tough on you guys. Their record last year was the same as Memphis and Seattle. They were worse than the Saints last year and the Bills are not likely to be much better this year. They might even be worse."

Walker seemed to be suffering from a memory lapse. I recalled all through the previous week his references to Buffalo as "tough" despite its record from 1976.

"There is no reason for you to get excited about beating the Bills. You may have beat these clowns by 24 points but you really didn't play that good of a game."

I also recalled Walker praising our performance only two days before.

But that's the way things were sometimes. Walker didn't want our egos swelling up because of our victory over the hapless Bills. I do believe, however, that he may have gone a little further than necessary with his denunciations.

During the films Walker wasn't as hard on us as I thought he was going to be. Too many guys had simply played too well. A victory is a victory.

The defensive film session ended at least a half-hour before the offense's did. That is because the offense spent a lot more time on the field than the defense did. That was a sign that both units did their jobs well. The defense shut down Buffalo's drives in timely manners while the offense sustained drives. Buffalo's only score was by its defense on an interception return.

"This breaks my heart," Walker said mournfully when the interception came up during the film session. "I know that interceptions have to happen on occasion but this one could have been avoided."

Walker froze the projector where Bender had his arm cocked, then restarted it. The interception was the result of a good play by the cornerback although it was arguable whether Bender should have passed to Grummon. The runback showed only Scott having any chance to tackle the ball carrier until Marv caught up with him near the end zone. As Walker ran the film back and forth we saw Larry seeming to try to tackle the ball carrier by butting him with his shoulder pad without trying to grasp him.

"Larry, were you ever a two-way player?" Walker asked as many of us stifled giggles.

"In high school I was."

"Really? Where was that?"

"Shreveport, Louisiana," Larry answered.

Walker sighed. He said it was probably a good thing that the game wasn't shown in that part of the country.

"Your old high school coach would be embarrassed to say he knew you if he ever saw that pathetic exhibition of tackling."

For a moment Walker seemed to have forgotten about the 107 yards Larry gained on the ground. Larry may have forgotten as well.

That was about as harsh a criticism that Walker doled out during the session. He actually threw out a lot of compliments including a few to Larry. He didn't want us getting cocky but I also believe he was being careful not to break our momentum.

When our film session ended the defensive unit joined us. Walker went over our itinerary for our trip to Miami so that we would know three days in advance to tie up any loose ends.

"We have two victories and no defeats," Walker stressed. "I don't want to burst your bubble but the two teams we beat were out of contention long before we were last year and they might even be out of contention now. You can bet your schedule is only going to get tougher."

Walker mentioned that Miami finished just below .500 in 1976. He said he expected the Dolphins to be a much better team than that.

"We've got a chance to be three and oh but if I know Don Shula, he is going to have his team well prepared," he continued. "Treat the Dolphins like champions and prepare yourselves like champions. If you play as well as I know you can we'll have an unblemished record when we get home Sunday night. That'll give us the momentum we need for the Ram game."

Walker paused. He grimaced a little.

"Never mind the Rams," he directed, slightly embarrassed about breaking his own rule against looking beyond the upcoming opponent. "Beating the Dolphins will give us the momentum we need for the Rams but I don't want you looking ahead. The only opponent we need to worry about now is the Dolphins."

Since I would be traveling on Friday, Carol and I went out on Thursday evening. We didn't do anything spectacular since we couldn't quite make up our minds about what to do. We wound up going for a simple dinner at the Bob's Big Boy in Mapunapuna.

It surprised me that this was the first time Carol had ever been to a Bob's. Being from Southern California, which was where Bob's Big Boy originated in 1936, I took it for granted that everybody was familiar with the eatery. The local Bob's Big Boy was a frequent hangout for my colleagues and me when I was in high school.

But there were no Bob's Big Boy's in Canada and none in Hawaii when Carol moved to the islands in 1968. Bob's finally reached Hawaii's shores in 1975 while Carol was in exile in Hilo.

I guess it was nice to introduce Carol to something new, especially since it was essentially a local version of something from my youth. In retrospect, perhaps I should have introduced her to myself instead of remaining behind the invisible wall that stood between us.

Not that Carol didn't know me or that we weren't civil to each other. We got along very well but the full commitment wasn't there yet. We held hands in public or she would hold the crook of my arm, giving the impression of a committed couple, but we hadn't actually reached that pinnacle yet. We had also kissed each other several times since our reunion more than three months earlier, yet we were both holding back emotionally. It was more of a friendship, which included a certain amount of affection, than a romance. I had yet to take her in my arms and hold her there.

It was frustrating. Often when Carol and I were together I wanted to hold her and I knew that she would not have objected. It seemed so natural and right to want to do that but I forced myself, often subconsciously, to hold back. Some diabolical force seemed to perpetually remind me that she had disappeared once before and might do the same thing again. If the force was Satan himself, the last thing that force wanted was for Carol and me to find happiness together.

Carol didn't force the issue. She had to have wondered, though, when I was finally going to open up. I somehow sensed that she wanted to break down the barrier but I wasn't totally sure.

The problem was, I wouldn't allow myself to trust her that much. I looked at her and saw all of the wonderful things I'd had with her a few years earlier. That was superseded by the fact that she was nowhere to be found when I returned to Hawaii after my first pro training camp and didn't turn up again for three years. Nobody would have blamed me if I simply wrote Carol off.

Yet I knew, at least subconsciously, that nobody was more right for me than Carol. People might criticize me for taking back a woman who left so abruptly a few years earlier but I knew. I was firm in my conviction that nobody but Carol could fill her role in my life. Although there was much that I didn't understand, something inside me told me I couldn't be complete with any other woman.

So there we were sitting across from each other in a booth at Bob's Big Boy. We talked about the university, the Hawaiians, the classes she was teaching and my weekend excursion to Miami. They were very topical subjects. It still would not have hurt for me to finally start opening up and discussing things pertinent to us as a couple. Although I was genuinely thrilled to have Carol back in my life, I had yet to say so. I never told her that I was glad she was back or that I missed her when she was gone or that I wanted us to go for it all.

It would take some time.

We wound up with a good week of practice. Kerner was back at full strength so that was good although Collier had done a pretty good job of filling in for him. The few signs of injuries among the active players were very superficial. It looked like we were going to be playing with a fully healthy roster.

Our flight to Miami would be about our longest of the regular season. Before Friday's workout Walker went over our itinerary again and then reminded us that we were going to Miami solely to play football.

"There are all kinds of distractions in Miami," he said. "It's a tropical resort area with beaches and nightclubs and. . . ."

Walker suddenly stopped. He almost blushed. Such talk might have been appropriate for teams from locales such as Detroit, Buffalo or Minnesota. Our team didn't have to fly to the southeastern tip of the United States to be distracted by a tropical resort area with beaches and nightclubs.

After Friday's workout we got in our cars and left the Marine base and drove to the airport. We flew out of Honolulu in mid-afternoon. As our flights went, this one was fairly typical with guys mingling and trying to entertain themselves. Excepting the rare occasions when we stayed on the mainland between games, we never had a flight of less than five hours. A five-hour flight was a long one for teams such as the Rams, 49ers and Raiders but for us it was a puddle jump. Our flight to Miami was more than double our minimum flight time. At least the extra fuel tanks on our chartered aircraft prevented the need to stop somewhere to refuel and add more time to our lengthy commutes. All of our flights were nonstop regardless of distance.

Along the way I had a nice conversation with Russ Allen. Being from Glendale, California, he was a Dodger fan although he didn't follow baseball as closely as I did. We were both exultant that the Dodgers became the first team in the majors to clinch their division a week and-a-half earlier. They got off to a fast start and never looked back. It was almost as if the National League West race was over by the end of April.

Russ was an interesting contrast. On the field he was as fearsome a middle linebacker as one could hope to find. I never saw Dick Butkus or Ray Nitschke play in person but I find it hard to believe that they could have been better or hit harder than Russ. Perhaps I could make a comparison had I seen Russ on the field at the same time as Butkus and/or Nitschke but, believe it or not, the first NFL game I ever attended was one I was playing in a little more than a year earlier. Butkus and Nitschke had retired by the time I began my pro career.

It was always very interesting to watch Russ from the sideline. There was something about his mannerism which made it easy to see that he was the veritable anchor of the defense. He was the epitome of confidence when he went about his business starting from the way he stood while calling the play in the huddle to the way he chugged in place waiting for the snap of the ball. He really seemed to love his work.

Russ wasn't as big as the prototype middle linebacker. His attributes were he was quick, strong and tough. I don't believe I ever saw anybody

162

who could shoot through the line and sack the quarterback as quickly as Russ could.

And he *loved* to hit.

But he was also a gentleman. He played to win, yet he played clean. He liked to hit ball carriers hard enough to intimidate them but he didn't want to injure them. He understood that injuries were risks we took to play this game and he didn't beat himself up if a player he hit was hurt in the process but any injuries he caused were never deliberate. He was a very brutal football player and a very kind man. He would rattle a ball carrier's bones before extending his hand to help the man up after the whistle blew. If a man he hit had to be removed from the game he would inquire about the player after the game, if possible.

What was it *really* like to have been hit by Russ?

More than two decades have passed since Russ and I were teammates and my recollection is still vivid. Not only do I recall what I saw on the field, I recall the hits I took from him during full contact workouts. He wasn't one to let up, even in practice.

Through the course of my career I was hammered by some of the hardest hitters in the game. Jack Tatum, Jack Lambert, Fred Dryer, Mean Joe Greene, Jack Ham, Brian Bosworth. . . .

The list goes on. The aforementioned, and others, were among the hardest hitters I recall. They didn't play dirty as far as I could tell. They definitely rang some bells including mine.

It's still hard for me to believe that any of the aforementioned hit harder than Russ did. Perhaps it is simply my perception as a teammate. I saw Russ hit opponents so hard that I could almost hear their bones rattle.

And yet Russ was one of the most disciplined players I ever saw. I doubt that he was ever called for a late hit. When the whistle blew he hit the brakes and then conducted a huddle for the next play. He had inflicted his punishment and silently looked forward to the next poor sap who was assigned to try to run through him. One sportswriter wrote that trying to run through Russ "made as much sense as trying to fly a kite in an electrical storm."

Off the field Russ was a model citizen. He was good about signing autographs, especially for the kids, and did so with a smile and even a few words for the recipients. He had a great sense of humor and rarely got angry. He was also very devoted to his wife who had been his sweetheart since elementary school.

We arrived in Miami at about seven o'clock on Saturday morning. We left Honolulu in broad daylight, watched night fall and arrived in broad daylight. Along the way I read, played penny-ante poker, ate a nice beef dinner and occasionally looked out the window to watch various parts of the Pacific Ocean, North America and the Gulf of Mexico far below. I even tried to sleep by stretching out over two seats but managed only catnaps.

The rest of Saturday was familiar. Check into the hotel, nap, eat a bite and then a light workout at the Orange Bowl.

Put another way; same routine, different city.

I had dinner with Marv and Ed.

At least we started as a trio. When we spotted Rossi in the hotel lobby we invited him to join us. We found a place that served a fairly decent steak.

It was a pleasant experience. We avoided the topic of football initially since we weren't among those who lived and breathed football 24/7. Ed talked a little about meeting his girlfriend while in college at California. I talked a little about Carol, whom they didn't know especially well yet.

"So she's been your girlfriend for four years now?" Rossi asked after I explained how she and I first met in August, 1973.

"No, we were apart for three of those years," I explained evenly. "She moved back to Honolulu in June and I happened to run into her a few days later."

I didn't feel the need to explain that Carol's departure was totally unplanned and left me in shock. I didn't know how to explain it. I still didn't understand it myself.

Later that night I took a walk. It was the same old scenario where I was aware of what city I was in but felt no significance. Whatever attractions Miami had, I wouldn't see them. I was there to play football. I might just as well have been in Baltimore, Green Bay, New York or Cleveland. Regardless of where I was, I was there with a singular purpose.

I imagined what it must have been like for the Bills to come to Hawaii the previous week. Later in the season the Vikings, 49ers, Rams, Saints, Falcons and Jets would arrive on our shores. They would not likely be visiting Sea Life Park, the Polynesian Cultural Center, Waimea Falls Park or any of the other tourist attractions. There might be a little time for a quick dip in the ocean or to check out Waikiki but that would be it. Their mission would be to play football.

Carol was on my mind. I still had mixed feelings of elation and fear. I was elated to have her back in my life and would choose her over a harem of hundreds of the world's most beautiful women. I still couldn't quite shake the fear that she might suddenly disappear again.

I actually slept late. It was almost seven before I rolled out of bed. I showered, dressed and went to the lobby. Bender, Marv, Clint, Shuford, Black, Gilbert, Ed, Rossi and McWherter were all having coffee. We were soon joined by Pratt, Hasegawa, Roberts and Dubois.

Same routine, different city.

164

The pregame breakfast was at 8:30 followed by a meeting. We then had a little time to kill before checking out of the hotel, boarding the bus and going to the Orange Bowl.

Of course I ran my laps. At precisely eleven o'clock, two hours before kickoff, I was running around the perimeter of the field. I would not have felt right had I neglected to run my laps.

Walker stood in the middle of the locker room a few minutes before we were to take the field. He had on brown slacks, brown shoes and an orange polo shirt with the Hawaiians logo on the breast. He smiled and asked for a volunteer. Ken Gilbert raised his hand.

Some guys knelt. Some stood. Some, like me, remained seated although reverently. I folded my hands and bowed my head as I joined my teammates in reciting *The Lord's Prayer*. There was so much that I had to learn about the way God worked but I was too ignorant to realize how little I knew. I did believe in God and in the resurrection of His Son Jesus Christ but I was pretty much in the dark about everything else. A few years later I would be more enlightened.

"Okay!" Walker exclaimed after the prayer. "We came here for one purpose. What it boils down to is 60 minutes of good solid football. Be alert. Be smart. Don't give anything less than 100 percent. Play hard and play clean. Now let's go get 'em."

I straggled out with most of my teammates. The defense would hang back in the end zone to be introduced. I jogged toward our bench alongside Kerner.

"How's the foot?" I asked as we neared the sideline.

"Great," he replied. "I don't think it'll give me any trouble."

"Good, good," I said.

As the defense was being introduced I did some stretching. It seemed as if I was more anxious than normal to get started. I was psyched to go home 3-0 and the sooner we got started, the sooner we could achieve that objective.

Kickoff still wouldn't happen until one o'clock. That was seven o'clock in Hawaii since Miami and most of the rest of the country were still on daylight time. Loyal football fans in Hawaii had bounced out of bed and were putting together their gametime refreshments. During the week they had to charter bulldozers to drag themselves out of bed to go to work but it was worth it to pop out of bed for a football game.

No doubt Carol was up. She was a very organized individual. My guess was she rose at about six and took a shower, put on something casual and got the coffee brewing before she blow-dried her hair. Then she put on just the right amount of makeup to enhance her natural beauty, put together a modest breakfast and was sitting in front of the TV waiting for CBS to cut to Miami.

Thinking about what Carol had probably done over the previous hour, and I was sure I wasn't off by much, enabled me to survive another 30 seconds or so while I anxiously waited for the game to start.

We won the toss.

"All right!" I exclaimed, glad that I wouldn't have to wait to get my first licks in.

After a few words from special teams coach Ken Holcomb I stood on the goal line. Hasegawa was with me, of course. We exchanged our customary slap fives.

"Let's do it, Jay," Rich said. "Let's stick it to these guys. That's what we came almost 5,000 miles to do."

"Right on," I replied, too hyped to come up with something more profound.

Miami's kicker got the game off to a dull start. He kicked the ball out of the end zone. I didn't think anything of it at the time. Apparently it was a sign that things were going to go Miami's way for a little while.

"Waimanalo right," Bender called in the huddle. "On three. On three. Ready?"

"Break!"

I had the honor of carrying the ball on our first play from scrimmage. I took the handoff and charged through the right. I was met by a solid wall of Dolphins. No gain.

Scott fared a little better off left tackle. He was hit at the line but still managed to get to the 23. Third and seven.

Naturally we went to the air next. . . .

Or so we tried. A perfectly timed blitz ended the play immediately. Bender had dropped back only about two steps and was sacked at the 20. The crowd roar reminded us that we may have been in a tropical setting but it wasn't *our* tropical setting.

Our drive, if we were justified in referring to it as such, lasted three plays and netted us no yards. In our first two games we dominated so much that our punter never got on the field until the second half. Now Jablonski was on the field less than two minutes into the game.

At least Jablonski did his job. He got off a decent punt that was fielded at the Miami 40. The Dolphins got a decent return to their 48. With that kind of field position they were expected to at least get to within field goal range unless our defense shut them down.

Offensive line coach Jerry Meacham held a small chalkboard in his hand. He called a meeting of the linemen. The purpose was. . . .

There wasn't time. Miami went for broke on the first play. One of the Dolphin receivers got a step or two on Blakely and made a clean reception at about the 20, drawing a huge roar from the Miami faithful. He was untouched the rest of the way.

166

We were in shock. We were trailing 7-0 with 12:51 left in the first quarter. The Dolphins were determined. We had to destroy their momentum.

It wasn't going to happen on the kickoff. I caught the ball four yards deep in the end zone. Hasegawa was signaling for me to down the ball. The determined charge of Miami's kicking unit convinced him and me that I would not get anywhere near the 20. I dropped to one knee.

"All right, all right," Bender commented in the huddle. "It's discouraging but we'll be okay. There's a lot of football left to play."

Unfortunately this drive proved to be only marginally better than our first drive. Bender got two passes off but both were incomplete; the second of which was to me and batted down by a defensive back. Our only sizable gain came prior to the next play when the Dolphins got called for encroachment. It was third and five.

The Dolphins were looking for a pass. Bender called a 3 kama'aina left. It looked like we had a shot at picking up a first down as Scott followed a convoy of blockers which included yours truly.

Unfortunately Stanek got tied up and Scott got tangled in Stanek's feet. He went down at the 27.

I was trying to block a defensive end when I heard the whistles blowing and the crowd cheers. My heart sank when I turned and saw Scott on the ground a few yards short of where he needed to go for the first down.

"What the hell is going on?" I sharply asked Kerner who had responded to the whistles when I did.

"I'm not sure," he replied mournfully. "It looks like we didn't get even close to the first down, though."

Just in case I needed more proof, I noticed the Dolphin defensive unit running off the field in exultation while their punt return unit took the field. I ran off the field while thinking that it didn't look like it was going to be our day. The only positive thoughts I could muster up was that we were still only in the first quarter and trailed by only a touchdown.

Jablonski was back on the field. Already he was matching his appearances from the Buffalo game. One more appearance and he would equal his total appearances from the Buffalo and New Orleans games. That's not the way to win football games.

At least Jablonski continued to do his job. His punt went out of bounds at the Miami 27; a 46-yarder. He was outshining the offense which had picked up seven yards on six plays (two yards if you throw out the penalty) and the defense which had surrendered 52 yards on one play. We were looking like an expansion franchise and that was not only frustrating and disgusting but also embarrassing.

The Dolphins opened by trying to complete another home run ball. Fortunately none of the receivers were open and the ball was overthrown.

Had the Dolphins come away with another score Walker might have put the entire defense on waivers on the spot.

After a four-yard rush we did our part to help Miami's cause. Richards got called for encroachment. The Dolphins made good use of our philanthropy by going two yards up the middle to give them a first down at the 38. With 8:41 left in the quarter it was the first first down by either team.

The Dolphins picked up two more first downs and faced a second and five at the Hawaii 29. They were going to the air.

Allen, Jennings, Pratt and McDaniel all had shots at the quarterback as he scrambled in the backfield. I watched in horror and disbelief as the quarterback continued to stay on his feet and move forward after tucking the ball away. It wasn't until he reached the 18 that he stepped out of bounds. It was another Miami first down. The home crowd was going wild while Walker was going ballistic.

"Whoever said these idiots could play football?" Walker bellowed to nobody in particular before turning his attention back to the field. "Do you guys want to get in the game? The game started about ten minutes ago?"

No doubt the offense was in for a similar verbal shellacking if we didn't get our act together.

After a two-yard rush the Dolphins returned to the air. The quarterback hit a receiver in the right corner of the end zone. With the extra point we were down 14-0 with 4:23 left in the first quarter.

"This is last week in reverse," Walker muttered, turning away from the field and shaking his head in disbelief. "It looks like our team isn't so damned good after all. We sure traveled a long way to find that out."

I took my place with Hasegawa on the goal line. Neither of us was smiling as we slapped fives. Rich had a very troubled look on his face. I probably did, too.

"If it comes to me, I'm running it out no matter what," I stated brazenly, feeling the need to be a catalyst to turn our fortune around.

"Same here, brah," Rich replied.

It was a commendable but risky attitude. If the kick was deep enough in the end zone it also increased the possibility of getting pinned back. That could only work to Miami's advantage.

The ball was coming my way. I fielded it six yards deep in the end zone. True to my word, I charged forward. I could see that the Dolphin kicking unit was coming hard. I didn't care.

My blockers were doing their jobs. I was focused only on the 20-yard line but I could also see some good blocks ahead of me. It was a great relief to reach the 20 since that was how far I had to go to justify the runback. Rossi played a role since he leveled a guy who was just about to bear down on me somewhere between the 15 and 20. He didn't play much but he didn't waste the opportunities whenever he was in there. I was brought down at the 23.

168

It was somewhat satisfying. My first kick return of the young season went for 29 yards. The gamble paid off. It was justified by a mere nine feet but that was enough. I think the other guys on the kick return unit were grateful for the opportunity to throw some blocks instead of running off the field on a touchback.

"All right, we've screwed around long enough," Bender said in the huddle. "Let's go to work."

Scott got us off to a reasonably good start by going up the middle for four yards. I was then the recipient of a pass at our 44. The ball was slightly behind me so I had to slow down and turn to catch it. That enabled a defensive back to hit me at the point of the reception but I still managed to hold on. Our first completion of the day also gave us our first first down.

Grummon was next. He caught a pass at the Miami 43. It was in tight coverage and he was hit immediately but we had another first down.

"Okay. It's our game now," Dietrich commented as we were forming our huddle. There was an air of positive excitement in the huddle.

A short pass to Dietrich only got us to the 40. Scott then ran around right end for a mere yard. We followed that up by transgressing with a delay of game penalty which gave us a third and eleven at the Miami 44.

This is where it got interesting. Bender's pass to Grummon was intercepted at the 31. As the crowd roared in anticipation of a three-touchdown lead the defensive back got to the Miami 45 where he was hit by Shuford. He fumbled the ball which was recovered by Abraham.

Technically we lost a yard on the play. However, the ball had changed hands twice. That meant that we had a first down at the 45 with 14 seconds left in the quarter.

The sporadic booing told me that some of the crowd didn't understand the rule regarding possession. Either that or they were simply unhappy that the Dolphins didn't get to keep the ball. I was simply relieved and somewhat overwhelmed by the bizarre chain of events.

Bender hit Scott with a swing pass at the 42. Scott took a step or two before being dropped at the 40. We had second and five as the quarter came to an end.

"What do you think, Jaybird?" Shuford asked as we moved to where we would huddle on the 50 while Bender headed to the sideline to converse with Walker.

"I think we're not playing very well," I replied evenly.

"Hey, we'll be all right," Marv said. "The Dolphins are just more ready for us than the Saints and Bills were. We'll adjust."

There was no doubt about that. What we needed to do was get into a groove and stay there. No matter how we tried to rationalize, we were down by two touchdowns. We needed to make something happen and hang on to the momentum. It would also speak volumes for the Hawaiians if we could come back from a two-touchdown deficit and pull the game out.

When play resumed it appeared that we were in that groove. Bender hit Grummon near the left sideline at the 28. Grummon's momentum caused him to step out of bounds but we had a first down.

"Okay, we're coming around," Bender remarked in the huddle. "We're going to be all right. Let's keep it up."

Kerner plowed off right tackle. He got to the 21 to give us second and three. We then wound up with *third and three* when Kerner's rush up the middle on a 2 Mililani right went nowhere.

I got the call next on a Moloka'i option left. I was hit in the backfield but stayed up. When I couldn't find an open receiver I kept running. I got to the 14 to give us a first down. It took a very determined effort to pick up those seven yards since it seemed as if I had about 100 Dolphin hands molesting my body the entire time.

It took us only one play from there. Bender fired a strike to me at the goal line. I was on a dead run and stepped untouched into the end zone to give us our first touchdown of the game and my first touchdown of the season.

I was exultant running to the sideline and accepting the congratulations of my teammates and coaches. We seemed to have finally gotten our act together. I was still aware of the deficit of eight points.

Guinn reduced the deficit to seven points with his PAT. We were down 14-7 with 13:39 left in the half.

I felt great and not simply because I was the one to score the touchdown although that didn't hurt. Our ability to cut the lead in half rejuvenated my confidence. We had proved over the previous two weeks that we knew how to put points on the board. Now we had to show that we could come from behind.

The kickoff boosted my confidence even more. The kick was fielded a yard deep in the end zone and returned. Dubois quickly made the ball carrier regret his decision to run the ball out. Henri met the ball carrier at the 14 and saw to it that he went no further.

"Yes!" I cried, thrusting my fist in the air.

At that moment I figured the best Miami would achieve was a three and out. We had the momentum and it was easy to see that everybody was fired up. I was hoping the Dolphins would cough the ball up before running those three plays. The thought of anybody believing we could lose this game was an insult.

The Dolphins were determined to levy the insult. A quick mix of rushes and passes moved the Dolphins past midfield. We even helped them a little when Gilbert got called for encroachment to give them a second and two at the Hawaii 43. One play later they picked up two yards to give them a first down at the 41.

That was when our defense dug in. After a rush of two yards Black deflected a pass that gave them a third and eight. The Dolphins attempted to pass again but Richards sacked the quarterback at the Hawaii 44. It was fourth and 13. Norm's play was exactly what we needed.

It was time for me to return to the field. Walker stopped me on the way.

"If you believe there is any chance at all for a return, go for it," Walker instructed. "Even if you are inside the ten. Use your judgement but see if you can get us some field position. I won't hold it against you if you wind up not getting a good return."

That was what I wanted. I loved returning punts. I had returned five thus far in 1977 for 59 yards. That was an average of 11.8 yards per return.

I wouldn't be padding that total this time. The punter kicked it low and well to my right so there was no chance for me to field the punt. I managed to lay a pretty good block on one of the wideouts to prevent him from downing the ball deep in our territory but another got through. He downed the ball just shy of the goal line.

It was going to be tough but we could do it. We all wanted it. The first thing we had to do was give ourselves some breathing room.

Kerner carried up the middle. He was hit while still in the end zone but refused to go down. He was hit by three Dolphins before finally going down at the five. Kerner was the type of guy who could hold his own while playing chicken with a steamroller.

Unfortunately Kerner's was the most impressive effort of the drive. Scott went off left tackle for a mere yard and Bender's pass to Dietrich while under a heavy rush was slightly underthrown for an incompletion. For the third time that day Jablonski was running on the field. Also for at least the third time that day I wanted to puke.

It wasn't so much that we couldn't move the ball that bothered me. It was the field position. Unless Jablonski could really boom one that got behind the return man the Dolphins would start with great field position.

Jablonski punted. It wasn't quite what I was hoping for. The return man caught the ball at the Hawaii 45. He sidestepped Hamer and got to the 35 before being tackled by McWherter. Miami was already in range for a long field goal.

I feared another two-touchdown deficit as the Dolphins cut through our defense. After two rushes they had a first down at the 22. They picked up two more yards to the 20 as the clocked moved toward the three-minute mark.

Our defense decided that enough was enough. The Dolphins decided to go to the air and Jennings prevented that from happening. He got the quarterback in his grasp. Gilbert came along to assist in sacking the quarterback at the 27. It was third and 15.

To the air again. This time the quarterback got the pass off. It was picked off by Black at the 14.

"Yeah! All right, Mark!" I cried out as my teammates and coaches expressed similar sentiment. Our sideline was about the only place in the stadium where people were cheering.

Black danced a jig in eluding a tackle by the intended receiver. He took a few steps forward and was brought down at the 19. It was a lot of dancing and twisting for a mere five-yard return but that was okay. We denied them a score and had the ball again.

"Offense!" Walker barked as if any of us needed prompting. We had the ball with 2:05 left in the half.

We got off to a promising start. Scott ran a sweep around left end to the 25. The clock stopped for the two-minute warning with 1:59 left in the half.

If there was anything I knew, it was that we were capable of going the remaining 75 yards in the time we had left. That would not have been unprecedented for us. As Bender talked to Walker on the sideline, I visualized us scoring a touchdown as time ran out. We could go into the locker room tied and have the momentum.

Things went our way when play resumed. Bender hit Dietrich near the right sideline. Ted immediately stepped out at the 32 to give us a first down and stop the clock with 1:52.

We went into our double-double formation. Rossi and Schary entered the game while Grummon and Scott went out. Schary would be wide to the left on the line while Rossi would be in the left slot. Dietrich would be wide to the right on the line while I would be in the right slot.

A pass to Schary near midfield was batted down but Bender hit Schary on the next play at the Hawaii 46. Schary advanced to the 50 before being brought down in bounds. We called time with 1:34 left.

Bender attempted to hit Rossi near the left sideline on the next play. Unfortunately Steve met a heavy rush and the pass was tipped upward. A linebacker caught the ball at the Miami 49 and got to the Hawaii 44 before Kerner brought him down.

"(Expletive deleted)!" I exclaimed while my teammates concurred with expressions of their own.

I was heartsick. How quickly fortunes can change. A moment earlier we were driving for the tying touchdown. Suddenly we were in jeopardy of going into the locker room down by two touchdowns. I stood in the middle of the field with my hands on my hips and eyes downward as if I could make the previous play go away. When I looked up the sight of the Dolphins offensive unit enthusiastically charging on the field, coupled with the ongoing roar of the crowd, told me that nothing had changed.

At least the defense did its job. Three consecutive incompletions and I was back on the field.

The punter went for the coffin corner and succeeded. The ball went out of bounds at the one. We had 53 seconds to travel 99 yards.

To the surprise of nobody, we didn't bother. Bender ran a quarterback sneak to the two to prevent downing the ball in the end zone for a safety.

Even that produced its share of excitement. Tempers flared in the interior line. Abraham, who was generally low key, actually threw a punch at one of Miami's linemen and was charged with unsportsmanlike conduct. That moved the ball half the distance to the goal line from the original line of scrimmage. That meant we were 18 inches from a safety.

The clock had stopped to assess the infraction and spot the ball. Once that took place the clock started with 47 seconds left. We broke the huddle and casually strolled to the line. Bender ran another quarterback sneak to the three and that was it for the half.

There was a sense of non-fulfillment as I ran off the field to the locker room. We simply weren't playing very well. I realized that our 2-0 record was misleading since we hadn't played anybody who was considered to have been a challenge. Now we were playing a team whose 1976 record showed one fewer victory than us and that team was clearly outplaying us.

Or else one could say our opponent wasn't beating itself the way we seemed to be doing with ourselves. Regardless of whether our opponent that day was the Cowboys, Dolphins or Buccaneers, we were gift-wrapping this game.

At least the defense had adjusted. After surrendering two consecutive scores to start the game the defense had contained the Dolphins. If the defense could continue to do that and the offense could consistently keep its act together we could pull the game out.

I thought about Honolulu as I went to grab a cup of Gatorade. We had traveled such a long way. I thought about Marv's remark in New Orleans two weeks earlier about not traveling this far to lose. I dreaded the thought of a long return flight if we lost, especially if we didn't get our game plan together. It wasn't so much our being outplayed as our inability to execute.

As I took my seat in front of my locker I noticed Walker in the middle of the room. I always knew he was there, I suppose, but hadn't been able to get myself to look at him. When I finally did look at him he had his trademark scowl that meant that all was not well with the Hawaiians.

The room was silent. Players and coaches surrounded the room. I sensed that we were all bracing ourselves for an explosion.

"You look like hell!" Walker finally remarked. "It's amazing that you're only down by a touchdown. You're too erratic; too inconsistent. You need some fire out there."

Of course Walker was right. We did have our bright moments. Overall we were as flat as a dead cat on the freeway.

Walker never raised his voice. He was just as effective without raising his voice as he continued his tirade. If how I felt was indicative of the rest of the team, we all felt like effluent.

173

"I know you men," Walker said just before we were to return to the field. "I know what you're capable of doing. Let's go out and do it."

Normally during halftime we made a few adjustments before Walker climaxed halftime with his remarks. This time Walker did his monologue through the entire ten minutes that seemed more like six hours before being advised that we had two minutes left. A lot of our problem was mental, I believe, so the mental adjustment was what we needed most.

Miami received the kick to start the second half and returned it from the goal line to the 21. The Dolphins then picked up a couple of first downs and crossed midfield. On third and five at the 43 Miami got called for delay of game but Allen countered by getting called for encroachment to return the ball to the 43. The Dolphins followed that up with an incomplete pass.

I was finally on the field in the second half. I stood on the ten in anticipation of the punt. I wanted a return but Walker told me not to try it if the ball came down inside the ten. From where I stood if I had to take a single step backward to field the ball I would not make the attempt.

Naturally the Dolphins went for the sideline. The punt didn't pin us as far back as the punt near the end of the first half. It was still very effective. The ball came down well to my left at about the eight. It went out of bounds at the six.

The crowd roared its approval. I couldn't deny that the punter had done his job. Having been a punter in high school, I knew that a punt like that was a punter's version of a touchdown.

We were undaunted. With 94 yards to our objective there was still an air of confidence in our huddle. Regardless of how poorly we played in the first half, we were still down by only seven points.

Kerner got us started by going off right tackle to the 12. Scott went through the same hole to the 16.

The referee waved his arms over his head while blowing his whistle before pointing to himself. Time was called for a measurement. The chain was brought out. We had a first down by about two inches.

"Right on. We're on the move, baby," Marv remarked.

The drive continued. Scott picked up four yards around left end. It was second and six at the 20.

It was to the air next. Bender threw a pass to me that was on target but sinking. I had to go into a slide to get to it.

I caught the ball cleanly at the Hawaii 47 and popped up the way I did when sliding in baseball. I managed to sidestep a defensive back and take off, crossing midfield. I was at about the 45 when I straight-armed another defender and knocked him out of the play.

All I could see ahead of me was end zone. It took me by surprise when I was caught from behind at the 39.

Whistles were blowing. My tackler was on top of me and popped up. He helped me up and whacked me on the rear before heading to his defensive huddle.

"Great play, Jay," Grummon remarked.

I nodded and smiled but was somewhat annoyed with myself for not getting further. I was hit at about the time I figured I was a sure bet for my second touchdown of the game. It was still a 41-yard gain that got us great field position. From what Carol and a few others told me later, CBS showed the replay of my sliding catch and popup slide three times.

Suddenly I noticed how quiet the Orange Bowl was. This was another obvious sign that we were playing away from home since things were going our way at the moment. Weather conditions were similar to those in Honolulu although the game time temperature was 88 which was high for Honolulu in October and we were also playing on grass. Things would have been raucous at Aloha Stadium but the fans at the Orange Bowl sat quietly with the realization that we were knocking on the door. I was hoping we would play the local crowd into silence for the rest of the game.

Miami's defense wasn't surrendering. A short pass to Grummon was batted down by a linebacker. Scott then went off left tackle for five yards to give us a third and five at the 34. A pass to Schary was batted down near the 20.

Reluctantly I ran off the field as the field goal unit ran on. I rarely liked having to settle for a field goal when my heart was set on a touchdown. It was still far better than having to make way for the punting unit. Jablonski could shower and dress and watch the rest of the game from the bleachers as far as I was concerned.

Arroyo's snap was on the mark and Billingsley put the ball down quickly. Guinn approached the ball and put his foot into it, causing the ball to arch up as it headed toward the end zone. From where I stood it appeared that the ball split the uprights with yards to spare. The two officials under the goal posts agreed and raised their arms. It was a 51-yarder that narrowed our deficit to 14-10 with 5:16 left in the third quarter.

I was satisfied for the moment. A touchdown on our next possession would give us the lead. The Dolphins scored on their first two possessions but the defense had shut them down since then. I was confident that our defense would continue to hold the Dolphins at bay.

"How are you feeling, Jaybird?" Hayer asked as he and I helped ourselves to the Gatorade.

"Okay for now," I replied. "I'll feel a whole lot better when we get on the right side of the scoreboard."

The huge tackle from Washington smiled in agreement before we returned our attention to the field. Guinn put his foot into the ball on the kickoff that was fielded at the four.

It wasn't our best effort. The reason, I believe, was that Miami's kick return unit rose to the occasion. Several blockers knocked our men out of the play. Gilbert finally brought the return man down at the Miami 34.

Our defense continued to contain the Dolphins. Miami managed one first down but never crossed midfield despite starting with decent field position. On fourth and eight at the Miami 46 I returned to the field. I was determined to not be denied a return this time.

The punt was up. Once again an attempt was made to keep me from fielding the punt. It was near the sideline to my left but I still managed to catch up to it on the 13 and head upfield. After a few steps I was pushed out of bounds at the 18.

That wasn't what I had in mind. I was somewhat angry that I hadn't gotten very far. At the time I didn't know exactly where I had fielded the punt but I knew where the ball was being marked. My goal was to get to the 20 and I came up two yards short.

Bender seemed to read my thoughts.

"It's all right, Jaybird," he said, giving me a reassuring smile. "Every yard we pick up is important."

Whether Steve's words consoled me, I don't know. I only knew that I couldn't dwell on it. We had to focus on our objective of moving 82 yards to take the lead.

The Miami line plugged the holes pretty well on our first play. Scott went up the middle but managed only a yard.

I was the recipient of a pass on second down. Bender hit me at the 35 where I was hit and dropped immediately. We had a first down. I had forgotten my substandard punt return.

Walker sent Rossi in. That was the first time of the young season that Rossi was sent in for me when the outcome was still in doubt. It wasn't that he didn't deserve the opportunity but it simply hadn't happened until this point. He had played only on special teams and in our double-double formation while the game was on the line.

"Stand by," Walker said. "I just thought I would show a little confidence in Rossi."

I didn't complain. I was actually a little happy for Rossi although I was itching to get back out there. I also knew that Rossi, despite his brash behavior, needed to have his ego padded occasionally.

Bender hit Dietrich past midfield at the Miami 48. Ted was hit quickly but managed to spin his way to the 45.

Rossi was the intended receiver on the next play. Unfortunately he was denied his first NFL reception when a defensive back knocked the ball away near the 25. It was second and ten.

"Ready to go back in?" Walker asked.

"Of course," I said.

"Okay, tell Bender to run a Waimanalo left."

"Right," I replied. "Rossi!"

Rossi was probably disappointed to come out after only two plays although he didn't show it. He and I slapped fives as our paths crossed.

Bender handed off to me and I shot through the hole opened by Stanek and Hayer. Protecting the ball with both hands, I put my head down and managed to get to the 37 before going down. It was third and two.

We didn't have to put forth much of an effort to get the first down. The Dolphins gave it to us by getting called for encroachment. We were 32 yards from taking the lead.

Unfortunately we didn't get much further. Scott went up the middle for two yards but then Bender was sacked at the 36. Bender then met another heavy rush and got a quick pass off to Dietrich but Ted only managed to get to the 32. It was fourth and ten and the field goal unit was heading out again.

Of course I wasn't feeling good about this but I did try to look on the bright side. After this field goal we would only need another field goal to take the lead.

The final seconds of the third quarter were counting down as Arroyo snapped the ball. Billingsley put down another good hold and Guinn got his foot into it. It looked like we were going to begin the fourth quarter down by a mere point.

From where I stood the kick looked good. Unfortunately the officials under the goal post had a better view. They drew a roar from the crowd as they waved their arms in front of them. The kick didn't miss by much but it was wide to the left. Whether it was wide by a few inches or a few feet, the end result was the same. We were still down 14-10. We had 15 minutes to take the lead.

A foreboding came over me. It was dawning on me that we might have to settle for a defeat. We had one quarter left to put together the decisive score while hoping that the defense would continue to hold the Dolphins. It seemed to me that those yards to the end zone would become more and more difficult.

I felt bad for Eric Guinn. Nobody expected him to convert on every field goal attempt. Just the same, it wasn't easy for him. No doubt he felt as if he let his teammates down. Kickers are pressed into service primarily when the points are very crucial. It is never easy for them to accept failure.

In 1977 the rule regarding missed field goals meant that the Dolphins began the fourth quarter with a first down at their own 32. Perspiring profusely, I sat on the bench to drink my Gatorade and try to conserve my energy.

The Dolphins went to the air on the opening play of the fourth quarter. They completed the pass near midfield. Black put a brutal hit on the receiver.

"Fumble!"

I jumped from my seat. I no longer felt the urge to conserve my energy. I only wanted us to get the ball back so that my offensive colleagues and I could get back on the field.

Unfortunately the Dolphins recovered. They had a first down at the Hawaii 49. I sat back down.

The Dolphins continued to move. After two plays they picked up another first down at the 34. They then rushed to the 30 before two incompletions gave them a fourth and six.

Make that a fourth and eleven. The Dolphins got cited for illegal procedure, moving the ball back to the 35. The Dolphins replaced their field goal unit with their punting unit, surprising everybody including me and leading to some major booing from the crowd.

As I took my place I thought about what the Dolphins had been doing. They had been trying to sustain their drive simultaneously with milking the clock. After plays where the game clock continued to run they ran the play clock down to no more than three seconds before snapping the ball. One could consider it a coincidence except that after the two incompletions where the game clock stopped they did not bother running down the play clock.

This could be construed as a smart move although it could also come back to haunt them. If we scored the clock would start working against them. They were obviously counting on their defense holding us regardless of whether they scored.

The Miami punter helped the Dolphin cause. He went for the coffin corner and succeeded again. The ball went out of bounds just before it reached the goal line. Such a punt could be considered justification for not attempting the long field goal. If the Dolphins held on to win the punter should have gotten serious consideration for the game's most valuable player. He was having a very good game.

We were dangerously close to losing the ball and adding two points to Miami's total. The rear of the ball was spotted no more than an inch from the goal line. However, we were almost certain to chew up most of the clock if we were to march 99 yards to a touchdown. The Dolphins' strategy of punting instead of going for a field goal would have backfired.

Our first order of business was to move a little way forward.

"Dotted I, 4 Wahiawa right. On one. On one. Ready?"

"Break!"

It was up to me to find the hole up the middle. The opportunity excited me. I just hoped I didn't blow it by doing something that tipped the play off.

I took the handoff. Amid the crash of equipment colliding I managed to get to the two. The immediate mission was accomplished but we still had a long way to go and still were reasonably close to surrendering a safety.

178

Kerner got us a little more breathing room by going off right tackle. He got to the five and earned every inch of those three yards. The fierce determination of both sides was turning this into a mongoose and cobra act.

After five hard-fought yards over the first two plays Bender couldn't find an open receiver and his pass was incomplete. It was another three and out for us. The offense yielded to the punting unit and the Dolphins were virtually guaranteed excellent field position. It was safe to say that their strategy of punting had been successful.

Punting from the end zone, Jablonski's punt was fielded at the Hawaii 41. The return man got as far as the 34. Miami had sensational field position to start their drive.

The Dolphins returned to their clock game, snapping the ball near the three-second mark on the play clock. I had told Walker about my observation and he relayed the information to defensive coordinator Max Crawford. Crawford reported observing the same thing but there was nothing we could do since the Dolphins weren't always snapping at the same point on the play clock so our defense couldn't anticipate the snap. The most he could do was advise the defense to be ready to charge once the play clock was down to four seconds which he had done during our ephemeral possession. Given the fact that the Dolphins had the lead and great field position, their tactic was a stroke of genius.

As the clock wound down the Dolphins continued to move a few short chunks at a time. Along the way they picked up two first downs before the drive stalled. It was fourth and three at the Hawaii seven.

The field goal attempt was good. It was only a 24-yarder. The Dolphins held a 17-10 lead with exactly four minutes to play.

What worked to our advantage was limiting the Dolphins to a field goal. It was still a one-score game. What was working against us was the clock. We were very capable of scoring in four minutes but probably not twice. We had to go for a touchdown and that would mean overtime unless we could recover an onside kick and score quickly. An onside kick after we tied the game would also put us at risk since the Dolphins would have good field position if we didn't recover the kick.

But I'm getting ahead of myself. We were still chasing a touchdown.

Hasegawa fielded the kickoff at the goal line. It was a decent return to the 25. Seven seconds were whittled off the clock to 3:53.

As we went to the line for the first play the crowd put out a sustained roar to try to prevent us from hearing our signals. This wasn't a surprise to anybody. It was exactly what we would have wanted when the Dolphins went to the line in this situation had we been at Aloha Stadium.

The crowd roared louder when Bender was sacked at the 16. As the clock continued to tick we had second and 19.

We showed that we weren't going down without a fight. Bender hit me near the right hashmark at the 38. I ran around a defender before two defensive backs got me down at the Hawaii 45.

Our next play only produced a yard and I took that away from us. Bender hit Dietrich with a quick pass at the 46 and he got no further. I had gone into motion on the play and turned slightly toward the line just prior to the snap. That nullified the play and gave us first and 15 at the Hawaii 40.

The play ended with 1:58 showing on the clock. We were at the two-minute warning.

While Bender conversed with Walker the rest of the offensive unit knelt silently in the huddle. We were all tired and perspiring profusely. There was no doubt that we were involved in one of the more intense football games in the team's brief NFL history. If I could have disregarded the scoreboard I would have been having a fun afternoon.

We may have only had a brief history but we played with the determination of champions when play resumed. Bender hit Dietrich at the Hawaii 43. Ted got to the Hawaii 48 before being brought down in bounds. We called time with 1:49 left. It was second and eight.

Grummon was next. Bender hit him near the left hashmark at the Miami 42. Rich picked up three more yards to the 39 before going down in bounds. I looked at the clock when it showed 1:38 and continued to run.

We quickly got set at the line. This was in the era prior to when a quarterback could simply take the snap and spike the ball to stop the clock. We had to run a play.

I went deep and Bender spotted me. He tried to hit me near the 15 and was nearly intercepted. A defensive back jumped up simultaneous with me and got his hands on the ball. I managed to swat the ball away before he could get a firm grip on it. We had second and ten at the 39 with 1:22 left.

We were more successful on the next play. Bender hit Dietrich near the right sideline at the 29. Ted advanced to the 25 before stepping out of bounds. The clock showed 1:15.

The fans were still vocal but they had to have been worried. I could almost feel their tension in the air although some of it was ours and some belonged to the Dolphins. We were 75 feet from sending the game into overtime. If we scored we would have the momentum although that factor can be extremely overrated. Momentum changes hands without warning.

Momentum did slightly change on the next play. Bender took the snap and found himself under a heavy blitz. He scrambled and wound up running out of bounds at the 28 to stop the clock at 1:05.

Another heavy rush forced Bender to hit me with a safety valve pass. I made the reception at the 26 and got to the 22 before stepping out of bounds. We had 57 seconds left.

We tried to get a first down on the next play. Bender spotted Grummon inside the 15. Unfortunately the pass was batted away.

It was fourth and seven. Nails were being bitten on both sides. There were 49 seconds left but that was not a major concern. We had to get at least a first down or else the game was as good as over.

Bender called the Waipahu. This was a play where all receivers ran to just past the first down marker and turned around. That meant crossing to just inside the 15.

Amid the raucous crowd we got the play off. I ran to the 14 and turned around. Bender was under a heavy rush but he still got rid of the ball. I was the intended receiver.

Unfortunately it was overthrown. I leaped up but the ball was about five feet above my raised hands and dropped untouched further downfield. Miami was taking over on downs with 39 seconds left.

There was nothing more to do except run off the field. Miami's quarterback took a snap and dropped to a knee. Although we had one more timeout there was no point in using it. The clock ran down and we left the field.

I understood that the Dolphins only did their job. I made it a point to shake hands with some of them as well as Coach Don Shula as I headed to the locker room. There was no doubt that I had been in a very intense game and a few of our opponents expressed the same sentiment. I was drained. There were also scrapes on both of my arms from sliding around on the Orange Bowl grass.

Allen gave the postgame prayer. Afterward Walker stood in the middle of the room for a long moment. He seemed to be having trouble knowing what to say.

"It was a tough game," he finally said. "We've got another tough game next week. We've got to find the keys. We'll work through this. I know we have a good team. We'll make sure we're ready for the Rams."

Walker didn't say much else. He knew we were hurting. He was also hurting.

As I shed my perspiration-soaked uniform that seemed to stick to my skin I tried to make sense of it all. Although we had fought hard, there always seemed to be something missing on this day. Whether it was something we were lacking or something the Dolphins simply took from us, I couldn't tell.

What I found out later was how well the Dolphins had stopped our running game. As a team we had 21 carries for 74 yards. Scott had eleven carries for a modest 33 yards.

Our passing game wasn't too bad. Bender broke even by completing 17 passes in 34 attempts for 240 yards. I had six receptions for 123 yards while Dietrich had six receptions for 55 yards. Unfortunately the Dolphins also picked off three of our passes.

Losing is a part of the game. It is something that has to be accepted although not necessarily cheerfully. What makes it extra hard is losing after such an effort to win. It isn't like in baseball where even the best teams are expected to lose two or three times a week. In football a victory or defeat represents an entire week's effort.

Two victories and one defeat. That didn't say much about us. We still hadn't played anybody who had a winning record in 1976. The first real test of how good we could be based on our opponents' 1976 record would come in Los Angeles.

I respected the Dolphins and suspected that their 6-8 record in 1976 was a temporary dip in fortune, not part a perpetual decline. Their victory over us got them halfway to their 1976 win total. They joined Dallas, Denver, Baltimore and Oakland in being undefeated after three games. At 2-1 we were tied for our division lead with the Rams and Falcons.

Nobody expected us to go undefeated. It wasn't because of our status as a second-year expansion team but because it wasn't realistic for any NFL team to go a full season without a defeat. It obviously wasn't impossible but the competition is simply too intense. It had last been done only five years earlier by the same team which had just toppled us from the ranks of the undefeated. The 1977 season would be the last opportunity for any team to duplicate Miami's 1972 17-0 record since the regular season was being expanded to 16 games in 1978.

The thing I hated as much as anything about this loss was the flight home. A flight from Miami to Honolulu is obviously not a puddle jump, especially after a tough loss.

Understand that a DC-8 is not comparable to a psychiatric ward. It was simply an aircraft transporting football personnel who weren't as happy as we would have been had we won. Guys played cards, guys read, guys engaged in conversation and guys smiled. Some guys even laughed a little. It wasn't a raucous flight but it also wasn't a flying morgue.

We were fed top sirloin during the flight. It was good. It would have tasted a lot better had we won.

Walker, as he always did, made a trip down the aisle to talk to his players. Usually he would ask each player how he was feeling and if he needed anything. Occasionally he would engage in a lengthier dialogue.

"So whaddaya think, Jay?" Walker greeted with a congenial smile when he approached where I was conversing with Allen.

"I just want to put it behind us and move forward," I replied evenly, as much because that seemed like it was what Walker wanted to hear as because that was the way I felt. "I know we've got to lose occasionally. I don't have to like it."

"No, you don't," he said with the smile still visible. "Neither do I. We can learn from it, though."

182

"I pity the poor Rams," Russ added. "I think this team will be more of a threat to them than we would have been had we won today."

"I hope so," Walker said. "We can beat them if we don't get wrapped up in the revenge aspect. If today's loss makes us concentrate more it may be a long Monday night for the Rams."

Of course the Rams would know that we would be extra hungry after a loss. They would prepare as if we were a championship caliber team if they knew what was good for them.

It was around almost midnight when we arrived in Honolulu. People in the locale from which we had just arrived were rising to begin their days. I was looking forward to a good night's sleep.

CHAPTER NINE
Homecoming

At least the Dodgers were in the playoffs.

That was the only positive thing I could think of after losing in Miami. The Dodgers were preparing to square off against the Phillies for the right to represent the National League in the World Series. At about the time we were losing to Miami, the Dodgers were on the losing end of a 6-3 score against the Houston Astros in a game that meant nothing more than closing out the regular season. The Dodgers finished with a ten-game lead over Cincinnati in the National League West. They also set a major league record with Reggie Smith, Steve Garvey, Ron Cey and Dusty Baker each hitting at least 30 home runs with Baker joining the 30-homer club during the final game. No other major league team had ever had four players reach that pinnacle.

On the American League side, the New York Yankees clinched the American League East over the weekend. They would be duking it out with the Kansas City Royals.

At least Hawaii's football weekend hadn't been a total loss. Under new head coach Dick Tomey, the University of Hawaii Rainbow Warriors scored a 20-6 upset victory over Southwest Louisiana. That raised their record to 2-2. The Bows were one victory away from equaling their win total from 1976.

As for my teammates and me, we focused on putting Miami behind us after a flight that seemed to take three days. We had to prepare for our Monday night game in Los Angeles.

Walker didn't get too ballistic during the films on Tuesday. There were moments because we made mistakes that were costly but he tried to keep it under control by not nitpicking. He knew how bad we felt. The loss itself was tough enough. He knew we tried very hard to pull it out and simply wound up on the wrong end of the scoreboard against a team that was expected to be much improved over 1976.

A tough loss is hard to swallow. No matter how good you are, there will still be mistakes. Sometimes you get away with them. Sometimes you don't.

"All right," Walker said as he turned off the projector. "This shows what happens when you don't play as well as you're capable of playing. Now we face a test of your resilience against a team that is favored to win our division. Let's work on what we can do in Los Angeles."

That was it. After the projector was shut off it was all about the Rams. The Dolphins were history.

Walker made a decision early in the week that surprised a few of my teammates and me. Since our game in Los Angeles was a night game he didn't feel it was necessary for everybody to spend Sunday night in the hotel.

Those of us with families in the area could spend Sunday night with family. We were only required to be in the hotel in time for the pregame meal at one o'clock on Monday afternoon.

This concerned a few of us. Abraham was from Compton and would stay with relatives there. Billingsley would stay with his in-laws since his wife was from Canoga Park. Allen and Richards would be staying with family in Glendale. Malick had family in Pomona.

I called my parents early Tuesday evening before doing my TV show and asked if they minded if I spent Sunday night with them. Of course they had no objections but it never hurt to be sure. I also told them that Walker was offering the Gatorade coach position to my brother Craig. If my parents could get him to the Coliseum by about five o'clock Monday afternoon he would be given a pass that would allow him to spend the game on our sideline and could earn some generous tips.

We had a good week of practice. I suppose losing in Miami motivated us to avoid consecutive losses. Since we would be playing on grass once again our practices were held on the Marine base.

Everybody was encouraging each other. Compliments were enthusiastically given when a teammate did something well. When somebody made a mistake he was encouraged to do better. There was absolutely no friction.

Of course I also kept some of my focus on the baseball playoffs. Since I was doing my TV show on Tuesday night I already knew the outcome of the first game of the National League playoff. The Phillies scored two runs in the top of the ninth to secure a 7-5 victory over the Dodgers. It was the Phillies' first postseason victory since 1915.

The game was shown by satellite delay that night. I watched the first part of it before going to the TV studio where I found out the final score. Although the delayed telecast was still going on after I did my show, I didn't bother watching. Had the Dodgers won. . . .

On Wednesday night I had no obligations. I was free to watch the game without any distractions. Carol came over and fixed a fried chicken dinner for us and we watched the game together. Dusty Baker's grand slam home run led the Dodgers to a 7-1 victory to even the series.

Unfortunately game 3 was not shown locally. The game was played in Philadelphia and began at about ten o'clock on Friday morning in Hawaii. I was able to catch the end of the game via radio while I drove home from our workout. The Dodgers scored three runs with two outs in the top of the ninth to secure a 6-5 victory.

That led to Saturday night's contest which was Saturday afternoon in Hawaii. Hawaiians majority owner Cec Heftel, who still owned KGMB-TV, arranged to have the game televised on his station. Tommy John pitched the Dodgers to a 4-1 victory in a game which included about two hours worth of rain delay and ended well after midnight in Philadelphia. My guys were heading to the World Series.

But against whom? Would the series begin in New York or Kansas City.

That question hadn't been answered by the time we held our final practice prior to our departure to Los Angeles on Sunday. The Yankees and Royals were deadlocked at two games apiece. The final showdown would be Sunday night. The winner would be determined while we were over the Pacific somewhere between Hawaii and California.

Our Sunday workout was held at Aloha Stadium. Although we would be playing on grass the next night, this was a simple walkthrough. Walker saw no harm in practicing on artificial turf.

It was a little after nine o'clock, Pacific Daylight Time, when we arrived in Los Angeles. My parents and brother were waiting. I introduced them to some of my teammates and coaches. As soon as my suitcase was unloaded we drove to Montebello. I would spend one night in the room I had slept in through high school.

Craig seemed very impressed with the Hawaiians blazer I was wearing. My mother was impressed with my overall look. The blazer, aloha shirt, slacks and dress shoes made for a very snappy ensemble.

"I just can't think of you in anything but blue jeans," she commented as we headed toward Montebello on the Pomona Freeway. As I had gotten older, I had developed fewer aversions to dressy attire and even enjoyed getting dressed up occasionally although I hated having to wear ties. I was still most comfortable in blue jeans or shorts.

We got to the house and talked in the family room until about midnight. It was going to be a very fast family reunion. My dad had to work in the morning and Craig had school. At about noon my mom would drive me to the team's hotel in Los Angeles where I would rejoin my teammates.

On the shelves in the family room three pictures caught my eye. Two of them were snapshots of Annica and me.

"You can take those down if you want," I said. "I doubt that I'll ever see Annica again.'

"I know," my mom said, "but those are nice pictures."

It didn't matter to me by this time. Almost six months had passed and all animosity was out of my system although I had no immediate plans to ever see Annica again for any reason. Had I last been to my old home just after my visit to Canada, instead of just before it, I probably would have torn those two pictures into a thousand pieces.

The other picture I noticed was one my parents had taken almost four years earlier. It was a framed 5x7 photo of Carol and me at the 1974 Hula Bowl. At the old Honolulu Stadium fans were allowed to walk across the field after baseball and football games and the picture was taken in the

186

Diamond Head end zone. She was in her cheerleader uniform and I was in my football uniform. We looked very happy together.

Of course we *were* very happy together.

My parents were happy to learn that Carol and I were seeing each other again. It was something I hadn't mentioned up until this point simply because I wasn't sure of whether or not it would last. I was a little more secure with it by this time although not enough to suggest that Carol and I would be forever. The barrier between us was weakening but it was still there.

In 1974 my parents, brother and sister spent less than 48 hours in Hawaii. They arrived the day before the Hula Bowl and left the day after. That was still enough time for them to get a favorable impression of Carol. Carol was so well-mannered and beautiful that they probably fell in love with her sometime between the time they got off the plane and got to baggage claim.

I rose just before seven o'clock on Monday morning. I took a shower and got dressed. My mom made me a breakfast of bacon and eggs.

"Did you sleep well?" she asked.

"Yeah I did," I replied.

And I had. A major advantage of playing a night game was not having to deal with the pressure of rising early for a game. With a late starting time there was no sense in getting hyper.

The disadvantage of playing a night game is having to spend the day being anxious to get started. One could drain oneself if one wasn't careful. Throughout my career I found it almost impossible to relax on days of night games.

I made my customary visit to South Valley High School after breakfast. I needed to see my former football coach. Since my move to Hawaii I never failed to call on Coach Marcus Farnwell whenever I returned to Montebello. If school wasn't in session I dropped by his house and was always welcomed warmly.

If Farnwell wasn't the biggest influence in my life, he was close to it. Each day it seemed that I became more acutely aware of what he was to me. He was the first devout LDS member I ever knew and used his religion's influence in handling his players and other students he taught without actually invoking religion.

Farnwell had some very strict rules although he didn't make rules merely for the sake of asserting his authority. The rules were simply for our own good and the good of the athletic program. Anybody caught smoking, drinking or ditching school was suspended from the team. Repeated infractions meant expulsion.

If a player was in jeopardy of losing his eligibility because of academic problems, Farnwell would try to help him by arranging for tutorial assistance or even doing the tutoring himself. One thing he wouldn't do was try to persuade a teacher to give a struggling athlete a grade other than what he had earned. There were high schools where coaches reportedly did arrange to have grades changed, just as some universities did. Farnwell refused to do that on moral as well as ethical grounds.

"You are students first," he emphasized several times. "Football is an extracurricular activity. Your academic performance will mandate whether you will be allowed to continue playing football. If you are struggling academically and would like some help, let me know."

During my tenure at South Valley there were three players removed from the team for disciplinary reasons. One was an academic casualty who worked his way back to the team the following season. One was suspended twice from school for smoking in the bathroom and was suspended from the team for the first infraction and expelled from the team for the second. The other was arrested for drunk driving and possession of marijuana and was expelled for the first infraction. Any arrest meant a suspension, pending the outcome of the judicial proceeding, with a conviction meaning an expulsion.

Farnwell still never closed his door to those three as people and students. He simply could not allow them to remain with the team.

I was no choirboy. I had my indulgences. I was simply fortunate enough to have done my misdeeds with impunity.

One high school tradition that I'm glad Farnwell did not invoke was the tradition of football players shaving their heads to play on the team. Some high school coaches, at least in Southern California during the 60s, forced players to cut their hair to crewcut length or even shorter. From what I was told, some coaches insisted it was necessary for the sake of unity. Others claimed it instilled a sense of pride while others claimed it was for sanitation purposes. I thought it was stupid.

Some of our opponents had this requirement while others did not. Some of those teams had winning records while others did not. From that I can deduce that a shaved head did not mean the difference between winning and losing. I would definitely like to see tangible proof that a team that was required to shave heads and wound up winning only one game would have lost that game had the players had longer hair. My teammates and I carried combs and went to the CIF Playoffs all three years that I was on the varsity.

Although I had access to a car, I decided to walk the mile to my old high school. It was something of a tradition whenever I visited my old home. I didn't necessarily always walk to the high school but I usually took a walk somewhere to check out the old landmarks.

I left early enough so that time was not a critical factor. Along the way I was able to recognize the homes of old friends. There was no point in knocking on any doors since my friends were not likely still residing at their former homes and I still had to be conscientious about the time even though I had a reasonably large cushion before having to rejoin the team. My walk through my old hometown was primarily an opportunity to reminisce.

The walk tradition began with my first visit after I transferred from USC to the University of Hawaii. On a few occasions there were arbitrary encounters with old friends. By this time more than seven years after my high school graduation such arbitrary encounters were virtually non-existent.

Unlike most of my classmates, I didn't move to Montebello until just before high school. When I first set foot on the South Valley campus I was joining a group of virtual strangers. Virtually everybody else in my class was entering South Valley with peers from their elementary and junior high schools. The only people I knew at all on the first day of school were those I met two weeks earlier when football drills started.

It struck me as funny that I didn't feel the same sentiment for Azusa even though I'd lived there roughly three times as long as I lived in Montebello. I wondered if it was because Azusa was where I was stabbed when I was 12, then realized that wasn't the reason. The high school years are considered to be the most formative and therefore have more sentiment attached. I felt some emotional attachment to those I had known in elementary school and junior high in Azusa but it wasn't the same. It would have been nice to visit Jim Martinez who had been in Hawaii as a member of the Marine Corps in 1976 and was now a civilian playing football at Citrus Junior College but there wasn't time.

Despite the fights and the stabbing, I had a lot of fond memories of Azusa including my friendship with Jim's brother, David. Montebello still had the majority of my heart for a variety of reasons. I suspected that the reverse might have been true had I lived in Montebello during my elementary and junior high school years and then moved to Azusa. High school was far more critical.

The walk through my old hometown was actually a very relaxing way of killing time. That night's game was on my mind but this made for a nice diversion. It gave me something to do with several hours still remaining before kickoff.

At this point in my career I didn't fully appreciate the diversion. This was only the first Monday night game on the Hawaiians where I could browse through my old neighborhood on gameday. Prior to this we had only had the Monday night game in Oakland the year before although it also wasn't unusual for us to have night games in the WFL days. In cities other than Los Angeles, including Honolulu, I spent the majority of the day of night games essentially counting the very long hours before kickoff. There were other things to do like read, watch TV or take walks but it was hard to concentrate on those things in the other cities. Walking through my old neighborhood was more of a mentally relaxing diversion since I was able to savor the memories that were there.

When I got to South Valley the student body was on its brunch period. I happened to run into my brother and a few of his friends who were fraternizing with a few girls. Craig was a lot like I had been although I was more jaded and flippant as a high school sophomore. Craig had the luxury of growing up in a neighborhood more tranquil than the rough section of Azusa I lived in for most of my first 15 years. Our parents had also learned from the mistakes they made with my sister and me so Craig didn't have to spend his formative years fighting for his right to live his own life.

Craig introduced me to his friends. A couple of them asked for autographs which started a chain reaction. I was in my fourth season as a pro football player and second in the NFL but still felt strange signing autographs, especially outside of Hawaii. This was especially true on the campus where I recalled spending weekends and vacations running on the rooftops, riding motorcycles and sneaking into the swimming pool. I also recalled sliding in the mud in my gym trunks with some of my colleagues during and after rainy periods and frequently sneaking off campus for lunch without ever getting caught.

"Are you going to beat the Rams tonight?" asked Lyle Bruce, one of my brother's "B" teammates and a friend of his since kindergarten.

"What do you think?" I replied wryly.

"Uh . . . ," he said, raising his eyebrows to avoid making a commitment. "I hope you win but I also like the Rams."

I nodded and smiled. I had successfully avoided a commitment. I knew we could win. I also wasn't about to make any brash predictions, even among high school students. Those things often find ways to haunt prognosticators.

The bell rang and the students headed to their classes. That got me off the hook since I didn't have much time. I didn't want to hang out at the school so long that I had just enough time to return to my parents' home before my mom had to drive me to Los Angeles.

Fortunately I knew exactly where to find my former mentor. I went into the boys' locker room and spotted him inside the door to the coaches' office. The sandy-haired, physically fit fiftyish man was decked out in his usual bermuda shorts and maroon polo shirt with the circular *SVHS Athletic Department* printed on the breast around three gold lightning bolts identical to the lightning bolts worn on the helmets of the South Valley Chargers.

"Well, well," he greeted cheerily, extending his hand simultaneously as I extended mine. "One of my favorite players. Are you ready to square off against your former teammate and his Rams?"

"Oh, I'm as ready as I'll ever be, I guess. Are you going?"

"I am. Normally my wife and I have Family Home Evening on Monday nights but we wouldn't miss an opportunity to see you and Lance play. We'll miss the first part of the game since we've got practice and game films. We should be there at least by halftime. Have you talked to Lance since you got into town?" he asked, meaning Lance Redmon, my former high school teammate who was a tight end with the Rams.

"No. We just got here last night. I'm sure I'll meet up with him tonight. I talked to him after our exhibition game against the Rams last year but that was the only time I've seen him since just after high school."

We didn't have much time to talk since Farnwell had to conduct his physical education class. He almost bowled me over when he asked me if I had married "the Canadian girl" I was going to see the last time I saw him.

"No, that's over," I replied, chuckling at the recollection of my previous relationship with Dr. Jekyll and Miss Hyde. "It actually ended about two days after I told you about her. I'm back with my college girlfriend now."

"Oh, I remember her. You showed me her picture once. Pretty girl."

There was some irony there. When I showed Farnwell Carol's picture I didn't know that my relationship with her was about to come to an end, at least for a few years. When I showed him Carol's picture and told him about Annica a few years later the last thing I expected in both cases was that the relationships were about to come to a shocking conclusion.

I walked out with Farnwell as he prepared to conduct the class for his students who were formed up in their gym clothes on the asphalt basketball courts outside the locker room. He told me he was proud to have two former players in the NFL although that night's game would be awkward for him.

"I'll be sitting on my hands," he said. "I can't root for either team. I just hope that you and Lance have good games."

I thought for a moment and nodded. I admitted that I also hoped my former teammate would have a good game.

But not *too* good.

It would be easy to assume that I was a personal favorite of Farnwell's. That was not the case. As a teacher, coach and athletic director he took his work very seriously, doing as much as he could for all of his students. No doubt there were countless others who far surpassed anything I might have done. I simply got more notice since my career happened to put me on *Monday Night Football* on occasion.

Farnwell was proud of me and that meant a lot. It wasn't because I was a pro football player that he was proud. It was because I had found something worth doing, worked hard at it and excelled. He would have been just as proud had I given the same dedication to being a teacher, a bricklayer or managing a McDonald's. He was equally as proud of a former teammate of mine who turned his life around after spending three years in San Quentin.

In 1977 my career was in its early stage. I wasn't especially well-known at the time. Ultimately I wound up in the Hall of Fame.

Being enshrined in Canton, Ohio, is a thrill beyond description. The thrill would have been slightly tarnished had Farnwell and his wife Judy not attended the induction ceremony. I almost choked when I looked at him from the podium and almost lost it completely when I referred to him in my induction speech. He was the one who planted the seed which led me to high school football, college football and a pro football career which included Pro Bowls and Super Bowls before climaxing at the Hall of Fame. I would never have played a single down of football anywhere had it not been for him. After my volatile beginning which compelled me to quit in a huff, he showed an interest and seemed to believe in me. That was all I really needed.

That was veritably Farnwell. He could bring out the best in people. I recall a linebacker we had my senior year who didn't appear to be much of a player. He was told as much by some of his teammates including, I am ashamed to admit, myself. That aided in his discouragement and he simply went through the motions at practices. Farnwell finally asked him why he didn't work harder.

"What good would it do?" I overheard the discouraged linebacker reply in a voice that did not betray his hurt feelings. "Everybody says I'm no good. If they're that sure, what good would it do for me to go all out? You're not going to play me anyway."

Farnwell took the player aside just as he had done with me a few years earlier. That player came out with a new attitude. It turned out that he wasn't a bad football player at all. He simply needed some encouragement to offset the discouragement. Although I don't recall him ever being in the starting lineup, he got his share of playing time and did well when given the opportunity.

Through it all Farnwell remained humble. Earning a reputation for getting the most out of his players, Farnwell was often recruited by junior colleges and small four-year colleges. Perhaps he could have gone from there to larger schools and a national championship before leading a pro team to the Super Bowl.

The recruitment efforts were unknown to most of his players. I never knew about them until his wife mentioned them while speaking at Farnwell's funeral in 1996.

"He never gave a second thought to turning those offers down," Judy Farnwell reported from the pulpit before an overflow crowd at the ward where the Farnwells worshipped. "He wasn't interested in making a lot of money or becoming famous. He just wanted to be where he felt he could do the most good for people."

192

I spent the rest of the morning at my family's house watching TV and talking to my mom. I actually looked at my mom with admiration. She had never worked outside the home after she married my dad and she was very content with her *housewife* status. She was very happy to be married to my dad dating back to his tenure as a soldier. She was proud of him for his willingness to risk his life for his country, as was I although I hadn't really expressed myself that way since I was in elementary school. I suspected that she was only taking my dad's side when I refused his effort in persuading me to make some branch of the military my career but that she could secretly, at least a little, see my point of view when I vehemently refused. By 1977 my dad had come around to accepting me as a perpetual civilian and I was sure that Mom's persuasion helped to change his attitude.

Mom was physically very beautiful. She and I shared many of the same features although she had a darker complexion. One might find it hard to believe that she was 50 percent Caucasian. Her complexion was naturally tan which could have come from her Seminole blood or her Hispanic blood. The only physical traits that suggested that she had Caucasian blood were her blue eyes and blonde hair. However, her natural hair color was dark brown but she maintained it so well that few people knew that she wasn't a natural blonde.

I am 75 percent Caucasian. My natural complexion when I'm not spending time at the beach isn't especially fair but it is light enough that it isn't mistaken for tan. I have dark brown hair that is the same shade that my mother's would be if she didn't dye it, the same blue eyes that she had and I have her high cheekbones.

While enjoying the time I was spending at home with my mother, my mind still rotated between the activity there and that night's game. We won our only Monday night game in 1976 and this was our only Monday night game in 1977. I desperately wanted to have a 2-0 record in Monday night contests.

Of course I didn't like losing under any circumstance. I would also be playing with family and a few old friends in attendance that night so that was another reason to dread losing. A nationally televised Monday night game against the team that was favored to win our division would prove to any doubters that the Hawaiians were not to be taken lightly if we could pull the game out.

At one o'clock I had rejoined my teammates in Los Angeles. We ate our pregame meal, had a brief meeting, lounged around a little and then departed.

There were changes in our lineup. One was that Jim Morrissey would be starting at right cornerback. There was nothing physically wrong with Henri Dubois. Morrissey had simply beaten him out for the week. Dubois would try to win the starting job back the following week. This was something that could go back and forth throughout the season.

Also, backup center Stuart Arroyo hadn't quite healed from his shoulder injury suffered in the Miami game. He had been listed as *probable* but wasn't quite ready. Kevin Zanakis, who had been a center in high school, would be our long snapper. He would also fill in at center if Dave Shuford went down.

As I took my pregame laps I took in the ambiance of the Los Angeles Coliseum. It had an impressive history dating back to its grand opening in 1923. In 1977 it was still home to both USC and UCLA football. The Los Angeles Dons of the All American Football Conference had called it home during their brief existence from 1946 to 1949. It became the home of the Los Angeles Rams after their move from Cleveland in 1946. It was even home to the Los Angeles Chargers of the American Football League during their inaugural season in 1960 before they moved south to San Diego.

This was my first trip to the Coliseum since I attended USC as a college freshman. Back in those days freshmen at Division I schools were relegated to junior varsity squads but I got to attend the varsity's games. One moved up to the varsity as a sophomore and played only three years on that level.

I never saw a football game at the Coliseum until I started getting free tickets from USC and UCLA as a high school prospect they were trying to entice. The first professional football game I would see there was the one I was about to play in. I had very little interest in pro football until I went to college. As a kid I was a fan of USC but I only had passive interest in the Rams and knew names such as Bill Wade, Roman Gabriel, Ollie Matson, Jon Arnett and Jack Snow. I was willing to beg, borrow and steal for baseball on all levels but pro football meant very little to me.

My first few trips to the Coliseum were to baseball games. The Los Angeles Dodgers used the Coliseum as their home from 1958 until Dodger Stadium opened in 1962. I was present the night Sandy Koufax struck out 18 San Francisco Giants, tying what was then a major league record set by Bob Feller. I also recalled going to a game where Koufax got knocked out in the second inning. He was a very sporadic pitcher at that phase of his career.

Despite the imminence of a football game on the turf where I was running my laps, I allowed my mind to recall the baseball memories as I usually did at a facility where professional baseball had been played. I was running on the same turf that legends such as Duke Snider, Gil Hodges, Wally Moon, Maury Wills, John Roseboro and Carl Furillo had played on. Being a loyal Dodger fan, I also had fond memories of the lesser knowns such as Rip Repulski, Charley Neal, Norm Larker, Danny McDevitt and Joe Pignatano. I also recalled "cup of coffee" players like Ed Palmquist and Fred Kipp. They were all heroes to me while I was growing up. It seemed most appropriate that I was running in my traditional Dodger T-shirt and Dodger cap.

As I finished my final lap and headed for the tunnel behind what used to be home plate it dawned on me that my last visit to this facility was to attend a high school championship football game. Bishop Amat squeezed out an overtime victory against Lakewood High School. Ironically Bishop Amat's quarterback would be one of my opponents that night.

I was on the field warming up with my teammates when my parents and Craig showed up. Craig had his sideline pass while my parents had to remain in the bleachers. For this rare opportunity Craig was excused early from his "B" football practice. No doubt this opportunity to spend the game in our bench area gave him upper class status among his peers.

Also to attend were my Uncle Robert and Aunt Shirley whom I barely knew since Robert had been a career Army man stationed in various parts of the world while I was growing up. I also scrambled to get tickets for a few old friends with whom I had maintained contact.

In the locker room prior to kickoff assistant coach Greg Wilson led us in *The Lord's Prayer*. Walker followed with a concise pep talk.

"Okay, man. This is a Monday night game. The whole country and a large part of the rest of the world will be watching. This is your time to shine. Last year you came through with flying colors on Monday night. Let's rise to the occasion again."

Walker started to motion us to head to the field, then stopped himself. A strange smile crossed his face.

"Cosell's up in the booth," he added. "He loves to find fault. Don't let the loudmouth do that to you. That's my job."

We broke up and Walker gestured for us to take the field. The offensive unit hung back in the end zone since we were going to be introduced individually. Everybody else moved to the sideline.

I am not sure what kind of reception I got when I was introduced as I ran toward the center of the field. I was actually too nervous to notice. It wasn't as if I hadn't played pro football in front of my family before. They had seen me play the year before in San Diego. They had also seen me play at Anaheim Stadium against the Southern California Sun during my WFL days.

This was somehow a much bigger stage. It was a combination of my family, old friends, my old high school coach and *Monday Night Football*. It would also mark the first time I faced my former high school teammate in a game that meant something. Lance was a very intense competitor.

So was I.

After the *National Anthem* our captains went to midfield for the coin toss. We won the toss so I wouldn't have to wait to take the field. I would get my first licks in right away. That would knock the butterflies out of my system.

"Ready to go?" Hasegawa asked me as we exchanged our slap fives on the goal line.

"I'm more than ready. I need to get started now."

Conditions were perfect. The temperatures would be in the mid-60s throughout the game and there was no precipitation. We would also be playing on natural grass which is what I preferred by a wide margin after noting how much more taxing artificial turf was on my body. We played on grass in Miami with the only other regular season games being played on grass would be in Atlanta and Tampa. This was in the wake of all six preseason games on artificial turf.

I still had to wait for ABC to come out of commercial. As I stood on the goal line which was in what had once been right-center field during the Dodgers' tenure at the Coliseum I stole a glance into the bleachers behind our bench. It meant a lot to see my parents there. Previously when they went to my pro games it seemed more like an obligation to them. For the first time since I was in high school they seemed to genuinely *want* to see me play.

There wasn't much time to focus on my parents' newfound acceptance of my career choice. Before I knew it the kickoff was heading our way. It was heading toward Rich so I ran forward to intercept anybody in a blue jersey who was thinking about pinning us back. I met up with one such Ram and laid into him, knocking him to my left. He kept his feet but I hit him again. He stumbled and I laid into him a third time, knocking him and me both to the ground.

By this time Rich had already run past. He managed to get as far as the 32 before going down, giving us relatively decent field position. It was a 30-yard return.

The butterflies were gone. I felt great. The first licks made me forget that I had ever been nervous.

Scott opened the drive by carrying twice for a total of three yards. The Ram defensive line seemed almost impossible to break. Fortunately the Rams got called for a facemask. We had a first down at the 50.

Scott carried again with more success. A sweep around right end netted us 15 yards. I managed to keep a linebacker out of the play by throwing my shoulder into his midsection. Thus far I was enjoying myself on the hallowed ground where the likes of Gil Hodges, Don Newcombe, Charley Neal and John Roseboro once tread.

We went to the air next. I lined up on the left wing, then went into motion to my right. On the snap I ran forward in a post pattern.

I wasn't the primary receiver but Bender saw that I was open. He threw a near-perfect pass that I simply had to reach slightly in front of me for at

196

the 15. I straightarmed one defender and outran the rest. Nobody laid a hand on me as I crossed the goal line.

There are few things more gratifying in sports that one's own teammates congregating to offer congratulations after a touchdown. Dietrich and Grummon were first on the scene with wide smiles on their faces. They were followed by the rest of the offense before we ran off together as the PAT unit ran on.

More teammates offered their congratulations on the sideline. At the same time Guinn was splitting the uprights. We had a 7-0 lead with 13:02 left in the first quarter.

I took off my helmet and went to the Gatorade table. As I grabbed my cup of refreshment I looked into the face of my 15-year-old brother. He was beaming. I guess it meant a lot to him to see his older brother score a touchdown.

"There's still a long way to go," I reminded him. A lot could happen in 58 minutes and two seconds. A lot of it was bad. The Rams were one of the last teams who would surrender over a touchdown in the opening two minutes.

I was still pumped. This was a much better way to start a game than the previous week. In Miami we were down by two touchdowns before we finally got started. I felt that we were on track to beat the Rams.

Henri Dubois seemed to feel the same way. On the ensuing kickoff the Ram return man fielded the kick at the two. Dubois shot through and brought him down at the 15.

"Yeah, baby!" I heard Allen exclaim while several other teammates offered their approbation. The momentum was going our way. We needed to keep it that way.

The defense was charged. An incomplete pass and a four-yard rush gave the Rams a third and six at their own 19.

"Let's hold 'em, guys!" I called as the Rams headed up to the line. "Get the ball for us!"

No doubt the defense wanted to comply. The Rams weren't going to make it easy. They completed a pass at about the 30. The receiver got to the 36 before being pushed our of bounds by Black.

They didn't get much further. After two plays they had a third and three at the 43. The Ram quarterback then dropped back and met a heavy rush. He spotted a receiver before being hit by Richards but the ball was off the mark, dropping untouched. I ran on the field to field a punt.

"Yeah! Way to go, defense!" I exclaimed as I crossed paths with the defensive unit.

I stood on about the 15 and watched as the Ram punting unit headed up to the line. Their field position was such that a fake was a distinct possibility. Those up front were going to focus on stopping a fake instead of trying to block the punt.

197

They punted. I was in pretty good position to field it. I caught it at the 17 and took off.

One wideout had gotten downfield in a hurry. He was coming from my right and I knew he was not coming at a very good angle. He managed to lunge, however, and momentarily grabbed me around the ankle, causing me to lose my balance. I managed to keep myself up by pushing my right hand against the ground as I went forward. Unfortunately my knee touched down at the 24. It was only a seven-yard return.

I was frustrated but there was nothing I could do. The defender barely got a hand on me but it was enough. Had he not touched me I could have gotten up and picked up a few more yards. I was hoping the officials didn't notice that I had been touched. The whistles as soon as my knee hit told me they weren't fooled.

The optimistic attitude in the huddle helped. Without anybody saying anything, I sensed that everybody was confident. We were ready to play some serious football.

We started with a slant pass that got us only a few yards. Dietrich caught the pass at the 28 and was immediately hit and dropped.

I was next. Bender hit me over the middle at the 38. I managed to fight for four more yards before going down at the Hawaii 42. It was first down.

Kerner next plowed the road off right tackle. He fought for six yards before going down at the Hawaii 48.

The Rams tightened up after that. A pass to Grummon was nearly intercepted to give us a third and four. Making matters worse was that Scott pulled a hamstring. He had to be helped off the field. He would not be able to return until the second half.

We tried to rush for a first down. I ran a sweep around right end. I got past midfield before I was hit. I fought the best I could and lunged forward. I believed I had a first down by at least a foot or two.

"Good job, Jaybird," Kerner said as he and Marv helped me to my feet.

I felt pretty good about myself. As I headed toward our huddle I heard Walker start yelling at the official.

"What do you think you're doing? You're spotting the ball too far back! He was at least two feet ahead of that!"

My heart sank. The officials had their reasons for spotting the ball where they did. Human error seemed to be the primary reason. I believed Walker was right although I was also a biased source.

The chain was brought and stretched out. We were short by about six inches.

"Let's go for it," I suggested although I was merely thinking out loud. Walker was calling for the punting unit. I had no choice but to leave the field.

198

"I know I had it," I said as I passed Walker. He nodded with his jaw clenched. It was going to take a little time before he was going to eradicate any negative feelings for the officiating crew.

I grabbed a cup of Gatorade. My brother Craig had a very inquisitive look on his face. All I could do was shake my head and went to sit on the bench. I was slightly upset but felt it was necessary to let it go as soon as possible. I didn't like to be visibly upset in a game, especially in an away game since that would rile up the crowd. I also didn't want to put on a display of anger in front of my brother.

Jablonski got off a pretty good punt. It was high so it had a long hang time. The return man held up his arm to signal for a fair catch. He was inside the ten so I figured he was trying to decoy the wideouts so that they could slow up while the ball hit the ground and bounced into the end zone for a touchback.

Much to my surprise, the return man caught the ball. He was on the seven.

"Man, that guy's crazy," I said to Rossi. "You don't make a fair catch inside the ten. You let the ball go into the end zone."

"I hear ya. I wonder why he did that."

I shrugged.

"He must not have known where he was," I said.

The Rams were 93 yards from the end zone. I was arrogant enough to believe it would be impossible for them to score. We were capable of going that far for a score but that was a different matter. We didn't have to do it against our defense.

Blakely wasted no time in trying to prove my theory correct. The Rams began their drive by completing a short pass inside the 20. Blakely hammered the ball carrier almost immediately.

"Fumble!"

"Loose ball!"

"Let's go! Get the ball!"

"Get it, get it, get it!"

Those were a few of the cries from our sideline as a large group in blue jerseys and white jerseys scrambled after the ball. Like the rest of my teammates on the sideline, I was on my feet hoping that the verdict would go our way. I wanted a two-touchdown lead before the Rams touched the ball again.

Unfortunately things didn't go our way. The Rams recovered on the 21. First down.

The Rams continued to move. They picked up a first down at the 36. Two plays later our defense seemed to have them at bay, limiting them to three total yards for a third and seven at the 39.

It didn't surprise anybody that the Rams went to the air. My high school teammate Lance Redmon made the reception near midfield. Naturally he was nearly impossible to bring down. He fought his way down to the Hawaii 42 for a first down.

"Just like I remember him," I muttered to nobody in particular.

"Hm?" asked Grant Collier who was sitting a few feet to my right.

"That receiver, Lance Redmon. He and I were high school teammates. He was a bull then and he's a bull now."

The march continued through the waning minutes of the first quarter. The Rams efficiently mixed a series of rushes and passes to tear up chunks of real estate. Suddenly it was first and goal at the eight.

Or I should say it was first and goal from the 13. An overzealous tackle jumped prior to the snap, setting the Rams back five yards.

I couldn't sit any longer. It amazed me that I had stayed seated for as long as I did. I finally stood as if I could aid the defense by standing.

A pass was caught at the three where Black shoved the receiver out of bounds. That stopped the clock with 43 seconds left in the quarter. The Rams picked up two more yards up the middle to give them a third and goal at the one.

The next snap was just before time expired in the quarter. The quarterback rolled out and found a receiver in the right corner of the end zone. The Coliseum crowd erupted as the receiver clung to the ball.

I resisted the urge to swear. I resisted the urge to slam my helmet down. I reminded myself that the Rams were expected to score along the way. I was hoping we would have a five-touchdown lead before that happened but I had to accept the fact that they scored a little ahead of schedule. The key was to score again ourselves.

The PAT was good. We had a 7-7 tie at the end of the first quarter.

"It's going to be a long night," I said to Hasegawa as we did our slap fives on the goal line. We had a little time to kill since ABC was showing commercials.

"Not if we win," Rich countered.

"Win or lose, it's going to be a long night. Nobody's going to run away with this one."

I was pretty firm in my conviction. The Rams were favored by a touchdown. I didn't believe the margin of victory either way would be much more than that.

The time had come to try to start retaking the lead. The kick came right to me. I fielded it on the goal line and ran forward. I hurdled a fallen Ram and maneuvered around another. I was brought down at the 23.

There were 77 yards to go for the score. The Ram defense wasn't going to make it easy. They came hard on the first play, perhaps reading the pass. Bender had to scramble and did manage to get away, stepping out of bounds at the 25 to give us second and eight.

We stayed on the ground on the next play. Ozzie Roberts, filling in for Scott, carried up the middle and picked up about five yards.

200

"Fumble!"

I was throwing a block when I heard that. I looked down and spotted the ball a few feet to my right. I made a desperate dive and got my hand on it but wasn't able to control it. The ball was pulled from my insecure grasp.

The Rams recovered the ball on the 32. I had risen to my knees in time to see the referee point in their direction. The next thing I saw was a linebacker holding the ball up and flipping it to an official as he practically danced his way to the Ram sideline. All the while the crowd was roaring.

Dejectedly I jogged off the field. The Rams were in great shape to take the lead. I expected at least a field goal attempt on a drive that was beginning 96 feet from the end zone. It would then be a test of our resilience.

After a two-yard rush and an incomplete pass the Rams had a third and eight at the 30.

Jennings dashed the Rams' hopes for even a field goal. He charged in on the snap and forced the quarterback to scramble.

"Get him, Ed!" I barked, jumping to my feet.

The quarterback hunted for a receiver but couldn't find one. He tucked the ball away just as Ed bore down on him. It was a nine-yard sack at the 39.

"Yes!" I cried, thrusting both fists in the air. "Yes! Yes! Yes!"

A field goal was still possible. In this case it would have been about 56 yards.

The Rams surprised me a little by sending the punting unit on the field. The Rams also seemed to surprise much of the crowd. There was a lot of booing when the punting unit took the field.

This meant that I was back on the field. I took my place on the ten. Anything that would pass over my head I was going to let go.

The punt wasn't going to be over my head but it was well to my right. The ball landed between the right hash mark and the sideline at the 12 and bounced toward the end zone. I tried to throw a block but it was all in vain. Another Ram wideout caught up with the ball and downed it not more than two inches from the end zone.

That brought the crowd back into it. After the Rams missed out on a golden opportunity to score at least a field goal, the Rams produced a perfectly executed punt. Had I been a spectator I would have been very impressed with the effort. The crowd, part of which had been booing a minute earlier, was very quick to forgive and roared its approval. It wasn't nearly as loud as it would have been with a touchdown but it was conspicuous.

No doubt the crowd was hoping the defense would force a safety. Kerner had other ideas. On a 2 Mililani right he charged up the middle and broke no fewer than three tackles between the line of scrimmage and the ten where he was still driving forward. It wasn't until he got to the 16 that he was dragged down.

"All right, Jeff!" I cried out as I offered my hand to help him to his feet. "That was the best impression of a Sherman tank I've ever seen."

A rush for no gain and an incomplete pass left us in a third and ten. On the next snap I ran toward the right sideline a few yards beyond the first down marker. Bender hit me with a perfect pass just before my momentum carried me out of bounds. It was first down.

Our momentum continued to build. After a four-yard pass to Dietrich, Bender hit Grummon at the Hawaii 45. Rich picked up four more yards before going down at the Hawaii 49.

I was feeling great. We were almost halfway to the end zone from where we started. We seemed to be doing pretty well against one of the most formidable teams in the league on *Monday Night Football*.

"Dockman!"

Rossi was coming in with a play. I would be relegated to the sideline for a play or two. I slapped hands with Rossi as our paths crossed.

Whatever play it was that Rossi brought in, it didn't work although it wasn't his fault. Bender's pass was tipped up. A Ram linebacker caught the ball at the Los Angeles 49. He got to the Hawaii 44 before Bender and Kerner teamed up to bring him down.

I was standing right behind Walker. When the play was over I probably rolled my eyes and shook my head before heading back to the Gatorade table. From the opposite side of the table my brother bore another inquisitive look.

"We knew they were going to be tough and they definitely are," I told him.

"You can beat them," Craig said hopefully as I took a sip of Gatorade.

"We have to come up with a couple of big plays," I replied. "We get moving and they come up with big plays to stop us. Our defense is doing the same thing to them right now. We have to make something happen on offense."

For the moment we had to rely on our defense making the big plays. Thanks to a big play by the Ram defense the Rams were 44 yards from taking the lead.

The Rams wasted little time. After two first downs they had first and goal at the eight. I tried to prepare myself emotionally to concede the score. I just hoped it would only be a field goal.

Richards pushed the Rams back a little on the next play. He shot into the backfield and dropped a running back for a two-yard loss.

The Rams went to the air next. A wide receiver slanted in and caught a pass at about the four. Rodgers and Blakely teamed up to slam the receiver down at the one. It was third and goal.

It was another pass. The quarterback, under a heavy rush from Allen, got the pass off. Fortunately Rodgers batted the ball down. It was fourth and goal at the one.

202

Nobody was sitting on our sideline. I was flanked by Bender and Kerner as all eyes were directed toward the end zone opposite the main scoreboard.

The Ram field goal unit never budged. The Rams were going for the full seven. The fans roared when the offensive unit broke out of the huddle and headed toward the line.

Most of us were yelling. I think we were all prepared to concede the touchdown if it was absolutely necessary. We preferred not to.

"I bet they go up the middle," I said.

"Me, too," said Bender.

"Nah. I think they're going to pass," Dietrich replied from the opposite side of Bender from me.

We were all wrong. They decided to shoot around right end. McDaniel got the ball carrier in his grasp and Black came up to help bring him down. From our vantage point it was impossible to ascertain how close to the goal line the ball carrier had gotten. All I know is the officials still hadn't raised their arms.

Finally an official raised one arm. That meant the play was dead without a score. Several of us jumped in exultation.

"Yeah!" I exclaimed as I leaped in the air before putting my helmet on and heading to the field.

"Let's go, offense!" Walker barked, smiling broadly and making a sweeping motion to direct us to take the field as we headed toward our huddle in the back of the end zone.

What was odd was that I happened to glance into the bleachers behind the Ram bench. Normally I try to avoid that type of thing, especially while on the field, but the bleachers seemed to be a magnet for my eyes. About halfway up I saw Coach Farnwell and his wife Judy arriving at the game. They were taking seats not too far from the tunnel from which they emerged. It was good to know that they were there.

Ozzie got the call on the opening play and got to the three. That was nullified because Stanek got called for holding.

It amazed me that the Rams accepted the penalty. It only moved us back half-a-yard since the penalty could only go half the distance to the goal line. Apparently the Rams were dead set on getting a safety out of the deal and this would make it easier.

I smelled a blitz coming. So did Bender. He had called a draw play but lunged forward on the snap. He got to the three to give us a second and eight. That is exactly what would have been had the Rams not accepted the holding penalty.

Ozzie carried again, this time off left tackle and getting up to the nine to give us a third and two. I then ran a sweep around left end to the 13 to pick up a first down.

Time was winding down toward the two-minute warning so we tried to pick up the pace a little. We picked up a first down but then the drive appeared ready to stall when we faced third and seven at the 32. We needed to get at least to the 39 or else punt the ball away and give the Rams an opportunity to go into the locker room with the lead.

We were going to the air. Naturally the Rams were expecting it. They came hard at Bender.

Bender miraculously avoided the sack. He tucked the ball away and charged forward. He got all the way to the 42 before finally stepping out of bounds. We had another first down.

That fired us up. We were clapping our hands and slapping Steve on the back as we headed to our huddle.

We let the clock run down to the two-minute warning. Steve went to the sideline to converse with Walker.

"Gentlemen. We are going all the way this time," Marv stated, keeping his voice low enough to prevent the Rams from hearing his brash prediction.

"You tell 'em, Marv baby," Kerner answered. "There is no way they are going to deny us this time."

It was exhilarating. I felt incredibly excited and confident. The Rams had risen to the occasion before. I wanted to believe that this time would be an exception.

Bender returned to the huddle. He was looking directly at me. I sensed that I was about to be a major player on the first play.

I was wrong. Ozzie went off right tackle to the 47. It was second and five. The clock wound down to 1:49 before we called timeout.

An incompletion followed. We had to do something now or else turn the ball over to the Rams. Anything short of first down yardage was not in field goal range.

"Split right, east Moloka'i left," Bender called, sending a chill up my spine. This was a brand new play in which I would be the passer. Although I would be running to my left and Dietrich would be split to the right, he would be my primary receiver since he would be running a post pattern. That would take him more toward my side of the field.

Bender took the snap and pitched out to me. I ran to the left as if I was going to be running a sweep. I looked downfield and slightly to the right and spotted Dietrich. I also saw that the defensive back guarding him had taken the bait and was moving in to defend against a rush.

I turned slightly and fired to Dietrich. He caught the pass cleanly at the 30. He was untouched all the way to the end zone. It was a 53-yard touchdown.

As soon as Dietrich caught the ball I leaped up and pumped my fists in the air. I knew he was going all the way. I ran downfield to join my teammates in offering congratulations.

Ted spotted me and ran up to me at about the 15. We were so exultant that we simultaneously wrapped our arms around each other and jumped up a few times.

"Great pass, Jay! Great pass! That was perfect!" he exclaimed.

"Hey, it was a great play all around," I replied.

We ran off the field together, slapping fives with some of the PAT unit. Walker had one of his broad smiles on his face as Ted and I approached him.

"That's the way to play it," he said, slapping me on the rear as I went by. "Good catch, Ted."

Feeling pretty content, I watched as Guinn's kick split the uprights. We led 14-7 with 1:23 left in the half.

I went to the Gatorade table. Craig was filling Gatorade cups and trying to look nonchalant. I tried to play it cool but he caught my eye as he looked up. His face broke into a broad smile.

"Great pass," he said although he told me later that he didn't see anything after I got the pass off. From his post his view was blocked by players jumping up. The reaction of my teammates told him the result of the play.

Guinn's kick was fielded three yards deep in the end zone. The Rams made no attempt to run it out. That enabled them to have a first down on the 20 without burning any time off the clock. They needed to work the clock properly to have an opportunity to score.

That was exactly what they did. Amid some incompletions they managed to complete two passes. One of them gave them a first down at their own 47. The other gave them a first down at the Hawaii 33.

My heart was pounding. If the Rams got a touchdown they would tie the game and have the momentum. They would also be receiving the opening kickoff of the second half.

Time was on our side. The Rams used their final timeout. They had 21 seconds to move 33 yards.

Two incompletions later they hadn't moved an inch. They also didn't get the passes off as expeditiously as they probably wanted. It was third and ten but there were only six seconds left. They sent their field goal unit out.

This was certain to be the final play of the half. The snap was made and the holder got the ball down. The kicker got the kick off and the ball headed toward the uprights. The officials under the goal posts raised their arms as time ran out. They had narrowed the gap to 14-10 at halftime.

I sat quietly in the locker room, drinking two cups of Gatorade while I smoked a cigarette. Some players were discussing plays with coaches but I was left on my own most of the time. I took note of my perspiration-soaked jersey which included patches of dirt, grass stains and chalk and smiled contentedly. I was having fun and we were winning. There was still a long way to go.

"Let's suck it up, men," Walker announced from the middle of the room before we were to return to the field. "There are only 30 minutes to go. Let's pull away. We can take these guys."

We all got up and headed back to the field. I was anxious to play the rest of the game. Adding to the excitement was playing so close to where I had excelled as a high school player.

Scott was cleared to resume action. That was good news for us. Ozzie had done all right but Scott was clearly the better running back. We needed our best as much as possible.

After I reached the sideline I looked at Craig and raised my eyebrows. He smiled and nodded, then resumed filling Gatorade cups.

"Whaddya say, Dave?" I said to Rossi. "Ready to go?"

"Ah'm ready, Jay. Let's beat them guys."

Guinn put his best foot into the kickoff. The return man fielded it four yards deep in the end zone. He didn't bother attempting a return.

"Aw, what's the matter with him?" Black asked jocularly to nobody in particular as he prepared to take the field with his defensive colleagues. "Is he afraid of our kicking team?"

After two plays the Rams had a first down at the 31. Following a four-yard rush around left end they tried a short pass to my old friend Lance in the flat.

Jennings cut in front of Lance and picked the pass off at the 39.

"Go, Ed!" I yelled, jumping to my feet.

Ed was untouched most of the way. He was finally brought down by the fullback at the eleven. We were 33 feet from another score.

"Offense! Let's go! Take it in!" Walker commanded.

As I ran out on the field toward where we would huddle I watched as Black and McDaniel pulled Ed to his feet. The trio ran off together. Ed even seemed to be including a few hops in his run. He normally wasn't that emotional.

We were determined to take it all the way in. The Rams showed that they were at least as determined to prevent that. They started out by sacking Bender at the 18.

Since the pass didn't work we decided to utilize our ground game next. Scott carried on a Kailua right. He got exactly nothing. It was third and 17.

It was back to the air again. Bender rolled to his right and spotted Dietrich open in the corner of the end zone. As Steve was unleashing the ball a defensive end charged in and batted the ball away. After starting our drive with outstanding field position we were facing a fourth and 17.

206

I understood why Walker was sending the field goal unit on the field. I didn't like it but I didn't blame Walker. We had moved the ball seven yards in the wrong direction.

"Three points are better than nothing," I muttered to Scott as he and I helped ourselves to the Gatorade.

I turned and watched as the ball was snapped. Billingsley set the ball down on the 25. Guinn put his foot into it and it was up and. . . .

Unbelievable! It was wide to the right. We started our drive with seven points written all over it. We wound up not even getting *three* points. The Rams would have a first down at their own 20 as they did when the third quarter started. It was as if our first series and their first series never happened.

Guinn was visibly shaken as he sat on the bench a few feet away from me. He had missed field goals before. I just couldn't remember him missing from this close since the team's inception a little more than a year earlier.

I was upset but forced myself to recall a few things. During my senior year in high school I was my team's placekicker and could recall missing at least a couple of field goals I knew I should have made. What came most readily to mind, though, was our game in Philadelphia the year before when I dropped what would have been the winning touchdown pass on the final play of the game. That play seems to be foremost on my mind whenever one of my teammates falters. "It's okay, man," I said to Guinn. "It's okay. Don't worry about it. We'll make it up."

Guinn looked at me with a trace of gratitude although he still looked somewhat distraught. I probably would have been the same way had our roles been reversed. When I dropped the pass in Philadelphia I was grateful for the teammates who told me to shake it off and even stood up for me. It was still a horrible experience.

I focused on the action on the field. The Rams ran off left tackle to the their own 26. They then went around right end to the 30. Zanakis caught up with the ball carrier and whirled him around.

"Fumble!"

Zanakis hit the man near our sideline. Unfortunately for the Rams the ball did not go out of bounds. The way Zanakis twirled the ball carrier around caused the ball to come loose and head toward the center of the field. Blakely was right there to fall on it at the 30. It appeared to me that Blakely had it all the way but a couple of Rams jumped into the vicinity.

The referee pointed toward the end zone with the primary scoreboard. We had the ball. For the second time that quarter we had excellent field position. This time I hoped we would wind up with something to show for it. If our defense was forcing turnovers the least the offense could do was answer by putting points on the board.

Bender opened up by trying to hit me inside the 15. The pass was slightly off the mark since it was too far in front of me. I made a diving attempt but was still about two feet short of where the ball hit the gound.

A pass to Grummon was more on target. Bender hit Rich at the 16. Rich was immediately hit and dropped but we had a first down.

"All right. We're looking good. Looking good," I remarked while clapping my hands as we formed our huddle.

The Rams were still determined to make us earn every yard we got. Scott went off right tackle and fought for three yards to the 13. Bender then attempted a pass and was forced to scramble. Although he was in the twilight of his career and had lost a step or two, he had an uncanny knack for getting away. He managed to get to the eleven to give us a third and five.

Kerner went up the middle on the next play. He was hit simultaneously by two Rams at the line of scrimmage. He practically carried them until they finally succeeded in bringing him down at the seven. That was still a yard short of what we needed for a first down.

This time I hoped the field goal unit would stay off the field. It wasn't that I lacked confidence in Guinn since I didn't. I simply wanted to get that yard we needed for a first down and see if we could punch it in for seven.

It didn't surprise me that the field goal unit ran on the field. It was probably even the right decision. We were almost guaranteed the three points. We needed to put points on the board, especially since it was still a one-score game. If we got a touchdown on our next possession without the Rams scoring first it would become a two-score game.

Guinn's attempt was from 24 yards. The ball sailed through the uprights.

As the ball was being snapped a yellow flag shot up in the air. It appeared to me that the Rams were offside.

"Let's take the penalty," I said, primarily thinking out loud but a couple of teammates heard me and nodded in agreement. That would give us a first down and another opportunity to go for the full seven.

It turned out that we were offside. Rookie guard Larry Westfall had lined up a little too far forward. The ball was moved back to the 12.

We replayed the entire sequence, this time with the attempt being from 29 yards. The end result was the same. Our lead had expanded to 17-10.

"All right. Good job. Good job," Walker remarked to the members of the field goal unit who came to the sideline who were not part of the kicking team. He looked at Westfall with a wide grin and shook his head. It was fortunate for Westfall that Guinn was successful on the second attempt. The end result of Westfall's faux pas was simply that a few more seconds were taken off the clock.

Guinn kicked off. As the ball rose up another yellow flag shot up in the air. That would indicate that somebody was probably offside but it was hard to ascertain who.

The kick was fielded a yard deep in the end zone. The return man charged forward and broke a couple of tackles. James Malick brought him down at the 28.

But now the penalty. Was it against us or them?

It was against the Rams. One of their front men was offside. We accepted the penalty and lined up to kick again, this time from the 40.

Guinn outdid himself this time. The kick sailed out of the end zone. The Rams would have a first down at their own 20. Their five-yard offside penalty wound up costing them eight yards.

The Rams were undaunted. They showed once again why they were favored to win our division. After two first downs they were in Hawaii territory. One first down later they were on the 36. A touchdown would tie the game.

"You can't be giving up all of this yardage!" Walker hollered. "You've got to stop them now!"

Our defense stopped them on the next play but only after the running back had picked up seven yards up the middle. A rush off right tackle picked up three more yards to the 26. The officials called timeout to measure.

I saw the gesture I least wanted to see. The referee stood erect and sharply pointed, indicating that the Rams had another first down. The only thing I would have hated more was seeing him raise his arms straight up in the air. The Rams were 78 feet away from that.

The Rams stayed on the ground. They rushed for four yards and three yards, respectively. It was third and three at the 19 with less than a minute left in the third quarter.

They were going to the air. The quarterback wound up under a heavy rush. Jennings and McDaniel seemed to hit him simultaneously. The quarterback was sacked at the 27. The crowd seemed to express a simultaneous groan.

"All right! That's the way to play it, defense!" I cried out while my teammates expressed similar sentiment from the sideline.

"Tackle by Ed Jennings and Jim McDaniel at the Hawaii 27," called the baritone public address announcer voice that I recognized as John Ramsey. He was completing his 20th season as PA announcer for the Dodgers and was now the PA announcer for the Angels, Rams and USC." "Fourth down and eleven for the Rams."

The Rams played it smart by sending the field goal unit out. A field goal would mean that a Ram touchdown later would give them the lead, assuming that we didn't score.

I was willing to concede the field goal. I put my helmet on since I would be taking the field to receive the kick after the inevitable three points. I watched with my arms folded as the ball was snapped, placed and then kicked. The kick was on its way. . . .

The ball hit the left upright! It bounced back on the field!

"All right!" I cried out as my teammates expressed similar glee for our good fortune while the crowd let out another collective groan before seeming to fall silent.

It was the final play of the quarter. We still held a 17-10 lead.

I ran on the field with the rest of the offense except for Bender who momentarily conversed with Walker. I allowed my mind to wander to the significance of this game. It was a tight game; the kind ABC wanted for *Monday Night Football.* I just hoped that we would still be on top at the final gun.

We began the fourth quarter by sending Kerner up the middle. The three quarters hadn't worn him down. He fought his way to the 33. It was second and four.

Scott ran around right end but wasn't quite so fortunate. He was caught in the backfield and dropped for a two-yard loss.

We went to the air on third down. Unfortunately Bender never got the pass off. The Rams went at him hard. As the crowd roared its approval Steve was sacked by a trio of titanic Rams at the 17.

I stood near midfield with my hands on my hips reluctantly conceding the fact that we would have to punt.

"Penalty marker down," I heard John Ramsey report over the PA system.

That gave me a glimmer of hope. Was it too much to ask that the penalty be against the Rams?

The Rams were offside. That nullified the entire play. Instead of being forced to send our punting unit on in a fourth and 19 situation, we had third and one at the 36.

Walker would never have forgiven us had we not taken advantage of this new life. I would be among the first on his hit list since I was designated to carry the ball. We did a sweep around left end. I managed to get to the 43 to get us the first down.

"Dockman!" I heard as I headed toward our huddle. Rossi was coming in. I didn't really feel like sitting anything out but I wasn't going to argue.

"Good run," Walker said when I reached the sideline. "Stay close. I'll put you back in in a minute."

It was good for Rossi to get in for a couple of plays. He had earned his spot on the team. Although he wasn't as good as my backup from the previous year, Walker wanted to give him the opportunity to feel like he was a part of the team on something other than special teams whenever he felt that I could use a breather. He did the same thing with the backups at the other positions. Virtually all of our backups often saw at least a little action from scrimmage during virtually every game.

Scott rushed for five yards to the Hawaii 48 and Walker sent in Ozzie to give Scott a breather. Ozzie picked up three yards to the Los Angeles 49 to put us in a third and two.

"Okay, Jay," Walker said as he turned to me. "Tell Bender to run a Kaneohe right."

"Right," I said as I ran on the field. "Rossi!"

Rossi looked up when I called his name and headed toward the sideline. We slapped fives, as usual, when our paths crossed.

The play worked well. Kerner picked up six yards to the 43. We had another first down.

"Roberts!"

Scott returned to the field. His rest period was over. Ozzie returned to the sideline.

Before we could get off another play the Rams' left end jumped the gun. I was lined up on the right wing obliquely behind the right tackle and he came right at me. He tried to hold up but bumped me, almost knocking me down. A penalty flag shot up in the air.

"He moved. He moved," he cried out, pointing at me.

"Like hell I did," I said evenly.

I didn't necessarily blame him for trying that tactic although at the moment I was a little annoyed with him. The officials were on my side and assessed five yards against the Rams, giving us a first and five at the 38.

Bender hit Dietrich over the middle at the 28 on the subsequent play. Ted turned toward the end zone. He was hit and dropped at the 19. It was another first down and we were smelling seven points.

We were hungry and were going for the jugular on first down. Bender spotted me in the end zone. I was covered but Bender threw the ball far enough in front of me to where only I would be able to catch it. Unfortunately it was a little too far out in front and I had to dive for it. I got a hand on the ball while in midair but wasn't able to get a grip on it. As I was hitting the ground the ball was heading upward after bouncing off my hand. It hit the crossbar of the goal post and came down in the middle of the end zone.

Another pass followed. This one included a heavy rush. Bender spotted Grummon and threw the ball his way.

Unfortunately this pass was deflected. The ball caromed off the defensive lineman's hand and was picked off by a defensive back at the one. He got to the seven where Scott wrestled him down.

It wasn't bad enough that the pass was intercepted. As we ran off the field we also had to listen to the crowd cheering its approval. The whole thing was creating an epidemic of being sick to stomachs on the Hawaiians' side of the field.

"Just when we were about to put them on the ropes," I muttered on the sideline to nobody in particular.

The Rams immediately showed that they were determined to cash in on the turnover. They picked up a couple of quick first downs. This included a third and six at the eleven where the quarterback was flushed out of the pocket and forced to rush. He got to the 18; one yard more than he needed for a first down. A rush and a pass later they had a first down at the 32. A rush and a pass after that they had another first down at the Hawaii 46.

"This is killing me," I muttered as I looked down at my white Puma cleats while sitting on the bench. I was getting a major anxiety attack. I'm sure it was another common problem on our sideline.

Two more rushes put the ball on the 36. The officials called time to measure.

It was short by about four inches. The Rams then ran up the middle and managed to pick up a yard to give them another first down.

"Come on, defense!" Walker barked. "Tighten it up! Let's go! Tighten it up!"

The partisan crowd was noisy. Los Angeles crowds had a reputation for being very laid back. Apparently this crowd did not care to live up to its apathetic reputation. The fans were really into it.

Our defense decided to try to silence the crowd. A rush off right tackle led to a rude reception by Richards. Norm dropped the ball carrier for a two-yard loss. It was second and 12 at the 37.

Allen decided to upstage his childhood chum in the stadium where he and Richards had excelled as collegiates. Allen and Pratt blitzed the quarterback. They combined to sack him at the 45. It was third and 20. They were no longer in reasonable range for even a long field goal unless they wanted to challenge the existing NFL record.

Most of the noise now seemed to come from our sideline. We were all standing. Most of us were cheering on our defensive colleagues.

The Rams attempted a pass but it dropped untouched. I detected a smattering of boos as the Rams' punting unit ran on the field. I took my place at the ten to field the punt.

I wanted a big return but knew that there was no way the Rams were going to give me a chance to get it. The punt was directed well to my right. It was determined that the ball went out of bounds at the eight. The clock showed 3:58 left in the game.

We began an extremely conservative game. Our objective was obviously to score since any kind of a score would put the game virtually out of reach. We would accept not scoring if we could run out the clock.

Kerner started things off by going up the middle to the 13. That was nullified by the Rams being offside. By taking the penalty we still had the ball on the 13. The difference was we had first down on the 13 instead of second down.

Scott went up the middle for four yards to the 17, putting us in a second and one. I then finished the first down quest, going off left tackle to the 19.

A 3 kama'aina left was called. Scott carried around left end for two yards. We allowed the clock to run down to the two-minute warning.

Two minutes, I thought while Bender conversed with Walker. They would be a very long two minutes. We had to keep the ball. If the Rams got possession they were more than capable of picking apart our defense and scoring very quickly.

Ozzie came in and ran off right tackle to the 23. It was third and six. The Rams called timeout with 1:53 left.

This created an interesting scenario. Third and six usually meant a pass was forthcoming. In this case we were trying to run down the clock. An incompletion would stop the clock without the Rams having to burn one of their two remaining timeouts. If we kept it on the ground the Rams would be forced to use one of their timeouts unless they opted to allow us to milk the clock down before calling a timeout just as the play clock was about to expire. That would run the game clock down to about 1:15.

We went for the pass. I don't believe the Rams were expecting it and Dietrich caught the ball at the 33. He maneuvered around a couple of defenders and headed upfield. He was finally forced out of bounds at the Hawaii 40, stopping the clock with 1:37. This prevented the Rams from having to use one of their timeouts but we had a fresh set of downs.

"Okay, good job, men," Walker remarked. Most of us heard him clearly since the play had gone to our sideline. "Keep playing it smart."

Kerner played it not so smart. He got a little anxious and jumped prior to the first down snap, setting us back to the 35. Scott followed by rushing up the middle to the 41, giving us a second and nine. The Rams used their second timeout with 1:28 left.

A Waimanalo right was called. That meant that I would be carrying off right tackle. I was hit at the line but somehow managed to squirm away. I spun around another would-be tackler and continued upfield. I got just past midfield to the Ram 49 to give us another first down. The Rams used their final timeout with 1:16 left.

"That's it. Run it out," Walker directed from the sideline. "They don't have any timeouts left."

Bender took three snaps and dropped to his knee each time.

When the final gun sounded we were officially 3-1 on the season, tied with Atlanta for first place in the NFC West. It was our second victory on Monday night in as many tries. The pain of the loss in Miami was completely behind us.

I shook hands with a few of my opponents before Lance and I found each other. For the first time ever an opposing player and I hugged each other. I later learned that the scene appeared live on national television. Apparently it was mentioned at least a few times during the course of the game that Lance and I had been high school teammates.

"You guys had the hot hand tonight," Lance remarked as we started walking toward the tunnel together.

"It wasn't easy," I replied. "You guys came at us with everything you had. It's amazing we managed to pull it out."

It sounded like two opponents trying to butter each other up. In this case we both meant it. It was a hard-fought game on both sides. We turned the ball over more than we should have but most of the turnovers were forced by the Ram defense.

Backs and receivers coach Greg Bennici gave the postgame prayer. Afterward Walker held up a football.

"I'm going to give three of these tonight," Walker announced. "There were a lot of good performances so it was all I could do to narrow it down to three."

Walker paused and looked around. I realized his eyes were fixed on Bender.

"One man had the Rams in his face all night long. He showed extraordinary poise and scrambling ability and that was one of the keys that kept us alive."

Walker tossed the ball to Bender. A rousing cheer ensued before Walker held up a second ball.

"One man sacked their quarterback twice and picked off a pass," Walker explained. "That is worthy of a game ball."

Walker tossed the second ball to Jennings. That was also succeeded by a rousing cheer. Walker then held up the third ball.

"We scored two touchdowns tonight," Walker reported. "One man caught a pass for one touchdown and threw a pass for the other."

Walker tossed the ball to me. I was taken by surprise, holding my jersey in one hand and a cup of Gatorade in the other. I dropped the ball and splashed the Gatorade all over myself while I got the customary round of cheers as well as a few laughs from my teammates.

I looked down at the ball and then up at Walker. He stood in the middle of the room with an amused grin on his face.

"The important thing is you make great catches on the field," Walker chuckled. "You can drop the ball all you want in here."

Walker said a few more words and then left. I showered and dressed as quickly as possible so that I could spend as much time as possible with family and friends before the team bus left for the airport. There were reporters who came around to ask me a few questions while I was shedding my uniform since I had figured prominently in our two touchdowns. I answered them politely but while hurrying to get out of my uniform and into the shower.

"I'm not trying to put you guys off," I politely explained off the record. "I'm just in a hurry. I have family and friends waiting outside and I'd like to spend a few minutes with them before we head to the airport."

214

I got along with most sportswriters, as opposed to Howard Cosell who didn't seem to like any of them. There were still those I didn't care for. I wasn't going to condemn an entire profession based on the actions of a few.

Outside there was a semblance of a reunion. My parents and brother were waiting, as were my aunt and uncle whom I had seen only on rare occasions. Lance also joined the group, as did his parents and two sisters whom I had known in high school. Also with us was Coach Farnwell and his wife.

Probably the best part of the reunion was seeing Lance's wife Darlene. She and I were close friends all through high school, having met when we sat next to each other in a freshman English class. Although the statuesque girl with long dark blonde hair and sweet blue eyes which matched her disposition was very beautiful, she was somebody I never considered dating for some reason. She was usually not romantically attached to anybody in high school, even Lance although she knew him, but she and I were never more than close friends.

Darlene and I hugged when we saw each other for the first time since our high school graduation night more than seven years earlier. Seeing her took me back nearly a decade. We had classes together, studied together in the library, gave each other rides to and from school, occasionally danced together at school dances and were often part of the same social clique. I even recalled one lunch period when she and I snuck off campus together; more for the sheer sport of it and not because we preferred Big Macs and fries over what they were serving in the cafeteria.

More than seven years after our last encounter I was still playing football except I was getting paid for it in a more advanced, rougher, more intense version. She had put her songleading days behind her and was carrying a beautiful baby girl who was not quite six months old. Also with the Redmon entourage was a three-year-old boy.

Darlene went from South Valley High to Rio Hondo Junior College for two years. She then transferred to UCLA where she began dating Lance. They were married after his rookie season during spring break of her senior year.

"This was the hardest game I've ever been to," Darlene remarked. "I was rooting for Lance while he was on the field and rooting for you while you were on the field. I don't know what it would have been like to have had you two on the field at the same time."

"I think you would have given Lance the nod," I retorted lightly.

"Well, yes, but I'm glad you had a good game although I'm not glad you won. It would be a lot easier for me if you and Lance were on the same team."

There wasn't much time to socialize. Introductions between the members of my family and the members of Lance's family who had never met, a few words, a few laughs, a few photos and then it was time to board the bus. I gave Lance my phone number so that he and I could link up when the Rams visited Hawaii about six weeks later and climbed aboard the bus that would transport my teammates and me to the airport.

It was a pleasant flight home. It was not necessarily festive since everybody was fairly tired but we were happy. The salmon was delicious; much better than the steak we had the week before on our flight from Miami. Food always had a way of tasting better after a victory.

CHAPTER TEN
The Vikings Come Ashore

It was not quite 1:30 on Tuesday morning when we touched down in Honolulu. By the time we taxied and unloaded at Air Service it was after two o'clock. I stayed and chatted with a few teammates but not for very long. At a little before three I entered my Hawaii Kai condo, set my suitcase down, got undressed and went right to sleep.

There wouldn't be much rest on my day off. I got up at about nine and took a shower before unpacking my suitcase. I drank some coffee and ate an apple while I did a little cleaning and vacuuming, watched a little TV, then went to the university to have lunch with Carol.

It wasn't easy sitting with Carol in the dining room of the student center. By this time I had become very recognizable. It was hard to eat and have a nice conversation with the woman I was trying to get to know again when there seemed like a perpetual flow of well-meaning students and faculty coming over to tell me what a great game it was the night before.

I understood.

Or at least I *tried* to understand. I smiled, gave the concise appropriate replies and tried to carry on. All the while I hoped the attention would not make Carol uncomfortable. It was almost as if she was invisible.

Carol had a bemused smile on her face. It was a new world for her, I suppose. As popular as she had always been, she wasn't one who craved attention. Her students addressed her as "Mademoiselle Lafayette" or simply "Carol." She was also commonly known around campus as "Jay Dockman's girlfrlend."

"You're a star," she remarked as I walked her to Moore Hall where she would teach a class a few minutes later.

I shook my head in bewilderment. Having scored a touchdown and passed for another the night before on national television, I suppose I was considered one of "the stars" of my team. I was concerned, though, that this might impede the chances for Carol and me to get our relationship on solid ground. We were doing fine together but it still seemed as if one negative experience might blow the entire thing. We were still walking on eggshells.

I spent a large part of the rest of the day at the TV studio. I suppose this was about the time that I began thinking of my show as a burden instead of an asset. If it had been a show where I had a special guest to ask questions to it would have been much more simple. Since it was a *sports highlight show* it took an awful lot of preparation which made it a distraction during the football season.

Of course this week's show would include highlights of our game from the night before. There would also be snippets of the University of Hawaii's game at Pacific. A large portion would also be dedicated to the baseball playoffs.

Videotaped highlights had been prepared. My job was to narrow it all down to fit into my show. We had very little available from the University of Hawaii game so their segment was a mixture of taped highlights and a preview of the upcoming game against Southern Mississippi. There wasn't much scoring between the Hawaiians and Rams so that wound up being five minutes of highlights and a minute of talking about the upcoming Viking game.

Each of the two baseball playoffs got six minutes. Another minute combined for my intro, close and introductions to commercial breaks. The remaining six minutes went to commercials.

I finished preparing with time to spare. I relaxed a little, got made up, did the show and then washed the makeup off. I then went down to the Columbia Inn, which was a block away, to have dinner while watching the end of the first game of the World Series which was satellite delayed. I already knew the score since I had been at the station and even had a segment where a graphic with the score appeared. I still felt compelled to watch. The Yankees beat the Dodgers, 4-3, when Paul Blair singled Willie Randolph home in the bottom of the 12th but it was only the first game. The game had its historical significance since it was the Yankees' 100th World Series victory. Unfortunately 28 of those were at the expense of my beloved Dodgers.

We had just won a hard-fought game. Walker wasn't too hard on us during Wednesday's film session. It was a huge test we'd passed by coming back after a tough loss to be a serious contender for the Super Bowl. It was also our first game against a team that had a winning record in 1976.

Walker pointed out mistakes. There were even times when he briefly became irritated. He also seemed to make a special point to point out good things.

"Wow, Marv. You really stuck it to that linebacker," Walker commented on a play where Marv moved a linebacker out with the ease of a pickup truck pushing a Volkswagen. "That's what I call an All-Pro block."

Shuford received an accolade a few plays later. One of his attributes was that he was very quick after snapping the ball.

"That's great, Dave!" Walker cried out. "Way to hustle off that snap!"

Hayer let a man through. Bender wound up scrambling for his life.

"Carl, I know it's got to happen like this on occasion," Walker said evenly. "I just hate to see it happen to you. You've been in the league too long."

It didn't make sense although Walker said it in a way that shouldn't have bothered Carl. Even the best linemen are going to get burned. To tell Carl that he'd been in the league too long to allow a blitzing defensive back to

218

penetrate is tantamount to telling Tommy John he'd been in the league too long to give up a home run. It happens.

"Look at this coming up," Walker directed as we prepared to receive a kickoff. "Watch Rossi . . . number 45."

Rossi turned in a highlight reel performance. He intercepted a Ram who was streaking downfield at a full clip. Rossi met him head on and threw a block that literally flipped the defender on his back. The Ram probably tried to vault over Rossi but it was hard to tell at the camera's angle from the top of the Coliseum.

It didn't hurt my ego when Walker gave glowing approbation to my touchdown pass to Dietrich.

"Beautiful, Jay! Beautiful! I've never seen you throw a more perfect pass. Ted," Walker continued lightly, "Jay made that catch too easy for you."

Walker was obviously happy with the way things went although his previous comment might have stung Ted a little even though he didn't mean it that way. It is obviously better to win a tough game than to lose one. This game was extremely tough. The Rams did not take us lightly.

When the film sessions ended the entire team got together, as always. Walker was still in a good mood but he still had a job to do. He gave us a sobering dose of reality.

"I was very impressed. You guys came back from a tough loss and beat the Rams."

Walker pointed out that we had a tougher challenge ahead.

"What you have to do from here on out is come back from Monday's victory. It is something you'll have to deal with all season long. Almost everybody from the 28 remaining teams was watching you on Monday night. You looked good and, believe me, they noticed. Everybody we see now from the Vikings to the Jets knows that they have to play you like it was Super Bowl Sunday if they want to beat you."

Walker paused. I wasn't sure if he was thinking of what to say next or if he was simply allowing his words to sink in. The room was silent until Walker spoke again. Nobody dared to even cough or clear his throat.

"Twice in your brief existence you have risen to the occasion on Monday night. Last year you beat the team that eventually won the Super Bowl on Monday night. Two nights ago you beat a team expected to be in the hunt for the Super Bowl. Everybody is impressed. I mean the entire NFL is impressed . . . and everybody who takes you on is going to turn up the heat. It'll be tougher now but I believe you can continue to win. Do you believe you can continue to win?"

We all responded with various enthusiastic words in the affirmative.

"Let's get to work," Walker directed.

It was only a light workout. It was, however, a very enthusiastic one. A lot of guys were emotionally ready to take on the Vikings that day.

I let go of football that evening. I spent the evening at Carol's. She made lasagna and we watched the second game of the World Series together.

The Dodgers put a smile on my face. They knocked Catfish Hunter out of the box in the third inning. It was almost as if they were getting back at Hunter for the 1974 World Series when he was still with Oakland. Ron Cey, Steve Yeager and Reggie Smith all hit home runs to do Hunter in. Steve Garvey added an anti-climactic home run later off of Sparky Lyle and Burt Hooten went the distance with a five-hitter.

It was a pleasure to watch. The series was tied at one game apiece and would be heading to Los Angeles. I figured the Dodgers could take at least two of the three games played in their home stadium. If they took all three it was all over. The notion of the Yankees winning all three at Dodger Stadium wasn't even remotely considered.

With a shortened week we only had two contact workouts. In my opinion they were very good workouts. Half-a-dozen workouts during the week would have been meaningless if we didn't execute well. We seemed very much in sync with a minimum of mistakes.

Walker seemed pleased. He criticized at times but not in a demeaning way. Primarily he encouraged us.

More specifically, he called on us to stay focused. That seemed to be the phrase of the week.

"Stay focused," he stressed more times than anybody could count. "Remember, stay focused."

As is always the case, injuries are a part of the game. Blakely was going to be out for a few weeks with a neck injury. Hasegawa would start in his place.

Jim McDaniel was listed as questionable with a sprained ankle. He would ultimately not play against the Vikings. Gavin Pratt would start at left defensive end with Jon Jurgens back in the starting lineup at right end. Safety Jim Vorsino, our ninth round draft choice from Indiana, would be activated from the taxi squad.

Scott's hamstring problem resurfaced. He was also listed as questionable and would wind up not playing. Ozzie would start in his place.

The team had its share of permanent changes. Joe Slater was being activated after being injured through the first four games. Schary, who had four receptions for 25 yards through the first four games, was waived and ultimately relegated to the taxi squad.

Also being activated was Hank Prendergast. He had also been injured through the first four games of the season. He would start at right defensive tackle against the Vikings.

Heading home was rookie defensive tackle Jess Palumbo. He had been signed as a free agent out of Texas and saw action on a couple of special teams but there was no longer any room for him. It was unfortunate although he could have accepted a post on the taxi squad when he cleared waivers but declined the offer.

"I guess I can say that I at least got here," he said in resignation, seemingly grateful for the opportunity. "I'll have to see if I can hook on elsewhere."

There were no takers, it would turn out. His NFL career lasted a total of four games. He wouldn't have even had that much had Prendergast not injured himself during the exhibition season. He wasn't a bad football player but only good enough to catch on if he got a lucky break. He ultimately became a minister in his hometown of Brownsville, Texas.

My old roommate called me on Thursday night. Bill and I talked frequently although we didn't see much of each other since we were no longer even living in the same part of town, let alone in the same condo.

This was a little more than a social call. Bill was from Burnsville, Minnesota, which was just south of Minneapolis. Since we were playing the Vikings on Sunday he had arranged to have the day off and needed a couple of tickets.

"Well, I don't know," I said lightly. "You're not going to be rooting for the enemy, are you?"

"Nah, I couldn't do that. I've got a couple of old teammates on the Hawaiians. I don't know anybody on the Vikings but I do like to see them play, even when I'm rooting against them."

"All right then. That sounds reasonable. Two tickets?"

"Yeah, two. I'll be taking Cherie."

I didn't want to judge but it amazed me that Cherie was still with Bill. I supposed their relationship had become more tranquil since it had become more casual. Cherie was no longer clinging to Bill like flypaper. He was no longer trying to get rid of her.

Just the same, I thought they would terminate their relationship before the end of the 1976 season and here it was a third of the way through 1977. Bill liked Cherie okay but didn't want anything permanent with her. Cherie was a very sweet, attractive young lady who could have had her choice among several good men but was madly in love with Bill. She backed off some because she knew that clinging to Bill would cause her to lose him completely. It still had to have torn her up to know that Bill was seeing other women.

Assuming she did know. I knew because Bill told me he was dating other women but I'm not sure Cherie knew.

It wasn't my place to tell Cherie what to do. I honestly believed, though, that she would have been a lot happier had she made a clean break from Bill and found somebody else.

Carol and I stayed in on Friday night. Normally we would have gone to a movie or something. This time we broiled a couple of steaks at my place. There was no way we were going out when the World Series was on TV.

Especially with the Dodgers involved.

The Dodgers' Dusty Baker lifted my spirits. His three-run home run in the third inning tied the game, 3-3.

Unfortunately that was essentially the extent of the Dodgers' offense. The Yankees picked up a couple more runs to give Mike Torrez a complete game victory. Tommy John pitched six innings, giving up all five Yankee runs in taking the loss for the Dodgers.

"They'll do it tomorrow," Carol said hopefully.

I looked at her and smiled. I had to believe she was right.

Throughout the week Sportswriter Ferd Borsch from the *Honolulu Advertiser* recruited players to take part in his World Series pool. The pool was for Sunday's game at Dodger Stadium which would run concurrently with our game against the Vikings. That way the winner could be announced after our game, assuming that the Dodgers and Yankees were finished with their game.

Ten dollars enabled an individual to arbitrarily choose a square on a sheet with ten squares vertical and ten horizontal to make 100 squares. When the sheet was finished numbers between zero and nine were drawn and lined up horizontally and vertically in the order they were selected. The winner would get 500 dollars and 500 dollars would go to charity.

The squares were completed by the end of our workout on Saturday. About 60 of the squares were purchased by players, coaches and staff members of the Hawaiians including our play-by-play duo of Les Keiter and Earl McDaniel with a few purchasing two or three squares. The remainder went to various members of the media and a few other people whom Borsch could recruit.

"Wow, look at the names of the people in on this," Hasegawa remarked. "Dave Donnelly, Aku, Tom Moffatt. . . ."

"Hey, Ted Sax," I added. "If he wins I hope he buys himself a new toupee."

"What? You don't like his current toupee?" Ferd asked jocularly, knowing as virtually everybody else did that the local radio personality's toupee was more like a hat of jet black hair that simply sat on his head and didn't fool anybody.

"Are you kidding?" I replied. "His toupee looks like something he got for 49 cents at Woolworth's. He could have found a more realistic toupee at a swap meet."

It might have seemed somewhat callous. Still, if Sax wanted a toupee to make people believe he wasn't bald he was going to have to spring for a much better toupee than the one he was wearing. He drove a luxury car but it was as if he only had pocket change for the toupee.

Ferd chose and arranged the numbers in front of us in the locker room. Marv cheered when he saw he had a three and a two since that seemed like a realistic score, at least if the Dodgers won since the Dodgers were on the horizontal section where Marv's three appeared. Bender groaned when he drew a one for the Dodgers and a nine for the Yankees since neither 9-1 nor 11-9 seemed likely. My square showed a zero for the Dodgers and a four for the Yankees.

"Geez, man," I groaned. "That means the Dodgers have to win 10-4 for me to win."

"Or the Yankees can win 4-0," Ferd suggested.

"Don't even joke about that," I replied half-facetiously. "The whole thing is worthless if the Dodgers don't win."

I also bought a square for Carol although I didn't plan to tell her right away. She drew an eight for the Dodgers and nine for the Yankees. I was hoping she wouldn't win unless the Dodgers actually managed to win by an 18-9 score. That seemed even more unlikely than the 10-4 that I needed.

After I showered and dressed I went to the hospitality room where a TV was set up. I was able to watch the second half of game four of the World Series which the Dodgers lost, 4-2. The Dodgers were down three games to one.

"I don't care if I win the pool or not," I said, knowing that a 10-4 score was almost hypothetical. "The Dodgers had just better win tomorrow."

How did I often spend the night before a home game?

Surprisingly enough, I usually went to University of Hawaii football games if the Rainbow Warriors were playing at home. I even had season tickets. If there was no other obligation Carol and I went whenever the Hawaiians were not on the road. If we were on the road Carol would still go, inviting a friend along.

Why did I go to football games that would end about 12 hours before the opening kickoff of games I was scheduled to play?

It sure beat sitting at home. I was going to have difficulty sleeping anyway. I might as well spend some time at Aloha Stadium watching my alma mater's team.

Had I played my home games in places such as Dallas, Los Angeles, New York or St. Louis I probably would have spent my Saturday nights involved in other activities. University of Hawaii football games, at least on a per capita basis among the local population, were significantly larger events.

Besides, this was the school where I had earned my bachelor's degree and was in the process of earning my master's. My girlfriend, who had once been a cheerleader at this same school before transferring to the University of Hawaii at Hilo, was employed as a French teacher at this school. We were indelibly connected to the university and fiercely loyal.

It wasn't unusual for me to run into teammates at these games. Bender and his wife were season ticket holders. Marv and his wife occasionally went, as did a few others.

The Rainbow Warriors were trying to rebound from their 3-8 1976 campaign. They were on the rise but still having a rough go. Against Southern Mississippi they were trying to overcome a 28-26 deficit in the final seconds. They lined up for a 27-yard field goal attempt.

It was no good. The kick was partially blocked. The Rainbow Warriors went down to defeat, proving that the rise to prominence would not come easy.

I left my place at a little before seven on Sunday morning. Depending on how many red lights I encountered on Kalanianaole Highway, it took 15-20 minutes to get to Carol's place.

It took about 15 minutes to get from Carol's place to the stadium. That contrasted the roughly ten minutes it took to get from the stadium to Carol's place. The reason for the difference was that one got right on the freeway from the stadium and the exit was right by Carol's condominium. Going to the game there was no onramp to the freeway by Carol's condo so I had to take Beretania to Punchbowl Street to get to the freeway.

Not that it was an inconvenience. It was simply the way it was. Carol happened to live right by the offramp but the nearest Ewa bound onramp was a few blocks, and a few traffic lights, away.

Of course my mind was on football. It was also on the World Series. The Dodgers had to win three in a row to win the championship. While the odds were against them, such a comeback was not unprecedented.

The Vikings won the toss. They chose to receive.

"Ah, what the hell," I said under my breath. I figured that someday I would learn to be more patient although probably not until after my career was over.

There was an air of confidence on the sideline as Guinn teed up the ball. I figured I might as well simply enjoy the experience. I was a pro football player. The fans in attendance had come to see my teammates and me play. I was there to entertain them by playing to the best of my ability.

Guinn kicked off when given the okay from the referee. The ball was fielded three yards deep in the south end zone. The return man did not hesitate to run it out.

I watched in horror as the return man ran freely up the field. Viking blockers were knocking my teammates out of the play. Before I knew it the return man was to the 30, then the 40 and then to midfield.

224

Suddenly the return man was hit from the side by Gavin Pratt. As the return man went down the ball squirted loose. Pratt lunged for the ball, as did a couple of Vikings.

It appeared to me that Pratt got to the ball first. It was primarily a matter of whether he maintained possession. As I nervously jumped up a few times the referee briefly sifted through the pile of humanity to. . . .

The referee stood erect and pointed toward the south end zone, producing a huge roar from the crowd and our sideline. Pratt had recovered the fumble that he caused at the Hawaii 47.

"Offense! Let's go!" Walker barked with a huge smile on his face as I was sprinting past him. It was as if I had to hurry on the field in case the officials changed their minds.

We broke out of the huddle smartly. We were 53 yards from an early lead. Dietrich was wide to the right. I was wide to the left a yard behind the line.

On the snap I ran a cross pattern. Dietrich ran a post. Bender set up in the pocket and got the pass off.

The ball was overthrown and intercepted at the Hawaii 29.

"Oh (expletive deleted)!" I said out loud near the Minnesota 40 before moving into position to encounter the enemy ball carrier.

The defensive back's momentum carried him back a few yards and then he charged forward. He managed to elude Dietrich's tackle attempt.

A defender tried to block me near the 40. I shook him off and then hammered the ball carrier at the 36. I hit him hard but clean.

I got up. As frustrated, if not angry, as I was, I still decided to be a good sport. I extended my hand to the defensive back whom I had just leveled and helped him to his feet. I really wanted to punch him out but. . . .

As I ran off the field I happened to notice the clock. There was 14:33 left in the first quarter. The game was 27 seconds old and already there were two turnovers on as many plays. If this was the beginning of a trend we may have been in contention for the sloppiest game in history.

The Vikings made good use of their first play from scrimmage. They completed a pass at the 50. The receiver got to the Hawaii 46 before Hasegawa brought him down.

They went to their ground game next. Up the middle for seven yards to the 39. That was followed by a sweep around left end. Jurgens caught the ball carrier two yards behind the line to make a third and five.

We went into a nickel defense with Dubois entering the game as a fifth defensive back. It was a pass situation but close enough to the first down to make a run a possibility. That was why we didn't go to a dime defense.

The Vikings went to the air. The quarterback spotted a receiver near his right sideline inside the 30 but Black picked the ball off at the 27, bringing the crowd and our sideline to our feet as we roared our approval.

"Yea, Mark!" I called. "Go, baby, go!"

Black picked up 12 yards to the 39. Five plays and three turnovers was the story of the game to this point.

"Let's do something with it this time," Walker directed somewhat sarcastically as the offense ran on the field. I silently concurred, hoping that this time we would be on the field for more than one play.

I was on the field for a total of *three* plays. A two-yard run by Ozzie was sandwiched by a pair of incompletions. In no time at all I was running off the field while the punting unit ran on. I hadn't shed a single drop of perspiration since the pregame warmup. Were we really the same team that outlasted the Rams six nights earlier?

Walker didn't say anything as the offense reached the sideline. He didn't have to. He stood with his jaw clenched as he glared at us. That said it all. The only thing noteworthy was it was the first possession by either team that didn't end with a turnover.

"What's wrong with us?" I asked Marv rhetorically at the Gatorade table.

"Nothing, really," He replied. "We've just got to wear them down. They're up for us but the heat and humidity will work against them. We'll be all right. Just be patient."

I don't know how accurate Marv's projection was that the heat and humidity would work against them. It didn't seem like something they could prepare for in Minneapolis but it seemed like something they should find a way to do the way we had to prepare to play in frigid conditions. The bottom line would always be which team had the better game.

Jablonski got off a decent punt. It was fielded at the 20. The return only went to the 25 before Eric Hamer brought him down.

The less than average yardage on the return was very encouraging. Unfortunately the Vikings took it in stride. Every other play netted them a first down. After three first downs they had the ball on the Hawaii 35.

They went to the air. Pratt jumped up and batted the ball forward. The ball hung up to give him a shot at an interception. He lunged and then stumbled forward but came up about a foot short, narrowly missing out on causing the Vikings' third turnover of the game and second caused by him less than halfway through the first quarter. Second and ten.

The Vikings passed over the middle next. The receiver caught the ball at the 22. He managed to run around Rodgers and was unmolested the rest of the way to the north end zone. With the extra point we were down 7-0 with 7:26 left in the first quarter.

Allen looked incredibly dejected as he left the field. It was understandable in most cases but not with Russ. He was the defense's holler guy who kept everybody fired up with his perpetual optimism. It was very unusual to see him hanging his head.

"We'll get it back," I told Russ before I ran out to take my place for the kickoff. After a quick huddle Hasegawa and I ran to the goal line of the north end zone.

226

"How're ya feeling?" I asked as we did our slap fives.

Rich shook his head.

"We gave them too much," he said. "They made it look too easy."

"We'll get it back," I said for the second time in about as many minutes. Although I was reasonably confident, I had to wonder if it was myself whom I was trying to convince. So far this game was incredibly bizarre.

The kick came my way. Barring a sudden stampede of buffalo coming out of the tunnel behind me, there was no doubt that I was going to run it out. I caught the ball a yard deep in the end zone and shot forward.

Good blocking helped justify the return. Hasegawa made a great block just inside the 15. He practically tackled a very swift Viking by lowering himself into the opponent's midsection without wrapping his arms around him so the block was perfectly legal. The Viking went down with Rich almost on top of him. I hurdled over both of them and was tackled at the 21.

On the surface it wasn't the kind of return that would compel me to write home. It was only a 22-yard return that was a mere yard longer than needed to justify the run from the end zone. I still felt as if I may have sparked something.

A short pass on the opening play produced four hard-fought yards. Bender hit Dietrich at the 22. Ted, with a cornerback and linebacker right there, got to the 25.

The Vikes gave us a nudge. A defensive tackle jumped and bumped Stanek. The encroachment penalty gave us a second and one at the 30. With the way we had been playing to this point we were grateful for the charity.

They still weren't going to make it easy on us. Kerner carried to the 31 but it took a herculean effort. No fewer than three white jerseys with purple and gold trim went down with Jeff.

"First down," I called, pointing toward the south end zone but the officials didn't seem to trust me. Time was called and the chain was brought out.

"I think they did a good job of spotting it this time," Bender remarked, recalling the times when we felt shortchanged.

The chain was stretched out. We were about two inches from a first down.

It was up to Ozzie. He carried up the gut. He was hammered at the line but, to his credit, his second effort got him to the 32. We had the first down. A few more of those and we could seriously consider the possibility of scoring.

We decided to grab a large chunk of the necessary yardage right away. Bender hit me near the left hashmark at the Hawaii 47. I was hit immediately but still managed to pick up two more yards. It was our best field position of the day to this point.

Ozzie got us to midfield on a 3 kama'aina left. He was having a hard time picking up yards although the game was still young. On three carries he had gained four yards.

We went back to the air. Bender hit Joe Slater on a slant at the Minnesota 45. Slater dodged his way to the 38. It was another first down; the third of the drive. As we headed to the huddle I took note of the enthusiastic cheers from the crowd.

A Kailua right produced nothing. Ozzie slammed into a solid wall for no gain. As frustrating as it was for my teammates and me, I really felt for Ozzie. He was getting a rare opportunity to start and was having little success. I didn't know it at the time but he was averaging exactly one yard per carry.

"It's all right. You'll get it next time," I told him as we moved to our huddle.

Ozzie said nothing. He didn't talk much anyway, rarely smiled and always looked angry. I could see and feel his frustration intensifying. One solid run and he should be cured.

A sweep around right end was solid since it gained seven yards. Unfortunately it was yours truly, not Ozzie, who carried. Ozzie threw a pretty good block that helped me get to the 31. I am sure he would have given anything to have had me throw the block while he picked up the seven yards.

"Good block, man," I said, slapping Ozzie on the back as I took my place next to him in the huddle. I hoped it helped lift his spirits.

Dietrich ran another slant pattern. He was actually at about the 26 when he caught the ball. Unfortunately his instincts caused him to arch back a little to try to get around a defender. He was hit and dropped at the 28.

Once again time was called to measure. Once again we were short. It was fourth and about a foot. Had Ted not arched back we would have had another first down. No doubt Ted was going to hear about it by Walker during Tuesday's film session.

About half-a-dozen of us made gestures to suggest to Walker that we wanted to go for it. The crowd got into it, too, when the animated cheerleader appeared on the scoreboard waving her pompoms from side to side over her head.

"Go! Go! Go! Go! Go! Go! Go! Go!"

Despite the substantial practice Guinn had been getting in kicking the ball into a portable net on the sideline, Walker decided to let us go for it. We went into our tight dotted "I" formation since it was obviously a run situation. Chester McCracken came in to be our left tight end and Dietrich went out. Grummon was tight on the right.

Kerner carried up the middle. He broke a tackle at the line. He broke another tackle at about the 25. He broke at least a couple more inside the 20 before going the final 15 yards untouched.

Nobody expected that. A single yard would have been fine. I ran through the line behind Kerner and laid a block on somebody inside the 25. By the time I could look up and see where Jeff was he was running the final ten yards to the roar of the crowd.

"Wow!" I cried out, raising my arms even before Jeff reached the end zone.

Guinn's practice session wasn't wasted. He split the uprights to tie the game at seven with 1:01 left in the first quarter.

The perspiration felt good. It was a top-quality drive. I helped myself to the best tasting cup of Gatorade I had had that day.

"Looking good. Looking good," Bennici commented, slapping some of us on the shoulder pads. "Just remember, there's still a long way to go. Offense, take it easy. Get some refreshment and take a seat. You need to conserve your energy."

It was sound advice, especially with the temperature in the 80s. After starting the season against two proverbial doormats we were squaring off against the better teams in the league. The Viking players watched us beat the Rams six days earlier and they were probably impressed, just as Walker said they would be. They were ready for us but I was hoping we would prove to be even more ready for them.

Guinn kicked off. The ball was fielded at the three. Our kickoff unit showed that it was ready. Westfall nailed the return man at the 13. It was another play that got the crowd to its feet and roaring.

That's not to mention Westfall's teammates and coaches.

"All right, Westfall!" was Walker's remark.

"Way to go, man!" Marv offered.

"That's the way to do it, rookie!" Dietrich remarked.

There were other compliments including my own. Westfall's play was truly a shot in the arm.

A one-yard rush and an eight-yard pass gave the Vikings a third and one at the 22. That ended the first quarter.

Allen came to the sideline to converse with Walker while the two teams switched ends of the field. The Vikings would now be moving toward the south end zone.

I took a moment to relax. From my seat I looked at the opposite side of the stadium. It was another sold out crowd with very few no shows, it seemed. The fans in the seats displayed a wide assortment of colors. Unlike the way the fans would have to dress in Minneapolis, a lot of our male fans were shirtless while some of our female fans wore bathing suit tops. The rest were in other attire befitting a tropical environment with not a single jacket, sweater, pair of gloves or wool cap in sight.

When play started in the second quarter the Vikings seemed rejuvenated. They picked up two first downs on four rushing plays, the latter of which had them at their own 36.

Pratt was shaken up on the preceding play; a rush up the middle that got them the yard the Vikings needed for the first down after a measurement following the previous play came up short. Pratt got the wind knocked out of him. McWherter replaced him for a few plays.

Our defense decided that the Vikings had gone far enough. Calling for a pass, the quarterback was forced to scramble when Jennings and Zanakis put on a heavy rush. The fullback blocked Zanakis out of the play but Jennings caught the quarterback and brought him down at the 28. Second and 18.

That's the kind of play the crowd loves. One could hear the crowd roaring its encouragement while Ed chased the quarterback. There was a dramatic crescendo when Ed caught up with him and took him down.

The drive was essentially over. Two incompletions and I was back on the field. I stood at about the Hawaii 30 to field a punt.

It was a better punt than I anticipated. I had to back up a little to get under it. I caught it at the 27 and charged forward.

I made a good return. I dodged a few opponents as I headed toward midfield. One Viking finally came up on my right and tackled me but I had already gotten to the Hawaii 41. It was a 14-yard return.

The punt return, unfortunately, was the highlight of the drive. Three plays later we had fourth and two at the Hawaii 49. I ran off the field with the rest of the offensive unit while the punting team ran on.

"We sure screwed that up," I said bitterly after I grabbed a cup of Gatorade and sat on the bench next to Scott who was watching the game in street clothes except for his game jersey.

Larry shook his head and then smiled.

"You've got to try to look on the bright side," he said. "If Jablonski does this right you'll have them pinned back inside the 20."

Jablonski did his job right. He punted away from the return man and really got his foot into it. The ball went out of bounds at the six. The Vikings definitely had their work cut out for them.

The defense did it right, surrendering only five yards on three plays. Before I knew it I was back on the field near the Hawaii 45 anticipating a punt return.

There wouldn't be a return. The punter accidentally kicked the ball off the side of his foot. The ball went out of bounds at the Vikings 39. Perhaps that was a sign that we were going to start pulling away.

As soon as it was obvious that the punt was shanked the crowd let out a huge roar. It was great to have the crowd in our corner. It also suggested that our fans would never forgive us if we didn't score this time. It was bad enough starting a drive at the Hawaii 41 and going nowhere like we did before. This time we were 20 yards closer to the end zone and not scoring would mean being shut down on two consecutive series which started with outstanding field position. We absolutely had to score.

Two incomplete passes later we faced third and ten. There was an air of frustration in the huddle. That air of frustration was probably also prevalent in the bleachers. We were on the threshold of doing the aforementioned unforgivable.

Bender brought the crowd back to life when he hit Slater with a pass at the 18. Joe scooted to the eleven where he was brought down.

"Okay, that's just what we needed. We will take it all the way in this time," Bender encouraged confidently before he called the next play.

Kerner carried up the middle on that play. He could only managed one hard-fought yard.

It was back to the air again. I was nine yards deep in the end zone when Bender hit me with a perfect spiral. I was hit simultaneously by a defensive back but managed to hang on to the ball. We had the lead for the first time that day.

I bounced up and spiked the ball, then got bear hugs from Dietrich and Grummon. We ran off the field in triumph as the crowd continued to roar.

"Good job, men," Walker cheered as we reached the sideline. "Marv, Dave, good job. Great catch, Jay. Jeff, Ozzie, Clint, good job."

The PAT was good. We led 14-7 with 4:11 left in the half.

I felt good. I also knew I had to guard my optimism. The Vikings were more than capable of tying it up before halftime. They were also more than capable of *taking the lead* before halftime.

Guinn's kick was eight yards deep in the end zone. The return man didn't bother.

"No guts. No guts," Kerner said lightly. He didn't realistically expect the return man to try to return a kick so deep in the end zone. It was simply indicative of how having the lead enabled us to be not quite so tight.

The Vikings picked up a couple of first downs. They crossed midfield and had a second and seven at the Hawaii 41 as we neared the two-minute warning. They went to the air.

Dubois picked the pass off at the Hawaii 31. He made a diving catch and managed to get up before being touched. He got to the Hawaii 44 before being hit and dropped.

This had us hyped. It was a great way to kick off the final two minutes of the half. We could go into the locker room with a two-touchdown lead if we didn't screw it up. Officially there was 1:51 left in the half.

Bender conversed with Walker and then presided over the huddle. We were going to start by going to the air.

The Vikings seemed to know that. They put a hard rush on Bender. I ran downfield and turned to look for the ball. Instead I saw Bender trying to scramble. He was finally run out of bounds at the 39. It was second and 15. There was 1:40 showing.

We more than made up for the sack on the next play. Bender had to scramble again although this time he got away. He hit me at the Minnesota

49. I danced a slight jig to get past a defender, then dodged and weaved around a couple more. I ran out of bounds at the 41 to stop the clock at 1:26. We had a first down.

Ozzie swept around right end. He picked up four yards to the 37. We called timeout with 1:18 left.

That was as far as we got. Heavy pressure led to a pass to Dietrich that was batted away. Bender was then sacked at the Minnesota 44. This being fourth and 13, the Vikings called timeout. There was exactly one minute left.

The punting unit ran on the field. I ran off with the rest of the offense. I felt frustrated by our inability to blow the Vikings away. I sometimes found it hard to accept the fact that we weren't going to score touchdowns every time we had the ball.

Jablonski did his part. His punt hit the ground inside the ten. As the crowd roared its approval, Hasegawa downed the ball at the one. There were 53 seconds left in the half.

That may have made the Vikings sorry they called timeout. They were obviously pinned back. Unless they could get at least one first down, we were certain to get the ball back in good field position. We had two timeouts left.

The Vikings went up the middle and managed only a yard. We called timeout with 46 seconds left.

A rush off right tackle produced no gain. At the same time the tight end started mixing it up with Zanakis. The Vikings were cited for unsportsmanlike conduct. Since the infraction took place while the play was going on it was not a dead ball foul. We declined the penalty since accepting it would have set them back only a yard and given them another down, destroying whatever hope we had of getting the ball back.

The clock was running. The Vikings would still need to get a play off. If we could stop the play quickly enough we could get a punt return since we had one timeout left that we could use after the following play. Depending on how much time was left after we called time, it was possible to simply make a fair catch of the punt and try a *Hail Mary* pass.

What we were hoping was that the Vikings would attempt a pass. Their quarterback was very quick and agile but we still wanted a shot at sacking him in the end zone. It would only be two points but that would make it a two-score game. The two points could very well be the difference at the final gun.

The Vikes ran up the middle. Allen was waiting for the ball carrier.

"Fumble!"

This was better still. If we could recover this close to the end zone. . . .

The Vikings recovered at the three. It was fourth down. We called time with five seconds left. Special teams coach Ken Holcomb called the punt return unit together.

"I want an all-out blitz," Holcomb directed. "Every lineman and linebacker shoot through as fast as you can. We've got nothing to lose if we get called for roughing the punter."

Holcomb looked at me.

"Jay, if they get the punt off you've got to bring it all the way back. The odds are against it but it can be done. Give it your best shot."

We ran on the field. I stood near the Minnesota 45. My adrenalin was pumping. I couldn't stand the thought of going into the locker room with a mere 14-7 lead. One way or another, I felt that we had to score at least a safety on this final play.

"Hukilau! Hukilau!" I could hear coming from my teammates near the line of scrimmage, suggesting to the Vikings that a blitz may be coming. In this case it was definitely true.

The snap was succeeded by our blitz. The Vikings anticipated the blitz and provided good protection for the punter. McWherter still managed to get through and made a diving attempt to block the punt. He barely missed but also did not draw a foul.

I backed up a couple of steps and caught the ball at the Minnesota 48. I managed to run away from one white jersey inside the 45 but more were on the way. There were eleven men of various sizes with a single objective to pulverize the guy with the ball. That would be me.

Somehow I managed to break a tackle near the 35 and continue my quest to reach the north end zone. I was hit again and fought to remain upright. While in the grasp of the man who hit me I was aware of being hit again and again. I was helpless as I went down at the 30.

Two of my tacklers bounced up and ran toward their locker room. The third rose more slowly and reached down to take my hand. I didn't notice anything about him except that he was Black and the size of a lineman. He pulled me to my feet and whacked my derriere.

"Good try, man. That was a great effort."

"Thanks," I replied as the Viking left to join his colleagues.

"Are you all right?" Zanakis asked as he reached me on his way from the line of scrimmage to the locker room.

"Yeah, I'm okay," I replied somewhat wearily. "I sure wanted to take it in, though."

Zanakis and I joined the rest of our teammates in heading toward the south end zone where the tunnel to our dressing room was located. Our fans gave the team a warm round of applause.

After relieving myself and drinking a cup of Gatorade, I opened a Dr. Pepper that I found and drank it while sitting in front of my locker. The Vikings were proving themselves to be a very tough opponent.

Of course it made sense. The Vikings to this point seemed to have been the most formidable team in the NFC if not the entire NFL in the 1970s to this point. Of the eight Super Bowls played in the 70s, including the 1970

Super Bowl for the 1969 season, the Vikings represented the NFC in half of them. Naysayers would point out that the Vikings lost all four of their Super Bowl appearances. Veterans of teams such as the Lions, Bears, Chargers, 49ers and Rams, as well as the Hawaiians, would point out that at least the Vikings got there.

Although past history should not be a factor in what is going on currently, the Vikings were displaying the talent that made them one of the NFL's most elite teams. While we were thrilled to have broken even in our maiden season, the Vikings finished that same season at 11-2-1. That was the best record in the NFC and second only in the NFL to Oakland's 13-1. It seemed fitting that Oakland was the team to beat them in Super Bowl XI.

It was going to be a tough second half. At least we knew we were capable of beating the tough teams. We proved that six days earlier in Los Angeles. To prevail against the Vikings would prove that Monday night was no fluke.

"Men, you know what you have to do," Walker reminded us just before an official came in to let us know we had two minutes left in halftime. "You've played them tough through the first 30 minutes. You need to continue for 30 minutes more. I want them to leave here believing that Hawaii isn't a very nice place to visit. Let's go get 'em."

I stood on the goal line of the south end zone as I awaited the kickoff to start the second half. The attendance would be reported to be 49,443. I looked around the stadium and marveled at how this was possible a little less than two years after pro football seemed to be completely dead in Hawaii. We were no longer battling the Southern California Sun or Jacksonville Express or Portland Storm in the struggling World Football League. Hawaii's pro football entity was now battling the best the NFL had to offer. That meant the best any football league had to offer.

On the opposite side I could see the large scoreboard that hung directly above the blue level of the north end zone. The scoreboard showed Hawaii leading the Vikings 14-7. Such a display could have meant the University of Hawaii was leading the Portland State Vikings and the Rainbows would be playing Portland State at Aloha Stadium six nights later. In this case it meant Hawaii's NFL entity was leading the defending NFC champs.

A wave of well-being swept over me. I was part of an organization providing entertainment for almost 50,000 on hand. That's not to mention the millions watching throughout Hawaii, Minneapolis and several other locales. With our Monday night victory over the Rams complementing our status as the *expansion wonder team* and Minnesota's status as the defending NFC champs, this game was very much in demand. We were televised in several markets, especially those with no other NFL teams in the vicinity.

This was one of those moments when I truly appreciated the significance of being a pro football player. It had nothing to do with winning or losing. It was simply about giving my best and savoring the moment.

I saw the red shirt pinwheel his arm in a small circle to let the referee know that CBS was back before returning to the makai sideline. The referee blew his whistle. The Viking kicker approached the ball.

It was coming my way. I called for it while Hasegawa ran ahead to block. I caught the ball three yards deep in the end zone and brought it out without a second thought.

At about the 15 I spotted a couple of white jerseys on my right and cut left. It was enough to get past them. As I crossed the 20 I met a white jersey I couldn't elude. I was brought down at the 22.

The Vikings wasted no time in showing why they were in contention for their fifth Super Bowl. Kerner went up the middle and received a rude reception of white jerseys for no gain.

Abraham, who spent five years with the Vikings before being taken in the 14th round of the expansion draft, helped his former teammates by jumping prior to the next snap. It was second and 15 at the 17.

Ozzie picked up four yards on a sweep around left end and then we went to the air. Bender hit me near the right hashmark at the 39. A defensive back made a desperate dive at me. He caught me just right, flipping me over at the 42. The films would indicate that had he not caught me I probably would have gone all the way.

A seven-yard completion to Dietrich, a batted down pass to Grummon and a nine-yard sack climaxed the drive. It was fourth and 12 at our own 40. The offense was forced to surrender to the punting unit.

"I know we can't go the distance every time," I remarked in exasperation to Shuford by the Gatorade table. "We still need to do it once or twice more if we want to win this game."

"I hear ya," he agreed. "These guys are no slouches. We'll just have to find the key during the next drive."

Jablonski got off a good punt. It traveled 41 yards to the 19. The Viking return man headed upfield. He got past Hasegawa and Hamer before McCracken drove him down at the 31.

Whatever well-being I was feeling a few minutes earlier was forgotten. I had confidence in our defense. I also knew that the Vikings were capable of moving against anybody.

A pair of rushes gave them a third and three at the 38. Whatever hope I may have had of our defense preventing the first down were dashed when Pratt got called for encroachment. That gave the Vikings a first down at the Minnesota 43.

"Dammit, Pratt! What the hell kind of football is that?" Walker bellowed. "We could've stopped them if you hadn't given them a free pass!"

No doubt Pratt felt pretty bad anyway. Walker's impetuous words did not lift his spirits. Pratt was a very aggressive player and sometimes aggressiveness can be an impediment.

The Vikings completed a pass at about the Hawaii 45. The receiver straight-armed Morrissey and got to the 39 before Hasegawa brought him down.

"Come on, defense!" I barked although I almost felt like a hypocrite. I felt as if my words might be taken as critical of the defense after the offense failed to score. Of course I was actually trying to encourage the defense but it may have sounded like criticism under the circumstances.

Regardless of my intentions, our defense dug in after that. The defense limited the Vikings to four yards on two rushes, giving them a third and six at the Hawaii 35. A pass inside the 20 fell incomplete when Hasegawa hit the receiver just as the receiver got his hands on the ball, forcing the receiver to lose control.

"Fumble!"

Rodgers fell on the ball near the 25. At the same time there were officials blowing whistles and waving their arms in front of them to signal an incomplete pass. They ruled that the receiver never had possession. From where I stood it appeared that the officials had called it correctly. I had simply hoped that they would blow the call.

Suddenly my eyes fell on a yellow flag near the line of scrimmage. Somebody had committed an infraction. It was simply a matter of who.

It was against the Vikings. A wide receiver had lined up too far forward. The referee was explaining it to Allen who looked over at Walker.

Walker waved his arms in front of him to indicate that we should decline the penalty. On fourth down the Vikings could either attempt a field goal of about 52 yards, punt to try to pin us back or try to pick up the six yards they needed for a first down.

They sent their punting unit out. I was sure they would go for the field goal. My next guess was that they would go for the first down but they opted for my third choice.

Which brought up another possibility. Just because their punting unit was on the field didn't mean they were going to punt. There was a good possibility of a fake.

I took my place at the ten. Walker considered not sending the punt return unit out, then thought better of it. He told me to charge in the very minute the punter showed a sign of a fake. If he did punt he wanted me to return it if I could. Otherwise he wanted me to try to prevent the Vikings from downing the ball near the goal line.

The Vikings surprised me by not faking the punt. It was a deliberately short punt slightly to my left in hopes of pinning us back. I held my arm up as a decoy, then let the ball drop behind me. I laid a block into the mid-section of the wideout as he charged downfield, knocking him to the side and causing him to lose his balance and fall. I looked back and saw the ball bouncing out of the back of the end zone. We had a first down at the 20.

We had the lead and needed some insurance. It was important that the offensive unit hunker down and travel the 80 yards. Not only would that get us another score but it would give the defense an opportunity to rest.

Bender got us off to a good start in a strictly unplanned fashion. He dropped back to pass and met a heavy rush. Somehow he managed to scramble away and pick up six yards before being forced out of bounds.

After an incompletion Bender hit Grummon at the 28. Rich made a very determined effort to get all the way to the 41 before being brought down. We were on our way.

Or so I believed. Bender dropped back on the next play and met another heavy rush. He scrambled again but was sacked at the 38.

Bender never let a little thing like a sack get to him. He came out firing on the next play, hitting me at the Hawaii 48. I scooted past midfield to the Minnesota 47. We had another first down.

Ozzie followed with his best run of the day. He went off right tackle and barreled through the defense. He wound up with a 13-yard gain to the 34. We were in field goal range.

Needless to say, the crowd was impressed and very vocal in its support. I suppose the fans had been cheering all along but this was the first time I noticed it during this drive. It was the type of thing that happened throughout my entire career where my focus would be exclusively on the field and all of a sudden it would dawn on me that we had the crowd behind us.

I also caught a glimpse of the Minnesota sideline. There were several bewildered expressions among players and coaches.

The Viking defense wasn't throwing in the towel. It put a hard charge on Bender. Steve got a pass off toward Grummon in front of the Viking sideline but it fell incomplete.

Bender rebounded and hit Dietrich at the Viking 24 near the right sideline. Ted was hit immediately but his second effort got him to the 22.

I tried to block them out but again couldn't help noticing the crowd. The cheers washed over me. The fans I happened to see had radiant expressions on their faces. We were giving them what they paid for.

The following play humbled the crowd a little. Ozzie went up the middle but was dropped a yard behind the line.

Kerner raised the crowd's hopes again. He went off left tackle and plowed the road. He was finally tackled at the 12. A measurement showed us with another first down. Kerner absolutely amazed me sometimes.

Following an incompletion out of the end zone Bender attempted another pass and was forced to scramble. He was hit pretty hard and dropped at the eight. The crowd let out a very conspicuous gasp at the sight of the tackle but Steve bounced up. It was third and six.

We were virtually guaranteed a field goal. At the risk of sounding redundant, I didn't want to settle for a field goal.

Perhaps that was what motivated me when I ran a sweep around right end. I was determined to take it all the way. A cornerback hit me head on, keeping me a yard short of my goal. We still had a first down at the one.

I guess my ego was bruised a little. Once I got to within three feet of the end zone I felt obligated to score. Although I didn't show it, I was frustrated about not making it.

Whatever frustration I felt was erased on the following play. Ozzie got another call. Straight up the middle. . . .

Touchdown!

I leaped with joy when the officials' arms went up. Our fans also leaped up, roaring their approval. A round of cannon fire would not have been as loud as our crowd.

Ozzie had done a great job of leaping over the goal line. He jumped up, spiked the ball and almost seemed to actually smile as he ran toward the sideline with the rest of the offensive unit. There was 1:37 left in the quarter.

We were exuberant on our sideline as we watched Guinn split the uprights. Our lead had expanded to 21-7. It was now our well-rested defense's turn to shine.

I grabbed a cup of Gatorade and stood next to Shuford.

"We have to hold 'em for 16 minutes and 37 seconds," I remarked.

The tall baby-faced center from Notre Dame looked at me and smiled.

"I think our defense can hold 'em off," he said.

"Me, too. If we can score once more we can just about put them away."

The clock was becoming a factor. Even if the Vikings scored a sustained drive by either team would knock a lot of time off the clock. If we could score again it would also force the Vikings to focus on one extra score even if we had to settle for a field goal.

Guinn's kick was four yards deep in the end zone. The Vikings didn't bother trying to return it.

"Ah, come on!" Shuford and I cried out in unison. We looked at each other and momentarily broke up.

The Vikings still weren't laying down. By the time the third quarter ended they had rushed for seven yards to the 27, picked up a first down on a 14-yard pass to the 41 and rushed four yards to their own 45. They would start the final quarter with a second and six.

I was feeling antsy. I sat on the bench next to Marv as I wiped the perspiration off my face with a towel.

"You'd think I'd get used to this," I remarked. "My stomach is tied up in knots."

"I hear ya, brother. I feel the same way. I keep looking at that scoreboard and wish the time would suddenly run out. We're still in a lot

238

better shape than the Vikings, though. It's better to be leading by two touchdowns than chasing two touchdowns."

Marv was obviously right. The Vikings were still one of the teams one did not count out when trailing by two touchdowns at this juncture but it was a lot better to be on our side of the scoreboard.

To start the fourth quarter the Vikings managed to rush for a mere two yards to their own 47. They then passed over the middle to about the 45. Hasegawa brought the receiver down at the Hawaii 43. The Vikings had a first down. The clock was ticking but there was still a little more than 14 minutes left.

"Please, turn it over," I muttered softly. Marv still heard me.

"Hang in there, Jaybird," he said with an amused grin on his face. "They're not going to catch us."

"Are you sure?" I asked lightly.

Marv looked at me, still sporting the grin.

"Not completely," he admitted. "We're still in great shape."

A rush up the middle netted only two yards. The Vikings then decided to go to the air.

Zanakis charged in. The quarterback rolled to his right. As the quarterback was about to cock his arm Kevin nailed him from behind at the Hawaii 47. It was amazing that the quarterback held on to the ball.

Had I not been watching the play I still would have known something special had gone our way. The sudden roar of the crowd would have tipped me off.

The quarterback survived Zanakis's charge. There was a question of whether Zanakis had survived. He was limping a little as he headed to the huddle.

"Zanakis! Are you all right?" Walker called.

Zanakis casually waved in Walker's direction and took his place in the huddle. It appeared to be something one could simply walk off. I'd had more than my share of those little dings in both football and baseball.

On third and 14 we knew a pass was coming.

"Hukilau! Hukilau! How about a little Hukilau?" Allen called out.

In this case it was a decoy. There was a rush but no blitz. The quarterback got the pass off over the middle. Rodgers was there to knock it down near the 30.

There was 12:47 left. We were about to get the ball back while still holding a two-touchdown lead. Jubilantly I took my place on the ten.

Walker had told me to play conservatively. That meant not attempting to return anything inside the ten and not attempting to field anything I wasn't certain I could field cleanly. It was common sense but sometimes a coach has to point out the obvious in order to do his job properly.

The punt was well to my left. It was a soft punt that bounced near the sideline inside the 15. I ran up and blocked one man but another got through. The ball was downed at the five.

"(Expletive deleted)," I muttered. "I guess I'm going to have to figure a way to block two men at once."

It was frustrating but I accepted it. The important thing was we had the ball and having to start so deep in our own territory could work to our advantage. A good drive would chew up a lot of the clock. We were reaching that point where the clock was becoming more and more significant. If we managed to score on a sustained drive the game would be all but officially over.

"Let's put it away," Bender said as we formed our huddle. "A 95-yard drive would pretty well do it."

It didn't appear as if we would chew up much of the clock. Kerner managed only a yard up the middle and I picked up five off right tackle to give us a third and four at the eleven. That changed to third and nine at the six when Hayer jumped too soon.

Nobody felt worse than Hayer. The trick was to get the first down and put the faux pas behind us. Otherwise the Vikings would have an opportunity to get back into the game with pretty good field position.

We achieved our objective on a play-action fake. Bender faked a handoff to Roberts and then hit Dietrich on a cross pattern over the middle at the 28. Ted turned upfield and got to the 34 before going down.

That was a huge relief. A sustained drive, even if we didn't score, would not only consume a lot of time but it would frustrate the Viking offense which was dying to get back on the field.

Ozzie showed his potential with runs of seven and three yards.

"Good job, Ozzie," Kerner lauded as he and I helped Ozzie to his feet.

"Way to fight your way forward," I chimed in.

The clock was stopped for a measurement. We wound up with a first down at our own 44.

Kerner went off right tackle to the 50. I then went around left end to the 47 to put us in a third and one. We figured the Vikings would be looking for Ozzie on the next play.

"Two Wahiawa left," Bender directed.

Bender handed off to Kerner. The Viking defense plugged the middle pretty well. Kerner spotted a slight opening off left tackle even though it was not his primary target and shot through. He got to the Viking 45 to give us a first down with a yard to spare by running to daylight.

We had the momentum. It felt great. The longer we held the ball, the more that time would be on our side.

The Vikings had other ideas. This was not a team that came to Hawaii wearing pink panties. The defense stopped Ozzie up the middle for no gain.

240

They then put a heavy rush on Bender but Steve still got a quick pass off to Grummon at the 39.

A cornerback brutally leveled Grummon on the spot. Third and four.

We went to the air one more time. Bender fired a pass to me near the 25. I went up for the ball on the run and collided with a safety who also wanted the ball. I managed to get my hands on the ball but couldn't control it. The ball and I hit the ground simultaneously and rolled in opposite directions.

Dietrich was the first one to me. I was lying on my back and looked straight up into his face.

"Are you all right, Jay?" he asked.

"I can't believe they let a tractor-trailer rig on the field," I remarked dryly as I rose to my feet.

The field goal unit ran on the field. The offensive unit reluctantly ran off.

"It's all right," Walker said as we reached the sideline. "It was a good drive. They did a good job in stopping you but you gained a lot of yards and chewed up a great deal of the clock."

That was, once again, a critical point. What we needed was for Guinn to convert on the field goal attempt. That would make it a three-score game. It wouldn't slam the door on the Vikings but it would bring us closer to that point.

Billingsley knelt down at the 46. It would be a 56-yard attempt. If he converted it would be Guinn's longest field goal of the season by four yards.

Arroyo snapped the ball right on target. Billingsley got it down. With the wind at his back Guinn got the kick off toward the south end zone. The crowd roared as if to encourage the ball on its course.

"Go! Go! Go!"

The latter exclamations came from my mouth. I suppose I thought that the ball would listen to me. If Mark Fidrych could talk to baseballs, why couldn't I talk to footballs?

The kick had the distance. Unfortunately the officials waved their arms in front of them. The ball was wide to the left. The Vikings would take over on their own 39. They had 6:58 left to try to put together two scores but they had to be touchdowns. A field goal would be of no use to the Vikings unless they got a third possession.

"It's okay, man," I said to nobody in particular as I stood by the Gatorade table. "It's still our game to win."

My morale had dropped substantially. I wasn't angry at anybody but was extremely downtrodden about our inability to ice the game away. A two-touchdown lead at this point was very reassuring but had we made that field goal it might have sunk the Vikings' ship.

A pair of incompletions stopped the clock and left the Vikings in a third and ten. If we could stop them we could run almost all of the time off the clock. We may have already wore down the Viking defense so extending the lead was a possibility.

The Vikings played it correctly. They sent their receivers out to just beyond the first down marker. The quarterback hit a receiver at the 50 in front of our bench. Black hit him immediately to prevent him from going out of bounds to stop the clock.

Minnesota decided to mix it up. The Vikings rushed three yards off left tackle to the Hawaii 47. They came back with a pass over the middle at the 35. The receiver picked up two more yards before Rodgers and Hasegawa teamed up to bring him down. They were 99 feet from a score. The clock was running and showed less than four minutes.

We had been in our 33-nickel defense. Walker called the 23 dime as further protection against the pass. Black, Morrissey, Dubois, Hasegawa and Rodgers manned the defensive backfield in the nickel with Jurgens, Richards and Pratt on the line and Jennings, Allen and Zanakis at linebacker. With the switch to the dime Eric Hamer went in and Norm Richards came out.

The Vikings hoped to take advantage of our depleted line by rushing off right tackle. Jennings stopped the running back at the 29.

My heart was pounding. A Viking score would still have us leading by a touchdown. I preferred to keep our lead as it was. The missed field goal could prove to be critical.

We switched to the 32 dime with Prendergast going in and Zanakis coming out. Prendergast wasted no time in making his mark and drawing approbation from the crowd. He sacked the quarterback at the 36. It was third and 13.

"Yeah! Way to go, Hank!" I yelled.

"Yea, Hanky baby!" Marv cried out.

"Way to hustle, Hank!" Bender called.

The Vikings used their first timeout. The clock was down to 2:44.

I was jittery. I was also having the time of my life. Although the outcome was still in doubt, I became more confident in our chances the more the clock wound down. That made me feel progressively more giddy.

We went to our 31 quarter to make it even harder for the Vikes to get a first down through the air. Jurgens, Prendergast and Pratt stayed on the line while Allen was the lone linebacker. The newly activated safety Jim Vorsino joined the other defensive backs.

The Vikings tried a pass underneath over the middle. Allen leaped up and got a hand on it, knocking the ball to his right. The ball dropped incomplete to stop the clock at 2:37. It was now fourth and 13.

Our fans were enjoying the game. They were still very vocal in their support. Of course they were always happy when we won. This was one of our more exciting games.

Since we were at the point where we could eat up virtually all of the clock if we got the ball back, the Vikings had no choice but to try to go for the first down. As was mentioned previously, a field goal was of no use to them and they knew it. They didn't get to the most recent Super Bowl by being stupid.

I think everybody on our sideline was standing. Several of us on the sideline and on the field flapped our arms up to encourage the crowd to let out a raucous roar to make it hard for the Vikings to hear their signals. Our fans were only too happy to comply.

The snap was made. The Viking receivers ran to near the 20. With Allen putting pressure on the quarterback the quarterback tried to hit a receiver near the left sideline. Dubois knocked the pass away, drawing another huge roar from the crowd.

"Yeah!" I cried out, jumping in place.

"Offense!" Walker called.

As the offensive unit ran to the field, slapping fives with any defensive colleagues who crossed paths with us, Walker briefly conversed with Bender. With 2:29 left Walker was probably reminding him that we still needed to pick up a couple of first downs to manage the clock effectively. The Vikings had two timeouts and the two-minute warning in their corner.

Kerner managed only a yard off right tackle. The Vikings called time with 2:23 left.

Ozzie went off left tackle when play resumed. It was a very inspiring effort. He broke two tackles before going down at the Hawaii 46.

Time was called by the officials. We were close to a first down. The chain was brought out. It came down about a third of the way from the rear of the ball. The referee majestically stood erect and pointed toward the south end zone, producing another roar from the crowd.

The Vikings used their final timeout in what now was a virtually hopeless case for them. The clock showed 2:14.

Bender went over to the sideline to talk to Walker. I looked at my colleagues in the huddle. Although we were not incapable of screwing things up and blowing the game, nobody seemed to believe it was possible. There were about ten smiles in the huddle.

I glanced up in the bleachers and spotted Carol. She looked absolutely beautiful, as always. She was very casually dressed in a pair of blue denim shorts, a blue women's T-shirt and her hair held back with a barrette. I still found it hard to believe that my college girlfriend was back in my life.

Sitting two seats away from Carol was my former college teammate, and former roommate, Bill Trimble. I was hoping the Minnesota native was enjoying our apparent conquest of the team he had rooted for ever since its inception in 1961. He seemed to be engaged in conversation with Carol and his girlfriend Cherie who sat between Carol and him.

When play resumed Ozzie went up the middle for two yards to the 48. The clock ran down to the two-minute warning.

"Keep it cool," Marv reminded everybody in the huddle while Bender talked to Walker on the sideline again. "We haven't put it away yet."

What Marv was also saying was to not gloat. It was tough on the Vikings. We didn't need to rub their noses in it.

On the first play after the break I ran a sweep around right end. Thanks to a convoy of blockers I crossed midfield to the Minnesota 46. I also made it a point to stay in bounds to keep the clock running. It was third and two.

Grant Collier, in for Kerner, went off right tackle for two yards. Time was called with 1:22 left to measure.

It seemed anti-climactic this time. For the record, we had the first down. The clock started up again.

"That's it," Bender reported in the huddle. He took three snaps and dropped down to run out the clock.

As our fans counted down the final ten seconds we shook hands with our opponents and their coaches. They were gracious. I didn't envy them their long flight to Minneapolis.

It was a good victory. Any victory is good, of course, but this was a little extra special since we had played one of the NFL's best and we had to win without our primary running back. Ozzie filled in adequately and everybody hoped that would give him the confidence he needed if called upon again.

Vorsino gave the postgame prayer. Walker then held up the game ball.

"It's not easy having to fill in," he said. "It's very gratifying to press somebody into service and see him do a good job."

Walker tossed the ball to Ozzie amid the usual chorus of cheers.

Ozzie's stats weren't spectacular. He had 15 carries for a reasonably respectable 50 yards. Scott would have had better stats although Ozzie did have some quality carries that were keys to our success. Nobody could say he didn't play an overall good game.

Kerner had an excellent game. He carried ten times for 55 yards. That was an average of 5.5 yards per carry compared to Ozzie's 3.3 yards per carry.

As for me, I had five carries for 28 yards. I also led the team with five receptions for 83 yards. Dietrich also had five receptions for 54 yards.

At 4-1, the Hawaiians were off to their best start ever including the two seasons in the WFL. We all savored the opportunity to be in high spirits since we knew the coaching staff would probably humble us during Tuesday's film sessions.

Members of the media came in. As was my custom whenever the Dodgers played at the same time as us, I asked the first media representative I encountered if he knew how the Dodger game came out. In this case it was Earl McDaniel, the general manager of KGMB Radio who was doing color commentary for our games. Unlike 1976, he was also going on the road with us.

"The Dodgers won," McDaniel replied happily, knowing me well enough to know that he was giving me the news that I wanted to hear.

"All right!" I replied exuberantly. "What was the score?"

"Uh, ten-to-four."

"Great," I said.

Suddenly it hit me. I had won the pool.

"Ten-to-four?" I asked, making sure I had heard correctly.

"Ten-to-four," McDaniel repeated.

Ferd Borsch suddenly appeared. He handed me an envelope with 500 dollars inside.

"Jay won the pool?" Rodgers asked rhetorically before loudly announcing, "Hey! Jay's taking us all to dinner."

"I'd avoid Harry Lyons for a few days," Borsch said lightly.

"Why?" I asked.

"Because he had ten and two. That was the score going into the eighth and it looked like it would be the final. Harry was already doing his Christmas shopping in his head when Jackson and Munson hit back-to-back solo home runs in the eighth. He feels like Don Sutton conspired with you against him."

"Ah, bummer," I said lightly. "Next time I see him I'll buy him a couple of left-handed martinis. That'll make him feel better."

What did I do with the money?

Let's just say I didn't spend it on myself and let it go at that. I was paid handsomely to play football and didn't need the 500 dollars as much as others did. I gave the money back to Borsch with instructions on what to do with it.

Carol and I didn't bother with the postgame buffet. Instead we went out to celebrate. It wasn't an elaborate celebration but it was nice to be able to get out.

We ate at Buzz's which was across the street from Kailua Beach Park. I made a reservation under the name of John Stuart since John was my legal first name and Stuart was my middle name. The name Jay Dockman was a little too conspicuous since I was the only person on the island with that name as far as I knew. This way we had an opportunity to get to the restaurant before anybody knew we were coming.

If we were recognized we were still left alone. Carol and I had a nice quiet dinner.

"What are we celebrating?" Carol asked somewhat lightly.

"What do you mean?"

"Are we celebrating the Hawaiians' victory or the Dodgers' victory?"

I shoved a forkful of baked potato in my mouth and thought it over, then swallowed.

"Both, I guess."

Shortly after that the subject of the baseball pool came up. I told Carol that I had won 500 dollars but gave it back to Borsch to donate to somebody less fortunate.

"I also bought a square for you?" I casually mentioned. "You had nine for the Yankees and eight for the Dodgers."

"Really? Why didn't you tell me?"

"Because I didn't want you rooting for the Yankees," I replied sardonically.

After dinner Carol and I took a walk on the beach. It was a very romantic experience, as walks on the beach are apt to be. We held hands and listened to the sound of the waves breaking near the shore.

Carol looked so beautiful. Before we left the stadium she changed into a lavender skirt and a blue floral blouse. Her golden blonde hair, which was down almost to her derriere, was now worn loosely and flowed freely in the breeze.

This would have been the night to tell Carol exactly how I felt about her. I was madly in love with her and believed the feeling was mutual. There was a very warm, peaceful feeling I got whenever I was with her.

The monkey was still on my back. I didn't say anything at all about love. Somehow all of the good things were superseded by the recollection of her surprise disappearance more than three years earlier. The fact that I wanted to put it behind me and believed she felt as I did meant little at the moment. A very annoying voice in my head insisted that she would disappear again if I gave of myself too freely. I knew better but. . . .

I was a total schmuck.

CHAPTER ELEVEN
In General Sherman's Shadow

Our 4-1 record seemed pretty impressive. At this point of the season we were among the NFL's elite.

On Monday afternoon Carol and I happened to drive by the former location of Honolulu Stadium. We sat at the light at King and Isenberg streets and stared at the hallowed ground.

Carol shook her head. She recalled the nights four years earlier when she bounced, danced, kicked and performed other maneuvers with her cheerleading colleagues while I closed out my college football career.

"I'll always miss it," Carol remarked, more to herself but loud enough for me to hear.

"So will I," I said although I wasn't thinking as far back as she was. I was recalling the day the WFL Hawaiians were practicing at the stadium and then were advised that the league no longer existed.

The second anniversary of that difficult day was the following Saturday. That would be the day we would touch down in Atlanta. In less than two years I had gone from believing that pro football in Hawaii was dead to playing on a team in Hawaii that was among the NFL's best. We were only three victories shy of our win total for all of 1976 and there were still nine games left.

Being 4-1 meant that Walker desperately wanted to be 5-1 after our trip to Atlanta. Of course we all did. Walker simply had a way of always wanting things worse than everybody else did. Sometimes it seemed as if the more we won, the more he pushed us. He had an uncanny fear of his players becoming complacent.

From the time Walker turned the projector on we discovered we should count on a very long day. On the opening kickoff Walker was breathing fire. Westfall, filling the vanquished Palumbo's old spot, broke through the wedge and was in perfect position to make the tackle.

Unfortunately Westfall committed himself too early, enabling the ball carrier to make a slight cut. He looked helpless as he went down with his arms out. He tackled nothing but air, causing almost everybody in the room to stifle giggles. It looked comical to everybody but Westfall and Walker.

Walker ran Westfall's non-tackle back and forth about half-a-dozen times.

"What the hell was that, Westfall?" Walker called lividly. "You pull an idiotic stunt like that and you call yourself a pro football player? How in the hell did you get through training camp? Did you play college football? How in the hell did you even survive high school football?"

There was absolute silence. All we could do was sit and stare straight ahead at the screen which featured a frozen frame of Westfall sprawled face down on the ground as his would-be victim was posed nearby. Sometimes when a play like this turns up we practically rolled on the floor. Walker's mood told us that this was not the day for that although we all wished we could get away with rolling on the floor. It was a perfect scenario for somebody's blooper reels.

"Geez," Walker muttered as he started the film again. "I can't believe we actually won on Sunday."

With Walker's reaction before we had even seen the outcome of the opening kickoff we found it hard to believe it ourselves.

Of course the rest of this session was this way. There was no way that Walker was going to read somebody the riot act on the opening kickoff and be sweet and lovable the rest of the way.

There was an unintentional moment of levity later. Hasegawa missed a tackle on a punt. He did a little better job than Westfall since he actually got his arms around the ball carrier. The ball carrier still managed to slip away.

"What the hell was that, Hasegawa? What do you have to say for yourself?"

There was a moment of very uncomfortable silence. A few of us, myself included, had to utilize every ounce of internal strength to keep from busting out in laughter.

"Dammit, Hasegawa! Where the hell are you?" Walker demanded.

There were a few more seconds of silence before Marv replied, "He's watching films with the defensive unit, Coach."

That loosened things up a little.

At least for a moment. Even Walker cracked a smile before returning to his merry martinet demeanor.

The only way to have escaped Walker's wrath was to have not played. It seemed like everybody was yelled at for one thing or another. Bender got it for throwing a pass that was nowhere near a receiver. Dietrich was lambasted for dropping a pass. Linemen were hammered for blocks that didn't satisfy Walker. We found it hard to believe that this was the same coach who was congratulating us for "such an outstanding performance" on Sunday.

Of course I took my share of abuse. On a short pass to Dietrich I blocked a defender but he slipped away and made the tackle.

"What the hell was that, Dockman?" Walker barked, utilizing what was ostensibly the phrase of the day since he used it at least two dozen times throughout the course of the film session. "Dockman, what the hell kind of blocking is that? Was your mind on the World Series, Mr. Dodger?"

There was no way to respond except by meekly shrugging my shoulders. I made it a point not to look at Walker. I was hoping he would simply move on so that he could marinade his next sacrificial lamb.

248

"I just can't believe we won that game," he muttered for the nth time.

Walker's tactic was to make us play better. We understood and accepted it. Just the same. . . .

At least Westfall redeemed himself. That was on the kickoff later in the first quarter when he sidestepped a would-be blocker and pulverized the ball carrier at the 13-yard line.

"Now that's what I like to see, Westfall," Walker said enthusiastically. "You definitely gave that man something to think about next time he sees you coming."

It was vintage Walker. Earlier he had ripped Westfall to shreds and probably even made him wish he had taken up tennis or even tiddly winks. Now Walker was rebuilding Westfall's confidence.

There was a collective feeling of relief when the film session ended. It was amazing that Walker didn't go hoarse from yelling.

"Man, I thought that session would never end," Kerner said wearily in the locker room.

"I hear ya," Shuford replied. "Walker missed his calling. He should've been a warden over at Halawa."

"I just can't believe we won that game," I added, mocking Walker.

"Are you sure we did?" Marv asked, cracking everybody up.

At least our workout was more civil. Walker wasn't congenial the way we knew he would be as the Atlanta game approached but we were no longer mistaking him for Joseph Stalin.

At six o'clock I was prerecording my TV show. This was an extremely rare occurrence when I was free on a Tuesday night. For purely selfish reasons I asked for permission to prerecord. That enabled me to watch the sixth game of the World Series.

"Don't tell me anything about tonight's game if you know anything about it," I instructed to virtually everybody I saw. It was a common sentiment in Hawaii since sporting events played during the week were shown on a delayed basis for the benefit of the working stiffs with banker's hours. This meant *Monday Night Football*, the World Series and any other weekday major sporting event shown on one of the three networks. People in Hawaii adopt painstaking tactics to avoid hearing final scores of games being televised later.

My show was divided into three, not necessarily equal, parts. I began with highlights of our game against Minnesota, referring to them as "highlights" despite any feigned objections Walker might have had. That segued into highlights of the University of Hawaii's game against Southern Mississippi and then there were highlights of the first five games of the World Series.

"And finally we come to tonight's game," I said as I moved into the closing segment of the show. "We won't tell you the score because you may

249

be planning to watch the game. If that's you, close your eyes for a few seconds while we flash the score on the screen."

I paused and counted silently to five.

"Okay," I said. "That score is no longer on your screen."

A technician would be putting a graphic of the score up after I told viewers to close their eyes. She would take the score off as soon as I said "Okay."

It seemed somewhat ludicrous to go to that trouble since my show would run right in the middle of the World Series telecast. Anybody who wanted to watch the game would already be tuned in. We still decided to play it safe for the benefit of anybody who, hypothetically speaking, might actually cut away from the World Series to watch my show before returning to the World Series.

With the show successfully prerecorded and me succeeding in knowing nothing about a game that was probably already over, I left the studio. Since I wanted to catch as much of the game as possible I didn't go home. It would have taken me at least a half-hour to get to Hawaii Kai. Since the telecast was already beginning I took the ten minute commute downtown to Arthur's. I would nurse a couple of beers and watch the game with my friends there.

Don Simmons was there which wasn't exactly a surprise. He was the one who introduced me to the place shortly before my miserable sojourn to Canada. His office was in the same building.

"Jay," Don greeted cheerily as I took the stool at the bar next to his. "Aren't you doing your show tonight?"

"It's in the can. I just finished taping it so that I can watch the Dodgers beat the crap out of the Yankees. What's the score?"

"It's three-to-nothing Dodgers, bottom of the first."

"Right on," I said as I turned my attention to the TV screen. Burt Hooten was pitching to Thurman Munson. The TV was hoisted high in this section of the lounge. Those of us sitting at the bar had to turn 90-180 degrees away from the bar in order to watch the game comfortably, depending on where at the bar one sat.

"Whaddya have, Jaybird?" Keith the bartender asked.

"Bud, please," I replied to the man who had been a star baseball and football player at Punahou School before going to Colorado State on a baseball scholarship. "And I'll buy everybody at the bar a drink."

"Right," Keith replied cheerily as he got everybody at the bar a refill. I normally wasn't one to buy the house a round or otherwise get cocky with my money but there were only three other people sitting at the bar and I knew them all fairly well. Besides Don, there was a stocky blonde man known as Moloka'i Mike who turned profits in various types of novelty sales. There was also an artistic but generally unmotivated individual named Terry Cheff.

250

"You're drinking with Jay," Keith told the beneficiaries of my philanthropy as he placed beers in front of Mike and Terry and a martini in front of Don. It was the Arthur's standard vernacular for informing somebody that another patron was buying the drink. If a drink was on the house it was, "You're drinking with Arthur's."

Arthur's was one of the classiest places in Downtown Honolulu. It had one of the best lunches available, making it ideal for local business people to entertain clients. When lunch service ended one could still get a meal by simply placing an order with the bartender. The bartender would pick up the phone to place the order with the adjoining Flamingo Coffee Shop and the meal would be brought over when it was ready.

It was an elegant establishment with red carpet running throughout the two sections. The bar section also contained a few booths and a juke box. On one wall was a large painting of a woman who was posed somewhat provocatively. One another wall was a painting of three monks enjoying glasses of wine together. The expressions on their smiling faces suggested that they had already had at least a few.

The adjoining section was a dining room although one could still get drink service. In serving trays during the late afternoons and early evenings there was a generous supply of hot snacks, known in Hawaii as "pupus," which were free to Arthur's patrons. One could grab a small plate and load up on beef, pork, fish, veggies or whatever were the pupus du jour.

"How about if I buy you a drink, Keith?" I offered discreetly as I began my second beer.

"Wow, Jay, thanks," Kevin replied in amusing mock enthusiasm. "I thought you'd never ask."

Kevin poured a shot of his choice into a glass, gulped it down and then quickly put the glass in the dishwater directly in front of him. He had to be discreet and quick because it was illegal in Hawaii for a bar employee to drink while on duty. Immediately dropping the glass in the dishwater tainted the evidence.

I continued to cheer on the Dodgers. I watched as Reggie Jackson hit a home run for the Yankees in the fourth.

And then another in the fifth and another in the eighth.

Despite Jackson's heroics, I continued to hope for a comeback even though it was the bottom of the eighth and the Dodgers were on the wrong end of an 8-4 score. The game had ended a few hours earlier but the Arthur's contingent, like most baseball fans in Hawaii, did not know the outcome yet. If anybody in Arthur's knew the final score, they had the decency to keep it to themselves.

There were only a few of us left by this time. Don and I were the only ones sitting at the bar. A couple of men occupied the booth directly across from where I sat. Two women watched while sipping drinks in another booth. That meant that there were seven of us, counting Keith who watched the game as he filled drink orders.

A man in his mid-20s suddenly walked in with an attractive young woman. He stood in the middle of where everybody watching the game was seated and looked up at the TV screen.

"What're you watching this for?" he asked loud enough for everybody to hear as he and his companion prepared to sit in a booth next to the juke box. "The Yankees already won."

Whoever this individual was, he made the enemies' list of at least seven people. He actually looked surprised by the loud expressions of contempt.

There were a few times in my life when I had to work hard to resist the urge to take somebody outside and beat the living daylights out of them. This was one of those rare times. It wasn't just that he gave the outcome away but he acted so smug about it.

I fought to quell my anger by facing the bar. I placed my hands over my face and took deep breaths. I couldn't remember the last time I was that angry.

"You just ruined it for these people," Keith calmly informed the intruder although it was obvious that he was also irritated.

"How could I have ruined it? The game ended hours ago."

"But these people didn't know the outcome," Keith explained diplomatically although he was probably also tempted to take this individual out and teach him a lesson in etiquette when entering a bar where people are watching a satellite delayed sporting event. It was lucky for this clown that Keith kept his cool since Keith was big and strong and probably didn't lose too many fights. "They were watching the game as if it were live."

The intruder merely shrugged.

"That's what you get for watching the game in a bar," the rude patron said flippantly.

The last remark almost pushed me over the edge.

"Tell me, Don," I whispered. "Why wouldn't it be a good idea for me to take this jerk outside and beat the crap out of him."

Don knew that I knew the reason. He also knew that I needed him to confirm it.

"Because you could get arrested and it would be on the front page of the paper and it could ruin your career," he replied discreetly.

"Thanks. I needed that."

And I did.

By this time Keith had utilized a less pugilistic method for dealing with the big mouth. He informed him that there was no way he was going to be served. Our intruder and the young lady were reluctantly walking out as the Dodgers prepared to bat in the top of the ninth.

I watched as the Dodgers mounted a semblance of a rally, then fell short. I knew the outcome, much to my chagrin, but still had to watch the final pitches of the 1977 baseball season. The New York Yankees were World Champions for the first time since 1962.

"Good morning, Jay," Walker greeted when I arrived at the Marine base where we were going to be practicing since our game in Atlanta would be on grass. It was as if he hadn't spent the day before haranguing my teammates and me. "Did you watch the game last night?"

"Yeah," I sighed in mock despair. "It didn't turn out the way I was hoping it would."

"I know. I don't know if we have any Yankees fans on the team but I know that you and a few of the other guys like the Dodgers. I was hoping that they would come through for you. That Reggie Jackson was really something, though, wasn't he?"

"That he was," I agreed wearily. "Someday I'll forgive him. For now I'll just take it out on the Falcons."

Despite his sympathetic greeting to me, Walker was still wearing his martinet hat on Wednesday. He was downright brutal during our workout. Since our focus was on the offense 90 percent of his tirades were directed at the offense.

Nobody was immune, naturally. He was never one to discriminate. He laid into me when I dropped a pass. The ball wasn't quite on target but it was one I normally would have caught.

"What's the matter with you, Dockman?" Walker barked as I trotted toward the huddle. "The World Series is over! Your team lost! Get over it! Focus on football!"

Man, that was a cheap shot! Of course the World Series played no role. I believe even Walker was aware of that but he simply believed he had to throw it in. I dropped the ball because I dropped the ball. No excuses.

Things didn't get any better the following day when the emphasis was on the defense. At one point Walker was giving Hasegawa an earful for getting beat on a pass pattern. Pratt casually walked over to a few Marines who were watching the workout.

"If you guys ever decide to become drill instructors, there's the man to emulate right there," Pratt said, nodding toward Walker.

Walker heard Pratt's remark. He didn't say anything but I could tell that he heard every word.

Revenge came at the end of the workout. Walker didn't give a specific reason aside from the fact that he didn't like our attitudes. We were certain it was because of Pratt's remark that we ran extra sprints and did extra grass drills.

Pratt was a little embarrassed by what he had allegedly caused. He was a cocksure individual who took the game seriously but the expression on his face was one of somebody who wanted to hide.

Grummon went over to Pratt in the locker room. He tapped him on the shoulder a couple of times.

"Don't sweat it," Grummon said to the second-year defensive end out of Arkansas. "You spoke for all of us out there."

That eased the tension. We didn't like having to do the extra sprints and grass drills but Grummon was right. Some of us even laughed under our breath at Pratt's remark.

On Friday Walker was returning to his Mr. Congeniality identity. It was part of the process to get us in the proper frame of mind. He criticized us but in a more constructive manner. Primarily he encouraged us and dished out compliments.

There were injuries with which to deal. Kevin Zanakis's slight injury on Sunday turned out to be something more than slight. He was going to be out for several weeks. Richards also would be out with a shoulder injury.

It was about seven o'clock on Saturday morning when we arrived in Atlanta. Another city, another routine of get on the bus, check into the hotel, take a nap, get on the bus to go to the stadium for a workout, get on the bus to go back to the hotel and then amuse ourselves on Saturday night.

This was my first trip to Atlanta. What did I think of the city?

As usual, what I saw could have been anywhere. It could have been Chicago or Detroit or Philadelphia or Tokyo or Bangladesh or any other large city. There were a few attractions that seemed veritably Georgia although nothing especially noteworthy from what little I saw. I was somewhat put off by the site of the state flag that included the Confederate Stars and Bars in its design which was an ugly reminder that Georgia had been a slave state more than 100 years earlier. For the most part it didn't seem like any other large city.

Shuford, Marv, Kerner and I went out for dinner. I had fried chicken that wasn't very good. Marv had roast pork that he said wasn't any better. We all made a mental note to not patronize that particular restaurant the next time we played in Atlanta. If it kept serving food like that it probably wouldn't be there when we returned anyway.

After dinner we went to a cocktail lounge for a drink. We were quietly listening to a couple of guitar players when at least one of us, and possibly all of us, was recognized. A couple of guys from a few tables away were obviously drunk and cut loose with some very abusive remarks about the Hawaiians.

We didn't go to the lounge to become celebrities and we didn't intend to disrupt anything. All we wanted was to relax with a drink. Instead two drunks spouted off loud enough so that even the musicians had stopped playing.

None of us said anything. Jeff, Marv, Dave and I looked at each other and tried to carry on as if we weren't the center of attention. Two dozen or so patrons knew that the Hawaiians were represented so it wasn't easy to be inconspicuous.

What blew us away was that the manager didn't 86 the disorderly drunks. Instead he insisted that we leave.

"Why?" I asked harshly.

"What kind of a place are you running here?" Jeff asked in an angry tone.

"I'm sorry," said the manager. "Your presence here is just too disruptive."

"You're blaming us?" Jeff asked; his anger building even though he was somebody who rarely got angry. "We were just sitting quietly."

"I know. I'm sorry," the manager replied. "These are my regular customers. If I throw them out I lose their business."

"If their demeanor tonight is typical then you don't need them to be your regular customers," Marv pointed out.

It didn't make any sense. We left but with a few more choice words to the manager.

It was probably Jeff whom the hecklers recognized first. He had played in Atlanta before Hawaii took him in the expansion draft.

I wondered, though, if Marv was the real reason we were kicked out of the facility instead of the hecklers. We were definitely in the Deep South where anything was possible and the manager seemed to be deliberately avoiding eye contact with Marv. The manager could not legally throw Marv out because of his color. The hecklers ostensibly just gave him the excuse he needed.

If that were the case. We'll never actually know. Either way, there was no reason to 86 us from the cocktail lounge.

"Another reason to beat the crap out of the Falcons," Dave suggested facetiously.

I jumped out of bed at a little after five. Kickoff was almost eight hours away. I was ready to go.

It was a great day, I believed. I even sang in the shower; something I would not have done had anybody else been around. I had absolutely no aptitude for singing. I was surprised that the soap didn't walk out on me.

My mood continued to soar. I felt great while drinking coffee with my teammates and during the pregame meal.

It was my 26th birthday but that had nothing to do with it. I gave it practically no thought and wasn't about to mention it to anybody. I still remembered my birthday disaster from the year before.

On second thought, I *didn't* remember. . . at least not the end of my birthday disaster. One minute I was throwing down a shot of Jack Daniels after more than a few beers. The next thing I knew I was waking up in my own bed the following morning.

It was stupid of me. It was also an example of how alcohol can take control of one's common sense. That kind of drinking wasn't for me. I still drank a little, obviously, but I vowed that I would never go to excess again and I kept that vow. Life is best when one maintains control.

As we were boarding the bus to the stadium Walker slapped me on the back.

"Are you ready to play some football?" he asked jubilantly.

"Hell yes!" I replied with enthusiasm that was not feigned. "I'll go both ways if you want."

Walker looked pleasantly startled. I think he understood that I would have been willing to go both ways if he would have allowed me to. That was still more than he was expecting.

My mood continued to soar through the bus ride, through my pregame laps and through our warmup. On the 26th anniversary of my birth I was set for some serious football.

Grant Collier led us in *The Lord's Prayer*. Walker followed with his pep talk.

"I know you're ready to play," he said. "I can see it in your faces. There's a game out there to be won. All you have to do is want it. Everybody work as a unit. Block, tackle and run. Execute, execute, execute. You do your job and you'll be another step closer to a division championship. Let's do it."

I noticed that the entire team was really up; that it wasn't just me. Our confidence level was high. I believed that there was little chance for us to lose.

The defense was introduced. It was good to see McDaniel back in action. Pratt would be starting at right end with Jurgens standing by ready to step in. The absences of Richards and Zanakis would be painful but Ken Gilbert and Chuck Hebron were expected to fill in admirably.

I took a moment to look the stadium over. There wasn't much of a sense of history since the Falcons were a reasonably recent addition to the NFL and the Braves had moved to Atlanta only a little more than a decade earlier and hadn't been in the postseason since 1969. At the time the Braves were not serious contenders.

This was where Hank Aaron hit his 715th home run off of Al Downing of the Dodgers about three and-a-half years earlier. Aside from that, there wasn't much else worthy of note. The Braves were still in Atlanta but most Atlanta residents didn't seem to know or care. Attendance at Braves games was often very sparse.

But it was October 23 and baseball for 1977 was forever a memory. It was time to focus on football.

This was a showdown beyond preseason projections. The Falcons and Hawaiians were in a division expected to be won by the Rams. While the Rams were only one game out of first place, so were the Falcons with their 3-2 record. If we kept winning neither team would ever catch us. Who

256

knew that in week six we would be battling the Falcons to maintain sole possession of first place? If we lost and the Rams won there would be a three-way tie for the top spot.

Bender, Marv, Rodgers and Allen met at midfield with the Falcon captains. The coin was tossed. Atlanta won. The Falcons would be receiving. The crowd cheered as if the Falcons already had the game won.

"What're they cheering for?" I muttered facetiously, standing next to Jennings and Black. "I guess they have to get their cheering out of the way now. Tonight they're all going to go home and cry themselves to sleep. They'll think of all the money they wasted expecting the Falcons to win."

Ed chuckled while Black smirked and shook his head. They knew that I was up for the game. I had no doubt that they were. I wanted to play the game of my life and enjoy a festive flight to the middle of the Pacific.

The kicking unit took the field. The red shirt wearing a headset stood with his arms folded on the field near our sideline to indicate that CBS was still in commercial. The game had been sold out long enough to televise locally. Since it was a battle of two division contenders it was one of the marquee games televised in several markets. Naturally it was also televised in Hawaii as all of our road games automatically were.

Finally the red shirt waved his arm in a circle and stepped to the sideline as the referee blew his whistle. Guinn raised his arm and dropped it, then approached the ball. It was a good long kick.

The ball was caught four yards deep in the end zone. The return man briefly hesitated and then ran it out. He maneuvered his way toward the 20. Jim Vorsino brought him down at the 21.

When the defense took the field Gilbert was apparently a little too anxious to get started. He got called for encroachment. The Falcons had first and five at the 26 before the first snap.

"Just take it easy, Gilbert," Walker called out. "Wait for the snap. You'll do all right. Shake it off."

No doubt Gilbert was anxious to rise to the occasion. The second-year free agent out of San Diego State had started our first four games at right tackle while Prendergast was on the shelf and did a good job, then served as a backup against the Vikings. Now he wanted to take advantage of another opportunity to start while filling in for Richards at left tackle.

The Falcons completed a pass to the 38 for a first down on their first play from scrimmage. A short pass underneath gave them a second and three at their own 45. Dubois was right there to prevent any further advancement.

Dubois was shaken up on the play. He limped off the field, having twisted his foot. Morrissey went in for him. Dubois would return a little later.

A rush off left tackle got the Falcons past midfield. They had a first down at the Hawaii 49.

Five plays and two first downs later the Falcons were on the eleven. They were proving that they were ready for us, turning my stomach in the process. I couldn't stand the thought of the Falcons drawing first blood.

The Falcons picked up four yards on a sweep around left end to give them a second and six at the seven. They tried the same thing around right end and McDaniel hammered the ball carrier at the four.

"Fumble!" I heard Walker bark.

I leaped up from the bench. The commotion near the goal line verified Walker's remark. A group of white jerseys and a group of red jerseys were clamoring for the ball.

"We've got it!" Walker cried out just before the referee pointed toward our end zone to concur with Walker. "Offense!"

What a fantastic break, I thought as I ran toward where we could huddle in the back of the end zone. When I got down there I was surprised by how close the ball was to the goal line. There was only about an inch of space between the rear point of the ball and the goal line. Had Black been able to let it travel another inch or so before recovering the ball it would have been a touchback and we would have the ball on the 20.

One couldn't blame Black. He saw a fumble and had to go for it. Had he tried to wait until the ball rolled into the end zone a Falcon might have recovered it and possibly for a touchdown. Instead the Falcons had a long, time-consuming drive that put nothing on the scoreboard. We were about to execute our first snap of the game with 7:41 left in the first quarter.

It was imperative that we get some breathing room so that we could open our game up. We felt no choice but to start with something very basic. Kerner was given the ball up the middle. He was tackled a yard deep in the end zone, causing the recently shellshocked fans to erupt into a huge roar. The Falcons had a 2-0 lead.

I was angry as I ran off the field with the rest of the offense. I wasn't angry at Kerner or anybody in particular. I was simply angry that things were not going our way. Even the fumble recovery, seemingly so pivotal at one point, was backfiring on us.

It had to have frustrated the Falcons to have driven downfield and then coughed the ball up. One play handed the momentum back to them. Not only did they have two points on the board one play after they lost the ball but they would be getting the ball back. If they had a drive as time consuming as their first drive our entire offense for the first quarter would consist of exactly one play.

"I wonder how prominent those two points will be at the end," I said in exasperation to Marv.

Marv shook his head gravely. He seemed to share my frustration.

Kerner walked by. I slapped him on the shoulder pad as he passed.

258

"We'll get it back, Jeff."

Kerner stopped and looked at me and nodded softly. Jeff was a truly good guy. He had a good sense of humor, a warm heart and he was also one of those athletes who actually went to college to get an education. He was also one of the better fullbacks in the game.

We had a free kick. Our regular kicking unit was on the field except it would be Jablonski, not Guinn, kicking the ball since the kick would be done as a punt.

Jablonski skied the ball which was caught at the 27. The return man then caused me to momentarily panic since I feared that he was going to take it all the way. He scampered 32 yards to the Hawaii 41 where he was finally tackled by Rory Manwaring. Something told me we were in trouble.

The fans were happy and were very vocal in expressing themselves. While the Braves hadn't been giving Atlanta much cause to cheer over the previous few seasons, the Falcons were filling that void at the moment.

After two rushing plays the Falcons had gained about ten yards. The clock was stopped to measure. They had a first down at the Hawaii 31. The crowd reaction was another reminder that we were far from home.

The Falcons chipped their way to two more first downs. It was first and goal at the five. It was another one of those times when I wished I could revert to my high school role as a two-way player. I felt incredibly helpless standing on the sideline.

Our defensive line was a solid wall on the first down play. A running back got to the line where he was gang tackled.

The Falcons went to the air on second down. The quarterback found a receiver just inside the end zone. It was 8-0 with 3:48 left in the first quarter.

And then it was 9-0 with the PAT. After eleven minutes and 12 seconds the Falcons had two scores. In that span the Hawaiian offense had run exactly one play.

It was one of those flukes that the Falcons' fumble had worked to their advantage. They picked up a safety on the play after and then got the ball back, ultimately leading to their 9-0 lead. Thanks to their own lost fumble they had a two-score lead.

Somewhat overwhelmed, I took my post on the goal line and did the traditional slap five with Hasegawa. Rich had been on the field for all but one play thus far and had worked up a pretty good sweat. Had I been a spectator I would have seen more action going from my seat to the men's room than I had to this point in the game.

"Let's turn it around," I suggested.

"Right."

The kick was up. It was coming my way.

"Run it, Jay!" I heard Rich direct.

I fielded the ball three yards deep in the end zone. With Rich directly in front of me I could see that I had room to run. Rich fought off a red jersey near the 15, enabling me to shoot past. Before I knew it I was at the 20 and then the 25.

There were good blocks ahead of me. Rossi forced a red jersey to the left. Collier literally knocked an opponent down. Slater upended a man by throwing himself into his midsection.

One man met me at about the 35. I wasn't able to cut around him so I lowered myself and slammed into him. I started to lose my balance and was slowed a little but I got past him. I was finally caught and dropped at the 43.

Whistles were blowing. Although I came up 57 yards short of the goal line, I rose with a feeling of satisfaction. The kick return unit had pulled together extremely well. The end result was good field position.

Kerner once again had the honor of carrying on the first play. The former Falcon didn't get caught behind the line this time. He picked up four yards to the 47.

Scott was next. He went off left tackle across midfield to the Atlanta 46. It was first and ten.

"Okay, we're moving," Bender said in the huddle. "Let's keep up the good work."

It was Scott again on the next play, this time through the middle. He got six yards. I believed we were on our way.

I was next and learned not to be so cocky. Off right tackle I picked up a yard before a linebacker blocked the road. It was third and three.

It was time for our first pass of the day. Bender took the snap and dropped back. The roar of the crowd before I could turn and look told me we might be in trouble.

Before Bender could find an open receiver he was sacked at the 47. So much for things going our way. This may have been our most futile first quarter, or any quarter, in our abbreviated NFL history.

The punting unit ran on as the clock reached the final 30 seconds of the first quarter. I ran off feeling unfulfilled. The drive once had promise. Just as one tackle behind the line killed what little we'd experienced on our first drive, a sack destroyed our second drive. We were simply going to have to stop getting tackled behind the line of scrimmage.

Jablonski got off a good punt. He kicked it toward the right side to prevent a return. The ball came to rest on the five. Time had run out in the first quarter.

I went for the Gatorade. Abraham and Grummon were also at the table.

"We're flat," Grummon remarked.

"You're telling me," I said. "I don't know what it is but we just can't get going. They're running all over the defense and shutting down the offense."

The three of us looked at each other as if one of us would come up with a profound solution to our troubles. Nobody seemed to have an answer.

At least the defense finally came up with a solution. The Falcons netted only one yard on their drive to start the second quarter. Before I knew it I was standing at midfield to return the punt. I was greatly relieved that we weren't chasing three scores.

It was a short punt since the punter had to get it off in a hurry to avoid a block. I had to run all the way up to the Atlanta 38 to field it although that gave me a better head of steam. I actually managed to run between two men who reached out and got nothing but air. Another defender dragged me down at the 25. We were a mere 75 feet from a score.

For the first time that day we got a pass off. Bender tried to hit Dietrich inside the ten but the ball was slightly overthrown.

Our first completion followed. I ran a cross pattern and caught the ball at the 15 while going into a slide. An Atlanta defensive back touched my right shoulder before I could pop back up and run. I tried to run anyway but the whistles persisted. I knew that I had been touched but had hoped that the officials didn't. Unfortunately they seemed to have been paying attention.

Time was called. The officials wanted to measure. They seemed to spot the ball well and I believed it was enough for a first down. The referee pointed to prove me right.

That was good for us at the moment. The Atlanta defense then dug in. Scott was stuffed at the 17 for a two-yard loss. Scott then picked up four to put us in a third and eight at the 13.

We tried to slip one past them underneath. Bender hit Grummon on a slant pattern at the eight. That was also where a cornerback and linebacker hit Grummon. We were three yards shy of the first down.

I was disappointed but not surprised to see the field goal unit running on the field. Once again it was a situation where we needed to get something on the board even if it wasn't the entire amount we were going for. Just as the safety could prove critical in the end, the field goal could also prove critical.

Guinn had no trouble. His 25-yard attempt was right on target. Atlanta led 9-3 with 10:07 left in the first half. The field goal made it a one-score game.

"Now we've got to hold 'em and get you guys the ball back," Allen said to Dietrich and me as we grabbed our Gatorade. "I don't know how these guys are going to wind up at the end of the season but right now they're playing like they want to go to the Super Bowl."

"So do I," I replied.

There was little doubt that the Falcons were fired up. I wondered if it was because we were now considered to be one of the better teams in the league. Perhaps it was because we were still considered to be an expansion team and they didn't want to lose to one of the new kids on the block.

Or maybe they were simply that good in 1977. That was always a possibility.

Guinn kicked off. The ball was taken a yard deep in the end zone. Just as I had done, the return man ran out without hesitation.

Just as I had also done, the return man was making a huge gain. The Falcons were cutting our defenders down at every turn. The return man didn't seem to be even touched until he was at about the 30. He broke that tackle and stayed on his feet until Gilbert and McWherter teamed up to bring him down at the Atlanta 44.

"Damn! What's going on here?" Walker loudly inquired to nobody in particular. "Let's go, defense! Shut 'em down!"

Things seemed to go our way initially when the Falcons broke their huddle and went for a long count that got them cited for delay of game. I was hoping that technical penalty would place enough doubts in their heads to prevent them from going anywhere.

Apparently not. They completed a pass at about the 46. The receiver picked up five more yards to the Hawaii 49 before Hebron drove him down. It was second and three.

A rush up the middle got them close to the three yards they needed. The ball was placed on about the 46. Time was called to measure.

It was short. The quarterback held up his thumb and index finger. He was either letting the coaching staff know how close they were to a first down or else taking advantage of the TV cameras to audition for a revival of the old Post commercials that boasted their cereals of being "just a little better." Regardless, his quarterback sneak got them the first down they needed at the 45.

Two plays later they had a first down at the 20. I was getting antsy.

So was Hebron. He got called for encroachment. It was now first and five at the 15.

It was that helpless feeling again. I was part of the offense. I couldn't do anything while the defense was on the field. What I wouldn't have given for telekinetic powers that would have caused the Falcons to turn the ball over.

A rush off left tackle picked up six yards. That gave the Falcons a first and goal at the nine.

"(Expletive deleted)," I muttered. It seemed to be a common sentiment among my teammates on the bench.

The Falcons ran a sweep around left end. Their execution was superb. There was great blocking and the ball carrier broke a couple of tackles. Dubois finally tackled the ball carrier but it was simultaneous with him crossing the goal line.

I jumped out of my seat. I expressed a few more thoughts that I would rather not repeat. I hated the thought of Atlanta, or anybody, sticking it to us like this. .

The successful PAT didn't help my demeanor. It was 16-3 with 4:49 left in the half. The noisy fans were glad that they paid whatever their tickets cost.

262

I started to head to the field. Special teams coach Ken Holcomb stopped me.

"You and Hasegawa," he said, "you have to make something happen. We need a big return out of you guys. Block like hell if it goes to him. Tell him to do the same if it goes to you."

It seemed like wasted words. Did he think I didn't understand the benefit of a long return opposed to a short return? Did he think that Rich or I didn't understand that whichever one of us didn't get the ball was expected to block? Did he think that if Rich got the ball that I would go into the bleachers to patronize the peanut vendor?

But I understood where Holcomb was coming from. As blatantly obvious as his advice was, he was simply caught up in the moment. We were in a desperately difficult situation. We had to make something happen. I probably would have given the same advice had I been in his shoes. It's just that with the foul mood that I was in Holcomb's words were almost taken as an insult. It took some restraint to avoid asking him not to insult my intelligence.

The kick came my way. Hasegawa opted to block instead of going into the bleachers to seek out a sushi vendor. I fielded the ball on the two and tried to make something happen.

Of course I wasn't alone. Had I not had ten men blocking for me I would have been lucky to get beyond the ten-yard line. My teammates were doing their part and I did mine by following their leads, dodging a couple of red jerseys, hurdling a red jersey, straight-arming a red jersey and breaking a tackle. I was at the 38 before I was brought down.

Rossi and Collier arrived simultaneously to pull me to my feet.

"Way to go, Jay," said Collier.

"Great runback, man," Rossi added.

"Good blocking, you guys," was my not especially profound, but honest, reply. Game films and what I observed in front of me indicated that they were both excellent blockers on kick returns.

While Collier and Rossi headed to the sideline, I headed back to where we were to huddle near the 25. I arrived at about the same time as Bender.

"Good runback," he said. "It's a good start for getting back into this game."

I was all for that. We were down by 13. Very rarely in our brief history did we trail by that many points, especially this early in the contest as far as I could recall although it was something that actually happened three weeks earlier in Miami. The Falcons wanted to blow us out of the water. We were determined to fight our way back.

We wasted no time. Scott went off right tackle to the 43. Bender then hit Dietrich at the Atlanta 39. Ted scooted around a defensive back while a second defensive back managed to bring Ted down at the 34.

"Helluva job, Ted," I remarked as I helped our blonde receiver from Washington to his feet. Ted had to leap a little to make the catch although it wasn't a difficult task for somebody like him.

It was my turn next. Bender tried to hit me over the middle at about the 25. A defensive back practically crawled up my back to get his hand on the ball to knock it down. He and I both went down in a heap.

As I rose up I couldn't believe that I couldn't see a flag somewhere on the ground. All I saw were officials waving their arms to indicate an incomplete pass.

"Hey, that was interference," I said to the nearest official who turned out to be the umpire.

"He was going for the ball," the umpire said.

I couldn't believe it. When I saw the game film a couple of days later it proved that the officials had made the call correctly. At the time I honestly believed the Falcons had gotten a break.

Slater came in and Grummon went out. We were in our double I right formation. That meant two wide receivers in the I formation with me on the right wing.

Bender hit Slater near the left sideline at the 13. His momentum carried him out of bounds at the eleven where we had another first down.

On a play-action fake Bender hit Kerner over the middle at the five. Jeff fought his way down to the one. The measurement proved that we had a first down with about six inches to spare. We had four plays to travel three feet.

Collier came in for Kerner and carried through the middle. The Falcons stopped him just shy of the goal line.

Scott took care of the rest. He leaped up and over. We had our touchdown.

"All right! All right! Way to go, Larry!" was my enthusiastic remark as I whacked Larry on the back.

"Great leap!" Shuford remarked.

Suddenly we were a part of the game again. It was a great feeling as we reached the sideline and watched Guinn split the uprights. It was 16-10 with 2:04 left in the half.

Now it was a matter of holding the Falcons. We were finally in a groove. If the Falcons managed to score before halftime it would be hard for us to rebound. We had to hope that our touchdown stole their thunder, not fueled their fire.

Guinn kicked off. It was a deliberately low, bouncing kick that was fielded at the seven. The return man shot forward untouched until James Malick brought him down at the 27. The clock was stopped at 1:58 for the two-minute warning.

I suspected that the Falcons were not going to simply run out the clock. With a little less than a minute left they might have been able to get away

264

with it. To do that with almost two minutes left would have been virtually sacrilegious. This was an opportunity for them to widen their lead to as much as 13 points, leaving us with virtually no opportunity to come back until the second half.

As I knew they would, the Falcons tried to make it happen. A long bomb was overthrown and then a shorter pass was also off the mark. That left them in a third and ten while automatically stopping the clock which could work in our favor. One more incompletion and I could go on the field to return a punt and possibly get something going for my team that could ultimately help us take the lead at halftime.

My teammates and I weren't going to be so fortunate. The Falcons completed a pass to the Atlanta 39. The receiver spun for another couple of yards, giving them a first down at the 41.

Another incompletion was followed by a completion to the Hawaii 41. The Falcons called time with 57 seconds left in the half.

Allen came over to the sideline to converse with Walker. It was easy to see that Walker was livid. I couldn't hear what was being said but it was pretty obvious with the way Walker was jerking his head around that he was very unhappy with the way things were going. This was not the time to be asking Walker for a favor unless one had a death wish.

When play resumed the Falcons opted to pass. McDaniel charged in. The quarterback tried to flee but McDaniel was relentless. He sacked the quarterback at the 50.

"Yea, Jim!" I cried out while my teammates on the sideline expressed cries of ecstasy of their own. "Way to go, baby!"

Although the Falcons still had one timeout left, they wisely opted to save it. Instead they went for a deep pass to try to at least get to within field goal range.

The pass was thrown near the 20. It was close to the receiver but Rodgers was right there to tip it away. It was fourth down with 18 seconds left in the half.

It was a great relief. I felt as if I was breathing for the first time in five minutes. I headed to the field.

I stood at the ten believing that I would not get a punt to return. I had told Walker and then my colleagues in the huddle that I was going to return the punt if there was any chance of fielding it cleanly. I didn't want to try to handle one I wasn't sure of because fumbling it away would give the Falcons another shot at a score. If I could make a clean grab I was going to go for it and see if I could at least get us a shot at a field goal.

There wouldn't be any return. The punt was deliberately kicked away from me which was no surprise. It went out of bounds at the 22. With eleven seconds left in the half Bender took a snap and dropped to one knee.

I ran off the field in utter disappointment. We had just defeated two of the NFL's most elite teams. I couldn't figure out why we were having such a tough time against the Falcons. Although the Falcons had an identical record to the Rams and Vikings, I wasn't in awe of them the way I had been with the Rams and Vikings. The Falcons were simply on the rise while the Rams and Vikings were traditionally near the top of the heap.

When I got to the locker room I drank a cup of Gatorade and smoked a cigarette, then ate a Hershey bar and drank a Dr. Pepper. Things just didn't seem to be right. It wasn't so much that we were trailing the Falcons. It was that we were not playing well.

What a difference 30 minutes of football can make. Being hit for a safety on our first offensive play seemed to have knocked off the entire team's equilibrium. Although we had kicked a field goal and scored a touchdown since then, we still seemed out of sync. The collective mood in the locker room seemed to reflect that. Everybody appeared to be more downtrodden than they normally would have been.

Walker, naturally, could be counted on to lift our spirits.

"What the hell are you doing out there?" Walker chided in the locker room. "Do you call that football? Defense, you're pathetic! Offense, you're no better! They're beating the living daylights out of you!"

It was almost funny. The Falcons led by only six points. It wasn't as if it was a rout.

Yet it did almost seem as if it was a rout. The scoreboard told only a little of the story. All through the first half, even when things seemed to be going well, we were getting our posteriors kicked.

Hasegawa and I did our slap fives on the goal line as we prepared to start the second half.

"Let's blow these guys away," I said.

"Hell yes," Rich replied.

Our dialogue was hardly profound but we were only football players. In this case we were football players who had spent virtually all of halftime being chewed out by a cantankerous head coach.

The kick came my way. I fielded it at the goal line. I ran forward behind the interference my colleagues were running.

Out of nowhere I was hit from behind and went down at the 30. Although I was taken by surprise and have no idea how the defender could have gotten behind me, let alone tackled me, I didn't fumble. It was a decent return.

Not that we did much with it. Three rushes and an encroachment penalty netted us slightly less than ten yards. That brought out the chain and we were about a foot short, setting up a fourth down. The punting unit immediately ran on the field.

I would much rather have stayed on the field with the punting unit than be near Walker. His face was flushed with anger as we ran off.

266

Suddenly Walker's countenance seemed to change. Apparently he decided that he wasn't helping us by being angry. As the offense settled on the sideline he turned to face us.

"Hang in there, men," he said. "I know you can break through. Don't get discouraged."

I don't believe we were discouraged. Frustrated, yes, but not discouraged. I wanted to shove it down the Falcons' throats for having the nerve to believe they had a legitimate right to beat us.

Jablonski's punt was caught at the 23. The return man picked up only four yards before Hamer brought him down.

The Falcons appeared ready to go for the jugular. After a three-yard rush to the Atlanta 30 they completed a pass that took them to their 49.

"They're playing like a team that's determined to beat us," Shuford remarked on the bench.

"And we're playing like a team that's determined to let them beat us," Marv replied bitterly from his seat between Shuford and me. "I can't believe we're not playing better. We've got to get on track and now."

The Falcons ran off left tackle. Prendergast had the ball carrier in the backfield but then lost his grip. The ball carrier scooted around for four yards. It was second and six at the Hawaii 47.

"Geez," I muttered.

"Well, hell. The offense isn't doing its job," Marv commented bitterly. "Why should the defense do its job?"

Marv was visibly upset. I suppose I may have been as well. Having the unflappable Shuford sitting with us helped to neutralize the mood.

The Falcons went to the air. Dubois, who had beaten Morrissey out for the starting job this week, picked the pass off at the 29. He actually leaped up in front of the receiver who seemed to be frozen in shock after the interception. Henri returned the interception to the Hawaii 45. He was tackled practically at Walker's feet.

"Helluva pick, Henri!" Walker exclaimed as he helped Henri to his feet. "That's the way to play it! Who says Canadians don't play real football?"

Of course the interception silenced the fans although they remained hopeful. Scott did what he could to dash those hopes. He went off right tackle and refused to go down despite being hit three or four times. He got all the way to the Atlanta 32, then carried up the middle to the 27.

A short pass to Grummon went practically nowhere. Bender hit him a yard beyond the line of scrimmage where he was immediately hit and dropped.

Our next pass produced a better result. Bender hit me on a quick slant at the 25. I fought my way to the 21. First and ten.

Suddenly it was first and 15. Hayer jumped prior to the snap to move us back to the 26.

"It's all right, Carl. Shake it off," Bender said to sooth Hayer's feelings as we moved back to huddle. It was the kind of thing we all say. Sometimes I wonder if the reason we say it is because we are truly compassionate or because we understand how futile it would be to cuss out the offending individual.

Possibly a little of both although I would like to believe the overwhelming majority is for the former reason and not the latter. It is irritating when a teammate screws up but it happens to everybody at one time or another. I was always grateful when my teammates stuck by me during my faux pas moments.

A pair of rushes by Scott picked up a total of seven yards. That was followed by an incomplete pass. This is where the penalty was critical. Had we not lost the five yards we might have done another rush on third down instead of attempting the pass. The rush might have gotten us the first down.

Instead it was fourth and eight. The field goal unit came on.

"It's all right. It's all right," Walker said as we reached the sideline, trying to keep us believing in ourselves. "We're moving the ball."

That was a good point although I wasn't totally convinced. Despite the fact that we were moving the ball, it still seemed as if we were out of sync.

At least the field goal attempt was good. That cut Atlanta's lead to 16-13 with 6:13 left in the third quarter. The Falcon fans had every reason to be nervous.

"Maybe they're out of gas now," I suggested to McDaniel. "Maybe our refusal to let down will discourage them. Then we can score a touchdown or two and come away with another victory."

"Maybe," McDaniel replied thoughtfully. "I don't think they're discouraged but I believe we can overtake them."

If our field goal that narrowed the gap to three had a demoralizing effect on the Falcons, they recovered quickly. Guinn's kick was fielded three yards deep in the end zone. The return man got to the 24 before Malick brought him down.

The Falcons wasted no time in moving upfield. After two plays they had a first down at the Hawaii 49. Three first downs later they had a first and goal at the seven. They were cutting through our defense like a sharp knife cutting through cheese. Thoughts of them being discouraged were totally forgotten.

After two rushes they had third and goal at the one with less than a minute to go in the quarter. On the very next play they went up the middle and into the end zone. The crowd roared its approval while I felt nauseous. It was now a two-score game again with 32 seconds left in the third quarter.

"There's a penalty flag!" I heard Arroyo call out.

I looked up and there it was. It appeared to be in the vicinity of the line of scrimmage.

268

Atlanta was cited for holding. Instead of a touchdown, the Falcons had third and goal at the eleven. We were still only chasing three points.

"This could be exactly the break we need," I said to Shuford.

"As long as our defense can hold them," he replied.

"If we can take it all the way in after that it could mentally knock them out of the game," I added although I wasn't totally convinced that it would be that routine.

The Falcons went for a short pass. The receiver caught the ball at the four. Black pushed him out of bounds just shy of the goal line as time expired in the quarter.

As the ball was moved to the opposite side of the field I realized that one way or another I was going to be on the field after one more play. It was simply a matter of whether I would be fielding a kickoff or participating in a play from scrimmage. For the moment I wondered if the Falcons would go for the TD, giving our defense a chance to hold them, or a field goal.

My guess was that the Falcons would go for the TD. That was what I would want to do if I were in their shoes. With a field goal it would still be a one-score game. They were also so close to the goal line it would be hard to resist the urge to go for the full six. They were only a few inches away.

When the fourth quarter started the Falcons confirmed my belief. They lined up for the touchdown, utilizing two tight ends.

"Hold 'em, defense! Don't let 'em score!" Rossi called while other teammates offered similar encouragement. My heart pounded while the quarterback called the signals.

The quarterback took the snap and rushed forward. Our defense tightened up in the middle of the line. I believed we had succeeded in our goal line stand although there was no signal from the officials. Some of the Falcons were raising their arms up while some of our players were waving their arms in front of them but there was still nothing from the officials who had the only vote that counted.

Suddenly the officials started raising their arms. The quarterback apparently crossed the line. It might not have been by much but it was enough. It was like comparing a home run that lands in the front row of the bleachers or out in the parking lot. Both read the same in the box score.

With the touchdown came the inevitable extra point. We trailed 23-13. It was getting under my skin that we couldn't break through and overtake these guys. I didn't believe they were better than us and, therefore, they did not have the right to beat us.

That sums up my mindset. I always took the field believing that our opponent was inferior to us. Whether that was naive or simply dedication, I don't know. All I know is I was always surprised whenever anybody beat us. I truly believed in my team.

"We've got to put these guys away," I said to Hasegawa, showing my proclivity for the obvious as we exchanged our traditional slap fives before the kickoff.

"They're tough," Rich replied. "They were ready for us. We can still take them."

The crowd was loving it, of course. The fans were out en masse. At this juncture the Braves played primarily before thousands of empty seats. As soon as I finished doing my pregame laps in the still empty stadium I jocularly told Russ Allen that I had a pretty good idea of what it was like to be on the field during a Braves game. Being a loyal fan of the Dodgers who narrowly missed becoming the first team to top the three-million mark in attendance in 1977, he appreciated the joke.

But the Atlanta fans were at Fulton County Stadium on this day. The Falcons had been playing some good football and that was putting people in the seats.

The kick was up and heading Rich's way. I was actually glad that I wouldn't be returning the ball. I was so angry that I wanted to take it out on the first red jersey that came my way and I had to avoid contact if I was carrying the ball. I threw a block although I didn't get to pulverize the man the way I had hoped since the man tried to fight me off and sidestep me. At least I kept him out of the play.

As for Rich, the film would show him fielding the kick a yard deep in the end zone and about two yards from the sideline. He returned the kick to the 26.

"All right. Let's get those points back," Bender suggested in the huddle.

We got off to a dubious start. Scott went off right tackle for nine yards to the 35 and then fumbled. Fortunately he recovered his own fumble.

I was next. I went off left tackle and was hit about a yard beyond the line. I still managed to fight for two more yards. it was first and ten at the 38.

It was Scott's turn again. A sweep around right end produced only two yards.

Much to my surprise, my number was called again. I took the handoff and went off right tackle. Unfortunately I wasn't able to get a secure grip on the ball. As I tried to adjust my hands I was hit at the 41 and the ball was knocked loose.

A mad scramble ensued. Eleven players in white jerseys and eleven players in red jerseys ran, jumped and dove after the ball. The ball seemed as elusive as a greased pig. It was gradually knocked backward from where I fumbled. The Falcons finally recovered at the Hawaii 29.

It is impossible to express how I felt as I headed toward the sideline and I won't repeat the words that I was thinking and saying. Despite the encouraging words and pats on the back from my teammates and coaches, I couldn't shake the feeling of having been slammed in the gut with a

270

sledgehammer. It wasn't the first time I'd fumbled and wouldn't be the last. That didn't take the sting away, especially since we were desperate to make up a ten-point deficit with time running down.

I grabbed my Gatorade and sat on the bench. I wanted to cry. I wanted to puke. I wanted to jump up and curse. I wanted to go into the bleachers and beat the daylights out of every man, woman and child who cheered when the Falcons recovered the fumble. I wanted to quit football.

Somehow I knew that none of the aforementioned was a practical solution. The only solution was for us to hold the Falcons and then come back and beat them.

The Falcons were having no part of that idea. Of course it would be inexcusable for them to get the ball at the Hawaii 29 and not put something on the board. From the very first play they were in field goal range.

They were determined not to settle for a field goal. After six consecutive rushing plays they were at the eight. A measurement showed that they had their second first down of the brief drive.

Two rushes later they were on the one. It was third down. They were three feet from a touchdown. That definitely didn't make me feel any better about the fumble that started this drive.

Atlanta tried to get in by way of left end. The Falcons gained a little ground but didn't cross the goal line. Pratt was blocking the road and prevented the ball carrier from completing his mission. It was fourth and less than a yard.

The Falcons called timeout to discuss the matter. There was little doubt again that they would go for a touchdown. A field goal would bruise us but a touchdown might virtually lock the door.

They were going for it. The field goal unit never even budged. The Falcons lined up again with two tight ends.

"Let's go, you guys," I said softly as if to will our defense.

On the snap the quarterback turned and handed off to a running back. The running back leaped and collided with Prendergast. The crowd was yelling although it was hard to discern if the crowd was cheering or simply making noise. A few of the Falcons had their arms raised.

But not the officials. Once again they seemed to be trying to determine where the play ended. Finally the play was blown dead.

They didn't make it!

"Yeah!" I cried out, jubilantly putting my helmet on and running toward the end zone where we would huddle. I slapped fives with as many of my defensive colleagues as I encountered. I was feeling not so bad now although I hadn't totally forgotten that it was my faux pas that put the defense on the field in the first place. Thanks to our stiff defense my faux pas wound up as a simple setback and not a gamebreaker.

When I got to the end zone and saw where the ball was spotted I realized how fortunate we were. The tail of the ball was only about two inches from the goal line. I just hoped that our defensive stand would not lead us to another safety.

Scott carried to the two to give us a little breathing room. Bender then hit me with a pass at the 14. I managed to scamper up to the 20, keeping a very firm grip on the ball the entire time. First down.

We continued to move. In five plays we had two completions each to Dietrich and Slater with Bender forced to scramble and take a two-yard sack on the second of those five plays. On of the fifth of those plays Slater went out of bounds to stop the clock with 2:08 left. We had a first down at the Atlanta 35.

Bender was pressured on the following play. He still got the pass off. He tried to hit Grummon but the pass was off the mark and fell incomplete. The clock stopped with exactly two minutes left.

As Bender conversed on the sideline with Walker I tried not to think about the negatives. I was sweating pretty hard even though the temperature was in the upper 60s. I had played such a hard game that my jersey was soaked with perspiration. Since the game was being played on natural turf I noticed grass stains, dirt and chalk on various parts of my uniform.

Suddenly I felt very confident. I knew we were going to win this game. It would prove to be the greatest comeback in our brief NFL history. I wanted a flight home so festive that we would almost regret touching down in Honolulu.

Oddly enough, my thoughts shifted to Les Keiter doing the play-by-play for Hawaii listeners. I had never heard him do football games but I had heard him do Hawaii Islander baseball games several times. He had a very friendly but authoritative voice with original terminology that captured the excitement of each game and held the listeners' attention. It suddenly occurred to me that the way for Hawaii listeners to get the most out of our road games was by turning the sound down on their TV sets and listening to Keiter's accounts on the radio.

Unless Vin Scully was calling the game for CBS. Nobody, even Keiter, could match Scully for broadcasting excellence.

When play resumed we let everybody know that we were determined to pull it out. Bender hit Dietrich at the 23. Ted immediately stepped out of bounds to stop the clock at 1:53.

The next play chewed up a few extra seconds because Bender had to scramble. He got the pass off to Grummon at the seven. Rich ran down to the two before stepping out of bounds. The clock showed 1:39. We had all three of our timeouts left so time was still on our side if we could score quickly and get the onside kick.

It took only one more play. Bender dropped back and spotted Slater. Despite a diving effort by a defensive back to knock the ball away, the pass hit Slater on the numbers about eight yards deep in the end zone. The score was 23-19 with a PAT virtually assured. The clock showed 1:32.

We were hyped as we ran to the sideline. While the crowd sat quietly we were clapping, yelling, slapping each other on the back and slapping fives with the PAT unit as our paths crossed.

I grabbed a quick cup of Gatorade and chugged it down. I knew I'd be back on the field after Guinn's PAT. Guinn put the ball through the uprights, as expected, to pull us to within 23-20 and I huddled with my colleagues on the onside kicking unit around Holcomb.

We actually had two onside kicking units. One was our regular kicking unit for onside kicks when the onside kick was not an absolute certainty. The other one was the unit where everybody including the least knowledgeable of football fans knew that the onside kick was coming. The unit was comprised of those experienced at handling the ball. To not try an onside kick in this situation would be tantamount to shaving points.

I took my place. I was next to Rodgers who was just to the left of Guinn. Vorsino was to my left. Also on the field were Dubois, Morrissey, Hasegawa, Rossi, Hamer, Dietrich and Roberts.

Guinn approached the ball. He kicked it to his left. That was on my side. Like everybody else, I ran like crazy after the ball.

The Falcons were not able to field it cleanly. I kept my eye on the pigskin as it rolled and bounced around while I charged after it. As I dove for the ball I even nudged somebody in a red jersey out of the way.

I got a hold of the ball and held it tight as I moved into the fetal position. Suddenly there were two or three bodies on top of me. I could hear whistles blowing and players from both sides claiming that their team had the ball. At this point I was the only person in the entire world who knew the absolute truth. The news would bring elation to all of Hawaii.

"Come on, men. Let's get off of there," I heard the referee directing. The weight of the other bodies was being lifted. As I was finally able to glance up I saw the referee point to indicate that we had the ball. That was accompanied by a groan from the crowd. I was only too happy to help screw up their day. My recovery almost made up for my fumble.

I bounced up and flipped the ball to the referee. Rodgers and Guinn were right in front of me to offer their congratulations before they headed to the sideline. Rossi arrived and slapped the top of my helmet.

"Way to go, Jaybird," he said before he also went to the sideline.

It was our game to win. Four seconds had been burned off the clock, giving us 1:28 to move 49 yards.

Scott was the surprise recipient of the first pass. Bender hit him over the middle at the 39. He scampered to the 27 before going down in bounds. We used our first timeout with 1:17 left.

Two passes would fall incomplete. Slater lunged for one near the ten that was in his hands but he couldn't hang on. Dietrich made a diving attempt for a pass in the end zone that he also got his hands on but lost it when he hit the ground. It was third and ten with 57 seconds left.

It was still our game to win. Now, though, we were one misplay from having to go for the tie.

The Falcons gave us a boost. A linebacker decided to blitz before the ball was snapped. The encroachment penalty moved the ball to the 22.

They blitzed again. This time they waited for the snap. Bender scrambled but couldn't get the pass off. He was buried by a pair of red jerseys at the 29. It was fourth and 12.

I looked at the clock and saw it ticking down toward 40 seconds. With it being fourth down there was no question that we were going for a field goal. By the time the ball was deemed ready to play there was a little less than 30 seconds left.

We called time just before the play clock expired. The game clock showed five seconds.

The field goal unit came on, crossing paths with the offense. I happened to catch Billingsley's eye as he ran on and gave him a nod to encourage him. The primary pressure was on Guinn but it was still up to Billingsley to do a good hold as well as Arroyo to make a good snap.

That's not to mention the blocking that was expected of everybody else.

I went to the Gatorade table and grabbed a cup of refreshment. I was resigned to our first ever overtime game. The 46-yard field goal would use up the remaining time in regulation.

As the field goal unit got set I stood in front of the bench casually sipping my Gatorade. I watched as Guinn put his foot into the ball, then as the officials waved their arms in front of them and then signaled that the field goal was wide to the left.

I plopped down on the bench in disbelief. The crowd was roaring. Although I tried not to look at the crowd, in Atlanta's cookie cutter facility I couldn't help but notice the fans standing, jumping and cheering. The missed field goal, and all that preceded it, enabled the Falcons to move into a tie for first place with us.

Guinn looked understandably dejected as he approached the sideline. Walker was going to midfield to shake hands with his counterpart. He stopped momentarily to console Guinn.

Although it came down to the final play, Guinn did not lose the game for us. I also didn't lose the game for us even though my mind was on my fumble. It seemed like a pivotal moment even though the Falcons ultimately did not score from it since their drive used up valuable time. My fumble and Guinn's errant kick were only two in a series of miscues that cost us the game and sole possession of first place in the NFC West.

I ran off the field to the baseball dugout that would lead to the locker room. Normally after a game I shook hands with my opponents and exchanged a few pleasantries regardless of the outcome. I simply wasn't in the mood this time. Something was gnawing at me. I was furious.

It wasn't anything on the field as far as I could tell. Nothing out of the ordinary had happened. I was hit pretty hard but there weren't any shots that I could conclusively classify as cheap. One of the defensive backs had taunted me a little. That wasn't anything I hadn't experienced before. It was part of the game.

Perhaps it was simply the loss. No athlete likes to lose. We are expected to accept losing as a consequence of the competition. We're still not required or expected to like losing.

I had been involved in organized athletics dating back to my first year in Little League in 1960. I had played on some very good teams over the years and a few that weren't so good. At no time did I play on a team that went through a season without at least one defeat. It wasn't as if I hadn't learned to accept defeat.

As our plane took off for Honolulu I tried to recall a time when I felt so much anger after a defeat. The only time I could think of was after a baseball game my freshman year in high school. We were battling another school's freshman team for first place and lost in a seesaw battle. I was never certain if I was angry because of the loss of a tight game or because I had lined out deep to right with the bases loaded and two outs and killed a late-inning rally. All I know is I was furious.

When I got home I was still livid. After I snapped at my younger sister for having the audacity to say "hi" to me I went into my bedroom and actually broke down and cried.

That embarrassed me even though nobody saw me. At 15 in our society where women were allowed to cry simply because they were women and men cried only if they were "big babies," I thought crying for any reason at all was beneath me.

Somewhere along the way I decided it wasn't the loss to Atlanta that angered me. I wasn't happy about losing but we were still 4-2. Not only was that very good, especially for a second-year NFL team, we were in the thick of the postseason hunt as we approached the season's halfway point.

It was my 26th birthday and I was angry for no apparent reason. I actually wondered if the game was part of some enigmatic birthday curse. The year before the curse was self-inflicted when I allowed myself to drink way too much. The year before that was the day after the World Football League officially folded.

By the time our DC-8 was over the Pacific I had the anger out of my system. If there was something specific that set me off, I still don't know what it was.

CHAPTER TWELVE
A Test of Resilience

Watching the game films was hardly a day at the beach. Walker didn't yell too much. He normally wasn't one to kick us when we were down. It was simply punishment enough to have to watch plays that were pivotal in our defeat.

Of course our first offensive "series" resulted in a score for the other team. We were well-rested by the time we finally got to run an offensive play with us so deep in our own territory that the rear end of the ball was only about a half-inch from the goal line.

One play and we were back on the sideline. It was after a safety blitz. The safety shot through Shuford and Nelson, who were doing their jobs by blocking other men, and got just enough of Kerner to bring him down about a yard into the end zone. That was the entire story of our opening "series."

Walker ran the play back and forth about half-a-dozen times. I could see Kerner grimacing in his seat near me.

"I've watched this sequence about a dozen times," Walker finally announced after he froze the film at the point where the safety crossed into our backfield and turned toward Kerner. "I don't see how we could have played it any better. You've got to credit their safety. He made the play. He was awfully quick."

It was good that Walker didn't harangue anybody on the play. He would get plenty of chances for it later.

Of course there was my fumble late in the game. I didn't realize until I saw the film how hard I had been hit although that was aided by me not having a very secure grip on the ball. I was pulverized by a linebacker. That still didn't make me feel any better about my fumble.

Abraham was the one who should have blocked the linebacker. The films showed that he stumbled while coming out of his stance. By the time he recovered the linebacker had read the play, sidestepped Abraham and threw his entire strength into me.

"I don't know what you were doing there, Abraham," Walker said in a voice that was not congenial.

"I stumbled, Coach," Abraham replied remorsefully.

"Yeah, well, your stumble cost us the ball. It's amazing that Dockman was able to walk off the field under his own power after that hit."

The truth be told, the hit didn't seem nearly as intense at the time as it appeared on film two days later. That's the way it often was.

Ultimately the films came to an end and the two units got together. Walker said that the game should have served as a learning experience for us.

"They were up for you. They wanted to beat you. A few key mistakes hurt us but it was primarily a matter of them getting fired up more than us for this game. That's the way it's going to be the rest of the way. Everybody we play is very impressed with us and will come at us with their best stuff. The 49ers are probably one of the worst teams in the league but they'll go at you on Sunday like Super Bowl champions. It's up to you to be ready for each and every game."

I really had to push myself beginning on Wednesday. When I woke up I could tell that I was developing some kind of bug.

It could have been worse, I suppose. I could have begun feeling the effects of the malady closer to gametime. My timing was perfect since I felt fine when I did my TV show the night before (although the *highlights* of Sunday's game in Atlanta made me sick) and there were still four days before our next game. I was reasonably confident that I would be okay when we squared off against San Francisco.

What I had was some type of flu virus. I practiced hard on Wednesday and Thursday although my condition continued to worsen. The team physician gave me some medication which didn't cure anything but kept my condition more under control.

I knew I would be ready to go at gametime. My fear was spreading germs to my teammates. I stayed away from them as much as possible and even considered using a surgical mask. It wasn't easy to avoid my teammates. Walker went so far as holding me out of contact workouts. Rossi filled in for me.

"Are you going to be ready to go?" Walker asked after Thursday's workout.

"I'll be okay. I don't get sick very often and when I do I'm not sick for very long."

"That's good to know," he said.

I honestly wasn't trying to impress Walker. I was simply being honest. Occasionally there will be a player who uses some type of frivolous complaint to get out of work but that wasn't me. There were a few times when I felt under the weather during my career but I never had anything to incapacitate me enough to keep me from the team's workouts. In this case I took part in everything except the contact workouts.

A few of my teammates expressed sincere hope that my malady would be gone soon. Rossi's expressions of good wishes were especially noteworthy.

"Hey, man. This bein' sick has got t' be a real bummer for ya," he remarked as we were leaving the Aloha Stadium turf following Thursday's workout to give me the impression that he was my best friend in the entire world. "You do what you hafta do to get yourself well, man. The team really needs ya."

277

Rossi's compassionate words might have carried more meaning had he not also been suggesting to some of our teammates that he figured to start in my place on Sunday. It was going to take a lot more than a flu virus to get me to willingly surrender my starting spot. Rossi may have been able to fill in for me in practice but there was no way I was going to give up my spot at gametime. Rossi was going to relegate me to backup status only by outplaying me.

Not that I blamed Rossi for wanting to start and preparing for the possibility of doing so. I wasn't holding anything against him. I simply had no intention of doing for him what an erroneous legend had Wally Pipp doing for Lou Gehrig.

I was slightly better by Friday and even engaged in contact workouts although I was not well enough to go through anything but my normal routine away from the team. Normally Carol and I went out on Friday nights when the team was at home. I had to beg off this time.

After I got home on Wednesday, Thursday and Friday I became a recluse. I talked on the phone occasionally but had no human contact aside from that. I wouldn't even let Carol come over because I didn't want to spread my germs to her.

During the evening hours I watched a little TV and did some work toward my master's. At least I wasn't wasting my idle time. I also drowned myself in orange juice to help wash away the germs.

Actually on Friday night I switched to two or three cups of coffee marinated with a shot of Canadian Club whiskey and wound up feeling better. I'm still not sure if the booze killed the germs or simply made it so that I didn't care about my virus anymore.

By Saturday I was just about ready to go. I wasn't 100 percent but was pretty close to normal. There was no doubt that I would be at full strength by Sunday.

On Saturday we also confirmed a couple of lineup changes. Hebron and Scott had both been listed as questionable for our encounter with the 49ers. Hebron's ankle would keep him out so Malick would start at right outside linebacker. Scott's hip was still sore so Roberts would start at tailback.

I gave Saturday afternoon and evening to Carol. I wanted to make it up to her by doing whatever she wanted to do as long as it wasn't something too strenuous. We laid on the beach at Malaekahana, renewing memories of our second date together since this was where we spent that date in August, 1973. We even capped the day off with a pizza at the Shakey's in Kaneohe like we did in 1973.

None of this was done deliberately to renew memories of our earliest days together. It was still somehow a sign that we were growing closer.

But there was still a way to go before we truly connected again.

I woke up exactly at three o'clock on Sunday morning. Then I woke up at 3:55, 4:27, 5:08 and finally 5:14. At least I stayed in bed until almost a full 45 minutes before my alarms were set to go off. Out of habit I set them for just before six. I forgot about our later starting time resulting from the rest of the country returning to standard time. Kickoff wasn't until eleven.

Carol and I were heading down the freeway by 7:45. As was usually the case, I was very quiet. My mind was on my driving and the game.

"Are you ready?" Carol asked. She understood how I was before a game and had no objections. She also knew that I wasn't averse to having a conversation although I wasn't really willing to talk about anything but the game.

"As ready as I'll ever be," I replied. "I just hope the rest of the team is ready. This game is almost a no-win situation for us."

"Why do you say that?"

I explained that we were playing a team whose place in the standings suggested that they weren't very good. If we beat them we simply beat a team we were supposed to beat while losing to them would suggest that we weren't as good as we thought we were. The only worthwhile difference it would make was if we won it would be another victory in the win column.

"That's better than another mark in the loss column," I added as I exited the Moanalua Freeway at the Halawa exit.

The facts about this no-win game were on my mind as I did my pregame laps. A loss would get a lot of attention that wouldn't work to our advantage. I also knew that the 49ers were not incapable of beating us or anybody else. As hackneyed as it may seem, any team can beat any other team on any given day.

Strange things can happen in sports. There were still people left in a state of disbelief from when we beat the Raiders in 1976. Three weeks later nobody expected the Eagles to beat us. In both cases the unexpected happened with our victory over the Raiders being infinitely more amazing since we wound up being the only blemish on the Raiders' record. As we prepared for the 49ers I fervently hoped that this would not be one of those days of the unexpected.

"How're ya feelin', Jaybird?" Rossi asked as the captains went to midfield for the toss.

"Great, man, great," I replied.

"The bug's gone?"

"All pau. I'm 100 percent," I said brightly. "I'm ready to give those 49ers a thrashing."

"Good, good. We need a good game from you. I'm glad you're okay."

I nodded and looked at Jennings who was standing close enough to hear the exchange. Simultaneously Ed and I raised eyebrows. Rossi's alleged concern over my well-being may have been genuine to a point. A few days after he unilaterally reported to teammates that my malady put him in the starting lineup made it a little hard to believe.

But this game was probably special to Rossi. This was not only the team that cut him in training camp in 1976, this was his hometown team. He would have relatives watching in the San Francisco area. I hoped he would get a chance to do something noteworthy.

We won the toss. We would be receiving. Those of us on the kick return unit huddled before taking our places.

"This is your time to shine," I said to Rossi as we trotted to our respective spots. "I'm counting on you to throw a helluva block. That'll look good for your friends and family watching in Frisco."

"Ah, screw the relatives and friends. I just wanna win," he said good-naturedly as he stopped near the 15 and I continued to the goal line.

The kick was up. It was heading my way. I caught the ball a yard deep in the end zone.

There were good blocks ahead of me. Rossi blocked a man in a way that wouldn't make a highlight reel but was adequate enough to prevent the man from getting to me.

I was untouched until about the 25. From there I broke a couple of tackles, dodged and weaved a little and even spun around once. A 49er finally tackled me at the Hawaii 42.

"All right, Jaybird! Helluva runback!" Rossi remarked as he helped me to my feet; probably ensuring that he would appear on TV in his hometown although that wasn't necessarily his motivation. In the background I noticed the roar of the crowd. The fans were also impressed. I got credit for a 43-yard return but I couldn't have done it without the help of ten teammates.

We went right to work. Our strategy was to come out charging and never look back.

Ozzie went off right tackle to the Hawaii 47. It was second and five.

Before we could get off another play we were back at the original line of scrimmage. After I went into motion Ozzie gave back the five yards he picked up by jumping before the snap.

We were undaunted. Bender completed a pass to me near the mauka sideline at the San Francisco 35. My momentum took me out of bounds at the 33.

The drive continued. Bender hit Dietrich at the 23. Ted picked up three more yards to the 20.

Kerner electrified the crowd with a rush up the middle. Defenders seemed to literally bounce off him. He wasn't dragged down until he reached the six and then he was tackled by committee. We had our third first down in as many plays.

"All right. We're hot. We're hot," Bender remarked in the huddle.

280

Ozzie climaxed the drive with a sweep around left end. He just barely managed to dive in near the pylon but that was good enough. With the extra point we had a 7-0 lead. It was our first lead in two weeks.

We were jubilant although guardedly so. There was still a lot of football left to play and little doubt that the 49ers were thinking upset. A one-touchdown lead meant nothing.

I personally felt a semblance of a letdown. At the time I thought it was the after effect of my recent malady. Later I realized that it had to do with the fact that were playing against a team going nowhere. A football player is expected to take everybody seriously. Some times are easier than others. There was a stark contrast between the 49ers of 1977 and the 49ers who would be a formidable force during the following decade.

Not that I wasn't aware that the 1977 49ers were very capable of beating us. It was simply easier to get fired up against a team like the Rams or Cowboys than it was to get fired up against a team like the 1977 49ers. One really had to push oneself.

The 49ers of 1977, not surprisingly, did not seem convinced that they couldn't beat us. They took the kickoff two yards deep in the end zone. Rather than down it like a defeated gladiator, the return man brought it out. He got all the way to the 25.

They didn't stop there. Ostensibly unaware that they were 17-point underdogs, or possibly very aware of it, they moved the ball. Twice they converted on third down. They wound up with a first and ten at their own 49.

It's funny how it is from a player's perspective. Everybody knows that no NFL team is going to be held to no yards. Everybody knows that no NFL team is going to be held to no first downs. Just the same, a player cringes when watching an opponent gaining yards and picking up first downs.

The 49ers went up the middle. They got past midfield to the Hawaii 49 before the ball carrier had a violent rendezvous with Allen.

"Fumble!"

I couldn't see the ball. All I could see were white jerseys and brown jerseys moving toward the opposite sideline near midfield.

Black leaped in the air a couple of times, frantically pointing toward the north end zone. The referee, forced to be less biased than Black and showing no emotion, also pointed toward the north end zone and drew a roar from the crowd.

"All right!" I exclaimed, putting my helmet on and running onto the field.

It was McDaniel who recovered the fumble. As our paths crossed I noticed that he was smiling so broad that he might as well have scored a touchdown.

"All right," said Bender in the huddle. "The defense got the ball for us. Let's thank them by taking it in."

I had the honor of catching the pass on the first play. Bender hit me at the 49er 37 near the right hash mark. I was hit immediately but managed to stay on my feet until I got to the 33.

Grummon was next. I had the honor of delivering a pass to him that wound up a strike near the left sideline at the 13. After taking the pitch from Bender I waited an extra second or two to fool the defensive backs into moving in for a run before I passed and Rich was unmolested the rest of the way.

A few seconds later I was in the north end zone greeting Rich while the crowd roared. It was a few seconds before we realized that the scoreboard hadn't changed. Rich had inadvertently stepped out of bounds at the 12. It was one of those rare moments when a first down was a negative.

"Hey, we'll get it," Bender said in the huddle.

Ozzie got a huge chunk of the necessary yardage himself. He went up the middle and fought his way to the four. He was making some quality gains during the early part of the game.

Two incompletions followed. None of the receivers could get open and Bender was forced to throw the ball away. The field goal unit was dispatched on fourth and two.

I wasn't happy about that. It hurt, especially since I knew we would have had a touchdown had Grummon stayed in bounds although I wasn't belittling Rich for what could have happened to anybody. A field goal was better than no score at all.

Guinn split the uprights with very little effort. We had a 10-0 lead. There was 4:40 left in the first quarter.

"This is just the beginning, boys," Allen said gleefully as he walked behind our bench. "Only the beginning."

"Only the beginning, baby," Abraham remarked. "We are gonna put these suckers away."

Suddenly it didn't seem so tragic that we had to settle for a field goal. There were at least a few more touchdowns in our arsenal, I figured, and then we'd come back for a few more in the second half.

Guinn's kick was taken eight yards deep in the end zone. The return man opted not to run it out.

"Aw, come on," I said lightly and in a normal conversational voice so that only a few teammates heard me. "Run that sucker out and show us what you've got. Be a man."

Of course the few teammates who heard me were certain to needle me the next time I downed a kickoff deep in the end zone.

Having the ball on their own 20, the 49ers continued their determination to make a game of it. Two first downs later they were at their own 46. Two plays after that they had third and two at the Hawaii 46.

282

Before they could run another play they got another first down when Prendergast got called for encroachment, moving the ball to the Hawaii 41.

"Let's settle down out there!" Walker called. "Make them earn it! You're making it too easy for them!"

It was annoying to see the 49ers moving on our side of the field. Richards seemed to share that sentiment. He didn't push them back to their own side of the field but he did sack the quarterback at the Hawaii 47.

"Fumble!"

Another scramble for the ball. Suddenly there were three Hawaiians pointing toward the north end zone. The referee followed suit.

It was McDaniel again. He had two fumble recoveries in the game and we were still in the first quarter.

More jubilation. For a guy who was struggling through workouts a couple of days earlier, I was feeling practically invincible if not immortal. The 49ers so far had put together two drives where they moved the ball reasonably well and then coughed it up near midfield. That had to have crushed them mentally.

Of course we still had only a ten-point lead. I figured that we had no choice but to focus on increasing that lead by at least three points but preferably seven.

Kerner picked up four yards off right tackle to the Hawaii 49. That was where the first quarter ended.

We changed sides. That meant moving the ball roughly six feet. We would now be heading toward the south end zone.

I couldn't wait to resume play. I wanted to ring up another score.

And another and another and another and. . . .

Although I had nothing personal against anybody on the 49ers, I felt compelled to show them no aloha. It was the price they would have to pay for having to face us a week after our tough loss in Atlanta.

Had we beat the Falcons I naturally would have found another excuse to want to bury the 49ers. In either case I wanted them sorry they came to Hawaii. That was the way I always felt about my opponents. We wanted to be very rude hosts.

To kick off the second quarter I was the recipient of a Bender pass at the San Francisco 27. I had to make a leaping grab but came down with it. I was off balance when I came down, though, and fell at the 26. A 49er touched me before I could get back up again.

Apparently the 49ers weren't quite ready to wave their white flags. Bender dropped back to pass and wound up sacked at the 33. It was second and 17.

We retaliated, stubbornly fighting to show the 49ers which was the better team. Bender hit Dietrich on the numbers at the eleven. Ted got to the six before finally going down.

The fans smelled blood. They were getting raucous. It was as if they were ancient Romans rooting for us to do for the 49ers what the lions did for the Christians. I was feeling sadistic and loved the idea.

Ozzie got us three feet closer to the end zone on a sweep around right end. Kerner covered the last five yards when he went off left tackle. He was touched a few times but nobody was able to make solid contact. He went into the end zone standing up.

A sold-out crowd of 48,753 was elated. That's not to mention a large group of players and coaches on the mauka sideline. The offensive unit didn't simply run off the field. We included the occasional hops, skips and jumps as well as back slapping, fist thrusting and hand clapping.

Guinn's extra point was good. We led 17-0 with 13:02 left in the first half.

"All right! We're on a roll here," Hayer remarked, walking along the sideline and slapping his teammates on the backs or shoulders. "Let's keep it up."

We were all smiles on the sideline. With 43:02 still left to play in the game we were already smelling victory. I just hoped it was confidence and not cockiness that motivated us. It wasn't as if we were playing the Cowboys or Raiders or Steelers but even against teams that are struggling one should never assume that a 17-point lead, especially in the first half, guarantees victory. It is even possible to make up a 17-point deficit inside the two-minute warning.

The 49ers didn't seem to be conceding that the game was over. After downing the kick in the end zone for a touchback they started a drive from the 20. After two third-down conversions they had a first down at the Hawaii 45. While our 17-point lead remained intact, the 49ers were determined to take a bite out of it. There was a lot less smiling on our sideline.

A rush off left tackle produced three yards to the 42. That was followed by a pair of pass attempts. In both cases the quarterback was forced to scramble under heavy rushes. Neither rush produced a sack but both passes also fell incomplete.

It was fourth and seven. I took my place to return a punt.

As I stood on the ten I looked around at the stadium. I could feel the crowd's elation. So far we were giving them exactly what they wanted. We had scored on all three of our possessions. I figured that we still had time to score two or even three more touchdowns before halftime although I didn't honestly believe we would strike quickly enough to do that. One more touchdown would have been perfectly acceptable and two would have been great.

The punt that was about to be made would climax the 49ers' best drive of the day. In all three of their possessions they wound up in roughly the same area past midfield. This was simply the first possession where they turned the ball over on downs and not fumbles.

Suddenly the punt was in the air. The punter was going for the coffin corner which surprised nobody. I ran only casually toward the ball on my right since there was no way I was going to catch up to it. The ball came down inside the ten and bounced out of bounds at the six.

I looked up at the clock on the large scoreboard in the north end zone. There was 8:19 left in the half. I figured that was perfect. We could chew up the clock over 94 yards and go into the locker room with a 24-0 lead.

Our opening play was a Waimanalo right. Marv and Clint opened a hole the size of the Diamond Head crater for me to run through. I was touched once or twice but still managed to get six yards to the 12.

Ozzie went up the middle in a gritty effort. The hole wasn't quite as generous as the one I got but he showed a lot of determination as he fought his way to the 15. It was third and one.

It was going to be up to Ozzie to pick up the first down. We then discovered that his services would not be needed. A linebacker, ostensibly knowing that we were going up the middle again, jumped prematurely and ran into Shuford. That gave us a first down at the 20.

"All right. We'll take the freebie," Shuford remarked as we formed a huddle near the ten. "What's the Hawaiian word for thank you?"

"Mahalo," Grummon, Marv, Kerner and I replied simultaneously.

The penalty wound up being the highlight of the drive. Rushes by Ozzie and Kerner followed by an incomplete pass gave us a fourth and three at the 27.

"Damn!" I muttered on the sideline, possibly visibly irritated.

"Don't let it get you down, Jaybird," defensive coordinator Max Crawford said soothingly. "We know we're not going to score every time we get our hands on the ball. You're playing a good game. Don't lose your focus."

I hate to admit it but I didn't respect the 49ers. As I have been stressing, their record indicated that they weren't a very good team in 1977. When that happens it sometimes causes a player to forget that the team is comprised of genuine professionals who simply aren't having things their way. Not only did I have to remind myself that they were not incapable of beating us, they were also not incapable of coming back from a 17-0 deficit.

Jablonski did his part to make things difficult for the 49ers. His punt got past the return man. Hamer touched the ball down at the 19. It was officially a 54 yard punt with no return.

I sat on the bench and watched the 49ers resume their familiar pattern. After two first downs they were at the Hawaii 48.

A rush up the middle got them to the Hawaii 44. They decided to go to the air next. Their deepest penetration had been to the 41 and they apparently wanted to get beyond that.

Richards dashed that hope. He fought off a block at the line and another in the backfield. He sacked the quarterback at the 50.

That drew a roar from the crowd as well as from our bench. All the while Richard got up and walked away as casual as a stroll in the park. Sack dances weren't his style. His way, like that of his lifelong friend Russ Allen, was to outplay the opponent but not taunt the opponent.

The clock ran down to the two-minute warning. The break was followed by an incompletion and I returned to the field. With the clock stopped at 1:52 I felt it was imperative that I try to have a sizable return to help our chances of getting at least a field goal before the clock ran out.

The 49er punter tried to foil my runback plan by punting to my left. I raced over and managed to catch the ball on one high bounce at the 14.

I immediately had to sidestep a white jersey. After a few more yards I straight-armed another white jersey. Hasegawa also blocked a white jersey out of the play and I managed to elude another white jersey before I was knocked out of bounds at the Hawaii 26.

We had 1:38 left to move 74 yards. At the very least, we needed to pick up about 40 yards to have a legitimate shot at a field goal. As we huddled I noticed Guinn on the sideline kicking a ball into a small portable net.

The 49er defense was determined to make us earn what we got. Bender met a heavy rush as he dropped back. He scrambled a little and then got the pass off to Grummon. A defensive back batted the ball down near the Hawaii 45. That stopped the clock at 1:28.

There was another heavy rush on the next play. This time the pass was completed. Slater caught the ball at the Hawaii 37 near the left sideline. He ran out of bounds at the 39 to stop the clock with 1:19 showing.

Bender was forced to scramble again on the next play. Just as he was going to be sacked he got a pass off to Dietrich near the San Francisco 40 in front of the 49er bench. A defensive back jumped in front of Ted and juggled the ball. Before he could gain control of it I tackled him, causing the ball to drop incomplete.

Another 49er pounced on the loose ball. I looked up and got a sick feeling as a couple of 49ers jubilantly pointed toward the north end zone.

Fortunately the officials disagreed and were waving their arms in front of them. The defensive back never had possession. The play was ruled an incomplete pass. The clock was stopped at 1:08.

We fared better on the next play. Bender hit me over the middle at the San Francisco 43. I ran a slightly oblique pattern toward the makai sideline. I had to fight off two tacklers in the process.

They finally brought me down just as we were going out of bounds at the 39. The clock was down to 56 seconds.

I bounced up and headed toward where we would huddle near midfield. At the same time I noticed Walker turn and gesture to Rossi. Walker gave Rossi a play to take in and then Rossi ran on the field.

"Dockman!" Rossi called.

Obviously Rossi was sent in to replace me. Initially I wasn't sure since there were formations we used with both of us on the field.

There wasn't much I could do. Although I considered myself to be a team player, I wasn't devoid of an ego. I also knew that it was simply Walker's way to send a backup in on occasion to give the starter a breather before sending him back in.

"Helluva play," Walker complimented as I reached the sideline. "Stay right here. You're going back in on the next play."

Bender dropped back. He was under moderate pressure this time. He got the pass off to Slater.

The pass was intercepted at the 23. A defensive back picked the pass off, stumbled and fell to one knee, then got back up before anybody could touch him. He got to the 28 before Rossi brought him down.

Had I not been so upset about the turnover during a golden scoring opportunity I would have been more impressed with Rossi's tackle. He had been a linebacker in high school but that was six years earlier. Without any hesitation he made a textbook tackle. It was obvious that he hadn't forgotten how it was done.

For Rossi the play could have been classified as a blessing in disguise. By making the tackle he got to do something noteworthy while relatives and friends watched the game on television in the San Francisco area.

Overall there were eleven disappointed faces as my offensive colleagues came to the sideline. The interception appeared as if it was simply a good play by the defensive back and not the fault of Bender or Slater. Nobody seemed to be blaming anybody but we were all still disappointed.

What surprised me was that the 49ers didn't try to make something happen. There were only 44 seconds left but they also had two timeouts. With some well-orchestrated short passes to the sidelines they could still take a shot at a field goal and maybe even a touchdown. Instead they took two snaps and let the half end.

"I don't believe this," I remarked as I watched the 49er quarterback drop to a knee after the first snap. "They ought to be trying to put a drive together."

"Yes they should," Grummon replied, standing next to me in front of our bench. "But I'm glad they're not."

"So am I," I concurred. "Still. . . . "

It didn't make any sense to me. Most of my other teammates were just as surprised. It was also disappointing since this also virtually eliminated any hope for forcing a turnover. The virtual surrender to end the half could also prove to be critical if the 49ers got to within a touchdown of us in the second half.

The final seconds ticked off after the second snap. The crowd gave us a nice round of applause as we left the field. The applause warmed me but I was still feeling incomplete. I believed we should have had a bigger lead.

As soon as I reached the locker room I wanted to return to the field. Although our final drive of the half left me feeling frustrated, I realized I was having an enjoyable day. Football was fun, at least with a 17-0 halftime lead.

I forced myself to take it easy during the 12 minutes. I visited the little boy's room, drank a cup of Gatorade and sat in front of my locker while consuming a Hershey bar and Pepsi. Offensive coordinator Jim Potter came over to discuss our plans for the second half and then Walker stood in the middle of the room.

"I have no doubt that you can bury these guys," he said. "I also have no doubt that they are going to make a very determined effort to bury you. They may have some success but I know that you can put them away. Just remember to stay in focus. Don't be laying back but also don't get too hyped. Just do your jobs and everything will fall into place. Let's go."

"Let's go!" about half of the team, myself included, echoed in unison. We got up and returned to the field amid enthusiastic cheers among the 48,753 not still on the concourse relieving themselves, buying dogs and beers, or simply kicking back.

Guinn kicked off toward the south end zone. The return man caught the ball at the three. I watched in horror as the 49ers effectively cut down my teammates while the return man shot past the 20 . . . the 30 . . . the 40. . . .

Rory Manwaring got the return man in his grasp. The two of them went down at the San Francisco 42.

"All right! Let's go, defense!" Walker barked, casually waving his arm to guide the defensive unit to the field but with a look of exasperation on his face. At the moment the kickoff team was on the top of Walker's list.

I sat on the bench to force myself to patiently wait. The good field position told me that the 49ers were more likely to finally score. I reminded myself that we would still have a two-score lead if they did score. I didn't want to panic over their stubborn refusal to play like the doormats they were supposed to be.

The 49ers started to move. After only two plays they were at the Hawaii 39. That was their deepest penetration of the day.

They continued to chip away. Going a few yards at a time, they picked up three more first downs. They had first and goal at the two.

It took only one play from there. A rush around right end put the 49ers on the scoreboard. With the extra point they cut our lead to 17-7 with 8:33 left in the third quarter.

"We should score on this drive. The offense has had plenty of rest," I said to Marv in both a serious and light demeanor before taking my place

288

on the kick return team. As I stood on the goal line in the north end zone I reminded myself that we still held a ten-point lead. The 49ers came to Hawaii determined to win. I knew we could send them home empty handed if we played our game for the remaining 23 minutes and 33 seconds.

Of course it would help if we could counter their touchdown with a touchdown of our own.

The kick was up.

"Run it out, Rich!" I called to Hasegawa before running forward to fight off the enemy. I managed to head off a white jersey near the 15, knocking him down while keeping my feet.

Hasegawa was running past by this time. He had taken the ball two yards deep in the end zone. I started to head back upfield to help him out but he was hit and dropped at the 24.

I reached Rich just as he was getting up.

"Good job," I said, whacking him on the rear.

"Great block," he replied before tossing the ball to an official and heading to the sideline.

We were 76 yards from a touchdown. I began the drive by running a sweep around right end. Following my blockers and doing a fair job of eluding tacklers, I got to the 31 to give us a second and three.

Ozzie got the next two carries. The second one gave us a first down at the Hawaii 37.

We went to the air. Bender hit me over the middle at the Hawaii 43 and I shot upfield. I got to midfield before anybody even got a hand on me and I still managed to break away while the crowd roared its encouragement. I was finally hit simultaneously by a pair of defensive backs and dropped at the San Francisco 38. It was a 25-yard gain.

One of my tacklers helped me to my feet. He didn't say anything or make eye contact. His expression was one of frustration. He obviously preferred that I not have been able to pick up the yardage but he still conceded to sportsmanship.

"Dockman!"

I looked in the direction of the voice and saw Rossi running on the field. I ran off, slapping five with Rossi as our paths crossed.

Walker had a big smile on his face when I reached him.

"Good play, Jay. How do you feel?"

"Great," I said. "I'm ready to go."

"Okay, hang back a few seconds. I just want to give Rossi a couple of plays."

After a pair of incompletions Walker sent me back in. In this case Rossi stayed in since we were going to our double-double on third down. Joe Slater went in with me while Ozzie Roberts and Rich Grummon came out.

Bender hit Slater near the left sideline at the 32. Joe rushed forward to the 27. That was one more yard than we needed for a first down.

"Okay, we're definitely back to playing our game again," Bender remarked in the huddle. "Let's take it all the way in and knock the life out of them."

Prior to the next play Grummon came back in but Ozzie stayed on the sideline. Walker apparently decided to experiment with our single-double formation. This was comprised of one wide receiver on the line and two halfbacks. The halfback on the side of the wide receiver, yours truly, would line up in the slot. Rossi would line up in what would be the slot if there was a wide receiver on that side. It was primarily a passing formation but we had several rushing plays designed for this formation.

Kerner picked up four yards off left tackle and then I picked up four yards off right tackle to the 19, having gone in motion from the slot and taking a handoff behind the interior line.

Ozzie came back in and Kerner went out. Still in our single-double but with a tailback instead of a fullback, Ozzie picked up four yards up the middle to give us a first down at the 15.

We tried going through the air again. Bender spotted Rossi about five yards deep in the end zone. Unfortunately the pass was batted down, leaving Rossi still looking for the first reception of his career.

"Rossi!"

That was from Kerner as he ran back on the field. We were returning to our more familiar formations.

Bender hit Dietrich at the five. Ted bellied back a little to try to elude a tackler. His effort was unsuccessful and he wound up being tackled at the six.

It was third and one. Dietrich was certain to hear about his effort at Tuesday's film session since he already had the first down, then lost it when he bellied back. He was an All-Pro caliber receiver but he seemed to get burned by bellying back more than any other receiver.

Kerner got us the first down, taking some of the heat off of Dietrich. Going off right tackle, he barreled his way to the two.

That was when I started noticing the crowd again. The fans were screaming and yelling and having a great time. I even noticed three young women wearing shorts and bathing suit tops dancing at their seats in the first row above the visitors' baseball dugout in the south end zone. The whole thing almost gave me goose pimples.

Bender tried to hit Grummon in the left corner of the end zone. The pass was knocked away.

We were going to the air again. This time there was a heavy rush. Bender was forced to scramble to his right. He tucked the ball away and crossed the line of scrimmage. He managed to continue until he reached the right front corner of the end zone, being tackled as the officials were raising their arms.

"Yeah, Steve! Way to go!" I exclaimed as I ran over to him from the back of the end zone. Marv and Clint were helping him to his feet. We all ran off the field together. The crowd was roaring.

"Good job, men," Walker remarked as we reached the sideline. "Great run, Steve."

Guinn came through with the extra point, as expected. We held a 24-7 lead. It was a three-score game again with 2:13 left in the third quarter.

The game was as good as over at this point. Whatever momentum the 49ers may have picked up was ostensibly crushed when we answered their touchdown with a touchdown of our own. They had a modest drive which carried into the fourth quarter and ended with a punt that I fair caught on the Hawaii 15. We then drove 85 yards on seven plays that ended with a 33-yard touchdown pass from Bender to Grummon to give us a 31-7 lead with 11:28 left in the game.

Any thoughts the 49ers may have had about overcoming a 24-point deficit were forgotten on the ensuing kickoff. The return man got to the 21 where he was hammered by Hasegawa. The ball came loose and was recovered by Hamer at the 19.

We decided to ice the game once and for all. We weren't interested in running up the score. We simply wanted insurance.

On the second play from scrimmage Bender hit Slater with a 17-yard touchdown pass. Unfortunately that was nullified by a holding penalty, giving us a second and 18 at the 27.

It only took one play from there. Bender hit me near the right sideline at the seven. I straight-armed a defensive back and ran in for a touchdown. That gave us a 38-7 lead which ultimately proved to be the final score.

My touchdown was the last play I was in. Walker went to the backups at that point. I spent the final minutes of the game talking and joking with my teammates, casually looking into the crowd and being a good team player by cheering on the backups. Rossi still didn't get his first reception of his NFL career since the only pass Billingsley threw fell incomplete. The primary concern was running out the clock.

At one point I looked up in the bleachers and gave Carol a smile and wave. She was happy that we won. She was even happier that I didn't get hurt. She was a great lady.

McDaniel gave the postgame prayer. Afterward Walker did as he always did after a victory, holding up the game ball.

"Two fumble recoveries in the first quarter set the stage for us," Walker said while tossing the ball to McDaniel who received a rousing ovation.

"You guys looked pretty good out there today," Walker said, leading to another roar from his players and virtually guaranteeing that he was going to change his mind before showing the game films on Tuesday. "We just hit the halfway point with a five and two record. We're halfway to a playoff berth."

That produced another roar. A playoff berth was obviously what we were after. From there we would focus on winning a trip to New Orleans. It would be great to end the season in the same place our season began, especially if we could end it with a victory.

"Let's not look too far ahead," Walker cautioned. "We're off to a great start but we still have seven steps to the playoffs. In each of those steps you'll be meeting teams that very badly want to beat you. For today we'll enjoy this victory. After that we'll focus 100 percent on Tampa Bay. Don't look beyond that because if you do you won't be at your best in Tampa. That's how you get beat."

Walker wrapped up his talk with a few more compliments about the day's game and then let the media in.

I knew I had played a reasonably good game. I was still surprised by my receiving statistics which were much better than I imagined. I led the team with seven receptions for 159 yards. Dietrich was next with four receptions for 54 yards while Grummon also picked up 54 yards on two receptions.

Kerner led the team in rushing with eight carries for 53 yards. Ozzie had eleven carries for 40 yards which wasn't bad although those stats would also never put him in the Pro Bowl. I was a very distant third with three carries for 17 yards.

Everything seemed to click. Our offense moved with great precision down the field. Our defense shut the 49er offense down almost completely, making several big plays when a big play was desperately needed.

Our tough loss in Atlanta was history. It was a blemish on our record and would be there for the rest of the season. It would still be a very insignificant blemish if we continued to win.

Needless to say, we were very full of ourselves in the locker room. There was a lot of laughing and back-slapping. Even our mistakes didn't come back to haunt us.

Did we make mistakes?

Of course we did.

So we celebrated now. We knew that within 48 hours we would be watching the films which would leave us as revered as what a passing dog leaves on the lawn. Walker, and Crawford who would be running the defensive film session, would use the literal translation of the allusion when describing our performances during the film sessions.

"Somebody's got a very long flight to San Francisco," I overheard Blakely remark.

He was right and we were allowed to celebrate. Sunday was a day of celebration. Tuesday was a day to be charred by fire-breathing coaches.

We continued our festivities in the hospitality room. That gave the wives, girlfriends, children and other guests an opportunity to feed the egos of a

292

group of football players whose heads barely fit through the door. We won big as a unit. On Tuesday we would be raked over the coals and cut down to size as a unit.

Nothing alleviates the sting of a loss like a victory. The season was half over and we were 5-2. That's not a bad record at all although the losses could prove to be critical, especially the loss in Atlanta since the loss was to a team in our own division as well as our conference. The Miami loss was less likely to figure in a tiebreaker situation since Miami was in the AFC. It could still prove to be critical in some way.

Looking at the standings, how would we fare in the playoff structure if the regular season were only seven weeks long?

It just so happens that the Falcons and Rams both lost. The Falcons fell to the Vikings and the Rams were shocked by the Saints. That meant that we had sole possession of first place in the NFC West again.

I would presume that we would have the home field advantage in the opening round. That's because the Central Division leader, Minnesota, had an identical record to ours but I would quickly give us the tiebreaker by virtue of the fact that we beat the Vikings in our lone encounter with them. There may have been other factors involved but the head-to-head was the factor I chose to use.

We would still be the second-place team in the conference. That's because the Cowboys were leading the Eastern Division and the NFC with a perfect 7-0 record. They were the only undefeated team in the NFL at this point. That means that if the season were seven weeks long and we and the Cowboys won our opening round games we would have to play in Dallas for the conference championship. If we won in the opening round and the Cowboys lost the conference championship game would be at Aloha Stadium.

But, of course, the season was 14 weeks long. We had to take the season one game at a time. Tampa Bay was next and that was a very hungry team, having lost to Memphis that day for its seventh consecutive loss on the season and lowering its overall record to 0-21. If we took the Bucs lightly and/or looked ahead to our game the following week in Chicago we were going to have an even more miserable trip to Florida than when we played in Miami, becoming the first team in history to lose to the Buccaneers.

For the moment I savored our victory over the hapless 49ers. Carol and I joined most of the rest of the team, wives, girlfriends, children and other guests at the postgame buffet in the hospitality room.

It was a festive atmosphere without it getting out of control. There was a lot of laughing and joking. Walker did his part, going around the room to slap his players on the back and exchange pleasantries with the guests. He was especially good with children.

Carol and I went to my place and soaked in the jacuzzi. After that I took her home. She still had some midterm exams to grade and wanted to get it done that night.

Since I still felt hyper, partially because of our victory and partially to celebrate not being plagued by the bug that had slowed me down for a few days, I drove to Waikiki and went up to the Nest.

I didn't get to Waikiki much anymore. It was no longer convenient. Parking could be atrocious for nonresidents. I still liked to visit there on occasion.

On *rare* occasion.

This was actually my first trip to Waikiki since I moved to Hawaii Kai about four months earlier. I was sold on the more tranquil environment of Hawaii Kai. That was after six years of having Waikiki as my primary hot spot.

"Hey, stranger," my old friend Roy Mulligan greeted when I came through the entrance at the Nest. "It's about time you showed your face in here again."

"I know. It isn't as convenient as it used to be, especially during the season," I replied, occupying the bar stool next to where Roy was sitting during a break. He was the entertainer in the Nest on Sunday and Monday nights and performed Thursday, Friday and Saturday nights at *The Toilet* although Davy Jones Locker really wasn't that bad a dive. Roy was actually half of a duo but his partner entertained only as an avocation and focused primarily on his work as a record producer and concert promoter. This forced Roy to often perform solo, which he didn't mind although he did enjoy working with his partner.

Roy and I first met in this same nightclub five years earlier. At the time I was a college junior on a Sunday night date with a young woman I met a few nights earlier at the Blue Goose. Roy was performing as part of a trio that was about to break up since the other two members wanted to take the act to Los Angeles to try to make it big. Roy opted for the relative comfort of his lifelong home in the islands.

The other two members vanished into obscurity. It may sound funny when expressed that way. Who can really blame them for making the effort to live their dream? At least they had the guts to try.

I didn't get to really know Roy until the summer after our initial encounter when we were both working as bartenders at the Rose and Crown in King's Alley. Roy was performing only occasionally at the time. I was simply working a summer job to earn extra money to stash away for my senior year at the university.

"That was a great game you guys played today," Roy said.

"Thanks. Were you there?"

"No. Myra and I wanted to go but we found out the game was already sold out. We had to watch it on TV."

"It's amazing what a winning record will do for attendance. All three of our home games so far have sold out enough in advance to televise locally. Last year we always drew good crowds but the only sellouts we had were the opener against St. Louis and the Oakland game. The Oakland game didn't sell out until the day before so they couldn't televise it here."

"Yeah, I remember. I went to the box office and the last ticket was sold about ten minutes earlier."

"Why didn't you say something?" I asked. "I don't know what the odds were but I might have been able to get something for you and Myra. The team might have had a couple of unclaimed tickets available."

Roy said he wasn't sure why he didn't contact me. He said he probably figured there wouldn't have been anything left. It was also the day before the game and he figured I would have other issues on my mind.

"We've got the Rams in three weeks," I said. "That's our next home game. Do you want me to see about getting you and Myra tickets?"

"Do you think you can?"

"It shouldn't be any problem this far in advance. I'm allotted two anyway so I'll only have to dig up only one more since Carol's the only one I automatically give a ticket to. I'll put the request in on Tuesday. I may have your tickets in hand that day."

"Great," said Roy. "That'll be a really good game."

"I think so. The Rams'll definitely have revenge on their minds."

Roy had to excuse himself to perform another set. I drank a beer and listened to my friend perform songs by the Kingston Trio, the Byrds, Gordon Lightfoot, Johnny Cash, the Beatles and a few others. When he finished the set we talked for a few more minutes before I excused myself and finally went home.

CHAPTER THIRTEEN
Keeping Tampa at Bay

Tuesday morning we met at the Marine base. First on the agenda was our film sessions. The offense went to the room it met in during training camp while the defense went to its room.

Walker entered and took his place at the projector. He was motionless for about a minute. Anybody who looked back at him saw a man with a disgusted scowl on his face.

"What's up with Walker?" Rossi whispered to Grummon, thinking that only Grummon would hear him.

"Shut up, Rossi!" Walker barked. "You're what's up with Walker! I can't believe you made this team! It amazes me what you clowns got away with Sunday!"

I'm not sure of how long the film session lasted. It was allegedly about an hour. It seemed like about eight or nine.

Rossi, who was in Walker's doghouse before Walker even turned on the projector, missed a block on our second kick return. He lunged for a defender who simply sidestepped him as Rossi went face first in the turf.

"What the hell was that, Rossi?" Walker asked belligerently, running the sequence back and forth a few times. "You're supposed to block the man, Rossi. Instead you turned yourself into a human doormat."

Nobody was immune. The team's top choice in the 1976 expansion draft, Marv, had trouble blocking the left defensive tackle on one play. The defender stuffed Ozzie near the line.

"What's the matter, Nelson? You getting tired out there? Is that the way they taught you to block in New Orleans? I can't believe you went to the Pro Bowl last year."

If there was a play where Walker didn't lambaste at least one person, I don't recall it. If the camera had zoomed in on our feet at some point during the game Walker would have criticized the way we tied our shoes. It was our reward for one of the biggest routs in our brief history.

"This was scarier than *The Exorcist*," Walker remarked when he mercifully turned off the projector. "It's lucky for you guys that the defense didn't allow too many points. They really saved you guys."

Of course it was also lucky for the defense that Walker didn't preside over their film session. Then it would have been lucky for the defense that the offense rang up 38 points.

"You guys looked better in Atlanta," Walker continued abrasively; a comment that stung a little although that was primarily because I didn't care to think about the Atlanta game. "The 49ers must really stink if they couldn't even beat you. If you play like this on Sunday you're going to make history by becoming the first team to lose to Tampa Bay. When the Bucs watch the films that we just watched they are going to be rubbing their palms together. I envy John McKay right now."

That was a huge stretch. We all knew that. His words still stung despite the fact that we all knew better.

Walker dismissed us to get dressed for our light Tuesday workout, apparently so worked up that he forgot that we normally meet as a single unit after the film sessions but he dismissed us just as the defense was coming to our room. In the locker room we looked at each other and shook our heads in amused disbelief.

"How'd your session go?" McDaniel asked Grummon.

"Oh, you know. We sucked."

"Yeah," Dietrich chimed in. "According to Walker, we would have had trouble against a Pop Warner team."

"I'm going to have to rewrite tonight's show," I added, referring to my TV show. "I've actually got it written that we won on Sunday. I'll have to correct that."

"Yeah, the newspaper also said we won," Kerner said. "They must have gotten our game mixed up with somebody else's."

Our jocular remarks were a good way to ease the nervous tension. As anticipated, we did not leave the film session on top of the world.

There were two primary reasons for why Walker ripped us to shreds. The most obvious reason was that we had won so handily that he had to bring us down to earth. The other reason was that we were playing Tampa Bay next; a team which had existed for exactly a season and-a-half and still hadn't won. Walker didn't want us getting complacent.

"Fortunately you guys saved the game for us," I added lightly.

"Yeah," said Grummon. "Walker said we definitely would have lost had the defense not jumped in to save us."

"That's funny," Jennings replied. "Crawford said it was the offense who saved *our* sorry butts."

We had our typical week of work. Walker ranted and raved on Tuesday, Wednesday and Thursday. He became more chummy on Friday and Saturday. After our workout at the Marine base on Friday we drove to Air Service at Honolulu International and caught an overnight flight to Tampa on our chartered DC-8.

At least Scott would be back in action. Nothing against Ozzie but Scott was better.

Hebron would be out for another week. That meant Malick would start in Tampa.

Morrissey spent the entire week officially listed as doubtful because of a shoulder injury. By the time we got to Tampa it was obvious that he would not be able to play. Dubois would get the start although he might have anyway since he and Morrissey competed each week for the starting post. Starting or not, Morrissey wouldn't be available.

We also had a casualty on the offensive line. Carl Hayer had been listed as questionable because of a sore hamstring. He would suit up for the game but would not start. Vince Daniels would start at left tackle in his place. Carl would play only as a last resort.

During the flight to Tampa I mentioned to Ed Jennings that the NFL schedule makers were responsible for a dramatic waste of aviation fuel.

"How so?" Ed asked.

"Two weeks ago we played in Atlanta," I replied. "And then we flew home to play the 49ers."

Ed nodded and then his eyes lit up. I could tell that he understood what I was saying.

"What you're saying is that they should have had us play Atlanta and Tampa back-to-back instead of scheduling the 49ers in between," he said.

"Exactly. Tampa and Atlanta are less than 500 miles apart but they are both about 4500 miles from Honolulu. If they had scheduled Tampa and Atlanta in consecutive weeks we could have just stayed on the mainland instead of flying back to Honolulu to play a single game in between the Falcons and Bucs."

"Right," Ed agreed thoughtfully. "And we also played Miami earlier this year. Perhaps they could have scheduled us to play in Miami, Tampa and Atlanta in consecutive weeks."

"Oh, yeah. I forgot about the Dolphins. That could have saved the airline thousands of miles in aviation fuel if we stayed in the area for three games."

Ed nodded and looked thoughtful.

"For reasons that are purely selfish," he added after pondering for a moment, "I would just as soon go back to Hawaii after each game."

"Same here," I concurred. "There will still be times when we'll have to stay for back-to-back games."

"I know. I can handle that when it happens. I just hope we don't stay for three consecutive games."

I nodded in full agreement.

"What surprises me is that we're going back to Honolulu after we play the Bucs," I added. "I would have thought that we would go up north somewhere to get used to the cold weather before we play in Chicago next week."

"You're right. Don't say anything. We don't want to give Walker any ideas."

"Yes, absolutely. It's not too late for him to change our itinerary."

Ed and I were actually being jocular. Walker wouldn't change our itinerary at this point. It would create too much of a distraction.

At least that is what we thought.

There are people who would laugh if I were to suggest that our next game was one that had me at least as nervous as any other contest that year. As I mentioned, the Tampa Bay Buccaneers at this juncture were 0-7 on the season and 0-21 in their entire existence while we were 12-9 over the same period. Why would such an apparent pushover make me nervous?

Because the Bucs *weren't* pushovers. Their record was humiliating but most of my teammates and I believed that they were better than that. They had good coaches and good players. They simply hadn't gelled. All it would take was a slight change in fortune and their momentum would shift dramatically.

Since we were the Buccaneers' next opponent that meant that we had the best chance of becoming the first team in history to lose to them. That was a dubious distinction that everybody on the team wanted to avoid. We wanted to make history but not that way.

"They're going to be tough," I said to Ferd Borsch of the *Honolulu Advertiser* and I meant it. I still made it a point to not belittle them to the media because that was the kind of thing that would fire them up. My teammates and coaches were equally cautious.

It was obvious when we did our light workout in Tampa on Saturday that we couldn't have been more up if we were preparing to square off against the Steelers. Had the Bucs already won a game or two we probably would not have been as psyched. The Bucs were still winless and we were determined to keep them that way. They would play the Giants the following week. Our philosophy was to let the Giants be the first to lose to the Bucs.

Being as psyched as we were was also scary. Getting too psyched up causes critical mistakes. One does not want to play a game lackadaisically but one also needs to avoid being so intense that we lose focus.

"Now take it easy," Walker cautioned at the end of the workout. "We all know what's at stake here. Don't play the game with the attitude of being afraid to lose. Play good, hard, clean football the same way you would against anybody else. That's the way to play winning football."

I relaxed on Saturday afternoon and evening. I took a walk and thought about things other than football as much as I could. For dinner I went with Marv, Clint and Ed to a restaurant near the hotel. The lasagna was exquisite.

Clint didn't care to play poker but Marv, Ed and I were up for a game. We knew that all we had to do was find Shuford's room. When we got there we found Dave, Grummon, Hamer and Jablonski already involved in Dave's customary low stakes game.

"Hey, we've got room for three more," Dave announced cheerily.

Seven of us spent the rest of the night playing poker. By the time we had to go to our rooms for curfew I had lost a whopping 20 dollars. The enjoyment and relaxation made it well worth the price.

Kickoff was at one. Breakfast was at 8:30. I was out of bed at a little before six.

As I usually did, I took a shower to kill time. Also as I usually did, I decided to head downstairs.

"Ready for some coffee, my man?" Marv asked good naturedly when we ran into each other in the hall.

"Sure," I replied lightly. "There's nothing like a good stimulant to calm your nerves before a game."

We weren't the first ones downstairs. Jennings had an uncanny knack for being first and this week was no exception. Also present were Allen, Richards, Black, Rossi and Dubois.

Bender, Abraham, Stanek and Dietrich soon showed up. That brought the total of athletic looking men to an even dozen. The other patrons and employees seemed to know who we were and we did have to sign a few autographs. Most of the people left us to ourselves.

For the most part we were quiet. We also had our giddy periods. We made comments that would probably not have been funny to anybody but ourselves since we were hyped with nervous energy.

"How many yards you gonna gain today, Jay?" Stanek asked.

"Gee, I don't know," I replied lightly. "How well are you going to block?"

Roughly half of us were smokers. That was not unusual in 1977. It was 13 years after the Surgeon General's conclusion that cigarettes were connected to lung cancer but it still didn't have that big of an impact on our society. One could still go to a bank or grocery store or most other public facilities and openly smoke. The only place I knew of in Honolulu to ban smoking was the Blaisdell Arena and that went into effect only the previous year. Smoking was still commonplace including among professional athletes.

Allen was a very dedicated non-smoker. He seemed puzzled every time one of us lit up. When Jennings lit a cigarette he finally commented.

"How do you guys smoke and play football?"

"We don't," Marv replied jocularly. "We keep our cigarettes in our lockers while we're playing."

"Yeah?" Hayer added. "And what are you going to do when your cigarettes give you cancer?"

"Die," Black retorted.

It was not especially funny. We laughed primarily from nervous energy. Our demented senses of humor loosened us up.

We had won the toss. My butterflies were racing at an unbelievable rate as I exchanged slap fives with Hasegawa at the goal line.

"Let's kick their butts," Rich commented.

"Yeah, let's do it," was my uneasy reply.

It was a day similar to what we were used to. The temperature was in the upper 70s. It would be humid, especially with only light winds and no precipitation to cool things off.

Fear swept over me as I waited for CBS to come out of commercial so that we could receive the kickoff. Mentally I was committing one of the most egregious of sins in sports. My fear of losing was so intense that I may have been playing *not to lose* instead of playing to win. As long as the flights from Miami and Atlanta had seemed after losses in those locales, the flight from Tampa would seem at least three times as long if we blew this one.

A good crowd augmented the fear. I didn't know if the game was sold out or not but it was a good crowd. The hometown team had lost all 21 games in its existence but it still had fan support. The fans probably knew, as I did, that the Bucs would eventually get the monkey off their backs and the fans wanted to be there when it happened. I fervently hoped that I wouldn't be.

On the Tampa Bay sideline stood an old friend. Dressed in white pants, a pumpkin-colored shirt and a white beach hat with an orange band was John McKay. Less than a decade earlier he was personally recruiting me to play football at USC. There were other schools that recruited me just as hard as USC did but he was the head coach who put the most individual effort into me. He visited me at my home, at school and even dropped in at my workplace. He was aware of the problems I was having with my parents who stridently believed I owed it to the United States of America to bypass college in favor of a military career. While being careful not to interfere in my domestic disputes, he told me he believed my parents would eventually come around to accepting my decision to go to college.

And they did although not until after the Vietnam War ended. They probably didn't fully accept my decision until after I graduated from college.

The red shirt signaled that we were live on CBS. This game was shown in Hawaii but possibly nowhere else. Any game involving Tampa Bay at this juncture would not be a ratings bonanza outside of the opponent's locale. If CBS showed the Bucs anywhere else it would prove to be a ratings coup for NBC and ABC.

As the kicker approached the ball I silently hoped that he wouldn't kick it my way. My fear of failure was making me nauseous. It was also making me pretty disgusted with myself.

Naturally the ball came my way. I caught the ball on the goal line.

Suddenly I forgot my fears and ran forward. I got all the way to the 30 before going down.

That did it. Perhaps I still feared losing but no more than usual. The success of the first play put me in the proper frame of mind. My focus was on winning.

Our first play from scrimmage made a statement. Bender hit Grummon near the left hashmark at the Hawaii 49. Rich broke a couple of tackles before going down at the Tampa Bay 43.

That was the highlight of our opening drive. Tampa Bay's defense made a statement that things were not going to be so easy for us. Scott's two-yard run was sandwiched between a pair of incompletions and we were forced to punt. The defense had shut us down.

"It's all right, men," offensive coordinator Jim Potter said as we reached the sideline. "We'll break them down. Just stick with it."

If the Bucs were going to score on their first drive, they would have to travel just about the maximum length of the field. Jablonski's punt bounced inside the ten. After another bounce Hamer caught the ball at the one and managed to freeze on the spot.

"Yeah! All right!" I hollered. I no longer regretted so much that we didn't score. Sometimes games are won by key plays such as that punt.

The Bucs weren't conceding. Utilizing the running ability of rookie Ricky Bell, they picked up decent chunks of yardage. Twice they converted on third down, once on the ground and once in the air, before a five-yard rush by Bell gave them a second and five at the Bucs 41.

USC alumnus Norm Richards got into the backfield on the next play. He brought Bell down for a two-yard loss. That was followed by an incompletion so I returned to the field to return a punt.

It was a bit of a disappointment that there wouldn't be a punt return since I was psyched to put together a good return. The punt was well to my left and not very long. It bounced near the left sideline at about the 30 and went out of bounds at the 24.

Unfortunately Tampa Bay's defense continued to be a virtual brick wall. Kerner picked up four yards off right tackle but Scott got nowhere around right end. Bender then dropped back to pass and was sacked at the 19. One would never know that this defense was part of a team that had never won.

As I dejectedly ran off the field I noticed the crowd. The fans were cheering wildly. The Bucs hadn't given their fans any victories but they did give them reason to cheer. This appeared to be a team with a bright future.

Jablonski continued doing his job well. He boomed a punt. It had a great hang time. The Bucs return man called for a fair catch at the Tampa Bay 38. For the second time that day Jablonski was given a semblance of a hero's welcome on the sideline.

This was indicative of how our game was going thus far. When high praise is offered only to the punter when one's team has the ball it is painfully obvious that the offense is not doing what it set out to do.

That was probably why Potter called the offense together to discuss how things were going. It wasn't a very long meeting because Tampa Bay followed our lead with a three and out. Following a two-yard rush, Prendergast and Jurgens combined on a seven-yard sack at the 33. That was followed by an incomplete pass and I took the field for another punt. At least our opponent's punter was also getting a lot of work.

"This time we're going to do something with it," I muttered to myself as I waited for the punt at about the 25. I was determined to be the catalyst if there was any possibility for a return.

The punt was slightly to my right and a few steps in front of me. I camped under it at the 28. Since I didn't believe anybody in enemy colors was near although I couldn't hear Hasegawa advising me for some reason, I didn't call for a fair catch.

I was correct. I had room to run although not much. I picked up eight yards to the 36 before I was brought down. It was a decent enough return.

Whether my return inspired the rest of the offense is arguable. It may have helped, I suppose, although not significantly since it was only eight yards. I believe it was our determination that caused us to move the ball.

Scott went up the middle to the 40 and then off right tackle to the 50. It felt good to have traveled 14 yards on only two plays.

We went 14 more yards on the next play. Bender hit me over the middle at the 37. I was hit immediately but managed to fight for another yard.

My adrenalin was pumping. We were on the move. As much as I loved and respected Coach McKay, he was my enemy at the moment. I wanted him to experience the agony of 22 consecutive defeats. I wanted him to spend the night regretting Commissioner Rozelle's decision to allow Hawaii to expand into the NFL. I wanted him to spend the forthcoming week asking himself why he thought he was ready to leave USC.

And then I wanted his team to beat the Giants the following week and everybody they faced afterward.

Scott went off left tackle to the 29. We decided to go to the air again, figuring the Bucs weren't looking for a pass on second and three.

Apparently the Bucs weren't fooled. They put a heavy rush on Bender. Steve still got the pass off but it fell incomplete.

Kerner was designated to give us our final three yards to avoid having the field goal unit sent out. He went up the middle and did exactly that with five yards to spare. We had a first down at the 21.

"I formation, wing right, four Waikiki left," Bender called in the huddle. It was a trap play and I was the ball carrier. It was a tricky play because I would be coming from the right side to run up the middle. Since it was a trap play Stanek would be pulling to the left. If the linebacker followed Stanek's decoy I would pick up a few yards. If the linebacker didn't take the bait the team would be flying to Chicago after my funeral.

As Bender handed me the ball it was a great relief to notice that the linebacker took the bait. I shot through the hole in a broad patch of daylight. I was gang-tackled at the 12 but it was mild compared to what I would have experienced had I collided with a ravenous linebacker who didn't have to bother fighting off blocks.

When I got up I happened to spot the newly burned linebacker. I was grateful that Bender was too smart to call that play twice in-a-row. It was probably a good idea not to call it two weeks in-a-row since the Bears would see it on film.

"Shall we run that play again?" Bender asked lightly as we formed our huddle.

"Sure," I replied equally as light. "As long as I get to be the quarterback and you carry the ball."

We did go up the middle again but not on a trap play. Scott picked up four yards to the nine. It was first and goal.

Two-thirds of the remaining distance we covered on the next play. Scott went around left end to the three. We were nine feet from drawing first blood.

We figured we would pick up the final three yards through the air. The Buc defense put heavy pressure on Bender. Steve got a pass off to Kerner but it was slightly tipped at the line. The ball arched up and back and a defensive back intercepted the pass nine yards deep in the end zone for a touchback.

Of course that got the crowd roaring and several guys in Hawaiians jerseys uttering expletives. The penalty marker quieted the crowd and the Hawaiians down.

"It's against them. It's against them," I said softly to myself. "It's got to be against them."

It was against us. The announcement that Dietrich had been offside got the crowd roaring again. Tampa Bay had a first down at the 20. There were 17 seconds left in the first quarter.

The expression on Walker's face was familiar. It was one of anger that he didn't want to show. He didn't want to discourage us.

"Don't let it beat you," Bennici directed as he met us near the Gatorade table. "It's a setback but I know you can rebound. They're playing you hard but you can break them down."

By the time I had my Gatorade and sat down the first quarter was ending. Bell had rushed for eight yards and the Bucs would be starting the second quarter at their own 28.

Daniels sat on the bench next to me. He looked at me and shook his head with a smile of resignation.

"They're tougher than people realize," he said. "Either that or I'm just getting old and weak."

Daniels was 28. That was not especially old and he did not appear to be weak. The problem seemed to be the former; that the Bucs were tougher than people realized.

The Bucs began the second quarter by rushing for a first down at the 32. That was followed by a three-yard rush to the 35 and then a one-yard loss where McDaniel caught the ball carrier behind the line.

304

McDaniel was slow in getting up. He was holding his wrist. Time was called while the trainer went out to meet the two-time Pro Bowler. It turned out to be just a minor ache but the rule mandated that McDaniel come out for one play since time was called for him. Kyle McWherter went in to replace him.

McWherter did not waste the opportunity. He broke through on the snap and forced the quarterback to rush his pass just as McWherter plowed into him. Hasegawa leaped up simultaneous with the intended receiver at the Tampa Bay 49 and came down with the ball.

That brought us to life. Those of us sitting on the bench jumped up in unison. Hasegawa's return was only three yards since he stumbled forward and fell down at the 46 where he was touched down but that was more than all right. The important thing was that we had the ball back.

Just prior to the play Grummon, standing in front of the bench, suddenly noticed that one of his shoes had come untied. He turned his back to the field and lifted his foot on the bench to tie his shoe. The play happened so fast that it was over by the time Grummon could turn around to see what we were reacting to.

"What happened?" Grummon asked.

"We're going to score a touchdown, that's what happened," I replied as I put my helmet on and raced to the field. Along the way I slapped five with Hasegawa who was getting a hero's escort off the field by Rodgers and Allen.

There was a newfound enthusiasm as we reached the huddle. We seemed to have emotionally recovered from the trauma of having our previous drive snuffed out three yards from the scoreboard. It was as if it didn't happen.

I was designated to carry on the first play. I swept around right end with the attitude of a bull. Thanks to that and superb blocking I got to the 40.

An incompletion followed and we decided to return to the ground. Scott, following a convoy of blockers which included yours truly, swept around left end. Not only did he pick up enough for a first down, he kept right on going. After breaking three tackles he had picked up 17 yards to the 23.

"That was awesome, Larry!" I exclaimed as I reached down to help him up. "Great job!" I added enthusiastically as he and I ran to where we would huddle.

I caught a swing pass on the next play which didn't produce much. I made the reception at the 22 and got only as far as the 20. Thus far that day our passing attack had been fairly anemic. It was only our third completion in nine attempts.

Our second and seven became second and 12 before the next snap. Grummon, perhaps still trying to figure out how we got the ball back in the first place, jumped prior to the snap.

"It's all right. It's all right," Bender said before calling the play in the huddle. "We'll make up for it."

Grummon himself made up for his own faux pas. On a post pattern he caught a pass at the eight. Maneuvering his way around the defensive back covering him, he hustled into the end zone and spiked the ball.

Our spirits were soaring. It was only the first score of the game. It was critical that we get it, though, against what had been a stiff, stubborn and resilient defense.

"All right, Rich," Walker greeted with a wide smile as we reached the sideline. "Every time you jump before the snap we'll expect you to score a touchdown on the very next play to make up for it."

"Okay," Grummon replied playfully. "But just remember you can't yell at me during game films when I do."

We were feeling good. We felt even better when Guinn split the uprights. We had a 7-0 lead with 9:43 left in the half. There was still a long way to go but it was okay to savor the moment.

It looked like we were going to maintain our momentum on the kickoff. The ball was fielded at the one. Black, filling in for Morrissey on the kicking team, cut the return man down at the 17.

"All right, Black! Way to go, baby!" Abraham exclaimed.

We all knew, though, that McKay wasn't coaching a group of quitters. After two plays they had a first down at the 29.

The latter play, a four-yard rush, proved costly for us. Malick injured his knee and had to come out. Although he would return after halftime, this would leave us short at linebacker since the only linebackers we had suited up were Allen, Jennings and Malick. We went to our 42 nickel formation with Hamer being inserted in the defensive backfield. As a proactive measure we did have somebody who had practiced at linebacker as a safety valve but that, unfortunately, was Morrissey who was on the sideline in street clothes. Walker would later start having Shuford get some practice in at linebacker since he had been a linebacker in high school.

Quickly the Bucs moved downfield. Before I knew it they had a first down at the Hawaii 37. I was now feeling insecure about our lead.

The Bucs went to the air. The pass was completed near the 20. The receiver was hit by Hasegawa at the 17. I saw the ball pop up as Rich and the receiver went down.

"Fumble!" I yelled as I jumped from my seat, causing a chain reaction as the rest of my teammates who had been sitting on the bench also leaped up and yelled enthusiastically.

The ball bounced and was picked up on the run by Dubois at the 13. He tried to advance it, getting only as far as the 15.

That was more than all right. We had the ball and the Bucs still had a goose egg.

"Let's get some insurance," Bender said in the huddle. We had 5:51 to move 85 yards.

We opened with a pass to Grummon. He caught the ball near the left hashmark at the 35. He picked up four more yards before going down.

Scott went off left tackle next. He broke a tackle at about the 45 and continued to the Tampa Bay 49 for our second first down in as many plays.

The stadium was fairly quiet, I noticed. The crowd was already stunned by the Bucs' drive ending with a turnover. The fans became even more stunned when we traveled 36 yards on the first two plays of our drive.

Scott went around right end with considerably less success. He picked up only one yard.

Tampa Bay's defense continued to dig in. It dropped Kerner for a loss of a yard to put us in a third and ten.

A short pass to Dietrich produced practically nothing. He caught the ball at the Tampa Bay 47. He was also hit and dropped at the 47 to put us in a fourth and eight.

We got a break. The Bucs had been offside to nullify the play. It was third and five at the 44.

"Okay, let's make 'em pay for that," Bender remarked in the huddle.

And we did. Bender hit Dietrich at the 29. Ted picked up four more yards to give us a first down at the 25.

That was about where the drive stalled. Kerner picked up two yards before a pair of incompletions put us in a fourth and eight at the 23. With 1:59 left in the half there was a pause for the two-minute warning. Naturally our field goal unit was dispatched.

I grabbed my Gatorade and waited for the break to expire. I silently hoped for Guinn to convert on the 40-yard field goal attempt and then for our defense to hold the Bucs.

Better still, I wanted our defense to cause another turnover and for us to rack up another score.

The timeout ended and our field goal unit got set. Before Arroyo could snap the ball the Bucs called timeout. It was obviously a psychological ploy to put more pressure on Guinn.

"Like Guinn hasn't seen this before?" Jablonski muttered.

Of course Ray also knew that it was a smart tactic. That was why we employed the tactic in that situation. Even the slightest distraction could be the difference between making it and not making it.

When play resumed Arroyo snapped the ball back to Billingsley. Billingsley got the ball down and Guinn got the kick up.

"Looks good. Looks good," Kerner remarked.

The ball hit the right upright and bounced back toward the field. Our lead was still a paltry 7-0. The Bucs had a first down at the 23 with 1:54 left in the half. The crowd was roaring.

"I don't believe this," I muttered.

The Bucs picked up a first down but that was all they managed before time expired. We went into the locker room still nursing our 7-0 lead.

As I entered the locker room and took care of my normal halftime business I noticed how drained I was. Statistically I hadn't done much with two rushes for 14 yards, two receptions for 17 yards, a kick return for 30 yards and a punt return for eight yards. I was still playing a hard game, doing everything I could do including blocking and decoying to try to help my team break through.

Throughout the week in Honolulu I overheard fans talking about how "easy" this game was going to be for us. They made it sound as if all we had to do was show up and the Bucs would lay down while we ran up and down the field unimpeded. I knew better than to adopt that attitude.

"You guys gonna win on Sunday?" I was asked by a stock clerk at the Hawaii Kai Foodland grocery store where Carol and I stopped to pick up a few things.

"I hope so," I replied.

"C'mon, man. It's Tampa Bay. They can't beat anybody."

"Sure they can," I said diplomatically while slowly breaking away, "and they will before too long. I just hope it's not us."

Every football fan in the country was aware of Tampa Bay's 0-21 history. Many of them were snickering if not laughing out loud.

But I wasn't snickering. Neither were any of my teammates as far as I knew. If any ever did snicker there was no snickering at halftime. The Bucs were obviously coming at us hard and playing to win. A victory on November 6, 1977, was still within reach.

"You're finding out that these guys are a lot better than their record shows," Walker told us before we returned to the field. "You were probably aware of that all along but now you're getting a taste of it firsthand. This is a genuine NFL team that you're playing that is capable of beating you. They're putting together a pretty good rushing game, they are capable of completing a few passes and their defense hits as hard as anybody we've seen so far."

I looked down at my white shoes. Walker's words were very true. Although the Bucs hadn't executed overall as well as some of the other teams we'd played, their defense seemed to be at least as tough as those of the Rams, Dolphins and everybody else we'd faced. Their passing stats and even their rushing stats were short of spectacular but their defense was stubborn. If the defense continued the way it was and the offense finally clicked we would be in for a very long second half.

"This is a hungry team," Walker pointed out. "They want to beat somebody. You're here now so you're the ones they want to beat. Their entire focus is on you. They're not looking ahead to next week. You are the target and they are zeroing in. They are making adjustments right now. They are very determined to beat you."

308

Walker paused. He looked us all over as if to ensure that he had our full attention. At this point an official looked in and notified us that we had two minutes left at halftime.

"I say we don't let that happen" he continued. "Let's play our game and blow Tampa off the map. Let's do it."

Malick was back in action and he wasted no time. The opening kick was fielded on the goal line. Malick broke through the wedge and nailed the ball carrier at the Tampa Bay 16.

Not surprisingly, the Bucs began their drive with the same determination they would have had had the return man been tackled on the Hawaii 16. A five-yard rush followed by a 29-yard pass completion gave them a first down at the 50.

Bell's three-yard rush followed and then Allen jumped too soon. That gave the Bucs a second and two at the Hawaii 42.

I looked down at my shoes again. I was feeling very uneasy. The Bucs were playing like a playoff contender, not a doormat.

Bell went up the middle. He met up with Allen. The two struggled almost as if it was a sumo match in football gear. The two went down in the vicinity of the 40.

Time was called for a measurement. The referee then pointed majestically as the crowd roared its approval. The Bucs had another first down.

"You guys had better be thinking about putting some points on the board when we get the ball," Bennici remarked as he turned toward the bench. "We may need every point we can get."

It was an obvious understatement. Nobody blamed Bennici for making it. We seemed to be in a precarious situation.

A four-yard rush and two-yard loss put them in a third and eight. Prendergast changed it to a third and three when he jumped offside.

"Knock off the charity, dammit!" Walker bellowed. "Make them earn it!"

The Bucs apparently thought we would be looking for a run. I know that I thought they would run. I was surprised to see the quarterback drop back in a play-action fake.

Fortunately the pass fell incomplete. Tampa Bay's field goal unit took the field.

It was a 50-yard attempt. The kick was short, touching down in the back of the end zone to suggest that the holder might not have set the ball down properly. We had the ball on our own 33 with our piddly 7-0 lead still intact.

I was relieved. I think most of us were. The time had come to start breaking the game open although nobody in a pumpkin-colored jersey was going to be laying down to pave the way.

Kerner opened the drive by going up the middle. He was hit at the 35 and the ball was jarred loose. In the scramble for the ball Tampa Bay defensive end Lee Roy Selmon picked it up at the 32. He was brought down at the 30 by Bender.

I felt sick. I am sure we all did. Tampa Bay's inability to score during a golden opportunity had briefly rejuvenated us. Now it was the Bucs who were rejuvenated in spades as the crowd continued to roar. My fear that we might actually blow this one scared me to death.

"You guys from Hawaii think you're so hot," a slightly inebriated male Tampa Bay loyalist called from somewhere in the bleachers.

"You guys are getting your asses whipped today!" cried an equally inebriated female loyalist.

At the time I wasn't sure the boisterous fans weren't correct. Victory was hardly out of the Bucs' reach. With the way things were going it was a very distinct possibility. The Bucs knew it, their fans knew it and we knew it, as did our fans watching in shock back in Hawaii. The Bucs were 90 feet from tying the game.

Bell went up the middle for three yards. He went up the middle again with such fury that he even broke Allen's tackle. Only the best running backs were able to do that and even then it was rare. A running back breaking Allen's tackle was like a catcher throwing Lou Brock out on a stolen base attempt. It happened but it was rare.

Hasegawa charged forward and tried to head Bell off at the 25. Bell maneuvered around him but Rich stayed with him. It looked like Bell was going to get away but Rich made a desperation lunge at him. He wasn't able to bring Bell down but he managed to knock the ball out of Bell's hands.

"Fumble!"

The ball was knocked behind Bell. An assortment of white jerseys and pumpkin jerseys dove after the pigskin. There was a pile near the 25.

Ed Jennings picked up the ball at the 24 and started to run with it. He was tackled from behind at the 31.

"Yeah!" I cried out, leaping to my feet before running on the field while putting my helmet on.

"Offense!" Walker called as if we needed prompting. I think we were all running on the field by this time. What we did with this opportunity would determine if we were experiencing a second chance or simply a stay of execution.

We started on a high note. Scott and Kerner both had good carries to give us a first down at our own 44.

The Buc defense gave the fans a glimmer of hope when it stopped Scott for no gain. I then went off left tackle to midfield to give us a third and four.

We planned to go to the air next. Bender read something he didn't like and called an audible. Scott carried around left end, picking up seven yards to the 43. We had another first down and were closing in on field goal range.

310

The Bucs were obviously aware that we were close to turning this into a two-score game and they turned up the heat. A pass to Slater was batted away at about the 30. They then put pressure on Bender, forcing him to scramble. Steve ultimately picked up three yards, going out of bounds at the 40 to put us in a third and seven.

Ozzie Roberts came in with a play, sending Scott to the sideline. Ozzie wound up on the receiving end of a pass over the middle at the 30. He twisted his way around a defender before going down at the 28.

I watched as Scott came in and Ozzie went out. They slapped fives as their paths crossed although I am sure that Ozzie would have liked to have stayed in a little longer. At the same time I thought about how important it was for us to put something on the scoreboard this time. At the very least, we owed it to the defense who got the ball back for us two plays after we coughed it up. We had also gone too far downfield to not pick up even a field goal. We had already blown two scoring opportunities and didn't want to make it three.

On the sideline I noticed Guinn kicking a football into a portable net. I didn't envy him at all. If our drive stopped at its current point all of the pressure would be on him. Most kickers are not otherwise cut out to be football players and Guinn was no exception although he had the guts and knowhow to make an open field tackle when he needed to. Regardless of whether they were true football players, kickers were an integral part of a football team.

We continued to move. I ran a sideline pattern and caught a pass at the 21. I abruptly hit the brakes, causing a linebacker to overcompensate and run right past me. I got down to the 12 before being hit and dropped.

I leaped up and clapped my hands. I was now extremely confident that we would score. I believed we were wearing down the defense.

It was still a seven-point game and Tampa Bay refused to surrender. The Bucs' defense was much tougher than the 49er defense a week earlier. The defense was probably tougher than those of most of our opponents that season.

A pass to Dietrich in the end zone was dangerously close to an interception. The defensive back got into position to make the pick so Ted had to impersonate a defensive back by swatting the ball away.

Another incompletion followed before Bender then hit Dietrich a yard deep in the end zone. Ted was hit but hung on. At long last it was a two-score game.

Our celebration as we ran to the sideline was very low key. I think we were simply relieved that we finally got that second score. This was one game where it seemed as if we were fighting for our lives against a very determined group of conquistadors.

Guinn's extra point attempt was right on target. We led 14-0 with 2:14 left in the third quarter. I went to the Gatorade table and then sat down to rehydrate myself. I was perspiring profusely, probably as much from nerves as exertion.

"What do you think?" Marv asked as he sat down next to me.

"I think we'd better score again," I replied, knowing the determination of our opponents. "I think they're not ready to throw in the towel."

"I think you're right," Marv agreed.

Guinn kicked off. The ball was taken two yards deep in the end zone. The return man shot forward to the 28 where he was tackled by Vorsino.

One of the Bucs made what can only be classified as a rookie mistake. Right about at the point where his teammate was being tackled he tried to block McWherter by hitting him in the back of his legs. McWherter went down although he was not injured. The clipping penalty forced the Bucs to start their drive at the 14.

It was a setback for the Bucs. It still didn't destroy their spirit. A five-yard rush and a ten-yard pass gave them a first down at the 29. Three plays later they had a first down at their own 45.

I started feeling nervous again and then forced myself to relax. We still had a two-score lead. That extra score worked wonders for my psyche, at least for the moment.

The Buc quarterback threw an incompletion. That stopped the clock with five seconds left in the third quarter.

Tampa Bay went to the air again. Pratt charged in and managed to get his hand on the ball. The ball arched up and back. Allen moved to his right and made a shoestring catch at the 50.

"Go, baby, go!" Abraham called as Allen moved forward. He broke a tackle near the 45 and another inside the 40. He was finally brought down at the 33. We would begin the fourth quarter 99 feet from making it a three-score game.

"Offense! Let's put it away!" Walker called although there was no need to rush. We were between quarters. CBS was showing commercials.

Only 15 minutes to go. It was a very comforting thought. A score would make it even more comfortable. With a two-score lead and excellent field position to start our drive it was definitely now our game to win.

Needless to say, Tampa Bay's relentless defense was not conceding anything. On the opening play of the quarter the defense charged hard and forced Bender to scramble. Steve still managed to pick up two yards to the 31 before going out of bounds.

The pressure was still on during the following play. Bender managed to get the pass off this time. He hit Dietrich near the right hashmark at the five. Ted was tripped up almost immediately but still managed to use his free hand to fight going down. He managed to cross the goal line before he finally fell.

We started to celebrate, then realized that our celebration was premature. Ted's knee hit the ground at the one before he crossed the goal line.

No problem. Kerner went off right tackle and was a yard deep in the end zone before going down. With the extra point we held a 21-0 lead with 14:18 left.

It was a three-score game. The Bucs still weren't likely giving up. I don't know what their psyche truly was but I believed they would play as if they believed they still had a chance.

The kick return was not impressive. The kick was fielded at the eight. The return man only got as far as the 19.

Just the same, the Bucs moved the ball. After two plays they had a first down at the 32. Two plays later they had the ball at their own 42 and time was called to measure.

It was short. Bell took care of it on the next play, picking up three yards off left tackle.

The Bucs next went up the middle. Bell crossed midfield to the 48 where he was hit by Vorsino.

"Fumble!"

There wasn't much of a scramble this time. Hasegawa quickly fell on the ball. One of the Bucs fell on top of him, ostensibly going for the ball but accomplishing only credit for the tackle. We had a first down at the 50.

That was pretty much it. Guinn ultimately kicked a 32-yard field goal to give us a 24-0 lead with 4:39 left. The Bucs finally got on the board with 1:13 left on a 34-yard field goal.

For the record, the Bucs didn't quit at that point. We knew they wouldn't so we utilized our hands kick return team. Rodgers fell on the onside kick at the Tampa Bay 46. After two snaps it was officially over; a 24-3 victory that was a lot closer than the score indicated.

When the final gun sounded we were officially 6-2 and very relieved. The Bucs were 0-8 and very frustrated.

Or at least I assume they were frustrated. We'd played a good clean game and beat them within the rules so I had no cause to regret our victory. When I shook hands with some of the Tampa players I was compassionate and sincere without being maudlin.

"You've got a good team," I said to one.

"Hang in there," I said to another. "You've got a lot of good people on this team."

I meant every word of it.

As I walked off the field I was approached by the man who had recruited me to play for USC.

"Don't let your good game fool you," McKay said good-naturedly. "I told my defense that you were an old friend so that they wouldn't tackle you until you'd picked up about 20 yards."

"So that was it," I retorted. "I thought I was just having a good game."

"Nah, I felt sorry for you. You transferred to Hawaii and missed out on the smog in Los Angeles."

That was one of many things I liked about McKay. He often invoked humor even in bad situations. He was a good man. My decision to transfer from USC to Hawaii after my freshman year was not a reflection on McKay. As I debated on transferring to Hawaii or staying at USC he represented a major point in favor of staying at USC.

It was a happy locker room although not especially jubilant. We were drained and relieved. The Bucs, desperately searching for that first big victory, came at us with everything they had. They may have been 0-22 in their brief history but their team was comprised of bona fide NFL football players, not Girl Scouts. Most of us were sure that the Bucs would get their elusive first victory sometime very soon.

For the record, Hasegawa was the recipient of the game ball. He was an easy choice. He caused two fumbles, recovered one fumble and intercepted a pass. I don't believe anybody else could have even been considered.

The roast beef we ate on the flight home was delicious. Food always tasted extra good after a victory. After a defeat we ate primarily as an obligation. After a hard defeat even the most epicurean of delicacies had the appeal of a plateful of sandpaper.

A group of us gathered in the aisle along the way. Hayer, who watched the game from the sideline because of his injury, was there. Also present were Scott, Malick, Dietrich and Prendergast.

"So what do you think?" Hank Prendergast asked.

We all pondered the question. I shrugged my shoulders.

"They were tough," I remarked.

"I can't argue with that," Dietrich concurred. "When I read the paper tomorrow I'm going to find it hard to believe when I see them listed at 0-8 in the standings."

"They definitely weren't intimidated by us," Malick added.

The scoreboard showed us as the victors by three touchdowns. It didn't show how the Bucs came at us as a team of destiny.

"They're going to start winning soon," Scott predicted while the rest of us nodded in agreement. "They're tough enough now but they're really going to crank it up once they get their first victory."

"That's what I've been saying," I replied. "The Bucs are likely to have a meteoric rise once they win a game or two. We've only played the Seahawks and Grizzlies in the preseason so it might not be a fair comparison but I think the Bucs will progress a lot faster than them once they get rolling."

"You're probably right," Prendergast agreed. "I'm really glad we played them before they finally found their groove."

"They're not too far from that," Malick added.

It isn't enough to say they were tough on us. They made us earn every one of our 24 points.

314

We were erratic at times. That was partially because they coerced us. It was also because I believe we played, at least subconsciously, to not lose instead of to win.

Grummon was our leading receiver. He had three receptions for 76 yards. I also had three receptions for 33 yards. Dietrich was next with two receptions for 31 yards.

Scott narrowly missed a 100-yard game on the ground. He carried 15 times for 96 yards. Kerner had seven carries for 24 yards. I carried three times for 20 yards.

Our next challenge would be a week later in Chicago. That meant another formidable running back for our defense to try to stop. Ricky Bell had been a handful. Our defense expected nothing less from Walter Payton.

CHAPTER FOURTEEN
The Bear Hunt

I felt sorry for Larry Scott. He had missed two of the three prior games because of injury. As was mentioned earlier, he rushed for 96 yards against the Bucs, narrowly missing his second 100-yard game of the season. One more carry probably would have done it for him.

Of course a 100-yard game is not a priority on the sideline. Any stats that the team keeps are unofficial anyway. Walker's focus is on winning. So is everybody else's but most of the rest of us would not hesitate to see if anybody is approaching any milestones.

Then again, is it worth it to risk injury so that a running back can pick up four more yards in a game where the outcome is no longer in doubt?

"I would hate to be Tampa Bay's next opponent," Walker remarked at the end of Tuesday's film sessions. "They have a good team and the barrier is going to break very soon. Mark my word, they're going to beat somebody this year. I believe they play the Giants next. It might very well be the Giants who become the first team to lose to the Bucs."

And that ended that. Tampa Bay was history. It was time to look to Chicago.

We would head to Chicago with a little more strength at linebacker. Marty Catron was signed to broaden the skeleton linebacker corps. He was a fourth-year pro out of South Carolina State, having played the previous three years with New England.

We worked hard, especially on Wednesday and Thursday. Walker was firm but civil.

There was a lot at stake. We were 6-2 and that was impressive but it wasn't enough. We had to keep winning, especially with two playoff contenders in a row with both in our conference and one in our division. We didn't simply want to secure a playoff berth. We wanted to win our division and, if possible, secure at least one game at home during the playoffs.

On Friday morning I left my place at 7:30. I had forgotten that it was a federal holiday. Getting the feds and whoever else didn't have to work off the road made a substantial difference in traffic. I reached Aloha Stadium at a little after eight.

Allen pulled into the parking lot directly ahead of me. We parked side-by-side and walked through the tunnel in the north end zone together.

"I guess we could've slept in today," Russ observed.

"I suppose," I said. "Of course if I had thought of that there would have been an accident on Kalanianaole that would have made me an hour late."

There was always something special about walking across the field of the virtually empty stadium. The tunnel connecting the parking lot and playing field functioned as a passageway to a world polarized from everything else.

Across Kamehameha Highway from the stadium was Pearl Harbor with those in duty status on ships, subs and other stations turning to. Somewhere nearby, I suspected, was a police officer writing a ticket for an overzealous driver while other officers patrolled the streets. In another part of town Mayor Frank Fasi thought about his agenda which probably included his hope of dethroning Governor George Ariyoshi in the Democratic Primary a year later.

Elsewhere in the country, President Jimmy Carter was working on ways to make his first year in office a successful one. His brother Billy was probably thinking that it wasn't too early in the day to crack open a beer.

About 4,200 miles away was another stadium. That was the stadium we would be in about 48 hours later. The weather was expected to be freezing or close to it. The empty seats that the stadium now displayed would be filled with hostile fans.

We weren't simply another opponent. We were a team competing with Chicago's beloved Bears for a playoff berth. Our primary objective was to beat out the Rams and Falcons for the division title while the Bears were hoping to win their division. If we both fell short of our primary goals then we would be competing against each other for the conference's lone wild card spot.

But a single game in Chicago came first. That was what we were preparing for that day. Russ and I headed into the locker room together.

Russ and I turned out to not be the first players at the stadium. Bender was there which came as no surprise. Also present were Hasegawa, Rodgers, Marv, Clint and a few others.

By 8:30 I was dressed and pumping iron. I lifted weights a minimum of three times a week but usually more. Often I lifted weights at home since there was a weight room, complete with a sauna and jacuzzi, in the complex where I lived. The weight sessions after training camp ended were highly recommended although not mandatory. Some guys lifted weights at home while others belonged to gyms. I had both options and was also a fulltime graduate student at the university so I could even pump iron in the athletic complex.

Our prepractice meeting produced nothing unexpected. It focused primarily on our itinerary for the trip. We were to meet at the airport at 3:30 that afternoon, board the plane, long flight to Chicago, bus ride to the hotel, light workout at Soldier Field in the afternoon, midnight curfew, team breakfast and meeting, game, fly home.

"Any questions?" Walker asked.

There were none.

317

It was a pretty spirited workout. We had won two in a row since falling on our faces in Atlanta. We were determined to keep the momentum going. The two most recent victories had been against teams going nowhere in 1977. We were about to face a team with high hopes although that didn't matter. Regardless of the opponent, our goal was to play 60 minutes of hard, smart football and come away as the victors.

"Are you guys going to win on Sunday?" Bill Kwon from the *Honolulu Star-Bulletin* asked me as we took the field to begin our workout.

"That's the idea," I replied evenly, "but the Bears have the same idea."

I had to be careful of what I said. The last thing I wanted to do was fuel Chicago's fire. Joe Namath was able to get away with guaranteeing a victory over the Baltimore Colts in 1969 but it was the kind of thing that was normally discouraged. Praise your opponent to death or say nothing at all. Don't give the opponent extra incentive to beat the crap out of you.

Our workout was the prototype limited contact workout. After calisthenics we broke up in groups. Offensive backs and ends in the south end zone on the mauka side, offensive linemen in the south end zone on the makai side, defensive linemen at midfield on the makai side and defensive backs at midfield on the mauka side.

After about 20 minutes a whistle blew and the two line units began working together near midfield on the makai side and the rest worked together on the mauka side. There was no tackling but contact for blocking and when two men went up for a pass simultaneously.

I made a miraculous catch that surprised everybody including me. I ran a post pattern and was defended by Rodgers. Billingsley threw a pass that seemed to float like a balloon and Rodgers and I went up simultaneously. We collided in midair, making a loud crack with the collision of equipment, and went down in a heap. Somehow I hung on to the ball even though Carl got his hand on it and thought he had batted it down.

Carl was face down about five yards from me as I raised to the sitting position. As he started to raise up he saw that I had the ball, something I didn't even consciously realize until after I hit the ground.

"Did you catch that?" he asked in disbelief.

"Do you believe that?" I responded in equal disbelief.

"Man, if that happens to me in Chicago on Sunday I am going to be very pissed."

"But if I make a catch like that in Chicago on Sunday I am going to be very elated."

Carl looked at me and smirked.

"So will I," he remarked as the two of us got up and returned to our positions.

After another 20 minutes or so a whistle blew and the entire squad met at midfield. We spent the next 45 minutes running plays. It was neither an offensive or defensive drill. Everybody took part.

318

I took some snaps at quarterback. There was nothing unusual about that. I spent the day primarily working out at halfback since that was my primary position. After Bender and Billingsley had run their share of plays I was inserted at quarterback for about a dozen plays or so. It was actually a normal part of our Friday workouts to keep me fresh in case I was needed.

With every successful play there was a lot of cheering by the team. Sometimes it was for an individual performance. Usually it was for an overall performance. Everybody seemed to be up.

On one play I rolled out to my right and fired a bullet to Rossi who was filling in at my halfback spot since that was what he would do if I was pressed into service as quarterback. He caught the pass cleanly despite being well-covered by Black. He turned sharply upfield until the whistle blew.

"Helluva pass!" he exclaimed as he returned to the huddle. "Helluva pass, Jay!"

During my snaps at quarterback Rossi was my most vocal supporter. I couldn't help but believe that Rossi was secretly hoping that Bender and Billingsley would go down so that I would have to take over at quarterback and he would be the starting halfback. I couldn't blame him for wanting to play but. . . .

We closed out the workout with special teams drills and then a series of sprints.

"Remember," Walker instructed us at midfield after we had gathered around him before he excused us. "Everybody be at Air Service by 3:30. We're cleared to depart at four if we can."

It must have been about 12:30 when I left the stadium. I had an overwhelming craving to swim. Perhaps it was the knowledge that I would be in Chicago in about 12 hours. I was enjoying a relatively comfortable tropical day in Hawaii and was destined to spend the weekend in frigid, windy Chicago.

Had Carol been teaching that day I probably would have gone home to take a dip or else taken a nice swim at the gym I belonged to in Pearl City. Since school was out that day I picked her up and had lunch with her downtown at Arthur's. We were seated at a table across from the bar, ensuring us a semblance of privacy. There were other patrons in the area but we were less conspicuous than we would have been had we been seated in the main dining room.

"You gonna beat them Bears?" asked a stocky man in a yellow aloha shirt who sat at the next table.

I raised my hands to the palms up position and smiled.

"They're a good team," I said. "I just hope we're better than them on Sunday."

The man nodded. Seeming satisfied, the man allowed Carol and me to go on with our conversation. I wish I could have thought of something to talk about besides football. Unfortunately my mind was on the Bears.

After lunch I took Carol home and headed for the airport. I was parking my car at 3:15.

Some of my teammates had preceded me. A steady stream followed. Everybody had arrived by 3:30, sparing them from the wrath of Walker.

"All right," said Richards, pumping his arms in triumph. "Let's go to Chicago, kick some okole and come home to get warm again."

We were airborne by a little after four. As our DC-8 ascended I observed as the island moved and shrunk underneath. In the days prior to the completion of the reef runway all aircraft took off over land. We flew over Honolulu Harbor, then veered to the right when we reached the Aloha Tower. As we passed Waikiki we were too high and too distant to see humans but I thought of the tourists taking advantage of the remaining sunshine to lie in the sand and swim. I was excited about playing the Bears. I just didn't relish having to travel to frigid Chicago to do it.

But that was the nature of the beast. Half of our games were at home and the other half were on the road. Over the course of my career I wound up playing in some very frigid conditions in not just Chicago but also Green Bay, Minneapolis, Denver, Cleveland, New York and in other locales whose winters mean cold and snow. The cold is an impediment although it doesn't have to be a major one. Except in the most extreme conditions, one focuses exclusively on his assignments while on the field.

I didn't get up from my seat during the first few hours of the flight. I had some research material which I worked on as I inched my way toward my master's. It helped me to get my mind on something other than football.

After a salisbury steak dinner I moved to the back of the plane to join Shuford's poker game. Hamer and Rossi completed the foursome while Black, Grummon, Richards and Abraham played a game of their own at another table.

This was the first time I had ever played poker with Rossi. Judging by the way he played, this was the first time *anybody* had ever played poker with Rossi. He never raised but called every raise, never folding regardless of what he had in his hand. This enabled him to win a few pots early on when it appeared that he was either holding a hot hand or bluffing.

Overall his careless play cost him. He lost about 75 dollars in about an hour, a phenomenal achievement with Shuford's penny-ante stakes where nobody normally lost or won more than 20 or 30 dollars. At that point Rossi surrendered his seat to Marv.

When Rossi quit I was up about 35 dollars. When the game broke up two hours later I was up about 20 dollars. The entire purpose for Shuford's games was recreation. I enjoyed poker but only when I didn't risk losing a large sum of money or taking a large sum from somebody else. I would have gotten sufficient enjoyment playing with pennies or matchsticks.

As for Rossi, he had a lot to learn. If he went to Vegas and played poker the way he did on the plane he would wind up leaving Las Vegas naked.

We landed in Chicago at about 4:30 on Saturday morning, Chicago time. About two hours later I was getting undressed in my hotel room to catch a few hours of sleep.

At noon I was on the bus that would transport us to Soldier Field for our light workout. Only 24 hours earlier I was approaching the entrance to the Aloha Stadium parking lot for that workout. It was a strange contrast of 4200 miles, four time zones and about 40 degrees.

It was a common part of the business. I made whirlwind trips to various cities across the country, played a game and went home. The weather in cities I played in was often in direct contrast to the weather in Honolulu.

It was slightly above freezing at Soldier Field. I was probably an interesting sight with my thermals underneath a pair of blue gym shorts and a Los Angeles Dodgers T-shirt.

But I guess I looked no more peculiar than some of my teammates. A couple of other guys wore gym shorts over thermals and a few others wore them under T-shirts. A lot of the guys wore sweatsuits and some wore ski masks or wool caps.

I couldn't wear either the ski mask or wool cap. Neither would fit underneath my LA Dodger baseball cap and I wasn't about to shed an integral part of my uniform just to keep my ears warm.

Although it was obviously cold, I didn't really notice it once the workout started. I did so much running that I was almost immune from the cold. I felt loose and ready to take on the Bears. The cold wind hit me in the face and made my nose run but I paid it no mind. The masochist in me found it appealing.

There were six of us having dinner together; Ed Jennings, Marv Nelson, Dave Rossi, Rich Hasegawa, Stuart Arroyo and me.

At least that's the way it started. When we got to where we were going we found Russ Allen, Norm Richards, Clint Abraham, Jim McDaniel, Ozzie Roberts, Jeff Kerner and Carl Hayer just barely there ahead of us. Kevin Zanakis, who was injured but able to travel with us, and Eric Hamer showed up before we were seated, bringing the total to 15.

Apparently we were all on the same wave length. This being Chicago, everybody felt obligated to head for the nearest pizza place. It ostensibly never dawned on anybody that there was actually a good chance of finding a decent steak in Chicago. It was as if eating pizza in Chicago was as vital as beating the Bears. It made me wonder if roughly one-third of the players on teams that visited Hawaii felt it necessary to go out for poi and pineapple.

Four tables were moved together to accommodate us. We ordered eight large pizzas with various toppings and five pitchers of beer.

"Are you guys with the Bears?" asked Marcy, an attractive waitress with dark brown hair as she set the beer on our tables.

"How dare you?" Allen replied jocularly. "Of course we're not with the Bears."

"Oh. Well you look like football players."

"Nah, we're FBI agents," Richards said. "We're here for an organized crime seminar."

"Oh," said Marcy, innocently seeming to believe Norm. To this day she probably believes we were with the FBI.

We were a loose bunch. We laughed through the meal, making fun of each other and creating banal topics to discuss. The most prominent subject was a light-hearted debate on whether the place in which we were dining was tied to the mob. At no time did we discuss football.

The five pitchers of beer lasted us. Everybody drank in moderation except for Rossi. He probably drank close to three full pitchers by himself.

"Take it easy, Rossi," Jennings advised as Rossi began his third beer before the pizzas had even arrived.

"That's all right, man," Rossi replied in contrived cocksurety. "Ah know what ah'm doin'."

I was asleep surprisingly early that night. It must have been shortly before 10:30. I fell asleep fully clothed with the TV on. I woke up a few hours later and saw nothing but a test pattern on the screen. I turned off the TV, got undressed and slipped under the covers to finish my night's sleep.

It was a little after six when I woke up again. I was anxious to play football once I took a moment to analyze the strange room and recall that I was in Chicago. However, I wasn't anxious to climb out of my nice warm bed in exchange for the Chicago November weather.

At least it wasn't cold in the room. That made it easier. I took a long hot shower and got dressed, then went down to the lobby for some coffee.

Of course I wasn't first. Jennings was sipping his first cup of coffee. A few other teammates were meandering about.

I ordered a cup of coffee and sat in a chair directly across from Ed. He produced his lighter and leaned over to light my cigarette for me.

"Have you seen Rossi?" Ed asked.

I shook my head as I exhaled a stream of smoke.

"Why? Should I have?"

"No, I was just curious. After all the beer he drank at dinner last night, he had a few more drinks in the hotel bar, then bought a six-pack and took it up to his room. I just wonder what kind of shape he's going to be in."

322

I shook my head. I couldn't imagine drinking as much as he did in the pizza place alone, let alone what he drank afterward.

"I guess I'd better be prepared to play every play," I said. "He probably won't be in any shape to fill in if I need a breather."

"Possibly not," Ed agreed, "although I've played with guys who could tie one on and be ready to go the next day. I don't know how they do it but they do."

The team breakfast was at 7:30. Ed decided to go up to Rossi's room at 7:15. It really wasn't his responsibility but he also didn't want to see Rossi screw up his career for drinking too much. I suppose I felt the same way.

It was a good thing Ed went up to Rossi's room. Rossi was still sound asleep. It is very unlikely that Rossi would have woken up for the team breakfast on his own. He might not even have risen in time for the game.

The team left the hotel at nine o'clock. That was six hours after Rossi said he went to sleep after killing his six-pack. He looked horrible. His eyes were bloodshot, his hair was almost completely disheveled and his facial expression showed a weariness of somebody very under the weather. Occasionally he let out a groan as he rested his head against the window by his seat all the way to Soldier Field.

At Soldier Field I refused to break tradition. Two hours before kickoff I was running my laps around the field. Since it was extremely cold I wore my uniform pants instead of gym shorts. I still wore my very important Dodger T-shirt and hat. My only upper body concession to the cold was I wore thermals underneath the shirt.

The weather wasn't quite as frigid as the day before although that wasn't saying a lot. Saturday's weather was right around the freezing mark while Sunday's weather was slightly above it; rising up to slightly below 40. What made it seem much colder was the wind that would be running between 10-15 miles an hour, bringing the wind chill to below freezing.

This wasn't my first visit to Soldier Field. I had been there before during the Hawaiians' tenure in the WFL. The team was the Chicago Fire in 1974, then became the Chicago Wind in 1975.

Why the change?

The concise explanation is that these were actually two different teams. The Fire disbanded after forfeiting its final game at the end of the 1974 season, three weeks after being routed, 60-17, by the Hawaiians in the Fire's final home game at Soldier Field. The Wind was a totally different team that lasted a total of five games, including a 28-17 loss in Hawaii, before folding during the 1975 season slightly less than two months prior to when the entire World Football League folded.

We sat in front of our lockers in the moments prior to taking the field. There was very little noise except for Allen talking to Jennings, Richards,

Malick and Catron about some defensive tactics. Billingsley was reading scripture, Grummon sat ponderously while puffing on his pipe and Dietrich sat in reverie with his eyes closed, giving the impression that he was asleep.

Rodgers, as always, occupied the locker next to mine since our lockers were always arranged in numerical order. He offered me a Marlboro. I accepted it and produced my lighter to light his cigarette and then mine. I didn't think much of my nicotine addiction at the time. I would conquer it a few years later. After going a few years without a cigarette I wondered what had appealed to me about smoking. I recommend to anybody that they never start smoking. With nicotine being even more addictive than heroin, quitting is every bit as difficult as it is said to be.

Walker stood in the middle of the room. We started our pregame meeting with Hayer leading us in *The Lord's Prayer*.

At the completion of the prayer Walker silently looked around the room. I took one final hit off of my cigarette and snuffed it out in the ash tray Rodgers and I shared.

"Men," Walker finally called. "We are here as guests of the city of Chicago and the state of Illinois. Let's make them sorry they invited us."

That was it. Walker motioned that he was finished. He had a way with these pregame pep talks. Some were long and some were very concise. They almost always seemed appropriate.

Everybody went to the sideline at their own pace except for the starting defense. It was the defense's turn to be booed during pregame introductions.

As I stood on the sideline I thought about the fact that we were going for our seventh victory. We didn't go for our seventh victory the previous season until the final game. Our fellow expansionists in Memphis, Seattle and Tampa Bay weren't even closing in on their seventh victories over *two seasons*. We had a chance to win our 14th game over that same period, equaling our entire win total from the year before with only two losses. We could wind up the regular season 12-2.

But I was getting too far ahead of myself. The Bears were now. The Rams, Saints, 49ers, Falcons and Jets were later. Any and all were capable of outplaying us if we didn't stay focused. We could just as easily finish 6-8 as 12-2.

Some of the spectators behind our bench tried to alter our focus. We were from the tropics and Chicago was definitely not tropical, especially in November. The fans made sure we didn't forget that.

"Is it cold enough for you, Hawaii?"

"Hey, it must be about 40 below here. What's it in Hawaii? About 80?"

"Oh boy. It sure is cold here. Wouldn't it be nice to be in Hawaii where it's nice and warm?"

This would go on throughout the entire game. I heard it throughout my career whenever we played in a cold climate. When teams from cold climates played in Hawaii our fans reminded them of how hot it was. It's an innocuous part of the game.

Did the taunting affect me?

Of course not. I already knew that it was cold.

We lost the toss. I was a little chilly, even with my parka, and wanted to get started but I accepted it. I did some stretching exercises.

I spotted Rossi on the bench. He didn't look too well. He was bent over looking down at the ground while resting his elbows on his thighs. I wondered if he was going to get through the game without tossing his cookies.

This wasn't like my boozed body from the Oakland game the year before. I admit to being reckless and stupid but my drinking binge had been two nights earlier. Rossi had been drinking heavily until about nine hours before kickoff. He may still have been intoxicated.

I turned my attention away from Rossi and focused on the field. Guinn was about to kick off.

The kick was up. It was fielded about two yards deep in the end zone. The return man looked as if he was going to run, then bobbled the ball. He downed the ball for a touchback.

"Let's go, defense!" Walker called.

The Bears wasted no time. Payton went off right tackle. He got all the way to the 37 before Black and Hasegawa teamed up to bring him down. That was hardly the auspicious beginning I was hoping we would have.

It got a little more difficult for them after that although not by much. Five plays later they had already picked up one more first down and time was called to measure for another first down at the Hawaii 42.

The referee stood erect and pointed, drawing a huge roar from the crowd.

I shook my head and sat on the bench. I forced myself to relax. I knew that I would get on the field eventually.

Our defense tightened up. There was a rush for no gain and then an incomplete pass.

Vorsino went in and Malick came out. We were in our 42-nickel.

The heat was on. Jennings shot through, forcing the quarterback to scramble. That led to a rendezvous with Jurgens who beat Pratt out for the starting job at right end for the second week in a row although Pratt would get his share of playing time. Jurgens sacked the quarterback at the Chicago 48. It was fourth and 20.

"Right on," I remarked primarily to myself.

I shed my parka and ran on the field, then took my place near the ten for the punt return. I was excited that I was about to get my first licks in. I was hoping that the punt would be something I could return.

The punt was up. I ran up a few steps and got under it.

"You're got room, Jay!" I heard Hasegawa call from several yards directly in front of me.

I caught the punt at the 16 and headed upfield. I was past the 20 before I came close to a dark blue jersey with orange trim and all I had to do was keep running to get past him. I used a straight-arm near the 25 and was brought down at the 29.

Whistles were blowing. I bounced up. I was hyped and confident. A 13-yard punt return was not a bad way to start.

As the Bears had done, we started fast. Bender hit Dietrich at the Chicago 49. He was hit immediately but hung on.

"All right, Ted," I said as I reached down to help him up. "Way to go, man. Way to hang on to the ball."

Scott went off left tackle on the next play. He fought his way down to the 42 to give us a second and three. It almost seemed too easy.

It was Scott again on the next play. He went up the middle to the 38 for another first down. On three plays we had traveled 33 yards and picked up two first downs.

A rush around right end was less productive. Scott managed only one yard.

It was time to go back to the air. I ran a post from the left slot. Somewhere between the hash marks I made a leaping catch at the 17 and turned toward the goal line. A pair of defensive backs were in hot pursuit and brought me down at the nine.

"Nice one, Jay," Grummon remarked as he and I headed toward the huddle.

"Helluva catch," Bender said.

"Good job, brother," Marv added.

The approbation was nice. What felt better was knowing that we were a mere 27 feet from drawing first blood.

Bender hit Scott with a swing pass at the seven. Scott took it all the way in. We were on the board.

Or were we?

I hesitated in my celebration. There was a yellow flag near the line of scrimmage.

The Bears were offside. We obviously opted to decline. Guinn kicked the extra point to give us a 7-0 lead with 7:20 left in the first quarter.

There were a lot of happy faces on our sideline. We also knew that there was a long way to go. We were still allowed to be happy with the way things were going so far.

But, again, it was only the beginning. One week earlier a very determined team in Tampa came at us with everything it had and made us feel fortunate that we secured a victory. Now we were facing an equally determined, more seasoned team in Chicago.

Guinn kicked off. The ball was caught at the goal line. The return man was gang tackled at the 22.

Two plays later the Bears had third and four at the 28. We weren't certain if they would rush or pass. Often this is a passing situation but the Bears' strength was its running game. We kept our regular defense in instead of something specifically designed to defend against a pass.

The Bears went to the air. The quarterback spotted a receiver near midfield along the left sideline.

Morrissey played it perfectly. He stepped in front of the receiver and picked the pass off at the Chicago 47. The primary receiver tried to step between him on the spot but only got air. Morrissey headed down the right sideline.

"Go, Jim, go!" I called while other teammates offered their encouragement.

"Run, baby, run!"

"Move it, Morrissey!"

"All the way, man! All the way!"

"Go! Go! Go!"

Morrissey cut in to avoid a couple of linemen inside the 35. He suddenly appeared to be limping. He was knocked down by the quarterback at the 29.

We were 87 feet from making it a two-score game. It came with a price. Morrissey got up and limped off the field. He was grimacing in pain.

We had to go on. This was, after all, a football game. As long as we had eleven men capable of playing we had to continue.

And so we did. We began with a pass to Grummon that was caught at the 16. Rich picked up two more yards to give us a first down at the 14.

Dietrich was next although it would have been just as well had the pass been incomplete. He caught the pass one yard behind the line. He got only as far as the line of scrimmage.

We went to the running game. Scott picked up a yard to the 13. It was third and nine. The Bear defense was bearing down on us; no pun intended.

"Okay, gentlemen, we've got to do it this time," Bender reminded us in the huddle.

The Bears guessed correctly that we were going to pass. Even with Payton in the backfield they probably would have passed on third and nine and it stood to reason that we would pass since our running backs weren't up to Payton's level. They put a heavy rush on Bender. Steve still managed to hit me at the eleven. It was all I could do to get to the nine with a crowd of dark blue jerseys in the vicinity. With the heavy rush on Bender and the number of Bears around me it almost seemed as if the Bears had about 20 men on the field. We wound up almost five yards short of a first down.

Our field goal unit took the field. It was disappointing but the Bears had risen to the occasion. They didn't let down.

Before we could get the snap off a Bear linebacker jumped and bumped Arroyo. That would move the ball four and-a-half yards closer.

I put my helmet on in anticipation of returning to the field. I waited for the officials to signal a first down. Instead they called timeout to measure.

We were short. We were no more than a foot from a first down. I was sure that Walker would want to go for it. Instead he left the field goal unit on the field.

I still had my helmet on as I watched the field goal attempt that was only slightly longer than a PAT. I was hoping that one of the Bears would jump again and give us a first down. At the very least, I was hoping that one of our guys would jump to move the ball back five yards and justify the field goal attempt.

Guinn got the kick up but he hooked it. The ball just barely got inside the upright. Had the attempt been slightly longer than the 21 yards it would have missed. Fortunately it didn't and we led 10-0 with 2:01 left in the first quarter.

"How're you feeling, Jay?" Bennici asked me.

"Okay, I guess."

"Are they playing you pretty tight?"

"Yeah, pretty much so. They're doing a pretty good job of keeping on us," I said.

"Well don't worry. We'll force them to loosen up before too long."

Bennici moved on to converse with Scott. I stood and watched as Guinn kicked off.

The kick was up. It was fielded at the one. The Bears put up a pretty good wedge. The return man got to the 28 before McWherter brought him down. Although McWherter rarely was a starter for us, he was a very valuable asset to the team. After he was cut during the previous season it was fortunate for us that nobody picked him up before he sought another shot with us in 1977.

Chicago made a statement on the opening play. Payton rushed off right tackle and picked up 14 yards to the Chicago 42.

The Bears crossed midfield on the next play. A pass was completed near the Hawaii 40. Rodgers brought the receiver down at the 37. Two plays had netted 35 yards and two first downs, causing the fans to jump out of their seats in exultation.

Chicago got called for illegal procedure and then threw an incompletion. It was second and 15 at the Hawaii 42 with the clock stopped with 23 seconds left in the first quarter.

On the final play of the quarter the Bears picked up another first down. The Bears completed a pass near the right sideline at the 23. Black hit the receiver immediately but the receiver hung on to the ball.

"I'm getting worried," I said wearily to Grummon who was sitting next to me on the bench.

"We know they're going to score on us," Grummon replied.

"I know. I was just hoping we would score three or four touchdowns first."

I looked over at Rossi who was sitting about 15 feet to my right. He was looking at what was going on in front of him instead of keeping his head down but he still looked miserable and still in no shape to play.

Walker had to have known about Rossi's condition. Nothing got past him. I doubted that Walker was going to send Rossi in for even a couple of plays unless I got injured. I wondered if Rossi's inebriation meant that we wouldn't be running in our double-double or single-double formations in obvious passing situations. Rossi had his post on the kick return team but that would probably be the only action he would see.

One thing I observed was that none of my teammates sat near Rossi or spoke to him; at least as far as I could see. I think everybody was pretty disgusted with him for showing up for the game not ready to play. Injuries and illnesses were understandable but Rossi's malady was self-inflicted. Even a party animal like Mark Black who was known for sneaking out after curfew never showed up for a game in anything less than peak condition.

When play resumed our defense was more in control. The Bears gained five more yards only because Richards jumped offside. Aside from that it was three incompletions. The field goal unit took the field with the ball on the 18.

The ball would be spotted at the 25, making this a 35-yard attempt. The kick was up and through the uprights to cut our lead to 10-3.

As Grummon said, we knew they were going to score. None of our six victories had been by shutout. I always wanted our defense to hold the opposition scoreless on every series the same way I wanted our offense to score on every series. In both cases it wasn't going to happen exactly the way I wanted it to.

I savored the experience as I lined up to receive the kick. I noticed Rossi several yards ahead of me. This was his first action of the game. If the Bears had any idea of how much he had had to drink only hours earlier they might have kicked the ball directly to him.

Instead the kick was to Hasegawa. It was a little short so Rich was going to have to run up a little to catch it before it hit the ground. I charged forward to head off a Bear or two.

I headed off a dark blue jersey near the 20. The defender did a pretty good job of fighting me off as I lowered myself into his midsection. He used his hands to knock me away. I still held him up long enough to keep him out of the play.

"Loose ball!"

Those words tied my stomach in knots. I ran toward where the action seemed to be. I couldn't see the ball but I could see Hasegawa raising himself to his knees. He did not have the ball.

329

By the time I reached the area the play was over. Hasegawa had caught the ball at the ten and reached the 33 before taking a hit that caused his fumble. The ball was picked up by one of the Bears at the 36 and returned back to the 33 where Grant Collier brought the ball carrier down.

The raucous cheers worked to exacerbate my ill feelings. At the moment I felt as nauseated as Rossi probably did. I had no choice but to run to the sideline. Although my ephemeral tenure on the field did nothing to dehydrate my body, I grabbed a cup of Gatorade. I suppose I believed it might wash the bad taste away.

I put my parka on and sat down and took a deep breath. I knew that fumbles happened. In high school, college, the WFL and the NFL I had fumbled. I just hated to see it happen to us.

Of course nobody felt worse about it than Hasegawa. The previous week he had caused two fumbles and recovered one other. It was as if fate was making him give something back.

The Bears opened with a short pass underneath. The receiver caught the ball inside the 30. He was brought down at the 23.

Time was called. The officials wanted to measure. The Bears had enough for a first down.

Two Payton rushes later the Bears were down to the 13. Time was called for another measurement. This time they were short.

It only took a run of one yard to give the Bears another first down. That was followed by a run to the nine.

A flag shot up. Payton was mauled by a host of tacklers. Apparently Black was a little late with his contribution. That moved the ball half the distance to the goal line.

Two plays later the Bears had first and goal at the one. Payton's rush around right end got them that final yard.

(Expletive deleted)!" I muttered.

The extra point tied the game with 8:08 left in the first half.

"(Expletive deleted)!" I repeated.

We knew all along it wasn't going to be easy. We were playing a contender for the first time in three weeks and were simply going to have to suck it up. This game may have been a matter of who outlasted whom.

I figured the best thing for us to do was milk the clock to use the remaining time to give us a halftime lead without giving the Bears another opportunity. That would start with a good kick return. Field position would carry a lot of weight. A good long series could prevent the Bears from getting the ball again.

The Bear kicker refused to cooperate with my hope for a long return. The kick came down six yards deep in the end zone. Hasegawa downed the ball for a touchback.

"Okay, we've got eight minutes to go 80 yards," Bender said in the huddle. "That will be a good way to end the half."

330

A short pass over the middle gave us five of the 80 yards. Scott caught the pass at the 22 and made his way to the 25.

The Bears smelled pass on the following play and put on a heavy rush. Bender scrambled and managed to elude his pursuers, even picking up a yard to the 26 before going into a slide. It was third and four.

I was running a post pattern on the next play when Bender hit me over the middle at the Hawaii 43. I tried to elude the defensive back who was covering me. I swung around him but he managed to get a grip on me and brought me down at the Hawaii 45.

At least we had our first down.

Unfortunately our drive stalled at that point. Three plays produced a total of three yards to the 48. The punting unit came on.

I heaved a deep sigh of frustration when I reached the sideline and grabbed my parka. The lead I was hoping for at halftime seemed very unlikely unless our defense forced a three and out or a turnover. I focused on hoping that the Bears wouldn't take the lead and pick up the momentum that would go with it.

Jablonski's punt wasn't what we normally expected of him. The punt was off the side of his foot. It didn't have much distance and was downed at the 20.

"Three and out," I said to Kerner after I grabbed my Gatorade. "If we get a three and out we'll still have time to put together a drive and have the lead at halftime."

Three plays later the Bears' punting unit was still on the sideline. They had picked up two first downs and had moved to their own 45. Three plays after that the Bears had another first down at the Hawaii 39.

"So much for three and out," I muttered and rose from my seat. I needed to walk around a little on the sideline to ease the building tension.

Payton ran around left end. Jurgens appeared out of nowhere and dropped him for a two-yard loss.

Like my teammates, I expressed a few enthusiastic words of approbation. I still didn't dare get my hopes too high on second and 12.

The clock wound down to the two-minute warning. That actually took me by surprise. I had been so intent on trying to will our defense into stopping the Bears that I paid little attention to the clock. It appeared to me that we needed to get the ball back in one or two plays in order to have a realistic chance of scoring.

Of course time heavily favored the Bears. They were close to at least field goal range if not already there. They could milk the clock before shooting for the uprights if they couldn't manage a touchdown instead.

When play resumed the Bears went to the air. The quarterback had good protection. He spotted a receiver around the left hashmark near the 20.

Dubois was nearby. He tipped the ball forward. The ball was still in the air and he lunged forward for it. He got his fingertips on the ball but couldn't hold on.

"Good effort, Henri!" Marv called out.

"Way to go, Henri!" I cried. It was third and 12.

We went to the 33 nickel. The Bears tried another pass. The quarterback dropped back. He suddenly found himself being chased by Allen.

The quarterback started to scramble. He managed to elude Allen. Unfortunately for him he ran into Richards who sacked him at the Hawaii 48. It was fourth and 19.

So much for being in field goal range. A field goal attempt would be about 65 yards. The Bears prudently sent their punting unit out.

I took my place on the ten. The clock was running. I realized that there would be less than a minute left when we got the ball and couldn't understand why nobody on our side was calling a timeout until I remembered that we had used them already. I figured I had better put together a good return or else we wouldn't even run a play. I figured I had to get at least to the Hawaii 30.

The punt was up. It was also well to my left. I ran toward it but saw that I wouldn't be able to field it cleanly. I wisely allowed it to bounce.

I blocked one wideout and even knocked him out of bounds, hoping to prevent the Bears from downing the ball. I figured if we got a touchback we still might try to make a go of it. Unfortunately another Bear shot through and downed the ball at the six. There were 52 seconds left in the half.

We didn't try to do anything, of course. Bender took two snaps and dropped down to run out the clock. We left the chilly confines of the field and entered the more comfortable confines of the locker room. I preferred to stay on the field and do some damage.

There was nothing spectacular about halftime. I drained my bladder and drank some Gatorade. We discussed some plays and then Walker gave a concise pep talk before we returned to the field for the second half.

In retrospect, it may have been fitting that we were tied at halftime. We were probably equally matched. There were areas where one team was stronger than the other but overall we came out pretty even. The oddsmakers favored the Bears, perhaps by virtue of their home field advantage, but only by a field goal.

When we reached the sideline I noticed Rossi again. His eyes were bloodshot and he took on the general appearance of a walking cadaver. He had been uncharacteristically taciturn throughout the entire game. Normally he was very vibrant and talkative on the sideline, almost to the point of being hyperactive. On this day he sat quietly on the bench wrapped up in his parka, obviously nursing a hangover. The only time I noticed him not sitting was when he was on the field for kick returns.

332

We would begin the second half by receiving the kick. I took my usual spot with Hasegawa on the goal line. Rossi was directly in front of me near the 15.

I don't want to sound overly critical of Rossi. He was far from the first player to overindulge the night before a game. He was a decent football player but far from indispensable. Too many experiences like his would be a sure ticket to the end of his career.

The kick was up and I disregarded my thoughts about Rossi. I caught the ball at the three. Following my blocking which, I assume, included Rossi although I couldn't see him, I managed to reach the 25 before going down.

As the offense ran on the field I sensed an abundance of enthusiasm. I suppose the Bears also had their share of enthusiasm although I didn't consider it at the time. I grinned like a cat cornering a canary as I moved into the huddle.

Two plays later I probably wasn't grinning. Kerner went up the middle for a mere yard. Bender was then sacked at the 16. It was now third and 19.

Walker sent Slater in but not Rossi. We were going into our double-single instead of our double-double which we would normally use in a blatantly obvious passing situation. Although neither Walker nor anybody else ever said so to the best of my knowledge, it was another obvious sign that Walker knew about Rossi's beer consumption into the wee hours of the morning.

At least that is what I have always suspected.

Whatever the reason, we had to travel at least 19 yards to avoid being forced to punt. We got eleven of those yards when Bender hit Dietrich over the middle at the 27.

Dietrich was hit immediately but somehow spun his way out of being tackled. I hit a defensive back in the midsection and kept him out of the play near the 30. Dietrich was hit again near the 35 but managed to lunge forward to the 36. As miraculous as it almost seemed, we had our first down with a yard to spare.

Unfortunately Dave Shuford was down. He was on his knees but doubled over before trying to get to his feet. Time was called so the trainer could run out to him.

Dave simply had the wind knocked out of him. Since an official timeout had been called he had to sit out at least one play. The trainer escorted him off the field to polite applause. Stuart Arroyo entered the game in his place.

Scott carried twice for four yards apiece. I then got the call on a Waimanalo right and managed only one yard. It was fourth and one.

As I was getting to my feet I noticed the punting unit running on the field. It was a pretty brutal hit I took although there was no physical pain. I only hurt because I only got half of what we needed for a first down. Whether it was because of a missed block or something, I didn't know or care. All that mattered was that we came up about three feet short of our goal and I blamed myself.

Jablonski got off a booming punt. It was long and had great hang time. I believed we had a good chance of pinning the Bears back against the goal line.

The Chicago return man suddenly seemed to appear out of nowhere. He caught the punt at the seven and shot forward. He actually managed to run between Hasegawa and Hamer who were probably taken by surprise that he opted to field the punt inside the ten. He was tackled by McCracken at the 17.

Unfortunately for the Bears the punt return comprised the only highlight of the drive. Two rushes sandwiched around a short pass left them a yard short of a first down. It was going to be that coveted three and out. I suddenly found myself standing near the Hawaii 35 in anticipation of a punt to return. I was determined to avoid a fair catch or having a punt I couldn't get to although I didn't have much control over the latter situation.

I got exactly what I wanted. The punt had a pretty good hang time but I felt secure in attempting to return it. Officially I caught the ball on the 36. I was down a couple of seconds later. I gained only six yards which made it only a so-so return in my book but the Hawaii 42 still wasn't bad field position.

"Let's go to work," Bender said in the huddle.

That's what we did. We began with a short but effective pass. Dietrich slanted in and made the reception at the Hawaii 46. He crossed midfield to the Chicago 48. After the measurement we had a first down.

"All right. Now we're rolling. Let's keep it up," Bender said in the huddle.

Scott went up the middle but managed only two yards. He then went off right tackle for six more yards to the 40.

Kerner got the call and was as easy to bring down as a charging rhino. Going off left tackle, he must have broken at least four tackles. He was finally brought down at the 28. With the way he was running it was hard to believe anybody could have brought him down without a tranquilizer dart.

I reached down to help Jeff up. He had an aggravated look on his face and was shaking his head.

"Damn, I should have gone all the way," he said.

"You got about ten or 12 yards," I responded. "That's not bad at all."

I almost laughed when I silently compared Jeff's reaction to something athletes occasionally do when they do something really well but act somewhat disgruntled because they felt they could have done better. In some cases they are trying to impress some girl who is watching. I wondered if Jeff was secretly trying to impress his wife who was watching the game on TV in Hawaii.

334

My number was called next. I went around right end but wasn't nearly as effective as Kerner. I picked up three yards to the 25.

The Bear defense bore down on the next play. Bender's pass over the middle was batted back. Bender nearly caught the ball as it shot back in his direction, narrowly missing a rare opportunity to officially pass and receive the same pass. It was just as well that he didn't catch it because he was ten yards behind the line and surrounded by Bears.

Bender was blitzed on the next play but that was anticipated. Steve got a quick pass off to me at the 23. I was immediately transformed into Goldilocks encountering three Bears but was quick enough to get to the 20 before they brought me down. We were still two yards short of a first down.

As I was getting up I looked in the direction of our sideline. It was not a shock to see the field goal unit running on. It was a disappointment that we wouldn't be getting a touchdown. At least we would be reclaiming the lead with a field goal.

It would be a 37-yard attempt. Billingsley knelt down to spot the ball at the 27. He started calling the signals.

Suddenly a defensive lineman jumped. A flag went up. Either he bumped one of our linemen or else somebody on our side flinched.

The infraction was against the Bears. The lineman bumped Pete Kimmitt; our top draft choice out of UCLA. The five yards put the ball at the 15.

"Offense!" Walker barked although I don't think anybody heard him. He could have called for the cavalry and the offense still would have run on the field. We wanted that touchdown.

"Okay, the Bears gave us a second life," Bender said in the huddle. "Let's show our appreciation by scoring a touchdown."

We went to the air. Bender's pass to Grummon fell incomplete.

Bender tried to pass on second down and dodged a blitz; forced to scramble. He got away and tucked the ball away. He got all the way to the four before stepping out of bounds. We had another first down.

It was amazing. Bender was 37 years old but somehow still found ways to elude predators. He took his share of sacks but avoided several others because he was often still able to shift gears and avoid losses when he needed to.

The final 12 feet of the drive were extremely difficult. We actually covered twice that amount but only because Bender was sacked at the 12. The sack was sandwiched between two incompletions. It was fourth and goal at the 12.

Once again the field goal unit came on. This time a penalty wouldn't give us a first down. After getting second life while the field goal unit was on the field earlier, I felt as if we had cheated our second chance by not getting the full seven.

The Bears didn't jump this time. Guinn's 29-yard attempt split the uprights. We led 13-10 with 2:54 left in the third quarter.

I began to realize that if we were to win this game it wouldn't be by much. I figured ten points at most. The Bears were up for this one. They also had the crowd on their side.

The weather was also a factor in the Bear's advantage. It wasn't a major impediment to us although it was still a factor. It was simply something the Bears were accustomed to. We had to adjust.

Guinn was unimpeded by the weather. His kick sailed out of the end zone. The Bears would start this series at the 20.

Four plays later the Bears had moved 61 yards, thanks largely to a 40-yard run by Payton. It was first and ten at the 19. I was getting worried.

Payton rushed five yards to the 14. That was when the drive stalled. Two incompletions later and the clock was stopped with three seconds left in the third quarter. Chicago's field goal unit took the field.

It was a 31-yard attempt that split the uprights to climax the third quarter. We would enter the final 15 minutes in a 13-13 tie.

I was so bummed out about losing our lead, especially less than three minutes after we got it back, that I almost didn't notice that special teams coach Ken Holcomb had called Hasegawa and me. He gave us a pep talk and sent us to the field to try to get our drive off to a promising start.

"This is one helluva game," Hasegawa remarked as we exchanged our slap fives at the goal line.

"Really. Why can't they be more like the 49ers?" I responded.

"For starters, the 49ers don't have Payton."

"That's true."

The truth is, I was having fun. The fan in me loved tight games while the athlete in me loved the challenge of trying to pull it out. The game was shown in several markets and nobody watching our game was changing the channel to see if NBC had a better game. I just hated not knowing if we were going to win. That was why a large part of me was wishing we had about a four-touchdown lead.

I focused on the task at hand as soon as CBS had cleared us to play. The kick was up. It was heading my way.

"Go for it, Jay!" I heard Hasegawa call.

I caught the ball four yards deep in the end zone and charged out. The first thing I saw was Rossi throwing an awesome block on a dark blue jersey. At least the beer didn't prevent him from doing his job on one of his cameo appearances that day. Although it was several yards ahead of me, I could hear the pop of football pads colliding.

All the while I ran. I was to the 25 before anybody touched me and that was to no avail. I got to the 34 before I was brought down. It was a 38-yard return.

I immediately popped up. It may not have been my best return but it was a darn good one. It was a good start toward retaking the lead.

"Now this is the way it ought to be," Bender remarked enthusiastically in the huddle. "We've got the momentum that should sustain us through this drive."

Scott almost killed that momentum on the first play. He went up the middle to the 37 and fumbled. Fortunately he managed to recover his own fumble on the spot. It was second and seven.

It was Scott again, this time off left tackle. He managed only two yards to the 39. The Bear defense was giving yardage the way "Papa Bear" Halas was reputed to give away quarters.

There was a penalty marker down. That lifted my spirits until I discovered that it was against us. Grummon had lined up a little too far forward and was called for offside.

The Bears declined the penalty. It was third and five.

And then it was fourth and five. A pass into and out of Slater's hands led to that. The promising start that I thought we had led only to a three and out. The offense ran off and the punting unit ran on.

It seemed especially imperative this time that our defense prevent the Bears from scoring. It was bad enough when they countered our previous score with a score. This time it would be up to us to *chase them* if they scored.

Jablonski got off a pretty good punt. The return man fielded it at the 20 without calling for a fair catch.

"Get him! Get him!" I called.

It was like a slow-motion horror epic. The return man eluded Hasegawa and broke Hamer's tackle. He weaved his way through white jerseys while I watched in disbelief. Finally Collier brought him down at the Chicago 42. Had he got past Collier the only man left to beat would have been Jablonski.

The Bears obviously had good field position. It is funny the perception one has about 58 yards. It seems like a much longer distance when your own side has the ball.

I sat on the bench and tried to relax. I tried to will our defense into holding the Bears to a three and out. A turnover would be better still.

Two rushes of three yards apiece gave the Bears a third and four at the Chicago 48. That would normally suggest a pass but four yards to go did not eliminate the rush with somebody like Walter Payton in the backfield.

Walker opted to try to defend against a pass with the 33 nickel. We still had enough manpower up front to contain a run.

The Bears passed. It was complete over the middle near the Hawaii 40. While the crowd roared and the Hawaii sideline expressed various examples of frustration and dismay with an assortment of expletives, the receiver maneuvered his way to the 31 before his former Bear teammate, Carl Rodgers, brought him down.

"They're in field goal range now," I said rhetorically to Grummon who nodded out of reflex as he sat on the bench between Scott and me.

"A couple of sacks will fix that," Grummon added wearily.

"An interception would also be nice," I added.

"Anything," said Scott, "just so long as they don't score."

The Bears picked up three yards on a sweep around right end. Jennings then helped the Bears' cause by jumping prematurely and winding up in the Bears' backfield before the snap. He possibly brushed against the right guard who did an Oscar winning performance of leaping backward more violently than he would have had he been shot from close range. It was second and two from the Hawaii 23.

My stomach seemed to turn. I looked at the clock and noticed it was moving toward the nine-minute mark. At least there was still plenty of time regardless of what the Bears did.

Payton's rush off left tackle was fruitless for the Bears. Prendergast and Allen were there to throw Sweetness for a one-yard loss. That was followed by a pass that was completed at the 22. Jennings hit the receiver on the spot to prevent the first down. It was fourth and one.

The field goal unit ran on. It was a relief in some ways. I could concede the field goal. A sustained drive for a touchdown on our part could just about kill the clock.

At least in a perfect world.

There was also the possibility that the Bears would miss the field goal, meaning that we could win it with a field goal of our own.

And then there was the possibility of a fake field goal. The Bears might pick up a first down and. . . .

Or come up short. . . .

I stopped trying to analyze the possibilities and focused on the action on the field. While I was doing that the Bears went to the line and didn't try a fake. The field goal attempt was good to give the Bears a 16-13 lead with 8:13 left.

"All right, gentlemen," I said as I shed my parka and put my helmet on before returning to the field. "It is time for the winning touchdown drive."

The frigid weather, the hostile crowd and the three-point deficit did not discourage me. We had beaten the Rams. We had beaten the Vikings. We could beat the Bears.

For the moment I focused on the task. The kicker kicked off. It was close to Hasegawa.

"Go for it, Rich!" I called, taking a moment to look upfield to ascertain the feasibility of a return before running up to block.

Rich took the ball a yard deep in the end zone. I met a dark blue jersey inside the 20 and hit him in the numbers. My counterpart was knocked back a little but didn't go down. He caught up with Rich and brought him down at the 22.

338

That wasn't a bad start. It was actually a great start if we were guaranteed to go the distance. Too long a return would mean a shortened drive, giving the Bears more time to respond.

At least that's the way I chose to look at it. Had Rich actually gone all the way I would have been elated.

"Okay, this is it," Bender said optimistically as we formed a huddle near the ten.

We opened the drive with a pass. Bender dropped back and spotted Dietrich near the right hash mark.

The ball was slightly underthrown. A defensive back picked it off at the 37 and took off.

I was near the 35 at the time. I immediately began my pursuit. Shortly thereafter I was knocked on my derriere by somebody in a dark blue jersey. I got back up but the ball carrier was too far gone.

It was Bender who brought him down. By that time the ball carrier had returned the interception 25 yards to the 12.

I took a moment and stood with my hands on my hips to analyze the obvious. We were down by three and the crowd was roaring. Something told me that we were in peril.

There was nothing I could do on the field. It was up to the defense. If the defense could hold the Bears to a field goal we would still be a touchdown away from victory.

"It's all right, Steve," I said to Bender at the Gatorade table.

Bender simply shook his head. He was inconsolable. I would also be inconsolable if I were in his shoes. He was still my teammate, a darn good quarterback and a good person. I wasn't about to condemn him for being as imperfect as the rest of the human race.

Payton went up the middle on the opening play. He picked up three yards.

I sat quietly on the bench huddling inside my parka. I silently tried to will the Bears into coughing up the ball.

The quarterback took the snap and rolled to his right. McDaniel was in hot pursuit.

"Get him, Jim!" I called out.

The quarterback got the pass off. He hit a receiver on the numbers near the back of the end zone. Black made a desperation lunge to try to deflect the ball but to no avail. The officials raised their arms as the crowd roared.

Suddenly the possibility of losing this game seemed very real. I still wasn't ready to surrender. The extra point had us trailing 23-13 with 7:11 left. That was enough time for a couple of scoring drives if we used the clock wisely. The game was no longer about milking the clock on a long drive.

But therein was the key. We needed a *couple* of scoring drives. One scoring drive would only determine the winners among those who bet on this game. We had to score at least twice to win this game and both of those scores had to be touchdowns. A touchdown and field goal would also be acceptable since it would send the game into overtime but I preferred to win it in regulation.

I took my place for the kickoff. I tried to ignore the fans as Rich and I exchanged our slap fives. Neither of us spoke.

"It's all over, you guys!" I heard one fan call from the bleachers.

"Enjoy your flight to Hawaii!" called another.

"Tomorrow you can lay on the beach! You should have stayed home and done that today!"

There were other remarks including those laced with inebriated obscenities. I did my best to shut them out. I was committed to ruining the fans' day. It would be especially sweet if we could actually do that since their hopes were currently very high so our victory would lead them to a very long fall.

The kick was made. It came my way. I caught it at the three and charged forward. I had good protection ahead of me and got past the 20. I was finally stopped at the 28.

As discouraged as I may have felt, I fought to appear optimistic to my teammates by jumping up and enthusiastically clapping my hands. I was probably also trying to convince myself that it was still our game to win.

"We've got plenty of time," Bender calmly said in the huddle. Like the rest of us, he had to put the interception and ensuing touchdown behind him.

On the opening play I caught a pass near the right sideline at the 39. I turned upfield and saw that I was about to be hit. I tried to straight-arm the defender but it wasn't enough. I was tackled at the 41. It was still more than enough for a first down.

Bender hit Dietrich on the next play near the right hash mark of the Chicago 40. He picked up two more yards to the 38 before he went down. We had another first down after picking up 34 yards on two plays. We were well on our way.

We went to the ground next and weren't quite so fortunate. Scott headed off right tackle and was dropped a yard behind the line.

A 4 kama'aina left was called. I got good protection as I raced around left end. I picked up six yards to the 33 to give us a third and five.

We were in field goal range. A field goal would have been all right although not our first choice. A field goal was simply a last resort. We preferred to pick up the full seven and simply utilize the field goal if it became necessary on the subsequent drive.

I lined up in the slot on the right as part of our double-single. I wasn't sure if that was what Walker would have called in this situation anyway or if he considered Rossi to be useless. All I knew was we needed at least five yards.

340

On the snap I ran a sideline pattern to about the 25. As I looked back I saw Bender trying to scramble. There were three Bears in hot pursuit as if he'd been caught sleeping in their beds. He was mauled at the 47.

It was fourth and 19. We were no longer in field goal range and a punt would have been equated with surrender. A field goal would have been about 64 yards. That was a yard longer than the NFL record. I couldn't recall Guinn attempting something that long even in practice.

We remained in our double-single. I was now convinced that Walker was either punishing Rossi or that he simply believed that Rossi wouldn't be effective in his condition. As I ran to my position in the slot I happened to look toward our bench on the opposite side of the field. Even from a distance I could see that Rossi was fuming. He stood with his helmet on as if he had expected to be sent in. I could see slight jerkings of his head as he appeared to be uttering expletives to himself.

I ran a post and looked in. Bender was under pressure but got the pass off quickly. I made a leaping grab of the ball and held on. As my feet hit the ground I was hammered.

It was a good play but not good enough. I was hit and dropped at the 30. I was trying to get further downfield but Bender had to get the pass off quickly to avoid the sack. I was two yards shy of what we needed for the first down.

As soon as the fans grasped the situation they let out a loud roar. The sound had the same appeal as the sound one would hear while stranded in the middle of a rattlesnake den.

It was now up to the defense to work quickly. There was 3:13 left. We also had all three of our timeouts and the two-minute warning.

Payton picked up four yards off right tackle. We used our first timeout. The clock was down to 3:05.

I tried to sit but couldn't. I gulped down a cup of Gatorade and stood as far forward as the league rule allowed. The closer I was to the field, the more I felt I could will the defense to get the ball back for us.

They went to Payton again. I wished they wouldn't but I suppose they wanted to win as badly as we did. Payton went up the middle to the 38. It was third and two.

We called timeout. The clock showed 2:58. We had one timeout and the two-minute warning. Our two scores were doable but it was imperative that we stop the Bears now.

They sent Payton around left end.

"Isn't he getting tired by now," I muttered under my breath in frustration.

Payton broke a tackle at the line. Malick and Morrissey brought him down but not until he reached the 44.

The game was virtually over. We were still alive but our heartbeat was very faint. We used our final timeout with 2:48 left. Our best hope was to force a turnover.

Two rushing plays netted the Bears two yards. One the second play the Bears were called for holding. Needing to get the ball back ASAP, we declined the penalty since accepting it would have given the Bears an extra play. The clock ran down to the two-minute warning.

"Damn," I muttered.

I slowly paced in front of our bench with my parka flapping in the wind. I also looked at the scoreboard. It was as if I believed I could change the 23-13 deficit like I could if this were an adventure of *The Twilight Zone*.

Each time I looked at the scoreboard it looked the same. It was 23-13 with two minutes to play. It also didn't help that the Bears still had the ball. We would get it back if our defense could hold the Bears to fewer than eight yards on the next play but time was obviously not on our side.

When play resumed the Bears stayed on the ground. If they couldn't pick up a first down they were still going to eat up as much of the clock as they could.

The Bears picked up only three yards to their own 49 to create a fourth and five. Most importantly, and most unfortunately for us, the clock continued to run.

I took my place at the ten in anticipation of the punt. We had to score almost immediately if we were to have a chance. Walker told me not to return a punt unless I was sure I could get at least ten yards in short order. That would be hard to determine while looking straight up at a descending football although I would count on Hasegawa to guide me.

The punt was up. It had a good hang time. Not wanting to catch the wrath of Walker by picking up fewer than ten yards, I raised my hand and made a fair catch at the nine. I was hoping that one of the Bears would clobber me so that we could pick up 15 yards toward our impossible dream.

As I caught the ball I braced myself for the hit I was hoping for but it didn't happen. We had 91 yards to go for our first of the two scores we needed. We had 1:16 left to get those scores.

Walker remained relentless. Rossi remained on the sideline. It was an unofficial suspension since Rossi technically hadn't broken any team rules since there were no rules against drinking in your hotel room after curfew and no rules against being stupid. We formed up in our double-single. I'm not sure I agreed with Walker in this situation.

Bender dropped back. He didn't have much pressure since the Bears were in a prevent defense. It seemed that everywhere I ran there was a defensive back nearby.

Slater appeared to be open. Bender fired the ball. A defensive back cut in front of Slater and intercepted the pass at the 36. He returned it all the way to the five before Kerner brought him down.

342

That was it. The game was as good as over. I trotted to the sideline and tried to accept it.

At least the Bears didn't try to run up the score. They were only 15 feet from another touchdown but they didn't bother. Two snaps and two drops to the knee and then it was officially over. There was nothing left to do but graciously shake hands with the victors and move on.

"Losing that game really sucked," Jennings muttered as he took the seat next to me on the bus to the airport.

It was a tough loss. The Bears had simply been the better team that day. They weren't better by much but it was enough.

The flight home was long; perhaps about 30 hours.

At least it seemed that long. Many of us replayed the game over and over in our heads and attempted to find the key that would have changed the scoreboard. When we touched down in Honolulu at shortly before eleven o'clock that night the scoreboard still hadn't changed.

What had changed was our hold on sole possession of first place. While we were losing to the Bears, the Rams were beating the Packers. Their victory enabled the Rams to tie us for first place in our division.

It was a pretty tight race. The Falcons beat the Lions that day. At 5-4, they were one game behind the Rams and us.

Naturally we had the next day off. I wanted to go surfing in the worst way. I actually pondered the possibility, knowing the odds were against me getting caught.

In the end I let my alleged integrity prevail. I didn't go surfing.

I thought about swimming in my complex's pool.

No, I decided.

Too many people would be down there. Most would want to talk about the game. I didn't want to talk about the game.

I grabbed a basketball and drove my car up to the North Shore. There was a basketball court at the beach at Pupukea. As the waves broke nearby I shot hoops. For a few hours I alternated among basketball, walking and watching the surf. It was R&R from the world of professional football. I clearly felt better when I got home at about five o'clock that afternoon.

But still not nearly as good as I would have felt had our sojourn to Chicago been more successful.

CHAPTER FIFTEEN
Rocky Mountain High, Lance and the Rams

Rossi rode to practice with Jennings. Apparently Rossi spent the trip berating me for "hoggin' all the playing time." I would have gotten most of it anyway but occasionally Walker would put Rossi in for a play or two if Walker simply wanted to give him an opportunity and me a chance to rest.

I might not have known about Rossi's tirade had Rossi not still been fuming after he and Ed arrived at the stadium. Unbeknownst to Rossi, Dietrich, Grummon and I were walking a few yards behind them. We could hear Rossi as he and Ed proceeded through the tunnel to the field. The tunnel had wonderful accoustics.

"So who does Dockman think he is, man? I coulda filled in and done real good."

"Hey," Ed replied. "Jay played a good game. It's not his fault that you didn't get in except for a few kick returns. It's Walker who orders the substitutions, not Jay."

"But he coulda got Walker to let me in for a few plays. He's done that before, man. Why didn't he have them guys give me a chance?"

"When did Jay ever tell Walker to put you in? I've never seen him do that. Even if he did, Jay knew how much you drank Saturday night and Sunday morning and he could see what a wreck you were at the game. You drank a whole keg by yourself, Rossi."

Dietrich, Grummon and I found this exchange amusing. I also found the allegation that I had ever gotten Walker to let him in for a few plays interesting. Ed was correct when he said that I had never done that. Whenever Rossi came in to replace me it was only because Walker sent him in. I was never so generous when it came to playing time that I would tell Walker to give somebody a few plays in my place. I never did it for Gary Giametti in 1976 and I wasn't about to do it for Rossi.

Of course Rossi didn't literally drink an entire keg by himself except when compared to what everybody else drank on Saturday night. If I had ever considered asking Walker to send somebody in to relieve me, this game was too tight to ask to be relieved by a man who had pickled himself the night before and was still drinking about nine hours before kickoff. Had I not known about Rossi's beer consumption I still wouldn't have volunteered to come out

But Walker knew about what Rossi had done and that was the key. Walker never said that he knew but he knew. Walker had a virtual omnipresence that meant that virtually nothing got past him. Santa Claus even contacted Walker if he wasn't totally sure about who had been naughty and nice.

As we sat in the hospitality room we all dreaded the game films. The offensive and defensive units dutifully sat with their respective units on opposite sides of the room. I was sitting next to Dietrich and behind Marv who turned to talk to us before Walker and his staff entered the room.

"I know Walker's going to put my butt in a sling," Marv said wearily. "I missed a block and the defensive tackle nailed Larry at the line."

"Yeah, I'm going to get it, too," Dietrich added. "I turned too late on a pass. It bounced off my chest before I even saw the ball."

That was the way it was; the way we were programmed. When it came to game films, all we thought about were our mistakes. Marv could have knocked his opponents clear to Lake Michigan or Dietrich could have caught 12 passes for 300 yards and 12 touchdowns. We went into the films dreading the plays we missed. The entire team was of that mindset.

But it wasn't that bad. Walker knew we were hurting. We had lost a tough game. Had it been a rout either way he would have read the riot act for each semblance of a mistake. In this instance we were wounded soldiers. Walker wanted us to get up and heal our wounds to fight another battle.

Of course Walker didn't simply let things slide. He chewed us out for our mistakes. He simply didn't nitpick the way he would have had we not lost such a hard-fought contest.

The play Marv was waiting for came up. It was a 3 Wahiawa right where Scott ran up the middle between the center and right guard. Marv went for the left defensive tackle but seemed to stumble just enough to allow the tackle to stuff Scott near the line of scrimmage.

"Marv, you missed the block," Walker called as he ran the play back and forth a few times. "The key in this play is you and Shuford making your blocks. Shuford handled the middle linebacker well enough but. . . ."

Walker paused while we got another look at Marv missing the defensive tackle who shot past and stuffed Scott.

"Larry might've picked up five yards on this play," Walker continued. "A missed assignment can be the difference between a first down and having to punt. Ultimately it can even be the difference between winning and losing. This play is not the reason we didn't win but we do win when we keep our mistakes to a minimum."

Walker moved on, much to Marv's relief. It doesn't matter how thick skinned one is. Nobody likes being singled out during films.

Still, we're human. We make mistakes. The mistakes always show up on the films. Walker always made sure we heard about our mistakes. At least Walker didn't run Marv's mistake back and forth half-a-dozen times. Had we routed the Bears that is exactly what he would have done.

Eventually Dietrich's miscue came up. I knew it was coming because Ted was sitting next to me. He muttered, "Here it comes," under his breath when the play was about to show up.

"What was this, Dietrich?" Walker asked as he ran the play back and forth a few times to repeatedly show the ball hitting Dietrich on the chest.

"I turned around too late, Coach," Dietrich replied diplomatically. "It was my fault, not Steve's."

Walker hesitated with the screen frozen where the ball was against Dietrich's chest and his arms not in position to grab the ball.

"That's right neighborly of you, Ted," Walker responded sarcastically. "I'm sure that Bender's very relieved that you aren't blaming him. The ball hit you right in the numbers. What quarterback in his right mind would want to throw the ball there?"

This produced some muffled laughter. I was fighting hard to keep from laughing out loud. I thought I was going to draw blood in my lower lip.

"Ted," Walker continued. "You've played with Bender for three different teams every year since 1969. I would think that you would be in sync with him by now."

The fact is, it actually could have been Bender's fault. Dietrich was running a hook pattern and the films showed that Bender was not under pressure. It could have been that he threw the ball too quickly by not making sure that Ted was looking in his direction.

We'll never really know.

We had a good week of practice. Everybody was up for the Rams. We had beat them in their facility after we lost to the Dolphins. Now we could take our loss to the Bears out on them, taking sole possession of first place again in the process.

After our practice on Friday I lifted weights at the gym in Pearl City and indulged myself with a swim, jacuzzi, ice plunge, sauna and steam room. I then showered and got dressed with anticipation. I had something very special planned for that evening.

"You're really going to see John Denver, huh?"

That rhetorical question came earlier that day from my good friend and teammate, Eric Hamer.

"Sure, why not?"

"Geez, man. John Denver?"

Knowing Eric the way I did, I knew that this was nothing to take personally. He was simply one who liked to needle those whose tastes differed from his own. We had a similar exchange two years earlier when we were teammates on the WFL version of the Hawaiians and John Denver came to town.

Denver packed the Neal Blaisdell Arena just as he did two years earlier at the same facility which was then known as the Honolulu International Center. My seats were behind the stage as they had been two years earlier since I bought my tickets too late to get anything better but at least I was closer to the stage than I was two years earlier when my seats were at the very top. Much to Hamer's surprise, Denver was very much in demand in Honolulu and the choice seats went quickly.

It was an outstanding performance. Denver sang all of his big hits, had a good rapport with the audience and even displayed a sense of humor.

When Denver played his last song and left the stage we all stood and cheered for more. Denver complied.

"I was coming back anyway," he announced when he returned to the stage. "It's a little game I play. I run back and touch the wall and try to get back before the applause dies down."

Don Simmons and his girlfriend Eileen were supposed to attend the concert with Carol and me. They had to cancel because of a minor emergency in Eileen's family.

Surprisingly enough, Bill, my former roommate, agreed to attend the concert with us even though he was more the Jethro Tull type. Bill admitted that Denver was quite a performer.

Ben Blakely was being activated. That was something we knew all week long but it was good to have it finally confirmed the day before our game with the Rams. He would be activated in time to face the team he had played for during the two years prior to coming to the Hawaiians in the expansion draft. He would also be playing against the team he was playing against when he got injured in the first place.

Blakely still wasn't totally recuperated. He would get his share of playing time but Hasegawa would still start, having done a commendable job in Blakely's place. Blakely was expected to be ready to start the following week against New Orleans.

Of course Blakely's activation meant that somebody had to step aside. The most likely candidate seemed to be Jim Vorsino, the ninth round pick out of Indiana. Vorsino began the season on the taxi squad and was activated when Blakely went down.

Apparently Walker didn't want to lose Vorsino who had already been waived once.

The team put Hamer on waivers. Nobody saw that coming. He was primarily a special teams player but filled in well in the defensive backfield when needed. It was simply one of those cuts that had to be made even though Walker didn't want to make it.

"Walker told me not to go away," Eric said after he got the news prior to Saturday's workout, hopelessly optimistic. "He said I am still part of this team and could be brought back at any time if nobody else signs me."

I felt bad for Eric although I was not necessarily surprised. He was a borderline player; good enough to make the team with no guarantees that he would. Although he wasn't the first person I thought of when I considered my best friends on the team, or elsewhere, he was still someone I referred to as a friend.

After our light workout on Saturday about a dozen of us went to the hospitality room to watch the end of the Michigan-Ohio State game. Michigan was holding a 14-6 lead with about four minutes left and Ohio State with the ball.

Ohio State fumbled and Michigan recovered. That pretty much iced the game away.

And yet the most dramatic moment of the game was about to happen. The sideline camera caught a live shot of Ohio State Coach Woody Hayes slamming down his headphones. The expression on his face immediately afterward indicated that he knew he was seen on national TV.

"Uh-oh! Woody's going to do something he'll regret later," Rich Grummon remarked.

Hayes suddenly charged the camera in full view of a national TV audience. On TV it appeared as if he had pushed the cameraman. It was reported that he had actually punched him in the stomach.

"Wow, man" Hasegawa said amid the other murmuring going on in the room.

"Unbelievable," said Bennici.

I said nothing but shook my head in disbelief. That sure looked like the soft-spoken guy with the two-handed handshake who came to my house to recruit me almost nine years earlier but he sure didn't act like him.".

"I think Woody's gotten himself in some hot water," Marv remarked with the rest of us nodding in agreement.

The victory assured Michigan of a trip to the Rose Bowl. About all some people remembered from that game was Woody's sideline volatility.

We were 6-3.

The Rams were 6-3.

We were division rivals. We were battling it out for the title with the Falcons hot on our heels.

So why was I fraternizing with the enemy?

Because my *enemy* had also been my high school football and baseball teammate.

The Rams arrived in Honolulu late Friday afternoon after working out earlier that day in Los Angeles. Lance called me just before I left for the John Denver concert. He and I agreed to meet at five o'clock on Saturday afternoon at the Ala Moana Hotel where all visiting teams stayed.

Lance had never been to Hawaii but there wasn't time to give him the grand tour. Carol and I treated him to a prime rib buffet dinner at the Flamingo Chuckwagon on Kapiolani Boulevard. We took Carol's Datsun since I still had my Porsche which seated only two people.

Over dinner the three of us chatted about a plethora of things. High school, college, Lance's wife and kids, Carol's job, the John Denver concert and President Carter all received mention. The one subject we avoided was the next day's game. About the only time we referred to the game was when we were ordering drinks at dinner.

"Now this is all on me," I said, "but don't be shy about ordering drinks. I figure about 20 or 30 might help your game."

"Wow, I was thinking the same thing about you," Lance cracked back. "I'll even carry you back to your car so you won't have to walk."

"Or crawl," Carol added lightly.

Since it was still fairly early when we finished dinner and since none of us had more than one drink, Carol and I took Lance to the Columbia Inn which was just a couple of blocks away.

The bar was crowded but we found a table in the middle of the room. On a high shelf behind the bar a TV was on. *Wonder Woman* was being shown.

"This is Hawaii's unofficial Los Angeles Dodger headquarters although it caters to sports fans in general," I told Lance.

Since we came in through the side door Lance didn't see the sign by the front door which clarified my statement. It was a large metal sign in the shape of a baseball. The baseball read *LA Dodgers Fever.*

We were approached by a short bespectacled Japanese man with an impish smile. The facility's proprietor, Tosh Kaneshiro, was arguably Hawaii's biggest local celebrity who didn't sing, dance, hold public office, play sports, act, get arrested or appear regularly on radio or TV. He was simply a fun-loving individual who got along with everybody and was a regular fixture at local sporting events. While he gave his undying loyalty to the local teams, the team he loved most was the Los Angeles Dodgers.

"You guys gonna win tomorrow?" Tosh asked.

"Well I hope so," I replied, "but my old friend here is hoping we don't."

Tosh eyed Lance bemusedly. Lance bore a mischievous grin.

"You a Ram fan?" Tosh asked in mock disgust.

"He's a Ram," I said.

I introduced Tosh and Lance. We talked for a few more minutes and then Tosh excused himself to mingle with some of the other patrons.

"That guy's a character," Lance observed.

"Yeah, he is. Sometimes during baseball season I'll come in here for a beer. He and I will talk for an hour or so about the Dodgers. He really loves the Dodgers."

The walls were covered with photos of primarily sports figures. Vin Scully, Sandy Koufax, Mickey Mantle, Stan Musial and a plethora of others were displayed around the room. Lance spotted a photo of me straight-arming a defender during our previous year's game against Houston. I also pointed out a photo of me running at the old Honolulu Stadium during a 1974 WFL game against the Jacksonville Sharks.

349

As we were getting up to leave Tosh came over to us. He had a business card which he gave to Lance. He asked if Lance minded sending an autographed photo of himself.

"Sure, no problem," Lance replied. "I'll try to have it in the mail during the week."

We dropped Lance off at his hotel and then I took Carol home, got in my car and went home. It had been an enjoyable night with Lance. There was no awkwardness even if he was my opponent the next day.

Of course it might have been less comfortable if one of us was a defensive player. Lance and I would never be on the field at the same time.

Carol and I arrived at Aloha Stadium at a little after eight. We crossed the field and went under the bleachers to the hospitality room as we always did. About eight or nine teammates were already present along with a small assortment of wives, girlfriends, children, coaches and guests.

I couldn't help but notice the assistants huddled with Walker in a corner of the large room. They appeared to be having a very serious discussion.

Paying it no mind, I got myself a small plate of fruit and a cup of coffee while Carol helped herself to some scrambled eggs, bacon, fruit and coffee. I was rarely tempted by the pressure of the large spread of food. I was always too wound up this close to gametime to eat much of anything regardless of its appeal.

Carol and I sat at a large round table that was already occupied by Jeff and Susan Kerner, Ed Jennings and his girlfriend Jennifer, and Clint Abraham.

"Did you see Billingsley?" Jeff asked.

"No. Why?"

"He sliced up two of his fingers."

I sat stunned for a moment. I couldn't fathom how he could have done something like that since I last saw him at our workout the day before.

"How'd he manage that?" I asked.

"He dropped a jar of mustard last night," Clint replied. "He tried to catch it before it hit the floor. The jar shattered on his right hand."

"Wow. How bad is it?" I asked.

"He won't be suiting up today," Ed answered. "It looks like you'll be calling the signals if Bender goes down."

At that moment the queasiness in my stomach tightened another notch or two. I finished the last of my fruit although it didn't go down easy. As I was taking a sip of my coffee I noticed Billingsley sitting at a nearby table with his wife. The index and middle fingers on his right hand were heavily bandaged. I found out he had eight stitches in his index finger and six in his middle finger.

I went over and spoke to Billingsley for a moment. Primarily I asked him how he was doing and told him I hoped his fingers would heal quickly. Since he and I weren't especially chummy our conversation was limited.

Walker intercepted me as I headed back to where I had been sitting. He looked agitated.

"I guess you already know that you're the backup quarterback today," he said.

"I know. Not that I expect to be used but I'll be ready."

"Good," Walker said and started to walk away.

"Hey, Coach," I called.

Walker turned around.

"Who's going to hold on the PATs?" I asked.

"The PATs. Geez, I didn't even think of that," Walker responded ponderously. "Do you think you can handle it?"

"Well, I did it my sophomore and junior years in high school. I suppose I remember how it's done."

"Okay, Jay," Walker replied, smiling for the first time since I first saw him that morning. "You've got the job. Just try to take a little time while the defense is on the field and take some snaps to get the feel for it, okay?"

I told Walker I would and sat back down at the table. I was growing more apprehensive since more responsibility was being dropped on my shoulders.

"I'm curious," Jennings said suspiciously. "I heard you tell Walker you held the snaps on PATs your sophomore and junior years in high school."

"Yeah, so?"

"So why didn't you do it your senior year?"

"Yeah," said Clint; his eyes getting bigger as if he was suddenly struck with a startling revelation.

I could tell that Ed and Clint were expecting me to recall having muffed too many snaps. I almost hated to disappoint them.

"Because I was my team's placekicker my senior year."

Ed and Clint nodded slowly. They both appeared surprised by the answer.

"Really?" Ed replied. "Could you do it now?"

"I don't know. I really haven't tried since I was in high school. I suppose if we didn't have anybody else I would give it a shot. I just wouldn't count on any 50-yard field goals if I were you. I think my longest in high school was 38 yards."

The Rams arrived as I was completing my pregame laps. Lance and I exchanged nods but didn't speak.

One thing I remembered about Lance was that he almost never spoke this close to gametime. In high school he was always one of the earliest arrivals in the locker room. He quietly got dressed in the varsity locker room and then would sit by himself outside until it was time for the team's pregame briefing.

If we played an away game he was an interesting sight on the bus. He always sat by a window on the right side directly across from the emergency exit. He rarely made eye contact with anybody. He probably never even knew who occupied the seat next to him.

I usually wound up sitting two or three seats behind Lance. As we headed toward our destination he kept his gaze fixed out the window. He had probably played the entire game in his head by the time we arrived at our game site.

When I saw Lance at Aloha Stadium I could see that he had his game face on. It was the same expression I had seen in high school. He was in reverie and didn't want to speak. I had to respect that.

Of course I spoke very little before a game myself. In high school and college I spoke very little in a locker room or on a bus before a game, saying only what was absolutely necessary. I continued saying very little as a pro, speaking when necessary but engaging in very little banter.

Compared to Lance, though, I had always been a veritable chatterbox.

I did very little out of the ordinary during our pregame warmup. During the last few minutes before we went into the locker room prior to the start of the game the coaches had me throw some passes. It was essential that I get a feel for the range and loosen up my arm in case I was needed at quarterback.

It was unknown if the Rams were aware of my status as the number two quarterback that day. It probably depended on how well they were paying attention to us. Billingsley's misfortune was a last-minute ordeal so the Rams might not have been aware of it unless they happened to notice Billingsley walking around in street clothes and his game jersey. Since Bender was healthy he was their primary concern anyway. I was, at most, an afterthought.

The truth is, I didn't believe I would ever play quarterback in a regular season NFL game. Billingsley was out only because of a freak accident. I believed that Bender was simply too durable to ever go down.

The defense was introduced and then the Leilehua High School Band played the *National Anthem*. I was about as excited as I had been all season. We were at home and playing the team I considered to be the primary obstacle in our quest to win the division.

First place!

That seemed like a lot to expect from a second-year expansion team, especially this late in the season.

Yet we were in the thick of the hunt. For the moment we were tied for first place with the very team we were playing. Barring a tie, one of us would wind up in sole possession of first place after this game. We wanted it.

Of course there were other obstacles in the forthcoming weeks which would affect how we finished in the standings. They came in the form of the Saints, 49ers, Falcons and Jets. It wouldn't be enough to beat the Rams if we didn't properly prepare for the ensuing games. If we beat the Rams but didn't do well against the other four teams on our schedule we would wind up with another mediocre season.

But first on the agenda was the Rams. Something told me that this game would not be a rout. It would probably be a very exciting matchup that may go down to the final tick of the clock.

Our fans seemed to anticipate as much. Attendance would be reported as 49,877, not counting the members of the Leilehua High School Band who would not be occupying any of the stadium seats. The bands always sat in folding chairs directly in front of the bleachers in the north end zone. There was enough space between the end zone and where the band sat to minimize contact with players. Occasionally an errant football would wind up in the vicinity but nothing else to speak of.

Among those in attendance were those for whom I provided tickets. Besides Carol, there were Roy Mulligan and his wife Myra. Don Simmons was stag since his girlfriend was working. Also showing up stag was my former roommate and teammate, Bill Trimble. He was stag because I was only able to scrape up one ticket for him and he was gradually phasing his girlfriend out of his life.

Or so he said. He was saying the same thing a year earlier.

Our captains went to midfield. Under the guise of stretching, I casually looked around at the crowd. Carol sat between Don and Bill. I don't know what they were talking about but one of them seemed to have said something funny. They all seemed to be chuckling.

Suddenly there was a roar from the crowd. We had won the toss. We would be receiving.

The captains returned to the sideline. Walker had the entire team gather around him. It wasn't something we normally did. This was actually the first time ever. Usually his pep talks were held in the locker room.

"All right, men. You beat these guys once already and you can do it again. This time you have your home crowd behind you. You men know what you have to do to pull this one out. Do it and you'll have sole possession of first place. Let's get it done!"

With that we expressed various calls of approbation and broke the massive huddle. We were ready although we weren't at full strength. Aside from Billingsley's freak injury, Westfall was out because of an injury suffered during our light workout the day before. During a kicking drill he turned too abruptly and sprained his ankle. He didn't think anything of it and went through the rest of the workout believing he had suffered only a minor sprain that could be walked off in short order. When he showed up for the game his ankle had ballooned and turned blue. He was given a pair of crutches to watch the game from the sideline in street clothes. He would undergo tests the next day at Queen's Hospital.

Clint Abraham also didn't suit up. He had a sore elbow that was expected to heal in time for the game and had him listed as probable. By Sunday morning he was still in intense pain but offered to play. During pregame warmups it was obvious to Walker that Clint was hurting so he ordered him back into street clothes. He would also be tested the next day at Queen's. Vince Daniels would start at right tackle.

At least Dietrich was able to play. He had been listed as questionable because of damage to his leg suffered in Chicago. He was deemed well enough to play against the Rams.

We took the field to receive the opening kickoff. Hasegawa and I didn't dare to break tradition. We exchanged our slap fives on the goal line of the south end zone.

The kick was up. It was heading Rich's way.

"Go for it, Rich!" I called before running ahead. I tried to block a white jersey but didn't get a very good piece of him.

Hasegawa didn't get very far. The film would show that he caught the ball two yards deep in the end zone. The man I had tried to block made a desperation lunge at the 12 and managed to trip Rich up by getting a piece of his ankle. Rich tried to use his free hand to bounce himself up but he fell at the 16.

This was one of those times when I wasn't thinking like a team player. Rich had an 18-yard return that brought him down inside the 20. All I was thinking about was how my inability to block the man who got credit for the tackle was going to mean Walker yelling at me during the film session on Tuesday. Forget the not very good field position. Walker was going to yell at me right at the beginning of the film session.

"Okay, men. Let's go," Bender said in the huddle. "We've got a lot of football ahead of us."

We came out hard and fast. Bender hit Grummon near the left sideline at the 36. He fought for two more yards to give us a first down at the 38.

The Rams turned up the heat on the next play. We were going to the air again. This time the Rams put a heavy rush on Bender. Bender still got a pass off before he was hit. The pass fell untouched in the *general vicinity* of Dietrich on the mauka sideline in front of our bench. I had run a pattern on the makai sideline near the Ram bench.

"Grounding! That's grounding!" one of the Ram coaches called.

"Oh, for cryin' out loud," I muttered under my breath. "Knock if off, will ya?"

A couple of the Ram players got involved in calling for grounding but no flag was thrown. The film would show that the Rams may have had a

354

case. Dietrich was the closest receiver to the ball but he was about ten yards to the right of it.

Kerner shot up the middle on the next play. Bulldozer that he was, he broke two tackles. He got to the Hawaii 45 to give us a third and three.

We went to the air. . . .

At least we tried to. The blitz was on. Bender dropped back and scrambled and avoided a large loss by running forward. He was still brought down for a three-yard sack at the Hawaii 42.

At fourth and six it was no enigma when our punting unit ran on the field.

Our fourth and six became fourth and eleven. Jim Vorsino, assuming Eric Hamer's position as a wideout, jumped before the snap. That moved the ball to the Hawaii 37.

Jablonski got off a good punt. It was one of those sky jobs that produces a collective "ooh" from the crowd. It had a great hang time that usually leads to a fair catch.

The Ram return man took a chance. He fielded the punt at the 20. He danced his way around Hasegawa but was hammered by Vorsino at the 26. Vorsino's hit was enough to make everybody forget his faux pas that set us back five yards.

Since I was no longer on the field I decided that this was a good time to get the feel of taking snaps. In the area between the bench and the bleachers Arroyo sent a few snaps my way about seven yards behind him. I fielded each one cleanly and set the ball down smartly. Although nine years had passed since I took a snap for a PAT or field goal, it felt very familiar.

I was feeling good. It was one of those rare times when I let go of stewing over whether we won or lost. I took a moment to simply revel in the excitement of being a pro football player.

This was a marquee game. Two first place teams doing battle meant viewers in several markets across the country. Of course it was also being shown in Los Angeles. My own family was watching as well as several old friends and high school teammates.

Even my former high school coach was watching. As a devout member of the LDS Church, Marcus Farnwell normally didn't watch football on Sundays. He made an exception, I found out later, since he had two of his former players in the game just as he did when he attended the game between us and the Rams in October.

The Rams opened with an incomplete pass. Going to the air a second time, Allen charged in. Just as the quarterback was getting set to pass he was mauled by Allen at the 19.

"Yeah, Russ! Way to go, man!" I called, jumping to my feet. There were similar cries of approbation from the sideline and the crowd was definitely vocal in expressing its approval. It was third and 17.

The Rams weren't among the NFL's elite during the '70s by surrendering in difficult situations. They needed to get to their own 36 for a first down and that was about where the receiver caught the pass in the middle of the field. He was brought down by Black and Blakely at the 39.

"Geez," I muttered under my breath. I sat back down on the bench.

"Hang in there, brother. They'll play us tough but we'll play them tougher. We'll get it back," Marv said confidently.

I forced myself to accept it. Perhaps it was easier for Marv because he wasn't on the punt return unit and wasn't anticipating taking the field after one play or maybe it was because he had seven more years of pro experience than me. I reminded myself that the Rams were going to pick up first downs, even in situations that didn't look good for them, and they were likely to score once or twice.

The Rams carried up the middle, picking up three yards to the 42. They then decided to go back to the air. The pass was fairly deep.

Rodgers leaped in the air in front of the intended receiver and picked the ball off at the Hawaii 33. After a few steps he was on a collision course with my old friend Lance. Rodgers cut sharply to his left and avoided contact, continuing upfield.

We were all jubilant on the sideline. We were on our feet and yelling while the crowd throughout the stadium followed suit.

Carl dodged and weaved his way past midfield. He showed some pretty nifty moves as he seemed to be virtually untouched by the time he got to the Los Angeles 40. The only man left to beat was the quarterback who had air mailed the package to Carl.

It was no contest. One more cut to the left and the Ram quarterback came up with nothing but air. Carl was on his way, galloping with nothing but end zone ahead of him to the 30 . . . 25 . . . 20 . . . 15 . . . .

Touchdown!!!!!

"Way to go, Carl! Way to go!" I hollered while my teammates offered similar praise. It was an outstanding play by the ninth year pro out of Oregon.

I watched as the extra point unit ran on the field. As the unit huddled there seemed to be some confusion. Malick, McWherter and Guinn all started gesturing toward the sideline. I also noticed Arroyo putting his hands in a "T" before the officials signaled a timeout.

"Dockman!"

That was Walker. In all of the excitement I had forgotten that I was the holder. When we were on offense I continually reminded myself to stay on the field if we scored or were going to attempt a field goal. While the defense was on the field I let go and functioned out of habit.

I ran down to the huddle near the north end zone with egg on my face.

"Sorry, guys," I said before leading the huddle. "Okay, PAT on three. On three. Ready?"

356

"Break!"

For the first time since late 1968 I knelt down to hold for a PAT. It seemed both familiar and strange. I looked around and saw my teammates ready in their half-upright stances.

"Blue, Chicago, 45!" I called, which meant nothing because we weren't going to audible on a PAT since this was long before the NFL implemented the two-point conversion. "Blue, Chicago, 45! Set! Hut! Hut! Hut!"

The ball shot back from between Arroyo's legs. I caught it cleanly and set it down. With good protection up front Guinn put the pigskin through the uprights.

At least my absence of brain activity didn't cost us a point. All it cost was a timeout that I hoped wouldn't prove to be critical. I was still a little embarrassed but ran off the field as if nothing out of the ordinary had happened except that I did try to avoid eye contact with Walker and got beyond him as quickly as possible. From what I was told later, he was laughing because of how obvious it was that I was trying to avoid him.

It was 7-0. There was 9:21 left in the first quarter. That meant 54:21 to try to stave off a very tough opponent.

After being on the field only for as long as a PAT I grabbed a cup of Gatorade. It was a subconscious superstition, I guess. I really wasn't thirsty.

Besides, I loved Gatorade. The lemon-lime was delicious. Even later when Gatorade came up with a variety of flavors the original lemon-lime remained my favorite.

Guinn kicked off. Despite kicking against the wind the ball didn't come down until it was six yards deep in the end zone. The Ram return man caught the ball, hesitated and then gently knelt down. First and ten at the 20.

I suppose the wind at Aloha Stadium wasn't as critical a factor as it might have seemed for football. On a normal day Hawaii features northeast trades from between about 15 and 25 miles an hour. That meant that there was an advantage to kicking and passing toward the south end zone but I didn't notice any major discernible difference most of the time.

A more glaring difference showed during baseball season. Drives to deep right got hung up in the jetstream, making it extremely difficult for left-handed hitters to pull the ball into the bleachers. Balls driven to left took off like rockets and immediately left no doubt that the ball would leave the park. Balls driven to right with the same intensity suddenly ran out of fuel and usually dropped for long outs.

Our defense got off to a good start with the help of a Ram faux pas. A three-yard rush was nullified by a holding penalty. The Rams had first and 20 at the ten.

It didn't take the Rams long to eradicate their miscue. After one pass they had second and three at the 27. That was followed by a rush around left end that got them a first down at the 32.

Two rushes later the Rams had a third and one at the 41. They tried getting the yard they needed up the middle. Allen not only headed the running back off but dropped him for a yard loss. It was fourth and two at the 40.

"Punt return unit! Let's go!" Walker called.

After a brief huddle I assumed my post just inside the 20. I looked forward to a drive that would put us ahead by two scores. It would be far from an insurmountable lead, especially against a team of this caliber, but every score would be vital to our quest.

The punt was up. It wasn't especially long but it was pretty high. That gave it a good hang time and plenty of time for the coverage to get downfield. I prudently held my hand up to signal for a fair catch and caught the ball at the 25. It was a mediocre 35-yard punt.

"Okay, gentlemen. Let's move to the end zone," Bender stated coolly as we began our huddle.

We moved a large chunk toward that goal on the opening play. Bender hit Grummon with a pass near midfield. Rich had to leap and bobbled the ball a little but managed to secure it at the Hawaii 48. He broke a tackle at that point and got to the Ram 38 before being hit and dropped by a pair of defensive backs.

On the next play we tried a pass underneath. Bender faked a handoff to Kerner as Kerner headed up the middle, stepped back and then flipped a pass to Kerner at the 36.

A linebacker jumped in front of Kerner and picked the pass off. It happened so quickly that the linebacker had no trouble running past the linemen who were still in the process of blocking. That left only Bender in his path.

The linebacker bowled Steve over at about the Ram 45.

I was about ten yards downfield when the interception was made and immediately gave chase. I managed to fight off a block near the line of scrimmage and eventually caught the linebacker from behind. I wrestled him down at the Hawaii 43.

Whistles were blowing. With the way I had to tackle the linebacker he wound up lying on top of me with the back of his blue and gold helmet pressed against my facemask. A few of his teammates quickly arrived and helped him up.

"Great play, man!" I heard as the weight of his body was lifted from me. "Way to go!"

As I started to raise up I noticed a black hand reaching down to me. I grabbed it and saw myself being helped to my feet by Larry Scott.

"Good job, Jay," Scott said although devoid of the enthusiasm expressed by the Rams as they helped their teammate up since the play had a negative outcome for our side. "You probably prevented a touchdown."

358

I hoped he was right. The rest was up to the defense. The Rams were starting a drive only 43 yards from the goal line. Already they were close to field goal range.

"Good job, Jaybird," Rodgers said as our paths crossed.

I appreciated the compliments but obviously didn't feel like celebrating. I ran off the field and went straight to the Gatorade table.

Bender was standing in front of the bench a few feet away from me. He was trying to appear stoic. It was obvious that he was irritated with himself.

The Rams opened with a four-yard rush off right tackle. They then completed a pass just inside the 20. The receiver ran past Rodgers toward the left sideline. He was brought down at the 12 by Morrissey.

A moment earlier I had been looking forward to a two-score game. Now a tie game was a very distinct possibility. The Rams moved five yards closer to that possibility with a rush up the middle to the seven.

The Rams then went to the air. The quarterback fired to a receiver in the right corner of the end zone. Black got his hand in and knocked the pass down. Third and five.

"Yeah, way to go, Mark!" I cried out as I jumped up from my seat.

We went to the 33 nickel. The newly reactivated Blakely went in and Prendergast came out.

The Rams didn't pass. Instead they ran a sweep around left end. Malick and Morrissey teamed up to tackle the ball carrier but not until he was crossing the goal line. The Rams were a PAT away from tying the score.

A few moments later the Rams had their PAT. The score was tied with 2:14 left in the first quarter.

Interceptions were the story of the game to this point. We intercepted a pass and scored a touchdown on the same play. The Rams intercepted a pass and that set up a touchdown.

I took my post on the goal line of the south end zone. Rich and I did our slap fives. Neither of us said anything. We communicated by nodding, both seeming to be thinking the same thing. It was imperative that we get the momentum back.

Before CBS came out of commercial I quickly scanned as much of the stadium as I could by simply turning my head without moving the rest of my body. We had the crowd on our side. It was definitely our home field advantage. That encouraged me.

The kick was up. It was heading away from me to my right.

"Take it, Rich!" I called and ran forward.

I put a pretty good block on a white jersey near the 20. I caught him by sticking my right shoulder into his gut, knocking the wind out of him. A split second later we were both on the ground.

Rich had taken the kick at the two. He got up to the 24 before going down.

It wasn't a bad start. After our huddle we lined up for our opening play of the drive.

Kerner carried off right tackle. He fought his way to the 31.

"Loose ball!"

The ball had popped loose. A Ram defensive back caught the ball in the air at the 34. He returned it to the 30 before being brought down by Marv. I had gone after the ball carrier but was cut down by somebody in a white jersey.

As I rose to my feet I noticed the eery silence of the crowd. The Rams were jubilant and the other sound I heard was the public address announcer describing the play. The crowd was stunned into silence. That was how I felt.

A kickoff and a single play from scrimmage and I was back at the Gatorade table. A few plays earlier we were not only protecting our lead but trying to expand it. Now we were in jeopardy of falling behind.

The Rams obviously hoped that they would take the lead. They began their drive with a quick slant-in pass to Lance. Lance caught the ball at about the 24. He got to the 20 before being brought down by Rodgers and Hasegawa.

Time was called. The chain was brought out. The Rams had a first down by about an inch.

Two plays later the Rams had a first down at the seven. That became a first and goal at the 12 when they got cited for delay of game.

"Maybe that'll screw up their momentum," I remarked hopefully to Kerner who was sitting on the bench next to me. "That might force them to settle for a field goal."

Kerner, no doubt smarting from having the fumble which enabled the Rams to start their drive 90 feet from the end zone, simply nodded. Nobody wants to fumble. Nobody especially wants to be responsible for the fumble that leads to a score. Unfortunately the only football players who never fumbled are those who never carried the ball.

The Rams picked up eleven of the necessary yards on a single play. A wide receiver caught a pass at the one and the angle he was running caused him to immediately step out of bounds. That was the final play of the quarter.

I got up and walked around in front of the bench. The break was unsettling as the referee moved the ball 98 yards toward the north end zone. Since a touchdown seemed imminent I wished the Rams would simply get their score and then we could get the ball back.

It took only one play. The Rams went off left tackle and penetrated just enough into the end zone to climax the drive. With the extra point we trailed 14-7 with 14:55 left in the half.

"I guess we'd better get something going," I remarked as Hasegawa and I did our thing on the goal line of the north end zone.

"We'd better," Rich agreed. "We're giving this game away."

We wanted to win. We were simply playing as if we didn't. The offense had had one semblance of a drive that ended with a punt. Our other two drives ended with turnovers. Our only touchdown was scored by the defense but, compared to what had happened since then, our touchdown seemed like something from the previous season.

For the moment we had to forget everything, good and bad, that had already happened and move forward. The kick was up and heading toward Hasegawa.

"Take it, Rich!" I called before running forward to block.

Rich returned the kick from the goal line but only got to the 18. That was followed by Scott's seven-yard rush being nullified when Grummon was cited for holding and the Rams being cited for a facemask to offset the penalty. It was still first and ten at the 18.

For the second time in three drives a short pass to Kerner was picked off. A linebacker snagged the ball at the 28. He returned it to the five before being brought down by Marv.

"Fumble!"

The return man coughed up the ball. Unfortunately his teammate fell on it at the five. The Rams were 15 feet from another score and I was feeling nauseated.

I think the crowd was too stunned to boo. Our fans had never seen us so inept. We simply could not hang on to the ball.

"What's going on, offense?" Walker asked tersely as we reached the sideline. "Why are you giving the Rams all of this charity?"

It was best to keep my mouth shut and proceed to the Gatorade table. I hadn't worked up much of a sweat since our drives were over quickly. I suppose the taste of Gatorade was better to focus on than the 77-7 score we seemed destined to experience.

After an incompletion and a short completion the Rams had third and goal from the one. Rory Manwaring then moved them half-a-yard closer by jumping offside.

I looked at Walker. His perfunctory response was to freeze like a glacier with his trademark scowl and folded arms. I wasn't sure he was even breathing.

The Rams tried going up the middle. The ball carrier got a rude reception from our defense. It would have been easier to plow through the Berlin Wall. The Rams were stopped for no gain.

I looked across the field to the Ram sideline. The field goal unit was making no effort to run on the field. The Rams were going for the full seven.

Our two backless aluminum benches were empty. Everybody was standing. It was very important that our defense rise to the occasion.

The Rams broke their huddle and headed to the line. That seemed to be the cue for our fans to start screaming at the tops of their lungs to make it hard for the Rams to hear their signals. In case anybody in the crowd didn't know to do that, Black started waving his arms upward to get them to turn up the volume. Some of us on the sideline did the same.

I watched breathlessly as the ball was snapped. The quarterback wheeled and handed off to a running back. The running back leaped up. . . .

Too many brown jerseys in the path. Leading the charge were Richards and Jennings. The crowd roared as the play was blown dead for no gain.

"All right, offense! The defense just saved your sorry asses! Do something with the ball besides give it away this time!" Walker barked.

It was new life.

Or perhaps it was borrowed time.

All I knew was I wanted to do something with the ball this time other than simply hand it back to the enemy. So far in this game we seemed to be awfully philanthropic.

Scott went up the middle. A linebacker and safety wrestled him down at the five.

"Fumble!"

I was a few yards beyond the five when I heard that cry. When I spotted the loose ball I uttered a few things I would rather not repeat as I ran toward the point of infraction.

Whistles had been blowing frantically. Scott was ruled down by contact before the ball came loose. It was second and six.

That was a relief beyond description. If we lost the ball again so early in the possession our fans were going to go ballistic. I wouldn't have blamed them if they ripped the seats out and threw them at us. At the very least, they would go to the parking lot and resume their tailgate parties.

Fortunately it was ruled no fumble. We were still in good shape.

We went right back to Scott. He went off left tackle, giving us a first down at the 13. The crowd cheered the first down although I couldn't help but wonder if some of them were sarcastically cheering the fact that we didn't turn the ball over this time.

After an incompletion I carried off left tackle for three yards to the 16. That gave us third and seven.

We went to the air next, feeling as if there wasn't much choice. Bender hit Dietrich over the middle at the Hawaii 35. He took another step or two and was hammered at the 37 while securely holding the ball against his gut. We had another first down.

"Okay, gentlemen. We're finally getting it together," Bender remarked in the huddle. "We've got to make everybody including ourselves forget how we were screwing everything up. Let's take it all the way."

362

After a 20-yard pass play to Grummon was nullified by offsetting penalties we ran two plays that got us nowhere. It was third and ten at the Hawaii 37.

It was an obvious pass situation. We could have tried to cross them up with a rush but the odds were that we couldn't get the ten yards we needed. We went to the air.

Bender hit Dietrich at the Hawaii 49. Ted had to lunge forward to catch the ball and fell down but still managed to get up before a Ram touched him. He crossed midfield and got to the 45 before being grabbed from behind, picked up and brought down.

"Fumble!"

I was trying to throw a block near the 40 when I heard that.

"Oh, geez," I muttered as I tried to turn back.

The table turned. As I turned back toward the loose ball the man I had been trying to block threw a block at me. It was quick thinking on his part since I had a clear shot at the ball. This enabled one of his teammates to recover the ball at the Los Angeles 42.

I rose to my knees. Believe it or not, tears clouded my eyes. It was the frustration of fighting hard and still not being able to play well. We had seven points on the board only because the defense made a big play and it was because of that same stubborn defense that we trailed by only a touchdown. All the offense was able to do was reek so badly that it permeated everything from South Point to Hanalei. They were probably even booing us on Ni'i'hau.

It wasn't as if Aloha Stadium was a massive boo festival. Most of our fans, I believe, did not boo. There was simply enough booing to notice.

Still, it wasn't the booing that bothered me. I was in too much shock to really notice anyway. It was the futility of our effort. Nobody fumbled because he wasn't trying. Bender's incompletions were not deliberate. Our miscues were coerced, at least in part, by the outstanding effort of the Rams. They wanted to pay us back for what we did to them at their venue. They also wanted sole possession of first place in the division. With our four turnovers they were well on their way.

On the sideline Potter called the offense together. He got down on one knee while the entire offense, backups included, huddled around him.

"What the hell is wrong out there?" he asked rhetorically. "Looking at you guys today, I can't believe you're the same team I see listed on top of the standings. With the way you're going right now, you couldn't beat a high school team."

That didn't make me feel any better. I also can't say we didn't deserve the admonition. I stood in the huddle with a cup of Gatorade in my hand, not daring to raise it to my lips for fear of Potter accusing me of not paying attention.

"If you're going to get beat, get beat," Potter went on, "but don't beat yourselves. You can't win every game but you are still expected to play as if you want to win. With the way you're playing now it is hard to believe you actually care. We've turned the ball over four times and we're still in the first half. We normally don't turn the ball over that much during an entire game."

Potter had remained composed to this point. As he continued he got more heated, the language became more colorful. He was not a happy camper.

By the time Potter finished the Rams had a second and six at the Hawaii 20. After two incompletions they kicked a 37-yard field goal. That gave the Rams a 17-7 lead with 2:43 left in the half.

I felt that it was especially important that we use the 2:43 to put something on the scoreboard. Up until this point it had been a wasted half on the offense's part. Football is a team game and it was imperative that our offense finally come together. If we didn't it might cause the defense to lose heart.

The kick came my way. I caught it four yards deep in the end zone and paused to consider my options.

It seemed prudent to simply down the ball. I could probably have gotten to the 20 which would normally justify the return. At this juncture it was better use of the clock to simply down the ball and automatically start at the 20.

We started with a quick short pass. Bender hit me near the right sideline at the 24. I immediately stepped out of bounds to stop the clock with 2:35 left in the half.

The next play took a little longer and was less successful. Bender dropped back and was under a heavy rush. That forced him to scramble until he spotted Dietrich near the 40. The pass was batted down to stop the clock at 2:25. It was third and six.

Bender was rushed again and forced to scramble. He broke away after a few seconds and spotted Slater near the left hash mark. Joe caught the ball at the Hawaii 43 and headed for the sideline. He was tackled a few feet in bounds at the Hawaii 45.

The clock continued to run. We could have used a timeout but decided to save them. Since there wasn't time to organize a play in the days before the rule allowing the quarterback to simply take a snap and spike the ball we let the clock run down to the two-minute warning.

As Bender went to the sideline to converse with Walker the remaining ten players in the offensive unit went down on one knee in the huddle. Nobody said a word. We could have talked about the dire need to go 55 yards in two minutes but that would have been redundant. Any other topic would have been inappropriate.

After a Rams encroachment penalty and an incomplete pass when play resumed we had a second and five at the 50. Bender hit me with a pass near the right hash mark at the 39. I ran obliquely toward the sideline and was hit as I was going out at the 35. I had made it to the sideline.

Or did I?

As I looked up I noticed an official pinwheeling his arm around to keep the clock running. I was surprised but the replay I would see later showed that my knee touched down in bounds before the rest of me went out.

Marv was slightly injured. One of the Rams fell on his ankle. The clock stopped for that but we had to hurry because the clock would start up after Marv was off the field. He hobbled off to a round of applause and would be back after a couple of plays but the clock was running again. At least was in the days before an injury inside the two-minute warning would cost us a timeout.

We worked quickly and Bender hit Grummon at the 24. Rich spun his way out of a tackle, then broke another tackle before going down in bounds while still at the 24.

"Timeout!" about half-a-dozen of us, myself included, cried out.

The officials blew whistles and waved their arms over their heads to stop the clock. There was 1:20 left in the half. We had only one timeout left because we lost one when I neglected to take the field for our extra point. My negligence was appearing more likely to prove to be critical.

"There is no way in hell that we are going to be denied this time," Scott remarked in the huddle while Bender conversed with Walker on the sideline.

"Damn right," Abraham responded.

"We've come too far," I added.

"We've got too much going for us to not make it," Scott said. "We can't afford to let them stop this drive."

The Rams showed that they were determined to do exactly that. Bender met a heavy rush and was forced to scramble. Not only were we in danger of losing yardage but the scramble was also using valuable time.

Steve was finally caught from behind and dragged down by the shoulder pads at the 28. It was a four-yard sack and the seconds were ticking down.

We got to the line quickly. It was fortunate that two plays had been called in the previous huddle. It still took a little time to get set but we saved at least a few seconds by not having to huddle.

At the snap I ran a flag pattern. Bender threw me a high pass so that either I would leap up and catch it or else the ball would sail out of bounds to stop the clock.

I made a leaping catch at the ten. Unfortunately I was hit and dropped immediately so I wasn't able to get out of bounds. The clock continued to run, heading down toward 30 seconds.

Bender gave a signal that we would run our Ka'ena Point. This was named for an area between Makaha and Mokuleia that is virtually impossible to maneuver around without a four-wheel drive vehicle. Without four-wheel drive you essentially go nowhere and that was essentially what the play was designed to do.

We lined up quickly and all of the receivers ran straight to the end zone at the snap. Unless somebody got wide open Bender was to fling the ball out of the end zone. That was what Bender did to stop the clock with 24 seconds left in the half. We got nowhere but at least we stopped the clock.

The crowd was with us. For the first time that day the offense was giving the fans reason to cheer. If we scored even a field goal they might forget that they had been booing us earlier.

Bender dropped back on the next play. I ran deep but couldn't shake the defensive back. That was also the case with Dietrich. Bender decided to hit Scott who was near the right sideline inside the five. The ball was batted back at the line of scrimmage and fell incomplete.

It was third and ten. There were 17 seconds left in the half. It was still technically possible for us to pick up a first down but only by inches. Given that and the limited amount of time, it was imperative that we score on this play. Otherwise the following play would be a field goal attempt.

McCracken and Rossi came in while Grummon and Scott went out. McCracken brought in the play while Rossi was dispatched so that we could work in our single-double formation. It would be Rossi's first appearance on a play from scrimmage since our game in Tampa two weeks earlier.

The Rams were in a nickel defense. On the snap I ran to the end zone near the goal post but was double-teamed. As the films would show, Dietrich was also double-teamed in the right corner. A single defensive back guarded Rossi near the left corner.

Bender was under pressure and had to scramble a little. He spotted McCracken who seemed to have an opening despite being guarded by a very determined linebacker. McCracken caught the pass near the goal line and took one step forward.

Touchdown!

The crowd erupted. I leaped in the air and ran toward McCracken who was spiking the ball a few yards away. This was the way we needed to end the second half. We seemed to be back in the game.

I was so happy that I almost forgot that I needed to stay on the field for the PAT. Fortunately I had taken only a couple of steps toward the sideline before it hit me. I rerouted to where I would be presiding over the huddle before anybody noticed that I almost screwed up again.

Everything went right. The snap, the hold and the kick and we left the field in triumph. It was 17-14 with eight seconds remaining in the half.

The ensuing kickoff took care of the remaining time. The ball was fielded at the four. The return man chewed up a couple of seconds when he bobbled the ball. He managed to get to the 25 before going down. Time had expired.

366

We left the field. Our fans gave us generous applause. After such a horrendous performance which earlier earned us some boos we had finally come to life and narrowed the gap. Our fans were with us.

Thanks to our final drive we had some reasonably impressive passing numbers. Bender completed only ten of 21 with two interceptions but the completions covered 173 yards and included a touchdown. Prior to the final drive Bender had completed only four of ten for 98 yards.

A more telling statistic was our rushing total. As a team we had five carries for 23 yards. Scott was our leading rusher with two carries for 13 yards. Not good.

"I'd like to believe we've finally got the momentum," Walker said as we prepared to return to the field. "We've just got to knock off the turnovers. We finally got it together at the end of the half and that's good but we have to keep it up."

Walker paused. He drew into his cigarette and pondered, looking around the room. At the same time an official entered and held up two fingers. Walker nodded.

"Defense, you've been pretty solid so far. You've kept us in the game. Keep it up," Walker continued. "Offense, I don't know what you were doing through most of the first half but at least you finally cleaned your act up at the end. Let's erase that pathetic showing and move forward. Now let's go get 'em."

I was hyped. Normally at the start of the second half I had gotten a few licks in and was poised to be patient. I suppose it was our overall inept play from the first half that gave me the hyperactivity I often experienced at the start of the game. I wanted to be on the field immediately.

But I had to defer to the Rams. We received the game's opening kickoff. The Rams got to start the second half with the ball.

Guinn teed up the ball and kicked off toward the south end zone when the referee gave him the okay. The ball was fielded at the two and returned to the 24.

"Defense! Let's hold 'em!" Walker called.

After two plays, the second of which would have given the Rams a first down at the 35 but was nullified by a holding penalty, the Rams had second and 13 at the 21. That was when Lance was on the receiving end of a pass near the sideline just inside the 35. He got to the 40 before Morrissey wrestled him down. First down.

The Rams continued to move. Whatever we were prepared for, they had something different. After three more first downs they had the ball on the Hawaii 20. That obviously meant that they were 60 feet from making this a two-score game again. Equally as important, it would mean that they had regained the momentum.

As our defensive unit huddled I took note of the way Allen was presiding. The way he was pounding his fist into his open palm told me he wasn't simply calling a formation. He seemed to be trying to fire up the unit.

I stood up. I needed the best possible vantage point to see if our defense was going to catch fire.

The unit broke its huddle with a very spirited "Break!". It awaited the Rams offense.

The Rams tried a sweep around left end. It was to no avail. Jurgens fought off a block to stop the ball carrier for no gain. It was second and ten.

Apparently the Rams decided to table the ground game for a moment. They went to the air.

At least they *tried* to go to the air. McDaniel chased down the quarterback and brought him down at the 28.

That brought the crowd to life. Sometimes a sack is just as exciting as a touchdown.

"Great job, Jim! Way to go!" I called although I knew McDaniel wouldn't hear me over the roar of the crowd. I still had to express my enthusiasm.

We went to our 32 dime defense. A pass seemed to be a virtual certainty. This would enable us to defend against it while still having enough muscle to prevent a ball carrier from picking up a first down if the Rams decided to run.

This formation included a cornerback blitz. Black shot in from the left. The quarterback was setting up when he spotted Black bearing down on him. He backed up a couple of steps and then accepted the inevitable. The quarterback hunched over to protect the ball just as Black gave him a hit guaranteed to give him nightmares for the next three nights.

It was a ten-yard loss. The Rams had fourth and 28 at the 38. A field goal attempt would be 55 yards against the wind. The Rams sent their punting unit out.

I took my post. I was just inside the ten, then moved back to the five. Walker wanted me to use my discretion and not necessarily go by the book. If I believed the ball would bounce into the end zone I would allow it to. Anything else I felt I had a shot at returning, even inside the ten, I would do.

The punt was up. It was well to my right. It flew out of bounds at the eight.

"Hokay," I said wearily under my breath. The Ram punter had done his job. He could have done it better but it was good enough. We had 92 yards to travel.

"Let's take it all the way," Bender said confidently as we huddled in the north end zone.

As I took my post in the right slot and got ready to go in motion I felt surprisingly confident about our chances. I figured that the *turnover monster*

368

was gone. There was no way that I could have fathomed how major a role I was fated to have in the outcome of this game.

We didn't exactly get off to a flying start. Scott went off left tackle. He didn't fumble, thank God, but was brought down at the six. We were moving toward the wrong end zone.

Scott got us moving in the *right* direction with a sweep around right end. He picked up seven yards to the 13.

Unfortunately there was a yellow flag on the ground near the line of scrimmage. Daniels was called for holding. That moved the ball half the distance to the goal line. It was second and 15 from the three. We were still moving toward the *wrong* end zone.

"Don't get down. It's out of our systems now," Bender calmly commanded in the huddle. "We're going to move forward now."

That was a good idea. Another nine feet in the wrong direction and the Rams would be the recipients of two freebie points with a bonus of getting the ball back.

At least we did as Bender said we would. Bender hit me in the center of the field with a perfectly thrown pass at the 17. I picked up a few more yards before being hit and dropped from my right side at the 21. First down.

There was another yellow flag. This time it was holding against the Rams. We declined the penalty but time stayed out because of an injury. Bender was in excruciating pain. He had been hit as he released the pass and went down hard on his right shoulder. Apparently he jammed it.

Initially I didn't think about how prominently this affected me. I watched from a few yards away while the trainer helped Bender up. He tried to hide it but his face cringed in pain.

"It looks like you're the man," Marv said to me.

"Huh?" was my scholarly reply before it dawned on me what he meant.

Bender looked at me as he walked past.

"You can do it, Jaybird. You can pull this one out."

As the crowd gave Bender polite applause I happened to look toward our sideline. Although the clock was stopped, it would start again as soon as Bender had cleared the field. Walker was gesturing for us to call timeout.

"Time!" I said to the first official I saw, making a "T" with my hands. He blew his whistle and waved his arms over his head. I ran to the sideline to engage in a confab with Walker while Rossi ran on the field to fill the vacated halfback role.

Walker put his hand on my shoulder. He had a paternal smile on his face. He wanted to build my confidence.

"I know you haven't really played quarterback except at practice lately but I know you can do the job. You excelled at this position in high school and you even did well when we put you in during an exhibition game last year. As I recall, it was also against the Rams. I guarantee you it's going to feel very natural after a play or two."

369

Whether Walker actually believed what he was saying or was simply blowing smoke, I didn't know. The important thing was that I believed his words. I was nervous. I also believed that I could get the job done.

"The Rams will expect you to be conservative," Walker continued. "We're not going to be conservative. We're going to play it as if you are our regular quarterback. We'll have our share of rushing plays but we're also going to make good use of our air attack. Judging from what I've seen in practice, your passing ability is at least as good as most NFL quarterbacks. You've also shown that you're a very capable passer from the halfback position. The only difference now is you are going to be throwing your passes from the quarterback position."

Most of our fans, as well as the Rams, were probably wondering what was going on. Billingsley's mishap happened so close to gametime that there was very little pregame publicity. Only those in attendance with radios would know since Les Keiter and Earl McDaniel, as well as the Rams broadcast team, mentioned it during the broadcast and I did find out later that those watching the game on television were apprised of the situation. The rest were probably wondering why number 12 hadn't even taken the field for our extra point attempts. Billingsley was wearing his jersey but those not especially close to our sideline might not have noticed that he was also in street clothes.

I returned to our huddle and called the play, then headed toward my post directly behind Shuford.

"Jay Dockman now at quarterback," I heard the public address announcer say. I was too focused on my job to notice anything else. Carol later told me she heard some audible gasps and murmurs from some of the fans. I didn't hear anything except for a few remarks from one of the Rams:

"Dockman? What happened to that Mormon guy? What's his name? Oh yeah, Billingsley."

In retrospect, it was amusing. At the time I was too focused on what I was doing to give it any thought.

There was a slight change in our standard formation. Since I was left-handed Dietrich would usually be split wide to the left instead of the right. Grummon at tight end would usually line up on the right.

It didn't seem to matter much. On the first play I hit Dietrich right on the numbers on a cross pattern. He caught the ball at the 31 and turned upfield. Ted was brought down at the 39.

The crowd, which probably had been holding its collective breath, roared its approval. That and the overall success of the first play convinced me that I was capable of getting the job done. The butterflies were gone. I no longer felt like a misassigned halfback. For the moment I had the confidence of a bona fide NFL quarterback.

A pass to Rossi was a little too far ahead of him and fell incomplete. That was followed by Scott running a sweep that produced only two yards.

Third and eight meant my biggest test thus far. My initial completion was on first down and served as an ice breaker. This play would indicate whether I could convert on third and long.

On the snap I rolled to my left and saw a linebacker coming after me. I shifted direction, rolling to my right. I spotted Grummon and shifted slightly forward, then unleashed the ball.

The pass was on the mark. Grummon caught it easily at the Ram 40. He picked up seven more yards before going down. It was first and ten at the 33.

As a quarterback I had engineered a drive covering 46 yards in four plays. Although I wasn't thinking of how many yards in how few plays at the time, the fact that we were moving had my confidence soaring. I could also tell that our fans were loving it and that also meant a lot to me.

It was a totally different type of game. Just the same, it was similar to the way things were when I was in high school. After the first snap or two in every game I played I felt as if I was in complete control. Although I never even practiced at quarterback in college and never took a snap in any kind of a game as a pro except for the one 1976 exhibition game, ironically also against the Rams, it all seemed very natural to me.

A pass to Slater was off the mark and then Scott picked up two yards off right tackle. Once again it was third and eight, this time at the 31.

We were in field goal range. A field goal would tie the game but my greed was running rampant. What better way to make a statement than by picking up the full seven?

I took the snap in the shotgun formation; something we still rarely used except in obvious pass situations. I had good protection as I dropped back a few steps. I spotted Rossi.

Dave had to jump but he still caught the pass at his chest. He was hit immediately at the ten. It was another third down conversion.

This was probably the first time I ever saw Rossi try to appear nonchalant. I expected him to jump up, clap his hands and then do a few cartwheels in exultation. Instead he did like some players who make big plays but want to appear as if it was simply part of the routine. He quietly got up and tried to appear stoic as he headed to our huddle. It was very unRossilike.

Jubilantly I whacked Rossi on the shoulder.

"Way to go, buddy. That was a great catch," I told him, forcing him to break into a beaming smile.

It was a significant milestone in Rossi's career. I didn't know at the time that it was his first reception of the season. He had caught passes in the preseason and possibly one or two during the 1976 preseason when he was with the 49ers but this was his first reception in a regular season game.

Now I was more determined than ever to take it all the way in. On a play-action fake I hit Scott over the middle at the five. He fought for three more yards to give us a second and goal at the two.

We finished the job on the next play. On the snap I took one step back and leaped up. Before the defense could react I fired a bullet to Dietrich who was running a slant pattern to the inside. He caught the ball just as he was crossing the goal line.

Hawaii still had the momentum. Even the loss of Bender didn't kill it.

More importantly, we had the lead. The extra point gave us a 21-17 lead. There was 1:49 left in the third quarter.

After the PAT I ran off the field in triumph. Walker was there to greet me when I reached the sideline. So were Hasegawa, Jennings, Allen, McDaniel, Slater and several others. Our ability to score without a regular quarterback seemed to have everybody pumped.

As I got my Gatorade Bender met me at the table. Using his left hand, he slapped me on the back.

"Good job. Good job," he said with a sincere smile.

"Thanks," I replied. "I appreciate your support."

Bender and the trainer then headed to the locker room. I found out later that he had refused to immediately leave for treatment on his shoulder. He insisted on staying on the sideline to give me moral support even though he was in pain.

Coaches Bennici and Potter came over to discuss some things with me on the bench. By the time we finished our discussion the third quarter expired and the Rams had a third and four at their own 44. Along the way our defense had burned a timeout, leaving us with only one. That could prove critical although only if we surrendered our lead.

An 18-yard pass play to open the fourth quarter gave the Rams a first down at the Hawaii 38. I was starting to worry. I liked looking at the scoreboard and seeing Hawaii on top. I wanted to build our lead, not get into a seesaw battle.

A pass to Lance near the 30 was knocked down by Morrissey. That was nullified because the Rams got cited for holding. They had a first and 20 at the Hawaii 48.

The penalty seemed to do the Rams in. A four-yard rush was followed by a pair of incompletions. I took my place on the ten to field the punt. I was anxious for another series at quarterback.

Once again the Ram punter went for the sideline. The ball bounced to my right near the sideline at about the two. I started to clap my hand in gratitude since the ball seemed destined for the end zone until the ball took a backward bounce and was downed at the five. It was a lucky break for the Rams.

"Okay, let's get some insurance," I said to begin the huddle, emulating Bender as if I was undaunted by starting at the five.

372

The series would not be my finest hour. We got off to a rocky start on a 2 Wahiawa left. Kerner and I were not in sync and we missed the handoff. Still holding the ball, I turned around and ran back toward the line. I managed to pick up one yard.

We went to the air next. I dropped back and discovered that the entire defensive line wanted a piece of me. I got the pass off just as I was being hammered in the end zone. The pass to Dietrich was just a little short and it dropped in front of him. Third and nine.

It must have been quite a shot that I took. As I waited for a big defensive lineman to get off of me I happened to look into the bleachers. I could see Carol holding her hands over her mouth as she waited to see if I would get up.

I wasn't hurt. I barely felt the impact of the collision. When I watched the films, though, I was better able to see it from Carol's perspective. The hit was clean but not especially subtle.

We went to the air again. From the shotgun I took the snap. Slater was open near the 20. With good protection I was able to get the pass off. The ball was thrown almost perfectly.

Slater dropped the ball!

It was right in his hands. Unfortunately the Baylor alum apparently had too much time to think about it. The ball hit him in the hands and he dropped it. He leaped up in frustration as the crowd collectively groaned in disbelief.

This was when it paid that I was primarily a receiver. I understood exactly what Slater was feeling. He would have felt less humiliated had the Ram defense teamed up to pull his pants down in the middle of the field.

Understanding what Slater was going through didn't change the scenario. I had no choice but to run off while the punting unit ran on.

"Sorry, Jay," Slater said dejectedly on the sideline.

"Don't let it get you down. We'll put it away on our next drive," I replied.

"That was a perfect pass. I can't believe I didn't hang on to it."

I understood. He felt the way I would have felt had I been in his shoes.

"Let's forget about it and move forward," I said, patting him on the shoulder.

Jablonski got off a pretty good punt. It had a great hang time and was fielded at the Hawaii 46. The return man saw Vorsino coming at him and moved laterally to his right to avoid him. He wound up being tackled instead by Hasegawa at the Hawaii 47.

Obviously it was a great play. The Rams still had excellent field position. If we could hold them to nothing more than a field goal we would still have the lead and try to run the clock out while trying to put together another score.

Of course the Rams were thinking in terms of a touchdown. Our defense was thinking in terms of preventing the touchdown or at least making it hard for them. The Rams showed signs of making it hard for themselves.

The Rams put together rushes of three and four yards, respectively. The latter was nullified by an illegal procedure penalty that gave them a second and 12 at the 49.

Undaunted, the Rams went to the air. The quarterback hit Lance at about the 37. He picked up three more yards to give them a first down at the 34.

Two rushes later they had a third and two at the 26. A rush off left tackle seemed to give them a first down at the 22. During the play a yellow flag shot up near the line.

"Holding," I mumbled hopefully as I stood on the sideline in front of our bench. "Let it be holding against the Rams."

It was holding against the Rams. Lance was the guilty party. He apparently contained Jurgens by grabbing him. It was third and 12 at the 36.

"That's a break, defense. Let's hold 'em," Marv said softly as he stood next to me.

"An incompletion would force a field goal attempt of about 53 yards," I added. "If we sack the quarterback they'll have to punt."

Against the 1977 49ers the odds against our opponent rebounding were more substantial. The 49ers were a substandard team in 1977 and we controlled virtually the entire game against them a few weeks earlier. The Rams were heavily involved in the Super Bowl hunt and played accordingly. They completed a pass just inside the 25. The receiver fought his way to the 19 before Blakely and Hasegawa brought him down. It was another first down.

"(Expletive deleted)!" I said.

I was getting a bad feeling. The Rams seemed determined to overcome anything and everything. I got the impression that it would take a fourth and 50 to stop them.

After a three-yard rush the Rams went to the air. A receiver managed to get a slight lead over Hasegawa in the end zone. Rich lunged to try to deflect the pass but to no avail. The receiver made the catch to give the Rams the lead again.

"(Expletive deleted)!" I said again.

I shook my head. Just the same, the score didn't change my intentions. I wanted to score a touchdown on our next drive anyway. The Rams' touchdown simply made our touchdown more imperative.

"If they miss the extra point we can still beat them with a field goal," I said, thinking out loud.

They didn't miss the extra point. We could only tie with a field goal which was an acceptable option if it came down to that. It was 24-21 with 6:07 left.

374

"Mix it up," Walker directed me before I took my post for the kick return. I had been asked if I still wanted to return kicks and punts. I eagerly consented to continue in my regular role. "We need to keep them guessing."

But first came the kick. Hasegawa fielded it four yards deep in the south end zone. He took it to the 21 before going down. It was hardly worth the effort although we had no way of knowing it would work out that way. We had gained only one more yard than we would have had he downed the ball. It was still far better than going down inside the 20.

Kerner carried up the middle for two and then Scott swept around right end for seven. It was third and one at the 30. I wondered if Walker wanted this to be a time to mix it up. The Rams were sure to be looking for the run.

Walker sent Slater in with a play. We were staying on the ground with a Kaneohe right. Kerner took it to the 37 to get us our first down.

"All right. We're rolling," I said confidently as we prepared to huddle.

The key on the latter play was that the Rams actually seemed to be looking for a pass. They allowed us space in which to run while focusing on preventing more sizable gains through the air. The yardage would be tougher as we moved upfield. For the moment we took what the Rams gave us.

Two carries by Scott gave us a first down at the 50. The clock was running with more than three minutes to go. That was plenty of time but not much for the Rams unless we took it in after only one or two more plays.

The crowd was loving it. The fans were cheering every yard. I had no doubt that the outer concourses were deserted. The concessionaires might just as well have closed up shop. At the same time the restrooms were only handling extreme emergencies.

Kerner went up the middle to the Los Angeles 46. Scott then managed only one yard off right tackle. It was third and five.

It was an obvious pass situation although the Rams couldn't bank on that. The Rams were thinking we had to pass now although they wouldn't eliminate the possibility of the run.

I lined up directly behind Shuford st center and took the snap. I rolled to my left.

Dietrich was running a cross pattern. I hit him on the numbers at the 38, then noticed the eruption of the crowd. Dietrich picked up three more yards to give us a first down at the 35.

The seconds ticked down to the two-minute warning. I trotted over to the sideline to converse with Walker. He looked a little nervous as coaches are apt to do in this situation. He still smiled in an apparent effort to keep my confidence up.

I tried to look cool. I tried to make it appear as if it were the most natural thing in the world for me to be an NFL quarterback at the two-minute warning with the game on the line. I doubt that Walker was fooled.

There were no profound revelations. We discussed the need to pass a little more. Our running game was working well but it was chewing up too much of the clock. It took us four minutes to travel 44 yards and that included a ten-yard pass play. We needed to strategically pick up larger chunks of yardage while also working the clock.

We wanted a touchdown but a field goal would be okay. We were now in Guinn's range. We still needed to get as close as we could to give Guinn a better opportunity.

When play resumed I took the snap and dropped back. I suddenly had white jerseys coming at me and had to scramble a little. I spotted Slater downfield and prepared to fire on the run. Just as I was releasing the ball I was hit from behind and slammed face down into the ground.

The hit knocked the ball slightly off course. It also took some of the velocity off of it. The pass was intercepted at the 15 and returned to the 20.

I was down on the ground inside the 45 and didn't see the outcome of the play. As I rose up I noticed some kind of commotion downfield. When I noticed the Ram defense jumping exultantly and running in triumph off the field I knew we had turned it over. I didn't know if it was an interception or fumble although I suspected the former. It didn't matter since the bottom line was that the Rams had the ball with 1:49 left. We still had a shot but. . . .

Lance looked at me as he passed while running on the field with his offensive colleagues. He was happy, of course, but careful not to make a big issue out of it in front of me.

"Are you okay?" he called as I slowly rose to my feet. I nodded my head because physically I was okay. I'm sure he knew I wasn't in my best mental state at the moment.

"Are you okay?" he asked again as he approached.

All I could do was nod weakly and head toward our sideline.

Tears stung my eyes as I left the field. I blinked the tears back. I was frustrated and sad and angry. I really wanted to pull this one out in a very bad way. Although football is a team game, the bulk of the responsibility seemed to be placed on my shoulders.

Walker understood how bad I felt. He gave me a slap on the back as I reached the sideline.

"Don't throw in the towel yet, Jay," he said. "If we can keep them from getting a first down we'll have time for a play or two."

Predictably the Rams stayed on the ground. A rush up the middle got them to the 24. We used our final timeout with 1:42 left.

Another rush up the middle only got the Rams to the 25. It was third and five. What was most critical was that the clock was running. The Rams were obviously going to run it down as much as possible before running a play.

We caught a break when one of the Ram guards jumped before the snap. That stopped the clock with 59 seconds. It also moved the Rams back to the 20.

A sweep around left end picked up only two yards. It was fourth and eight. The Rams were going to have to punt.

"Don't let the punt bounce," Walker told me as I prepared to run on the field. "That'll use up too much time. Return it if you can but don't run any fancy routes that take off several seconds. Run straight as far as you can and then go down quickly."

The Rams made one tactical mistake that could prove to be critical. They didn't let the play clock run all the way down. What they should have done was run it down and then call timeout. Even taking a delay of game penalty would have been acceptable since the clock was working against us, not them. If they didn't call timeout in time the five yards would have been a small price to pay for the amount of time they took off the clock.

I was near the Hawaii 30 when the Rams surprised me by snapping the ball with more than five seconds left on the play clock. As expected, the punt was away from me to try to prevent me from fielding it. That way the ball was not only most likely to bounce deeper but it would shave several seconds off the clock as Walker pointed out.

But the punter also had to be careful not to kick it out of bounds since that would enable us to start further upfield than the Rams wanted. The punter's prudence enabled me to hustle over and settle under the ball. I wanted to signal for a fair catch but was afraid that raising my hand would either slow me down or prevent me from fielding the ball cleanly. I caught the ball on the run at the 32 and ran obliquely before stepping out of bounds at the 38. We had 19 seconds to travel 62 yards.

One thing I noticed as I waited for the punt was that we had a few hundred empty seats that were previously occupied. Most of our fans were still with us and very enthusiastic but there were those who headed for the exits after I threw my interception. I was hoping to give them a grand finale that they would be sorry they missed.

My teammates were also very enthused. Everybody on the sideline was standing and cheering us on. The guys in the offensive unit were clapping their hands and talking it up as we prepared to huddle. I also noticed Bender watching from behind the south end zone near the Islander dugout.

"Let's do it," said Dietrich.

"We're gonna pull it out, man," was Rossi's remark.

"Let's go, Jaybird. Lead the way," was Marv's contribution.

I was also hyped. What a finish this was going to be. I just hoped that we would be the team on top when the final gun went off. I called the play and headed up to the line with my teammates.

Naturally the Rams were in a prevent defense. I was going to have to work through it by essentially threading the needle. We were in a double-

double with Scott in the right slot as a receiver since the individual who would normally be there was trying to impersonate an NFL quarterback.

I took the snap and dropped back. There was no discernible rush but I still had to work quickly.

Slater seemed to have a slight opening. I fired the ball to him near the left sideline. He caught the ball at the Los Angeles 32 and stepped out of bounds, stopping the clock with 12 seconds left. By working quickly we covered 30 yards in only seven seconds.

Of course the crowd roared. I was hoping that those loyal fans who had headed to the parking lot were regretting their decision. Regardless of the outcome, they were missing a very exciting finish.

We were in field goal range. We also had time for one more play before having to go for the field goal. Preferably we would get a touchdown and end the game that way. If I couldn't find an open receiver in the end zone I would look for somebody near the sideline to at least get us closer.

What was most critical was that we had to stop the clock if we couldn't go all the way on this play. We needed either an incomplete pass or a complete pass where the receiver stepped out of bounds quickly. A sack or anything else where the ball carrier went down in the field of play would end the game since there would be no way to stop the clock.

It was risky but we felt that we had to try. Since it was an obvious pass situation I was in a shotgun position. Kerner was directly behind me and would try to protect me if anybody penetrated into the backfield.

I took the snap. A blitz was on. Kerner could protect me from one white jersey but two were much harder and three were impossible. I was forced to scramble a little, fully cognizant that a sack was not an option. Only the Rams had a timeout left and I was pretty sure they wouldn't feel compelled to use it just to make the ending a little more dramatic.

After burning about three or four of our 12 seconds off of the clock to allow my receivers to get into position I noticed that Dietrich was open in the end zone.

I fired a pass in his direction. It felt right as I released the ball. If he caught it we would have the winning score. If it fell incomplete there would still be just enough time for a game-tying field goal.

What happened next was incredibly bizarre. At the last second a defensive back dove in and swatted the ball away from Dietrich. However, he knocked the ball up instead of down. Another Ram tried to pick it off but couldn't hang on, knocking the ball in Rossi's direction. Rossi dove for it but couldn't grasp it, knocking it back up toward Dietrich who was only a few feet away. Dietrich had to reach out with one hand and tried to hang on but couldn't. The ball arched up a little before it finally fell incomplete.

After a few seconds to get over the most improbable play I had ever seen I looked up at the scoreboard in the north end zone. My heart sank as I discovered that there was no time left on the clock. The impromptu volleyball game ate it all up. Had the ball not been knocked around so much we would have had time to try to send the game into overtime with a field goal. Instead we had our second consecutive loss.

Our fans were stunned. One could sense it on the field. We gave them the exciting game they paid for despite us committing a team record five turnovers. The ending was so bizarre that our fans stood in stunned silence.

Ultimately the impromptu volleyball game would wind up on sports blooper films that still turned up after I retired. They would include a variety of sound bites, making people laugh, myself included.

But I wasn't laughing on that afternoon in November, 1977. How does one laugh when losing a game that was so obviously within reach?

Obviously I wanted to pull this one out. I can't honestly discern if it was for the sake of the team or my ego. I would like to believe I was putting it all out for the team but I'm sure there was some ego involved.

Resigned to defeat, I shook hands with a few of my opponents. They complimented me on my performance, which was nice, and I was satisfied with my effort up to but not including the interception and the final pass.

Suddenly there was Lance. He wrapped his arms around me. He took me so much by surprise that I almost cried. I took a deep breath and composed myself.

"You really gave us a scare," Lance said sincerely.

"Well, you came out on top this time. We beat you on your field and you paid us back here," I replied, not able to think of something more profound to say.

Lance and I talked for a few minutes while standing in the south end zone. We were both among the last members of our teams to leave the field.

"Say hi to Darlene for me," I said as we shook hands one last time. "And Coach Farnwell, too."

"I will," he promised. "Give me a call if you get to LA in the offseason. We've got to get together."

"Sounds good. Of course we might square off one more time this season. It's possible we'll meet in the playoffs."

Unfortunately my playoff confidence was slightly bruised. Eight days earlier we were 6-2. That was an excellent record. Unfortunately we followed with two consecutive tough losses. At 6-4 we were slipping toward mediocrity.

"Okay, everybody's here now," Walker said when the entire team reached the locker room. "Who will volunteer to do the postgame prayer?"

Blakely volunteered and did a nice job, especially for somebody who wasn't known for having any religious convictions. He gave thanks for the team's strength to play the game cleanly. He even remembered to ask that Billingsley, Bender and others with injuries recover quickly. It made me wonder if I had misjudged the skylarking safety.

"Thanks, Ben," Walker said at the end of the prayer. He looked around as if trying to find the proper words. "It was a tough game to lose. A victory could have given us a bit of an advantage in the division race but . . . I guess they were really up for us. We'll just have to go from here."

Walker paused. He looked at me and took a breath.

"Jay," he continued, "you did a good job at quarterback. I was really proud of you."

I nodded my thanks for the compliment. I still didn't feel right. It felt good to be at quarterback when the heat was on but we still wound up on the wrong end of the scoreboard. I was happy that I gave it my best shot and happy that I played well and happy that my teammates gave me their unconditional support. There is still no satisfaction in not winning. I wanted to pull the game out for my teammates, for our fans and for all of Hawaii if not for my stupid ego.

When Walker finished addressing the team the media were invited in. It hadn't dawned on me that I was going to be the darling of the media that day. I didn't feel up to answering their questions but felt an obligation to do so. Had we won I probably would have been willing to talk all night.

"Were you nervous?" was one question.

"I suppose so. Who wouldn't have been? But once I got started I was okay."

There was a multitide of questions as I gradually peeled off my uniform and equipment. They were good questions. I still felt funny being the center of attention since I hadn't done anything especially heroic.

"I was a quarterback in high school," was one answer I had to give although I was certain that was fairly common knowledge.

As I stood naked except for a towel around my waste one sportswriter told me I did a good job.

"Thanks," I said graciously. "I appreciate it. Unfortunately it wasn't enough. I could have completed 30 out of 30 passes and it can never be enough if we finish on the wrong end of the scoreboard."

With that I headed for the showers. Most of my teammates were already getting dressed by this time. I envied them for not having to answer a lot of questions that day. It was always more fun when we won.

In the hospitality room I received more compliments from the guests and tried to graciously give them my thanks. It was awkward.

My quarter and-a-half at quarterback made me want to alter the plans that Carol and I had made. We had planned to spend the afternoon swimming and sitting in the jacuzzi at my condo complex.

"I just don't feel like being around a lot of people," I said. "Most of the people in the pool area will know that I played quarterback today. They're all going to want to ask a million questions."

"I understand. What shall we do instead?" Carol replied.

We bounced a few ideas off each other. We considered going to Waikiki and blending in with the tourists, taking a drive around the island, finding an uninhabited beach to sit on or having dinner in a quiet restaurant.

"Why don't we go to Burger King?" Carol lightly suggested.

"Now why would we want to go there?" I asked, knowing that Carol was only kidding.

"Because nobody would expect to find you there. If anybody sees you they'll think you're somebody else. They won't expect a pro football player to be there right after a game."

"Are you kidding? Norm Richards lives at the Burger King that's just around the corner from your place. He probably gets his mail there. If anybody ever needs to find him that's the first place they would look. They'd probably check there before they check his apartment."

Of course I was stretching things a little. Richards was still a Burger King fanatic.

"He's addicted to Whoppers," I continued. "All last year he kept saying that the only thing Hawaii was missing was Burger King. They finally opened that Burger King on Beretania in March or April and Norm thought he'd gone to heaven. He even likes Burger King better than In-N-Out."

"In-N-Out? What's that?"

"Now there's a place to get a burger," I said enthusiastically. "If Hawaii ever gets an In-N-Out, that's where I'll be hanging out."

Once we finished our giddy burger discussion we decided to start by seeking refuge at my place. The phone rang constantly. We let the answering machine handle the calls.

We started feeling guilty about ignoring the phone. We decided to spend the evening at a drive-in theater. We even picked up our dinner to enjoy during the movie . . . at the Burger King on Beretania Street which was just around the corner from Carol's place. Somehow it seemed appropriate. We even got to chat with Norm for a few minutes while they prepared our order.

The drive-in turned out to be a wonderful exile from football. We went to the Kailua Drive-In to see *Heroes* although it was the co-feature that caught our attention. Carol and I saw *The Sting* when we were together a few years earlier and liked it well enough to be willing to see it again. We weren't shocked by the ending this time but still enjoyed sitting through it.

A few times during the movies my mind raced to the game. Overall the drive-in proved to be a wonderful exile.

Both newspapers the next day said nice things about my performance. It's not a good idea to take your newspaper clippings seriously and I didn't but it was always nice to read nice things about myself. It beat the alternative.

The newspapers showed that Bender had a respectable game before he went down. He completed eleven of 22 passes for 195 yards and a touchdown with two interceptions. I completed seven of 12 passes for 115 yards with one touchdown and one interception.

Dietrich had the most receptions with five for 69 yards although Grummon led the team in yardage, picking up 96 yards on four receptions. I had four receptions for 55 yards.

And then there was our anemic rushing game. As a team we carried 15 times for a paltry 53 yards. Scott was our leading rusher with nine carries for 36 yards.

Of course the turnovers were the primary keys to our defeat. We turned the ball over five times with three interceptions and two fumbles. Those five turnovers made it seem miraculous that we were still in the game on the final play. They also made it hard to believe that we were a contender for a playoff spot.

Howard Cosell put in his input on Monday night. During halftime of the Monday night game between Green Bay and Washington Cosell narrated highlights of the Sunday games. Naturally this included highlights of our game:

"To the sunny shores of Hawaii. The Hawaiians host the Rams. The most veritable highlight came from the losing side. Backup quarterback Joe Billingsley was incapacitated by a freak domestic accident and starting quarterback Steve Bender was knocked out of action in the third quarter."

"Enter Jay Dockman, a veritable paragon among all-world performers who had been a quarterback in high school. He showed the world that he hadn't forgotten how it was done. He played heroically, undaunted by blitzes as he completed nine of 12 passes for 115 yards and a touchdown. An incredible performance by one of the NFL's preeminent performers but the Hawaiians still fell short, 24-21."

All of this was done with a collage of our game being shown. It was different from what Cosell normally did since he didn't describe specific plays during our segment of the highlights.

I sat on my couch somewhat shocked by Cosell's approbation. I was doing my best to remain humble although I have to admit that I enjoyed looking good during my moment in the spotlight.

Carol was sitting next to me. She suddenly started staring at me.

"What's wrong?" I asked.

"Oh, nothing," she said lightly. "I'm just watching your head swell."

I nodded to acknowledge the humor in the spirit in which it was intended as the phone rang. It was Don Simmons.

"Is this the paragon?" he asked.

No sooner did I finish my conversation with Don that the phone rang again. This time it was Bill Trimble.

"Wow, you still answer your own phone. I didn't think you would now that you're one of Howard's all-world football players."

"I don't normally. Unfortunately I gave the butler the night off."

The phone rang a few more times that night but I stopped answering. I let the answering machine handle the calls while I watched the second half.

CHAPTER SIXTEEN
The Saints March In

"Mr. All-World," McDaniel greeted as we arrived simultaneously at Aloha Stadium.

"I'm going to have Cosell shot," I muttered jocularly.

When we got to the hospitality room for the film session we found about 15 of our teammates had arrived ahead of us. All of them seemed to have seen the Monday night game and the halftime highlights.

"There he is!" Jennings exclaimed. "Our preeminent performer."

"Right," I replied dryly. "Cosell dished out all of that praise for a game we didn't win."

The latter, I felt, was a very compelling point. I also knew that Walker would not be happy if he showed up while everybody was laughing and joking after two consecutive tough losses.

Things had settled down by the time Walker and the rest of the staff showed up. I have no doubt that almost everybody knew that Walker did not want to walk in during a celebration. The flames spewing from the dragon would have been white hot.

Walker was firm but didn't really fly off the handle during the offensive film session. That took a lot of restraint since we did manage to turn the ball over five times and had a virtually non-existent running game. He wanted to avoid salting our wounds after a loss that was hard-fought. He didn't want to beat us down with the Saints coming up. The Saints at this juncture were 3-7. Everybody from Walker on down wanted the Saints game to shift our momentum.

Of course Walker criticized us. He just didn't yell much. He got on my case when I called for a fair catch on a punt in the first quarter. I was looking up and thought I heard the opposition nearby so I raised my hand up. What the film showed was no Ram within ten yards of me when I caught the ball.

"Oh, man," I sighed in exasperation when I saw how much space I had.

"What were you thinking, Jay?" Walker asked.

"I was thinking that somebody was too close and that I'd better call for a fair catch. Obviously I was wrong."

We used one deep punt returner and one semi-deep safety. Our semi-deep man was Hasegawa. He normally would have called out whether I should run or call for a fair catch once it was clear what the scenario was.

Unfortunately for me, Hasegawa was making the block of his life. He saw one of the coverage men streaking toward me and nearly knocked him across Kamehameha Highway into Pearl Harbor. He told me later that he called for me to return the punt while he went after his opponent. Obviously I didn't hear him.

Walker ran the film back and forth a few times. Hasegawa's block may have been the block of the year. The perfect combination of pursuit, speed and leverage sent our opponent airborne.

"I could watch that block all day and all night," Walker said joyously. "Rich, that poor sap is having nightmares about you."

"We'll let him know, Coach," Shuford responded lightly.

That produced a few laughs including from Walker. Hasegawa was watching the defense's films.

The star of our film actually turned out to be Rossi. Rossi got his first experience of being a regular part of the lineup for the final quarter and-a-half. Walker had much to say about his performance.

Rossi didn't play poorly. He never carried and caught the only pass that was thrown to him for 21 yards. Also his blocking wasn't bad.

While Rossi picked up 21 yards on the play, Walker apparently believed that he could have gotten a few more.

"The defensive back had committed himself in the same direction you decided to cut on your pattern before you caught the pass," Walker said. "If you had noticed that and slightly altered your pattern you could have had a larger gain. You might have even picked up the last ten yards to the end zone."

Walker never yelled at Rossi. He did call his name a lot. He pointed out his pass patterns, his blocks and once even the route he took when he went in motion.

I believe that there were three reasons why Walker dedicated so much of the session to Rossi. The first was to simply give Rossi a taste of what it is like to be a regular part of the lineup. There is a price to pay for the alleged glory. Part of that price is the scrutinization of the films.

The second reason, I believe, is because Walker wanted to conduct the session in a normal manner but he wanted to take the heat off the rest of us. Rossi was normally in very few plays from scrimmage so he was rarely singled out during films. Those of us who played on a regular basis were singled out, lectured, yelled at and/or cursed at. This time we could all settle back and listen to Walker pick on somebody else.

I believe timing was the third reason. The previous week Rossi had complained bitterly about not being in any scrimmage plays in Chicago. Walker's omnipresence enabled him to know that and he utilized the opportunity to put Rossi in his place. Walker's ears appeared to be normal size but he had a way of hearing everything.

Rossi was visibly shaken when the film session ended. He also used some very colorful language when he spoke of Walker in the locker room.

"Don't take it so hard," Shuford said.

"It's the price we pay for being in the NFL, brother," Marv added. "Would you rather be on the sidelines where it's nice and safe or would you rather be on the field where the camera is going to follow your every move?"

Rossi said nothing. He shook his head, ostensibly believing that Walker considered him to be the worst player on the team if not in the NFL.

During the session Walker didn't criticize my performance at quarterback. I think he was satisfied that I had done as well as could be done under the circumstances.

Despite the accolades, I honestly believe we would have pulled the game out had Bender been able to stay in. I had done a reasonably good job but Bender was an experienced NFL quarterback. Bender was certain to have found a way to get us that final touchdown we needed. Billingsley might have done the same.

Regardless, everything positive and negative about the Ram game was history as soon as the projectors were turned off. It was time to gear up for the Saints.

"You've got to see these guys," I told Carol. "This is a country band that really rocks."

"That good, huh?" she remarked laconically.

"They are so good that even people who don't like country music like these guys," I assured her.

Carol and I spent the night before Thanksgiving at, of all places, the Pearl Harbor Enlisted Men's Club. The featured attraction was a group from Texas known as The Yellow Rose Band and they were hot. If they ever cut an album they would have gone straight to the top of the charts.

Or so I believed.

The truth is, they didn't do anything original as far as I knew. The songs they covered sounded better than the original recordings.

I stumbled on the Yellow Rose shortly before my sojourn to Canada. I got tickets to see The New Riders of the Purple Sage at Pearl Harbor's Bloch Arena in a concert that was open to the public.

Unfortunately for the headliners, the Yellow Rose was the warmup band. The New Riders paled in comparison when it was their turn. My then-roommate Bill, Cherie, my then-girlfriend Annica and I left when the New Riders were only about halfway through their set. They were anti-climactic in the wake of the Yellow Rose's country-rock set.

The Yellow Rose played at Pearl Harbor on a regular basis but I didn't see the band again until early November at a place in Waikiki called O'Pehr's. This facility was about to close down so the Yellow Rose shut the place down in style. Don Simmons and I joined a small group of friends and enjoyed a few sets.

Unfortunately for its Hawaii fans, the Yellow Rose was preparing to return to the Lone Star State. I wanted to see the band one more time and take Carol with me. The night before Thanksgiving seemed perfect since

386

Carol would not be grading papers or preparing lessons or even having to get up in the morning to go teach.

I didn't have any connections to get us on base but Don did. He asked that connection to get him and his girlfriend Eileen, as well as Carol and me, on base. Don and I were somewhat conspicuous among the other men present since they all sported military haircuts.

"Hey, I know you," observed a partially tanked bearded sailor who walked by our table.

"Really?" I responded cheerily. "Have we met?"

"No, no. I mean, I know who you are. You're Jay Dockman from the Hawaiians, right?"

"Well, yeah," I admitted modestly, extending my hand to shake his. I was hoping he wouldn't ask for an autograph since I didn't want to be the center of attention. A pro football player should never be allowed to upstage the Yellow Rose. The New Riders of the Purple Sage, maybe, but never the Yellow Rose.

"Could I get an autograph?"

"Sure," I replied graciously, taking a dry napkin and pulling a pen out of my shirt pocket. "What's your name?"

"David."

As I signed he told me that he was from Oklahoma and a longtime Cowboy fan.

"But I like you guys," he added. "I got to go to the game on Sunday. You did a helluva job filling in at quarterback. I really wanted you to beat the Rams."

"Well, they were ready for us," I said as I handed him the autographed napkin. "They're tough and they wanted to get back at us after what we did to them on their home field."

"Yeah, that was a great game."

David thanked me for the autograph and headed to his own table. I was hoping I had signed the autograph without attracting attention to myself. Not too far away while the band was between songs I could hear David's voice.

"You know who that guy over there is?"

I did have to sign a few more autographs that evening. We still had a great time and my presence didn't upstage the Yellow Rose. Carol later told me that she was glad that I had persuaded her to go with me. She said it was far better than she'd imagined.

"Just about the best band I've ever heard," she said.

Thanksgiving never meant no practice. We were battling for a playoff berth and were determined to not be denied. It had been hard enough to accept losing on Sunday to the team that was favored to win our division.

We didn't want to follow it up by losing to the team that was favored to finish at or near the bottom of our division as well as the conference.

It was a full-padded workout and a good one. Walker's concession to Thanksgiving was that there was no accompanying meeting to precede the workout. Had our next opponent been the Rams or Cowboys or Steelers or somebody of that magnitude Walker might not have been so liberal. Since we were playing the Saints Walker apparently decided it was okay to deviate from the norm, just as we did on Thanksgiving the year before.

Since we didn't have to deal with rush-hour traffic we agreed to begin the workout at eight o'clock. That meant being finished by about ten o'clock. That would give us the rest of the day to spend with family and friends.

I had a good workout despite the fact that I didn't get home until about one o'clock that morning. I hadn't drank much since I was always very careful about that, especially after my 25th birthday fiasco the year before, but it was still a late night. I definitely wanted to sleep some more when my alarm clocks went off at a little before six. I was dutifully on my way to Aloha Stadium at 6:30, allowing me plenty of time to get suited up and on the field.

Walker offered substantially more praise than criticism. He even turned it up a notch by addressing everybody by their first names. That seems like a trivial detail but it was his way of getting the players to bond together. Never underestimate the need pro football players have to have their egos stroked.

"Great coverage, Mark!" he exclaimed a little more enthusiastically than normal when Black knocked down a pass.

"Right on the money, Steve! Right on the money!" he cheered when Bender fired a perfectly placed long pass to me, by this time completely recovered from his injury. Although Thursday workouts were normally focused on the defense, the offense got plenty of work in as well. While the offensive unit primarily represented the Saints offense, we also ran a few of our own plays.

"Great rush, Ed!" he told Jennings after a blitz which came up to but not including contact with the quarterback.

Of course being human, we made mistakes. Not too many but a few. His countenance didn't change.

"Remember, Joe," Walker calmly reminded Billingsley when he dropped too far back on a play where he was to pitch out to me, "if you drop back too far Jay will be in front of you and your lateral becomes a forward pass. That means that Jay won't be able to legally pass the ball himself."

That was Walker on his best "getting later in the week" behavior although he normally waited until Friday to become this congenial. I guess he was giving us another reason to be thankful on Thanksgiving.

388

The truth is, Walker wasn't too hard on us at all that week. Aside from the turnovers, we played a hard game on Sunday. He knew that we really put our hearts into the game and ultimately wound up on the wrong end of the scoreboard. He knew how tough it was to lose a game that went down to the final play.

After practice I picked Carol up. A large group of us from the Arthur's crowd was spending the day at a home in Hawaii Kai. When we got there most of those in attendance were, quite naturally, watching football. I had missed the first game between the Bears and Lions because of practice. The second game between the Dolphins and Cardinals was going on.

The earlier game affected us although it wasn't certain of how it would play out. Both the Bears and Lions were 5-5 going into their game, trailing the Vikings in the NFC Central. If we couldn't win our division one of those teams could wind up competing with us. At the moment we had a better record than both teams so all we had to do was win to stay ahead of them. As it worked out, the Bears won to raise their record to 6-5.

It was the game we were watching that had a more immediate impact on the Hawaiians fortunes. The Cardinals were 7-3 and trailing the Cowboys in the NFC East. That made the Cardinals a wild card contender at the moment and they had a better record than we did. We obviously had to pull for the Dolphins.

Fortunately the Dolphins were beating the daylights out of the Cardinals. If we beat the Saints on Sunday we would have an identical record as the Cardinals. That would also make the Cardinals and us the two primary contenders for the conference's wild card berth if neither of us could overtake our respective division leaders.

It was primarily non-football people at the Hawaii Kai gathering. There were about two dozen present. Most of those in attendance I had at least met if not known me personally. There were still a few whom I had never met before.

One of those I hadn't met was a stocky sandy-haired man named Jerry who was sitting about ten feet away from me. He was a city bus driver who had apparently tied one on the night before. There was nothing in his conduct that gave him away until a friend of his showed up.

"Hey, Steve," he called out lightly when his friend entered through the front door. "Did I have a good time last night?"

"Yes, you had a wonderful time."

"Oh, good. When I woke up this morning and forgot most of last night I was afraid I might not have enjoyed myself."

"Trust me. You had a ball."

Three of my teammates showed up. Marv and Karla Nelson were first. Rich Hasegawa turned up stag a few minutes later. He was followed by Ed Jennings and his girlfriend Jennifer.

"Oh, wonderful. There's a football game on," Karla commented in mock sarcasm. "That's something we can't get enough of."

"It's what we live for," Carol replied equally as light.

"You bet, honey," Karla said. "We watch our men bang into other men all day. They're happy when they win. We're happy if they make it through in one piece."

"Geez, Karla. You sound like my mother," Marv remarked.

My three teammates and I cheered wildly as the Dolphins continued to pile it on. So did almost everybody else. Almost everybody understood the impact of this game on the Hawaiians.

Don Simmons showed up stag. Since his girlfriend was a nurse, holidays were no different than any other days.

"Where's Eileen?" Carol asked as Don occupied the sofa seat on the opposite side of her from where I sat.

"Working," he replied. "She gets off at 3:30. I'll pick her up and have dinner with her family but I thought I'd come here for a while."

"What time did she have to be at work?" Carol asked.

"Seven-thirty."

"Seven-thirty? After she stayed out so late last night?"

"Hey, I got up at about six to go to practice this morning," I reminded Carol.

Carol shrugged. She had never been somebody to stay out late when she had an early commitment if she could possibly avoid it. Although there were times when she made exceptions, she was very disciplined when it came to getting enough rest. In college she was the type to ensure that she spent a sufficient amount of time studying before exams before making sure she also got a good night's sleep. I had been the type who studied just as much and then stayed up most of the night before an exam because I was afraid I might have missed something important.

In any large group of people watching football there will be three types of people. There are people who understand the game, people who don't understand the game and people who don't understand the game but pretend to be experts. As the game went on there were various cheers and groans, depending on what was going on.

Sitting on the floor nearby was a nerdy looking individual named Mark. He was about 5'6" with dark wavy hair and black-rimmed glasses. I had seen him a few times and talked to him a little at Arthur's. My opinion of him had generally been ambivalent.

Mark didn't comment much about the game in front of us. I barely noticed him until an upcoming game between Houston and Kansas City was mentioned during the telecast.

"Houston's gonna kill 'em," Don remarked.

"Like hell they will," Mark retorted.

"Come on, Mark," Don said. "There's no way that the Chiefs are going to beat the Oilers."

The record supported Don's claim although the Oilers weren't exactly tearing up the league. Houston was 5-5. Kansas City was 2-8.

"As an alleged expert on football, I contend that the Chiefs are not better than their record indicates," I said in mock bravado. That claim was backed by the fact that the Chiefs were dead last in their conference in both offense and defense.

"Right," said Don. "The Oilers are going to blow the Chiefs away."

"You wanna bet?" Mark challenged, indicating further that he either knew nothing about football or else was privy to a Houston conspiracy to throw the game.

"Twenty bucks," Don replied.

"Okay," said Mark casually, "and I'll give you 14 points."

This got everybody's attention if the fact that Mark was willing to bet straight up on Kansas City didn't already do it. Just about everybody in the room was looking at each other with bemused expressions. Mark was willing to spend 20 dollars to, at the very least, exploit his ignorance or, at most, make a total fool of himself.

"I won't accept the bet," Don said.

"Why not? I gave you 14 points."

"That's exactly why I won't take it. You obviously don't know what you're doing. If you followed football you would know better than to give 14 points when betting on Kansas City against anybody this year, especially since I didn't ask you to give me the points. It's a sucker bet. You might as well just hand me the 20 bucks right now."

Don was living proof that *ethical lawyer* was not necessarily an oxymoron.

Greg Wilson was an enigma. As a person away from football I honestly liked him all right. He was a nice guy and reasonably intelligent. There were those who considered him to be lacking in smarts but I never agreed with that. Occasionally he displayed a deplorable lack of common sense but he didn't lack intelligence.

As a football coach, that was another matter. He understood the game as well as anybody, I suppose. He simply didn't command much respect. He probably could have done well as an executive in the front office. He seemed out of his element in a coaching capacity.

Wilson was the one member of the coaching staff not personally selected by Walker. Wilson had a front office connection who persuaded Walker to take him on. His duties were few; primarily to be there and little else. His greatest responsibility was up in the press box communicating with Walker about his observations on the field. To his credit, he did that job well although I never forgot the time in Cincinnati the previous season when he accused me of costing the team a first down when the officials spotted the ball incorrectly after I had caught a pass just beyond the first down market.

Another example of why Wilson didn't command much respect took place before our Friday morning workout. Dietrich dressed in a hurry and was among the first on the field. He had been having problems with muscle pulls in his right leg and wanted to take some extra time to stretch.

Wilson was already on the field when Dietrich began stretching. Dietrich was in the south end zone and Wilson watched from about 30 feet away.

About 15 of us had formed up around Dietrich when Wilson finally approached him. I was sitting with my legs out at a 45-degree angle as I touched my forehead to my knees. My teammates were going through their individual routines when we discovered that Wilson seemed to believe he had a stopwatch inside his head. Dietrich had ostensibly used his allotted stretching time.

"That's enough stretching, Dietrich," Wilson said tersely.

"What?" Ted replied incredulously as he looked up at Wilson with his left leg curled under and his right leg stretched out.

"I said you've stretched enough and I mean it," Wilson said sternly. "You've been at it for ten or 15 minutes. That's plenty of time. You can move on to other things now."

Ted continued to stretch as he argued with Wilson. The one-time Lombardi player didn't feel like risking injury because he neglected to continue to stretch during Wilson's insipid argument.

"What would Vince Lombardi have said if he saw you spending so much time stretching?"

"He would've told me to take as much time as I need," Ted replied curtly. "Lombardi was a smart man. He knew that a player had to stretch to avoid injuries. I'm not about to injure myself on Sunday just because you think you know how much time I need to stretch."

By this time just about the entire team had emerged from the locker room. Everybody was in the vicinity of the south end zone. Those who still needed to were stretching but everybody's attention was on Wilson and Dietrich.

Some were fighting the urge to laugh. Others were shaking their heads in disbelief. Others bore expressions which suggested shock that anybody, Wilson included, could provoke such a ridiculous dispute. The workout hadn't begun yet and the whole team could have generated less controversy had we just been talking among ourselves.

"This whole thing's been a waste of time," Wilson said, pointing his finger at Dietrich. "In the time I had to spend chewing you out you could have been working on your sideline patterns."

Wilson stormed off. Most of the rest of us, including Dietrich and everybody all the way up to, and including, Walker stifled laughter. Wilson's tirade had been very entertaining, albeit annoying, for virtually everybody except Wilson.

Of course this carried into the ensuing period.

"How's your sideline pattern?" Ted would be asked mockingly.

"Is your sideline pattern okay?"

"Did you get enough work on your sideline pattern?"

During that day's workout we ran a play which required me to run a flag pattern and Ted to run a sideline pattern. Black covered Ted well and batted Bender's pass down.

As I ran back toward the line of scrimmage I heard Black say to Dietrich, "I never would have been able to bat the ball had you run a better sideline pattern. Better work on it."

Eric Hamer's tenure among the unemployed lasted all of one game. He told me later that when Walker put him on waivers it was with the intent of bringing him back at the first possible opportunity if nobody claimed him. Fortunately nobody did.

In Eric's case he was assured by Walker that he would be back in short order. if it was at all possible. I think Walker was waiting to see if Westfall's injury was substantial enough to place him on injured reserve. The injury was in the vicinity of his right elbow and they decided to wait before making a decision on what to do with him.

Westfall wound up on injured reserve. Eric was reinstated, giving us four cornerbacks and four safeties. In 1976 we had three at each position but Walker felt that the eight defensive backs in 1977 were too good to turn loose. Vorsino had already had waivers revoked and couldn't be waived again without losing him and was doing pretty well on special teams. Eric and Hasegawa were also valuable on special teams and filled in well when given opportunities to play in the defensive backfield.

Among the rest, Black played left cornerback as if he was psychotic. Morrissey and Dubois had an intense but friendly competition for who would start at right cornerback. Blakely, who was in his tenth season, was still a very effective safety and Rodgers still played free safety in All-Pro form.

With Westfall now out for the season, that left only Randy Hubert as the backup at guard for Marv and Stanek. That was not considered to be a major concern because of Walker's safety valve plan. Daniels was the primary emergency fill-in if we ever came up short. Allen could also play guard although only as an absolute last resort since he was the anchor for our defense.

Sunday, November 27, 1977.

It was nine o'clock in the morning. I was running my traditional pregame laps around the field. There was a feeling which swept over me that this would be a very good day.

In the movie *Eight Men Out* that came out about a decade later there was a scene in which pitcher Eddie Cicotte told Manager Kid Gleason that he couldn't lose. I knew exactly how Cicotte must have felt.

Nothing out of the ordinary took place that morning. It was the typical gameday when I rose well before the alarms went off and read the morning paper. I picked Carol up and focused just enough attention on the road and most of the rest of my mind on the game, meaning I spoke very little. I ate a small amount of fruit in the hospitality room, changed into my running attire including my traditional Dodgers T-shirt and hat, and was running my pregame laps.

There was something inside me. I was almost giddy in anticipation. I was as excited as I was when we opened the season against this same team in New Orleans.

"Bring on the Saints," I said softly to myself as I completed my second lap.

We had lost two tough games in a row. Supposedly that was a bad omen for the Saints. It has been alleged that the last thing a football team wants to do is face a good team coming off a defeat.

Of course the Rams may have been undaunted by that. The Saints were considered to be easier prey. They had flown more than 4,000 miles to square off against a team of angry Hawaiians. We couldn't get revenge against the Bears or Rams this week. The Saints would have to be their proxies.

As I ran along the home team's sideline on the mauka side I saw our opponents start to trickle in from the north end zone tunnel.

"Poor suckers," I whispered to myself and smiled broadly before reminding myself not to get overconfident.

I crossed paths with the Saints as they headed across the field to their locker room. I nodded to some and gave vocal greetings to others. For the moment they were fellow human beings in street clothes. Later they would be wearing uniforms that would designate them as mortal enemies.

To sports experts there is some incongruity about the fortunes of the Hawaiians and Saints. In only our second year in the NFL we were classified as one of the better teams. We were respected by all and even feared by some. Nobody was looking at our record and snickering. The victims of our most recent victory, Tampa Bay, began the day with an overall 0-24 record.

We were a combined 13-11. That is a winning record that lingers in the mediocre range but we had proven that we could compete with anybody. I was thinking about how in 1976 we managed a 7-7 record and along the

394

way we beat the team that eventually won the Super Bowl. We also had to win our final two games in cold weather to get to the break-even mark and in doing so we played a major role in dashing the playoff hopes of our final two opponents.

Some so-called experts say our unbelievably good second year performance is misleading. They point out that the Hawaiians spent two years in the WFL before being added to the NFL.

That is true but it wasn't at all like the AFL merging with the NFL. Hawaii and Memphis were added as expansion teams like Tampa Bay and Seattle, not as existing teams from one league merging into another league. Only a few of us from the WFL team were on the opening day NFL roster.

So the second year NFL Hawaiians came out swinging with players acquired the same way as any other expansion franchise. As was previously mentioned, and was often pointed out by the sports media, the other three expansion teams won a combined total of four games in 1976. We won seven by ourselves.

Our opponent on this day had once been an expansion franchise. In their eleventh season they were still experiencing the fortunes of an expansion team. Their record through the first ten games of 1977 was 3-7. Their overall record to this point was 39-106-5 with the Hawaiians having the honor of handing the franchise its 100th loss to kick off the season.

Put another way, the Saints won five games in 1969, 1973 and 1974. That was their highest win total ever.

Pity the poor Saints. We were licking our chops. We were not going to allow ourselves to become three-time losers in as many weeks. In our brief history in the NFL our longest losing streak was two. For a team like the Saints a three-game losing streak was normal. For us such a losing streak would be an unprecedented tailspin.

I could see that it wasn't going to happen. I sat in front of my locker and looked around the room as we waited for Walker to address us before we took the field. Carl Rodgers sat next to me; his arms folded and there was a very determined look on his face. Norm Richards pounded his right fist into the palm of his left hand over and over as he sat with a faraway look, obviously focusing on the competition. Nobody was listening to music, nobody was reading and nobody was talking. Everybody was focused.

My feeling was that the only way we would lose this game was if a few teammates had taken bribes. Since I didn't believe any of my teammates were that stupid there was no way we were going to lose. The Saints were our sacrificial lambs.

As focused as we were, I believed nobody could beat us this day. Not the Steelers, not the Cowboys, not the Rams, not the Raiders and definitely not the Saints. We wanted this one bad and were putting our feet down. We knew how to get it.

"All right, Hawaiians," Walker called as he moved to the center of the room. "Let's start by doing *The Lord's Prayer*."

In unison we recited the prayer. Nobody led us this time. We instinctively started together. That's how in sync we were.

"All right," Walker continued after the prayer. "I just want to know one thing. Are you ready to play some serious football?"

There was a roar in the affirmative.

"I think so, too," said Walker. "Something tells me you are physically and mentally ready. Let's get out there and make those Saints curse the day the NFL expanded into Hawaii."

We headed to the field. Everybody ran to the sideline except for the starting offense whose turn it was to be individually introduced.

As the offense stood in the end zone the Saint defense was introduced. As each Saint was introduced there were predictable sounds of dissension from the crowd. It was mostly boos although most of the fans seemed to prefer no sound at all. If anybody was cheering for the Saints, I didn't hear them.

No leis were given to the Saints who were introduced. Like all visiting teams, they were asked if they wanted the introduced players to be issued leis. The Saints were one of the few teams to politely decline the offer.

"And now, the starting offensive lineup for the Hawaiians!" the enthusiastic public address announcer called out, leading to a thunderous roar from the sold-out crowd of 49,727. "At wide receiver, number 80, from the University of Washington, Ted Dietrich!"

Ted was greeted by another roar; as was each subsequent player. We definitely had the crowd behind us.

"At halfback, number 22, from the University of Hawaii, Jay Dockman!"

The roar of the crowd was inspiring. As soon as I was to be introduced I began my trot from the end zone to midfield as my name and likeness appeared on the scoreboard. The route was lined by a row of a dozen cheerleaders on each side who waved their pompoms over their heads and jumped up and down. The alternate cheerleaders stood at the end of this passageway of vibrant pulchritude since they were in charge of handing out leis.

A beautiful Chinese alternate cheerleader with raven hair cut just above the shoulders draped an orchid lei over my head. I then slapped fives with the nine offensive teammates who ran to midfield ahead of me.

"At quarterback, number ten, from the University of California at Santa Barbara, Steve Bender!"

Our healthy again starting quarterback followed the path of his ten predecessors and slapped fives with us. We lined up in an "I" formation with me on the right wing and ran our standard quarterback sneak to our sideline.

396

I disposed of my lei by giving it a hard tug so that the string broke on the back of my neck. This was the method I began using in college. A couple of my teammates disposed of their leis in similar fashion while others simply lifted them over their heads and dropped them to the ground or threw them into the crowd.

The Waialua High School Band marched on the field and played the *National Anthem*. As the band marched off the captains of the two teams went to midfield for the toss.

I ran in place while awaiting the outcome. As usual, I didn't believe I could get on the field soon enough.

We won the toss. New Orleans would defend the north end zone and I wouldn't have to wait to get on the field. I was elated.

"The coin toss is going to prove to be the turning point in the game," Stanek cracked half jocularly.

"You think?" I responded.

"Yup. They screwed up the coin toss and blew their entire game plan."

I was hoping Stanek's prophecy would come true.

"Kick return team, over here," called special teams coach Ken Holcomb.

Dutifully those of us who were on the kick return unit gathered around the sandy-haired man just off the playing field.

"Okay, everybody ready?" he began rhetorically. "We need a good return to get this thing started. Let's make a good wedge for the ball carrier. Whoever gets the ball, look for daylight."

Our kick returns were usually pretty basic. The five up front generally blocked the first men to come their way. Those who got through became the responsibility of everybody behind the front line while the ball carrier simply looked for an opening and ran as far as he could. Occasionally we deviated from the basic by having the blockers switch assignments or we focused on moving to the left or right. Usually it was simply a very straightforward effort.

Hasegawa and I took our places on the goal line. As always, I was on Rich's left. About 15 yards ahead of me was Rossi.

Both teams' units were ready. All we needed was the signal from the red shirt who stood on the field near the makai sideline with his arms folded. From his headset he would be given the okay from CBS.

The red shirt waved his arm in a circle and moved off the field. The referee blew his whistle and we were about to get underway.

In 1977 the kickoff was from the 35. The Saints' kicker sent the ball up and it was heading my way.

"I got it!" I called, being very careful not to raise my hand the way I did when I called for a fly ball to the outfield in baseball. I didn't want to inadvertently signal for a fair catch which can be done on a kickoff although knowledge is esoteric since it is almost never done.

The film showed that my right foot was right on the five when I caught the ball. As the crowd roared its encouragement, which I didn't notice at the time but recalled later, I began racing up the field.

Hasegawa moved up and made a good enough block on the Saint who was furthest downfield. He didn't actually manage to knock him down and the Saint managed to get a hand on my left shoulder at about the 15 but I kept running. Rich's block was enough to prevent the man from making the tackle.

Directly ahead of me was Rossi. He lowered himself directly into the midsection of a would-be tackler. Dave may even have knocked the wind out of the defender because I heard a very audible "oof" when contact was made. The Saint wound up flat on his back.

"Thank you, Dave" I actually said although primarily under my breath as I ran past.

I was finally hit from the left side near the bottom of my rib cage as I crossed the 30. I had a split-second warning that I was about to be hit. That was enough time to protect the ball by moving it to my midsection and putting both hands over it. Had he come from my right side I might have been able to straight-arm him since I was carrying the ball in my left hand. I couldn't do that when he suddenly turned up on the same side as I had the ball since there wasn't time to make the switch.

"Okay, let's bounce up there," I heard one of the officials call.

The man who tackled me was raising himself up. I made eye contact with the young Black opponent.

"Nice tackle," I said evenly.

"Thanks, man," he replied and ran to the sideline.

The referee took the ball from me as I got up. He placed the ball on the 31.

"Jay Dockman with a kick return of 26 yards," I heard the PA announcer report before reporting the tackler. "First and ten Hawaiians on their own 31 yard line."

I spotted Rossi running toward me on his way to the sideline. I held my hand out to slap five with him.

"Helluva block, man! That was great!" I said enthusiastically as he was running past.

Rossi turned and waved with a broad smile as he continued toward the sideline. He lacked the discipline to be a better player but he had his moments. His block enabled me to pick up at least an extra five yards. Although Rossi didn't get much playing time, he was an asset whenever he kept his focus.

It probably helped that Walker had lifted Rossi's spirits. After nitpicking Rossi's performance during the film session on Tuesday, Walker gradually padded his ego through the rest of the week. By the time Saturday rolled around Walker had Rossi believing he was an All-Pro and Walker's best friend.

Which was what the cocky halfback seemed to believe all along anyway.

We began with a short pass. Bender hit Dietrich on a quick slant at the 33. Ted fought his way to the 36 to give us a second and five.

Just as quickly we lost the five yards. Marv jumped prior to the snap. As we moved back to the huddle Marv had a pained expression on his face.

"It's all right, man. We'll get it back," I said, patting him on the back.

Unfortunately we didn't. Kerner managed a mere two yards up the middle. A pass to me was batted down near the Hawaii 45. It was a three and out.

I focused on not letting it bother me. It was no surprise that the Saints were determined and would come out the gate hard. We were the better team, I believed, and we would beat them if we played up to our potential.

Jablonski got off one of his better punts. It bounced near the 20, having gone over the head of the return man. It took a couple of bounces and rolled to a stop at the eleven. Officially it was a 56-yard punt with no return.

As the Saint defense had done, its offense played with determination. The Saints began with an eleven-yard completion that gave them a first down at the 22. On a third and eight they completed another pass to give them a first down at their own 41.

Black came through for us on the next play. He picked off a pass at the Hawaii 48, returning it seven yards to the New Orleans 45. We had a first down with excellent field position.

"All right, offense," Walker called over the roaring crowd. "Black got you good field position. Do something with it."

We started with an incomplete pass when Bender underthrew Grummon. That probably wasn't what Walker had in mind.

Scott made up for it. Shooting through the hole opened by Stanek and Hayer, he fought his way to the 34. That gave us our first first down of the game.

We went to the air again. Bender spotted Grummon inside the 20 near the left sideline. Rich made the catch but one of his feet was out of bounds.

It was a costly play. Hayer went down. While blocking he got knocked back and seemed to twist his left ankle. He was helped off the field and taken to the locker room for examination and treatment.

Pete Kimmitt came in. Everybody probably expected to see Daniels but Walker apparently wanted to give the rookie from UCLA an opportunity to show what he could do in a semblance of a starting role. He was technically Hayer's backup anyway while Daniels worked out at right tackle to fill in for Abraham although Daniels was selected to fill in when Hayer was out previously.

When play resumed Scott ran a sweep around right end. He got to the 27 to give us a third and three.

"All right. We're going all the way," Bender remarked in the huddle, rubbing his palms together.

That prophecy almost died on the next play. Scott carried off left tackle and got to the 22. He also fumbled but managed to recover his own fumble. We had another first down.

The Saints gave us a hand when one of their linemen jumped and bumped Abraham. We now had first and five at the 17.

Kerner picked up four yards to the 13. Scott then charged up the middle to give us a first and goal at the six. Naturally our fans were offering very vocal support.

Kerner went off left tackle. He broke a couple of tackles and tumbled into the end zone.

"All right!" I hollered, thrusting my fists in the air.

Of course the fans erupted. Their spirits were dashed by a yellow flag. McCracken was cited for holding. Instead of going for the extra point, we had first and goal at the 16.

The Saints turned it up a few notches. They were all over Bender when he dropped back to pass. He got the pass off but it sailed out of the end zone.

We went to the air again. Bender hit me over the middle at the nine. I was hit and dropped immediately. It was another one of those hits that appeared more brutal than it seemed, I would discover when watching the game films two days later. It was third and goal.

Shuford helped me to my feet.

"We're on our way," Dave said discreetly to avoid firing up the Saints as he and I headed to where we would huddle.

The Saint defense charged hard again on the ensuing play. Perhaps they were insulted by being ten and-a-half point underdogs and our determination to beat them by at least double that. They forced Bender to scramble. Steve dodged and weaved his way to the six where we had fourth and goal.

There was no hesitation. The field goal unit came on the field. It was important that we put points on the board even if it was only three points.

I was frustrated. It was only a 45-yard drive and I believed we should have picked up the full seven. Never mind that the Saint defense dug in when it needed to. I believed we should have picked up the maximum benefit.

McCracken was sitting by himself on the bench. He appeared to be muttering quietly to himself. He was upset with himself since his penalty cost us a touchdown.

"Shake it off," I said as I patted him on the back. "It happens to everybody."

McCracken looked up at me with a trace of gratitude on his face. I patted him on the back again and turned my attention to the field.

Arroyo snapped the ball to Billingsley. Guinn stepped forward and then Billlingsley abruptly got up and ran to his left.

"Wow!" I cried out in amused disbelief when I saw what was happening.

With good protection and even Guinn running interference, Billingsley dove into the end zone for a touchdown.

Excepting the coaching staff, nobody on the sideline knew it was coming. It came as quite a shock to see Billingsley get up and run with the ball. Although we had been working on the fake field goal since the 1976 exhibition season, this was the first time we had ever attempted it in a game. It was fortunate that the gamble paid off.

"See?" I said to McCracken. "We got our touchdown anyway."

I was hoping the play would deflate the egos of the Saints defense. They were probably patting themselves on the back for limiting us to a mere field goal. The trick play put them in their place.

Or so we hoped.

The extra point gave us a 7-0 lead. There was 4:41 left in the first quarter.

Billingsley was radiant when he came to the sideline. It was the first big highlight of his brief career. While normally aloof, he was smiling broadly as he accepted the congratulations of his teammates. Aside from some work at quarterback in games whose outcomes were already decided, his only work was as a holder on extra points and field goal attempts. This play gave him a greater sense of purpose. I was very happy for him as well as the team.

"You couldn't have done it any better," I said to Billingsley before seeking out Guinn. "You were blocking like an All-Pro," I told Guinn, obviously embellishing a little but not in a way that was inappropriate.

The play actually lifted the spirits of the entire team. We didn't assume we had the game won but the play did give us the momentum we thought we may have lost. We were fired up.

And, of course, any thoughts any fan might have had of hanging McCracken in effigy were forgotten. His penalty that nullified our initial touchdown only delayed the inevitable. McCracken was off the hook.

At least until Tuesday's game films.

Billingsley, at least for the moment, was the most popular player on the team. The normally moody quarterback was grateful for the congratulations of his teammates. Even Black, who was known to refer to Billingsley as "the (expletive deleted) Mormon" whenever Billingsley wasn't around, greeted Billingsley enthusiastically.

The immediate concern was protecting our lead before having a chance to expand it. That began with the kicking unit. Guinn kicked off.

It was a good kick which briefly seemed to hang up in the jet stream. The ball was fielded four yards deep in the end zone. I expected the kick returner to accept a touchback. Instead he opted to run it out.

That was a mistake. Hasegawa shot through virtually untouched. He nailed the return man at the seven. Hasegawa's tackle was likely to have the return man hearing bells and whistles.

A blind man would have known what happened. He would have noticed the very abrupt roar of the crowd. Amid the roar were the enthusiastic calls of approbation on the sideline. It was another big play.

Yet the Saints, despite their record that suggested futility, were professional enough to give it their best shot. They opened with a four-yard rush around right end. They then completed a pass to the 19. Black was right there to prevent the ball carrier from going any further but the Saints still had a first down.

Four first downs later the first quarter ended. We still had our 7-0 lead but the Saints would begin the second quarter at the Hawaii 38. An eleven-yard pass over the middle had given them that fourth first down on the final play of the quarter; their fifth first down of the day.

Once the second quarter started the Saints continued their relentless pursuit of the goal line. They had a third and six and a third and 12 and both times converted to pick up first downs. The ball was now on the 14.

"These guys beat the Rams earlier this month," I said wearily to Bender on the bench. "They seem determined to do the same thing to us."

Bender shook his head.

"They won't beat us," he said confidently. "They're making the plays now but they're wearing down. Our defense is going to adjust and shut them down. I'll bet you they don't get a touchdown on this drive. They might get a field goal but not a touchdown."

Bender's confidence was reassuring. I was still worried. We needed to get back on track. I probably wouldn't have been quite so concerned had we not lost to the Bears and Rams over the previous two weeks. The thought of a three-game losing streak made me want to puke.

The Saints rushed up the middle and managed only two yards. They then decided to go to the air.

Jennings blitzed. The quarterback tried to scramble but couldn't get away. Ed got a hold on him at the shoulder pads to slow him up, then grasped him at the midsection. By this time McDaniel turned up and hammered the quarterback as well. It was a sack at the 21.

That made it third and 17. The Saints were within a reasonable field goal range. Sometimes in a situation like that a team will run a rushing play to simply get better position for the field goal as if they felt a touchdown was beyond reach. My guess was that the Saints would go to the air.

The Saints did exactly that. What they didn't expect was Dubois. He reached around the receiver near the five and tipped the ball up, then grabbed it and took off.

"I win," Bender said jubilantly as he and I spontaneously jumped up, referring to his claim a moment earlier that the Saints wouldn't score a touchdown on the drive.

As the crowd roared along with those of us on the sideline, Dubois headed in the direction of the south end zone. He charged past the 20, the 30, the 40. . . .

Henri reached the New Orleans 45. The very same receiver he had intercepted against caught him from behind. The two went down just as they were going out of bounds in front of the Saints' bench. Henri bounced back up and leaped in the air in triumph.

The offense charged out. We were out for blood. The Saints had just undergone a very demoralizing experience by driving almost the entire length of the field and coming up empty. Not only did they turn the ball over, we wound up with excellent field position.

"Let's not waste this," I said to whoever might have been nearby as we ran on the field.

"We're going for the TD," I heard Grummon respond.

A pair of rushes by Scott produced seven yards. I then got the call on a sweep around right end. I got us the three yards we needed plus four more. We had a first down at the 31.

We went to the air next. No receivers were open. Bender deliberately overthrew the ball to prevent an interception.

Bender called for Scott to run a sweep, then audibled at the line. He spotted something that told him he had a good chance to complete a pass.

I had a slight opening downfield. Bender spotted me and fired in my direction. I leaped up and reached over my head, catching the ball cleanly at the 13. As soon as my feet hit the ground I was hit from my left side and dropped. We had a first down at the 13.

Dietrich was there to whack me on the derriere as I rose up.

"Great catch, Jaybird!" he cried enthusiastically.

"Dockman!"

Rossi was on his way in. I didn't want to come out but what could I do? My adrenaline was pumping and I didn't want to cool it down. I was hoping I wouldn't be out for more than a play or two.

"Great catch. How are you feeling?" Walker asked when I reached the sideline.

"I feel great," I replied, trying not to sound annoyed or flippant.

"Okay. I'll send you back in after this play if we don't score."

We didn't score. Bender dropped back and was forced to scramble. He managed to go forward and stepped out of bounds at the nine.

True to his word, Walker sent me back in. We tried another pass.

Bender was forced to scramble again. He managed to move forward again but this time he was sacked two yards behind the line of scrimmage. It was third and eight at the eleven.

The Saints were looking for a pass. We hoped to cross them up by staying on the ground. Scott carried off left tackle but only got five of the yards we needed. It was fourth and three at the six.

I silently wished that Walker would let us go for it. It was no surprise that my wish didn't come true. The field goal unit ran on the field. It was important that we make this a two-score game.

A few of my teammates looked somber on the sideline, as I probably did. We hated not getting the full seven, especially after starting the drive with such great field position.

"Don't sweat it, guys," Bender said, reading our thoughts and slapping a few of us on the back as he walked past. "We're going to score at least one more time before this half is over."

Guinn easily made it a two-score game when his 23-yard field goal attempt split the uprights. It was 10-0 with 5:13 left in the half.

I grabbed my Gatorade and sat down. I hoped the Saints wouldn't have a sustained drive. If they had the ball too long, even if they didn't score, the clock would work against our quest to put together another scoring drive before halftime.

As Guinn approached the ball to kick off I stood up. The kick was fielded at the goal line. The Saint return man got to the 24 before being brought down.

"All right, defense!" I called as the defense ran on the field. "Let's have a three and out. Whaddya say?"

I sat back down and consumed the last of my Gatorade. I wanted to conserve my energy for the final drive of the half that I hoped we would have.

It wouldn't be a three and out. The Saints opened with a pass that was completed at the 38. The receiver took a step or two forward and was pummeled by Rodgers.

"Fumble!"

I stood and watched as a small assortment of white jerseys and brown jerseys chased a ball that was bouncing toward the opposite sideline. Morrissey suddenly dove and seemed to have it.

The officials fully agreed, much to the delight of our fans. We had a first down at the New Orleans 36.

"Yeah! All right!" I cried out as I put my helmet on and charged on the field. On the way out I slapped fives with about half-a-dozen defensive players as our paths crossed.

"Way to go! Good job, Ed! Nice going, Russ! Hey, Jim! That's the way to play!"

My adrenaline was pumping. Moments like this help make the overall game fun.

At least for us. I don't think the Saints were enjoying their visit to Hawaii at this point.

Our immediate concern was traveling the 108 feet we needed to get the score Bender had assured us we would get only moments earlier. I was looking for the full allotment.

We started by sending Kerner off left tackle. He managed only two yards to the 34.

Scott went off right tackle and got to the 30. It was third and four.

Suddenly it was third and nine. Abraham was overzealous and jumped before the snap.

We had to convert. If we didn't Walker was going to have Abraham's derriere in a sling. I didn't think about it at the time but it was definitely true.

Bender took the snap and dropped back. He spotted Dietrich over the middle. He threw a near perfect spiral that Dietrich caught at the 14. Ted got to the eight before going down.

Now we were extremely pumped, as was the crowd. Only 24 feet to go. A touchdown would make it a three-score game.

The eight yards wouldn't be easy. The Saints were determined to make it tough. Kerner fought for three yards up the middle and then Bender threw an incompletion. It was third and goal at the five.

As far as I was concerned, this drive had to culminate in a touchdown. A mere field goal would seem like no score at all and might even seem like a moral victory for the Saints. Three points can be the difference in a game but I didn't feel that I could settle for two consecutive field goals on two consecutive drives where we started in such good field position.

We went to the air again. It was a play-action fake. I was near the back of the end zone about halfway between the goal post and the right corner. I watched as Bender fired a strike that hit Kerner on the numbers about three yards from the back line of the end zone. We had our touchdown.

I leaped in the air and then ran over to Kerner, whacking him on the helmet. As the crowd held a sustained roar we ran off the field along with the rest of our offensive colleagues.

"Good work, men," Walker remarked as we reached the sideline. "Good catch, Kerner. Steve, that was a perfect pass. Abraham. . . ."

I turned and looked. Walker was waving his index finger at Clint and then busted out laughing. The touchdown seemed to have earned Clint a full pardon.

At least until Tuesday's film session.

As he normally did, Guinn drilled the PAT through the uprights. It was 17-0 with 2:11 left in the half.

"We are hot, baby!" Grummon remarked vibrantly on the sideline.

"Yeah, we're hot," Bennici concurred. "Just don't let down. These guys can still play. We've got to focus on scoring every time we get the ball. Keep scoring and they'll surrender."

I was feeling great. I hoped the defense would keep the Saints scoreless over the final 2:11 of the half. I didn't want the Saints to even get a field goal. My heart was set on going into the locker room halfway to a shutout.

Guinn kicked off. The ball was taken two yards deep in the end zone. The return man hesitated, then dropped to a knee for a touchback.

The Saints had two timeouts left. We had all three of ours although I doubted that we would use ours since we weren't likely. . . .

I changed my way of thinking. If we could force the Saints into a three and out or, better still, another turnover we would get the ball again. Our three timeouts could work to our advantage. As usual, there were no limits to my greed.

We were in our 33 nickel since we figured the Saints would pass a lot. The Saints opened with a pass and we put heavy pressure on the quarterback. The quarterback still managed to get the pass off which fell incomplete right at the two-minute mark.

When play resumed the Saints went to the air again. My hopes for a three and out were dashed when the pass was completed near our sideline at the Saints 37. Black was right there to bring the receiver down immediately without allowing him to get out of bounds.

The Saints opted not to use a timeout. They immediately went to the line for another play. The quarterback took the snap and was forced to scramble a little. He got the pass off that was caught in front of our bench near midfield but about two yards out of bounds.

It was second and ten. The clock showed 1:28. After another pass that was broken up by Dubois the clock was stopped at 1:21.

The previous play took its toll. Dubois ran off the field with a slight limp. Morrissey went in to replace him. Fortunately Dubois' injury was superficial. He would be back.

This is great, I thought, turning my attention back to the field. One more incompletion and we'll be getting the ball back. I figured that we'd have about a minute after the punt. That was enough time with our three timeouts to rack up another score.

The Saints had other ideas. They completed a pass at about their own 48. The receiver crossed midfield and was brought down at the 49. They had a first down and used one of their timeouts with 1:10 left.

I couldn't sit. The tension was too much. The Saints were close to field goal range. A touchdown was also a possibility. That would give them momentum and they would also be receiving the kickoff to start the second half.

They definitely had that on their minds. A score on this drive and a score on the opening drive of the second half would put them back in the game, especially if at least one of those scores was a touchdown.

The Saints moved to within field goal range with a pass to the 32. The receiver stepped out of bounds to stop the clock at 1:02.

I gave up any thoughts I was entertaining about one more score for us this half. I would be satisfied if we simply prevented them from scoring.

An incompletion stopped the clock with 56 seconds. The Saints went to the air again and this time the quarterback was forced to scramble. He got the pass off but the ball was tipped upward by McDaniel.

Jennings made a shoestring interception at about the line of scrimmage, setting off an explosive roar from the crowd as well as from my teammates and me on the sideline. Ed carried to the Hawaii 36 before a pair of linemen brought him down. We had 45 seconds and three timeouts to travel 64 yards.

We were going for it. That was obvious when Walker called for the single-double. Scott stayed on the sideline. Rossi joined Dietrich and me as receivers. I was even hoping, surprisingly enough, that Rossi would be the one to score a touchdown if we were going to get it.

The Saints wisely went to a prevent defense. That didn't stop Bender from finding Grummon at the Hawaii 47. Rich made the catch and got to the Saints 49 before going down. He was still in bounds.

"Timeout!" I called simultaneously with a few of my teammates and probably half of the crowd.

The officials who heard the multitude of requests waved their arms over their heads while blowing their whistles, then pointed in our direction to indicate that we were being charged with a timeout. The clock was stopped with 36 seconds.

As Bender went over to converse with Walker, Slater ran on the field.

"Grummon!"

Grummon went out. We would be in the double-double. I was surprised we weren't in that formation previously.

Of course we continued our air attack. This time the target was Dietrich near the right sideline. Ted made the reception at the Saints 39 and saw that he had room to run. As a defensive back closed in he stepped out of bounds at the 31 to stop the clock with 25 seconds.

The next play demonstrated why our timeouts were critical. The Saints blitzed. Bender dropped back but had nowhere to go. He was sacked at the 39. We used our second timeout to step the clock with 17 seconds.

Naturally Bender went to the sideline while the rest of the offense dropped to a knee. One could literally feel the atmosphere of confidence and enthusiasm in our huddle.

"Don't you just love doing so well against your former team?" Abraham subtly asked Marv, drawing chuckles from me as well as a few teammates.

"We're showing them how it's done," Marv replied lightly, again being careful not to speak so loud that our opponents could hear him.

Bender returned to the huddle. We decided to go for broke. Slater, Dietrich and I would all head straight for the end zone. Rossi was to run a post pattern. That way, if none of us could get open in the end zone, Rossi would at least be available to get us to more reasonable field goal range.

The Saints were in a dime defense. Dietrich and I were double-teamed. Slater had a defensive back sticking to him and the other defensive back was with Rossi.

Bender went for Rossi. The ball was way out in front of him but Rossi lunged and hauled it in at the 22. He was hit and dropped immediately but hung on to the ball.

The clock was running. With less than ten seconds left we knew we only had time for a field goal attempt. We let the clock run down to three seconds before calling timeout.

We ran off the field while the field goal unit ran on. Walker looked specifically for Rossi as we reached the sideline.

"Helluva catch, Dave," Walker remarked, giving Rossi a handshake and a pat on the back.

I grabbed a cup of Gatorade and chugged it down, then watched as our field goal unit got set. It was going to be a 39-yard attempt.

Not surprisingly, the Saints suddenly used their final timeout to put more pressure on Guinn. It would have been a surprise if they didn't call timeout.

Unfortunately for the Saints, the tactic didn't work. Arroyo's perfect snap and Billingsley's perfect hold helped Guinn to put the ball through the uprights. Our lead had expanded to 20-0.

We got a rousing ovation as we headed for the locker room. The fans smelled a rout and were loving it. They were almost sadistically out for blood.

So were we.

In the locker room I took care of business at the urinal and with a cup of Gatorade. After that I kicked back with a Mr. Goodbar and Dr. Pepper.

I was feeling extremely satisfied with the way the game was going. That was something that could prove to be dangerous. Although we had a 20-point lead and the momentum, if we got complacent we could very easily blow the entire thing. It was good that we had the lead. We needed to build it up even more to put the game away.

Walker seemed to feel the same way. He pointed that out when he addressed us prior to our returning to the field.

"Don't be satisfied with this. If you're satisfied you're in for a rude awakening. We've got them on the ropes but we're only halfway home. We still have 30 minutes of football left. Let's keep things going our way."

Walker waved his arm toward the exit and we filed out. We were greeted by a thunderous roar as soon as we emerged from the tunnel. The last thing we wanted to do was let our fans down.

I was hyped. I would have to be patient, though. The Saints would have the first possession.

"If we prevent them from scoring and we score on our first drive that ought to just about kill them," Bender said to Grummon, McDaniel and me.

"The pressure's on them right now," McDaniel responded. "They have to force something to happen. We have to dig in and frustrate them."

"Right," Bender agreed. "We hold them scoreless during their first two possessions and we score on our first two possessions and they'll be waving the white flag by the time the fourth quarter starts."

To start the third quarter Guinn kicked off toward the south end zone. The ball came down in the end zone and bounced out the back to the dugout seats between the two baseball dugouts. The Saints would start on their own 20.

The Saints were relentless. They ran six consecutive rushing plays. The end result was two third down conversions. They had a first down at their own 43.

They stayed on the ground. Perhaps they thought we were looking for a pass. Between two rushes they picked up three yards and then lost two of those yards. It was third and nine at the New Orleans 44.

For the first time in the second half they went to the air. Our 32 dime left them with very little hope. The pass fell incomplete.

"Punt return team!" Walker called.

I didn't hesitate. After a brief huddle I took my place inside the 15. I was psyched to put an exclamation point on this one. It was a major shot in the arm that we kept the Saints from scoring but only one of a few critical steps toward certain victory.

The punt was up. I couldn't hear Hasegawa's instruction but instinct told me I'd be able to run it back. I caught the ball at the 15. Breaking a tackle at the 22, I finally went down at the 25.

I was hyped even more and forced myself to tone it down. I didn't want to blow my assignments by being too hyperactive.

Kerner got us started by picking up three yards up the middle. Scott then fought for two yards off right tackle.

The latter was nullified by offsetting penalties. Shuford got cited for holding while one of the Saints was offside. It was still second and seven.

I got the call on a 4 kama'aina right. With impeccable blocking I managed to get to the 34 to give us a third and one. Scott then got us our first down by going off right tackle to the Hawaii 40.

It didn't look good for the Saints. They still didn't surrender. It was as if they represented a Confederate force nearly depleted of ammunition but continued battling a well-stocked Union force. They put a heavy rush on Bender before batting the pass away from Grummon.

We went to the air again. This time Bender hit me just past midfield at the Saints 49. I was hit almost immediately but managed to squirm my way to the 47.

Naturally the crowd was cheering. I felt confident but not overconfident.

Scott justified my confidence over the next two plays. He shot through the middle for nine yards to the 38, then went off left tackle and appeared unstoppable. He broke two tackles within the first five yards and then two more before he got to the 20. A defensive back finally wrestled him down near the left sideline at the eleven.

We were definitely pumped now and determined to take it all the way. Kerner and Dietrich helped Scott up with such enthusiasm that they practically threw him in the air. The fans were so loud that I swore that they could be heard on Maui.

"Way to go, Larry! Helluva run!" I exclaimed as I joined him and our other teammates in the huddle.

"Good job, Larry," Bender said more casually but sincerely, shaking Larry's hand before calling the next play.

The Hawaiians were the predators. The Saints were our prey. We were going for the kill.

Kerner got the call on a 2 Mililani right. He shot through the middle. He was hit a couple of times but didn't go down until he was two yards deep in the end zone.

The crowd exploded! As exciting as tight games were for our fans, they definitely loved the rout that was brewing. It almost seemed sadistic although those of us on the winning side had no objections. We weren't trying to run up the score. We simply wanted to prevent the Saints from catching us.

Guinn's extra point attempt was flawless. We had a 27-0 lead with 5:54 left in the third quarter. It was still possible for the Saints to come back. That would take a total collapse on our part.

That was pretty much it. After the Saints had a short series we chewed up the rest of the third quarter before Scott scored on a 12-yard rush to give us a 34-0 lead with 14:34 left in the game. After the Saints had another series which climaxed with a punt Walker put the backups in.

At this point the Saints were playing for pride. After Ozzie Roberts coughed up a fumble at the Hawaii 39, the Saints tried to drive the 117 feet to the end zone.

They got to the three. A measurement showed them inches from a first down. They went for it on fourth down.

Their quest came up short. We had the ball again with our 34-0 lead still intact.

As our backups on the offensive unit got some playing time in, the rest of us looked and acted like conquering heroes. There was a lot of smiling and laughing on the sideline. With victory secure the tension was gone. The only question was whether we would continue to hold the Saints scoreless.

Some of our fans opted to leave. The overwhelming majority stayed in their seats but there were those who couldn't wait to resume their tailgate parties or simply hit the road ahead of the crowd.

The Saints got the ball one final time. They began on the 50 and got to the 27 with four seconds left. Not wanting to be shut out, they tried a 44-yard field goal.

I didn't care if they made it. Probably subconsciously I wanted them to miss but it didn't matter. We were back in the win column.

The kick was up. It headed toward the goal posts of the south end zone. Wide to the right!

That was it. The game was over. For the first time in our 25-game NFL history we had a shutout. It was something very difficult to achieve in the NFL.

Twice we played the Saints and twice we made history. In both cases it was dubious history from the Saints' perspective.

It was already mentioned that we started the season by handing the Saints their 100th career loss. This time around they were on the receiving end of our first-ever shutout.

I couldn't believe it when they missed the field goal. I even felt sorry for them. The field goal attempt was one last gasp to salvage something for their pride and they missed. Although my vantage point on the sideline suggested to me initially that the kick would be true, an isolated shot of the kicker showed that he knew he had missed it from the moment he got the kick off. I think he simply wanted it too badly and wasn't able to focus properly.

This had been a critical game for us regardless of whether we got the shutout. The victory put us back on track. Had we lost this game I doubt that we would have fully recovered. It would have appeared as if we had run out of gas after a fast start.

We felt as if we were in good shape for a playoff berth. There were no guarantees. We were simply legitimate contenders in the hunt.

It was a milestone victory. We were 7-4. On our third attempt we finally matched our win total from 1976.

I recalled how thrilled we were with 7-7 in 1976. Such a record is almost like winning the Super Bowl when you're a first-year expansion team. At 7-4 with three games to play in 1977, the last thing we wanted was to finish 7-7.

"That was a helluva game we just played," Kerner said to me in the locker room as he puffed on a victory cigar.

"It sure was," I concurred. "Those Saints probably don't ever want to come here again."

"Even on their honeymoons," Rodgers added.

"But they're stuck with us," I said. "I doubt that the NFL is going to switch us to another division again. They have to come back and get their butts kicked again next year and the year after that and the year after that."

It was obviously a festive, if not presumptuously cocksure, locker room. We had answered the reporters' questions, showered and were getting dressed so that we could move to the hospitality room for postgame munchies.

"You know what else this means, don't you?" Kerner asked lightly.

"What?" I replied.

"It means that Walker's going to rip us to shreds during game films on Tuesday."

I thought for a moment, then shrugged.

"Who cares?" I said. "At least we're winning. I would rather have him berate us for winning than feel sorry for us for losing."

The mood was just as festive in the hospitality room. It stood to reason since the monkey was off our backs. We won for the first time in three weeks. It was a relief.

Carol was talking to Wendy Billingsley when I arrived. Wendy was a cute young lady with shoulder-length dark blonde hair. She was a tiny thing; barely five feet tall and had an inquisitive face with bright blue eyes.

After I fixed myself a mixed plate of mahi mahi and assorted side dishes I sat with Carol and Wendy. Unlike the other wives and girlfriends who were clad in casual attire, Wendy was wearing a red skirt and white blouse. She and her husband would soon be leaving for a three o'clock service at the Honolulu Tabernacle.

This was the first time I ever actually talked to Wendy except for an occasional greeting. Normally she and Joe left for church as soon as he was dressed. This time was no exception. Wendy would be leaving as soon as Joe was ready.

Wendy was a stark contrast to her husband. Joe was cocky, hot-tempered and aloof much of the time. Wendy was sweet and soft-spoken. She was actually fairly shy; a newlywed who had graduated from Brigham Young University only the previous May.

"That must've been hard on Joe not being able to play last week," I said.

"He was very upset," Wendy agreed. "He hated not being able to suit up. He felt like he let everybody down when Steve got hurt and he wasn't able to go in but he said you did a good job."

"I felt sorry for him. It would've been a good opportunity for him. Even if we hadn't won the experience would've been good for him . . . and good for us since he's expected to take over when Bender retires."

As Carol and I talked to Wendy I could see her husband come in before talking briefly to Bender and Hayer near the entrance to the hospitality room. Again I suspect that his jaded personality stemmed from his zealous

412

desire to be the starting quarterback. Some players handled backup roles better than others.

Joe Billingsley met Wendy Sorenson when they were both students at BYU. The brash returned missionary junior quarterback from Ogden, Utah, and quiet sophomore former high school cheerleader from Canoga Park, California, seemed like an odd match. They were actually very content together.

The test period came when Joe graduated and left to play his rookie year in Hawaii. They remained fiercely loyal to each other and got engaged during the few days we spent in Salt Lake City prior to our game in Denver although nobody knew about the engagement until after the season ended. They were sealed for eternity in the Salt Lake Temple shortly before the 1977 training camp got underway.

CHAPTER SEVENTEEN
Another Happy Reunion

"This thing's really running good now," I remarked to Marv after picking him up prior to Tuesday's film sessions and light workout, referring to my Porsche. "I was a little overdue for a tuneup. I took care of it yesterday."

"Where'd you go for that?"

"Jaymac," I replied. "It's on Waialae near Chaminade across from Chico's Pizza. They do great work over there."

"Really? Maybe I should take my car there. I've been going to this place on Queen Street but I don't really like their work."

"Unfortunately you can't take your car to Jaymac," I said. "They only do Volkswagens."

"Oh."

I had spent a chunk of my day off taking care of personal business which is essentially what a day off is for. I dropped my car off at Jaymac and then went up to the university which was only about a 15-minute walk away. I had lunch with Carol before walking back to Jaymac and picking up my car, then did a little grocery shopping at the Manoa Safeway.

Along the way I looked ahead to Tuesday. Having whitewashed the Saints 34-0, I suspected that we would be sentenced to a fire and brimstone film session on Tuesday.

"Walker's sure going to give it to us today," Marv remarked as we walked across the field toward the tunnel in the south end zone that would take us to the hospitality room.

I couldn't help but note the irony of hellfire film sessions in something referred to as a "hospitality room." During many of our film sessions I didn't care much for the quality of the hospitality.

We got pretty much what we expected while watching the films of Sunday's games. Walker did his best to keep us humble if not humiliated. He picked apart virtually every play.

It wasn't all negative. There was a handful of compliments. Walker couldn't have been too unhappy with Larry Scott if he rushed for 111 yards. Rossi also received a few words of approbation for his work on special teams as well as for his one reception. Walker probably felt he owed Dave a more tranquil film session after making him the sacrificial lamb the week before.

Walker even threw in a little levity. During the second quarter Dietrich couldn't quite reach a pass thrown in his direction. He barely got his fingertips on the ball and couldn't hang on. Walker ran part of the sequence back and forth about half-a-dozen times.

"You see, Ted?" Walker said in mock despair. "You really need to work on that sideline pattern."

That cracked us up. Overall, though, Walker opted to nitpick us to death.

Of course we worked off some of the tension in the locker room as we dressed for our light workout. In retrospect, I wonder if the reason Walker usually stayed out of the locker room after films was to allow us the opportunity to ease the stress brought on by the harsh critiques.

"If we didn't have such a lousy team we would win a game or two," Abraham said in mock frustration.

"Nah, the only way this crummy team will ever win is if Walker cuts the entire squad and starts from scratch," Daniels offered.

"It's not that, man," Kerner chimed in. "The Saints beat the crap out of us because they were so much better than us."

We laughed a little. The facetious remarks might not have been designed to have anybody rolling on the floor but they did lighten the mood.

Unfortunately we still had to deal with Walker. He was especially brutal on Tuesday, Wednesday and Thursday. I guess it was his way of dealing with football players who had just routed a team going nowhere and was about to take on another team heading for the same destination.

"The 49ers are going to kick your cans on Sunday," Walker predicted on Tuesday. "I don't know how you were lucky enough to beat them in October but they're not going to let you beat them again. They're going to knock you all over Candlestick Park on Sunday."

As usual, we practiced with emphasis on the offense on Wednesday. That meant that Walker vented his charm on the offense.

"What's with you linemen? Hit, hit, hit! Don't act like you're just getting out of bed on the snap. If you're going to do that you might as well not bother at all. Just get in your stance and stay there when the ball is snapped. The backs will thank you for it."

Naturally the opposite was true on Thursday when the defense was emphasized.

"If you can't move any quicker than that, Jurgens, I'll find somebody who can. The City Medical Examiner probably has a cadaver or two who'll move faster than you."

On Friday Walker started getting chummy to build us up. When I first saw him as I headed toward the prepractice meeting he greeted me with a smile as wide as a sumo wrestler's girth.

"All right, Jay. I can tell just by looking at you that you're going to have one helluva game."

I nodded and smiled. I was glad that Walker was exchanging his forked tongue for a halo.

"How about you, Mitch? Walker asked Mitch McGovern who was a few feet behind me. "Are you ready to go?"

"Uh, yeah."

Mitch was obviously tentative with his response. It had to do with the small matter of him having been on injured reserve and out for the entire season.

"Hey, Larry," Walker greeted when Larry Scott showed up a minute later. "How're you feeling? Ready to go?"

"Ready to go, Coach," Larry replied.

I'm sure Larry wasn't lying. Even if he was, it wasn't likely that he was going to call in sick on Sunday.

We arrived in San Francisco at about 10:15, Pacific Standard Time, on Friday evening. It was close to midnight when I got to my hotel room although I wasn't especially tired. After all, my body time was only about 8:15.

Of course Marv's body time was the same as mine.

"Want to go down for a drink?" I asked as Marv and I got off the elevator and headed for our rooms which were across the hall from each other.

"I was going to ask you the same question."

"Let's go."

"Right."

And so we did after we dropped our luggage in our respective rooms. We also made it a point to leave our team blazers in our rooms. We didn't expect to be anonymous but we didn't want to make it too easy for any drunken 49er fans to spot us. The blazers potentially meant trouble.

When we got to the hotel lounge we discovered that Kerner and Dietrich had beat us down there and invited us to join them. Abraham soon followed. Then came Hasegawa.

Before long roughtly one-third of the team was in the lounge. Teammates and coaches sat at various tables talking quietly among themselves. Other patrons of the facility seemed to recognize us although they left us alone.

At one o'clock on Saturday afternoon we had our walkthrough practice at Candlestick Park. It was somewhat loose although we were still very serious. After getting back on track with the previous week's victory we wanted to keep the momentum going by winning in San Francisco. A victory would be a great way to vault us into our final two games which would be at home.

We were 7-4. That was a slight improvement over the 5-6 we were after eleven games in 1976. We still weren't satisfied with that. Our focus was on getting into the playoffs. Even if we finished with a better record than we had in 1976 there would be an emptiness if we didn't make the playoffs and we knew it. The next step up was not to simply have a better record than 1976. It was to make the playoffs if not the Super Bowl itself.

416

It was inevitable that some adjustments would be made in our lineup. Catron would be out with bruised ribs. He started against New Orleans and aggravated his ribs during the game but never came out. He was listed as probable before having the problem exacerbated when he took a hit during our workout on Thursday. James Malick would start at right outside linebacker.

Mark Black was also out. He injured his ankle against the Saints and had been listed as questionable. The answer to the question was that he would be on the sideline among those wearing street clothes and game jerseys. Morrissey would start at left cornerback. Dubois would start at right cornerback.

I suddenly started wondering about Hamer's future with the team. I wondered if the writing was on the wall. Two weeks earlier he was placed on waivers with no takers. Although he was reinstated to the active roster a week later, being waived indicated that he was probably the most expendable of our defensive backs. With eight active defensive backs on our roster it appeared likely that Hamer would be the one cut loose if the coaching staff decided to beef up the offensive line to its former strength.

Or perhaps it would be Vorsino who had also spent time away from the active roster.

More than likely it would be Hamer. Hamer rarely played except on special teams. Vorsino went in ahead of Hamer if we went to a nickel or dime defense.

I suppose my concern for Hamer stemmed from him being my teammate longer than anybody except for Hasegawa. Hasegawa had been my teammate every year since 1971 while Hamer was with us in the WFL in 1975. He was a fun guy to know. Although he wasn't the first guy I would call if I wanted to go out on the town, we were on friendly terms. I hated the thought of losing him as a teammate.

But Eric was still with us and our prime concern was the next day's game. At the end of the workout we all gathered around Walker. The entire contingent of coaches and players, including those with injuries and those on the taxi squad since Walker wanted every player connected to the team to be at every workout and feel as if he was still a part of the team, huddled in. The players were clad in an odd assortment of sweatpants, shorts and various types of tops as they stood or knelt.

Of course I was wearing my traditional shirt and hat from the Los Angeles Dodgers. It was the kind of attire that could have gotten me run out of town, or at least tarred and feathered, had the more than 70,000 seats in the San Francisco Giants' home park not been empty.

"I think we're ready," Walker announced. "But that's just my opinion. You know the truth about that. I don't."

"What I do know is you're going to be taking on a team that wants to humiliate you in the worst way. You buried them at Aloha Stadium and

417

they're dying to return the favor here. At the very least, they want to beat you for the sake of their pride and because a loss might very well knock you out of the playoff picture. I personally don't want to see that happen."

Walker paused to look at his players and coaches. Everybody seemed to share his sentiment.

"I want you to have a good evening," he continued. "Loosen up a little in moderation. Just enough to come out fired up tomorrow but not wound too tight. Don't let San Francisco's nightlife throw your game off. Remember also that we have a midnight curfew."

Walker dismissed us. We showered, dressed and boarded the bus for the hotel. I couldn't project how we would fare the next day. I did know that the general attitude of the team and level of confidence seemed about right.

I would not be partaking in San Francisco's nightlife. I had another engagement. At four o'clock I stood at the curb outside the hotel and caught a ride to San Mateo.

Driving the car was Georges Lafayette. This was Carol's dad who unwittingly played a role in triggering my relationship with Carol by introducing me to her in 1973. Three and-a-half years had passed since I had last seen Carol's family. Her dad and I talked as if it had only been a day or two.

This meeting was officially set up a few weeks earlier although I knew back in training camp that it would happen if Carol and I were still together at this point. The arrangements were made primarily between Carol and her family. It wasn't until a few days earlier that I talked to Carol's dad on the phone to arrange our rendezvous time and point.

I was greeted almost like a conquering hero when I entered the house the Lafayette's moved into after Georges Lafayette's abrupt transfer to San Francisco while I was in training camp in 1974. Although the geography and the house itself were different, most of the furnishings were very familiar. During a tour of the house I saw many pictures I had seen before but had almost forgotten.

Among the pictures on the living room wall was a framed photo of Carol and me taken just a few days before I left for my first pro training camp. I had never seen the picture before and barely remembered posing for it. What I would find out later was that they had always kept the picture on display since they liked the picture and Carol never had any romantic interest to fill the void of our estrangement. Contrary to what the parents of some of the girls I had been with prior to Carol thought about how I fit in with their daughters, Carol's family actually thought I was a good fit for her. Despite the reputation I had in 1973, which Georges Lafayette was vaguely aware of, they saw me as someone who genuinely cared about Carol so I was never unwelcome in the Lafayette household.

The first order of business when I entered the Lafayette home was being reunited with the rest of the family. Carol's youngest sister Denise even let out a shriek of delight and ran up and threw her arms around me. She was only nine when Carol and I met and, after telling a neighborhood friend that Carol was going out with "some creep on the UH football team" as Carol readied herself for our first date, she supposedly developed a semblance of a crush on me.

Denise was now 13, in eighth grade and developing into a beautiful lady. I could still see a lot of Carol in her. She was almost a clone of a younger version of Carol except that she had blue eyes as opposed to Carol's green.

Carol's younger sister Michelle greeted me with just as much warmth although she was more contained. It was a trait that I vividly recalled from before. Denise was almost always vibrant. Michelle was friendly and warm but more on the taciturn side.

Michelle was now 18. She was a freshman at Sonoma State.

The most prevalent trait that all three Lafayette girls shared was that they were very unselfish. They were very grateful for what they had and understood that there were people in the world who had very little. They all hated injustice in any form. The sight of anybody suffering could move all three to tears.

No less warm in greeting me was Carol's mother. She looked exactly the way I remembered her right down to the golden blonde hair that, like that of her oldest daughter, was enhanced by the good people at Clairol.

"We missed you, Jay," Danielle Lafayette said as she embraced me.

It was a time capsule moment. The only thing that reminded me that I was not back in 1973 or 1974 was that Denise and Michelle were older and so much more mature. Looking into their eyes still took me back in time.

We spent dinner and the time afterward catching up. That was a tall order since this covered a span of three and-a-half years. They had followed my career pretty closely from the very beginning so there was no need to spend a lot of time talking about myself.

That is, unless they wanted to know about the ladies I was with between the time Carol disappeared and the time she reappeared.

Something told me that was not a subject that they wanted me to broach. It was also something I preferred to forget. I was sure that they knew that I developed a reputation as a bit of a lothario during Carol's absence although nobody was comparing me with Joe Namath. I also knew that they didn't expect me to spend my time alone. I missed Carol terribly during the three years that I didn't see her or hear from her. Despite the carefree ladies' man reputation that I reacquired, I only did what I did because I believed that Carol wasn't coming back and so I needed to let go.

Carol's dad drove me back to the hotel in plenty of time before curfew. Naturally I left the Lafayettes four tickets to the game. They would be a part of the minority in Candlestick Park rooting for the Hawaiians. I hoped that they would also be a part of the minority happy with the outcome of the game.

As I dressed for the game it surprised me how nervous I was. I always had butterflies before a game but this was beyond normal.

The game was important. We believed we had to win all of our remaining games in order to make the playoffs. One loss meant it was still possible but our best bet was to not lose again.

Still, the game itself had little to do with the excessive butterflies. My apprehensions were probably rooted in the presence of Carol's family.

They had seen me in Oakland the year before but I didn't know at the time that they were there. For the first time in almost four full years I would play with the knowledge of their presence.

Carol's family saw me in all but one home game my senior year at the University of Hawaii. The last time they saw me play when I knew they were present was the 1974 Hula Bowl. They were looking forward to seeing me play with the WFL Hawaiians but Carol's father's sudden transfer superseded those plans.

It never bothered me to have them at my games in college. I enjoyed having them there. Carol's parents gave me the support as a college football player that my own parents would not give.

This was different for some reason. It was as if I had to impress them all over again.

And yet I knew that they didn't care how good a football player I was. Carol's parents and two sisters were four of the most wonderful people I had ever known. They accepted me from our very first meeting together which is more than I can say for some parents I had met. It was as if the Lafayettes saw something in me that others didn't. I was all right with them as long as I was good to Carol.

As I took my place on the sideline prior to the start of the game I realized that all of the terrible things that were said about Candlestick Park were true. The temperatures in San Francisco were in the upper 50s but it was lower than that at Candlestick Point which was probably the worst place in the entire city to build a ballpark. Icy winds were blowing up to 15 miles per hour, bringing the temperature down. I wore a windbreaker when I wasn't on the field but the cold wind was enough to keep several of our noses running. It was still considerably worse in Chicago three weeks earlier.

San Francisco won the toss. I reminded myself that I would be on the field soon enough. I felt enigmatically at peace. This was something else I attributed to the reunion with Carol's family.

Rossi also had an entourage. His mother was there and also a few old friends. I wouldn't know who they were if I looked in the bleachers but I knew that Rossi had an entourage of about eight. I suppose if I really wanted to know I could try to pick out the eight people with the worst grammar and drinking the most beer.

420

It was a big moment for Rossi. This was his hometown team we were playing; the team that cut him the previous year before his mother and friends got to see him play in a regular season game. It was finally happening and Rossi was on a team battling for a playoff berth, not the hapless team that turned him loose in 1976.

Rossi was a screwball. As I said previously, I still liked him. I was happy for him and hoped he would have a chance to do something in front of his entourage. I wasn't going to volunteer to give up my playing time since I wasn't quite that generous. We still had our single-double and double-double formations where we were on the field at the same time. Perhaps he would get to catch a pass or two.

Kerner also had guests who had come down from Oregon. Others having friends and family on hand included Jennings, Bender, Daniels, Stanek and Guinn.

Guinn stood at the ready. When he got the signal to proceed he kicked off.

The kick was fielded at the four. The kick returner got reasonably good protection and got past the 20. He was brought down by Hamer at the 25.

That'll work to Hamer's advantage, I thought to myself. I was recalling how I had wondered what Hamer's chances were of staying with the team much longer. I was reasonably sure that my old WFL teammate would last the rest of the season. I simply wondered if he would survive into 1978.

Like the Saints a week earlier, the 49ers were determined to beat us. They opened with a 17-yard pass to the 42. Three plays later, one of which was nullified by a holding penalty, they had another first down at the Hawaii 45.

Three plays after that the 49ers had a fourth and one at the 36. They sent their field goal unit out.

"Are they going to strike first?" Shuford asked rhetorically.

I shook my head as I watched our opponent get set to attempt a 53-yard field goal. I was still very confident about our chances. I hoped that didn't mean complacency.

The kick was up. It was on its way. . . .

Wide to the left!

"Yeah!" I exclaimed, punching the air with my fist.

We had the ball on our own 36. It was still a scoreless game.

"All right! Let's put some points on the board!" I enthusiastically called as I put my helmet on, shed my windbreaker and ran on the field. I was raring to go.

We were going to the air on the opening play. I took my position in the slot and took off downfield on the snap.

Bender hit me at the 49er 39. I was hit immediately but still managed to spin for another yard. It was first and ten at the 38.

Just in case we needed any assistance, the 49ers gave us a boost. A defensive tackle jumped and nudged Stanek. That got us five yards closer.

We went to the air again. Bender spotted Dietrich in the middle of the field.

A safety jumped in front of Dietrich and picked the pass off at the 21. He returned it to the 28 before being brought down by Grummon and me.

Whatever optimism I might have had before, I lost. Not only were the 49ers coming at us hard, they were executing. That caused me to utter a few expletives I'm not proud to admit I knew on the way to our sideline.

"Shake it off. Don't worry about it," I overheard Kerner saying to Bender. "The fans here just needed something to cheer about. They won't get too many chances today."

I wanted to share Kerner's optimism. For the moment I couldn't. I probably simply wanted this game a little too badly. It seemed to affect my personal life as well as our playoff chances.

While I sought refuge on the bench via the Gatorade table, the 49ers needed two plays to pick up a first down at their own 41.

"They're determined," I remarked to Hayer on the bench. "We're just going to have to turn it up."

"The defense will stop them," Hayer replied. "The 49ers will pick up a few chunks but our guys will shut them down."

It didn't happen right away. Malick got called for encroachment. That gave the Niners a first and five at their own 46.

McDaniel set them back a little. On a sweep around right end he threw the ball carrier for a two-yard loss to the 44.

After an incompletion our defense went into the 33 nickel. A pass seemed imminent although not guaranteed.

The 49ers tried to convert with a short pass to their right flat. Jennings cut in front of the receiver and picked the pass off at the 46.

"Yeah!" I cried out, jumping to my feet.

"Go, Eddie, go!" I heard Rossi call out. He was the only person I knew who called Ed "Eddie."

Ed wasn't especially fast. He was still tough to bring down. He practically ran over the quarterback and broke one other tackle while other members of the defensive unit threw blocks. Ed didn't go down until he reached the 15.

"You can sure tell who has family in the crowd," I heard Hayer jocularly remark as he and the rest of the offense ran on the field.

Of course Ed would have made the play anyway. Having family and friends in the bleachers simply made it sweeter for him.

The presence of Ed's family notwithstanding, the idea was to score. We were 45 feet from paydirt. Anything less than a touchdown would almost seem like a touchdown for the 49ers.

"This is the turning point," Bender remarked in the huddle. "We're in the lead from now to the very end."

Of course we had to hope that another interception was not in the 49er defense's future. That would prove to be very demoralizing.

Scott took us almost halfway to our goal. He carried up the middle to the eight.

Unfortunately there were penalty flags lying on the ground.

Fortunately the 49ers were called for holding.

Unfortunately so were we. The penalties offset. We still had first and ten at the 15.

Scott got the call again; this time off left tackle. He got as far as the eleven.

A short pass followed. Lined up wide to the left, I slanted in on the snap and caught the pass just inside the nine. I outran a linebacker and straight-armed a defensive back before taking it into the end zone. We were on the board with 4:18 left in the first quarter.

I spiked the ball in triumph. It was my fifth touchdown of the season but first in more than a month. My previous touchdown was October 30 against these same 49ers. The touchdown at Candlestick ended a drought of six games for me although I did throw a touchdown pass against the Rams.

Whether I was the one to take it in or not was not significant as far as the team was concerned. The important thing was that we scored. Guinn's extra point capped the drive off to give us a 7-0 lead.

On the sideline I was greeted like a conquering hero before watching the extra point and going for the Gatorade. I suddenly thought of my own entourage. It felt good to have made such a good play in front of Carol's family. I wondered if I was subconsciously playing a little harder because of their presence.

Guinn kicked off to the one while I pondered. The return gave the 49ers a first down at their own 22.

"Now let's get the ball back and see if we can score another TD before the end of the quarter," I said to Marv as I sat down for what I hoped would be a very short rest period.

We wouldn't be getting the ball back as quickly as I wanted but it really didn't take long. After two plays the 49ers had a first down on their own 35. After a rush of three yards and two incompletions I found myself standing near the Hawaii 20 to field the first punt of the day.

There wouldn't be any return. The punt was kicked far to my right. It was downed at the Hawaii 18.

"Okay. No skin off my nose," I remarked to myself and then joined my offensive colleagues in the huddle.

Scott picked up four yards on a Kailua right before Dietrich picked up a first down with a reception at the 32 and then fighting for two more yards.

"All right. We're moving. We're moving, baby," I heard Marv remark as we formed a huddle.

After a pass to Grummon was batted down I caught a pass over the middle at the Hawaii 45. I managed to spin around to avoid being tackled until I reached the 47. We had another first down.

"Okay, you guys. Let's keep it going," I enthusiastically cried out as I bounced back up and headed to the huddle.

Scott went off left tackle and crossed midfield. Breaking two tackles, he managed to get to the San Francisco 45.

I ran over to where Scott was tackled. I extended my hand to help him up, then noticed a yellow flag. Something about the demeanor of a couple of 49ers told me the penalty was against us.

Hayer got called for holding. We had a first and 20 at the Hawaii 37 instead of being in 49er territory.

"Okay, forget it," Bender told us in the huddle before calling another play. It was a 4 kama'aina left. "On two. On two. Ready?"

"Break!"

It was up to me. . . .

I stand corrected. It was up to a convoy of blockers and me. I took the handoff and followed the convoy around left end. I was approaching the Hawaii 45 before I was hit and I simply kept going. I broke another tackle at the 50 and cut left to avoid another tackle. I was finally brought down at the San Francisco 44. It was second and one.

"Nice going, Jaybird," Grummon remarked as he helped me up.

"I had a lot of help," I replied, trying to maintain my humility after a 19-yard run that might even have made Walter Payton envious.

Scott went up the middle to the 42 to get us the yard we needed with one to spare for the first down. Bender then threw an incompletion which stopped the clock with two seconds left in the quarter.

"I was hoping we would score another touchdown before the quarter ended," I said to Dietrich as we headed back to the huddle from downfield. "We'll either have to make a big play now or settle for scoring it in the second quarter."

"We'll get there soon enough," Dietrich replied confidently.

I suddenly wondered if Dietrich was psyched up more than he would normally be. He had played seven years prior to being taken by the Hawaiians in the expansion draft. The last five of those years were in San Francisco. Ted may have been among those with extra incentive.

We didn't get the big play to end the quarter. Scott went off right tackle to the 37. We would begin the second quarter with a third and five.

As we changed sides of the field I glanced up into the bleachers. It amused me to see the fans wearing cold weather gear. Candlestick Park was hardly a tropical locale and was even known to be cold and miserable in the summer. I recalled watching televised Dodger-Giant games while growing

424

up and hearing Vin Scully facetiously refer to "the Candlestick Park we all know and love" when describing the strong winds off the bay.

"It's interesting to see these people all bundled up," I remarked to Dietrich.

"Yeah, I know what you mean. I never really gave it any thought while I was playing here. Now I'm used to home games where our fans come out in shorts and T-shirts."

"And, of course, we win a little more often," I added discreetly to avoid inciting the 49ers.

Ted smiled and nodded.

"We had some good teams while I was here," he pointed out. "Just not good enough. We won the division in '71 and '72. We were subpar during my last three years here."

Bender returned to the huddle as we prepared to start the second quarter. With the 49ers looking for a pass, Scott ran a sweep around right end. He got to the 30 to give us another first down.

"All right, gentlemen. Let's keep on moving," Marv remarked.

We kept moving although not always in the right direction. For the second time that day a pass to Grummon was batted down. It was a moot point since Abraham got cited for holding. That put the ball back on the 40.

For the second time this drive we had a first and 20. For the second time on this drive a 4 kama'aina was called in this situation, this time to the right. I wasn't quite as successful this time since I only picked up seven yards to the 33. It was second and 13.

Kerner next went off left tackle and got nowhere. Time was called because Shuford was down.

Dave would be okay and would even be back for the next series. He suffered a slight ankle sprain that he would be able to walk off. He got the predictable polite applause as he was escorted off the field.

We were in our double-double now. I got inside the 20 but was well covered. Dietrich was in the same situation.

Rossi was running a shorter cross pattern over the middle. Bender connected with him at the 26. Rossi maneuvered around a linebacker but still could only get to the 23. It was fourth and three.

"Good job, buddy," I said after running over to help Rossi up. "That was a good job of picking up a few extra yards."

"Yeah but it wasn't enough, dammit," Rossi said although he probably wasn't as bitter as he wanted to appear. "I shoulda got da first down."

"It's okay. We're doing all right."

Walker didn't hesitate to send the field goal unit out. I was disappointed although I didn't blame him. We needed to make it a two-score game.

Guinn would be kicking from the 30 to make it a 40-yard attempt. He would be kicking against the wind. He seemed undaunted as he routinely split the uprights to give us a 10-0 lead with 12:37 left in the first half.

"Don't let this bum you out," Bender said to a few of us at the Gatorade table. "We're going to blow these guys away."

Bender's confidence was reassuring. He usually did epitomize confidence although we didn't always win. I suddenly believed that the only way we were going to lose this game was if we beat ourselves.

I suddenly spotted Allen. He was talking to Malick as he prepared to take the field after the kickoff. He had a big smile on his face. That was also reassuring.

"I do believe we are going to win this game," I remarked to Shuford who was still walking off his sprained ankle.

"And I believe we're also going to beat the spread," he replied lightly; something that could raise eyebrows although Dave honestly never bet on sports of any kind as far as I knew. Small stakes poker or blackjack or a few coins in the slots in Vegas were his only known gambling vices. He avoided the high roller stakes and anything illegal but he often joked about gambling issues in ways that didn't incriminate him. He still needed to be careful.

For the record, we were favored by 17. I didn't care about that but it was hard to miss. The spreads were a regular part of the newspaper sport sections, TV sportscasts and conversations overheard among the public.

Guinn kicked off. The ball was fielded at the four. Hamer brought the return man down at the 20, adding a little more insurance to his chances of staying with the team for the rest of the season.

"All right, defense! Chaaaaaarge!" Allen cried out, waving his arm like a military leader leading his troops into battle.

The 49ers did not seem to be impressed. It took them two plays to pick up a first down at their 36. Two plays later a pass interference call against Blakely gave them another first down at the Hawaii 46.

"Let's play smart football out there!" Walker barked angrily. "We can't be giving away these chunks of yardage!"

Whether we were giving it away or not, the 49ers continued to move. After two first downs they had the ball on the Hawaii 20.

"Maybe we can shut them down now," I said to Scott who was sitting next to me. "Maybe we can force them to go for the field goal."

"And maybe they'll miss the field goal," Scott added.

"Now that's a nice thought. Maybe they'll just turn it over," I remarked hopefully.

That 49ers went to the air. A receiver caught the ball on the eight. He was hit immediately by Morrissey near the sideline.

"Fumble!"

It was a feeble effort to recover the fumble. There wasn't an opportunity for anything more. The ball hit the ground and bounced out of bounds. Although Morrissey hit the receiver almost immediately after the reception, the officials ruled that the receiver had possession. The 49ers had a first and goal at the eight.

426

Two rushes netted the 49ers two yards. It was third and goal. They had to have been frustrated.

I stood up. As confident as I was in my team, I dreaded the thought of them scoring. A ten-point lead was reasonably comfortable for the moment but we needed to expand on that. A 49er touchdown would give them a boost and put them a touchdown away from taking the lead or a field goal away from tying it up.

The 49ers went to the air. It was a quick pass that was caught just as the receiver was crossing the goal line.

Naturally the crowd roared. Quickly the roar died down. The fans were taking note of the yellow flag.

It was, as I obviously hoped, against the 49ers. A lineman got called for holding. The 49ers still had a goose egg on the scoreboard. It was third and goal at the 16.

My heart was pounding as I watched the two units huddling. I believe I did want this game a little too much. Normally I didn't like to see a score that narrowed the gap against us but I seemed to dread the thought more than normal this time.

We were in our 32-dime. That gave us six defensive backs.

That didn't stop the 49ers from attempting a pass. The quarterback hit a receiver in the middle of the end zone. The receiver was hit simultaneously with his reception by Rodgers and Hasegawa. He went down but still clutched the ball.

"(Expletive deleted)!" I cried out.

"(Expletive deleted)!" Walker cried out.

A few similar remarks were heard in various parts of our sideline.

But the fans seemed happy. The crowd was roaring. This time there was no penalty. With the extra point successfully executed the 49ers had cut our lead to 10-7. There was 2:28 left in the half.

"We've got plenty of time. We'll put up another score before halftime," Bender said as he walked in the bench area clapping his hands.

Suddenly I noticed that everybody seemed to be psyched up. We always were but this seemed extreme. The last time I recalled us being this psyched up was in Cleveland to close out 1976.

I took my place on the goal line. As Hasegawa and I slapped fives I noticed that he appeared to be slightly downtrodden. Being on the field while the 49ers scored left him feeling low.

"Hey, it's okay. They had to score sometime. We're going to bury these clowns and celebrate all the way home."

Rich grinned. I hoped that meant he believed me.

The kick headed Rich's way. He caught it six yards deep in the end zone. He started to run, then thought better of it and downed the ball.

We started the drive by showing the 49ers that we were willing to mix it up. With three timeouts and the two-minute warning we had plenty of time.

Scott went up the middle to the 24. We used our first timeout to stop the clock at 2:20.

As Bender conversed with Walker I glanced up in the bleachers. I caught sight of the Lafayettes several rows behind our bench. I suppose they were a large part of the reason why I was feeling so good about myself. My reunion with them went as well as could be imagined. They seemed to love and care for me in a way all their own. It was just like it was a few years earlier, yet somehow it was even better.

With my possibly future in-laws watching along with several thousand disgruntled and frustrated 49er fans I made a leaping catch of a pass in front of our bench at the Hawaii 44. Although I was only about a yard in bounds, I wasn't able to get out of bounds. I was hit as soon as my feet hit the ground and dropped on the spot.

It was still a good play. We decided to preserve our final two timeouts and let the clock run down to the two-minute warning. We had plenty of time to travel 56 yards.

We went back to the air when play resumed. Bender hit Dietrich on a short pass at the Hawaii 45. Ted crossed midfield to the 48 to give us a second and two. We used our second timeout with 1:51 left.

Although it didn't seem as critical, we had to be careful to avoid a repeat of what happened two weeks earlier at the end of our game against the Rams. We were hanging on to our final timeout in case we needed to stop the clock for a field goal. We still had to be judicious in our use of the clock even if we did still have a timeout.

When play resumed Grummon caught a pass at the line of scrimmage. He raced to the San Francisco 42 and stepped out of bounds. That stopped the clock at 1:44 and gave us another first down.

Bender was sacked at the Hawaii 49 on the next play. That got the crowd roaring. The clock also continued to run.

We lined up quickly. Shuford got a little too anxious and flinched before he snapped the ball. That cost us five yards to give us a second and 23 at our own 44. The crowd was roaring as we were showing signs of self-destruction.

Working quickly, Bender hit me near the right hash mark at the 49er 34. I ran obliquely before stepping out of bounds at the 29. We had another first down and quieted the crowd. The clock showed 1:12.

It only took one more play. Bender dropped back with excellent protection. He fired a perfect pass that Slater caught just short of the goal line. He was hit and wrestled down but not until his momentum carried him and his tacklers two yards deep in the end zone.

"Yeah! All right!" I exclaimed, leaping up with two clenched fists high over my head.

Triumphantly we ran to our sideline. Guinn did his job, putting the ball through the uprights to extend our lead to 17-7. It climaxed the perfect response to the 49er touchdown.

We were pretty loose. Perhaps we were a little too loose; too sure of ourselves.

"I hope Candlestick Park has good hot dogs. That's the only thing these fans are going to enjoy from now on," Prendergast remarked.

We had a ten-point lead. One would think we were up by 50 with the way we were acting. There was a lot of laughing and joking on our sideline. Did we really have a right to be that sure of ourselves with a mere ten-point lead before halftime?

I don't think we were overconfident. We were simply happy with the way the game was going at this point. We normally weren't this loose in this situation but I don't believe anybody really assumed the game was in our hip pockets.

Or so I hoped.

Guinn kicked off. The ball was fielded three yards deep in the end zone. The return man dodged and weaved his way to the 26. The clock showed 49 seconds.

The 49ers were going for it. Perhaps they wanted to humble us before halftime and then pull an upset. A long bomb downfield was overthrown, stopping the clock at 42 seconds.

They meant business.

But so did we. We switched to a 32 dime.

A pass on the next play was intercepted by Morrissey at midfield. As virtually everybody on our sideline cheered him on, Morrissey returned the interception to the San Francisco 38.

We were within Guinn's field goal range although it would be a low percentage attempt at this distance, especially since he would be kicking against the wind. We had 27 seconds to score a touchdown or move to the ball to a more comfortable range. We still had one timeout.

The 49er defense served notice that it wouldn't go down easy. A pass to me inside the 20 was broken up. That left us with 19 seconds.

It was the defensive line that foiled us on the next play. It forced Bender to scramble. He managed to pick up a yard before stepping out of bounds at the 37. That stopped the clock with 12 seconds.

Rossi and Slater came in. Grummon and Scott went out. We were going into our double-double.

"We've got time for one quick try for six," Bender said in the huddle. "Double-double Pearl Harbor on two. On two. Ready?"

"Break!"

I took my position in the right slot. The play Bender called meant all receivers were to go to the end zone. We would either score a touchdown or else use the remaining seconds to go for a long field goal.

As I got into position I flashed back. The 12 seconds were exactly what we had two weeks earlier in the fourth quarter against the Rams. The impromptu volleyball game in the end zone chewed up every one of those 12 seconds. I hoped that history wouldn't repeat itself.

From the shotgun formation Bender took the snap. He had to scramble a little while searching for an open receiver. He finally passed to Dietrich in the right corner of the end zone.

A defensive back tipped the ball up. He dove for it and got his hands on it but couldn't hang on. The ball hit the ground. There were three seconds left and I heaved a sigh of relief.

Our field goal unit took the field. I regretted not getting the touchdown but accepted it. The 49ers came through when they needed to the most.

It would be a 54-yard attempt. The field goal unit broke its huddle. Billingsley knelt down to take the snap at the 44 with Guinn positioned behind him.

"They're going to call a timeout," I said to nobody in particular.

The 49ers called timeout. It was a smart move. I only regretted that they were smart enough to know that.

We started over when play was ready to resume. Billingsley took Arroyo's snap and set the ball down. Guinn put his foot into it and got it up despite a diving effort by a 49er to block it.

"Looks good, looks good, looks good . . . ," I said, trying to will the ball on course.

But it was wide to the left. It didn't miss by much but it didn't matter. We would retreat to the locker room with a ten-point lead.

I relieved myself before grabbing a cup of Gatorade and a Hershey bar. I walked by Rossi who was sitting in front of his locker sipping Gatorade and smoking a cigarette.

"How's it going?" I asked.

Dave looked up and grinned.

"Ah'm doin' good," he replied. "Ah just hope ah get to catch a few more passes."

I nodded and grinned, then headed toward my locker. On the way I crossed paths with Dietrich.

"How's it going?" I asked. "Are you having any trouble with your sideline patterns?"

Ted broke into a broad smile and shook his head before heading toward his locker. A few of our teammates heard my inquiry and chuckled softly.

We were supremely confident although, the fact is, we should have had a bigger lead. At least Walker seemed to believe that.

"You're giving them too much," Walker told us just before we were to return to the field. "We have a much better team than they do but we're not playing like it. Execute! Execute!"

Walker bit down on his lip. He looked around the room.

"We'll be receiving to start the second half," he pointed out. "Let's waste no time. We're going to stick it down their (expletive deleted) throats!"

I got in position with Hasegawa on my right as we got set for the second half kickoff. I wanted to stick it down their throats like Walker described. We could start right with a good return.

As luck would have it, it was coming my way. I caught the ball at the one.

I wound up with a pretty good return. Good blocking paved the way. I also helped the cause with my own defiance; flat out refusing to go down. Twice between the 20 and 30 I broke tackles. I tried to cut to elude another red jersey but he managed to grab me by the shoulder pads and swing me down at the 37. It was still a good return.

Somebody in a red jersey reached down to help me up. Sportsmanship wasn't dead.

"Good run," the opponent said evenly and retreated to the sideline.

A five-yard rush by Scott and a 15-yard pass to Dietrich got us a first down at the San Francisco 43. That was followed by a pass near the right sideline to Kerner. Jeff caught the ball at the 35 and picked up three more yards to give us a first down at the 32.

Although we were moving pretty well on our own, accepting a little charity was not beneath us. We were only too happy to accept the five yards when the 49ers got called for encroachment. We had first and five at the 27.

Rushes by Scott and Kerner got us a first down at the 19. That was followed by a five-yard run by Scott and a pass that I caught while going into a slide on the one-yard line but on a bounce to give us a third and five at the 14.

We were going to the air. Bender hit me again at the one but this time while I was on the run and the pass didn't bounce. I was tripped up immediately but stumbled a few yards into the end zone before going down. Our quest to score on the opening drive of the half was fulfilled.

"Spike it!" I said when I got up, handing the ball to Shuford. The center from Notre Dame became one of the few linemen to have the opportunity to spike the ball after a touchdown.

It always feels good to score a touchdown.

At least if your side is winning or your score keeps your hopes alive if your team is behind. I stood aglow as I watched Guinn convert on the PAT. Our lead was extended to 24-7.

"Good job," Bennici said, patting me on the back. It showed how funny sports could be sometimes. On the drive I had a good kick return and caught the winning touchdown pass, picking up 50 of the 99 yards we had to travel from where I fielded the kickoff. Along the way there was outstanding blocking, quality rushes by Kerner and Scott, receptions by Kerner and Dietrich, and good passing by Bender.

431

Yet all it would say in the box score was that I had a 14-yard touchdown reception. Bender would get some credit for his effort but very little else would be reported about the drive.

But I was happy that we scored and also happy that I got to take it in. Marv was in his eleventh season and had never scored a touchdown on any level but he was also happy. We were both glad to have a 17-point lead.

Yet it wasn't enough. We weren't even halfway through the third quarter. Our victim was down but not quite ready for the count.

"It's not over yet," Bennici reminded us. "We've got to continue fighting when we get the ball back. No matter what the defense does, we've got to put more points on the board."

It didn't surprise me that the 49ers didn't run on the field with sad or scared expressions of those about to be ambushed by machine gun fire. After returning the kick from three yards deep in the end zone to the 23 they headed upfield. After two first downs they had the ball on the 50.

After a three-yard run around left end our defense decided that the Niners had gone far enough. The Niner quarterback took the snap and dropped back with Allen on his tail. He cut to his left and met up with Pratt who brought him down at the San Francisco 44. That was followed by an incomplete pass which produced a fourth and 16.

I took my place near the 15 to field the punt. I suppose the 49ers may have had a communication problem. Before they could get the snap off they got cited for delay of game. That made it fourth and 21 at the 39.

As the yards were being paced off Hasegawa drifted back toward me as I took a few steps forward. He had an amused look on his face.

"Gee, do you think they might try a fake?" he asked jocularly.

"If they do it'll explain why they are where they are in the standings," I replied lightly.

Under the circumstances a fake punt might not have been the worst idea in the world. They didn't have that much to lose by trying. If everybody on our punt return unit was taking the situation as lightly as Rich and me they might just pull off a successful fake.

Fortunately they punted. I caught the ball at the 22 and returned it to the 28; an unspectacular six-yard return.

Equally as unspectacular was our drive. A rush by Scott and a pass to Slater gave us a first down at our own 48. Unfortunately another rush by Scott, an incomplete pass on a hurried throw and a pass to Kerner only got us to the San Francisco 45. It was fourth and three.

I was annoyed at the futility. I hate to say it but I, at least subconsciously, was not taking the 49ers seriously. Instead of acknowledging the fact that they had capable NFL players, I led myself to believe that we could simply will touchdowns against these guys. It was another example of players on good teams having trouble getting up for a team that wasn't so good.

432

From the fans' perspective it probably wasn't a very exciting game. The margin was fairly wide. We knew, though, that the 49ers were capable of catching up.

Jablonski went for the coffin corner. The ball bounced inside the ten. Hasegawa raced down the left sideline. The ball had just barely reached the end zone before Rich could touch it down. The 49ers had a first down at the 20.

We were for the moment tearing up the middle of the field; at least as much as two teams could on artificial turf. The 49ers managed a first down but got no further than their own 38. Before I knew it I was fielding a punt at the 29 which I returned to the 37. There were 23 seconds left in the third quarter.

A sweep around right end by Scott picked up ten yards to the 47. As the seconds ticked down the officials called time with nine seconds left. A measurement showed that we had our first down and the clock started again to allow the third quarter to expire.

"We've got to hold them," Scott remarked as we huddled while Bender conversed with Walker on the sideline.

"I've got a better idea. Let's score first and then hold 'em," Marv remarked.

"My sentiments exactly," I said.

The brief exchange seemed frivolous. In retrospect, I think it charged us up.

After Scott charged across midfield to the 49 on the opening play of the final quarter Kerner caught a pass over the middle at the 49er 38. He fought for two more yards to the 36. We were within field goal range with the wind at our backs but we didn't want a field goal.

Scott managed only two yards up the middle and we went to the air again. Grummon got a step on a defensive back near the left sideline and made the catch at the 13. The defensive back wrestled him down at the eight. It was first and goal.

"All right! Way to go!" I exclaimed, slapping Grummon on the back as he rose to his feet while clapping his hands.

"Let's do it!" he called out, pumping his fists in the air as we ran to where we would huddle near the 20.

The 49ers bore down on us after that. Runs by Scott and Kerner produced only two yards apiece. It was third and goal at the four.

At this point the 49ers started showing signs of self-destructing. They got called for encroachment to put the ball at the two. They then sacked Bender at the six but got called for a late hit, giving us a third and goal at the one.

"All right. We're three feet away," Bender remarked in the huddle. "Let's do it in one play."

Scott went up the middle. He leaped up and managed about a yard. A few of us raised our arms to signal a touchdown.

But nobody wearing a striped shirt was raising his arms.

"He made it," I said although primarily to myself.

The nose of the ball was spotted about three inches from the goal line. I didn't know how tempted Walker may have been to go for the field goal. I refused to look toward the sideline, ostensibly believing that the field goal unit couldn't come if I didn't see it coming.

Only McCracken came in and it was with a play. Dietrich went out. We were going with two tight ends.

"Dotted I, double tight," Bender directed in the huddle, "Kailua left on three, on three. Ready?"

"Break!"

As I assumed my position directly behind Scott I knew that we absolutely had to score. With the clock ticking down with less than ten and-a-half minutes the 17-point lead seemed reasonably secure. A 24-point lead would seem like the perfect time for the 49ers to wave their white flags.

Bender took the snap. He faked a handoff to Kerner up the middle and then stretched to his left to hand off to Scott. I was running behind Scott so if Bender and Scott didn't connect I could take the handoff.

The handoff to Scott was flawless. He lunged forward.

Touchdown!

"Yeah! All right!: I cried out, leaping in the air with two fists thrust up. This time the officials agreed with us.

Those of us not on the PAT unit ran off the field in triumph, slapping fives with the members of the PAT team who crossed paths with us.

Walker was smiling on the sideline. He smacked a few of us on the back as we reached him. His smile appeared to be more out of relief than triumph.

Guinn's PAT attempt was true. We led 31-7 with 10:16 left.

I noticed a lot of fans making for the exits. The 49ers themselves weren't quite as ready to surrender as their fans were. They tried to narrow the gap and picked up one first down. Blakely then intercepted a pass at the Hawaii 44 and returned it to the San Francisco 23.

"Let's go, offense!" Walker called.

That surprised me. I thought that he would be sending in the backups. The only change he made was he put Billingsley in at quarterback.

After Scott picked up five yards off left tackle Walker replaced Grummon, Hayer, Shuford, Marv and Abraham with McCracken, Kimmitt, Arroyo, Hubert and Daniels, respectively. The only starting lineman still in was Stanek since Hubert was our only backup guard.

Scott ran a sweep around right end to give us third and one at the 14. I then went off right tackle and, possibly more because of a worn down defense than my own ability, got all the way down to the five.

A 49er generously helped me up. He whacked me on the rear.

"Good run, Dockman," he said.

"Thanks, man," I replied and noticed Rossi running on the field while calling my name. Also coming in were Collier, Roberts and Slater. Kerner, Scott, Dietrich and I ran off. We were given a warm reception on the sideline led by Walker.

Two plays later Collier took it in from the two. With the PAT it was 38-7 with 3:19 left.

Everything was over except the final 3:19. The 49ers picked up two more first downs but couldn't convert on the third one. Billingsley then took two snaps and dropped down to run out the clock.

I don't mind saying I felt pretty good. We now had one more victory than we had in 1976 and were very much alive in the playoff hunt.

Dubois said the postgame prayer. Walker then held up a football.

"Okay, game ball. For playing an all-around solid game and scoring two touchdowns. He also went past the thousand-yard mark in receiving for the season."

Walker then tossed the ball to me while my teammates cheered. I was very surprised but happily so. A game ball was always an honor. I was surprised, though, to get the game ball twice in the same season.

A victory is a victory and this was a good victory. We were 8-4, meaning that the absolute worst we could wind up was 8-6. We were gunning for 10-4 and a playoff berth but we didn't want to get too far ahead of ourselves. For the moment we savored our most recent victory.

Of course we were aware of our playoff standing. The Rams had just beat the Raiders to raise their record to 9-3, giving them a one-game lead over us for the division title. We had the upper hand in the wild card chase since the Giants beat the slumping Cardinals to drop them to 7-5. The Bears were also 7-5 after handing the Bucs their 26th consecutive defeat. Also still alive were the Redskins who seemed to come out of nowhere to appear with a 7-5 record. Regardless of what the Bears, who were still competing with the Vikings for their division title, Redskins and Cardinals did the final two weeks of the season, we were now guaranteed a playoff berth if we won our final two games.

The last two games wouldn't be easy. Our next opponent was Atlanta which was still technically in contention for the wild card although the Falcons' hopes were dimmed after losing to New England to drop to 6-6. The Falcons came out the gate fast at the start of the season but seemed to have reached their peak when they beat us in October. Although the Falcons had fallen on hard times, they would be heading to Honolulu with the knowledge that they had beaten us before and there was no reason for them to believe that they couldn't do it again.

435

But Atlanta was still a week away. I joined my teammates in savoring the day's victory.

As I had done several weeks earlier in Los Angeles, I showered and dressed quickly while answering reporters' questions. Carol's family would be waiting for a few final minutes with me before I had to board the bus to the airport.

We completed our reunion. I was in excellent spirits since we had won. Reconnecting with the four Lafayettes also had my spirits soaring. I loved them all and had missed them terribly. It wasn't until our reunion that I became fully cognizant of exactly how much I had missed them.

"Carol was so happy that you and she got back together," Carol's mother said somewhat emotionally just before I was to board the bus that would take my teammates and me to the airport. "She missed you so much while she was away. She was really afraid that you wouldn't want to have anything to do with her when she moved back to Honolulu."

The frankness of Danielle Lafayette's words and tone struck a nerve. Her comment made me finally believe it may have actually been for real this time. It had always been real, of course, but I was beginning to believe that Carol was now truly with me to stay.

Roughly six months had passed since that day when I found Carol at Kahala Mall. We were getting along great although we didn't seem to be growing closer as fast as we probably should have. I had been good to her but I had also been holding back. Perhaps it was time to bust down the barrier.

Initially after Carol's mother's remark I opened my mouth. I was tempted to give a very graphic account of how I felt. Despite knowing that there was a void in my life during Carol's absence, this experience told me exactly how miserable my life had been without Carol. I met several nice women, as well as a few who weren't so nice, during Carol's absence but even the best of the bunch couldn't hold a candle to Carol. I was truly blessed to have her back.

I wanted to tell the Lafayettes all of that but I didn't. It didn't seem appropriate since I hadn't told Carol yet. I was going to have to rectify that soon.

"I'm just glad that she's back," I said tentatively as I resisted the urge to unveil my most veritable feelings. "I really missed her but I . . . I think we're going to be okay."

I believe that concise account told the Lafayettes what they needed to know. It also told me what I needed to know. For the first time in more than three years I started thinking of the Lafayettes as my future in-laws. It was still presumptuous but I believed that Carol and I were destined to make it.

436

As our aircraft took off I recalled a flight from San Francisco earlier that year. As the aircraft ascended on my flight to Vancouver we flew right over Candlestick Park.

That's where we're going to beat the crap out of the 49ers, I thought to myself. I didn't necessarily believe we would rout them by 31 points. I was merely thinking positive. A mere one-point verdict in our favor would have sufficed.

Of course my trip to Canada was ill-fated. I was now heading home to what I finally accepted as the absolutely right woman for me. I was determined to find a way to eliminate the rough edges and break down whatever barriers that might have still stood.

It was a pleasant flight to Honolulu. Flights after victories usually were. This was our final flight of the regular season so it was good that our final road excursion was a positive one. Flights from Miami, Atlanta and Chicago hadn't been so pleasant.

I wasn't rowdy. I was simply at peace. The victory, the fact that I had played a good game, our playoff hopes, the reunion with the Lafayettes and my newfound optimism about my future with Carol were all factors. None of my teammates understood the significance of the perpetual smile on my face.

CHAPTER EIGHTEEN
Catharsis

Normally after we beat the crap out of an opponent Walker uses the film session as an opportunity to verbally beat the crap out of us. We can be full of ourselves immediately after the game and on our day off the next day but the day after that could be very humbling. Walker would become a fire breathing martinet to bring us down to earth.

Walker surprised us during this film session. He was downright civil. He pointed out mistakes but didn't rant, rave and belittle. Perhaps he knew what we were expecting and hated the idea of being so predictable.

In all likelihood, Walker simply didn't want to take the chance of bringing us down. This was a crucial game coming up. Our playoff hopes hinged on this game and we were playing a team that beat us earlier in the season. Walker seemed to believe it was best that he start building us up early in the week.

"There isn't much left for the Falcons except to play the spoiler," Walker stressed during our joint meeting after the film sessions on Tuesday. "They are still technically alive in the playoff picture but they need for you and a few other teams to completely collapse. They beat you once and want to beat you again, especially since they know that losing to you will kill any slim hope they might have to reach the playoffs. We're not going to let them beat us."

We were focused. Our workouts that week were well-structured and our execution was superb. We were confident but not cocky. That was a good sign.

Naturally Carol was on my mind. I wanted to find the right moment to break through whatever barrier was between us. I wanted to take care of it before the Atlanta game.

Tuesday night was out because I would be busy with my TV show. On Wednesday I was to be the keynote speaker at a football banquet in Waipahu. On Thursday we would be going to a concert together so that didn't seem likely even though we would be together.

Friday night seemed ideal. Carol didn't have to teach the next day and I only had a light workout. I figured we had much to discuss and could feel free to make it a late night.

For the time being I focused on football and my other commitments. Walker even decided to forgo the prepractice meetings on Thursday. He felt we deserved a shorter workday as a change of pace. All we had on Thursday was our regular workout.

On Thursday I left Aloha Stadium at a little after noon and headed toward home. One of the advantages of being a football player is there are some comparably shorter workdays. With as hard as we work, putting our bodies through some brutal experiences, we pack at least eight hours' worth into our compacted workdays.

Before I left for practice that morning Don Simmons gave me a call.

"What are you doing for lunch today?" he asked.

When I told him I had no specific plans he invited me to join him and Roy Mulligan for lunch at Jose's; a Mexican restaurant on Koko Head Avenue in Kaimuki. This was on my way home.

I had an assortment of errands to run that day. Taking the time for lunch caused my day to be scrunched together although it was well worth it. I valued my friends, especially those closest to me. Don may have been my business agent but he had also been a close friend in the years prior to that and remained a close friend. Roy was also a close friend.

One of the many advantages of playing football in Hawaii for me was that I could continue to socialize with people I had known while I was in college. I did not actually go to college with Don and Roy but I knew them in my college days. I could have made new friends had I played in Dallas, Houston, St. Louis or anywhere else. It would not have been the same.

After lunch I stopped in Aina Haina. My agenda that day included helping Marv move in some new furniture he had bought. I built up a pretty good sweat in the process. That cancelled out the shower I had taken at the stadium.

I barely had enough time to shower and dress when I got home. The climax of the day's schedule was the Fleetwood Mac concert at the Neal Blaisdell Arena. This was the second of two shows featuring Mick Fleetwood and company. My former roommate had gone the night before and assured me that I was in for a great show.

Stephen Bishop was the opening act and got the concert off to an excellent start. Normally performers who required an opening act had the local promoters find a local group to perform. Occasionally the opening act would be somebody less obscure. Bishop had been on the charts with his signature piece, *On and On*, rising near the top earlier that year.

At intermission Carol and I went to the concourse that circled the outside of the arena. I got a beer for myself and a wine cooler and popcorn for Carol. We stood at the railing which bordered the concourse and a fish pond that surrounded the concourse, talking softly to each other and saying hello to a few friends who happened by.

We were both casually dressy for the concert. I was wearing dark blue slacks, black dress shoes and a blue aloha shirt. Carol was wearing a pink skirt, pink medium heels and a white ruffled blouse. Her long blonde hair was worn loosely except for pink barrettes on each side of her head.

Carol turned to face the fish pond. She threw kernals of popcorn to the fish and ducks, lightly laughing to herself at the sight of dozens of fish and a few ducks lunging for the few morsels of food.

I subtly looked amorously at Carol. She appeared easily amused.

439

"You know it really is special having you back with me," I remarked impulsively. It was something I had obviously been wanting to say, especially since my return from San Francisco, but was trying to figure out a proper way to say it. When I finally did say it the words simply slipped out. I had honestly planned to save it for the next night.

Carol seemed to tense up and frowned as she kept her gaze fixed on the fish pond. I suppose I had taken her by surprise.

After several seconds she looked at me with a puzzled expression. She hesitated; uncertain of how to respond.

"I have no way of knowing how you feel," she replied in a tone that was blatantly honest without sounding angry or hurt. "All you seem to want to talk about sometimes are your playoff chances and Tampa Bay's losing streak."

Suddenly it was my turn to be uncertain about how to respond. She may not have been open about her feelings to this point but I definitely hadn't been.

"Perhaps we should talk," I said softly. "I mean *really* talk."

Carol nodded.

"Tonight?" she suggested. "After the concert?"

"After the concert if you're up for it. Let's open up."

Carol gave me a smile that seemed gratuitous. I returned what was probably a similar smile and gently stroked her hair a few times. We followed that up with a short tender kiss.

"We can make it work," I commented softly.

Carol nodded. She looked relieved. I probably did, too.

Fleetwood Mac put on an outstanding show. It was the best concert I had been to up to that point and I had seen some rocking good bands ranging from the Rolling Stones to Creedence Clearwater Revival to John Denver to the Yellow Rose Band.

In 1977 concerts did not normally include lavish props featured in later years which helped escalate ticket prices. Fleetwood Mac's show was simply rockin' good music.

The most visual effect of the show was a dance Stevie Nicks did during *Rhiannon*. Done during an extended guitar solo at the end of the song, there is no way to describe it that would give it an accurate picture and do it justice. It was simply extremely titillating and unforgettable.

Overall the entire group put its heart into the show and the music was flawless. The effort was well-appreciated.

After the concert Carol and I went down the road to the Columbia Inn to start sorting things out while enjoying a post-concert drink. That was not an especially smart move if we were serious about getting our relationship on track. Although we were speaking French in our quest to keep our conversation private, we had to guard our emotions since the facility was so crowded. We were also periodically interrupted by people who came over to say hello.

A few times we were interrupted by well-wishing strangers. They came over with the "Excuse me, aren't you Jay Dockman?" line which was succeeded by polite acknowledgement in the affirmative. They would leave quickly after getting an autograph and/or wishing me luck in Sunday's game.

After we finished at the Columbia Inn we walked back to Carol's place. We had walked to the concert since Carol lived only a couple of blocks from the arena. As we walked back to her place we held hands as if it were for the first time since we got back together. We had held hands several times in the previous six months but there was something very reassuring this time. Always before it was as if we were going through the motions while hoping to fully get on track. This time I felt as if we were a more committed couple.

Going to Carol's place was the right move. We had the privacy to open up and also speak English. We covered a lot of ground, discussing the earlier chapter of our relationship, the reunion six months earlier, all that had transpired since our reunion and even some things from the three-year estrangement. It was a veritably emotional experience for us both.

"I know how wrong I was to have run off the way I did," Carol admitted weakly. "It was probably the most stupid thing I've done in my life but it was a long time ago and we've been back together for six months. How much longer are you going to punish me?"

That struck a nerve. In keeping a little distance between Carol and me I honestly didn't realize that she might have been getting hurt. I put both hands on her shoulders and squeezed affectionately as I sat facing her on her living room sofa.

"I'm not punishing you," I replied in a manner I hoped she would see was sincere. "I was just afraid . . . afraid to knock down the barrier, I guess. I wanted to be sure that you were going to stay this time. A few years ago I was so in love with you and so grateful to have you and. . . ."

I was about to point out that I had even been looking forward to the day that I would ask her to marry me but I caught myself. I was never more sure that I was with the woman I wanted to marry; that nobody else could fulfill my life the way she could. It still seemed premature to mention any thoughts of marriage.

"You were the primary reason why I signed to play with the Hawaiians," I finally continued, recalling the calamity of having three professional sports franchises vying for my services with representatives from the Red Sox and Cowboys stalking me while the Hawaiians were more low key since they needed to fill a full roster and couldn't afford to put so much effort into a single player. "I probably would have signed to play for Hawaii anyway but what convinced me most of all that I needed to stay here was you. I dreaded the thought of signing with the Cowboys or Red Sox because it would have meant having to be away from you for several months. I was fortunate that the Hawaiians drafted me because it meant that I could stay here with you . . . and then I came back from training camp and discovered you were gone with virtually no trace. I can't begin to describe how painful that was."

Carol closed her eyes. She took a deep breath through her nose. She appeared to be fighting the urge to cry.

I tried to help. I pulled her close and held her. That was probably what caused her to cave in to the urge to break down but her tears were probably very cleansing for her.

The experience was probably also very cleansing for me. I didn't cry although I wanted to. Crying was not beneath me and I even admit to having privately cried at one point a few years earlier when I finally accepted the fact that Carol was gone. There was still the masculine mystique which mandated that a man must hide his emotions and I had practically taught myself not to cry.

"I didn't mean to hurt you," she sobbed while holding me as tightly as I held her.

"I know you didn't. I even knew it then. I knew you well enough to know you wouldn't do something maliciously. That's probably why I never really got angry. I still missed you. I missed you terribly."

"I missed you, too. The day that I decided for whatever the reason that I couldn't come back to Honolulu, I watched you play on TV. I cried through the entire game. I wanted to come back so bad but. . . ."

"I really wanted to find out where you were and go get you," I added. "I just wasn't sure if that was the right thing to do. If I had known you were in Hilo I would have gone to get you. If I discovered you were in San Francisco or Paris or Tokyo or . . . on Venus I would have gone to get you. I resisted the urge to find out where you were even though it would have been very easy for me to find out. Stacy would have told me. All I had to do was ask."

Carol took a deep breath and cracked a semblance of a smile.

"Good ol' Stacy," she said, referring to her best friend in whom she had confided prior to her departure for Hilo and with whom she kept in touch. "I told her not to tell you where I was but she would have been absolutely right to tell you. You had every right to know."

"It was very tempting to ask. I just figured that your need to be away might have superseded my need to have you with me so I didn't ask. All I could do was hope you would get everything straightened out and come back. While I was still at the Manoa Zoo every time there was a knock on my door or the phone rang I hoped it would be you. By the end of the year I figured you would never be back and I had to try to let go."

What also came up was my ill-fated trip to Canada. I had told Carol practically nothing about my experience with Annica to this point. I was

442

aware that Annica's antics had me somewhat skittish about romance. I didn't realize until this moment how substantially Annica figured in my reluctance to commit myself more openly to Carol.

"It's her loss," Carol pointed out half-seriously.

"Whatever," I said. "I was probably afraid to be as nice to you as I wanted to be because of her. If you don't mind my saying so, I was really good to her. She was naive and not especially well-educated but I didn't belittle her for it. I accepted her for what she was. The reason I went up to her place in British Columbia was because it meant so much to her and I wanted to keep the romance going if that was what was meant to be. It never dawned on me that she might use what I thought was a very noble gesture as an opportunity to accuse me of being. . . . "

I couldn't finish the sentence. What Annica did was extremely degrading although I knew that in the end it reflected on her, not me. It actually angered me a little that Annica had played such a role in the barrier that prevented Carol and me from getting closer. The barrier was justified initially, I believe, when Carol and I reunited after a three-year hiatus. Annica was simply part of the reason why the barrier was as strong as it was; why it took six months to raze.

"I suppose I should feel sorry for her," I said. "She seems to believe that a man has to be abusive to be a real man or else he deserves to be abused. I tried to treat her like she was an intelligent, worthwhile human being. She picked one helluva way to show her gratitude."

"You did the right thing," Carol replied. "She'll always miss out on something really wonderful as long as she has the wrong attitude about men. You've always treated me right. I've always been very grateful."

I told Carol that I was actually glad now that Annica and I didn't last although I would never be glad for the way we split up. Carol was a much better fit for me.

"If I had known that you would eventually be back I would like to believe I would have waited," I said. "I would like to believe I wouldn't have even dated. I was with a lot of women while you were gone although not nearly as many as people have allowed themselves to believe. Despite the reputation that I wound up having, I was actually looking for the right woman and was hoping to settle down in a monogamous relationship. Now I know what I knew my senior year in college. You are the right woman."

As Thursday evening turned into Friday morning our bond continued growing stronger. For the first time since we reconnected we were as comfortable together as we were in college. In retrospect, we had probably spent the previous six months acting like an old happily married couple who had lost the spark. We got along great and were happily committed even if neither of us said so. Unfortunately we both occasionally wondered when we would finally truly become an uninhibited couple again.

Or even *if* it would ever happen.

The three years without each other were difficult for both of us. Having experienced the sincerest form of love, I spent three years truly cognizant of what I was missing. Carol's absence drove home the adage that those who have the most also have the most to lose.

Although I had reacquired my college pre-Carol embellished reputation as a hustler and, I am sorry to say, sometimes lived up to that reputation, I actually went more than a year and-a-half without dating after Carol's enigmatic disappearance. The only time I took a woman out prior to that was at the very end of 1974 when I went to California and an old friend set me up on a blind date which I reluctantly accepted. My date was reasonably attractive but I didn't do her justice. Despite the fact that I was trying to get used to carrying on without Carol, I spent the entire evening trying to pretend that my date *was* Carol.

I couldn't fool myself. That is probably why I waited more than a year before I went on another date. I couldn't enjoy myself until I was ready to give my full attention to the ladies who were out with me. I literally went through all of 1975 without a single romantic encounter.

"I never stopped loving you," Carol said sincerely as she squeezed my hand. "I've loved you from the day we met."

As ashamed as I am to admit it, this was the first time either of us used the "L" word since the day we reconnected. When we were together previously it took us four months to say that we loved each other. This time around it took us six months to express what we always knew.

"I've always loved you," I said softly, nearly losing control of my emotions. As maudlin as it might seem, it meant probably more to me to tell Carol I loved her as it meant for her to hear it.

Carol smiled, then looked uneasy. It appeared that something else was on her mind.

"There is one thing we need to discuss that's very important," Carol said with a serious but uneasy expression. "I. . . . I won't be having sex until my wedding night."

Carol's feelings came as no surprise to me. The only thing that surprised me was that she thought it was necessary to broach the subject.

I was thrilled to death just to be with Carol and was equally thrilled that we were razing the barrier between us. I had no intention of trying to lure her into bed before she was ready.

"When have I tried to persuade you to have sex?" I asked evenly.

"You haven't," she replied, "and I'm grateful. I just wanted to make sure you know my standard. I have to stick by it because I won't be able to live with myself if I don't. I am not active as a Catholic anymore but my Christian values are still the same. I love God and want to live my life as much as possible according to how He wants me to live. Just because I don't go to church on Sundays doesn't mean that I'm not a believer."

444

I nodded slowly. I didn't believe Carol was telling me anything I didn't already know or at least suspect.

"If sex is important to you and you intend to fulfill whatever sexual need you believe you have by picking up other women, just say so now," she continued. "We can part as friends."

I was numbed by this. I was probably even slightly hurt that Carol suggested that I might put so much emphasis on sex that I would resort to getting it elsewhere.

"I don't. . . . I don't want to come across like I'm setting a series of rules for you to follow," Carol said after a long uneasy moment. "I just have to be adamant about this. I can't have sex until I'm married and I can't be with somebody who. . . ."

Carol didn't finish her statement but I obviously knew what she was trying to say. She probably stopped because she feared sounding like she was accusing me.

"During the earlier part of our previous relationship I cheated on you a few times," I said somberly. "I still recall how much I hurt you. Do you actually think I would do something like that again."

Carol shook her head slowly. I could tell that she was flustered. I squeezed her hands and gave her what I hoped was a reassuring smile.

"I cheated on you, as I recall, three times," I said. "At the time I wasn't sure where I stood with you and I . . . was very . . . stupid. Three times I had sex with other girls when we were together before. That was three times too many. You forgave me, didn't you?"

Carol nodded.

"And I never did it again," I added. "I promised you I would never do it again and I didn't. I figured that my sex life was over until you and I got married. I was more than okay with that. What was important was being with you; not getting you into bed with me."

Carol looked almost grateful. Suddenly her chin quivered. Somehow I knew what was coming next.

"But we did have sex together," she pointed out in a barely audible voice; a tear descending from each eye.

I felt bad about this recollection. I felt sorry for her. There still seemed to be only one retort to this.

"And whose idea was that?" I asked.

Carol nodded somberly at the rhetorical question. I took her in my arms to hold her close.

"I know it was my idea," she finally said once she had almost completely composed herself, still melted in my embrace. "I remember how hard you tried to talk me out of it . . . how you told me I would be irreversibly changed and that you didn't want me getting hurt. I remember being surprised by your reluctance because I figured you would be like most other men who would jump at the opportunity but you said it wasn't that

445

important to you. You were probably the only heterosexual man anywhere who would have tried to talk me out of it. I realized later that you were actually trying to protect me. You didn't know it but your love and concern for me made me that much more determined to go through with it. Everybody else was doing it and I figured it was okay for us since I had gotten an IUD and we were so much in love."

I wasn't sure how to respond. We had been very much in love and that, to me, had been justification although I had had sex with several girls with whom I was not in love dating back to my first time when I was 16. What heightened my concern was that Carol was still a virgin at the time. I knew she could not possibly fathom how she would feel once she sacrificed her virginity. I didn't want her doing anything she would regret later.

"That night I prayed for forgiveness," Carol continued, tilting back to look me in the eye. "I realized that I had been wrong to have had sex before marriage, especially since I was the one who initiated it and that I didn't heed your words when you tried to talk me out of it, and I wanted God to forgive me."

"I don't think you ever told me about that," I said.

"I'm pretty sure I didn't. It was between God and me. I did feel as if He had forgiven me even if I did give up something I couldn't get back. For the next few months our relationship was the way it had always been . . . and then we did it again."

Our second time was the night before I left for my first WFL training camp. In that case we spontaneously went into a sexual mode. Had we not had sex the first time roughly four months earlier I am positive that the second sexual encounter would not have happened. The first time, despite Carol's prayers for forgiveness and our discussion a day or two later about what we had done, made it easy to have sex the second time.

"Is that why you left?" I asked.

"That was part of it," she admitted. "I mean, there was a lot more to it than that. I was also upset about my family having to leave. Had they stayed in Honolulu I would never have left but I really was not feeling right about myself. I went down to Hilo to clear my head after my family left and intended to be back by the time you came home but I needed to sort things out. I missed my family and I missed you . . . and I was worried about you making the team. All of that stress made me wonder if I was being punished for. . . . Somehow I decided that the only way I was going to be forgiven was if I gave you up."

Carol's voice had weakened again. The recollection was hard on her. She wasn't crying at this point but her voice had a very mournful tone.

"I think it was the same day that I realized I wouldn't be returning. I cried my eyes out. I couldn't go home because I felt I had to show God that I was really, really sorry. He can accept us making normal human mistakes but sex is a more serious matter. It seems innocuous but He really takes a

446

dim view of sex that isn't between a married couple. You might not feel that way about it but I am absolutely certain."

I had no answer to that. At the time I didn't see it that way. Eventually I would.

"I'll tell you something I believe," Carol continued. "I believe that God guided us together when we met in college. I believe He was the one who gave us strength to work through our problems when we had them. You treated me very well, especially once we got on track, and I tried to do the same for you. Whether it was right for me to seek refuge in Hilo, I don't know. I probably never will know. I just know that I did what I thought I had to do."

Carol added that she believed that God was now giving her another chance but that she had to lay down one very specific ground rule.

"You can laugh if you want," she said, "but I honestly believe that that day at Kahala Mall was no accident. I never actually prayed to get you back but He still knew what was in my heart."

Carol was obviously much more into religious issues than I was at the time. I didn't necessarily believe that God brought her and me together. I did like the idea.

"I love you," I said.

"I love you, too," she replied with a warm smile that had a way of hiding the redness of her eyes. "I'll love you forever. But no matter how much I love you, I will always love God and His Son Jesus Christ a whole lot more. A lot of people would scoff at that and that's all right. I'm not going to pass judgement on anybody else but I hope you understand my convictions."

I said that I did.

"I want His blessings and I am not going to get them if I betray Him," she continued. "I can make all kinds of mistakes and be forgiven but we can't have sex unless we're married. If we get married you can take me to Maui or Tahiti or Paris or Tokyo or anywhere else in the world and I'll spend the entire time naked in bed for you without seeing any of the area attractions if you want."

The latter part of that spiel was meant to be taken lightly and it was. Another thought crossed my mind that I also found amusing.

"If we're going to lie naked in bed and do nothing more than make love through our entire honeymoon, what's the point of going to any of the places you mentioned?"

Carol laughed at this. She threw her arms around me.

"I'm glad you agree that there can be no sex," she said. "If we ever get married you can have all the sex you want as long as it's with me."

I wanted to tell Carol that I didn't want there to be an "if" regarding our future marital commitment. I was pretty sure we would eventually be married and had probably sensed that as far back as the day I met her. I wanted to tell her but it somehow didn't seem appropriate.

Which was stupid. It didn't hurt our relationship by not telling her how I felt but I still should have told her. An actual proposal would probably have been premature. Telling her that I hoped that sometime in the very near future that she would become my wife would have been very appropriate.

Carol looked lovingly at me. She threw her arms around my neck and hugged me. She kissed me a few times on the side of my face before we shared a long kiss.

"I promise I'll never leave you again," she whispered as we held each other close. "I'll only leave you if you tell me to. I'm so sorry for the way I suddenly disappeared. I honestly didn't mean for it to work out that way."

"I know that, honey. You did what you thought you had to do. We're human beings. That means we make decisions that aren't always right."

The fact is, I'll probably never know if I handled Carol's disappearance correctly. Perhaps I was right to have left her alone to sort things out. Perhaps I should have found out where she was and gone to try to persuade her to return.

All I really know is it seemed right to leave her alone. I did what seemed right even though it was in direct contrast to what I actually wanted. Whether it was right or wrong, I did what I did out of love for her.

Carol was, and is, a very intelligent, warm, witty, compassionate, vibrant, rational human being. Like anybody else, she makes mistakes. I don't believe it was necessarily a mistake for her to go to Hilo. She was mistaken when she feared that I wouldn't welcome her back after she wasn't around when I returned to Honolulu. I would have expected some type of explanation from her but I would have greeted her with outstretched arms. She may have convinced herself that I wouldn't welcome her back but I was waiting and waiting and waiting.

We touched on a variety of subjects. Our joint catharsis was very liberating. I felt a sense of peace now that we had opened up to each other.

Carol and I talked until close to three o'clock in the morning. That includes substantial time doing nothing more than holding each other. She had to teach in the morning and I had football practice so neither of us was going to get much sleep. Some things are simply more imperative. We truly were a couple again.

And we were thrilled!

CHAPTER NINETEEN
Must Win

With a little more than 24 hours to go before our rematch with Atlanta we were hyped. A year earlier we were hyped going into week 13 because a victory the following day would virtually knock our opponent out of the playoff picture and victories in our last two games would give us a .500 record in our first ever NFL season. A year later we were hyped because we were in the thick of the postseason hunt.

Our first choice obviously was to win our division. Not only was that more prestigious than the wild card but it would mean at least one playoff game at home if we had at least the second-best record in the conference. In 1977 with only one wild card team in each conference a wild card team could never have a home game during the playoffs. That would change the following year when a second wild card team was added for each conference and the wild card teams would square off against each other while the division champions had a bye week.

In order to win the division we had to win our final two games of the season and have the Rams lose at least one of their final two games. In that case we would wind up tied but we would get the tiebreaker nod since we would have more total points in our head-to-head competition.

It would get more complicated if we lost to the Falcons. If we lost to Atlanta and beat the Jets while the Rams dropped their final two games we would wind up in a tie for first place but the Rams would win the division by virtue of having a better division record. In that case the best we could hope for was the wild card. When I woke up on Saturday morning the wild card would be either the Rams, Cardinals, Redskins, Bears, Vikings or us.

But to hell with the wild card. We wanted the division. That meant winning our final two games with the Rams losing at least one. We were greedy. We wanted it all.

Our traditional Saturday light workout went well. Everybody who would be suiting up was ready to go. Walker told us to have an enjoyable day without overdoing it so that we would be physically and mentally ready to play.

At about the time our light workout was ending the Redskins were finishing off the Cardinals. That knocked the Cardinals out of the playoff picture while keeping Washington's slim hopes alive. If we beat Atlanta the Redskins would be virtually eliminated. We had the tiebreaker over the Redskins by virtue of overall point differential. It would take an unimaginable slaughter by the Jets in order for the Redskins to gain the point differential advantage over us.

But I put all of the playoff scenarios on the back burner and focused on having the enjoyable day Walker recommended. Having time to have a reasonable amount of recreation the day before a game was very soothing and conducive to playing a good game. Throughout my career I knew guys who lived and breathed football 24 hours a day. I was among those who preferred to let go and have a life away from football. I didn't mind talking football or watching football but it was all generally recreational except when I was watching teams who affected our standings.

Of course my life was dramatically changed. Carol and I were truly bonded now.

I picked Carol up and we went to Kailua. Don Simmons was hosting a beach party. It was primarily the Arthur's crowd but there were others present including a few teammates.

Naturally I had to be careful not to get sunburned. I buttered myself with sunscreen to be sure and also put on a shirt when I thought I had been bare-shouldered long enough.

Marv and I were opposing captains in a beach volleyball match. Ed Jennings was among those on my team while Hasegawa was on Marv's. It was a pretty good match. Marv's side beat us in a close game.

"I guess you did your best," I told Ed in a voice of mock despair. "I'll know more when I watch the game films."

The highlight was simply a walk I took down the beach with Carol. We didn't say much. We simply reveled in the joy of being together and holding hands. It might seem trivial, I suppose, but it wouldn't have been the same with some other female.

Our bond was not lost on Don. He and I had been friends since before Carol and I met so he was around during our college relationship. He approached me when Carol excused herself to go into the house.

"You two look like a nice couple," Don remarked in a tone of admiration.

"Thanks. I think we're going to make it," I replied.

Don nodded and looked thoughtful. I never told him that there had been a barrier between Carol and me but he seemed to have sensed it. Whether he did or not, it was probably obvious to him that Carol and I had reached another level.

"I'm glad I was right," Don said.

"Hm?"

"Do you remember what I predicted about four years ago?" Don continued. "It was just before you went to California for a few months."

I smiled and nodded my head. I never forgot what Don said while he waited with me in the boarding area prior to my flight to Los Angeles.

"I don't recall word for word but you essentially said that Carol and I would get back together someday," I said. "I don't remember if I believed it or not. I'm just glad you were right."

"She's a great lady."

Overall it was a great day of camaraderie among friends and an opportunity to meet people I didn't already know. After a dinner of hamburgers, hot dogs and various trimmings I was ready to annihilate Atlanta.

I was almost giddy on Sunday morning. I got out of bed at 5:29, took a shower and killed time until it was time to pick Carol up. My mind was primarily on football although not completely. There was a sense of peace that I hadn't known since. . . .

It may have been an unprecedented sense of peace. It intensified when I caught my first glimpse that morning of the golden-haired aphrodite in white shorts and a blue blouse with aloha print.

All seemed well with the world. The blue skies, the clouds against the Koolau Mountains, the warmth of the sun, the sight of the ocean and everything else seemed overwhelmingly beautiful.

The drive to the stadium was blissful. Football was on my mind and I was still relatively taciturn. Just the same, I had let go of some of my pregame psyche. There were other things in the world besides football.

Like Carol.

We talked some; more than during any previous drive to the stadium. Once we entered the freeway from Punchbowl Street and I had shifted the car into high gear we even held hands.

After we passed over Red Hill the stadium came into view. Visible directly on the other side of the stadium was Pearl Harbor. In the distance we could see the Waipahu Sugar Mill, the Ewa plain and the Waianae Mountains.

I was a man in love. I was also having a productive career. I had a lot for which to be grateful.

Christmas was exactly two weeks away. I already had what I wanted.

Well, there was that matter of a trip to the playoffs and even a Super Bowl berth. As happy as I was, I still had to be psyched to play football. I was in a frame of mind where I believed that I could rush for 100 yards and receive for 500 yards.

"Okay, men," Walker began after Jurgens led us in *The Lord's Prayer*. It looks to me like you're ready. You've won eight games this season. Today we go for number nine and another step toward the playoffs. All we have to do is execute. We block. We tackle. We run, pass and receive. What could possibly be more simple than that?"

Nobody had an answer to Walker's rhetorical question. Walker flashed a sheepish grin and then signaled for everybody to file out.

I headed out. The fans roared their approval as we stepped on the field. Two weeks earlier we took the field 6-4 and the fans were hoping we would snap a losing streak. After victories at home against New Orleans and in

San Francisco against the 49ers our fans were tasting playoffs. Our fans were very vocally behind us.

Black was back to close to 100 percent and would be starting at left cornerback. Catron's injury kept him out for another week.

As we stood on the sideline waiting for the introductions of the Falcon defense and our defense the public address announcer got our attention.

"This just in from New Orleans. The Saints, 14. The Tampa Bay Buccaneers . . . 33! Tampa Bay's losing streak ends at 26!"

At first there was a gasp from the crowd and then applause. It wasn't a raucous cheer but our fans seemed happy for the Bucs that their dubious streak had come to an end.

I looked at Slater and raised my eyebrows when I heard the announcement.

"Wow," I said, very happy for Coach John McKay and his Buccaneers and happier still that the streak didn't end until *after* our visit to Tampa.

"I have never been as glad to not be a Saint as I am today," I overheard Marv remark.

We won the toss. Feeling invincible, I took my place on the goal line of the south end zone.

"Let's kick okole!" Hasegawa commented enthusiastically as we exchanged our slap fives.

"Right on, brah! They got lucky in Atlanta. We'll bury them here."

As I awaited the kick I stole a quick glance into the bleachers. Carol was such a blessing to me. I realized again how incarcerated I had been over the previous six months and I was now completely liberated. Some guys I had known equated commitment with shackles. I saw it as freedom.

The kick was up. It was slightly to my right.

"I got it!" I called.

I took the ball at the two and charged forward as if possessed by a celestial force. I cut left near the 15 and forced a Falcon to reach out and grab air. While teammates did their jobs of blocking white jerseys, I managed to elude those who got close.

A couple of cuts and I was to the 30, barely conscious of the steady encouragement of the crowd. There was a straight-arm near the 35 and another cut after the 40. It wasn't until I got to the Hawaii 48 that somebody came from my right and grabbed me at the waist, bringing me down.

Whistles were blowing. I bounced up quickly. I had hoped to go all the way but a 46-yard return is certainly no cause for shame. As I would observe in the films, had I eluded the man who tackled me the only man left to beat would have been the kicker.

452

"All right! Let's go!" I said, clapping my hands a couple of times as I moved toward where we would huddle. "Let's go, Ted! Larry, Marv, Rich, Dave . . . !"

Scott got nowhere off right tackle but the Falcons made it up for us. Prior to the next snap they got called for encroachment, giving us a second and five at the Atlanta 47.

"Okay, if we can't do it ourselves, we'll let the Falcons do it for us," Bender lightly quipped in the huddle. "But let's focus on doing it ourselves."

The Falcons remained stubborn when the ball was snapped. Scott went up the middle and managed a mere yard. Thus far he had two carries for one yard. I was counting on his average per carry improving as the game progressed.

It could be argued that I lost a yard on the next play even though it was a 14-yard gain. Bender hit me over the middle at the 31. I tried to belly around a defensive back but he grabbed me by the lower part of my jersey and swung me down at the 32. It was still a first down but I made a mental note to stop trying to belly around defenders unless I was positive that I would gain yardage. That wasn't as easy as it seemed because bellying around was a subconscious reflex.

The Falcon defense continued to frustrate our running game, limiting Kerner to two yards up the middle. Bender then hit me near the right sideline at the 19. I picked up two more yards before being pushed out of bounds. First down at the 17.

That was as far as we got. A pass to Grummon in the end zone was nearly intercepted. On the ensuing two plays the Falcons blitzed. Bender managed to get the passes off before being sacked but both passes fell incomplete.

It's a fact of life. It was frustrating but I knew we weren't going to score a touchdown every time we had the ball.

Guinn did his job. He converted on a 34-yard field goal. We led 3-0 with 10:46 left in the first quarter.

"Okay. Okay. We got some points," offensive coordinator Jim Potter reminded us as the offense gathered around him to discuss future strategy. "Every point we rack up is critical. We'll get more."

As this was going on there was a huge roar from the crowd that got our attention. Initially we thought it was a turnover although it wasn't quite that good. What happened was the kickoff was fielded two yards deep in the end zone and returned only to the nine. Dubois shot downfield and made the return man regret his decision not to down the ball in the end zone.

Apparently our defense felt compelled to return the favors the Falcon defense did for us. McDaniel got called for encroachment to give the Falcons a first and five at the 14. After two plays and a measurement showed them inches short of a first down at the 19 a rush to the 20 for a first down was nullified when they accepted the offside penalty caused by Prendergast.

"Make them earn it, defense!" Walker called, cupping his hands over his mouth. "You don't have to give it away!"

The Falcons did manage to pick up a first down without us aiding them with penalties but they proceeded no further than their own 43. Before I knew it I was standing near the 15 waiting for a punt.

I was still on the 15 when I fielded the punt. I took it to the 24 for a respectable enough, but unspectacular, nine-yard return.

We decided to attack by air. Passes to myself and Grummon, respectively, being batted down by defensive backs put us in a third and ten.

"Okay, team. Enough of this crap. We'll get it right on this one," Bender seemed to promise in the huddle before calling the play. He seemed to know what he was talking about because he completed a pass to Dietrich at the Hawaii 37. Ted picked up six more yards to give us a first down at the 43.

It took us one play to pick up our second first down of the drive. I caught a pass at the Atlanta 37. There was a defender in my face but he seemed off balance. That enabled me to essentially run right through him, knocking him down and continuing to the 31 before I was finally brought down.

"All right! We're not settling for three this time," Bender remarked in the huddle. "We're getting it all."

Bender's confidence was inspiring. He wasn't always right when he made brash remarks like that. Usually, though, it seemed that he was.

We picked up our third first down in as many plays. This time we did it on the ground. Scott went up the middle on a draw play and shot his way to the 19. The boisterous cheers of the crowd was a reminder to the Falcons that we were not in Atlanta.

Three rushes later we had fourth and one. I sensed that Walker wanted to send the field goal unit out. Bender was gesturing that he felt that we could pick up the yard by pointing as if we already had the first down. Although it was next to impossible to hear anything but sustained noise from the crowd, I sensed that most of the crowd was calling for us to go for it.

Walker decided to go for it. He sent McCracken in. Dietrich went out. We were going with two tight ends.

Bender quickly called a play since the play clock was winding down. From the dotted "I" we were running a Waimanalo right. It was going to be up to me to hit the hole and get that yard.

I took the handoff and headed for the hole being opened by Abraham and McCracken. I had picked up a yard before a linebacker caught up with me. I spun off of him and fought my way to the six. It was first and goal.

"Way to go, Jay!" McCracken cried out enthusiastically as I rose up.

454

"Nice, job," said Scott, patting me on the back as we headed for the huddle.

"Dockman!"

The latter came from Rossi. As our paths crossed I slapped fives with Rossi and Dietrich who was sending McCracken back out.

"Good work, Jay," Walker said with a broad smile. "How're you feeling?"

"I feel great, Coach," I replied sincerely but with a little bit of an annoyed inflection to indicate that I didn't really need to take a rest.

"Okay, good. Stay behind me. I'll send you back in if we don't score on this play."

We didn't score. A sweep around left end by Scott picked up only a yard.

"Rossi!"

That was me after Walker sent me back in with a play. It was a quick slant that Dietrich caught at the three. He was brought down at the one.

Third down and three feet to go. Kerner got the call. He pounded his way up the middle and was brought down by four Falcons but not until he was a yard deep in the end zone.

"Yeah!" I called out, raising my arms over my head before running over to join my teammates in celebration. It was, as it turned out, the final play of the first quarter.

After we ran off Guinn converted on the extra point. We led 10-0 with exactly 45 minutes to go.

I was feeling invincible. To keep from getting overconfident, I thought back exactly seven weeks. I reminded myself that we were playing a team that had already beaten us. In that game they jumped off to a 9-0 lead and never looked back. They prevailed in the end when a 46-yard field goal attempt which could have sent the game into overtime was wide to the left.

That was essentially all I needed at the moment to keep things in perspective. Our opponent may have struggled of late but the Falcons had already proven that they were capable of beating us. We needed to pad our ten-point lead.

Our defense also seemed to recall the loss in Atlanta. After the kickoff to start the second quarter was returned from two yards deep in the end zone to the 20 the Falcons managed only one first down. That came after one play only because Malick got called for pulling the facemask. Our defense, despite its determined effort, couldn't seem to help being mildly philanthropic.

But the Falcons didn't take advantage of our generosity. Soon it was fourth and eight at the Atlanta 40. I was back on the field to return the punt.

I wouldn't be returning a punt. It was too far to my left. It bounced near the 20 and kept going. It was downed at the eight.

"First and 92," I said to myself. I figured we would methodically move the entire distance a chunk at a time and chew up much of the clock in the process, leaving the Falcons very little time to retaliate before halftime.

Or we could score quickly, hold the Falcons and put together another scoring drive before the half.

We started with Scott who picked up two yards on a sweep around right end. Kerner then went up the middle for about eight yards. A measurement showed that we were about two inches short of a first down.

I got the call. Outstanding blocking enabled me to pick up four yards off left tackle to the 22. It seemed as if everything I tried was sufficient to this point.

"All right, gentlemen. We are in business," Bender said in the huddle. "Let's put one in the air."

Dietrich wound up being the recipient. He made a diving catch at the Hawaii 41. A defensive back fell on him before he could get up and advance.

"It hit the ground first! It's incomplete!" another defensive back insisted.

"He didn't catch it!" an irate Falcon coach called from the sideline.

This was years before coaches were allowed to challenge close calls. Had the Falcons been allowed to contest the ruling it would have cost them a timeout. The TV replay showed that Ted caught the ball legitimately. I would see it that night on the news.

Scott got us our third first down of the drive one play later. He went up the middle and broke a tackle at the line of scrimmage. He broke two more tackles before finally going down at the Atlanta 45. It was a 14-yard gain.

Our fans continued to be very vocal in their appreciation. We were justifying their decision to purchase tickets.

Kimmitt got overanxious and jumped prior to the next snap, knocking us back to the 50. Scott then ran around right end to get us back to the 45 before going off left tackle to the 38 to make it a third and three.

"Okay, 'I' formation, slot left, 4 kama'aina right," Bender ordered in the huddle. "On one, on one. Ready?"

"Break!"

I would be lining up in the slot on the left and going in motion toward the interior. Bender would hand off to me and I would follow the convoy.

It worked well. My escorts got me to the 33. We had a first down.

"I do believe we're in field goal range, my man," Marv remarked jovially as he helped me up. "But to hell with the field goal. We're going for the TD."

Marv seemed uncharacteristically cocky, especially since we still had only a ten-point lead. I never asked him about it but I believe it had to do with him being a Hawaiian and not a Saint that day.

"You're darn right we're going for the TD," I said as we headed to the huddle. "We're only allotted one field goal today and we've already got it."

456

I suppose I was feeling a tad cocky myself.

At least we continued moving in the right direction to justify our brash attitudes. Grummon caught a short pass at the 30 and took it to the 24. We declined the offside penalty to be in a second and one.

Kerner barreled up the middle to give us a first down at the 15. Two Scott carries later we had first and goal at the three.

Sometimes you just know. I can't explain it but I knew we would get the full seven. Perhaps it was atmospheric. Perhaps it was the attitude of my teammates. Perhaps it was even something about the Falcon defense. I just somehow knew. The only mystery seemed to be who would carry the ball over the goal line.

I was elected on the first play. From the right wing I did a quick slant toward the middle. Bender hit me as I was reaching the goal line. I dove forward, coming down a yard deep in the end zone and cognizant of the sudden roar of the crowd.

Touchdown!

There was a Falcon on the ground nearby. I couldn't help but notice the look of frustration on his face. I couldn't conclude that we had the game won since the game wasn't even half over but we had the momentum and the Falcons knew it.

Guinn's PAT was a given. We led 17-0 with 4:27 left in the half.

"Offense, rest yourself," Potter directed on the sideline. "Get yourselves some Gatorade and sit down and rest. We want to put more points on the board before the half if we can get the ball back."

"All right," said Shuford as he took the seat next to me. "We're going for the jugular."

"Yeah, why not?" I responded in a cocksure tone.

"Yeah, baby," Clint added. "Nobody beats us twice in the same season."

Well, there was that team from Denver.

But that was 1976. That seemed light years away.

Atlanta started on its own 28, returning the kick from three yards deep in the end zone to that point. I figured the defense would give us the ball back with about three minutes left.

When the two-minute warning rolled around the Falcons still had the ball. It was second and six at the Hawaii 29.

"What's going on here?" I asked rhetorically. "We can't let them score."

It was a three-score game. I wanted to keep it that way if we couldn't extend it to four. The stubborn Falcons refused to cooperate.

When play resumed the Falcons ran a left end sweep that got them three yards. It was third and three at the 26. They called timeout with 1:51 left.

"Hold 'em, defense," I said softly as I watched Allen converse with Walker. At this point a field goal attempt would be about 43 yards. I was willing to concede that if I had to. Two touchdowns would still be a decent lead to take into the locker room.

The Falcons were going to try to pass for a first down. The quarterback dropped back. The receivers were well-covered.

Pratt broke through the line.

"Get him, get him, get him!" I barked in rapid fire fashion as Pratt went in for the kill.

The quarterback tried to run but it was too late. Pratt nailed him at the 35. It was fourth and 12.

Our fans roared. The Hawaiian sideline roared. Something told me there was cursing and other forms of discontent on the Atlanta sideline as well as all over Georgia.

"Okay, 32 dime!" Walker called, sending Hasegawa and Vorsino in while Malick and Prendergast would come out. It appeared that the Falcons were not going to try a field goal which would have been about 52 yards against the wind. They were also not going to punt to try to pin us back. They were going for it.

The clock was running. It was down to about a minute at the time of the snap. We had two timeouts but we didn't use one because we felt we needed them more on offense. Besides, if the Falcons picked up a first down our timeout would have worked to their benefit.

Not surprisingly, the Falcons went to the air. The quarterback fired a bullet right on the numbers of a receiver over the middle. He was hit and dropped immediately by Blakely.

I stood up. I wanted to get a better vantage point to see where the ball was being spotted. From where I stood near midfield it looked like they had enough for a first down.

The ball was spotted at the 24.

They needed to get to the 23!

"Offense!" Walker barked although he was almost impossible to hear over the roar of the crowd.

With unbridled enthusiasm I ran on the field. I held my hand straight out at my right side so that Blakely could slap it as he ran by. We had 51 seconds and two timeouts to travel 76 yards.

We got off to a slow start. Bender hit Dietrich with a quick pass at the 25. Ted got to the 30 and stepped out of bounds. It was second and four with 44 seconds.

Rossi came in and Scott went out. We had been in our double-single. Walker decided we weren't fooling the Falcons into thinking we might run by leaving Scott in so we went to the double-double.

We moved into Falcon territory on the next play. Bender hit Slater at the Hawaii 49. He got to the Atlanta 44 before being brought down in bounds. We called timeout with 33 seconds.

Bender met a heavy rush on the next snap. He still got the pass off to me. I leaped up near the 30 close to the right sideline. A defensive back went up with me and knocked the ball away. It was second and ten with 25 seconds left.

The defensive back had made an excellent play. I didn't feel like telling him that. My heart had been set on making the play that would have gotten us to within field goal range. I didn't do anything that would have labeled me a bad sport but by running back to our huddle and cursing under my breath I also wasn't being an especially good sport.

I was a safety valve on the next play. Bender was rushed and couldn't find an open receiver downfield. He hit me near the line of scrimmage. I picked up three yards before being tackled in bounds. We used our final timeout with 16 seconds.

The previous play could be called a tactical mistake. We were three yards closer to a score but the cost meant that it would have been better to allow the pass to fall incomplete. The three-yard gain might not have justified using our final timeout.

There were no receivers available on the next play so Bender threw the ball away. There were nine seconds left.

I suddenly noticed a yellow flag on the ground. We were being cited for illegal motion. Rossi had gone in motion and turned forward just prior to the snap.

The Falcons enigmatically declined the penalty. With nine seconds left the most we would have time for were two plays but the half could end after only one. The five yards to the 46 that the Falcons declined could have proven substantial.

I guess the Falcons were counting on keeping us to less than seven yards. I suppose it may have been a tough call. If we picked up the first down on the next play we would still have to get out of bounds to stop the clock. Declining the penalty also kept us five yards closer to the first down.

The Falcons weren't fools. They might have been willing to concede the first down but nothing more. Their defense included every defensive back on their roster.

On our end Dietrich and Slater were to run deep patterns in hope of beating the secondary. Rossi and I would be running sideline patterns of about ten yards so that Bender could hit one of us far enough downfield to get us in field goal range if Slater or Dietrich couldn't get open. It was also obviously imperative that Rossi or I step out of bounds immediately after a reception.

I ran to just inside the 30. Bender fired a pass my way near the right sideline. I had to leap to grab the ball but made the catch. I was hit at the same moment and came down out of bounds.

As I rose up I noticed that the pass was ruled incomplete.

"What happened? Why was that incomplete?" I asked the nearest official.

"You came down out of bounds."

"But he knocked me out of bounds."

"No, no. Your momentum would have carried you out anyway."

"Oh, geez," I said, throwing my hands up as if I was doing a John Madden impersonation. There was no way that I was going to win this dispute regardless of how vehement I was so I ran across the field to our sideline without arguing.

"What happened?" Walker asked, holding outstretched palms at his sides.

"He said my momentum would have carried me out of bounds even if the defender hadn't hit me."

"Would it have?"

I shook my head in exasperation and held my palms out.

"I don't know. I don't think so but the official thought so."

As much as I hated to admit it, replays I would see later showed that the officials made the right call.

There was one second left. The Falcons took a snap and dropped to end the half.

I guess our spirits were fairly high even though a 17-point lead at halftime was not necessarily a rout in the making. I happened to be behind Stanek when he pulled up next to Jablonski as we approached the tunnel.

"What are you doing in that uniform?" Stanek asked.

"What do you mean?" was Jablonski's puzzled reply.

"Well you're not going to play. Did you punt during the first half?"

"No."

"And you're not going to punt during the second half. Get dressed. You're not needed today."

Of course it was a good thing for Stanek that Walker wasn't around. Walker could get away with such a brash prognosis but for one of his players. . . .

"This is your game to win," Walker remarked as we prepared to return for the second half. "You outplayed them in the first half and you should be able to continue in the second half. Just remember that they still want to beat you and they're capable of doing that. It's up to you to play 30 more minutes of heads-up football to prevent them from achieving their objective. Now let's do it."

I wasted no time. I couldn't wait to return to the field. Even though we wouldn't be receiving the kickoff I couldn't wait to just be on the field.

"Let's do it," I said as I ran toward our sideline while the crowd roared our return to the field. "Let's blow these turkeys back to Atlanta."

As I approached our bench I caught a glimpse of Carol. I felt gratitude again that she was with me. My career could end that day and she would still be there for me. She loved me for me. Being a football player simply happened to be what I did for a living.

Carol was a very strong woman.

And yet she was very sensitive to the sufferings of others. It upset her that there were children in various parts of the world who couldn't get enough nourishment and that there was very little that she could do to change that. Video footage of wounded soldiers in Vietnam used to make her cry, as did the news that a neighbor whom she barely knew was killed in Vietnam. She was as opposed to that war as much as I was and never hesitated to express herself.

Nobody cared about me more than Carol did. Even during the three years we were apart she was probably my biggest supporter.

For the moment she was rooting for me (and my team, of course) to blow away the Falcons. She didn't want anybody on either side getting hurt. She still wanted the Falcons to go down in flames.

The Falcons made a statement on the opening kickoff of the half. The return man caught the ball at the five. By virtue of blocks, broken tackles and sheer speed he made it almost to midfield. The only man left to beat was Guinn and, fortunately, Guinn didn't shy away from contact. He managed to bring him down at the Atlanta 47.

"It looks like we'd better be ready," I remarked to Kerner and Scott on the sideline. "They're not going down without a fight."

The kick return could actually have worked more to our advantage than theirs. Instead of lulling us to sleep by chipping away before we finally caught on after they had substantially narrowed the gap and seized the momentum, we knew right away that the Falcons meant business. It was up to us to play as if it was still a scoreless game.

As it was, the Falcons managed a first down at our 31. After a five-yard rush and two incomplete passes they sent their field goal unit out.

Kicking against the wind which was not especially strong but enough to have an impact, the ball cleared the crossbar with about a foot to spare. Our lead was 17-3 with 13:13 left in the third quarter.

"It's all right. It's all right," Walker remarked calmly as I prepared to take the field for the kick return. "We've just got to counter that with a touchdown."

He made it sound so easy. My guess was that the Falcon defense would want to be a little more difficult than that.

The Falcon kickoff unit also didn't want it to be so easy. I took the kick at the goal line and charged forward. Before I knew it I encountered a white jersey that brought me down.

Normally when I return kicks and punts I don't know where I am on the field until after I have gone down. This proved to be the case here. My heart sank when I rose to my knees and saw that I was still inside the 20.

"You've got to be kidding," I said out loud although it was primarily an expression of my thought.

It was rare that I was caught inside the 20 on a kick return. I couldn't recall any previous time that it happened on any level.

The ball was marked at the 17. On the game's opening kickoff I had a 46-yard return. That meant that I had two returns for 63 total yards, giving me an average of 31.5 yards which is pretty darned impressive. For the moment I was kicking myself over the more recent effort although, the truth is, it was primarily because the Falcons made an outstanding play. To their credit, they were not throwing in the towel.

When we resumed play it no longer mattered. The bottom line was that we had to travel 83 yards. Scott erased six of those yards off right tackle when he fought his way to the 23.

There was a yellow flag. The Falcons were offside. We declined the penalty although I am not sure why. Had we taken the penalty we would have been one yard further back but it would have been a first down instead of second.

"Okay, let's go to the air," Bender said in the huddle.

I ran a post and caught the pass at about the Hawaii 40. I outran a defensive back but met up with two others who brought me down at the Hawaii 48.

"Way to go, Jay," Dietrich remarked, patting me on the back as we headed toward the huddle. I was so elated that I had already forgotten my subpar kick return.

"Dockman!"

Rossi was on his way in. I ran to the sideline where Walker was waiting.

"I want to give Rossi a couple of plays here and there since we've got a halfway decent lead and are pretty much in control of the game," Walker said. "This can give him a little experience and build his confidence in case he's needed in a more critical situation. Stay close."

Rossi got involved right away. Bender hit him with a quick pass at the 50. He picked up four more yards to give us a second and four at the Atlanta 46.

"All right, Rossi! Good play, babe!" I called out although I was probably just as concerned with showing Walker that I was a team player as much as I was with actually being one.

Scott picked up three yards on a sweep around right end. Walker turned to face me.

"We'll give Rossi one more play," he said.

As I watched the offense break out of the huddle I realized that I actually was genuinely happy for Rossi. An opportunity did make him feel like he was more a part of the team. It never really bothered me the year before when Gary Giametti came in to spell me. It even happened more often with Giametti than it did with Rossi so there was really no reason to begrudge Rossi.

Kerner went up the middle and immediately met a determined gang in white jerseys. He moved forward but was it enough?

Time was called. The chain was brought out. The referee then pointed toward the south end zone, drawing a roar of approval from the crowd.

"Okay, Jay. Go on back in," Walker directed.

"Rossi!"

Also coming in was McCracken. Walker wanted to give Grummon a rest.

As Rossi had been, McCracken was in the center of the action right away. He caught a pass at the 32 and then made his way to the 28. It was another first down.

"Okay, we're looking good out here," Bender remarked.

Two Scott rushes later it was third and three at the 21. I then got the call off right tackle.

It was a strange sensation. I charged forward amid the sounds of grunts and pads colliding. I practically closed my eyes as white jerseys reached out for me and brown jerseys tried to knock them away. I finally went down with at least a couple of bodies on top of me.

Whistles were blowing. Time was being called while the officials picked bodies off of me. There must have been six or so from both teams.

The ball was spotted at about the 18. The chain was brought out. The marker came down about two inches prior to the nose of the ball.

"All right!" I said, clapping my hands. That got the crowd roaring even before the referee even had to point southward.

Scott's subsequent sweep around left end got us to the 14. Kerner then went off right tackle and only got to the 13, giving us a third and five.

"Okay, they're not quitters," Bender remarked in the huddle. "That will make today's victory that much more fulfilling."

A quick pass to Grummon was caught at the eleven. He managed to fight for four more yards to give us a first and goal at the seven.

What made it extra special was that this was a home game. We had the crowd behind us. Our fans were having the time of their lives watching us wear down the Atlanta defense. The heat and humidity also had to have been working to our advantage.

"One play," Bender stated in the huddle. "We take it in on one play."

Bender handed off to Kerner who shot through the hole opened by Marv and Abraham. He was hit at the three, was still on his feet at the two, fought his way to the one. . . .

Touchdown!

The crowd erupted again. I leaped in the air and clapped my hands. Kerner spiked the ball. Scott raised a clenched fist.

And then we noticed the yellow flag. Dietrich was cited for holding. Instead of a three-score game it was first and goal at the 17.

"Shake it off. We're still going in. This just gives them less time to catch us," Bender said, showing that he could almost always see a silver lining.

Despite the heat and humidity, the Falcons hadn't completely melted into the turf. They charged hard when Bender dropped back to pass. He got the pass off to Slater but it was batted down inside the five.

We tried to sneak in on the ground. Scott did a sweep around left end. He managed only three yards to give us third and goal at the 14.

It was back to the air. Our fans knew it. The Falcons definitely knew it. It was simply a matter of who could take it all the way in.

Bender dropped back. He had good protection. I got to the end zone with two defensive backs stuck to me. I tried to run around to shake them.

Grummon had a slight opening near the left sideline. Bender hit him at the four. Rich shook off a tackler and made his way into the end zone. This time there were no yellow flags.

From my position in the end zone I raised my fists in the air, leaped up and nearly did a full 360 before I came down. I reveled in the score and the roar of the crowd.

"Way to go, Rich!" was my profound expression of approbation. I may have been a graduate student but that didn't mean that I had to quote Shakespeare. The same vernacular used by Pop Warner players was most appropriate.

Predictably Guinn split the uprights. I marveled at how much of the clock our latest drive chewed up. It was 24-3 with 3:41 left in the third quarter.

We cruised the rest of the way. The Falcons knew they were beat but they played for pride and respectability. This included their next drive which carried into the final quarter. They wound up with a 34-yard field goal to narrow the gap to 24-6 with 13:27 left.

It was still a three-score game. With the starting unit still in there we focused on milking the clock. The clock was just as much the Falcons' enemy as the scoreboard.

Our fortune turned ugly about halfway through the possession. Scott rushed up the middle for three yards to the 50. One of our opponents making the tackle accidentally came down hard on Scott's ankle.

"Aaaaaah!" Scott cried in agony.

Larry tried to get up and walk. His face cringed and he sat down in excruciating pain.

The trainer came out. He looked at Larry's ankle and almost turned pale.

"It doesn't look good," he said mournfully.

Larry was helped off the field to a rousing ovation. He was definitely finished for the day. Something told me he wouldn't recover in time for next week's game against the Jets. He had been looking forward to that game, having played for the Jets for three years before being taken by the Hawaiians in the 24th round of the expansion draft.

Ozzie came in at tailback. He did a respectable job. We continued to milk the clock.

On first and ten at the 17 Ozzie carried off right tackle. He got to the 13 where he was hit. The ball popped loose.

"Fumble!"

There was a scramble for the ball. I dove for it and got my left hand on it but the ball squirted away. It was finally recovered by Atlanta at the seven.

It was frustrating. The touchdown we were hoping for would have officially pronounced the Falcons dead. They were already in extremely critical condition with about a one percent chance of survival but they weren't dead yet. They needed three touchdowns with 4:38 left to play.

With as many backup defenders in the game as we had available, the Falcons managed a touchdown. They scored on a 12-yard pass with 33 seconds left. It was 24-13.

The Falcons tried an onside kick. Everybody and his brother knew they would. Our hands team was sent out. Rodgers recovered the kick at the 50. One snap and it was officially over.

We were 9-4. For the first time in our brief history we had a three-game winning streak over the course of a single season.

It was a good victory but a costly one. Scott's ankle was broken. He would be out throughout the playoffs. There was some chance that he would be activated for the Super Bowl, assuming we would get that far.

Larry narrowly missed a 100-yard game. He had 97 yards, giving him 782 yards for the season. In 1976 he rushed for 1,055 yards but his effort in 1977 included two earlier games he had to sit out because of injury and he was obviously going to miss one more regular season game.

Injuries are always a part of the game. We knew that and expected injuries. We felt bad for Larry and knew that his absence would hurt us. We were still in a festive mood in the locker room.

Collier gave the postgame prayer. Walker then announced that Scott would receive the game ball although he was not present to receive it. Larry was already at Queen's Hospital so Walker placed the ball in Larry's locker.

"He played a good game," Walker said solemnly, then brightened up. "You all played a good game. One more victory and we're in the playoffs."

As far as the playoff picture went, the Rams won that day. That enabled them to keep their one game advantage over us in the hunt for the division championship. Their victory guaranteed them at least the wild card berth.

That left the Vikings and Bears who were still battling each other for their division. The Bears beat the Packers while the Vikings lost to the Raiders, leaving the two teams at 8-5. If both teams won their final games the Vikings would win the division but if they both lost the division would go to the Bears.

The Vikings needed to win the division or else they would not be in the playoffs. We had the tiebreaker advantage over them since it boiled down to us beating them during the regular season. The Bears beating us during the regular season was also why they had the tiebreaker advantage over us.

Of course we didn't have to worry about any scenario as long as we beat the Jets. A win and we were playoff bound. It would simply be a matter of whether we would be division champions or the wild card.

Carol and I bypassed the hospitality room spread. We hung out with the team and guests for a little while before we celebrated over a more personal dinner at the Crouching Lion in Kaaawa. This was a beautiful restaurant on Kamehameha Highway with a romantic ambience overlooking the ocean.

I was elated to have this experience with Carol. There was a lot of security in knowing that we were at long last indelibly a couple. The food was delicious although I was so happy that the waitress could have given me a plate of dog food and I wouldn't have noticed.

CHAPTER TWENTY
Must Win Again

The final week of the regular season was upon us. A playoff spot was ours to win. We were favored to get it since all we had to do was beat a team with a 3-10 record.

Obviously our playoff hopes were on my mind on Monday. I also had other responsibilities. Since this was my only day off I took care of my personal business. That included standing in line at the post office with two packages. One was mine to my family in Southern California. The other was Carol's to her family in Northern California. Carol was teaching that day, heading down the home stretch before finals later that week, so I volunteered to mail her package. She rewarded me in advance with a breakfast of eggs, sausage, hash browns and toast.

The recommended deadline for packages to the mainland had passed. When one is focusing on strengthening his relationship with his significant other and trying to make the NFL playoffs the date for sending packages to the mainland was not a top priority. It was amazing that I actually found the time to buy the gifts, let alone mail them. It was fortunate that Carol volunteered to wrap the gifts since my wrapping ability was roughly comparable to a baby's ability to change its own diaper.

"There's no guarantee that these will arrive by Christmas," the postal clerk told me.

"I know. That's all right."

Both packages would ultimately arrive at their respective destinations before Christmas.

Much of the rest of the day was spent at the Pearlridge Shopping Center. I tried to do my Christmas shopping for Carol and a few other local friends. Along the way I ran into about half-a-dozen teammates who were also taking advantage of the opportunity to shop.

At this juncture it was uncertain where I would be on Christmas Day. If we won our division I would be home one day before we would be hosting the winner of the Central Division. If we had to settle for the wild card I would spend Christmas in Dallas since the Cowboys had already secured the home field advantage throughout the playoffs and would host the wild card team in the first round.

The odds of the Rams losing their regular season finale were about the same as ours. The Rams would be squaring off in Los Angeles against the Grizzlies. Memphis was 3-10, having just beaten the Browns.

What it boiled down to obviously was we desperately needed for the Grizzlies to pull an upset while we beat the Jets. That would entail Memphis having a winning streak longer than one for the first time in its brief history. As far as the Hawaiians and their fans were concerned, a

Memphis victory over the Rams would be bigger than Tampa Bay's victory over New Orleans.

Of course if we didn't make the playoffs I would be spending Christmas at home. If I had to choose between having to be in Dallas or staying home because we didn't qualify for the playoffs. . . .

There's a no-brainer for you. If I chose not making the playoffs over having to spend Christmas in Dallas then I had no business being a pro football player.

The one thing I was sure of was that this was going to be my best Christmas since 1973 regardless of how we fared in the playoff picture. Even if I had to spend Christmas in Dallas Carol was still back in my life and would be there when I returned. That made all the difference in the world. I never forgot how miserable I was on Christmas in 1974. I suddenly realized how unhappy I also was on Christmas in 1975 and even in 1976.

I would like to believe that Carol and I were the happiest couple at Arthur's on Monday night. They had a special Christmas party for their most loyal customers. We got casually dressy and joined a few dozen other invited guests for free drinks and pupus. My good friend and agent Don Simmons was there, which made sense since he was the one who introduced me to this reasonably new member of the local Flamingo chain several months earlier. Dave Shuford was the only other member of the team present since he was known to drop in for a beer two or three times a week.

Aside from Dave's presence, the night kept my mind off of football. Carol and I mingled and had a good time with good friends who didn't happen to be connected to football. Arthur's attracted primarily a very nice group of people.

Tuesday meant back to the world. Film sessions, light workout and TV show. The radio stations may have been playing Christmas music but earning a living dominated my agenda.

Walker was civil again during the film session. He raised his voice a few times but not too severely. Overall we played a fairly solid game. The Falcons were ready for us but we were more ready for them.

"We need this game," Walker announced at the beginning of the joint meeting after the films, referring to our forthcoming game with the Jets. "Everything rides on this one game now. We need this game. So do the Jets."

Walker paused. He seemed to be checking to see if anybody was taken by surprise. The Jets were closing out their season. They weren't going anywhere but home regardless of how they did on Sunday.

"The Jets are playing for pride," Walker continued. "They need this game more than you might imagine. If they beat you it will give them momentum for next year. They also know that they have a chance to

468

possibly knock you out of the playoff picture. Teams that are out of the playoff hunt love to play the spoiler."

That was a sobering thought.

But a truthful one.

"You control your own destiny. At least you control most of it. If you win you're in the playoffs. Whether you win the division or not depends on what the Rams do against Memphis. Let's just focus on the Jets and not think about the Rams. If you spend your time worrying about the Rams you'll be distracted."

It was difficult to be distracted with Walker around. That was like a Marine Corps recruit being able to focus on something else when his drill instructor was around. Walker worked us pretty hard on Wednesday, Thursday and Friday. He didn't belittle us too much but he pushed and pushed and pushed.

Wednesday evening I had time to myself. Carol was busy grading final exams and I spent the late afternoon addressing a youth group in the Salt Lake section of Honolulu. I was going to go home afterward and throw something together for dinner, then decided instead to dine at the Sizzler in the Salt Lake Shopping Center.

A wave of euphoria swept over me as I enjoyed my steak dinner. Being back on track with Carol was probably the primary factor. It also didn't hurt that the Hawaiians appeared to be playoff bound with a remote possibility of a division championship included. I was also thrilled to have been selected to the Pro Bowl.

But it was more than that. Although I wasn't consciously aware of the specifics, I was changing for the better as a person.

A year earlier I was looser. I wasn't a drunk but I drank more than I did in 1977; not really thinking of the consequences of having an extra drink or two.

Of course I was also with different women back then. I believed at the time that it was the way I was meant to be although I could never explain why. Although there were some very nice ladies who passed through my life, it was a miserable existence. I played the role of ladies' man but didn't prefer it.

Obviously Carol had much to do with my sense of well-being and not simply because she satisfied my ultimate desire to be in a monogamous relationship. She was simply the woman who was right for me. Even before we finally opened up and cleared the air I knew that she was the one. I probably knew it the moment I laid eyes on her at Kahala Mall the previous June. I probably even knew it during the three years of estrangement.

Carol's presence probably influenced my overall mannerisms. Although she had her imperfections, she was primarily a well-mannered, morally upright individual. I suppose she inspired me to be my best on and off the field. As the cliche goes, behind every great man there's a woman. How great I might have been was a matter of conjecture but there was no disputing that Carol was an extremely wonderful woman whose influence over me was positive.

"I never wanted to win a game so badly in my life," Walker told us at the end of Friday's workout. "I know you can beat those guys from New York. Let's do it."

Billingsley seemed to be the primary target for Walker during the week. I don't know if it was contrived or if Billingsley simply wasn't playing as well as Walker thought he should. Some of his passes were off the mark although that was never unusual. Bender's passes also missed the mark occasionally. So did those of Bart Starr, Terry Bradshaw, Y.A. Tittle and Ken Stabler.

The differences between Bender and Billingsley were overwhelming. As hackneyed as it is, comparing those two is like comparing night and day.

About the only similarity between the two is that they were both good natural athletes. Both had excelled in football, basketball and baseball in high school. Bender went strictly to football afterward although the San Francisco Giants made a modest pitch to sign him in the days prior to the free agent draft. Billingsley played both football and baseball at Brigham Young University while also playing basketball in a recreational church league.

Bender was a self-confident, quiet leader. He was friendly but reserved. He was very poised and dead serious about his life on and off the field. He had a sense of humor, yet he didn't laugh much. If somebody said or did something funny his concession to the levity usually was that he would grin and nod his head. If something was hysterically funny one might be able to get a chuckle out of him.

Perhaps it was that he was older than his teammates that detached him a little without causing resentment. He got along with virtually everybody although the only player he was truly close to was Dietrich. Dietrich played with Bender for two years in Washington and they were traded together to San Francisco where they played five more years before both were taken by Hawaii in the expansion draft.

Bender was aloof but not cold. He was actually the kind of guy who would go out of his way for anybody who needed it. I found out by accident that he and his wife spent a lot of time during and after his career working with the underprivileged. When he found out that I knew he made me promise not to tell anybody.

Billingsley was another matter. It wasn't that he wasn't a good guy. He definitely had a chip on his shoulder. He wasn't as big as Bender, wasn't as tough as Bender, wasn't as strong as Bender and wasn't as poised as Bender.

470

He was occasionally verbally abusive with his teammates and that caused friction.

I suppose Billingsley resented his backup role. That's understandable to a point. No self-respecting pro football player wants to be a backup. He can accept his role graciously but he should always work hard to try to overtake the incumbent.

Ironically Bender was the one teammate Billingsley seemed willing to listen to. Bender went out of his way from the very first season to help Billingsley prepare for his days as a starting NFL quarterback. When Bender retired concurrent with Earl McDaniel deciding to step down as the color commentator for our radio broadcasts, paving the way for Bender to replace him, he still tried to help Billingsley whenever possible.

But Billingsley's degree of difficulty for overtaking Bender rose up a few notches. For the first time in his career Bender was selected to the Pro Bowl. That was a powerful compliment for Bender. It showed how vital he was to the team's success and how much respect he had earned among his peers around the league.

Unlike 1976 when only Marv represented the Hawaiians at the Pro Bowl, this time we had more than one player selected. Besides Bender, Allen and Jennings were also selected, as was yours truly.

"Man oh man," Walker commented at the end of our light Saturday workout. "I wish we could kick off right now. I think you guys are ready to play some football."

That brought enthusiastic cheers from his players. Most of us were on one knee as we gathered around him in the south end zone.

"The Jets are in town," he continued. "They're a good bunch of guys but tomorrow they are your mortal enemies. I want you to stick it to them so bad that you ruin their Christmas."

Walker paused before adding, "Ruin their entire offseason."

Prendergast would be out. He had a pinched nerve in his neck. He was expected to be ready the following week. Ken Gilbert would be starting in his place.

Jerry Reiser was signed after being cut at the end of training camp. The tailback from Western Michigan would see his first NFL action since 1975 when he was with Houston. He was taken in the 23rd round of the expansion draft in 1976, one round ahead of Scott. He spent all of 1976 on injured reserve. He would be Ozzie Roberts' backup against the Jets.

On Saturday night I took Carol to the Chart House for dinner. It was a semblance of a celebration for her. Finals were completed and she would be free until the spring semester.

Our arrival coincided with that of Earl McDaniel and his wife Ellie. As was mentioned, Earl was the color commentator for the Hawaiians' radio broadcasts as well as the general manager of KGMB Radio. A few years later after the call letters were changed to KSSK he would persuade me to go to the studio on Kapiolani Boulevard the morning after each game to briefly discuss the just completed games. Initially I would be on with Aku and then, after Aku passed away in 1983, with Perry and Price. On the rare occasion that the Hawaiians were staying on the road after an away game I would phone the report in. I would continue this gig through the end of my career.

Earl invited Carol and me to join him and Ellie. Although I still didn't know him that well despite the fact that he had been the color commentator since the Hawaiians' first-ever game, Carol and I graciously accepted the invitation.

"So how do you think you're going to do tomorrow?" Earl asked.

I hesitated and looked around the room. The Jets were staying at the Ala Moana Hotel which was very near the Chart House. I didn't want to say anything that might be overheard to fire up the Jets. There didn't seem to be anybody from the Jets present but I couldn't be completely sure.

"All I can say is we appear to be ready to go," I finally replied. "Larry Scott and Hank Prendergast are going to be on the sideline in street clothes but we've got sufficient backups. Ozzie Roberts and Ken Gilbert are both very capable."

Earl looked thoughtful, seeming to hang on to my every word. I was under the impression that he would be quoting me the next day but what I had told him was public knowledge. I made a mental note to be careful about what I said; not that I didn't trust Earl but I had to ensure that I didn't say anything that Walker wouldn't want said, and attributed to me, over the air.

McDaniel was about my height with a thin build. He also had a good sense of humor with a face that reminded me a little of Spike Jones. His smile seemed to be almost identical to that of Jones, at least in my mind.

"You're from California, aren't you?" Earl asked.

"Right. I was born in Glendora, then lived in Azusa and moved to Montebello just before I started high school."

Earl told me that he was Southern California native himself, having been born in Santa Monica. During the 50s and into the 60s he worked on the air at a few radio stations in Los Angeles, most notably KFWB Radio beginning in 1961.

"That was before I started listening to anything but Dodger games on the radio but maybe my parents listened to you. They listened mostly to KMPC but I remember them listening to KFWB once in a while back then."

While in Los Angeles Earl had also worked as a promoter, an actor and even managed the Champs musical group which was best known for *Tequila*. It was a very colorful career which climaxed with his move to Hawaii in

472

1966 when Cec Heftel, the majority owner of the Hawaiians and owner of KGMB Radio, hired him to be general manager at KGMB.

Based on my own observations of Earl which would develop over the years and what those who worked under him told me, he was a very good man for whom to work. He was very self-confident and knowledgeable about how to go about his responsibilities. Like Heftel, he understood that it was the people at the station that made it successful and the staff was treated accordingly. I heard a few horror stories about how staffs were treated at other radio and TV stations in Hawaii but KGMB did not fall into that category. Most of the staff was very content, thanks largely to Heftel and McDaniel.

On the other hand, based on what I was told, if one ever got on Earl's bad side it was nearly impossible to get back on his good side. Fortunately not too many people seemed to get on his bad side.

It wound up being a very entertaining dinner with Earl and Ellie. We spent most of the evening talking about things other than football. By the time the evening ended I felt very relaxed and ready to take on the Jets.

I was ready to play as we went through our final rituals in the locker room prior to kickoff. For the eighth time in a row dating back to the 1976 home finale we had a sellout. For the seventh consecutive time we had sold out well enough in advance to televise the game locally.

Malick led us in *The Lord's Prayer*. Walker then looked us over with a funny grin on his face.

"I'm ready," he finally reported. "Are you men ready?"

We roared in the affirmative.

"I thought so," Walker continued. "You guys are going to make the Jets sorry they left New York. You can make beautiful Hawaii look so unattractive to them that they'll dread the thought of ever returning, even on vacation. Let's stick it to them."

I checked to make sure I had everything, chugged a cup of Gatorade and left the locker room. I joined my offensive colleagues in the south end zone.

"All right," I said, clapping my hands. "It's a great day to play football. Look at this crowd we've got. Let's give them what they want."

The crowd was going to be very vital in our effort. I could literally feel the fans' excitement about our regular season finale. A year earlier we were going nowhere but home after our final game but we had an opportunity to play the spoiler which we did not waste. Now we would advance as long as we didn't allow the Jets to play the spoiler role.

As I jogged in place in the end zone I knew that our playoff hopes could be assured at any time. Although I tried to avoid thoughts of the Bears, it was announced over the public address system that they were in a 9-9 tie with the Giants at the end of regulation. Since the Vikings won their game the day before to sew up the NFC Central Championship, the Bears' last hope was the wild card berth. If the Giants prevailed the Bears' season was over and we would be guaranteed at least the wild card berth. If the Bears came through they would be rooting like crazy for the Jets.

It was also announced that the Buccaneers had extended their winning streak to two games. They beat the Cardinals at home. Less than a month earlier the Cardinals were leading the wild card race. They then went into a tailspin and wound up with a 7-7 record.

I tried to distance myself from the rest of the league. I was giddy with excitement over the significance of the game I was about to play. In our brief two-year NFL history and during the two years of the WFL Hawaiians there was never a game with more meaning. Assuming that the Bears would get past the Giants, our playoff hopes hinged on this game.

Nobody expected the Grizzlies to beat the Rams. I figured that the Rams had the division in their hip pocket unless they got complacent.

But stranger things have happened. The Hawaiians themselves were living proof of that. We won at least four games in 1976 that nobody expected us to win. We weren't expected to win in our debut game against the Cardinals but when we did most people wrote it off simply as one of those flukes. When we later beat the Raiders, Bengals and Browns people were totally blown away.

I kept that in mind. The odds were very much against us winning the division. It still wasn't out of the realm of possibility. Like the Jets, the Grizzlies wanted to play the spoiler.

Of course it was also possible for the Jets to beat us. I reminded myself, again, to focus on the Jets. I had no control over what happened with the Bears and Rams.

The crowd gave us unbridled support during the pregame introductions. After the Damien High School Band played the *National Anthem* our captains went to midfield.

We won the toss. The crowd roared our first victory of the day. I hoped the crowd would be roaring its pleasure the rest of the day.

"All right, men! Gather round!" Walker called, calling for a pregame pep talk on the sideline for only the second time that season. Apparently he felt that what he said in the locker room wasn't quite enough.

"This is our finest hour to this point in our history," Walker remarked once we were all around him. "When you men are on your game there is nobody who can beat you. The Jets are determined to pull an upset and they'll have a few tricks up their sleeves to go with the extra motivation. Just hang in there and give the best you have with a minimum of mistakes and you'll pull this one out."

I took my post on the goal line of the south end zone. As I slapped fives with Hasegawa I noticed how overwhelmed with butterflies I was. It was normal for me to have butterflies before I got my first licks in but this was

474

extreme. It was at a level of my biggest games dating back to high school. The last time I recalled it being at this level was before the last game of my sophomore year at the University of Hawaii when we were to take on Nebraska.

The kick was up. It was heading toward Hasegawa.

"You've got it, Rich!" I called.

Forgotten were the butterflies. All that mattered was the job at hand. I ran forward and collided with a white jersey with green trim, lowering myself to just below his shoulder pads. I hit him hard enough to knock him down, then stumbled forward a few steps before going down myself.

Rich went past me. He was a few yards ahead of me before he went down at the 21. It was a 24-yard return.

I popped up and ran over to Rich. I reached down and helped him to his feet.

"Good job, Rich," I said, whacking my teammate of seven years on his derriere.

"Great block, man," he responded. "I thought you were going to break that sucker's ribs."

I honestly never played to hurt anybody. However, I wasn't averse to temporarily traumatizing my opponents.

We didn't start our drive like a team hoping to get into the playoffs. Ozzie picked up three yards off right tackle but that was nullified by Marv's holding penalty. We had first and 20 at the eleven.

Kerner went off left tackle to the 15 but then Bender got sacked at the ten. The Jets were obviously very determined to play the spoiler. We were going to have to suck it up and wear them down.

The Jets came hard at Bender on the next play. Before he was hit he found Dietrich over the middle at the 21. Ted turned upfield, breaking two tackles and dodging a couple of other defenders. He was finally caught from behind at the 38, giving us a hard-earned first down.

"All right. Good going, guys," Bender remarked in the huddle.

Slater came in for Dietrich. A pass to him was batted down. Ozzie then ran around right end for a mere two yards to the 40.

Obviously we were going to the air on third and eight. We just didn't go as long as the Jets anticipated. Bender took the snap and immediately hit me at the Hawaii 41. That was obviously well short of the first down but I had room to run. I maneuvered my way across midfield to the Jets 44 to the delight of the roaring crowd.

Plays like that really make you feel good about yourself. You have helped your team, electrified the crowd and also caught the attention of those watching on TV. It was a joint effort comprised of passing, running and blocking. It was still one of my better plays because it took some running and maneuvering ability to pick up 15 yards after I made the reception. God gave me the skills and I used them.

Since our opponent was an AFC team away from its home the game was being shown on NBC. Since the game figured prominently in the playoff picture it was shown in several markets across the country as well as Honolulu and New York. This included the Los Angeles market since it figured prominently in the Rams' fate if they actually managed to lose to Memphis so my family and old friends were able to watch. Since Memphis was in the AFC the Rams-Grizzlies game was also on NBC concurrent with ours but the Rams didn't sell out well enough in advance to be shown in the Los Angeles market so our game was shown instead.

Our drive stalled. Over the next three plays we managed only one yard. Jablonski came on to punt for the first time in two weeks and hadn't forgotten how it was done. His punt was downed at the six.

"All right. Be cool. Be cool," offensive coordinator Jim Potter said. "We'll wear 'em down. Don't lose your heads."

Although the Jets were hopelessly guaranteed a poor record, they understood their role and wanted to give it their best. They even arrived in Hawaii on Wednesday to try to get adjusted to the heat and humidity. It was commendable that they went to the trouble of arriving a couple of days earlier than most teams would have come although there was also little doubt that they took advantage of the local beaches. We still hoped to have them hopelessly weak and dehydrated as soon as possible. In the backs of our minds we were probably hoping that some of their key players were not only badly sunburned but spent the better part of Saturday night drinking mai tais.

The Jets started with a four-yard run that was nullified by a holding penalty. That gave them a first and 13 at the three.

I was hoping that the Jets would attempt a pass. I had no doubt that a pass attempt on this play would lead to a sack in the end zone to give us a 2-0 lead.

My wish came true; at least the part where the Jets attempted a pass. Unfortunately the Jets also completed the pass. It was a short pass and they wound up with a second and five at the eleven.

The Jets picked up a couple of first downs before their drive died at their own 41. I stood near the 15 to field a punt. I was determined that this drive would end with a better result than our previous drive. I had the opportunity to get it off to the start it needed.

It was a so-so punt. The distance was reasonable but there wasn't much hang time. I caught the punt on the run at the 23. I managed to outrun one defender and maneuver around another before being brought down at the 35. It was a good return.

"All right. Let's score on this drive," I said as I joined my colleagues in the huddle.

Ozzie managed only a yard up the middle on the opening play but Bender hit me near the left sideline at the Jets 45. I got four more yards before being pushed out of bounds.

It was essentially a battle of wills. The Jets, although having a season that would make one forget that this was the team that upset the Baltimore Colts in Super Bowl III, were comprised of genuine professionals. They followed my reception with a sack of Bender at the New York 48 to give us a second and 17.

"Okay, that's one for them," Bender remarked calmly in the huddle although I sensed that he was somewhat irritated about the sack. "Let's strike back with a vengeance."

And so we did. Bender hit Grummon near the left hash mark at the 29. That alone gave us another first down. Grummon fought for 12 more yards to the 17.

"We've got 17 yards to go," Bender reported in the huddle. "They're not going to make it easy for us but we can wear them down."

We picked up roughly six feet from that point. Ozzie got two yards off right tackle. That was followed by two incompletions; the latter of which was right to Slater in the left corner of the end zone but was batted away just as the ball was hitting his hands.

I stood in the middle of the north end zone with my hands on my hips as soon as the latter play was completed. I looked toward the sideline and noticed the field goal unit being dispatched to the field. I sighed and ran to the sideline.

"It's okay. We're wearing 'em down. We're wearing 'em down," Bennici was saying encouragingly as I reached the sideline. "This heat and humidity is the 12th man on the field for us. The crowd is the 13th man."

The temperature during the game was in the upper 70s which was fairly typical for Hawaii in December. There were also reasonably strong trades which would alleviate the humidity. It was hot and miserable compared to what the Jets left behind in New York but their early arrival should have enabled them to adjust. Bennici's pep talk was effective only if it helped to psych us up.

I was buying it. I think we all were.

Guinn did his job. His 32-yard field goal attempt was true. It was 3-0 with 1:37 left in the first quarter.

"All right. We've got three points," I said, deciding to do my part to keep everybody up. "Let's get at least 30 or 40 more before we're through."

Despite the fact that we didn't get the full seven we were hoping for, nobody seemed downtrodden. Also, nobody was satisfied so overall it was a very positive sign. There was an air of confidence without overconfidence. We were essentially analyzing what we could do to the Jets, figuring out their weaknesses so that we could wear them down.

In the meantime Guinn kicked off. The ball was caught a yard deep in the end zone. The Jet return man immediately dropped to one knee.

The crowd booed. The fans apparently wanted to see either Hasegawa or Hamer, or anybody else for that matter, pulverize the return man. They both got downfield so fast that they were both inside the 20 by the time the return man caught the ball. There were still blockers available but the return man apparently didn't trust them. The kick was, however, very high by kickoff standards so that gave Hasegawa and Hamer a few extra seconds to get downfield.

"Run it out, ya wimp!" Stanek called out when the play was officially blown dead.

There were several similar remarks from the crowd near our sideline. A few of the remarks were better left unsaid in such close proximity to children. Overall it was great having the crowd in our corner.

The Jets seemed undaunted. They picked up a first down on two rushing plays. When the quarter ended they had a second and six at their own 37.

On the first play of the second quarter the Jets appeared to have another first down. They completed a pass at about the Hawaii 48. The receiver got to the 44 before being hit by Dubois.

"Fumble!"

It was the usual scenario of bodies in brown jerseys and white jerseys scrambling for the ball. The referee stood above a small pile of humanity, waved his arms over his head and then pointed toward the south end zone. That drew a huge roar from the crowd.

"Offense!" Walker called.

For the record, it was Jennings who made the recovery at the Hawaii 46. He bounced up, flipped the ball to a nearby official and ran triumphantly to our sideline with the rest of the defense.

"Way to go, Ed!" I called out as I ran toward our huddle. "Magnifique, Henri!"

"All right, gentleman," Bender remarked coolly in the huddle. "This is opportunity knocking."

We went to work immediately. Kerner went up the middle and looked like a tank plowing through a group of Volkswagens. He got to the New York 44 before being dragged down.

Time was called. The officials wanted to measure. We were a little short. It was second and inches.

Suddenly it was second and five. Stanek jumped before the snap. That moved us back to the New York 49.

"That's not the way to win ballgames, you clowns!" Walker scolded from the sideline, looking at us scornfully with his hands on his hips.

478

Ozzie ran a sweep around left end behind a convoy of blockers of which I was proud to be a part. He got back to the 44. Time was called again to measure. This time we had the first down.

"Great job, Ozzie!" I said enthusiastically. I figured he had to have been nervous about suddenly being thrust into the limelight as our premiere running back spot with so much on the line. I wanted him to feel as if we had confidence in him.

Ozzie got the call again; this time up the middle. He picked up five yards to the 39.

As we were moving to the huddle we discovered that we absolutely had to win in order to get into the playoffs. The Bears kicked a field goal in the final seconds of overtime to secure a 12-9 victory over the Giants. The final score was announced over the PA system. I couldn't help but hear it even though I tried to drown everything out.

"Don't sweat it, men," Bender said amid the murmuring as the huddle was forming. "We're going to win this game. All the Bears did was buy themselves a little time. Now let's get back to work."

Bender, who called his own plays about 75 percent of the time, decided to go to the air. He hit me near the right hash mark at the 21. I was hit at the exact moment I got my hands on the ball but held on, giving us a first down.

The clip I would see on the news would show that it was a pretty brutal hit that I took. From my end it was another one of those hits that felt like nothing. I bounced right up and went to the huddle.

Kerner kept the crowd excited with his run up the middle. He blasted his way to the 13.

Unfortunately the Jets were determined to stop us. Our pass on the following play didn't get off. Bender dropped back and wound up sacked at the 23. It was third and 12.

"Well, we'll just have to show them what we're made of," Bender remarked somewhat flippantly in the huddle. What we didn't know as we were forming up was that there was a penalty marker down.

Unfortunately it was against us. Hayer was cited for holding. The Jets declined.

"How in the hell could we have been called for holding?" Bender remarked facetiously. "Their entire defense was in my face."

We were in field goal range. Something about Bender's demeanor told me a field goal would never be considered. I sensed that Bender would direct us to the full seven before Walker could send in the field goal unit.

It took one play. In our double-single formation Bender found Slater open near the left sideline. He hit Slater at the ten. With a few fancy moves Slater ran virtually unmolested to the end zone. He leaped up and tried to slam dunk the ball over the crossbar of the goal post. He wound up bouncing the ball off the crossbar.

"Don't ever take up basketball," Stanek said lightly as he shook Slater's hand.

"What? I did it that way on purpose," Slater replied equally as light.

"Sure you did," Dietrich said dryly.

It didn't matter. The touchdown was what mattered. We had a 9-0 lead with 11:23 left in the half. Guinn's extra point made it 10-0.

"We're on our way," I said to Hayer as we grabbed our Gatorade.

Suddenly there was a huge roar from the crowd. Instinctively Carl and I looked at the scoreboard. Across the Pacific Memphis was holding a 10-7 lead over the Rams at the end of the first quarter.

"Do we dare hope?" Carl asked.

"We can hope. Of course our first order of business is to beat the Jets."

As focused as I was on the Jets, I would still be thinking about the Rams. It was impossible not to. We would be happy just to get into the playoffs but even happier if we could win the division, especially since it would mean a home game in the opening round of the playoffs against the Vikings. We would also have the home field advantage in the NFC Championship if we beat the Vikings and the Rams could upend the Cowboys.

But we still had to force ourselves to focus on the Jets. We had to keep our scoreboard watching to a minimum or else we risked handing the wild card to the Bears. If we lost it was all over for us regardless of what the Rams did.

Guinn kicked off. The ball was fielded at the one. The return man got to the 26.

I sat on the bench and hoped the defense would make quick work of the series. I wanted to get back on the field and devote my full attention to the Hawaiians and Jets. I believed that being on the field would take my mind off of the Rams and Grizzlies.

The Jets opened with a four-yard rush to the 30. They then went to a short pass over the middle.

Gilbert reached up and tipped the ball up. Rodgers ran in and picked the ball off at the 33.

Carl was quick. Before any of the offensive linemen realized what had happened Carl had already passed them. The fullback, who had stayed in the backfield to protect the quarterback, gave chase. He brought Carl down but not until he was crossing the goal line.

"Yeah!" I exclaimed as I leaped up.

Needless to say, Carl was given an enthusiastic reception on the sideline. It was another milestone toward the wild card if not the division title. With Guinn's extra point we led 17-0 with 10:22 left in the half. We had scored two touchdowns in 61 seconds.

"Another nail in the Bears' coffin," Kerner said to Rodgers who had played seven seasons with the Bears. "That's a good way to get back at them for leaving you unprotected in the expansion draft."

Our attendance was 49,913. I snuck a peak up in the stands and caught a brief glimpse of Carol. She was flanked by Pam Bender and Don Simmons. Don's girlfriend Eileen was also present with my former roommate, Bill Trimble, next to her. They all seemed to be enjoying the game.

I had only been able to get two tickets on top of the standard two I was allotted. Don had requested a ticket for Eileen well in advance so that was no trouble. When Bill called me a few days earlier to request two tickets I really had to scramble. I was lucky to get one but the second one for his alleged girlfriend Cherie, or whoever it was he was planning on taking, was a dead end.

The 17-point lead looked pretty good. Naturally the Jets were still determined to retaliate. They began by fielding the kick at the three and returning it to the 23.

The Jets almost made things look easy immediately after the kick return. I would hate to think that our defense got complacent although the defense might have let up a little with a three-score lead. I prefer to believe it was simply good execution by the Jets which enabled them to pick up two first downs in four plays. Three plays later they had a first down at the Hawaii 29.

A rush up the middle got them six yards to the 23. That was when our defense finally bore down. A rush for no gain and an incomplete pass put them in a fourth and four. That sent their field goal unit out.

"I guess I can concede three points," I said to Prendergast who was standing behind our bench in street clothes and his game jersey.

"Yeah. You know they're going to break through and put some points on the board. As long as we continue to score we'll be okay," Hank replied.

It was an obvious fact. Primarily we were reassuring ourselves.

The kick was up and. . . .

Suddenly there was a roar from the north end zone. As the officials waved their arms in front of them and made a sweeping motion to their right sides there was a crescendo from the rest of the crowd. The kick was wide to the left.

"I can also concede a missed field goal. Maybe we'll just start putting it away now," I said to Prendergast with a huge grin before I put on my helmet and returned to the field. We had a first down on the 23. We had all three timeouts left. The clock showed 2:22 left in the half.

"This is perfect," Bender remarked in the huddle. We figured we could at least get a field goal if not a touchdown.

Our opponents weren't quite ready to lay down. The sufficiently rested Jet defense put a lot of heat on Bender as he dropped back to pass. Steve managed to scramble away and move forward, stepping out of bounds at the 29. The clock showed 2:09.

The heat was on Bender again on the next snap. He was again forced to scramble. This time he got the pass off. I caught the ball near the Hawaii 45 but not until I was about a yard out of bounds. It was third and four with 1:58 left in the half.

As Bender conversed with Walker on the sideline during the two-minute warning I seethed a little. I wasn't really angry at anybody. I was simply frustrated over the fact that we weren't cutting through the Jet defense as routinely as I thought we should.

Their season was virtually over. Why didn't they simply bask in the Hawaiian sunshine?

Because they were professional football players, that's why. They were trying to end an otherwise horrific season in a blaze of glory. A victory for them would speak volumes. We wanted to go to the playoffs. It was the Jets' job to prevent us from getting there.

We got on track when play resumed. I carried off left tackle. I was hit near the line but kept going. It was mind over matter, I believe, and I wasn't brought down until I had reached the Hawaii 37. It was a first down.

"Timeout!" I heard Bender call as I prepared to pick myself up. The clock was stopped at 1:48.

There was still a long way to go and the clock was a major factor. We still needed to pick up about 30 yards before we had a reasonable expectation of a field goal.

Bender's pass to Grummon was slightly overthrown and dropped untouched. It was second and ten with 1:41 left in the half.

On the next play Bender went for Dietrich. Unfortunately the pass was slightly underthrown and a defensive back picked the ball off at the New York 48. Ted managed to get his hands on him but wasn't able to grasp him securely. The defensive back was heading for the north end zone.

I was in pursuit. I began near the middle of the field as the defensive back moved toward the left sideline. He broke Kerner's tackle and maneuvered around Bender. That slowed him up enough to enable Marv and me to hit him simultaneously at the 27. The three of us tumbled out of bounds.

The defensive back bounced up in jubilation and was mobbed by his teammates. I raised to my knees and watched the celebration. The exultant Jets weren't rubbing our noses in it, I knew. There was no taunting or finger-pointing. It was a legitimate celebration.

Still, I felt violated. I felt as if someone had come into my home and committed a burglary.

I got up and ran across the field to our sideline. I also looked at the clock on the large scoreboard in the north end zone. There was 1:22 left and the Jets had all three of their timeouts. They had plenty of time to travel 81 feet.

We donated 15 feet. Jennings was a tad overzealous and got called for encroachment. It was first and five at the 22.

The Jets got the play off. There was pressure on the quarterback. He scrambled a little but found a receiver inside the 15 just as Jennings was about to nail him. The receiver got to the four before Black and Rodgers dragged him down.

"(Expletive deleted)," I said to myself although those standing in the same vicinity heard me. A few expressed similar sentiments.

The Jets called timeout. There was 1:08 left in the half.

"It would almost be worth it to concede the touchdown right now," I said discreetly to Shuford who was standing to my right.

"It would?"

"Sure. We get the ball back with, uh, two timeouts left. We put together a few big plays and score another touchdown in the final seconds to give us our 17-point lead back."

The Jets foiled my strategy. They went off right tackle to the one and didn't call timeout. With two more downs to try to punch it in before going for the field goal they were apparently planning to use a timeout after the next play and would take their final timeout when all they had left to try was a field goal.

It wasn't until much later that I wondered why we didn't call timeout. I suppose our focus was strictly on preventing the touchdown or forcing them to run out of time, not putting together a final drive.

The Jets ran around left end. Pratt lunged and tripped the ball carrier up. However, the ball carrier didn't go down until after he crossed the goal line.

I didn't say a word. I looked at Shuford and raised my eyebrows. He nodded slightly. It was probably our respective ways of conceding that our 17-point lead was down to eleven points.

The extra point reduced our lead to ten points. There were 23 seconds left in the half.

Those 23 seconds were enough time for the strangest decision of the half. I caught the kickoff six yards deep in the end zone and opted not to run it out. Bender then took a snap and dropped to one knee to run out the clock. I took a step or two forward toward the locker room.

"Timeout!" somebody called.

I couldn't believe it. With the clock ticked down to 14 seconds one of the Jets enigmatically called timeout. Nobody on either side understood why. Whoever it was who called timeout probably didn't understand it himself.

"This game is really getting weird," Marv muttered.

Although the Jets still had one timeout, they didn't bother with it after Bender took another snap and dropped to a knee.

"Are we finished?" Kerner asked lightly, looking at the defense as if to ask if they wanted to use their final timeout. Players on both sides cracked up and we headed to our respective locker rooms.

In the locker room I visited the little boy's room and drank a cup of Gatorade. I grabbed a Pepsi and Kerner offered me a Baby Ruth bar.

"We're halfway to the playoffs," I said quietly as I unwrapped the candy. "We've got to expand this lead to give us some breathing room."

"They're playing for pride," Jeff replied. "That makes them dangerous. They've got nothing to lose."

For the next few minutes the offensive and defensive units made a few adjustments with their respective coaches. Walker then stood in the middle to address us before our return to the field.

"You're lucky to be ahead," he said somewhat somberly. "You've got a ten-point lead but they're pushing you around pretty well. You've got to stick it to them."

I don't know if Walker honestly felt that way or if he was simply trying to motivate us to play better. I did not feel as if the Jets were pushing us around. They were motivated and hanging tough against us, turning this into a contest where we had to be at our best in order to beat them but that was not equated with pushing us around.

It could even be argued that the Jets had the momentum. What we had to do was continue to play to the best of our ability and wear them down.

The Jets would be receiving. As Guinn was getting set to tee the ball up I heard the public address announce address the crowd.

"At halftime, the Rams 27, Memphis 13."

That produced a groan from the crowd and even from our sideline but we couldn't dwell on that. We had to win regardless of what the Rams did. If we lost we'd be watching the Bears in the playoffs instead of them watching us.

Guinn kicked off. The ball was caught two yards deep in the south end zone. The return man didn't even bother looking. He immediately downed the ball.

The Jets were still thinking upset. Despite an illegal procedure penalty, they managed to pick up a first down after three plays. Two plays later they had another first down at the 50.

"The thought of these guys scoring on this drive makes me want to puke," I remarked while standing next to Slater on the sideline. Even a field goal would turn this into a one-score game.

The Jets went off left tackle to the Hawaii 45. McDaniel then got called for encroachment to move the ball to the 40.

Time was called for a measurement. The Jets were short. It was second and inches.

A first down seemed inevitable. They tried to get it by rushing off left tackle.

484

The running back received a rude reception from Gilbert, much to the delight of his teammates and the crowd. Not only did Gilbert prevent him from moving forward, he threw him for a two-yard loss.

Not bad for a substitute defensive tackle. It was third and two.

And then it was fourth and three. The Jets tried a sweep around left end. Jurgens was waiting to drop the ball carrier a yard behind the line, drawing another roar from the crowd. It appeared that we may have been regaining the momentum.

Suddenly I was on the field. A field goal attempt would have been about 60 yards against the wind. The Jets prudently opted to punt.

The punter predictably went for the coffin corner. The ball hit at the four, took a high bounce and came down in the end zone for a touchback. We had first down at the 20.

"Okay, let's start putting it away," Bender optimistically directed in the huddle.

Unfortunately the Jets didn't seem to want to see us in the playoffs. The linemen and linebackers came hard at Steve as he dropped back. He got a pass off toward Ozzie in the flat but it fell a little short.

Bender hit Grummon on the next play at the Hawaii 35. A defensive back was right there to prevent any further advancement. We still had a first down.

I got the call on the next play. Bender handed off to me and I headed through the left side. A wall of white jerseys with green trim prevented me from gaining any yardage.

There were thoughts that I don't care to reveal. At least I kept them to myself. I angrily bounced up and went to the huddle.

We couldn't wait for the next play.

Or at least Grummon couldn't wait. The snap was on three and he jumped on one. We had second and 15 at the 30.

"All right. Let's be cool. Everybody take a deep breath and focus on your assignments. We'll get it back," Bender said in the huddle.

It was back to the air. Bender threw a bullet into Dietrich's chest at the Hawaii 45. Ted had a defender on his tail but still managed four more yards to give us a first down at our own 49.

"Good job, Ted," I said, whacking him on the rear after Grummon helped him to his feet.

The crowd was cheering. It sounded great. We were 51 yards from expanding our ten-point lead.

Or perhaps it was the Jets who were 49 yards from dramatically cutting into our lead. A pass to me in the flat was nearly intercepted. A linebacker cut in front of me and got his hands on the ball, juggled and finally dropped the ball inside the 40. There was nothing but north end zone in front of him. The pained expression on his face indicated that he was keenly aware of it. He probably felt worse than I did when I rushed for no gain two plays earlier.

We were more successful on our next pass. I caught it over the middle at the New York 39, having to leap slightly to grab it. As soon as my hands were on the ball I was simultaneously hammered by a pair of defenders who flipped me over, causing me to land on my back. The hits were pretty brutal but I didn't remember them. I only remember catching the ball and hitting the ground. It was amazing that my wind wasn't knocked out when I hit the ground. It was even more amazing that I held on to the ball.

An incompletion and a rush by Ozzie for no gain put us in a third and ten. That was followed by another incomplete pass that was nullified by an offside penalty against the Jets. It was third and five at the 34.

Unfortunately we didn't convert. Another incomplete pass slightly out of Dietrich's reach sent our field goal unit to the field.

It was frustrating. I still tried not to let it bother me. The Jets were putting everything they had left for the season into this final game. If they had been this dedicated during their first 13 games they might have been in the AFC playoff hunt.

Arroyo's snap was fielded cleanly by Billingsley. Billingsley put the ball down at the 41, making this a 51 yard attempt. Guinn got the kick off.

It was on its way. It didn't seem to have the height one would expect. The kick split the uprights but passed slightly under the crossbar.

"Oh, geez," I said.

I wasn't angry at Guinn or anybody else. I was simply frustrated. We couldn't seem to expand our lead.

After grabbing my Gatorade I sat on the bench. Shuford sat next to me.

"This is '76 in reverse," I remarked.

"Hm?"

"This game. It's like it was for us at the end of last year. Remember?"

Before Dave could respond I realized that he couldn't relate to what I was talking about.

"Oh, I forgot. You were with the Colts then," I said. "We went into the last game last year as the most relentless team in the NFL. We knew that by beating the Browns we would knock them out of the playoff picture. That's what the Jets are trying to do to us."

While we did knock the Browns out on that final Saturday of 1976, their playoff hopes would have ended the following day anyway when the Steelers won. Our victory simply knocked the Browns out 24 hours earlier.

"There's other incentive for them," said Dave who was a very philosophical individual. "The Jets have only won three games so the front office might be considering some major changes. The players don't want to be cut in the offseason and the coaches don't want to be fired."

"Maybe," I replied. "However, I don't think a victory is going to save anybody's job. If they're going to make any personnel changes they have probably already made their final decisions."

Dave looked thoughtful and agreed that I may have been right.

During our conversation the Jets had picked up a first down at the Hawaii 47 on an 18-yard pass play. Two rushes later they had a third and five at the 42.

We went to the 33 nickel in anticipation of a pass. As predicted, the Jets were going to the air.

What the Jets didn't anticipate was a safety blitz. Hasegawa shot through the line. He was virtually unimpeded as he headed for the quarterback. The quarterback tried to backpedal but couldn't get away. Rich leveled him at the Jets 46, drawing a huge roar from the crowd and our sideline. It was fourth and 17.

"All right," I said as I put my helmet on and ran on the field. "Let's put some points on the board this time."

At that moment I didn't care about the Rams. I didn't care about the Cowboys. I didn't care about the Vikings. I didn't care about the Bears. I only cared about winning this game.

I caught the punt at the 13. I shot past a defender and got to the 20 before I was hit. I broke the tackle but stumbled in the process. I went down at the 22.

"Okay. There's no stopping us this time," Bender said in the huddle.

On the first play Bender hit me near the left sideline at the 32. I picked up seven more yards before going down. One play, one first down.

An incompletion followed before Bender hit Collier in the right flat at the Hawaii 45. Collier squirmed for three more yards to give us a third and one at the 48.

I got the call on a sweep around right end. I noticed as I crossed midfield so I knew we had the first down. I managed to get as far as the New York 46.

Ozzie followed with his best run of the day to this point. He went off right tackle and fought his way to the 31, showing that he wasn't incapable of making a big play. This brought his average up after his halftime stats showed six carries for 15 yards for a 2.5 average. This gave him eight carries for 30 yards and a 3.75 average.

Kerner got nowhere up the middle and then Ozzie lost a yard off left tackle. It was third and eleven as time expired in the third quarter. Both sides had goose eggs in the third quarter.

"We've got to do it on this drive," Marv said to Kerner and me as we headed toward the north end zone which would be our goal for the rest of regulation. "They're playing us hard but we've got to break their backs."

As Bender ran toward our huddle from the sideline I looked up at the large scoreboard. On the right side of the scoreboard was a digital clock mixed in with a replica of a pack of Salem. It showed an even 15 minutes. That indicated that we were 15 minutes from either the playoffs or heartbreak.

The Jets gave us a little help. One of their linemen got called for encroachment. Without a single tick in the fourth quarter we had picked up five yards to put us in a third and six at the 27.

On the first actual play of the quarter I ran a cross pattern. Bender hit me on the numbers over the middle at the 19. I looped around a defender and straight-armed another inside the 15. That slowed me up a little but not enough. I ran unmolested into the end zone.

Near the goal post I spiked the ball. As my teammates congregated to congratulate me, I basked in the roar of the crowd. The smell of playoffs was growing stronger.

By this time most of our fans were giving up on the idea of a home playoff game. I didn't know it at the time but the Rams had a 34-13 lead over Memphis after three quarters. Our hopes for a division championship were all but completely dead.

But we couldn't afford to worry about that. We had to beat the Jets or else we couldn't even count on the wild card berth.

Guinn's PAT got us a step closer. It was 24-7 with 14:46 left.

"They're down but not out," I remarked at the Gatorade table.

"You got that right," said Grummon. "We've got to move in for the kill. Let's put it away."

The Jets seemed to be running out of aviation fuel but they were still airborne. They got a good kick return from one yard deep in the end zone to the New York 24. They also picked up a first down at their own 43.

A rush up the middle got the Jets to their own 46. McDaniel then sacked the quarterback at the 40 to give them a third and 13. After a pass was batted down by Rodgers near the Hawaii 40 I found myself near the Hawaii 15 to field another punt. It was another critical step toward our objective.

The punt had a good hang time. I probably could have picked up a few yards with a return but I wasn't totally sure. Since there was no sense of urgency and I couldn't hear any instruction Hasegawa was giving me I raised my hand and made a fair catch at the 19.

We wanted to score. We also wanted to eat up the clock. We would still run some pass plays to prevent the Jets from focusing on the run but our primary objective was to run the clock down.

Rushes by Ozzie and Kerner got us to the 28 to put us in a third and one. I then went off right tackle, diving forward to the 30. We had a first down.

The Jets got called for encroachment to give us five free yards. Kerner then managed a mere two yards off left tackle. On a sweep around right end Ozzie got to the 41 to give us another first down.

"Good job, Ozzie," I said as I helped him to his feet and headed to the huddle with him. "You're playing a really good game."

I wasn't cognizant of what Ozzie's stats were. All I knew was he seemed to have a few quality carries when we really needed them.

It was Ozzie again on the next snap. This time he went up the middle. He fought hard but was only able to pick up two yards to the 43.

"I think it's time to show them they can't be keying on the run," Bender said in the huddle.

Our strategy worked. We lined up in the same rushing formation we had been running with me on the right wing. Bender took the snap and then rolled to his right, hitting Dietrich near the right sideline at the New York 40. Ted picked up four more yards before going down at the 36.

The crowd loved it. Our fans had been relatively quiet while we ran a succession of rushing plays on this drive. The pass brought them to life. They were out for blood.

We were 108 feet from turning this into a four-score game. We were also eating up a huge chunk of the clock.

Ozzie managed only a yard up the middle. The Jets seemed to have known we wouldn't pass two times in a row. Bender decided that we needed to loosen up the defense again.

Bender hit Grummon near the left hash mark at the 23. He was hit immediately but we had a first down. The clock was winding down to the six-minute mark.

We were making a more concerted effort to run out the clock. We stayed in our huddles a little longer and went to longer counts. Bender kept his eye on the play clock and called signals with such precision that the ball would be snapped just before the play clock ran out.

Rushes off right tackle by Ozzie and Kerner produced one and four yards, respectively. It was third and five.

Dietrich ran a short slant. Bender hit him at the 15. Ted was quick enough to elude a tackle until he got to the eleven. It was another first down. The crowd was getting louder and louder as we grew closer and closer to a date in Dallas.

Collier and Reiser came in to replace Kerner and Ozzie. Collier went up the middle for a yard.

Reiser was next, getting his first carry in two years. He managed a single yard off right tackle. It was third and eight.

We went to the air again. Bender tried to hit Dietrich in the end zone to seal the deal. A defensive back knocked the ball away to stop the clock at 2:06. It was fourth and eight.

The field goal unit ran on. It was disappointing, I suppose, but we had achieved our prime objective. There was no way that the Jets were going to pick up two touchdowns and a field goal in about two minutes. That was exactly what Hayer was saying on the sideline.

"Not unless NBC decides to preempt the last two minutes with *Heidi*," Shuford cracked.

If Guinn converted on his 26-yard field goal attempt the Jets would be forced to score three touchdowns to catch us.

Guinn converted. It was 27-7. The clock showed 2:02.

The Jets tried to get themselves back in the game. After downing the kickoff in the end zone they threw a couple of incompletions, then completed a pass to secure a first down at their own 39.

Hamer was down. He hurt his knee. He was finished for the game but would be back in action in time for the next game.

The next game. It felt great to know that there would be a next game. While the Jets tried to narrow our lead there was a carefree, if not festive, ambience on our sideline. There was a lot of laughing, a lot of joking and a lot of handshaking. Even Walker had loosened up, turning in our direction with a big smile on his face while still directing the action on the field.

After a short completion to the New York 43 Morrissey intercepted a pass at the Hawaii 40. I admit that I was so busy savoring the victory that I didn't see the play until the thunderous roar from the crowd turned my attention to the field. Morrissey returned the interception to the Hawaii 48.

Walker sent in as many backups as we had available. That included Billingsley, Collier, Reiser and Rossi in the backfield.

The Jets had all three of their timeouts left and were opting to use them. With 1:07 left in the regular season we ran a few plays to try to kill the clock without having to turn the ball over. As our crowd gave us a standing ovation to close out the regular season Reiser picked up seven yards off right tackle and Collier picked up one yard off left tackle. It was third and two with 46 seconds left.

Rossi got the first carry of his career. He picked up three yards to the New York 41, perhaps impressing a few friends and relatives since the game was shown in San Francisco. We had a first down.

Ostensibly because the Jets would not be getting the ball back, they didn't bother calling their final timeout. Billingsley took a snap and dropped to his knee.

I was all smiles as the crowd very enthusiastically counted down the final seconds. The Jets came at us hard that day and played a pretty good game. It wasn't until the final quarter that we knew we had the game locked up. The only way we were going to lose at that point was if we surrendered.

The Rams beat Memphis, 37-13. That meant that we had to settle for the wild card.

We weren't complaining. The wild card was better than what 22 other teams were getting. Players for those teams would participate in the playoffs vicariously in front of their TV sets.

490

The Jets were among those 22 teams. Their season was over but they had played hard and were gracious in defeat. As we shook hands some of them wished us luck in the playoffs.

As I entered the tunnel that would lead to the locker room I turned and looked at the field. I noticed the message on the scoreboard in the north end zone.

MAHALO TO THE HAWAIIANS FOR AN OUTSTANDING SEASON! CONGRATULATIONS FOR WINNING THE NFC WILD CARD! BEST OF LUCK IN DALLAS!

It was a pleasant dose of reality. Going to the playoffs in the NFL was hard to imagine.

But we were definitely going.

If there was anybody in the locker room who wasn't smiling, I didn't notice. Every active player, every injured player, every taxi squad member, every coach and every attendant was happy. Some contributions were greater than others but all were vital.

I passed Reiser on my way to my locker and patted him on the back.

"Good game, Jerry," I said.

Jerry looked a little surprised. He smiled and nodded to accept the compliment.

"I didn't do much," he replied.

"You did enough."

After spending all of 1976 on injured reserve and the first 13 games of 1977 out of work I think he was grateful simply to have an opportunity to play.

Amid all of the hooting and hollering was Walker. He stood in the middle of the room and held his hand up to quiet us down. He was as radiant as anybody.

"Okay, who's going to give the prayer?" Walker asked.

A few hands went up. Walker selected Larry Scott who watched the game on crutches.

Larry gave a good prayer. He gave thanks for the strength to play hard and for the absence of serious injuries. He also asked that blessings be administered to victims of poverty, violence and other world problems. It was another reminder that life didn't start and end on the gridiron.

"Thank you, Larry," Walker said at the end of the prayer, hoisting the football he had been holding. "Now . . . game ball. Carl?"

Walker tossed the ball to Rodgers. His interception return for a touchdown earned him the ball. His teammates roared their approval.

"I knew you could do it," Walker stressed. "Ever since training camp I knew we had a very special group of football players. All season I've been waiting to say . . . , 'the Hawaiians are in the playoffs!'"

That produced another round of cheers. It meant a lot to me to know that the regular season was over and we were advancing. That was why we played the game.

"Enjoy this," Walker instructed. "This is a very special reward that you earned with your hard work and overall good play. Savor the moment and be ready to go to work on Tuesday. We'll have to work hard if we want to get past the Cowboys."

That was just in case anybody believed our ticket to the Super Bowl was already punched. Walker was right about us having earned our playoff spot. That was also when the road was certain to get rougher.

The hospitality room was a festive place that afternoon. Amid the roast beef and chicken, assorted side dishes, desserts and beverages was a very vocal group of players, wives, girlfriends, children and other guests. Nobody was yelling or throwing food but people were chattering enthusiastically and laughing.

Our broadcast team of Les Keiter and Earl McDaniel came in. With them was Congressman Cec Heftel who was the primary team owner. Heftel stood at the buffet table but didn't eat. He chatted with the players and their guests as they filled their plates.

"You guys sure had a great season," he said to me.

"Thanks," I replied. "We're got some outstanding personnel."

"You most certainly do. I don't get to see you play very often but I am able to keep up with how you are doing."

What I learned later was that somebody from the front office or coaching staff would call Heftel in Washington after each game and give him a summary of how the game went. He kept a low profile, having enough confidence in his front office and coaching personnel to allow them to handle the team without him badgering them 24 hours a day. He had the addresses and phone numbers of all of the players so occasionally he would send out letters of congratulations after hard-fought victories. Occasionally he would call a player to chat for a few minutes and see how things were going with him. He even called me a day or two after our loss to the Rams.

Carol had a surprise guest with her. That was Stacy Miyamoto. She had been Carol's best friend since the day Carol moved to Hawaii from British Columbia when she was 14. Stacy was a year older and had lived two doors down from Carol. From the minute they met they were like sisters.

I had actually known Stacy before I met Carol. In each of the two semesters prior to when I met Carol I had classes with Stacy. We became good friends although we didn't normally socialize away from campus. It wasn't until the day after my first date with Carol that I learned that Carol and Stacy were neighbors when they came in together at the Rose and Crown in King's Alley where I was tending bar before the start of preseason football practices at the university. At the time they were both even working at the Ala Moana Center; Carol as a waitress at the Continental Coffee Shop and Stacy next door in the women's department at Sears.

I didn't even know that Stacy was in town. She was doing graduate work at Northern Arizona University. I hadn't seen her since our preseason scrimmage but didn't get to talk to her then.

Stacy played a vital role in my relationship with Carol in 1973 and 1974. She was a confidant for Carol. She was also a very compassionate friend when Carol unexpectedly disappeared.

I hugged my old classmate and friend when I saw her. I followed that up with a warm hug and assortment of kisses for Carol.

"This is what I've been hoping for the last few years," Stacy remarked. "It's so nice to see you two back together."

Several members of the team celebrated in Waikiki that night. Jim McDaniel and his wife, Bill Stanek and his wife, Ed Jennings and his girlfriend, Marv Nelson and his wife, Ray Jablonski and his wife, Dave Rossi, Rich Hasegawa and a pretty girl he was dating, Russ Allen although his pregnant wife opted to stay home, Dave Shuford and his wife, Eric Hamer, Larry Scott and his wife, Jerry Reiser and his wife, Clint Abraham and his wife, and James Malick and his wife.

That's not to mention Carol and me. Normally Carol preferred something on the private side but occasionally she liked to go out with a large group. We joined the group in Waikiki with the understanding that I would have her home by one.

We made for quite a group. We were comprised of 15 pro football players and 12 female companions. We began by eating pizza at the Red Lion on Kuhio Avenue, then went dancing at the Tiki in the International Marketplace.

Of course we were recognized. A few well-wishers came over to say hello at the Red Lion. In the Tiki the band pointed us out.

"Hey, that looks like some of the Hawaiians over there," the attractive Filipino female lead singer announced between songs. "Congratulations, guys. Way to go."

We didn't want to be singled out. We were also in too good a mood to really care. We had to sign a few autographs but were generally left alone to have a good time.

Carol and I danced a lot. She loved to dance as much as any woman I had ever known. She was naturally athletic so that made her very light on her feet.

We laughed and hugged a lot on the dance floor. Carol was having a great time. That meant a lot to me.

At one point Carol asked Rossi to dance. He was the heaviest drinker of the bunch and, without a date, there wasn't much for him to do except smoke and drink.

It was just like Carol to try to help Dave have a good time. She always hated to see unhappy people. I was sure that Rossi, beneath the facade of cocksurety and heavy drinking, was a very unhappy person.

I suppose I cared about Rossi, too. I wasn't sure how long my career would last but I figured it would be a lot longer than Rossi's. I was also continuing to educate myself to have something to sustain me after my career was over. Rossi only had football and wasn't disciplined enough to last more than a few years. Despite having spent two years as an alleged student at San Jose State after two years at a junior college, he had very little education and no discernible skills. Unless he changed his attitude and learned something, Dave would be in for some very hard times when his career ended.

"That was fun," Carol remarked radiantly as I drove her home. "We needed a night out with your teammates."

I had to agree. We usually went out by ourselves or one or two other couples when we went out. Going out in a large group was a refreshing change for us; something we would enjoy doing on occasion as long as it wasn't an especially rowdy celebration. Carol had never been a party animal and my days of hard partying were behind me.

"You're going to hate yourself when you wake up in the morning," I remarked.

"Why? I didn't have much to drink. I just had one beer in the Red Lion and a glass of wine in the Tiki."

That was another of Carol's traits. She rarely drank and usually only had one when she did drink. Her absolute maximum on any given day was two. Her biggest vice was smoking but even there she was more disciplined, limiting herself to two or three packs a week.

"I just meant that you'll hate yourself for staying out so late. You have a dental appointment in the morning."

"Oh, that. I can sacrifice a little sleep on occasion," she said. "Besides, I don't have to be there until ten."

I checked the newspaper on Monday. Primarily I wanted to see what kind of stats Ozzie had. He had 14 carries for 41 yards which was a yard shy of an average of three yards per carry. Kerner had seven carries for 33 yards. I carried four times for 16 yards.

As a receiver I had six receptions for 114 yards. Dietrich caught four passes for 75 yards. Grummon had three receptions for 58 yards.

Our stats for the season were also listed. Scott led the running backs with 168 carries for 782 yards for an average of 4.65 yards per carry. Kerner was second with 81 carries for 397 yards for an average of 4.9 yards per carry. I was third with 50 carries for 266 yards for an average of 5.32 yards per carry. Ozzie carried 61 times for 211 yards, averaging 3.45 yards per carry.

For the second consecutive year I led the team in receiving. I caught 69 passes, also for the second consecutive year, for 1,205 yards. Dietrich had 55 receptions for 804 yards. Grummon was next with 35 receptions for 574 yards.

Bender had a good enough year at quarterback to justify his selection to the Pro Bowl. He had 192 completions in 346 attempts for 2,897 yards. He threw 16 interceptions and 22 touchdowns.

I was second in passing with ten completions in 15 attempts. I also had one pass picked off and threw for two touchdowns.

Billingsley was obviously used only to mop up. He had three completions in six attempts for 20 yards with no interceptions or touchdowns.

Not surprisingly, Guinn led the team in total points. With 42 PATs in as many tries and 17 out of 24 field goals he had a total of 93 points.

What did surprise me was that I was second on the team in scoring. I had eight touchdowns for the second consecutive season for 48 points. This time all of my touchdowns were through the air. In 1976 one of my touchdowns was on the ground.

Kerner was third in scoring with five rushing touchdowns and two receiving for 42 points.

The most interesting stat was that Rodgers had only two interceptions. He was one of the most feared defensive backs in the league; one that quarterbacks tried to avoid. He broke up a lot of passes but only picked off two. Both of his interceptions were returned for touchdowns.

CHAPTER TWENTY-ONE
The Wild Card

Monday, December 19

Carol and I enjoyed a nice quiet Monday evening together at my place. We swam in the pool at my condo complex, had a nice baked mahi mahi dinner and watched TV while lying on the living room floor.

But it was now Tuesday and it was back to the world. I was a football player again. Five months, two weeks and one day (168 days) after the beginning of training camp I was still involved with football.

That was more than okay. In Detroit, New Orleans, St. Louis, Chicago and Kansas City the focus was on the Pistons, Redwings, Jazz, Blues, Bulls, Blackhawks and Kings. The 49ers weren't playing football anymore, nor were the Falcons, Bills, Jets and Giants. Our fellow expansionists in Seattle, Memphis and Tampa could only look on with awe and wonder how we had developed so quickly while mediocrity was still a huge step up for them.

I guess all of that was why I was smiling in the hospitality room prior to our film sessions. The alternative was to not have made the playoffs. I was ready to go to work.

Ozzie was the darling of the offensive film session. Almost everybody else got his share of criticism but Walker called Ozzie's name far more than anybody else's.

The fact is, Ozzie did not have an especially good game against the Jets even though he did make some key plays. Some of Ozzie's subpar day could be attributed to the linemen for not blocking as well as they should have. Other times the credit could have gone to the Jets' defense for making good plays.

Still, Ozzie wasn't the running back Scott was. Larry was virtually certain to have broken through for a total of 15-20 more yards than Ozzie. Larry was a lot better at breaking tackles than Ozzie was and he was quicker in getting through the holes. Some of it was because Larry was more experienced and still in his prime. Some of it was simply that Larry was naturally better.

The statistics were testimony to why Larry, when healthy, was our starting tailback and Ozzie the backup. Besides the previously listed statistics, Larry had two 100-yard games and came up just short on a couple others, rushed for four touchdowns and had two more touchdowns on pass receptions.

"Here's our itinerary," Walker announced during the joint session after the films. "Today, tomorrow and Thursday will be just like any normal Tuesday, Wednesday and Thursday during the season. Tomorrow, of course, we'll begin by watching films of the Cowboys game from the weekend. On Thursday we'll begin the day by watching films of our game last year against the Cowboys."

Walker reported that the routine would be different on Friday and Saturday. We had an extra day to prepare since we wouldn't be playing until Monday. That, to Walker, meant an obligation to have one extra padded workout.

"On Friday we'll spend half of the workout polishing the offense and the other half on the defense. Somewhere along the way we'll work some on special teams."

Walker paused. He lit a cigarette and looked at his notes. He then made some notations, ostensibly deviating from his original plan.

"Saturday is Christmas Eve," he reported. "It's also our day to travel. I want to give you as much time as possible with your families but we still have to prepare. There won't be any rush hour traffic on Saturday morning. Is there anybody who won't be able to be dressed and on the field by eight o'clock on Saturday morning?"

I looked around the room. Nobody had a hand up.

"Okay, good," Walker said. "We'll begin our workout right at eight. It'll be a limited contact workout so we'll be in full battle gear. We'll tie up whatever loose ends we have on offense and defense and then work on our special teams. If we get everything done quickly we'll hit the showers by about 9:30. That way you can spend a good part of the day with your families before we fly to Dallas."

Walker then went over our itinerary for the actual trip. Win or lose, we would return to Honolulu immediately after the game.

"You'll enjoy the flight home a lot more if you win," Walker added lightly as if he needed to remind us.

Walker felt compelled to discuss an article in the *Honolulu Advertiser*. A syndicated columnist wrote a piece on the teams in the playoffs. I hadn't seen the article since I subscribed to the *Honolulu Star-Bulletin* which was delivered in the afternoon. Apparently the columnist did not think too highly of our getting into the playoffs.

What irritated the columnist was our allegedly weak schedule. The overall winning percentage of our opponents was .442 which indicates that it wasn't an especially strong schedule.

Since we play our division rivals twice, we played a total of ten teams in 1977. Only four of those teams had winning records, one broke even and the other five had losing records. Of our five games against teams with winning records, counting both games against the Rams, we won only two of those games.

Put another way, the combined winning percentage against teams we beat was a paltry .383. The combined winning percentage against the teams that beat us was .661.

The writer was very direct. He said that the Hawaiians were the least likely of the eight teams in the playoffs to win the Super Bowl. It goes without saying that he didn't expect us to even get past the first game.

"Don't pay any attention to crap like this," Walker implored. "I've told you all along to not take newspaper clippings offering high praise too seriously. You should also not take the negative press seriously. This man writes garbage like this because he wants the nation to think he is an authority on football. His stats were accurate but they told only a small portion of your story. Ignore this article and just go out and play your game. I know what you men are capable of doing and this jackass obviously does not."

It was a great week of practice. Walker pushed us, naturally, but he was fairly civil. How angry could he get at a second-year team with a 10-4 record and a wild card berth?

Ozzie was still the one Walker rode the most. He was the key to how effective our running game would be. Kerner was a good powerful rusher but he wasn't one who would be as effective if he was expected to rush 20 times or more in a single game. I was nothing more than a receiver who was capable of picking up a few yards on the ground a few times a game. My average would also drop if I carried more often.

And then there was Reiser. One didn't have to be a genius to know that he was raring to go.

I couldn't say for a certainty but I suspected that Ozzie did not have the starting tailback job guaranteed. The second-year fourth round draft choice from Austin Peay was getting some serious competition from Reiser. Reiser was getting in a lot of work and looking pretty good.

Reiser was a classy individual. He was a very vocal supporter of Ozzie. If Ozzie hit a hole well or broke a tackle Reiser was among the first to offer his congratulations.

I don't know what Walker was thinking. I am certain, though, that he gave at least some thought to starting Reiser.

In the locker room after Wednesday's workout Rossi decided to offer Ozzie his own unique brand of support.

"Hey, man. It's really a bummer the way Walker gets on ya like that," Rossi said, bending over to look into Ozzie's face and patting him on the back while Ozzie sat in front of his locker. "If that was me Walker was getting on I'd. . . ."

Ozzie abruptly rose from his stool. He glared at Rossi, who had an incredibly startled expression on his face, then walked away. Reiser, Dubois, Allen and I and a few others stood ready to intervene in case it came to blows although I don't believe that was Ozzie's intention.

"Rossi, you need to learn to mind your own business," Marv said evenly.

"Geez, man," Rossi replied defensively. "I'm just tryin' t' help him feel good again."

"He doesn't need your help," Blakely interjected. "Just leave him alone."

Rossi shook his head. It was very befuddling to the man who seemed to believe that there wasn't a single player on the team who didn't need his help.

But I suppose he meant well.

Ozzie didn't care much for Rossi although he wasn't especially close to anybody on the team. He was a very somber and taciturn individual. My initial impression of him was that he was arrogant and I believe he probably was but he might actually have been shy.

Not that Ozzie was a troublemaker. He didn't mouth off or put anybody down. When somebody did something well on the field he didn't hang back. He was up there with everybody else to offer a handshake and/or words of congratulations.

It wasn't that Ozzie was incapable of opening up. I recall having a long conversation with him during our flight to Tampa. He admitted to me that he once had difficulty dealing with Whites but he came to understand that the White people who caused him grief in his childhood hometown in Mississippi were a part of an extremely small minority.

Ozzie's grandfather had been a pretty good athlete and even spent a few years playing professional baseball in the Negro leagues. When Ozzie was seven his grandfather was casually taking an evening stroll when about half-a-dozen known members of the Ku Klux Klan jumped out of a car, kidnapped Ozzie's grandfather, tortured him and hung him.

Obviously it was a hate crime. It ultimately came out that the crime was triggered by Bernard Roberts committing the *heinous* crime of sending his son to dental school. Ozzie's father, Willie Roberts, had an office which bordered a White neighborhood and a Black neighborhood. Some of the local Whites objected to having a Black man prospering in what they insisted was a "White man's profession."

Although Ozzie's father earned a reasonably good living as a dentist, it wasn't without difficulties. On a couple of occasions molotov cocktails were thrown into the office during nights when the office was unoccupied. On at least a couple of occasions White men showed up for appointments they had made by arbitrarily picking a dentist from the phone book and then refused treatment after discovering that the dentist was Black.

Amid the turmoil was a young White woman who moved to Mississippi from Indiana. She was hired by Ozzie's father to work as a receptionist. This caused friction from both races since there were Blacks who felt that Bernard Roberts was betraying his own race by hiring a White woman and boycotted Ozzie's father's practice.

The majority of the heat still came from the local Whites. The hiring of a White woman seemed to exacerbate the hatred. On a few occasions crosses were burned in front of the house the receptionist rented. Despite that and the verbal threats she was subjected to, the brave young woman refused to quit her job. In 1977 she was still working as the receptionist.

By Friday Ozzie was back in Walker's good graces. Walker was offering high praise to everybody but especially, it seemed, to Ozzie.

Of course it stood to reason. Our first ever playoff game as an NFL entity was only three days away. The last thing we needed was somebody in a Hawaiians uniform not believing in himself.

Final adjustments to the roster had been made. Prendergast was cleared to play and would start at defensive right tackle. Zanakis was finally activated again although he wouldn't start. Malick would start at right outside linebacker but Zanakis would get a lot of playing time and be a valuable addition. To make room for him, Catron was waived.

Friday was when Carol and I celebrated Christmas. She put together a nice little dinner. There was ham and an assortment of trimmings including a pumpkin pie for dessert. We also opened the presents we kept under the Christmas tree and sang Christmas Carols.

At least Carol sang Christmas Carols along with what was being played on her stereo. She had an unbelievably beautiful voice. Since I had a range of about three notes on my best days I opted to not adulterate the festive holiday atmosphere with my contribution.

"There are 30 teams in the NFL," Walker announced at the start of our workout on Saturday morning, "22 of which are finished for the season. In only your second season of existence you have joined pro football's elite."

One could literally feel the level of enthusiasm rising in the hospitality room. There is no such thing as making the playoffs on a fluke regardless of what at least one syndicated sportswriter ostensibly thought. We got exactly what we deserved and hoped to vault two formidable hurdles en route to New Orleans. Our season started with a victory in New Orleans and that was how we wanted to end it.

Walker quickly reiterated the itinerary. We would practice until about 9:30 and then be excused until 3:30. That was when we would report to Air Service and board our chartered DC-8.

And then it was on to Dallas. We would check into the hotel, get a few hours of sleep. . . .

Put another way, the routine would be pretty much the same as for any other road game. The only difference was that we would be doing everything a day later since our first playoff game was going to be on a Monday. We would have a light workout at Texas Stadium on Christmas Day, hopefully get a good night's sleep that night and have our usual road gameday routine on Monday.

500

Another difference was that it was mandatory for us to win. A loss and it was all over.

Win or lose, we would return to Honolulu after the game. If we won we would practice Wednesday at the Marine Base since our next game would be on grass regardless of the opponent. The Rams and Vikings would be squaring off in Los Angeles after our game so we would know who our next opponent would be by the time we returned home, if not by the time we left Dallas.

If the Rams won we wouldn't leave Honolulu until after Friday's workout. If the Vikings won we would leave after Wednesday's workout to give us a couple of extra days to adjust to a frigid climate although our first stop would be Madison, Wisconsin. Walker had already arranged for us to practice on Thursday and Friday at the University of Wisconsin. We would not fly to Minneapolis until after Friday's practice and have a light workout on Saturday at Metropolitan Stadium. The trip to Madison would drastically reduce the possibility of spies from the Vikings.

Regardless of whether we played in Los Angeles or Minneapolis, our conference championship game would be on New Year's Day. Winning a trip to Super Bowl XII seemed like a wonderful way to kick off 1978.

"But let's not get too far ahead of ourselves," Walker cautioned. "Our road to the Super Bowl goes first through Dallas. We have to get through that before we can be thinking about what comes next. Let's go out and have a good workout and be ready to battle those Cowboys."

It was an excellent workout. Everybody hustled, few mistakes were made and nobody suffered the slightest suggestion of an injury. I can't imagine how we could have been more ready for the Cowboys that day.

But this was Saturday, December 24. The game wasn't until Monday, December 26 almost 3800 miles away. We were reasonably sure that the Cowboys were spending as much time making themselves ready for us as we were readying ourselves for them. They were sure to take us a lot more seriously than a certain syndicated sportswriter and any other doubters did.

"I don't know about you guys but I'm up for kicking some okole in Dallas," Marv commented as we were undressing in the locker room.

"I'm up for that," Jennings replied enthusiastically.

"It would be quite a coup for you, Marv, if we go all the way to the Super Bowl," Richards added. "New Orleans let you go in the expansion draft and then you return two years later as a member of one of the Super Bowl teams. About the only thing the Saints have accomplished since you left is that they became the first team to lose to Tampa Bay."

Marv chuckled as he wrapped a towel around his waist and picked up his accoutrements for his shower.

"Yeah, well, I have nothing bad to say about New Orleans or the Saints," Marv replied good naturedly. "I sure do like winning better than losing, though."

"I'll give a big amen to that," said Prendergast who was taken in the 35th round of the expansion draft from the Saints although he only played one season in New Orleans. Prior to that he played four seasons in Philadelphia and one year in Baltimore.

I went to Carol's place after I left the stadium. We took a dip in the swimming pool at her building but otherwise took it easy inside her condo unit. It was primarily an opportunity to spend a little time together.

The original plan was for me to drive by myself to the airport but Carol wanted to go with me. Happy to have her along, I agreed to allow her to accompany me to Air Service and then drive my car back to her place.

Before we got out of the car I opened the glove compartment and pulled an envelope out. The envelope contained the epistle I wrote to Carol in June after our first date together after our three-year hiatus.

Dear Carol,

Today something wonderful happened to me. As I write this I wonder if you will ever read this. It depends on whether we stay together. Although I was thrilled to be with you for the first time in three years tonight, I still feel somewhat detached from you. It is as if it was simply a beautiful dream and I'll wake up the same lonely guy who is expected to pretend to be happy as a swinging bachelor.

I hope you do read this someday soon. It will mean that we have become a confirmed couple again. I know that there will be some difficult moments ahead while we get used to being together again, especially since training camp is less than a month away and I will be forced to focus my attention on football.

But we've gotten through that type of thing before. As you might recall, we met less than a week before we began preseason workouts in college. I think we both knew from the moment we met that we wanted a lasting relationship but we sure had some tough times in the early going. Somehow we managed to get through them and become a couple that people seemed to admire.

One thing I've always known is I never stopped loving you. I had to try to carry on as best I could without you but that didn't mean that I had to stop loving you. I didn't know where you were and even made it a point not to know since I was afraid I would drop everything and go to wherever you were if I ever found out. As much as I wanted you back, I tried to look at things from your perspective. Perhaps you were better off without me.

502

All I really know is I was thrilled to be with you again. I just hope that this was the beginning of something that won't end this time. I would like to believe that we are getting the proverbial second chance. If you ever read this it will mean that all of the dreams that I have on this night are coming true.

I love you,

Jay

"What's this?" Carol asked as I held out the sealed envelope.

"A very special Christmas present," I said. "You have to promise me that you won't open this until Christmas Day."

Carol gave me a gratuitous look. She sensed that the envelope contained something special. I was sure that she had absolutely no idea of how heartfelt the contents were. The simple epistle took me a few hours to put together. It did not do justice to how strong my feelings actually were.

In a few minutes we moved toward the aircraft on the tarmac at Air Service. At the base of the stairs leading up to the entrance to the DC-8 I took Carol in my arms and exchanged a long kiss with her.

"Have a good game," she said warmly.

"Thanks. I will," I replied, giving her one final kiss before I ascended up the stairs. Before I stepped inside the plane I turned and waved to her one more time while she stood and waved with the other wives, girlfriends and children of players and coaches.

I took a window seat on the left side of the plane. The left side was always my choice whenever I left Honolulu since I liked to watch the island as I flew away.

This time it also meant that I could look at Carol before we started to taxi. She was clad in a pair of blue shorts and a pink blouse and looked absolutely gorgeous with her long golden blonde hair that was worn loosely. As the aircraft started to taxi I thanked my lucky stars for the nth time that she had come back into my life. The difference in the quality of my life was phenomenal.

After a lengthy taxi the aircraft reached runway 8L and began speeding down. As the aircraft lifted off I could make out the group at Air Service. They were too far away for me to make Carol out but I knew that she was among those who stood by to watch us lift off. The next time we would set foot on land would be in Dallas.

It was a long flight but not unpleasant. The tension was thicker since this obviously was not our prototype road game. This was a playoff game where our options were win or else. Nobody wanted the season to end in Dallas.

503

Carl Rodgers occupied the seat next to me. He and I talked some but not much. The ninth-year safety out of Oregon whom the Hawaiians drafted from Chicago was somewhat aloof off the field. He and I were friendly although we didn't socialize together. Away from the team he was devoted to his wife Melinda whom he met in sixth grade in his hometown of Geneva, Nebraska, and his three daughters. Like me, he had also been a quarterback in high school as well as a defensive back.

It didn't really matter who sat next to you going to a game. We all had so much nervous energy inside us that we spent much of the flight mingling up and down the aisle. Since our flights were a minimum of five hours, meaning that our shortest flights were roughly the same length of the longest flights of any team not flying to Hawaii, there was plenty of time for socializing. During many flights I exchanged at least a few words with virtually everybody on board including teammates, coaches, media personnel and anybody else I could find.

Steak dinners were served during this flight. Normally we were served some type of fish, chicken or some other type of meat but on this flight we were served delicious sirloin steaks with baked potatoes, mixed vegetables, salad, rolls and ice cream. Obviously it paid to make the playoffs.

We landed in Dallas well before dawn. It was about six when I entered my hotel room. Within five minutes I was under the covers, sound asleep.

Although I had left a wakeup request for eleven o'clock, Marv rose at ten o'clock and somehow persuaded a maid to let him in my room. Seeing me still asleep when he came in, he naturally decided that I was being too lazy.

"Get your lazy bones out of bed, Jaybird," Marv good-naturedly called while repeatedly whacking me with a pillow. "How're you gonna play football if you sleep your life away?"

"Geez, man," I said, burying my head under my own pillow for protection. "What time is it?"

"Time for you to get your lazy body out of bed, little brother," he replied, still working me over with the pillow.

"Man, I don't believe you," I said, uncovering my head when Marv finally stopped hitting me. I sat up in the bed and pondered.

"What's wrong?"

I shook my head and hesitated.

"I was just trying to remember what city I was in. Dallas, right?"

"Oh, you're a veteran now," Marv commented while flashing a toothy smile whose whiteness contrasted his black face and waving an index finger. "The day you wake up and have to think about where you are is the day you know you've been a pro football player too long."

"Either that or your damned pillow knocked me senseless," I retorted in mock sarcasm. "What if I get hurt and can't play tomorrow because of your pillow? How are you going to explain that to Walker?"

"Hey, that would be something."

"It sure would," I said as I climbed out of bed and headed toward the bathroom. "It would definitely get the media's attention."

"Hey!" Marv remarked brightly. "So that's how an offensive lineman gets headlines."

I ran into the bathroom and closed the door just as the sound of a pillow could be heard hitting the other side.

Texas Stadium was only six years old. Somehow I still got a sense of history as I stood on its turf and sized it up while waiting for practice to start. There was something awe inspiring about the facility with the roof that covered every seat in the house but not the field. Perhaps it was because the team that played there had an annoying habit of winning the overwhelming majority of its games.

"Still hoping to play baseball, I see," Walker commented as he walked by and observed my traditional Dodger shirt and cap. "Are you going to be ready tomorrow?"

"Hell, I'm ready to go now."

Walker stopped and nodded.

"Don't get too worked up this far from kickoff," he advised. "I know how you feel. I'm ready to go now, too, but you need to relax some. Do something after practice that will get your mind off the game for a little while. Take a walk or read a book or something. Tomorrow will be here soon enough."

It wasn't bad advice although Walker also knew that a hyperactive player's nerves were hard to control. I always did try to control myself in the hours before kickoff. Often it was a herculean task.

The workout was a good one. We primarily worked out a few of the last-minute details, got the feel of the facility and worked off a little of the nervous energy that was certain to build back up.

After we returned to the hotel I ventured out by myself. Locals had their minds on the next day's game but they were celebrating Christmas as they normally would. With my mind on the next day's game and its significance it was hard for me to remember that this was Christmas.

The team had Christmas dinner in the hotel. Normally we were given a per diem to eat where we saw fit but this was a special occasion. Team majority owner Cec Heftel arranged for us to have a spread consisting of a turkey/ham buffet with an assortment of side dishes and desserts. It wasn't mandatory but I can't think of anybody who wasn't in attendance.

Marv, Manwaring, Slater, Walker, Black, Stanek and a few others had family members who were in town for the game and their guests were

505

welcome. Our broadcast team of Les Keiter and Earl McDaniel, other members of the Honolulu media, the flight crew and the rest of our entourage also joined us.

Most of the evening after the dinner was spent watching TV in my hotel room. Ed and Marv joined me, bringing a six-pack of beer to share. We talked very little. We kept our focus on the TV while we sipped our beers.

We were usually a little more loquacious but this was a playoff scenario. Marv's first playoff game didn't come until after he had been in the league eleven full seasons. Ed's first playoff game came at the end of his seventh full season. It was virgin territory for both of them. They had the nervous exuberance of a rookie.

I didn't think about it at the time but I knew something about being in the playoffs. During the only full season of the WFL the Hawaiians made the playoffs. We beat the Southern California Sun in Anaheim before flying to Alabama and losing to the Birmingham Americans in the league semifinal.

Those playoff games were exciting. They came nowhere near the magnitude of making the playoffs in the NFL but they were still exciting.

I couldn't tell you what time I went to sleep. I only knew that I fell asleep shortly after Marv and Ed returned to their own rooms. The TV was still on when I woke up the following morning.

I savored my steak and eggs. It wasn't so much the food although it was good. It was the fact that I was sitting in this Dallas dining room enjoying the pregame meal with an assortment of teammates and coaches.

Of the 30 teams in the NFL, 24 were finished for the year. The Steelers and Colts were eliminated on Christmas Eve, leaving the Raiders and Broncos to duke it out on New Year's Day for the trip to the Super Bowl. We were endeavoring to send the Cowboys home before taking on the winner of the Vikings-Rams game on New Year's Day.

I was rooting for the Rams. It wasn't because we would encounter more favorable conditions in Los Angeles than Minneapolis although that was definitely also a factor. It simply was more appealing to win the conference championship in Los Angeles. Since we obviously couldn't do it in my home locale of Honolulu, I wanted to do it in the place that I used to call home.

But first thing's first. We had to successfully complete our mission in Dallas. I continually reminded myself that we were among only six NFL teams with a shot at the Super Bowl.

That thought gave me a rush. On this date two years earlier I had only signed with the NFL Hawaiians about two weeks earlier. We had no idea of who would ultimately join me on the roster aside from Hasegawa and Hamer who had agreed to terms just before Christmas, 1975. Although I had the attitude that anybody in the NFL had a shot at going all the way to the Super Bowl, I knew that a minimum of four or five years to make the playoffs was much more realistic.

One year prior to this date I had a slightly different perspective. Having played well beyond what was expected of us in 1976, I knew that the playoffs might not take as long as what was previously projected. Of course I hoped to make the playoffs and contend for the Super Bowl in 1977 but merely finishing with a winning record regardless of whether we made the playoffs would have been another step forward.

Obviously we took that step forward and were on the road to the Super Bowl. The odds were still against us since we were the NFC wild card team. We were also a young team in terms of the short amount of time we had played together as a unit.

But we had overcome long odds several times before. Why not now?

Why not indeed? We were very capable of beating the Cowboys. It was simply a matter of doing it.

Game time was drawing near. I sat in front of my locker drinking a Pepsi and eating a Hershey bar and thought about all that I hoped to achieve that day. I wanted to rush well, I wanted to receive well, I wanted to block well, I wanted. . . .

The bottom line was that I wanted to win. No matter how well I played, it would mean little if the team didn't win.

It had been the typical game day. I rose early, took a shower, went down for coffee with some of my teammates and ate breakfast with the entire team. A short time later I took the team bus to the stadium, dressed, did my pregame laps, warmed up, put the pads on and returned to the field for more warmup.

This time it was different. In the majesty of Texas Stadium we would be competing for the right to play the following week. The only thing certain was that the NFC Championship Game would not be played at Aloha Stadium.

I gave Carol some thought.

Actually I gave her a lot of thought. She was hard to miss since I now kept a framed photo of her in my locker. A few of my teammates kept photos of their wives and girlfriends in their lockers. Bender, Hayer and Kerner were among those who kept a photo of their entire families in their lockers.

Carol's picture was a reminder of not so much what I was playing for but what I was living for. My career, as much as I dreaded the thought of it abruptly coming to an end, was simply what I did for a living. Carol was far more important. By keeping her picture in the locker I hoped to find an extra dose of inspiration and strength while being reminded of what was waiting for me in Honolulu regardless of the outcome.

"All right, men. It's just about that time," Walker called as he moved to the center of the room. "Every football fan in the nation is going to be watching you. It's another opportunity for you to show the world what kind of football is played in Hawaii. You've worked hard all season and your effort has paid off. Let's go put it to the Cowboys and have a festive flight home."

We won the toss. I was prepared to wait but was thrilled to have the opportunity to be on the field on the opening kickoff.

"This is it," I said as I slapped five with Hasegawa. "The second step to the Super Bowl is right here."

""The *second* step?'" Rich asked quizzically.

"Right. The first step was getting to the playoffs."

"Oh, right. Let's do it," Rich replied enthusiastically. "From UH to the Super Bowl."

That sounded good to me. It wasn't as if we would be the first alumni from the University of Hawaii to play in a Super Bowl. It still had a nice ring to it.

The kick was up. It was to my left. I caught it about two yards deep in the end zone near the sideline. I was itching to take it all the way but it appeared more prudent to down the ball.

"Okay. Eighty yards to our first score of the day," Bender remarked in the huddle.

The yardage wouldn't come easy. We opened with a short slant. I caught the ball at the 23 and was hit immediately by a linebacker. I managed to spin for an additional yard to give us a second and six.

Bender met a heavy rush on the next snap. Dietrich and I went long but Bender couldn't find us because he was busy dodging white jerseys. He threw a safety valve pass to Kerner at the line. Jeff fought for two yards to the 26.

We got some help on the next play. One of the Cowboy linemen jumped the gun and bumped Abraham. That cost Dallas five yards and got us a first down at the 31.

"All right. They gave us new life," Bender said in the huddle.

We went to our running game. Ozzie went up the middle to the 34 and then off right tackle to the 36. That gave us a third and five.

The Cowboy defense was relentless. Bender tried to get a pass off and met another heavy rush. He was smothered at the 30 to give us a fourth and eleven.

I don't mind admitting to feeling discouraged as I ran off the field. When the Jets came at us hard it was easy to believe that they were simply giving their all before inevitably running out of gas. In this case we were dealing with the Dallas Cowboys in their prime. It wasn't that we were

508

incapable of beating them but they were as formidable as anybody we had seen all season.

As if the Cowboys were incapable of picking up yardage on their own, we gave them a boost on the punt. Hamer jumped before the snap to move us back to the 25.

Jablonski was finally able to get the punt off and it was a pretty good one. The Cowboy return man got under it and raised his hand to signal a fair catch. He caught the ball at the 35.

"Defense!" Walker barked.

As our defense ran on the field I hoped that they would go at the Cowboys with the same relentless spirit as the Cowboy defense did against us. This promised to be a hard-hitting matchup. It was imperative that we go at them hard and heavy.

I got my Gatorade but I couldn't sit. I was too hyper.

The Cowboys opened with a rush of a mere two yards and then an incomplete pass. It was third and eight.

We went to the 33 nickel. Hasegawa ran in and Prendergast came out.

"Let's go, defense!" I called while other teammates on the sideline offered similar encouragement. "Let's hold 'em!"

As expected, the Cowboys went to the air. Their quarterback was forced to scramble and then got the pass off. Rodgers cut in front of the receiver near the Hawaii 40 and got his hands on the ball. The receiver alertly swatted the ball away before Carl had possession.

Enthusiastically I returned to the field. The three and out our defense caused boosted my confidence in our ability to win. I hoped to put together a long punt return to get us good field position to start our drive.

I didn't count on the Cowboy punter punting the ball away from me even though I had seen it countless times before. It was too far to my right. It bounced near the 25 and was ultimately downed at the 19.

"Okay, they can't all be returned," I muttered to myself and joined the rest of the offense as we formed a huddle.

We started with a Kaneohe left. Kerner managed two yards.

Walker sent Slater in with a play, sending Dietrich out. We were going to the air. I was the primary receiver but I was also double-teamed. Bender went to Slater instead near the Cowboy sideline at the 38. Joe caught the ball just before he went out of bounds.

"He didn't have possession!" I heard somebody yell from the sideline.

"He was juggling the ball!"

"No catch! No catch!"

What the Cowboys were claiming was that Slater didn't have possession when he went out of bounds. He did juggle the ball a little. The film clips I would see later suggested to me that Slater did have control just before he went out although it was an incredibly close call. My guess is that had this happened when challenges were allowed the replay would have been inconclusive.

Bender hit me over the middle at the Hawaii 48 on the next play. I turned upfield but was immediately flipped over at the 50. I found myself right in the middle of the star on the turf at midfield.

"All right!" I said enthusiastically as I bounced up and trotted to where the offense would be huddling. "We're on the move. Let's keep it going, guys."

Ozzie went up the middle and managed all of one yard. On top of that he seemed to hurt his ankle and limped off the field. Reiser was inserted in his place.

It was back to the air. Bender hit Dietrich at the Dallas 37. Ted actually caught the ball on his knees but was able to get up before anybody could touch him down. He picked up five more yards to the 32.

"Yeah, Ted! Great effort!" I remarked gleefully, reaching down to help him up. For the moment we were doing what we had to do. I was sure we were going to score on this drive.

Bender tried to hit me inside the 15 on the following play. It was a high pass and I leaped up for it.

Unfortunately a defensive back leaped up with precision timing. He tipped the ball up and dove forward for the ball. He missed making a diving interception by about an inch or two.

I heaved a sigh of relief. I was hoping that losing an opportunity like that would discourage the Cowboys. I also knew better than to actually believe that it would.

Ozzie came back in and we returned to our ground game. Kerner went off right tackle and picked up only one yard to the 31. It was third and nine.

"I'm not in the mood for a field goal yet," said Bender in the huddle. "Let's keep this drive going."

That's exactly what we did. Bender hit Grummon at the 20. It was a routine catch but Rich lost his footing and fell down. A defensive back touched him down before he could rise up. At least we had the first down.

"Dockman!"

Rossi was running on the field. That surprised me and I wasn't happy about it but that's the way it was and I no choice but to accept it, slapping fives with Rossi as our paths crossed before I muttered a few expletives that nobody else could hear as I headed toward the sideline. Walker wanted to send in a play and he used Rossi to bring it in. It isn't as if Rossi didn't deserve to get into the game. I was simply feeling selfish.

It was another pass. Bender hit Rossi at the six. Dave leaped over a defender and headed toward the goal line. He was brought down at the one.

"Okay, Jay. Go back in," Walker said to me.

"Rossi!"

As our paths crossed we slapped fives again. Rossi looked somewhat radiant. I couldn't really blame him. He had just made a big play for us, getting us to within three feet of our first touchdown.

The last yard wasn't going to be easy. The Cowboys served notice right from the beginning that they weren't conceding anything. We were going to the air and the end result was that Bender was sacked at the nine.

That was what the crowd wanted to see. The roar was a grim reminder that we were on Cowboy turf. I was hoping that in the long run we would royally tick the fans off.

The crowd also roared its approval on the next play. Ozzie ran around right end and wound up being dropped for a one-yard loss. It was third and goal from the ten.

Slater and Rossi came in. Ozzie and Grummon went out. We were going into our double-double.

Bender dropped back and unleashed a pass to Slater in the left corner of the end zone. A defensive back jumped up with Slater and got a grip on the ball but couldn't hang on. The ball dropped incomplete.

From my position in the end zone I looked toward our sideline and saw exactly what I expected. The field goal unit was running on the field. I joined the rest of the offense in running off.

I wanted to swear. I wanted to slam my helmet down. I wanted to kick something. I wanted to make obscene gestures.

Somehow I maintained control despite my momentary disconsolate feelings. I calmed myself down and watched the field goal attempt.

It was a 27-yard attempt. The snap was a little high but Billingsley did a good job of getting control and putting it down. The delay, however, caused Guinn to hesitate. He got the kick off but it was wide to the left.

Now I *really* wanted to swear. I *really* wanted to slam my helmet down. I *really* wanted to kick something. I *really* wanted to make obscene gestures. We actually picked up 80 of the 81 yards we needed and wound up with nothing. There was 3:03 left in the first quarter.

I grabbed my Gatorade and sat on the bench. Bennici seemed to read my mind or the expression on my face.

"You've just got to hang in there," he said as he leaned over and patted me on the shoulder. "There's still plenty of football left. Don't let it get you down."

Of course he was right. However, believing it and implementing it were two different things. I was still feeling down.

The temperature in Dallas at the moment was about 50 degrees. I was still perspiring. I had done a lot of running during our futile drive.

I watched from the bench, hoping that the defense would hold the Cowboys again. This time the Cowboys moved the ball, starting their drive from the 20 since the line of scrimmage on our field goal attempt had been from inside the 20. They rushed for seven yards on the opening play and then wound up in our territory. A pass was completed near the Dallas 45 and the receiver crossed midfield to the 42 before Black brought him down as the two tumbled out of bounds.

I hated to panic but inside I was doing exactly that. I had been through this type of thing several times before but this time seemed different. This wasn't just any game, this was an NFL playoff game. It also wasn't just any opponent, this was the Dallas Cowboys. This was the team that somebody dubbed "America's Team" as if the other 29 teams in the league were from the Third World. I believed the Cowboys were going in for seven. I hoped I was wrong.

Two plays later the Cowboys had a first down at the 28. That was followed by a short pass that got them to the 19.

"Let's go defense!" I called. Although I am sure that the defense did not hear me from my post on the sideline and had every intention of stopping the Cowboys anyway, I couldn't resist calling my encouragement. I suppose it may have relieved some of the tension I was feeling.

A rush off right tackle got the Cowboys nowhere. They even lost a yard. Richards dropped the running back at the 20.

"Way to go, Norm!" I cried out.

The Cowboys decided to go to the air. They tried a short pass to try to pick up a first down. McDaniel read the play and moved to his left. He dove toward the sideline as the pass was being released and managed to deflect the pass, causing the ball to veer off course and drop harmlessly to the turf. It was fourth and two with two seconds left in the quarter.

We knew the Cowboys would score points. We only shut out one team in 1977; something that is considered to be virtually impossible in the NFL according to some. Shutting out the Cowboys was among the least likely scenarios one could expect.

The Cowboy field goal unit was on the field. With seemingly little effort the kicker put the ball through the uprights. The Cowboys had a 3-0 lead as the first quarter came to an end.

I stood up and heaved a sigh of relief. The Cowboys had drawn first blood but only for three points. The solution, as I saw it, was to counter with a touchdown.

The second quarter would begin the same way as the first quarter; with us returning a kickoff. The only difference was that we would be moving in the opposite direction. Hasegawa and I did our slap fives.

"We need a touchdown on this drive," I remarked.

"We'll get it," Rich replied; an interesting response since he was a defensive back and would be on the sideline during our drive.

But we were on the same team. What the offense did reflected on the defense and vice versa. If the defense surrenders only three points but the offense doesn't rack up even that many the entire team loses.

The kick was up. It was heading Rich's way.

512

"Run it, Rich!" I called before charging forward to run interference.

I didn't get much of a block in. I spotted somebody in a white jersey charging my way and tried to head him off. The defender sidestepped me, even causing me to fall flat on my face. Fortunately it was enough of a diversion to prevent the defender from making the tackle. Rich had taken the ball two yards deep in the end zone and returned it all the way to the 29.

As I moved to where the offense would huddle I felt foolish about missing the block. Walker was certain to single that one out during our film session on Wednesday.

Suddenly I realized that I would be more than happy to have Walker point out that faux pas on Wednesday. He could ride me all he wanted. If we had a film session on Wednesday it would mean that we had beaten the Cowboys. If I was going to have to take a lot of crap from Walker, it would be a very small price to pay for the privilege of still being in the hunt for the Super Bowl.

We started the drive by sending Ozzie off left tackle. He picked up seven yards to the 36 but there was a penalty marker down.

It was against the Cowboys. A linebacker had tried to tackle Ozzie at the line by grabbing Ozzie's facemask. Ozzie broke away but the violation was not unseen. The Cowboys were assessed 15 yards from the point of the infraction to give us a first down at the Hawaii 44.

We went to the air next although we didn't get very far. Bender took the snap in the shotgun formation and immediately fired to Dietrich at the line. Ted sidestepped a defensive back but the defender still managed to hook on to Ted and bring him down at the 47. It was second and seven.

I was next, catching a pass near the right sideline at the Dallas 43. A defensive back was right there and steadfastly refused to allow me to break away. He brought me down at the 40.

"Okay, first down and 120 feet to go," Bender said in the huddle, referring to the distance we needed to cover for the touchdown.

Bender went for Dietrich again. He hit Ted at the 27. Despite the presence of a defensive back, Ted managed to pick up two more yards.

"All right! Here we go! Here we go!" Grummon cried out, enthusiastically clapping his hands.

Whatever discouragement I had felt earlier was gone. I was not only confident that we would score, I was absolutely sure of it. We had only 75 feet to go.

We returned to the ground game since we had loosened up the Cowboy defense. Kerner picked up three yards up the middle and then Ozzie went off right tackle and picked up seven yards to the 15.

"Great job, Ozzie," I said as I patted him on the back as we headed toward where we would huddle. As much for Ozzie's sake as the team's, I wanted him to have a good game. I didn't want him to be a bust as a starting running back.

Time was called to measure. The chain was brought out and stretched out. The referee then stood erect and pointed to indicate that we had a first down.

There wasn't much reaction from the crowd, of course. When the referee pointed I allowed my mind to drift back to Honolulu. I visualized Carol reacting happily as we got the first down. Hawaiian fans gathered in various homes and even in bars that opened up in time for the eight o'clock, Hawaii time, kickoff and cheered wildly.

I got my first carry of the game. Going off left tackle, I picked up three yards to the 12.

Ozzie then went to the middle and picked up three more yards. It was third and four.

Or was it?

There was a penalty marker down at the line of scrimmage. The placement suggested that somebody was going to be cited for holding.

That's exactly what it was. Grummon had held. Instead of having a third and four at the nine, we had a second and 17 at the 22.

"Okay, don't let it get you down. This kind of thing happens. Let's overcome it," Bender advised us in the huddle in his usual unflappable manner.

I ran a pass pattern toward the right sideline. Bender hit me at the nine. I had to hop a little but managed to get both of my feet down in bounds before going out of bounds. This time we were able to keep the third and four.

We were going to try for the first down on the ground. Bender handed off to Kerner who shot through the line off left tackle.

"Fumble!"

Kerner was hit and fumbled at the seven. I caught a brief glimpse of the ball and tried to dive over a Cowboy to get to it but didn't even get close. A Cowboy lineman had recovered at the seven, bringing the crowd back to life with a vengeance.

Dejectedly I slowly rose to my feet and ran to the sideline. For the second time in as many tries we had long drives that took us inside the Dallas ten and we apparently lacked the efficacy to get the job done. All we had to show for our effort were a missed field goal and a lost fumble while traveling long distances. I wondered how our next long drive would end.

At least we only trailed by three. If our defense could hold the Cowboys at bay, or at least limit them to another field goal, we could take the lead with a touchdown on our next drive. We had already shown that we could move the ball against this defense. Now we needed to focus on actually getting into the end zone instead of knocking on the door and shooting ourselves in the foot.

After two rushes the Cowboys had a third and one at the 16. They went up the middle and picked up a first down at the 20.

514

Four plays later the Cowboys had completed three passes in as many attempts and had picked up three first downs in the process. They were on the Hawaii 28. It didn't look good for us at the moment although there was still plenty of football left. If the Cowboys started running away with the game it was going to be a very long uphill battle for us.

A sweep around right end netted the Cowboys only two yards. They decided to go to the air on the next play.

The quarterback dropped back. He found himself under attack. He tried to scramble away but to no avail. He was sacked by Jennings and Allen at the 33. It was third and 15.

That brought our woebegone sideline to life. It had been pretty gloomy as we sat helplessly watching the Cowboys eat up huge chunks of real estate after we had squandered two scoring opportunities. Suddenly we were all on our feet and hollering encouragement.

"Okay," I said to Dietrich who was next to me. "If we can hold them to no gain it will be about a 50 yard field goal attempt."

Once again, this wasn't just any team we were playing. These were the Dallas Cowboys and they didn't want to have to settle for a field goal. Despite our switch to the 32 dime, they managed to complete a pass just inside the 20. The receiver was brought down by Rodgers at the 14.

First down, Cowboys.

I had a few words to say about this. Most of the words are better left unprinted. I was trying not to swear but I hadn't eradicated the expletives from my vocabulary completely. At times like this they flowed like the Mississippi River.

Two rushes later and the Cowboys had a first and goal at the two. They let the clock run down to the two-minute warning.

I stood up and walked around a little. I decided to grab another cup of Gatorade since it gave me something to do besides sit on the bench and feel helpless.

"What do you think?" Bender asked as he stood next to me.

I shook my head.

"I'd like to believe the defense will hold them or get them to turn the ball over," I said, "but we still need to score."

"We will," Bender said assuredly. "Even if the Cowboys get the full seven on this drive we'll still be within striking distance. If they leave us enough time on the clock we can go downfield and get at least a field goal."

The two-minute warning ended. The Cowboys rushed right up the gut and into the end zone.

"It's still a close game," I remarked to Bender. "We've got time to narrow the gap."

Bender nodded as the Cowboys converted on the PAT. It was 10-0 with 1:55 left in the half.

It was an interesting game to this point. Both teams were eating up the clock by putting together long sustained drives. That was pretty much the way the game was played in those days with more emphasis on the running game and passing games of 300 yards or more virtually unheard of. The difference between the way we ate up the clock and the Cowboys ate up the clock was the Cowboys were actually getting into the end zone to climax their drives.

I took my position on the goal line. Hasegawa and I did our slap fives and words of encouragement. I was determined that we would get the drive off to a flying start with an outstanding return. It didn't matter to me which of us did the return. I simply wanted outstanding field position if not a touchdown from this return.

It was coming my way. I caught the ball four yards deep in the end zone. Without a moment's hesitation I headed upfield.

There were some pretty good blocks ahead of me. Hasegawa and Rossi managed to keep a couple of Cowboys away. Reiser, giving his all after almost two full seasons of inactivity, leveled a defender near the 25.

I was past the 20 before anybody was able to challenge me. I kept on going, primarily by outrunning the defenders. I was actually almost to the 35 before anybody got a hand on me and I still managed to keep going. I was finally caught from behind and wrestled down at the Hawaii 43.

As I bounced up I was exultant. A 47-yard return was just what we needed to start our drive. We had all three of our timeouts so there was no reason to believe we couldn't beat the clock through the 57 yards to the end zone.

Three incompletions followed. Jablonski punted to the 17. There was no return on the punt. The Cowboys, who had their three timeouts, had 58 seconds to travel 83 yards.

I kept my mouth shut. I was angry but not at anybody in particular and I didn't want anything I said to be taken out of context. I got my Gatorade and sat on the bench, hoping either that the Cowboys would simply run out the clock or that our defense would not allow them to get anywhere.

We were in the 32 dime. We were willing to concede a certain amount of short yardage. We simply did not want to let them get into even field goal position.

After an incompletion the Cowboys completed a pass at their own 35. The receiver got to the 37 before being brought down in bounds by Hasegawa. The Cowboys used their first timeout with 40 seconds left in the half.

Two incompletions later it appeared as if we had a shot at escaping this drive unscathed. Before I could breathe a sigh of relief the Cowboys completed another pass near midfield. They had, at least, the first down but the receiver wasn't satisfied with that. The receiver got to the Hawaii 38

516

before Rodgers and Blakely dropped him. The Cowboys used their second timeout with 13 seconds left.

The Cowboys seemed to be gearing up to get into position for a field goal. From their current position a field goal attempt would be about 55 yards which their kicker was capable of doing although it was obviously a lower percentage distance. I figured they would try a pass about 15 yards downfield and then burn their final timeout to bring out their field goal unit.

As I knew they would, the Cowboys went to the air. We were able to put some pressure on the quarterback but he was one of the best scramblers in the league. He ran to his left and found a receiver inside the ten. By the time the ball got to him the receiver was crossing the goal line.

The crowd erupted. That coincided with my desire to regurgitate my breakfast. We were still in the game but the hill we were climbing just got steeper. It was a three-score game with two seconds left in the half.

For the record, the PAT was good. We were down 17-0.

As I headed to the field for the kickoff Walker gave me a look that told me everything. We both knew that we needed a return that would go all the way. Not only would it narrow the gap and give us some momentum going into the second half, it was also imperative because the Cowboys would be receiving the second half kickoff.

Of course Hasegawa and I did our slap fives. They and the words we exchanged seemed somewhat hollow. We were in trouble although we both knew that a big play resulting in a touchdown would get us back in the game.

What I actually hoped was that this would be the last time Hasegawa and I had these little encounters. For the rest of the day they would only happen if the Cowboys scored.

The Cowboys surprised me by doing a regular kickoff. I was expecting a squib but this was a high kick heading in my direction. I took it a yard deep in the end zone.

With the clock running as soon as I exited the end zone there would not be time for another play. What I would need to do was take the ball all the way in. I was brought down 73 yards short of my goal.

In the locker room I relieved myself at the urinal and drank a quick cup of Gatorade. The offense gathered around Potter for a few minutes to make adjustments in our game plan while I drank a Dr. Pepper and ate a few orange slices.

I sat in front of my locker and tried to analyze things. The fact was, we were simply being outplayed. We had two sustained drives to start the game and nothing to show for it. The Cowboys were doing what they had to do, especially in the clutch. Their ability to travel 83 yards in 56 seconds spoke volumes.

Walker stood in the center of the room. He looked shellshocked although he appeared to be trying very hard not to.

"This game is not over. Far from it. They've come at you hard so you've got to go twice as hard. They're making the big plays but there's no reason why you can't do the same. You have it in you to do it."

Guinn teed up the ball at the 35. I stood in anticipation as he prepared to kick off. I was hoping for a fast series, if not a turnover, on the Cowboys' opening series. I was hoping that our offense would then do its part to shift the momentum by actually scoring for a change instead of merely getting close. A field goal was okay but a touchdown would be infinitely better.

The kickoff was caught three yards deep in the end zone. The Cowboy return man charged out. He got as far as the 24 before Malick brought him down.

"Let's go, defense!" Walker barked as the defense ran on the field. "Let's shut 'em down!"

The Cowboys had other ideas. They began with a 17-yard completion which gave them a first down at the 41. They then rushed up the middle to their own 47.

"Fumble!"

"Get it! Get it!" I called, jumping to my feet.

In the brief scramble the Cowboys recovered their own fumble. It was Blakely who made the tackle that jarred the ball loose but the ball carrier managed to recover his own fumble.

"Just our luck," I muttered. It was second and four.

The Cowboys got past midfield to the Hawaii 49 on a sweep around left end. That appeared to take care of the final four yards they needed for a first down. The measurement showed that they were a little short.

No problem. The Cowboys got what they needed, rushing to the Hawaii 48.

Three first downs later the Cowboys had first and goal at the seven, much to the delight of the local crowd which I found annoying. I didn't want to give up too easily but it was starting to look like the only way I was going to be in New Orleans on Super Bowl Sunday was if I paid my own way.

A rush around right end got the Cowboys to the three. That was followed by a pass that was caught in the back of the end zone. It was a four-score game now and we looked like (expletive deleted)!

I was getting angry. The Cowboys were making it look too easy. Not only did they extend their lead but by grinding it out a few yards at a time they used up more than half of the third quarter in the process. The clock showed 7:14.

The PAT was true. We were down 24-0.

We were also determined to make a game of it. Bigger leads have been erased although not by us to this point in our brief history. A break or two in our favor and we were back in the game.

Of course there were slap fives exchanged between Hasegawa and me; something I had hoped we wouldn't be doing until the following week against either the Vikings or Rams. The Cowboys had used up their allotment as far as I was concerned and their return men had only had to take their positions once this game. I was hoping they would get a lot more work.

For the moment our kick return unit was getting a little work. I caught the kick about six yards deep in the end zone and decided not to run it out.

"Okay, let's get back in this game," Bender said in the huddle.

Kerner opened the drive by going off left tackle for three yards.

Time was called because Stanek was down. He pulled a hamstring and would not return until the fourth quarter. Randy Hubert, the only backup we had at guard who wasn't a safety valve from another position, took his place.

We went to the air. Bender hit me near the right hash mark at the Hawaii 43. I broke a tackle at that point and managed to get to the 48 before going down.

"All right, Jay! That was a helluva play! Keep it up!" Walker called from the sideline.

Suddenly I forgot the score, at least as much as I could. It was no longer a matter of how much we were losing by but what we needed to do to take the lead.

Ozzie went up the middle for a mere yard to the 49. I didn't do much better on a sweep around left end, getting only to the Dallas 49. It was third and seven.

We badly needed a third down conversion and we tried it by going through the air. Dietrich, Grummon and I were all to go just far enough for the first down.

Bender hit Dietrich at the 42. He was hit and dropped immediately.

It was close. The officials called timeout to measure. It was either first and ten or fourth and inches.

When the chain was stretched out it wasn't anywhere near as close as it appeared. We had a first down by the entire length of the football.

The Cowboy defense was determined to stop us. Bender was under a heavy rush on the next play. He unloaded a pass to Grummon who was at the line as a safety valve. Grummon fought his way to the 34 to give us a second and two.

"All right, Rich!" I called enthusiastically as Dietrich and I helped him to his feet. I was determined to not concede anything.

Ozzie secured the first down by going off right tackle to the 29. He then went up the middle to the 25. That was followed by a short pass to Slater where he made the reception and was dropped at the 21. Third and two.

"Okay, let's keep it going," Bender encouraged in the huddle. "There's still plenty of time."

Kerner got the call. He rushed off right tackle and blasted his way to the 17.

"All right!" I said, clapping my hands as we were forming our huddle. "We're almost there. Let's keep going."

The next play was very interesting. Bender was under a moderately heavy rush but managed to get the pass off to Dietrich in the end zone. Ted appeared to either fall or get knocked down as the defensive back covering him got his hands on the ball but failed to hang on. The pass was ruled incomplete.

"Wait a minute! He pushed off of me!" Dietrich insisted. "That should be pass interference."

While Dietrich was pleading his case, Bender was pleading a case of his own. He was hit pretty hard shortly after he released the ball. Bender claimed that the Cowboys should have been charged with roughing the passer.

The replays would show that Bender's case could have gone either way but the Cowboys definitely got a break on Dietrich's end. It was a pretty flagrant violation that the officials somehow missed. The end result was that the play was still officially an incomplete pass.

Another incompletion followed and then Marv jumped before the snap to give us a third and 15 at the 22. We then tried to sneak our way to a first down with Bender hitting Dietrich on a quick pass at the 19.

The Cowboys weren't fooled. Ted managed only two more yards before being hit and dropped. It was fourth and ten.

We needed a score. Any score would do so it was no surprise to see the field goal unit running on the field. It was frustrating but I dutifully ran off.

What surprised me was the amount of time our drive had consumed. I looked at the clock and noticed that there were less than 15 seconds left in the third quarter as the clock continued to run and the field goal unit broke its huddle. By the time the ball split the uprights time had completely expired in the quarter.

But at least we were on the board. It was 24-3. We had exactly 15 minutes to try to score at least three touchdowns. Field goals were no longer an option.

And then there was the small matter of the clock. The Cowboys didn't wind up with the home field advantage by not understanding how the clock worked in a situation like this. They were likely to run plays that would not stop the clock as much as possible. What our defense had to do was either hold them so that they would turn the ball over on downs or else force them to turn it over. After that we had to stick almost exclusively with our passing game since short gains on the ground chewed up too much of the clock. We had to really open it up and work fast.

Guinn's kick to open the final quarter was fielded at the goal line. The return man headed upfield. Malick cut the return man down at the 15.

"All right! Now we're cookin'!" Kerner exclaimed. Keeping the return man from getting as far as the 20 was a good start.

The Cowboys seemed to look at it another way. The more field they had to cover, the longer they would have the ball. Throwing only one pass along the way, they ran a series of rushing plays and flat out refused to run any play that would take them near the sideline. The clock continued to run as I sat on the sideline and helplessly watched the final minutes of our 1977 season tick away.

After five first downs the Cowboys had a second and six at the Hawaii 14. Any kind of a score including a field goal would make it a four-score game again. The clock was ticking down to the eight-minute mark.

For only the second time of the drive the Cowboys went to the air. It wasn't expected so there was little pressure on the quarterback. Unable to find an open receiver, he threw the ball out of the end zone. The clock showed 7:56 left in the game.

The Cowboys went to the air again. This time a receiver got open. The quarterback hit him at the one. Another step and he was over the line to officially rack up another score for the home team.

A wave of sadness swept over me. I suppose it was a pretty common feeling among those of us wearing brown jerseys. With just a little more than half of the final quarter left we would need something miraculous to bring us back into this one.

Naturally the PAT was done without difficulty. The Cowboys now led 31-3 with 7:49 left to play. We were looking like an expansion team that somehow got into the postseason by some enigmatic fluke.

That was pretty much the end of it. I managed a good return from a yard deep in the end zone to the 29. From there we put together a drive that ate up most of the rest of the clock. Playing primarily for pride although we weren't averse to a big play that would raise our hopes, Bender took the snap at the Cowboy three and fired a pass to Grummon in the end zone to finally get us a touchdown. The extra point made the score 31-10. There was 1:51 left of our season.

We were pretty much out of it, obviously, but we also didn't concede the game without one final effort. We tried an onside kick to see if we could throw together a quick score and try another onside kick. Unfortunately the Cowboys recovered the kick and ran out the clock.

With the exception of the small contingent of Hawaiian fans present, the fans at Texas Stadium were obviously not disappointed. Our Christmas present to our fans and ourselves was that we got to play in a playoff game. Actually winning one was still at least a year away.

Not winning was a huge disappointment. Contrary to what actors allegedly say when they don't win Oscars, it was not an honor just to have been nominated. We did not fly to Texas with the intention of simply being honored to have been in the game.

As I walked off the field I put on my facade of congeniality. I shook hands with some of the Cowboy players including one who had been a teammate at the University of Hawaii and another whose tenure at the university preceded mine. Some of the Cowboys offered nice compliments about the Hawaiians' overall season.

I smiled as I spoke with my opponents including Coach Tom Landry. What else could I do? I wasn't going to cuss them out for beating us fair and square. There weren't any cheap shots or any other forms of cheating or dirty play. We lost because the Cowboys were simply the better team that day.

A *much* better team. It was the most lopsided loss in our brief history.

When I got to the locker room I let my true feelings show. I didn't cry although I sure wanted to. My good friend Marv couldn't hold back a few brief tears and I smacked him on the shoulder and ruffled his hair a little as I walked past. Kerner also shed a few tears. So did Hayer, Allen, Hasegawa and a few others.

"Okay, men," Walker called although he seemed to be on the verge of tears himself and had trouble getting out even those first two words. "I need a volunteer for the postgame prayer."

Rookie tight end Chester McCracken raised his hand and got Walker's attention. Under very difficult circumstances, taking into account that our season was over before we wanted it to be and in such an ignominious manner, he gave a very nice prayer.

"Thank you, Chester," Walker said when the prayer was completed. "And thanks to all of you. This wasn't the way we wanted to end it but nobody can take away the fact that you had one hell of an outstanding season."

Walker paused while some of us nodded our heads. He was right but it didn't mitigate the sting of our defeat.

"Of course we can't be satisfied since we didn't win but I don't believe anybody gave less than 100 percent. When you give it everything you've got you do all that anybody can ever ask of you and have no cause for shame."

Walker took a deep breath. He was having as hard a time swallowing this defeat as anybody.

"For now, get showered and dressed. I'll come and talk to you individually on the flight home."

The shower was hardly refreshing. The previous week we had won our fourth consecutive game; a streak that made possible our trip to Dallas and

522

almost a playoff game at home had the Rams' fortune been slightly different. At that time the shower was like champagne. My teammates and I were singing and hollering and carrying on as if the world was absolutely perfect.

Eight days later the shower was simply water. Very little was being said. No singing, no dancing, no playful antics of any type in our locker room. The shower, with the aid of soap and shampoo, was simply a way of getting the body clean. It couldn't wash away the demons I felt from losing.

It was *just a football game.*

Tell that to somebody who didn't have his heart set on a greater athletic glory. Being human, one can't possibly be ambivalent about losing a tough football game. We play to win. Anybody who doesn't play to win or is satisfied in defeat has no business being in uniform.

I would get over it. We all would. For the moment, though, it was very difficult.

It was a long flight home, of course, but it didn't seem as long as it could have. As usual we talked quietly among ourselves while replaying the game we just lost in our heads.

Of course there were the "what ifs" on this flight but instead of stewing about them in our seats the team was bonded. My teammates spent a lot of time in the aisle talking to each other. We had every reason to be proud of our season. We couldn't be completely satisfied with it because it didn't include a victory in the Super Bowl or even a trip to the Super Bowl in a losing effort. It had still been an outstanding season. Nobody could take that away from us.

Absolutely nobody!!!

I sat next to Jennings although, like the rest of the team, he and I spent more time out of our seats than in them. He and I were not finished yet since we would be joining Bender and Allen at the Pro Bowl a month later. Selection to the Pro Bowl was an honor. It was still very small consolation for losing a game we very badly wanted and needed to win. At that moment it was no consolation at all.

Walker, as he said he would, made his way through the cabin. Ed and I were near the very back of the DC-8 so we could see Walker making his way down the aisle as he chatted with our teammates. He spent a few minutes at each set of seats, smiling in a paternal way which defied the martinet we often saw during the season and especially during training camp. After he finished talking to each player he moved on.

"How're you two doing?" Walker asked congenially when he reached Ed and me.

"What can I say?" Ed half-sighed.

"I'll live," I replied with very little conviction. "I just wish we could go back and do it all over again. Maybe we could change the outcome."

"Maybe," Walker said, his smile never leaving his face. "It's tough to lose a game like that. Still, we've had two seasons that were far better than anybody expected. A loss in the playoffs, even a lopsided one, doesn't change that. It just means that we have to learn from the experience and be better prepared next time."

Ed and I nodded our concession. A combined 17 wins and a playoff berth over two seasons was considered phenomenal for a second-year team in the NFL. Before we came along it was considered hypothetical.

"I just want to thank both of you for all you did during the season," Walker continued. "I can't recall a time when either of you gave less than 100 percent. That's why you're both going to the Pro Bowl and why you'll both help lead us to the Super Bowl eventually. Maybe next year will be the year."

Walker tapped Ed on the shoulder and smiled and nodded at me before turning to Marv and Clint Abraham who were sitting across the aisle from us. The loss still hurt but Walker's kind words deadened some of the pain. Only about six or seven hours after our season ended I couldn't wait for training camp. After Walker's display of compassion I would have been willing to do two-a-days in 12 hour increments.

"I've been thinking," I said to Ed near the end of the flight. "There are two reasons why we played so hard."

"Two?"

"Well, probably a lot more than two but there are two primary reasons. One is pride. The other is Walker."

Ed shrugged and grinned.

"Is that because we like Walker or because he'd kill us if we don't."

"Probably both," I responded lightly but truthfully. Most of the team revered Walker and nobody wanted to get on his bad side. He forgave us our mistakes. He was less forgiving of those who didn't put out.

A few minutes later I watched from my window seat on the right side of the aircraft as Oahu came into view. It was after eleven o'clock so it was dark. I could still make out the adjacent areas by virtue of their lights and my knowledge of Oahu's geography. We passed by Hawaii Kai, then Kuliouou, Niu Valley, Aina Haina, Wailupe, Kahala, Kaimuki and then Waikiki before we bellied out to the south and then back in a northerly route. We touched down on runway 4R before rapidly cutting our speed and turning right to taxi to Air Service.

We were home. Less than 55 hours earlier we began our sojourn from this same locale with visions of sugar plum Cowboys who were about to be stomped out by Hawaiians dancing in our heads. We fell way short but would survive.

"How ironic," Marv commented somewhat lightly as we stood to gather our overhead luggage. "Last year we were all jazzed up on our last flight because we finished seven and seven. This year we won ten games and we take our last flight not feeling so good."

It did seem ironic. In 1976 we had a record that would have done any expansion team proud and came home feeling almost as if we had won the Super Bowl. In 1977 we were among the elite eight and came home feeling flat as a pancake.

"Well," Ed responded as we began the slow sojourn up the aisle toward the exit. "Now that we know how much we hate to lose in the playoffs, let's win the Super Bowl next year."

"I can dig it," I said.

Once again it sounded so simple.

The long flight had done us good. We got off the plane in much better spirits than we were in when we boarded the aircraft in Dallas. As we descended the stairway of the DC-8 we were greeted by warm applause. Wives, girlfriends, children and a few others with connections to the team were allowed to park on the tarmac and greet us near the green hanger. Many greeted their defeated warriors with leis. Others were holding banners welcoming us home. There were even a few TV cameras and reporters.

In the midst of everybody was Carol. I went over to her and embraced her tightly, then accepted the orchid lei that she had for me.

"Thanks for that letter," she said softly, referring to the letter I gave her just before we left. "I was really moved by it. Did you really write that the night that we went out for the first time in June?"

I nodded.

"It wasn't easy to write," I told her. "I knew how I was feeling. It was just hard to put it into words."

"I'm glad you found a way. It really made this Christmas extra special. I love it when you speak totally from the heart."

Carol and I joined my teammates and their families. We clumped together and made small talk among ourselves while we waited for our luggage to be unloaded, occasionally answering questions posed by reporters. I answered a question by saying I was happy with our season but not completely satisfied because we didn't achieve our ultimate goal. I'm sure a few of my teammates answered that same question in a similar manner.

Gradually we picked up what belonged to us, got in our cars and left. Like the year before, we knew that the contingent would be slightly different when we kicked off the 1978 season.

"You okay?" Carol asked as we headed east on the H-1 Freeway.

"I'll live. You?"

"I'm sorry you didn't win," she said. "It doesn't take anything away from you guys. You had a great season."

Carol was absolutely right. Memphis, Seattle and Tampa Bay were fighting to reach mediocrity. We were respected and even feared.

After I dropped Carol off I went home. It was 12:30 in Honolulu; 4:30 in Dallas. That meant that I had been awake for 23 hours. I had no trouble going to sleep.

I took it easy for the first few days after our Dallas defeat and then started working out again. Normally I would have taken a little more time off but I wanted to be in top shape when I traveled to Tampa for the Pro Bowl. One never knew how many times the privilege of playing in this postseason game would come around. I always wanted to be at my best.

Carol and I watched the Super Bowl with a large group at the Sport Page. This was a facility which had recently opened up on Kalakaua Avenue under the ownership of an old friend, Carl Green. Being the disciplined football player, I nursed two beers to get me through the game. Carl and Keith Kasparovitch, one of the bartenders who also worked at Arthur's, tried to persuade me to drink some local moonshine that they had behind the bar. It was 196 proof!

"Thanks but no thanks," I replied lightly to my two good friends who had both been outstanding athletes during their school days.

While most of those watching the big screen TV favored one team or the other, I found it hard to take sides. In some ways I wanted Denver since it was the team's first Super Bowl and the Broncos were playing the team that knocked us out of the playoffs. On the other hand, I had complete respect for Dallas.

In the end it was Dallas. The Cowboys had about as much trouble with the Broncos as they had with us.

When the game was over I took Carol to her place. Along the way I had an amusing thought about my old friend and college teammate Chris Alexander who was last reported to be in Arizona. I recalled that he had had a very brief tenure in the Broncos' training camp a few years back until his mouth helped him to an excessively early departure. With the way the Broncos were routed by the Cowboys, Chris was probably thinking that it served the Broncos right. Knowing Chris the way I did, he would probably insist that the Broncos developed bad karma for putting him on waivers.

After dropping Carol off I went to the TV studio. I would be prerecording Tuesday night's TV show. With the Super Bowl finished the primary feature of the show was ready to go. Half of the show would be comprised of Super Bowl highlights. Most of the rest of the show would feature highlights of the University of Hawaii basketball team and a few NBA highlights. There would be no problem recording the show two days in advance unless there was a game that ended with a winning half-court shot at the buzzer later that night or the next day. The show would simply not be able to include it.

On Sunday night I picked Carol up and went to the airport. Jennings, Bender, Allen and I caught a redeye to Los Angeles. From there we would catch a connection to Tampa.

I thoroughly enjoyed my first Pro Bowl. Although I would have sacrificed the Pro Bowl for the Super Bowl, the Pro Bowl was a fulfilling experience. It was a good way to get to know some of the other players from both conferences in a more congenial atmosphere.

When it was over I looked forward to the 1978 season, working hard to stay in shape while also taking care of my other responsibilities and enjoying life with Carol. We would have only four exhibition games in 1978 since the regular season was being expanded to 16 games. The playoff format would also change since both conferences would have two wild cards, meaning that ten teams would reach the postseason.

I couldn't wait to get started.

About The Author

Jim Gardner grew up in West Covina, California, then moved to Hawaii after high school where he lived for 50 years. Like the main character in the trilogy, Gardner is an alumnus of the University of Hawaii, earning his degree in journalism before embarking on a career as a broadcast journalist and freelance writer. In 2021 he retired to Union, Missouri, to be closer to his son, Reggie, but his heart will always be in Hawaii.

Made in the USA
Monee, IL
05 February 2023

27175436R00295